THE
FIRST
BILLION

A NOVEL

CHRISTOPHER REICH

A DELL BOOK

THE FIRST BILLION
A Dell Book

PUBLISHING HISTORY
Delacorte hardcover edition published September 2002
Dell international mass market edition
published February 2003
Dell domestic mass market edition / August 2003

Published by Bantam Dell
A Division of Random House, Inc.
New York, New York

Library of Congress Catalog Card Number: 2002022254

ISBN: 0-440-23469-7

Manufactured in the United States of America
Published simultaneously in Canada

OPM 10 9 8 7 6 5 4 3 2 1

For my daughters, Katja and Noelle, with love

1

YOU ARE MILLIONAIRE?" she asked.

"Me?" Grafton Byrnes pointed a finger at his chest. "No. I'm afraid not."

"Yes," she insisted, adding a coy smile. "You are millionaire. I can tell. You have nice suit. Beautiful tie. You are confident. It is clear. You are millionaire."

Byrnes unglued his eyes from the leggy blond who'd taken a seat at the bar next to him and looked around the room. The place was called Metelitsa, and it was a restaurant, nightclub, and casino rolled into one, located on the Novy Arbat in the center of Moscow. Red curtains blocked out the summer evening's glare. White tablecloths, smoked mirrors, and croupiers in black ties lent the room a touch of class. But one sniff told Byrnes different: the smoke, the perfume, the heady mix of expensive liquor and easy morals. He could recognize a cathouse by scent alone.

"I'm successful," he said, curtly. "Nothing special."

"You are *very* successful, I think. Yes, a millionaire." She pronounced the word—*mee-lone-air*—and her Slavic accent and grave delivery lent the word a patina of its foregone luster. "You would like to buy me drink?"

"Sure," he said, before he could ask himself what he was getting himself into. "What'll you have?"

"Vodka. On rocks with twist of orange."

"Coming right up."

Byrnes was finding it increasingly difficult to keep his eyes off the woman next to him. To call her gorgeous would have been an injustice. She was no more than twenty-one, with white blond hair, satin blue eyes, and the kind of pouty lips that his ex-wife called "bee-stung" and that no amount of collagen injections could reproduce. Her dress was black, short, and tight; her nails were lacquered a rich maroon. But it was her bearing that Byrnes found irresistible: the inquisitive tilt of the head, the brazen posture, the adventurous twinkle to the eyes that seemed to say, "Dare me—I'll try anything." In short, she was every middle-aged divorcé's idea of a fitting companion.

"Bartender!" As Byrnes shifted on his seat to get the barkeep's attention, he inadvertently nudged the man next to him. "*Izvinitye*," he said, offering a smile. Excuse me.

The man looked Byrnes up and down, then rose from his stool. He was six four, about two twenty, with a Marine's crew cut and a neck the size of a fire hydrant. He had a buddy next to him who looked like he'd fallen out of the same tree. Byrnes had been warned about guys like this. "Flat tops," they were called. Enforcers for the Russian *mafiya*, or more politely, point men for the Russian business elite.

Be careful, Byrnes's best friend had told him. *Moscow isn't Paris or Zurich or Rome. It may look like a European city, but it's not. You're in Russia. The whole country is in the shithouse. Two percent of the people are making a fortune and the rest don't have a pot to piss in. It's dangerous over there.*

"Excuse *me*," the Russian replied, in decent English. "I hope I not disturb you and pretty lady."

"No," said Byrnes. "My fault. Again, I'm sorry. Let me buy you a drink. We'll call it even."

"No need," said the Russian, with grating politeness. "Have nice evening." He made a show of adjusting his blazer and retook his place. Only a blind man would have missed the nickel-plated revolver nestled beneath his arm—a .357 Colt Python with a pearl handle, if Byrnes wasn't mistaken.

Turning back to the girl, Byrnes found a round of drinks on the counter. Okay, he said to himself, let's start over again. And raising his glass, *"Na Strovye."*

"Na Strovye." She took a sip, then leaned forward and gave him a lingering kiss on the cheek. "My name is Svetlana."

"I'm Graf," he said, knocking back the entire drink. "Good to know you."

"You speak Russian. Why you not tell me so before?"

"Nemnogo," he said. Just a little. The Air Force would be proud of him for having remembered as much as he did. He also knew how to say, "I am an officer," "My serial number is . . . ," and a few choice obscenities.

"I no like Russian men," Svetlana confided in his ear. "So arrogant."

"Me neither," he complained. "So big."

She laughed. "Tell me, Graf, why you are in Moscow?"

"Business," he answered.

"Beez-ness? What do you do?"

Byrnes shrugged, looking away. "Nothing interesting. Just some routine stuff."

His response couldn't have been further from the truth. He'd arrived earlier that afternoon on an emergency visit. All very hush-hush. Forty-eight hours in country to check out the operating equipment of Mercury Broadband, a multinational Internet service and content provider his company was set to bring public in a week's time. Questions had surfaced regarding the firm's Moscow network operations center—namely, whether it owned all the physical assets it claimed to: routers, switches, servers, and the like. He was to find the facility, verify that it contained equipment necessary to provide broadband services to its publicized customer base of two hundred thousand people, and report back.

The IPO, or initial public offering, of shares in the company was valued at two billion dollars, and nothing less than his firm's continued existence depended on what he discovered. A green light meant seventy million dollars in fees, a guarantee of fee-related business from Mercury down the road, and a rescue from impending insolvency.

Shelving the offering meant death—defined either as massive layoffs, the sale of the firm to a larger house, or in the worst case, shuttering up the shop and putting a "Gone Fishing" sign in the window. Permanently.

"And what you do for business?" she asked.

"Investment banking. Stocks. Bonds. Like Wall Street, you know?"

"So, I am right," she announced proudly, dropping a hand onto his leg and allowing it to linger there. "You are millionaire."

"Maybe," he said. "Maybe not. Anyway, it's not polite to talk about money."

"I think you are wrong. Money is sexy," she said, winking. "Aphrodisiac, I think."

He ordered another drink, and when it came he took a greedy sip. He was getting that warm, fuzzy feeling, and liking it. From his perch at the bar, he overlooked a parquet dance floor and a small casino with slot machines and a half dozen gaming tables. A few flat tops had staked out positions at the craps pit. They were dressed to a man in snazzy black suits, open collars, and gold chains. Crisp American greenbacks were exchanged for stacks of blue and silver chips. No one was playing with less than five thousand dollars. Dice tumbled across the green baize tables. Raucous voices lofted across the room, spirited, cajoling, violent. The staccato shouts had a serrated edge and lent the place an aggressive buzz. At five past nine on a Tuesday night, the joint was beginning to jump.

"And why, Graf, you come to Metelitsa?" Svetlana's hand had moved higher on his leg. A single finger danced along the crease of his trousers. "To see me, maybe? See Svetlana?"

She was staring at him, the magnetic blue eyes commanding him nearer. Her lips parted, and he saw a moist band of pink flashing behind the dazzling teeth. He could taste her warm, expectant breath. The scent of her hair, lilac and rosewater, drifted over him . . . enticing him . . . seducing him.

"Yes . . . I mean, no . . . I mean . . ." Byrnes didn't know what he wanted to say. He wasn't sure whether it was the vodka or just Svetlana, but suddenly he was decidedly tipsy. He was having trouble focusing, too. Placing a hand on the bar, he stood up unsteadily, bumping once more into the thug next to him.

"Watch it!" barked the linebacker.

You're in Russia. It's dangerous over there.

"Sorry, sorry." Byrnes raised his hands defensively. He turned toward Svetlana. "Excuse me. I'll be right back." He mumbled the words "rest room" and "freshen up."

"I help you," she said, resting a hand on his waist. "We go upstairs together. I show you way."

"No, no. I'm all right, really. Where do I go?"

"Up. To right side." She pointed the way, then wrapped her arms around him. "You no leave Svetlana?"

Suddenly, she didn't look so much the unapproachable Russian ice princess as an insecure twenty-year-old frightened she might lose her evening's pay.

"No," he said. "I no leave Svetlana. I come right back." Jesus, now he was even talking like her.

He set off to the rest room, lurching along the bar before recovering his sea legs and guiding himself up the stairs. Inside the john, he turned the tap on full and took turns slapping cold water on his face and taking deep breaths. A minute passed and he began to feel better. That was some vodka he was drinking. Two doubles and he was on his ass. He promised himself he'd have a word with the hotel concierge, tell him he had something different in mind when asking about a place where a gentleman could get a few drinks and some dinner.

Laying both hands on the sink, he took a close look at himself in the mirror. "Come on, kid," he whispered. "Snap out of it."

Staring back was a vital, handsome father of two teenage children gracefully approaching middle age. Strands of silver streaked a generous head of black hair. Fatigue shadowed his flinty eyes. His bold, clefted chin, the brunt of a thousand jokes, evidenced a slight but noticeable sag. Squinting, he wondered what had happened to the gallant airman who had flown his nation's fighters in two armed conflicts, the able pilot who had deadstick-landed a flamed-out F-15 and bailed out over open ocean after he'd lost his hydraulics.

"Still here," tolled a fighting voice deep within him. "Just get lost once in a while."

"You are a huckleberry," he said aloud, angered by his lack of self-restraint. "Your little lady friend probably had your drink spiked. Five'll get you ten her big buddy is waiting downstairs at this very instant to give you his best regards. You came to do a job, not fuck around. Get thyself out of here. Now!"

Five minutes later, Grafton Byrnes left the rest room. His tie was straightened, if a little wet. His jacket was buttoned. His wooziness had faded, replaced by a whopping headache and an ironclad desire to get as far from the premises as possible. Walking to the head of the stairs, he glanced down at the bar. Svetlana was deep in conversation with the two bullies who'd been sitting next to him.

Idiot! he thought. It really was a put-up job.

Spinning on his heel, he headed to the dining room. An illuminated sign along the far wall read "Exit." He snaked through the tables, bumping into diners, slowing only to offer an apology. Reaching the emergency exit, he threw open the door and found himself standing at the top of a fire escape. He put a tentative foot on the rusted landing. The entire structure swayed and groaned. The thing had been built before Stalin had even thought of the words "five-year plan."

Retreat. Go to plan B.

But even as he turned to reenter the building, the door slammed shut. There was no handle or doorknob to gain entry.

Byrnes swallowed hard, a bolt of unease creasing his shoulders. He wasn't sure if he was frightened or exhilarated, but a moment later he was attacking the fire escape. Rung by rung, he descended the rickety structure, his steps cautious but not unsure. Six flights of stairs took him down three floors, and when he reached the ground he stood stock still, amazed the thing had actually held together.

He was still dusting the rust off his hands when the emergency exit flung open and his favorite flat top emerged onto the landing, six floors above. "*Allo*, Graf," the Russian called. "Stop. I want to talk. You owe Tatiana money."

Tatiana? What happened to Svetlana?

It took Byrnes less than a second to decide to get the hell out of there. He might owe Svetlana, or Tatiana, or whatever her real name was, an apology for his sudden departure, but he certainly didn't owe her any money. And even if he did, he didn't want to give it to her pimp. Somehow he didn't peg the guy as a believer in win-win negotiation.

A deep breath and Byrnes was off, running down the alley as fast as his Bally loafers would carry him. He didn't look back to see if the *mafiya* goon was following him—the angry creaking of the fire escape told him all he needed to know on that account. The sky was a pale blue, softening to azure. A crescent moon hung in the sky. The air smelled of fried potatoes and automobile exhaust. Rounding the corner of Metelitsa, he hightailed it through the parking lot toward the street.

The Novy Arbat had been built in the early sixties as Khrushchev's answer to Manhattan's Fifth Avenue. Four lanes of traffic flowed in either direction, lined by a succession of nondescript offices and run-down apartment buildings, the kind where air conditioners dripped coolant from jury-rigged perches and half the windows were caked with grime. Maybe the Bowery, carped Byrnes, but Fifth? No way.

Reaching the street, he raised a hand in the air. "Taxi!"

It was a Russian tradition for ordinary drivers to offer their services as taxis in exchange for a few dollars, marks, or francs. In a heartbeat, a red Lada had pulled over and Byrnes was in the passenger seat.

"Hotel Baltschug," he said, then a second later, "No, wait." Digging his hand into his pockets, he found the address of the network operations center he was supposed to visit. If this was Russia, he wanted to get the hell out of it as quickly as possible. He checked the sky again. Plenty of light remained to get his job done. Finish tonight and he could catch the first plane out in the morning. He'd be back in San Francisco at four and in the office by five. Plowing through his E-mails would never be so much fun.

"You know Rudenev Ulitsa?"

"*Rudenev?*" The driver appeared confused, then it came to him. "*Rudenev! Da. Da.*" He was a small man, near sixty, with a Tatar's eyes and a hairline that started t an inch above his eyebrows. Living proof the gols had reached the gates of Moscow.

"Rudenev Ulitsa 99," Byrnes said, yanking a hundred-dollar bill out of his wallet and handing it to the man. "And hurry!"

Five seconds later, the Lada was barreling down the center lane of the Novy Arbat. Byrnes looked over his shoulder out the back window. Late-evening traffic had already closed in around the car. For a moment, he was able to glimpse the parking lot in front of Metelitsa. A long line of cars was pulled up to the valet. Men and women ambled toward the entrance. He saw no sign of his newest friend.

"Rudenev. How long?"

The driver held up a finger. "One hour."

Byrnes sat lower in his seat, catching his breath.

He knew it had been a lousy idea to come to Russia.

2

THE EARLY-MORNING SKY WAS DARK, a low cloud cover threatening rain as John Gavallan backed his Mercedes 300 SL "Gullwing" from the garage of his home in Pacific Heights and accelerated down Broadway toward his office in the heart of San Francisco's Financial District. It was a short trip: eight minutes in good weather or foul. At 4 A.M., the streets were deserted. The night owls had gone to bed; the early birds were only just beginning to rise. A fat drop of rain plopped onto the windshield, and Gavallan shivered. A week into June and he'd barely seen the sun. He recalled Mark Twain's quote about the coldest winter he'd lived through being the summer he'd spent in San Francisco, and smiled thinly. Normally, the prospect of another dreary day would have soured his mood. Reared in the southernmost nib of the Rio Grande Valley as he was, his blood had been boiled thin by the Texas heat, his soul stone-bleached by the subtropical sun. This morning, though, the stormy skies suited him. What better companion to the acid drizzle corroding the lining of his gut?

Gavallan drove the Mercedes hard, shifting down through the gears, enjoying the engine's finely tuned growl, loving the communion of man and machine. He cracked the window an inch, and a blast of sea air freshened the car. Directly ahead lay the bay, and for a moment he lost himself in its blind expanse, wondering how much time had passed since so much had ridden on a single day's outcome. The answer came immediately. Eleven years and five months. It was the calendar against which he measured his life. There was before the Gulf War and after the Gulf War. And sinking deeper into the black bucket seats, he felt himself strapped inside the cockpit of his F-117 Nighthawk, the turbofan engine rumbling to life beneath him, G suit tight across the waist, hugging his legs and his back. He recalled, too, the shortness of breath beneath the confident smile, the tingling that had taken hold of his stomach as he gave the thumbs-up and taxied onto the runway for takeoff that first night.

A tingling not so different from the one he felt this morning.

Shaking off the memory, Gavallan drove his foot against the accelerator, taking the sports car to seventy miles an hour. The rain hardened and a gust sheeted the windshield with water. Blinded, he downshifted expertly, braking as he crested Russian Hill. "Instrument conditions," he whispered, eyes scanning dials and gauges. A moment later, the wipers cleared the screen. Off to his right loomed the Transamerica Tower, a pale triangular needle framed by a score of steel and concrete skyscrapers. The buildings were dark, except for random bands of light encircling their highest floors. He glanced at the mute forms a moment longer, feeling a kinship with those already at their desks. He'd always thought there was something daredevilish about starting the workday at four in the morning, something not completely sane. It had the whiff of tough duty that had always attracted him, the raised bar of an elite.

At age thirty-eight, John J. Gavallan, or "Jett" as he was known to friends and colleagues, was founder and chief executive of Black Jet Securities, an internationally active investment bank that employed twelve hundred persons in four countries around the globe. Black Jet was a full-service house, offering retail and institutional brokerage, corporate finance advice, and merger and acquisition services. But IPOs had been the ladder it had climbed to prominence. Initial public offerings. The company had made its fortune in the technology boom of the late nineties and, to Gavallan's dismay, it was still suffering a financial hangover from those halcyon days.

Nine years he'd been at it. Up at three, to work by four, finished twelve hours later, fourteen on a busy day. Once, the days had passed with astonishing rapidity. Success was an opiate and mornings bled into evenings in a hazy, frenetic rush. Lately, the clock had assumed a less benign stance. Time meant money, and every month that passed with revenue goals unmet was another inch cut from Black Jet's financial tether.

Dropping a hand to the stereo, Gavallan spun the dial to National Public Radio. The 4 A.M. business report was under way, a summary of action on the world's major markets. God, let it be an up day, he thought. In Asia, the Nikkei and Hang Seng Indexes had closed higher, both with solid gains. In Europe, markets were divided, with the London FTSE, or "footsie," strongly ahead and the German DAX and French CAC 40 *("cack quarante")* lagging only slightly below their highs. But what about New York? He'd been in the business long enough to know there was only one market that really counted. A moment later he had his answer. At seven-oh-five Manhattan time, the futures markets were up sharply, presaging a solid opening in just over two hours.

"Nice!" he said aloud, landing his palm against the

varnished oak steering wheel for good measure. It didn't take a genius to know it was best to sell in an up market. But just as quickly his exuberance faded, replaced by a cold apprehension. If all went well, he could celebrate at the end of the day. For now, though, he had to wait. Too many cards remained facedown on the table.

THE OFFICES OF BLACK JET SECURITIES occupied the fortieth and forty-first floors of the Bank of America Tower, a fifty-two-story slab of red carnelian marble not dissimilar to Mies van der Rohe's Seagram Building in New York. The elevator opened, disgorging Gavallan into a brightly lit reception area. Sofas and chairs upholstered in Corinthian leather offset terra-cotta carpeting. A combed birch counter stood to the left, and behind it a seven-foot wall of polished black granite bearing the firm's name in silver matte letters.

"*Six days!*"

Gavallan slowed, turning to meet the source of the words.

"Six days," Bruce Jay Tustin repeated, cresting the interior staircase that led from the trading room on the floor below. "The countdown for Mercury is on. T minus a hundred twenty-two hours. Fuckin' A, bubba!" Tustin was the firm's head of syndicates as well as a member of the executive board. He was forty-five years old, short, and svelte, a bantamweight clad in a Brioni suit. He had a boxer's mug, too—the broad forehead; the flat, broken nose; the sly, determined cast to the eyes.

"How's the book?" Gavallan asked. "Holding strong?" The "book" referred to the nimble piece of software that held all orders and indications of interest for the new issue.

"A few cries in the jungle, but we're working to calm the savages."

Gavallan sensed there was more to it. "Any of the major players backing out?"

"Just one so far. Mutual Advantage in Cincy canceled their order. Said they wanted to put the money into bonds. Doesn't look like anyone else is taking the rumors seriously. The market wants this deal to happen."

"Let's stop it there, Bruce. I don't want a snowball effect. We're standing behind the deal one hundred and ten percent. Keep putting the word out: Mercury is hunky-dory."

Tustin nodded obediently. "You find out who it is bad-mouthing us? Not one of your girlfriends, is it?"

Gavallan shook his head, thinking that someday Tustin's mouth was going to kill him. "Not yet. But we're looking."

"Ah, that's right, I forgot. *She left you.* Hang in there, kid. You're young yet." Tustin clapped Gavallan on the back. Features brightening, he added, "Opening's looking strong, *Jefe.* The market's getting primed for Mercury. Six days. Hoo-yeah!" And pumping his right fist in the air, he spun and bustled down the steps to the trading floor.

"Hoo-yeah," repeated Gavallan, but his parting smile disguised a pressing urge to get to his office. Walking briskly, he shifted his calfskin satchel to his left hand while withdrawing a set of keys from his pocket.

At first glance, he looked more the affluent bachelor than the driven executive. Tall and fit, he'd dressed for the day in his usual outfit: jeans, moccasins, and a faded chambray shirt, throwing on a navy cashmere blazer for good measure. He was finished with uniforms, be they dress blues or three-button worsteds from Savile Row. In the same disobedient spirit, he kept his sandy hair cut long, sure that it brushed his collar and hid the tops of his ears. His face was strong rather than handsome. Creases dimpled weathered cheeks. Wrinkles bracketed eyes hard and gray as agate. His nose was slim and straight, the boldest testament to his Scottish ancestry. His jaw was steadfast, and as usual raised an extra degree, as if he were trying to peer over the horizon. A pillar of the yacht club, you might guess. A regular at the nine-teenth hole.

But a second look would give you pause. His gaze was direct, and when not combative, confrontational. His gait was compelling and hinted at tensions simmering within, some urgent, inner purpose. You would never, for example, stop him on the street to ask for directions. It was his hands, though, that gave him away. They were the hands of a brawler, large and callused, the knuckles swollen from long-ago fights. No Ivy Leaguer he, you might say, and take a step back. This one was hewn from rougher stock. This one had required polishing.

Even at this hour, the hallways were abuzz. The day's first conference call originated at four-thirty. Everyone present in the office at that hour—usually about sixty traders, analysts, and brokers—gathered in the company conference room to share earnings announcements, an-alysts' reports, and street gossip with branches in New York and London. Video cameras, color monitors, and microphones linked the participants, and for thirty min-utes they hashed out anything that might boost a par-ticular stock's price or knock it down. Information was the market's universal deity—rational, impartial, and above all merciless—and it was worshiped accordingly.

Inside his office, Gavallan turned on the light. A glance at his watch gave him ten minutes until the conference call began. Not bothering to unbutton his jacket, he sat at his desk and checked his E-mail. Seventy-four new messages had come in since yesterday evening. Hurriedly, his eyes scanned the flat panel screen. The usual brokerage rec-ommendations: Buy Sanmina, hold Microsoft; so-and-so initiating coverage on Nortel. Delete. Delete. Delete. Notes from a few venture capitalists in the Valley. An invitation to a golf tournament in Vegas. "Don't think so," he muttered, hitting the delete key; he'd take his clubs out of storage when the world righted itself. A smattering of messages from his colleagues in the firm. He'd check these later.

"Byrnes, Byrnes, where are you, buddy?" He looked for Grafton Byrnes's handle but didn't see anything. "Damn it," he muttered, rocking in his chair.

He'd hardly slept, expecting his number two to call with an update on the trip to Moscow. At the least, he'd hoped for an E-mail. Finding nothing, he unlocked the top drawer of his desk and located a square slip of paper bearing the initials G.B. and a ten-digit number. He picked up the phone and dialed.

"Hotel Baltschug Kempinski. Good afternoon."

Gavallan snapped to attention. "Yes, good afternoon. I'd like to speak with one of your guests. Mr. Grafton Byrnes."

"One moment."

Where are you, my boy? he wondered, drumming his fingers impatiently on the desk. You're my ace in the hole. Pick up the goddamn phone and tell me everything's all right. Tell me I was a fool to worry and that we can put some champagne and caviar on ice for our European friends.

"Mr. Byrnes is not in the hotel."

"Very good," said Gavallan, though in fact he was curious as to why Byrnes hadn't finished his work yet. Drawing a manila file from his desk, he flipped open the cover. Inside lay the photographs—the reasons for Grafton Byrnes's last-minute trip.

The first showed the façade of a two-story building that could have been a warehouse or a manufacturing plant. A sign above the entry read "Mercury Broadband." The photo was captioned "Moscow Network Operations Mainstation." A second picture purported to show the building's interior: room after room packed with standard telephone switching equipment, circa 1950, gray rectangular dinosaurs sprouting black connector cables like unruly hair.

Founded in 1997, Mercury Broadband was the leading provider of high-speed Internet service in Russia, the Ukraine, Belarus, and the Czech Republic—an area that Gavallan, with his training as a Cold War jet jock, would forever think of as "the communist bloc." Through its network of coaxial cable, fixed wireless, and satellite relays, Mercury Broadband serviced over two million businesses and residential customers and had contracted rights to service an additional twenty-seven million. It also packaged and offered multimedia content and E-commerce in the form of Red Star, a multilingual portal similar to America Online that boasted over seven million subscribers.

But here was the good part: Not only had the company doubled its revenues each of the last three years, it had begun turning a profit as of third-quarter fiscal 2000. In six days, Black Jet Securities would take Mercury Broadband public on the New York Stock Exchange in an IPO set to raise two billion dollars. The seventy million in fees the deal generated was crucial to relieving Black Jet's worsening financial malaise. Every bit as important was the boost to the company's reputation a successful offering would bring. From regional mighty mite to international presence in one fell swoop.

Which brought Gavallan back to the photographs. He had another picture in his manila file, also purporting to show the interior of the Moscow network operations center. This one positively beamed with the latest in Internet hardware—Sun servers, Cisco routers, Lucent switches—and it was this photo he'd showed to his investors.

"I'd like to leave a message," he said. "Please tell him Mr. Gavall—"

"Mr. Byrnes is not in the hotel," the Russian operator interrupted.

"Yes, I heard you. If you don't mind I'd like to leave a—"

"No sir, you do not understand," cut in the operator again. "Mr. Byrnes has checked out."

"That's not possible. He's not due to return to the States until tomorrow. Please check again." And before the operator could protest, he shouted, "Do it!"

"Very well." The "sir" was distinctly missing.

Confused, Gavallan ran his eyes over the computer screen, reconfirming he hadn't received any E-mails from Byrnes. His instructions had been clear: Once Graf picked up something about Mercury—*good or bad*—he was to let Gavallan know. Immediately.

"Sir? Our records indicate that Mr. Byrnes checked out of the hotel yesterday evening at eleven-thirty."

"Eleven-thirty? You're sure?"

Moscow was eleven hours ahead of San Francisco; 11:30 P.M. in the Russian capital meant lunchtime in the office. Byrnes had called in four hours before that, at around eight yesterday morning, to report that he'd arrived safely and would start his investigations the next day. The notion that he'd checked out without spending the night was as unsettling as it was absurd.

"Mr. Byrnes is no longer a guest with us," replied the operator. "If you'd like to speak with our general manager, I'd be happy to connect you."

"No. That won't be necessary."

"*Po Zhausta. Da Svidaniya.*"

Gavallan put down the phone and strode to the window. For a long time, he remained still, looking out over the city. Through the rain, he could make out Telegraph Hill, and beyond it the bow lights of a supertanker advancing slowly out to sea. Farther to his left, pale red beacons glimmered atop the cable towers of the Golden Gate Bridge. Staring at the melancholy panorama, he experienced a sudden tremor, a shiver that rustled his spine and caused him to cross his arms and hug himself as if fending off a stern winter's breeze. It was the same yawn of anxiety that had passed over him two days earlier, when on a foggy Monday morning he'd first broached the idea of a trip to Moscow to Grafton Byrnes.

3

So you've seen it?" Gavallan had demanded as Grafton Byrnes entered his office.

"Yeah, I've seen it," answered Byrnes with a calm Gavallan did not share. "Not the best PR one of our deals has ever gotten, but not the worst, either."

"I'm not so sure. Timing couldn't be worse, that's for certain."

Byrnes strolled across the room with the easy authority that was his trademark. He was taller by an inch, dressed in a navy crew neck sweater over a white oxford button-down, brown corduroy slacks, and Belgian loafers polished to a spit shine. His face was craggy and lean, with eyes that appraised but never accused, and a smile that forgave all sins.

"Want something to drink? Pellegrino?" Gavallan spun in his chair and opened the compact refrigerator hidden in his credenza. "I've got one of those new lattes in a bottle. How 'bout that?"

Byrnes took up position behind him, peering over his shoulder. "Nothing with caffeine, thanks. I'll take a mineral water. No, no . . . one without any bubbles."

Gavallan handed him a bottle of Ozarka and selected an ice-cold can of Orange Crush for himself. He considered his teenager's sweet tooth his only vice. Vintage European automobiles, chilled Russian vodka, and Stevie Ray Vaughan playing the blues at excruciating volumes counted as passions, and were thus exempt.

"Skoal, brother," he said, lifting the can of soda pop.

"Skoal, my man."

It was a joke between Texans, "Skoal" being both an informal "Cheers" and the tried-and-true chewing tobacco of their youths.

Gavallan had known Grafton Byrnes his entire adult life. They had met at the Air Force Academy in Colorado Springs, where Byrnes had played regimental commanding officer to Gavallan's plebe. Every time Gavallan mouthed off, it was Byrnes who administered the punishment. A hundred push-ups on the deck. A thousand-yard sprint in shorts and tennis shoes through waist-high drifts of midwinter snow. Two hours of reciting the Uniform Code of Military Justice while doing Roman chairs against the commons room wall. If harsh, the abuse was well-intentioned. It was Byrnes's job to make sure Cadet John J. Gavallan made it through the Zoo, and to that end he tutored him in calculus, instructed him on how to properly hold his knife and fork, and taught him to iron a razor-sharp crease into his trousers.

Retiring from the Air Force a major, Byrnes had followed him to Stanford Business School, then to Black Jet Securities two years after its founding. He was pretty much Gavallan's older brother, and as close a friend as he could ever hope for.

"You know this guy, the Private Eye-PO?" Gavallan asked.

Byrnes shrugged, offering a wry smile. "I do now. Who is he exactly? Or should I say 'what'? Some sort of Internet gadfly?"

"You could say that. Calls himself the Robin Hood of the Valley's pink slip brigade. He spies on the rich to protect the poor."

"The poor being who?" smirked Byrnes. "The laid-off techies who can't afford their Beamer payments?"

"More like the average investor who lost his shirt when tech stocks took a beating."

"Oh, you mean our retail clientele. So he's the bastard responsible for the plunge in our commission revenues. Got it."

Outside, a blanket of fog sprawled across the Bay Area, a pea soup so thick Gavallan had trouble making out the gargoyles on the roof of the Peabody Building a hundred feet away. Rising from his chair, he circled the desk, swiveling the computer monitor 180 degrees so they could both read from the screen. As usual the Private Eye-PO's posting was written in a style somewhere between the Motley Fool and a fifties Hollywood tabloid.

For weeks now, Wall Street has been in a lather for the $2 billion Mercury Broadband deal being brought to market by Black Jet Securities. Well, kids, your own Private Eye-PO has learned that the offering is fully subscribed, with plenty of savvy investors looking to get in on the action. Caveat emptor. Mercury is not what it appears. My own no less savvy gum-shoes swear to me that Mercury is only a shadow of its trumped-up self, and Red Star, a sheep in AOL's clothing. What do you expect from Black Jet Securities, itself a pretender to the throne? When will Mr. Gavallan learn? Black Jet can never be white-shoe. But, hey, friends, why listen when you can look? After all, isn't seeing believing?

"You sure you don't know this guy?" asked Byrnes. "This stuff sounds almost personal. He had as much fun knocking you as he did Mercury."

"No one knows him," Gavallan replied testily. "That's his gig. He keeps a bag on his head while he goes around savaging companies. Mercury's not the first company he's skewered."

"I suggest we find him on the double and shut him up."

"I know a guy we can call. Does some work for the government. I'll get on it right away." Sighing, Gavallan turned away from the monitor, massaging the bridge of his nose with his thumb and forefinger. "Every time I read it I feel like I've been socked in the gut. This is not what we need right now."

"No, it's not," Byrnes agreed, "but it's what we got, so we deal with it and move on." His eyes narrowed with concern over a different matter. "You okay, kid? You look a little tired."

"Yeah, yeah, I'm fine. It's just this on top of all the other crap lately . . ." The words trailed off.

"If it's Manzini who's bothering you, forget it. You had to let his team go. They knew the rules. Around here you eat what you kill. We're not a bulge bracket firm that can rely on our granddaddy's clients to throw us some scraps. GM's not knocking down our door wondering if we might underwrite some debt for them. IBM isn't about to ask us to do a secondary offering. We have to go out and get it."

"Yeah," said Gavallan. "We make money the old-fashioned way—*we earn it.*"

"Damn right," said Byrnes emphatically. "Don't beat yourself up over it. They were lucky you kept them on as long as you did. Half those guys were earning a base of three hundred. Look, the Internet vertical was dying. They didn't produce, they got canned. End of story. We're not running a charity here."

A "vertical" was banking jargon for a particular industry segment. The tech sector was divided into E-commerce, web infrastructure, optical equipment, software, and so on. Each vertical was assigned a team of bankers to service businesses operating in that sector. The team consisted of an equity analyst, a few capital markets specialists, the investment bankers who actually drummed up the business, and two or three associates to do the grunt work.

"I'm well aware of that," said Gavallan. "Next time it can be your turn to fire the guy you've been going to Warrior games with for five years. Carroll Manzini's a friend."

But he could see from Byrnes's skeptical expression that he wasn't buying. Byrnes had a more unyielding attitude toward business. You performed or you got cut. That simple. He'd governed by the same draconian principles when Gavallan had served under him at Stealth training in Tonopah, Nevada, the two-thousand-square-mile cut of yucca and scrub known to conspiracy buffs as Area 51. The funny thing was that back then Gavallan had been happy to live by those rules. He was as confident of his own skills as he was disdainful of the saps who didn't make the grade.

Strangely, as chief executive of Black Jet Securities, he was unable to demand of his employees the uncompromising standards he asked of himself. He regretted the most recent firing of twenty-six of his executives and couldn't help but feel in some way responsible for their inability to generate income for the firm. So what if financing activity in the Internet sector had dried up as quickly as a summer squall? That not a single IPO had been done for an Internet play in months? Or that every other bank on the street had slashed their staffs long before?

Frustrated, Gavallan looked around his office. It was large but modest, with tan carpeting, textured ecru wallpaper, and comfortable furniture arranged to promote informal discussions with clients. A floor-to-ceiling window ran the length of the room and gave the office a stagelike feel. The plummeting vista was nothing short of spectacular, and nearing the window more than one client had professed an incipient acrophobia. A second glass wall ran along the interior corridor. When Gavallan was alone at his desk, he made every effort to keep the blinds open, as well as the door. He detested the trappings of authority and wanted everyone at Black Jet to know he was available at all times.

"Maybe you're right," he conceded. "I'm just lousy at that kind of thing. It's easier to hire a man than to kick him out on his tail."

"Oh, but if the world were a fair place," said Byrnes, bowing an imaginary violin.

"Get out of here," said Gavallan. "Come on, cut it out. You look really stupid doing that."

He knew his ideas about an employer's duty were old-fashioned, but he stuck with them nonetheless. His father had worked on the cutting line at Martinez Meats in Harlingen, Texas, for forty years. Forty years hacking the hindquarter off a flayed steer's carcass, eight hours a day, five days a week, in a fluorescent-lit factory that breathed blood and sweated ambition, where temperatures routinely soared to a hundred degrees during the six-month summer. The Martinez family might not splurge on luxuries like air-conditioning and they certainly didn't pay much. (Gus Gavallan's weekly salary of $338 came tucked in a wax-paper envelope delivered Monday mornings at nine o'clock sharp, so that the younger men wouldn't drink their paycheck over the weekend.) But neither did they fire their staff. In those forty years, Martinez Meats never let go a single man or woman except for absence, tardiness, or public inebriation, and his father's devotion to the Martinez family was nearly religious.

Black Jet had barely been in business nine years and Gavallan had already fired, let go, laid off, made redundant—however you wanted to put it—over a hundred men and women, including the latest casualties, Carroll Manzini's tech-team of banking superstars, twenty-six strong. The thought pained him. He wanted to believe that the bond between a man and his employer went beyond business to family. It was a social contract that exchanged loyalty and service for welfare and security. Maybe he was foolish. Maybe at seventeen thousand dollars a year you had a right to that kind of paternalistic relationship. At half a million bucks plus bonus you were on your own.

Byrnes laid a hand on his shoulder and gave it a squeeze. "Toughen up, kid," he said. "Look at you. Your chin's falling into your neck, your ass is dragging, and God knows you need a haircut. And that whining ... Christ, you sound like a dooly crying during Hell Week. The Gavallan I knew was a rock. You didn't say a goddamn word that day up at Alamogordo. Not before, during, or after. A fuckin' rock, man."

"Easy to be a rock when you're border trash that doesn't know any better," retorted Gavallan, but already he was smiling, feeling a little better. He was remembering the day in Alamogordo. August 2, 1986. Lead-in-Fighter Training.

THE WEATHER HAD BEEN PERFECT, hot and mostly clear, with only a few thunderheads to keep away from. The two of them were up in a T-38 jet trainer, Byrnes already a combat-tested pilot, the instructor, and Gavallan his student. After an hour of practicing basic fighter maneuvers, the two were heading in for landing, making plans to rendezvous at the O-club for a few beers and a steak after debrief. Then—*Bam!*—without warning, the jet's turbine engine had exploded, severing the hydraulic main, ripping off a chunk of the tail, and sending the plane into wild, uncontrollable gyrations at four hundred knots. One second they were flying level, the next they were pitching wildly, rolling and yawing, the burnt scrub of New Mexico changing places with the powder blue sky with sickening frequency.

Standing in his office, Gavallan jolted. Sixteen years

after the fact, he could hear the whine of the disintegrating engine, the whoosh of the violated air as it battered the jet. Mostly, he recalled the adrenaline rush, the iron fingers grasping his heart and crushing it mercilessly.

"Everything's copacetic," had come Byrnes's voice, calm as a Sunday morning. "Just let me take care of this fire and we'll be jim-dandy to land." And in the same unbothered delivery, he'd begun ticking off the measures to regain control of the plane—depress rudder, bring up left aileron, release the stick to let the nose find its way down.

But strapped into the front seat, Gavallan knew damn well everything was not copacetic. His eyes were glued to the altimeter, watching it tick down from four thousand feet at a hundred feet a second. He could feel the G forces increasing, driving him deeper into his seat, nailing his arms to his side. As he counted the seconds until they augered in, his hands automatically reached for the side of his seat, searching for the ejection handles. But when he found them, he immediately let them go. It was an act of betrayal. Of disbelief. No, it was worse. It was a pilot's cardinal sin: the acknowledgment of his own fallibility.

The altimeter spun merrily counterclockwise, passing eight hundred feet, seven hundred, six. . . . The plane came out of its death spiral, the nose pointed straight down toward the arid landscape. Gripped with a quiet terror, he waited for the nose to rise. A series of prayers stumbled from his lips. When that failed him, he swore silently. *Come on, you son of a bitch. Come up. Just a little, you mutha, just a little!*

Slowly, the plane righted itself. The nose inched up, the wings leveled to the horizon. And as the ground zipped beneath their wings close enough to slap a longhorn's rump, Byrnes chuckled, as if the whole escapade had been engineered for Gavallan's amusement.

"What'd I tell you, rookie?" he asked.

After landing, the two accomplished their postflight inspection of the debilitated aircraft. A four-by-four-foot section of crumpled metal dangled from the tail, secured by an aluminum thread no wider around than a pencil. Viewing the damage, neither Byrnes nor Gavallan commented. They simply exchanged glances and shrugged their shoulders. That night, "everything's copacetic" entered lore, meaning, of course, just the opposite—that nothing could be more screwed up.

"Okay, okay. I get the message," said Gavallan, walking to his chair and sitting down. "Slap me around a little if I start feeling sorry for myself again."

"Yes sir. You're the boss."

Gavallan eyed Byrnes suspiciously. Sometimes he wasn't so sure. "Look, the pictures of Mercury's network operations center are fakes. I know that company inside and out. The only question is what we're going to do about it."

"You've talked to Kirov?"

"He called me a few minutes ago. He was livid. Said the comments were nonsense. A ploy to drive down the offering price. He hinted it might be political. He wasn't sure, yet."

"Political? Come off it. If there's one thing I can tell you about the Private Eye-PO, it's that he's as American as apple pie. Still glad you crawled into bed with the enemy?"

"Kirov's hardly the enemy. We checked him out backwards and forwards. Even Kroll gave him a clean bill of health. No ties to the *mafiya*, no indentures to the government, no evidence of corruption or criminal activity. Konstantin Kirov's the first—"

"Stop right there," blurted Byrnes. "I know what you're going to say. He's 'the first truly Western businessman.' The *Financial Times* said that, right? 'The patron saint of the second Russian perestroika.' Remember, Jett, I read the prospectus, too."

Gavallan shook his head. Byrnes would always be an unrepentant cold warrior. "You know, Graf, you missed your calling. You should start up a new chapter of America Firsters. Bring isolationism back into vogue."

"Okay, okay," said Byrnes, lifting his hands palm up. "He's a wild card, that's all I'm saying."

"Well, he's *our* wild card, so you better get used to him. If the Mercury IPO goes well, we'll be doing business with Kirov for a decade. We're already talking a secondary offering in a year, and he's asked us to scout some acquisition targets for him. Mercury's a gusher waiting to be tapped, and we're darned lucky they chose us to do the drilling. He asked me if I wanted him to send over his jet to bring me to Moscow. He wants to personally show me the premises. He's worried about how the market's taking it."

"And how *is* the market taking it?" asked Byrnes. "What's the word from Bruce?"

"Too soon to tell, but this kind of thing is never good. We'll need to engage in some proactive damage control."

"So you believe Mr. Kirov?"

"A hundred percent."

"All right then. Let's look at this closer."

Digging his hands into his pockets, Grafton Byrnes began a slow circuit of the room. "This is an accusation of material fraud. The Private Eye-PO isn't just saying that Mercury isn't up to snuff, he's implying we knew all about it, too, and kept our mouths shut. If those photos are genuine, there's no way Mercury can be doing the business it claims. Two hundred thousand clients in Moscow? Hell, they couldn't service twenty with that stuff. These accusations are tantamount to saying the company's entire P&L is a bunch of garbage. We've got to imagine that most of our customers will either read this or get wind of it and come to the same conclusions themselves. In a few hours, every one of Bruce Jay Tustin's salesmen will be fielding calls asking for us to comment on the Private Eye-PO's claims. Whether we believe Kirov or not, we've got to check on Mercury."

"Agreed."

"And not under his personal auspices, I'm afraid. Tell him you'll pass on the jet. I'll give Silber, Goldi, and Grimm a call instead." Byrnes was talking about the Swiss accounting firm that had performed the due diligence on the deal. "They're in Geneva; it's only a two-hour flight for them. They can have this sorted out by the end of business tomorrow."

"No go," responded Gavallan. "I don't want to bring an outside firm into this. It's too late for that. We can't have anyone thinking we have even the slightest doubts about Mercury, not this far into the quiet period. One of us has to go. Like you said, our head is on the chopping block as much as Mercury's."

"One of us?" Byrnes did not look pleased.

"I'd go if I could, you know that. I've got the dinner on Wednesday."

"Yeah, yeah, I know. Since when did hospitals start honoring border trash as 'Man of the Year'? I'll miss heckling you. I had a few choice tomatoes saved for the occasion." Byrnes collapsed onto the sofa, resting his chin on folded hands. "And how will your friend Kirov feel about this? He's bound to find out."

"He won't like it, but he'll understand," explained Gavallan. "He knows what's involved to get a listing on the Big Board. In the end, he'll thank us for it."

"I hope so. I don't relish getting a guided tour of the Lubyanka."

Rolling his eyes, Gavallan opened the drawer and took out a plane ticket. He'd known all along the actions required of the firm. He'd just wanted Byrnes's opinion on the matter. "Flight goes at one," he said, waving the slim jacket. "Consulate opens at eight. You'll need a visa.

If you hurry, you might even have time to get home and pack."

Byrnes picked up the ticket off the desk, opening the sleeve and reading over the flight details. "You're a crafty prick, you know that?"

"What do you expect? I learned from the best."

RECALLING THE MOMENT forty-eight hours earlier, Gavallan caught his reflection in the glass. He was surprised at the man staring back. He looked tired and worn, older than his years. The weight of office, he told himself. The price for making a fortune before the age of forty. And the price for losing it? he wondered. What's that? Do you get some of your youth back? Learn how to take a few days off? Regain the affections of the woman you love?

Gavallan put a stranglehold on his thoughts. Self-pity was a loser's luxury. He heard Byrnes telling him to "toughen up" and felt the wise eyes boring into him.

Graf, where the hell are you? Give me a call and tell me everything's all right.

A minute passed as Gavallan considered taking a dozen actions: canvassing the larger hotels in the Russian capital, contacting the U.S. Embassy in Moscow, even calling the Moscow Police directly. All were premature. If Byrnes had checked out of the Baltschug, he had a good reason. It was silly to worry. He'd give his best friend until noon to call or check in, then reassess the situation.

A firm hand rapped on his door. "Morning meeting's about to start, boss."

"Yeah," said Gavallan, without turning. "Be right there."

Returning to his desk, he made a quick check of his agenda. As always, his schedule was packed to bursting. Quarterly earnings review at ten. A powwow to go over acquisition candidates for a new client at eleven. Round-table with the executive board to discuss new business opportunities at two. And, of course, the black-tie dinner that evening for which he had yet to write a speech.

But even as he catalogued his day's appointments, his thoughts vaulted six thousand miles to the onion domes and cobblestoned streets of a city he'd known forever, but never visited. Moscow.

Graf, he shouted silently. *Talk to me!*

4

GRAFTON BYRNES WAS STILL TRYING to figure out when exactly they had left the city and entered the country. It seemed like only five minutes ago they'd been barreling down the road to Sheremetyevo Airport, the driver busily pointing out Dynamo Stadium, home to Moscow's soccer team, the Ministry of the Interior building built by Stalin, the new Seventh Continent supermarket. Then they'd made a left turn past a car dealership, traveled a ways through a birch forest, and—*bang!*—they were in the Russian countryside. Eight lanes had dwindled to four, and then two, and now they were bouncing down a dirt road smack in the middle of a potato patch that stretched as far as the eye could see in every direction.

Byrnes took out the paper on which he'd written the address of Mercury Broadband's network operations center. "Rudenev Ulitsa?" he asked skeptically, gesturing at the road beneath them.

"*Da*. Rudenev," said his Tatar chauffeur. He blurted a few words in Russian that Byrnes caught as "Long street. Goes to city of Rudenev."

"*Eto Daleko?* Is it far?"

"*Nyet.*" The man shook his head emphatically. "Very close now."

Byrnes looked at him a second longer, wondering if he might be possessed of some criminal intent. He dismissed the thought out of hand. If the guy wanted to rob him, all he had to do was pull over on any side street and stick a gun in his face. A look over his shoulder confirmed they were not being followed. The road behind them was empty, desperately so. Svetlana's or Tatiana's—or *whatever her name was*—protectors were no doubt still at Metelitsa, concentrating their efforts on the next unlucky schlemiel. He stared at the setting sun, a dusky orange dome melting into the infinite plain. Russia, he thought, shaking his head. It was like watching a sunset on another planet.

They passed a row of dachas, small brightly painted cottages with steep, angular roofs. He'd always imagined dachas to be quaint, well-constructed cabins that lay hidden in pine glades. Maybe some were. These, however, were slapdash and garish, one plunked down next to the other with not a green tree in sight. The dachas looked uncared-for, as did the gardens and fences that surrounded them. In fact, his one overwhelming impression of Russia so far was of neglect. Offices with shattered windows, roads scarred with potholes, cars rusted beyond belief. He refused to think about the fire escape he'd climbed down an hour ago. He had a feeling the country was running as fast as it could just to stay in the same place. If he'd seen a mule pulling a hay cart, he wouldn't have been surprised. Somewhere back there he hadn't left just Moscow, but the entire twentieth century.

A half mile down the road, a blue strobe flashed urgently. Gripping his hands on the dashboard, Byrnes leaned forward, willing his pilot's eyes to focus. He made out a stubby automobile bestriding the narrow road. The car was white with green doors. The traffic militia, Byrnes groaned inwardly. On his ride in from the airport, he'd noted several similar automobiles parked in the center of tangled intersections. In each case, an olive-smocked policeman had stood nearby paying no mind to the horns blaring around him, doing damned all to right the congested thoroughfares. In a country famous for its corruption, the traffic militia had a reputation second to none. He didn't care to imagine what had brought them this far into the countryside a few minutes before nightfall.

"Shit," spat the driver, clearly sharing his anxiety. Shooting a worried look Byrnes's way, he braked to a halt and produced his papers.

A pug-faced militiaman approached the car. Ducking low, he peered into the windows, looking between Byrnes and the Tatar. The disparity between the two couldn't have been greater: Byrnes in his custom-tailored suit and five-hundred-dollar shoes, the Tatar in worn wool trousers and a frayed red pullover. The militiaman said a few words, then backed away from the car.

"A bad accident ahead. The road is closed," explained the Tatar. "We must go back. But first he wants you to get out and show him your passport."

"I have to get out? How come?" Byrnes didn't know why he was so surprised. In anticipation of the request, he'd already removed his passport and slipped a hundred-dollar bill inside the cover. Preparing a servile smile, he stepped out of the car and walked toward the militiaman.

"Good evening," he said in halting Russian, wanting to show he was one of the good guys.

The militiaman approached slowly, rolling his boots, thumbs tucked into a heavy utility belt. He was a block of a man, more chunky than muscular, heavy around the shoulders and neck. He was dirty. Visibly dirty. Dirt flecked his cheeks. His hair was greasy and uncombed, his mustard uniform dotted with stains. Deliberately, he slid his baton from its holster.

"Passport," he grunted.

Byrnes eyed the baton. Dents and chips and scuffs decorated its length. Losing the smile, he handed over the passport. The baton flicked through the air, so fast as to be a blur, cuffing Byrnes's wrist and sending the passport tumbling to the road. "Hey," he shouted, grabbing at his hand. "Watch it, you sonuva—"

The next blow was faster, if that was possible. Harder, too—a lightning-quick jab to Byrnes's unsuspecting gut. The baton disappeared into his midsection before caroming back a split second later, robbing Byrnes of his belligerence as well as his breath. He fell to a knee, eyes bulging as he prayed for his lungs to start working again.

The militiaman pointed at the hundred-dollar bill lying on the ground. "Yours?" he grunted in English.

"No," coughed Byrnes.

The militiaman motioned for Byrnes to hand it to him. Struggling to his feet, Byrnes picked up the note and his passport and handed them to the policeman.

"*Spaseeba.*" The unkempt cop stared at the passport for a few seconds. "What hotel, please?"

"The Baltschug. In Moscow." From the corner of his eye, Byrnes could see the Tatar, standing at the rear of the car, hands folded in front of him, eyes making a meticulous study of the rocks near his shoes. The militiaman returned to his car, placed a call on his radio, smoked a cigarette, talked a little more on the two-way, then came back. Curling a finger, he motioned for the Tatar to join them. He barked a few words, looking at Byrnes.

"You are not guest at the Baltschug," the Tatar translated. "The hotel does not know you. The officer would like to know where you are staying, please?"

"The Baltschug." Byrnes could not keep the irritation from his voice. "I checked in at four o'clock. Room 335. Look, I have a key." He delved into his pocket for the room key. Not finding it, he tried the other pocket, then his jacket. He remembered the tempting blond leaning close to him, rubbing his leg. "Please tell the officer that he can accompany me back to the hotel. I'll be happy to show him my room. My suitcase, my clothing, everything is there."

But the militiaman was already shaking his head. An amused grin said he'd heard this one a hundred times before. "No," he said in his brusque English before rattling off a few more bursts at the Tatar.

"We must go," said Byrnes's chauffeur worriedly, pulling at his sleeve. "The road is closed. A bad accident farther on."

"Go? Hold on a goddamn minute," cried Byrnes, freeing himself. "The guy still has my passport. I'm not going anywhere." He took a step toward the police officer, his ingrained belief in law and order overruling his common sense. "I'm an American citizen. You have no right to keep my passport. Please, I'd like it back."

"When you check into a hotel, you are to call police," explained the Tatar, scuttling back to the Lada. "They will bring you passport. Now please, we go."

"Ask him how much he wants for it. Here, here's another hundred." The militiaman feinted with the baton, and Byrnes jumped back. "You go," barked the policeman, ignoring the proffered currency. Then slipping the passport into his breast pocket, he ambled back to his beat-up patrol car.

Furious, Byrnes climbed into the Lada. The Tatar started the car, executed a neat three-point turn, then steered them back toward Moscow. Turning in his seat, Byrnes stared behind him. Fading into the distance was the same featureless vista that had played out before him for the past thirty minutes, a rutted, dusty road rolling like a draftsman's straightedge into the horizon. The Tatar began humming a tuneless melody, his breath whistling through chipped teeth. The car bumped along and Byrnes kept staring over his shoulder at the blinking strobes, feeling cheated and unjustly persecuted, asking himself what he might have done differently to effect a better outcome. He had no doubt he'd get his passport back—or that it would cost him another hundred dollars, if not more. He was sure the cop had never called the Baltschug. Of course, there was no accident, but his mind did not allow him to go any further. He waited until he could no longer see the militiaman, then said, "Stop."

The Tatar dashed an annoyed look his way. "We go home now. I take you to hotel. You sleep. I sleep. Okay?"

Byrnes slipped his wallet from his jacket and took out a hundred-dollar bill. "Stop," he repeated. "Please."

The Tatar sighed painfully, as if he knew what Byrnes was going to ask, then slowed the car.

"I must go to Rudenev," Byrnes said. Using his hands, he indicated his desire to make a bell-shaped detour around the militiaman. He was sure the Lada was sturdy enough to handle a few miles through hardscrabble fields. When the Tatar hesitated, Byrnes took out another hundred and pressed both bills into the man's creased palms. Two hundred dollars was probably double his monthly salary. "Please. It's important."

The Tatar stuffed the bills in his pocket and grunted as if Byrnes's request was but the final depredation forced upon him by a world going to the devil. Pulling off the road, he said, "I am Mikhail. Pleased to meet you. You are millionaire, maybe?"

Byrnes shook the callused hand. What was it about this place? "Graf. Likewise."

THEY DROVE THROUGH THE FIELDS for half an hour. The Lada bounced and groaned and rocked, keeping up a steady assault on the Russian potato industry. Never did the needle on the speedometer surpass twenty kilometers per hour. The sky was darkening quickly, and Byrnes thought if they didn't find the network operations center soon, he'd be spending the night in the countryside instead of in his four-hundred-dollar hotel room.

An outcropping of buildings came into shape a kilometer ahead. The silhouettes were low, right-angled, and unimaginative, no different than a strip mall or office park. He thought he could make out a satellite dish.

"Rudenev 99?"

"*Da.*"

Byrnes laughed, then clapped his hands and expelled a soft "Hooray!" He knew it was common for satellite downlinks and cable relays to be located at the periphery of metropolitan areas; land was cheaper there and it was easier to lay cable in undeveloped areas. He just hadn't expected to be so far outside the city. Only then did he make out the squadron of small trucks and automobiles parked in front of the buildings. Dark figures scurried like ants back and forth between the vehicles.

As they drew closer, he was able to discern four separate buildings, one at each corner of an intersection. The "ants" were workmen. Some were clad in overalls or jumpsuits, others in denim shorts and T-shirts. To a man, they were busy unloading large rectangular cartons from the trucks and carting them on dollies into the building with the satellite dish on its roof. No one paid the Lada any mind as it climbed onto the road and drew to a labored halt.

With a strong elbow and a few oaths, Byrnes opened the door. "Please wait," he said.

The driver got out of the car and lit a cigarette. Byrnes made a note to ask for his address so he could FedEx him a carton of Marlboros.

Buttoning his jacket, he set off through the throng,

intent on making his way into the building. He had only to glance at the cartons being wheeled inside to get a sharp, sick pain in his stomach. Now he knew what Jett had meant when he said he felt as if he'd been socked in the gut. Printed on the boxes were names like Dell, Sun, Alcatel, and Juniper—the brightest lights of the new economy. He walked stiffly, expecting at any moment to be stopped and asked who he was and what he was doing there.

The center of activity was a large warehouse painted a totalitarian gray, windowless and boasting double doors through which a nonstop stream of men filed in and out. Painted on the wall was the Mercury Broadband name and logo. He recognized the building from the picture the Private Eye-PO had posted on the web. No doubt about it: He was in the right place. Taking out his cell phone, he dialed the office. A recorded message informed him the call could not be completed at that time.

"Damn it," he muttered, sliding the phone back into his jacket.

Working to keep his gait slow, his bearing relaxed, Byrnes took up position by the front doors. Fluorescent lights blazed inside. The atmosphere was hushed, as reverential as that of a cathedral. The workmen kept to a long corridor, disappearing into another part of the building. What the hell, he said in a bid to buck himself up. You've come this far, why not go whole hog?

And tightening his tie, he ducked inside Mercury Broadband's Moscow network operations center.

HIS FIRST IMPRESSION was that the pictures were wrong.

The operations center was a model of its kind. Rack after rack of servers sat in black metal cages. Video cameras monitored every room. Liebert air conditioners kept the temperature an ideal sixty-five degrees. A corps of technicians manned a sophisticated console keeping tabs on the company's metropolitan operations. Every now and then a red light would flash on a map of the city, indicating a problem at a relay station or outlying node. Immediately, a technician would pick up the phone and attempt to solve the problem.

Byrnes slid from room to room, noticed but unquestioned, his suit and tie and confident posture as good as any E-ZPass. His relief in learning that the Private Eye-PO's pictures were bogus was outweighed only by his desire to know what in the world all the new equipment was being used for. He didn't remember reading any plans for a buildout of this proportion. As unobtrusively as possible, he followed the train of deliverymen through the corridors, passing from the main building to an outstation that had not been visible from the road. Just ahead, a security guard stood in front of a pair of swinging doors. He was holding a clipboard, and as each piece of equipment passed through the doors he checked both the item and the man's name against his list.

Byrnes allowed himself only a moment's hesitation. Then, hurrying his pace, he approached the security guard and handed him his business card. "Good evening," he said in English. "I'm a friend of Mr. Kirov's. He invited me to visit." And before the man could answer, Byrnes thanked him, smiled, and followed the next deliveryman through the doors.

He was standing inside a very large room, one hundred feet long and seventy feet wide. The floor was white. The walls were white. The ceiling was white, and from it hung rafts of fluorescent lights suspended by thin cables. Table after table ran the width of the room. On them was arrayed an army of personal computers: hundreds ... no, *thousands* of PCs arranged one after another in perfect rows. The screens blinked on and off. On and off. He walked closer. One screen read, "Welcome to Red Star. Please enter your password." The computer did as it was asked and the PC logged onto Mercury's signature portal. The welcome screen went blank, replaced a moment later by a familiar web page. Somewhere on the page, he read the greeting "Hello, Sergei Romanov," but a moment later the screen blinked and traveled to another electronic address. The PC continued its peripatetic iterations, bouncing from one site to another for a minute or two, then logging off. A few seconds passed, and it began the same trick again.

Byrnes advanced a few rows and watched another PC perform the same operations, only visiting different websites. He stood mesmerized, floating in a white universe of personal computers, wondering what the hell was going on. He took a few more steps and watched some more.

And then, it hit him.

Taking in the entire room at once, he whispered, "My God. It can't be."

WHEN HE EMERGED FIVE MINUTES LATER, his first act was to phone his office. It was near noon in San Francisco. This time the call went through.

"Yeah?" answered a familiar voice.

"Oh, it's you," said Byrnes, a little surprised that Gavallan hadn't answered his private line. "Where's Jett?"

"Not around right now. What's up?"

"Is he close by? It's important I talk to him."

Byrnes caught the sound of an engine revving hard and jogged toward the Lada. A gold Mercedes sedan was flying down the road, leaving a curtain of dust in its wake. No roadblock for him, Byrnes mused; no playing kissy-face with Uncle Vanya of the traffic militia.

"Where are you, Graf?" came the voice in his ear. "You sound a million miles away."

Byrnes tapped his foot nervously. No one but he and Gavallan knew about the excursion to Moscow. "Just get Jett. And hurry."

"Cool down. He's not here. I saw him a while ago, but he may have stepped out."

The Mercedes was a hundred yards away and showed no signs of slowing. Byrnes hesitated, hoping the sedan would pass through the intersection, knowing in his gut it was headed here, and that whoever was inside was looking for him. As the Russian police didn't drive late-model Mercedes that retailed for a hundred grand a pop, he had a feeling he was in for a rougher brand of justice. He looked around. It would be easy to duck back into the building, to hide among the workers. But why? He'd done nothing wrong. As Mercury's banker, he had every right to be here. His visit was unannounced, but not surreptitious. He had every intention of phoning Mr. Kirov once he assembled his findings. The thought of being found cowering inside an empty cardboard box decided the matter. Galvanized, his feet took firm possession of the ground, and he rummaged in his pockets for a business card.

"All right, all right, listen then," he said into the phone. "It's about Mercury. You have to tell Jett everything I'm about to say verbatim. You got that? Verbatim. You won't believe it."

And for the next sixty seconds he rattled off everything he'd seen inside the Moscow network operations center, stopping only when the Mercedes sedan had pulled to a halt ten feet away. "You got that?"

The voice sounded shocked. "Yeah, I got it. It just sounds a little crazy. I mean, that's not even possible, is it?"

But Byrnes didn't answer. By then, the door of the Mercedes had opened and Tatiana, or Svetlana, or whatever the gorgeous pickpocket with the satin blue eyes wanted to call herself, had stepped into the Russian night. In her hand she held her friend's nickel-plated Colt revolver, and she was pointing it at his chest.

"*Allo, Graf.*"

5

AT PRECISELY 7:15, Jett Gavallan ducked out of his office, took the elevator to the garage, and jumped behind the wheel of his Mercedes. The rain had stopped and traffic was light as he pulled onto the street two minutes later and accelerated east toward the Embarcadero. He didn't like being away from the office in the mornings; even the most important client meeting left him feeling like a choirboy locked outside of chapel. But today, there was nothing to be done. He had an appointment to keep, one that required discretion and a degree of stealth. One that on no account could be handled inside the walls of Black Jet Securities.

To his left, Chinatown passed in a blur of weeping pagodas and shuttered storefronts. Steering around slower cars, Gavallan made good time, managing to make every light on Pine Street without seeing so much as a hint of yellow. He did not notice the silver Ford Taurus tucked neatly into his lane three cars behind him, following at a discreet distance. If he had, he would have had no reason to be suspicious of it. The FBI was a professional organization. They had made it a point to change their tail car every day since taking up surveillance on Mr. John J. Gavallan ten days earlier.

Gavallan focused his mind on business. He had an earnings review at ten, and to prepare for it he'd spent an hour studying the firm's pro forma revenue estimates for the second quarter. The results were not encouraging. He was beginning to wonder if it wasn't the market that had gone sour, but his own touch.

"Nine years," he whispered to himself, recalling the arduous climb from one-man band to multinational touring act. Today, it felt like ninety.

GAVALLAN HAD FOUNDED Black Jet Securities one year out of Stanford Business School. He'd had offers from plenty of blue-chip firms—IBM, Goldman Sachs, Ford—but he'd turned them down. Six years in the Air Force had left him wary of institutional authority. Instead, he rolled up his sleeves, took a job with Sutro & Co., a smallish California investment bank, studied for his registered rep's license, and taught himself the investment business. Twelve months later, he quit his job and hung up his own shingle, taking with him a few of his largest clients and eighty thousand dollars in savings.

For a year or two, he was content to act as a broker-dealer, hiring registered reps and managing clients' money. But south of town, in Silicon Valley, things were happening that quickly caught his eye. Something called the Internet was springing to life, and overnight, companies eager to capitalize on its heralded, but unproven, potential were sprouting up like mushrooms. While their products and strategies differed wildly, they all shared one common trait: a dire, unquenchable need for cash.

It was into this market that Gavallan jumped headfirst in the fall of 1996. He didn't know much about initial public offerings, but that didn't matter. Nor did a lack of pedigree or track record. Jett Gavallan had something none of his rival investment bankers did. Something his business school profs would have labeled a "unique point of differentiation."

During the Gulf War, he had flown twenty-six missions at the controls of an F-117 Nighthawk, the angular black jet known to the world as the Stealth bomber. And there was nothing that a gaggle of laboratory-bred "techies" liked hearing better than what it was like to man the controls of the world's most technologically sophisticated aircraft and drop a laser-guided smart bomb smack on the top of a pack of kaftan-clad, Uncle Sam–jeering camel jockeys. Forget Quake. Forget Doom. Forget Tomb Raider. Here was the real McCoy. A first-person shooter with blood on his hands. And they would be proud to have him battle the wizards of Wall Street to secure funding on their behalf.

For two years, Gavallan traveled between the towns of San Mateo, Menlo Park, and Palo Alto. His first clients were small ones, rinky-dink start-ups happy to raise ten million dollars on the Pacific Stock Exchange. Computer jocks with dirty fingernails who worked in their pajamas. He did eight IPOs the first year. Twenty the second. In time his reputation grew, and with it the quality of his clients and his company's revenues. Black Jet's annual gross rose in a vertiginous spiral. Sixty million dollars, one hundred forty, four hundred. Amazingly, the firm managed to break a billion before the bubble broke and things went to hell.

Since then he'd been fighting to keep his head above water. The company was still making money, just not enough. He was sized for growth, not stasis. Euphemisms like "ramping up," "burn rate," and "top-heavy" and their connotations of boom and bust weren't solely the preserve of Silicon Valley.

He could imagine the earnings review later that morning. Retail brokering was coming back nicely, but nothing like it had been. IPO activity was only just recovering. M&A was off 20 percent the last two years. Only trading was making money, landing on the right side of the latest big leg up. As each managing director reported his or her results, their eyes would creep toward Gavallan. He knew the downcast glances, the uncomfortable silences, the nervous laughter by rote, each person wondering when the ax would fall, and whose head it would be thumping into the wicker basket. God, he hated being the executioner.

"We're not running a charity," Byrnes had said during their last meeting.

Gavallan was all too aware of the fact. Three times in the last year he'd dipped into his savings to fund increases in Black Jet's capital. He'd liquidated his portfolio of stocks, sold off a large chunk of real estate in Montana he'd been planning to build on for his retirement, and cashed out of a promising hedge fund. This morning, he would take the final plunge—a second mortgage on his home. After that ... An old adage about tapping a dry well came to mind.

Arriving at the Embarcadero, he was pleasantly surprised to find an empty space in front of the building. He parked hastily, telling himself that the space was an omen of good things to follow. Entering his attorney's office, Gavallan laughed at his desperation. He knew there was no such thing as good luck. Just good timing.

SPECIAL AGENT ROY DIGENOVESE, on temporary assignment to the San Francisco field office of the Federal Bureau of Investigation, double-parked the silver Ford Taurus a safe distance shy of Gavallan. Keeping the engine running, he rolled down the window and lit a cigarette. A glance in the side-view mirror confirmed that DiGenovese was Sicilian in looks as well as name. His hair was black, his eyes the color of midnight wine, his beard pushing up stubble three hours after he'd shaved. He had the brooding, patient gaze of a hunter, and a hundred years ago he might have been found wandering the rugged landscape of southern Sicily clad in chamois pants and a sheepskin vest, a *lupara* slung over one shoulder, tracking the wolves that regularly ravaged his family's flock. Today, DiGenovese might still be called a hunter, but his prey was decidedly human, and his arsenal more subtle than his ancestor's twelve-gauge shotgun.

Armed with a Juris Doctor and an MBA from New York University, a CPA's credential emblazoned upon his breastplate, Roy DiGenovese was the newest member of the FBI's Joint Russo-American Task Force on Organized Crime. Prior to his studies, he'd spent time in the U.S. Army, earning his Ranger's tab and serving with the 75th Ranger Regiment at Fort Benning, Georgia. Three years into what he hoped to be a lifelong career with the FBI, he was trim and muscular, and possessed of the same killer instinct as the wild-ass teenager who used to rappel out of helicopters in the dead of night, an M16 on his back and a K-bar strapped to his calf.

Setting the cigarette in the ashtray, DiGenovese picked up a scuffed Nikon from the seat beside him and brought it to his eye. The speed-wind whirred nicely as he fired off a dozen stills of Gavallan hauling himself out of the crazy old car with the gullwing doors. Even through the shutter, the man looked tired and in need of a break. It was easy to understand why. Seven days of following Gavallan had convinced DiGenovese he'd made the right decision not to take a job on Wall Street. Twelve hours a day cooped up inside a skyscraper was no way to go through life. The guy's desk might be made of mahogany, but the chain that tied him to it was pig iron, all the same.

As soon as Gavallan disappeared inside the sleek

office tower, DiGenovese exchanged the Nikon for a
two-way radio. "Zebra two, this is Zebra base, come in."

"Zebra two, roger."

"Maid gone?"

"Two minutes back. On her way to pew number seven
at St. Mary's as we speak."

"Good. Tell her to light a candle for us, we who are
about to sin."

Gavallan's maid, a middle-aged Guatemalan illegal
named Hortensia Estrada, hadn't missed morning mass
a single day that week. The service lasted between fifty
and sixty minutes, leaving DiGenovese's men plenty of
time to do their work.

"You're good to go, Zebra two," said DiGenovese.
"Time at target is thirty minutes. I repeat: three-zero
minutes. Are we clear?"

"Roger, Zebra base. Three-zero minutes. Walk in the
park."

ARE YOU SURE YOU WANT TO DO THIS?" Sten Norgren
asked, clutching a sheaf of manila folders, legal envelopes, and stray papers to his chest.

"Just give me the documents, Sten. It's not that big a
deal."

Hesitantly, Norgren laid the stack of papers on his
desk. "It's only for your protection," he pleaded in an injured tone. He was short and barrel-chested, with a florid,
cherubic face and curly blond hair. "Isn't it just a wee bit
crazy to stuff all your money in one investment?"

"Not if it's your own company," said Gavallan. "Besides, can I tell you a secret?" He motioned the attorney
closer. "That stuff about diversification? It's bullshit.
Just a ruse to bump up commissions. We can't have our
customers buying and holding the same stock for twenty
years at a time. We'd be bankrupt by Christmas. Sector

rotation, averaging in, market timing—that's the ticket. Churn and burn, Sten, that's the name of the game."

For a moment, Norgren didn't answer, and Gavallan could practically see the lawyer's analytical mind parsing over his statement, deciding whether what he said might actually be true. Then Norgren burst out, "Shut up, you bullshit artist. Sit your butt down in that chair, right now. I've got just the pen to sign your life away—a Mont Blanc that Sherry gave me for Christmas. Lousy thing cost more than my law school diploma."

Gavallan found his way to the chair and sat down. He had always hated lawyers' offices. He had only to set foot inside one for a feeling of imminent bad luck to creep into his neck and shoulders. Norgren's office was no exception, even with the Scandinavian furniture, the credenza packed with photos of blond, smiling kids, and the colorful modern art on the wall.

"Last chance," said Norgren.

"The pen, maestro."

Norgren took a beautiful onyx and gold fountain pen from his pocket and plucked off the cap. "She's all yours."

Recognizing the concern as genuine, Gavallan was flushed with a sudden fondness for the man. These days it was pretty hard to find a lawyer who gave a damn. "Thanks, man, but I know what I'm doing."

"I'm sure you do," said Norgren, a little too quietly.

The firm of Norgren, Piel, and Pine had done the majority of Black Jet's securities work for years: fairness opinions, registration statements for the SEC, legal analyses of all manner of financial instruments. At some point, Gavallan and Sten had become friends. They had dinner once a month and Gavallan took his kids sailing when the westerlies weren't too strong. Norgren had recently earned his pilot's license and was always calling Gavallan to ask his advice on one matter or another, begging him to come up with him for a short flight above the bay. Gavallan always declined politely, without offering an excuse. He hadn't taken the controls of an aircraft since the Gulf.

Gavallan spent a few moments reading through the documents. On top of the pile was a statement from Alameda Trust Corporation, granting him a second mortgage on his home in Pacific Heights in the amount of two million dollars. Beneath it were envelopes containing Gavallan's monthly bank and brokerage statements and the HUD-1 for the recent sale of his property in Montana—all the paperwork Norgren had needed to secure the loan on his behalf.

Gavallan's first action was to endorse the check made out in his name and hand it to Norgren. "You know where to deposit this."

"How much does this bring it to? North of twenty million, if I'm not mistaken?"

"Twenty-five point seven, to be exact," answered Gavallan, meeting his eye. "Don't worry, Sten, I am keeping track."

Black Jet's recent quarterly losses, combined with decreases in the value of securities the firm held for its own account and a certain fifty-million-dollar bridge loan he'd made to a less than investment grade customer, necessitated the capital injections. The Securities and Exchange Commission had strict requirements for firms underwriting new issues, especially ones valued at two billion dollars. Gavallan was not going to lose Mercury on a technicality.

"Why don't you let me make some calls," suggested Norgren. "I know some money center banks who could help out. Your reputation's sterling, Jett. You know that."

"I'm flattered, Sten, but it's hardly a good time. We're due to book our second quarterly loss in a row. We wouldn't get close to the price we deserve."

"I thought business was picking up. Markets are a

helluva lot stronger than a year back. I'm sure you could get a great price—two times book at least."

Gavallan wondered if Norgren had already placed a few calls on his behalf. Black Jet's book value was close to four hundred million dollars; two times book gave the firm a value of eight hundred million. Gavallan considered the price, but the prospect of vast riches left him unfazed. And then? he mused. What happens after that? Report to a drone three thousand miles away? Sit on a beach reading paperback novels? Work on his golf game for eleven years in hopes of joining the Senior Tour? Sell? *Never.* The word wasn't in his vocabulary.

"The problem's overhead," said Gavallan. "Business isn't too bad. Revenues might even inch up a little over last year."

"So fire some people, Jett. Come on. Rationalize, downsize, economize."

"Compromise, marginalize, capsize," countered Gavallan, firing off the words like bullets.

"Survive!" shouted Norgren. "Stop being so damned proud and do what everyone else in your place would have done a year ago."

"Proud? I've fired forty men and women so far this year. Is that 'proud' enough for you?"

"It isn't up to me to decide—it's up to the market. It's no sign of failure if you cut back a little, tighten your belt." When Gavallan didn't respond to his prodding, Norgren threw up his arms in frustration. "Whatever you say, Jett. I'm just your lawyer. You pay me to keep you apprised of your best options. Consider yourself informed." And sighing, he bent over Gavallan's shoulder and thrust out a beefy hand to indicate where he should sign. "Here. Here. And here."

Gavallan affixed his violent slash to the documents as indicated. "That it?"

"That's it, my friend." Norgren added his own signature as witness, then gathered up the papers and laid them neatly in the out tray. "First payment isn't for sixty days. After that it's twenty-five grand a month, *every month*. And that's on top of your regular nut. That's a lot for a guy who hasn't taken a salary since Christmas."

Gavallan figured that taking a paycheck was like robbing Peter to pay Paul. He was all too aware of his precarious circumstances. "Not to worry, Sten. I'll have the entire amount paid back by the end of the month."

"Thousand-dollar prepayment penalty, just so you know. Couldn't get them to drop it. Come on, I'll walk you out." When they reached the reception area, Norgren said, "Sorry if I'm being a nervous Nelly. It's just that you're cutting it awfully close this time—I mean putting it all on this deal. Frankly, if you weren't my friend, I'd tell you you were out of your blazing mind. You sure it's going to work out?"

Gavallan smiled slyly as he threw an arm over the attorney's shoulder. "You saying you don't want your Mercury shares? Is that it?"

"Jett, I'm serious. If Mercury goes south—even if you have to shelve it for a few months—you'll be feeling the pain. You and your company. Think about what I said. About cutting. Make it temporary. A three-month vacation."

"Relax, Sten. It's not that big of a deal."

"Better yet, let me make that call. I'm just wondering if it's wise to bet it all on one number. It is a big deal, Jett."

"Nah," said Gavallan, shaking his friend's hand. "Betting it all isn't such a big deal—losing it is. Anyway, didn't you know? The house always wins."

Waving good-bye, Gavallan strode confidently to the elevator. He pressed the button for the ground floor, and as the car descended, his stomach went with it.

Cutting it close? Norgren had no idea. Gavallan was down to three thousand dollars in his checking account, a hundred grand in certificates of deposit, and his prize Mercedes parked out front, its value beyond reckoning. He had a first mortgage of eighteen thousand dollars a month, a second of twenty-five grand kicking in in sixty days, and a quarterly tax payment of two hundred and eighty thousand dollars due on the twenty-first based on a salary he wasn't receiving—and that was before he put one foot out of bed.

Walking to his car, he considered his other obligations. To his three sisters and a widowed mother, all in Texas. To a club of broken and battered men spread around the world whom he'd adopted as his own. To a hospital that this very evening would fete him as its Man of the Year.

"And so, Mercury," he whispered, with a secret hope.

And so, seventy million dollars in fees and a spigot of related business to come down the pike.

And so, a twenty-first-century return to normalcy.

Gavallan started the motor. He had one more stop before returning to the office.

THE TEAM OF THREE MEN and one woman worked quickly, efficiently, and silently. They entered Gavallan's residence through the rear door, disabling the security system, then spreading out through the four-thousand-square-foot home to their assigned target areas. Each knew the house by rote. They had studied architectural drawings of the home as well as an electrical schema of its wiring. They carried the tools of their trade in black web belts hidden beneath striped cotton shirts declaring them employees of Pacific Gas and Electric.

It was a standard "look and listen" job. Two of the men, known in agency lingo as the "ears," planted ultra-high-frequency wireless listening devices in strategic locations throughout the house. Under the dining room table. On top of the refrigerator. Behind the headboard of Gavallan's bed. Each bug had been assigned its own frequency, so that there would be no risk of one transmission interfering with another.

A third man, "the eyes," installed the cameras. They were very small and designed to replace the screws securing the faceplates of standard electrical outlets. Where this proved impractical—in the study, for example, where it was crucial that the lens be granted an unobstructed view of any materials Mr. Gavallan might be reading—he drilled a hole the circumference of a surgical needle into a gilded picture frame and inserted an even smaller model. Afterward, he applied a coat of colored translucent epoxy over the pinhole, making it invisible to the naked eye.

The last member of the team walked straight to Gavallan's private office and installed herself at his desk. She was the only person that morning engaged in a function outside the scope deemed legal by the court order issued the previous day by the Eighth Circuit Court in Washington, D.C. In her belt she carried a set of Czech-made titanium alloy skeleton keys, a dozen picks, and two dummy credit cards. She didn't need any of them. Giving a gentle pull, she discovered the desk to be unlocked. Methodically, she withdrew the papers, set them neatly upon the desk, and photographed them with a digital camera. Once she was finished with the top drawer, she returned the contents to their place and attacked the two larger drawers to her right.

When the team departed twenty-two minutes and fifty-one seconds later, a total of eleven bugs and six wireless cameras had been planted throughout the house. Two hundred twelve photographs of the suspect's most confidential documents waited to be enlarged and scrutinized. Mr. John J. Gavallan, subject of federal warrant SJ-74A001, under investigation in connection with thirty-two counts of international fraud, larceny, and racketeering, could not crap without the FBI knowing exactly how much tissue he used to wipe his ass.

Walk in the park.

ROY DIGENOVESE WAITED until the Mercedes 300 SL had exited the office car park, then put the Ford in gear and pulled into traffic. He was not particularly worried about losing his mark. Gavallan was a steady driver, fast, aggressive, but safe. He used turn signals and didn't run red lights. A bakery truck pulled away from the curb, momentarily blocking Gavallan's car from view. DiGenovese didn't mind. He knew that when traffic picked up, all he'd have to do would be slide to the left and peek down the road. The white Mercedes, with its slot back and flat roof, would be there as usual, exactly three car lengths ahead of him, sticking out like a sore thumb.

"Zebra base, this is Zebra two, come in."

DiGenovese calmly picked up the walkie-talkie. "Roger, Zebra two."

"Went off like a charm. Target is wired for sound and light. Copy."

"Roger that, Zebra two. Rendezvous at the ranch at 1600. Drive on, Airborne."

DiGenovese put down the walkie-talkie and checked his watch. It was 8:07. In and out in under twenty-three minutes. "Outstanding," he murmured, remembering the long hours he'd put in on the case, the endless calls overseas, the numbing arguments with one after another federal magistrate to obtain his precious search warrants.

Setting up surveillance on Gavallan's residence was the final step in the casting of an all-encompassing electronic net over the suspect. Phone taps had gone into effect last night. Calls in and out of Black Jet, as well as his home, were screened for a succession of keywords and names. Mercury, Moscow, Novastar, Andara, Futura, and Kirov, Baranov, Tustin, and a hundred others. At the first mention of any of them, sophisticated computers at the National Security Agency would track and record the conversations.

Better yet was the second-generation Internet eavesdropping software being installed even as he drove. Nicknamed "Daisy," in deference to the flak brought down on their heads by its predecessor—the ineptly titled "Carnivore" system—the FBI's newest cyber-surveillance tool was housed in a black metal box no larger than a Palm personal assistant and powered by state-of-the-art software developed by the Bureau's in-house programmers. Installed at Gavallan's and Black Jet's wireless and Internet service providers, Daisy monitored every E-mail he or his executives received, their RIM Blackberries, cellular phones, or digital pagers for the list of keywords that DiGenovese and his superiors in D.C. had deemed likely to indicate conversations of a criminal bent.

All Gavallan had to do was breathe one word of his wrongdoing anywhere in his home, office, or car and DiGenovese and his superiors would know it. It was only a matter of time before the man slipped up.

DiGenovese waited a few more seconds, then edged the Ford over to the left, tilting his head to see around the bakery truck. A train of unfamiliar cars clogged the lane in front of him. The white Mercedes was nowhere to be seen. Panicked, DiGenovese craned his neck to the right and left, his eyes darting over every inch of the roiling cityscape. "Fuck," he muttered, chastising himself for his daydreaming. Signaling, he pulled into the fast lane and accelerated. He made it ten yards before a red light stopped him cold. Slamming his hand on the wheel, he swore again, this time loudly. He glanced to his right. There was Gavallan, a hundred yards away, trawling down Hope Street.

DiGenovese leaned on the horn, then jumped into the intersection, cutting off an oncoming taxi. He threw a hand out the window, showing his badge. Horns blared, voices shouted, fists threatened. In fits and spurts, he edged across the cluttered intersection. After what felt like a lifetime, he was barreling up Hope, the Mercedes no longer in sight.

He found Gavallan three blocks away, parked catty-corner to a playground next to St. John's Hospital. The guy was seated in his car, still as a bird. If DiGenovese wasn't mistaken, he was watching a couple of crips playing some early-morning roundball.

"Go figure," DiGenovese whispered. "Go fuckin' figure."

THE SCORE WAS 16–8, with Flint pulling away.

Gavallan sat at a distance watching the two soldiers battle each other on the basketball court, the men rolling this way and that in their graphite low-profile wheelchairs, chasing down rebounds, clearing the ball, making fast breaks. Flint was the quicker of the two and, with his arcing hook, a better shooter. A close look revealed he was missing both legs below the knees and most of his left hand. Jaworski had the better bank shot and was speedier off the mark, but he was going to fat and his stamina was weakening down the stretch. A sliver of shrapnel no bigger than a needle had severed his spinal cord at the twelfth vertebra. He hadn't walked or made love in eleven years.

Gavallan watched another five minutes, until Flint had roundly defeated Jaworski, then started the car and headed back to the office. Passing the hospital's entrance, he felt a jab of shame bow his shoulders. "Man of the Year." The words made him wince. And for the first time, he acknowledged that he might soon have to write a letter explaining why due to financial circumstances, wholly of his own making, he would be unable to meet the terms of his commitment to the hospital.

He drove faster.

He wanted to be back in the office.

Byrnes might have called.

6

STANDING ON A GRANITE PEDESTAL opposite Gavallan's
desk was an imposing four-foot statue of a shaman
carved from the wood of a Canadian maple by the Haida
tribe of the Queen Charlotte Islands, south of Alaska.
It was a strange-looking creature, with an abbreviated
torso, narrow neck, and large, grotesque head that was
all bulging eyes, flattened lips, and flared nostrils.

"The shaman is a mystical and omnipotent medicine
man," the dealer in Indian curios had explained to him
when he'd first seen the statue three years before. "He
knows all, does all, and judges all." Gavallan had locked
eyes with the carving and decided at once that he had to
have it.

Since then, whenever something unforeseen came up
in his life—good or bad, important or trivial—he consulted the shaman. When the markets caught fire or fell
in the dumps, when his putts rimmed out or his drives
sailed a mile, when his emotional entanglements threatened to suffocate him if his commitment to his business
didn't, he consulted the shaman.

The statue didn't offer any answers. He didn't speak
in tongues or send telepathic messages. He just looked
back, bored, impassive, and generally disdainful of all

things human, counseling faith in the grand scheme of things while reminding Gavallan that he wasn't as important a shit as he sometimes got to thinking.

Sinking into his chair, Gavallan gazed imploringly at the shaman. He didn't need any reminders about his human frailties this morning, no rejoinders about hubris, arrogance, or cocksureness. He simply needed its help.

Returning to the office, he'd found no messages waiting from Grafton Byrnes. Nothing on his E-mail or voice mail. No chits left with Emerald, Gavallan's secretary of seven years, to call him back at the Metropol or the National or any of Moscow's better hotels. Nothing. The harried executive in him told him to wait until noon before reacting and to concentrate on other matters. The concerned friend urged him to get on the horn with Konstantin Kirov, tell him of their plans to disprove the Private Eye-PO's accusations, and demand his help in tracking Byrnes down. Respect for his friend's judgment and Gavallan's innate discipline won out. He would wait.

"You take care of my buddy, okay?" he said, holding the shaman's eye.

Opening his satchel, Gavallan withdrew the copies of the documents he'd signed at Norgren's and filed them in his drawer along with the other markers routing his path to perdition. He folded the receipt for the two-million-dollar check in two and slipped it into his pocket. Then he leaned back his chair, kicked his feet up onto the desk, and laughed.

It was not a joyful laugh, nor one with any hint of amusement hidden inside its rolling baritone folds. It was a sad laugh, a mocking laugh, one tinged with doubt, disdain, and wonderment at his own folly. Oh yes, he was cutting it close this time. He was hanging it out there in the wind real far. He'd always been one to enjoy the roll of the dice, to crave the giddiness of a measured risk, but this time he had overextended himself. This time he'd bet on events that he could not control, only witness.

This time he'd been plain old stupid, and it was about time he admitted it.

Gavallan felt a wave of reckless anger build inside him, a steady roar expanding in his chest, filling his lungs, and scratching at his throat. If his rage was directed at himself, it was no less explosive for it.

In response, he made himself absolutely still. He slowed his breathing and laid his palms down on his desk as if he were about to stand. But he didn't move, not a muscle. Instead, he closed his eyes and began to count. He'd taught himself this trick years ago, when he was young and wild and given to bouts of unbridled fury. As a teenager he'd gotten into frequent fights. Not the clawing, awkward wrestling bouts of high school rivalries, but knock-down-drag-out, bare-knuckled exchanges with older, stronger men, the winner losing a tooth and the loser going to the hospital for stitches and X rays.

Gavallan didn't know from what spring the violence inside him flowed. His father was distant, but kind; his mother a fixture in the household; his sisters adoringly attentive. He himself was for the most part an obedient, dutiful, and undemanding youngster. Yet there was no doubting the wild streak, the inclination toward anger, the predilection for the nervy, rash act. Twice he was arrested for disorderly conduct. The first instance was when he beat the tar out of a Texas A&M lineman who'd stood up his oldest sister for her senior prom; the second and less valiant occasion occurred when, shit-faced in a Matamoros bar, he picked a fight with the biggest Mexican in the room just to prove he could whip him. He did, but he'd ended up with three broken knuckles, a cracked rib, and an eye swollen to the size of a grapefruit. Only through the benevolence of a local police officer had both acts been expunged from his record.

Aware of this flaw in his character and unwilling to allow it to defeat him, Gavallan had decided to isolate it and raze it from his behavior—or, at the very least, to keep it hidden from public view. Deep down, he knew his anger to be primal and lurking, and impossible to extinguish altogether. But slowly, and with an iron discipline new to him, he'd altered the way he acted.

He had always harbored ambitions, dreams of a life that would take him far away from the twelve-hundred-square-foot cinder-block home where he had grown up sleeping in the same bedroom as his three sisters, away from the unrelenting heat and humidity, from the mosquitoes that preyed on a man from dawn till dusk, from the bleak horizons of his parents' timid expectations.

By the age of fifteen, he knew what he wanted. He wanted to see the world as a pilot in the United States Air Force, and to be an officer and a gentleman in the best sense of the words. He wanted to be honorable, truthful, dependable, and courageous. He wanted to be respected not only for his skills as a pilot but for his integrity and character, and he expected to earn that respect. He wanted a wife and two children, and it was very important to him that he fall truly, madly in love. One day he hoped to wear a general's star on his shoulder.

To others, his dreams appeared fanciful or, worse, illusory. He had no money, no connections, no guidance but his own. But never did he doubt that he would gain his ambitions. He set forth a plan and he did not alter from it. He knew what he had to do. He must work harder than the rest, he must expect unfairness and some degree of intolerance. He must never complain. He must present the world a façade of unrelenting good spirit, equanimity, and drive. Above all, he must harness his rage.

To a large extent, Gavallan succeeded. He tempered his behavior. He fought down his rage and played up his humor. He showed the world what it most liked about itself.

Most of his ambitions were realized, though for a price beyond his reckoning. But deep inside him, the anger still burned, the rage still flickered, and he knew he must be ever watchful. For if he wasn't, one day it would surely rise up and destroy him. In the blink of an eye.

Reaching the count of one hundred, Gavallan exhaled audibly. For now, the anger was gone; the struggle for control won for another day. Happier, he turned and glanced at the pictures on his wall, wanting to share the victory, however minor. There was Gavallan and his father shaking hands on graduation day at the Air Force Academy. The old man looked as stern as ever, paying no mind to the fact that he was wearing his son's dress cap on his head. He never got over his boy's leaving the service, or the less than satisfactory general discharge that had made it official. Until the day he died, he insisted to his friends that his son had left the cockpit over the lack of decent pay.

"Money," sniffed Gavallan. "If only ..."

The true cause of his sudden, and not altogether voluntary, separation from the United States Air Force could be found on a ninety-minute videocassette kept shut in the bottom corner of his flight locker alongside his jumpsuit, his flying scarf, and his old Omega Speedmaster. The tape was dated February 25, 1991, and titled *Day 40—Abu Ghurayb Presidential Complex*. It had been made with an infrared camera mounted on the underside of his F-117. The tape was a copy, a pirated bootleg, and his possession of it was a jailable offense. The original was kept in a more secure location, most likely somewhere deep inside the Pentagon where the United States Armed Forces hid its dirty laundry.

Gavallan's eyes dodged his father, only to land on himself. There he was, a twenty-six-year-old superman gussied up for combat, strapped into his G suit, helmet in hand, standing beside the cockpit of his Desert Storm mount, an F-117 he'd christened *Darling Lil*. Look at that smile. Top of the world, eh, kid? The photo had been taken in a hangar at King Khalid Air Force Base in Saudi Arabia. A giant American flag hung from the rafters behind him. Beat that, Tom Cruise!

Another photo showed his mother and three sisters standing at the base of Big Tex, the 150-foot cowboy, at the state fair in Dallas ten years back. Mom, meek and gray, with her haunted smile, the woman who'd gifted him the name of Jett, not out of any premonition of the future, but because of her long-held crush on an unknown actor who'd visited her hometown of Marfa, Texas, one teenage summer, to stand before the cameras as Jett Rink, impetuous wildcatter who struck it rich in the glorious Technicolor Texas epic *Giant*. James Dean did a number on Marfa. Look in the phone book. You'll find a dozen men aged forty and up carrying the ridiculous name of Jett.

Above the photos hung two wooden plaques with attached miniature replicas of an A-10 bomber. Flowery script declared: "Captain John J. Gavallan, USAF, Squadron and Wing Top Gun at Red Flag '89 and '90." Red Flag was the annual competition staged at Nellis Air Force Base outside Las Vegas, where a pilot's proficiency was measured during several days of demanding flight exercises. As always, the mementos triggered a desire to fly, a yearning so strong he could feel it.

Trade your company, your career, to do it again? a skeptical voice demanded.

Any day, he answered.

To be at the stick of a jet was like nothing else in the world. To soar like an eagle and dive like a tern, while enveloped in the sky's royal blue cape. If there was magic in the world, Gavallan had found it in the cockpit of a jet aircraft.

Dismissing his longing, he continued on his nostalgic tour. There was only one place left to visit. Like any sentimental fool, he'd left his heart's graveyard for last.

Opening the bottom drawer of his desk, he rummaged through a dozen photographs, most framed with simple silver settings, a few loose, the dates and places written on the backs. Leaning to his side, he picked up one photo, then the next. With each, he stared into the woman's bold, ebullient green eyes, imagining the touch of her pillowed lips, sighing, smiling, longing, always wishing he could reshape the past. Flipping over the snapshots in turn, he read the inscriptions penned on the back: *Manhattan, Valentine's Day; Chicago, Xmas Eve; Hong Kong, Easter Sunday.* The script was looping and feminine, but never less than purposefully legible. Lingering over the words, he felt happily vulnerable, close to her again.

Cate who was kind but serious. Cate who was shy but sensual. Cate who was painfully honest yet a mystery even to those nearest to her. Cate who never raised her voice but let her eyes argue for her. Cate who declined his proposal of marriage with a single word and no backward glances.

Gavallan brooded for a minute or two, still in a kind of suspended state of disbelief that she'd turned him down. He hadn't seen it coming. Not after two years of dating and six months of living together. One moment, he'd popped the question; the next, she was out of there. Not a sock, stocking, or bobby pin left behind.

Cate who was gone.

The last picture in the stack had been taken just a few hours before he'd proposed, and showed the two of them at the rail of Sten Norgren's fifty-foot Wellington as it passed by the Presidio, San Francisco's oldest military installation. Cate's lustrous black hair, sparkling in the mid-morning sun, whipped across her face. Her eyes were partially hidden, but there was no disguising the smile or the quicksilver brilliance of the perfect white teeth. And no mistaking the unalloyed joy behind them.

Bringing the photo closer, he traced a thumb over her features, searching her obscured expression for a hint of what was to come. Looking past the hair into her eyes, checking her smile, he fought to glimpse a trace of discord, a measure of dissembling, some signal of the betrayal that lurked around the corner. He'd been doing the same stupid thing every day for a month, and every day he came away empty. She hadn't given him a clue.

This failure to foresee her actions had left him feeling powerless, the fool. Later, when she'd refused to explain her reasons, or to even speak with him, his emotions had hardened and he'd felt tricked and cheated and vengeful.

A few nights ago, he'd woken in a sweat, trembling, his heart racked with a terrifying anxiety. He hadn't suffered a nightmare. No subconscious spasm that his bet on Mercury would turn sour, no clawing certainty he'd lose everything he'd worked toward since leaving the Air Force, that he might end up penniless and without a means of supporting himself. The fear that stole upon him out of the darkness was deeper and more personal. It was fear sprung from his most desperate insecurity, more a premonition really, a merciless and exacting portrait drawn in black and gray of his life to come.

He saw himself in twenty years. He looked as he did now. He had all his hair, was trim and fit. He knew as you do in the subterfuge of dreams that he still had Black Jet, that he played golf once a week and went sailing on occasion, and that he was as well-off as he would ever need to be. Yet his image was surrounded by a naked aura of despair. Waves of loneliness rose from him like heat from the desert floor. Here was a man who had spent his life wedded to his business, involved in the stark, predictable activity of making money. Here was a drone who embraced repetition and success as a substitute for passion—and who, for all his effort and infinite industry, had no one.

Awake, perched on the edge of his bed in the dead of night, he'd suddenly realized that he had no possibilities without her, that he would never find someone to replace her, that there was no one in the world who could excite him and challenge him and thrill him as she had. No one who would own him so utterly.

Gavallan's phone rang. Bolting forward, he dropped the pictures into the drawer, slid it shut, and picked up the receiver. It was Emerald Chew on his private line.

"Yes, Emerald."

"Sorry to disturb you, but Tony's on his way in. He's very agitated."

"Agitated?" Gavallan dropped his feet to the floor and sat bolt upright. "Did he say what it's ab—"

Just then the door burst open and Antony Llewellyn-Davies, the firm's head of capital markets, rushed into the room.

"Tony, what is it? What's wrong?"

But one look had already told him everything he needed to know.

7

HE'S BACK," shouted Antony Llewellyn-Davies. "And he's calling our stock a 'scam dog.' Cocky bastard!"

Gavallan rounded his desk, confronting the anxious man in the center of the office. "Who's back?"

"Who do you think? The Private Eye-PO. He's worse than the bloody herp. But this time he's gone too far. It's slander. I swear it is, Jett. Mercury, a scam dog? Never."

Gavallan knew all too well what a scam dog was. Slang used by day traders and Internet stock junkies, it connoted a stock that was at worst a fraud—hence, "scam"—and at best an underperforming or poorly run company—hence, "dog." "Okay, Tony, let's calm down. Just give it to me from the top."

"If you'll step aside, I believe the expression is 'Better show than tell.' "

Llewellyn-Davies was a tall, thin man with wavy blond hair and a bobbing Adam's apple. An émigré from "the City," as London's financial district was known, he looked every inch an advertisement for the English upper classes. Gray slacks, white shirt, and navy pullover: It was his uniform, and he wore it every day. Add the apple blossom cheeks and the look of childish outrage and he was the old Etonian who'd never grown up. Just thirty-one, he was the youngest member of Black Jet's executive board, and its latest addition.

Gavallan allowed Llewellyn-Davies to pass, and a minute later the men were huddled over the monitor reading the Private Eye-PO's latest salvo at the Mercury Broadband offering.

Hi, kids! Surprised to hear from me again so soon? Don't be. News this sizzling pops right out of the pan and into your laps. Don't thank me. Thank our sponsors at Black Jet Securities. Last week, we showed you a pretty pic of Mercury Broadband's Moscow network operations facilities. Très déclassé, n'est-ce pas? This week, we go a step further. Your Private Eye-PO has come into possession of documents proving once and for all that Mercury is nothing but a hairy little scam dog with mucho fleas.

The Private Eye-PO went on to claim that Mercury Broadband had not purchased sufficient Cisco routers to service its two million business and residential customers in Central and Eastern Europe. (Routers formed what was known as the "IP backbone" and were basically sophisticated machines that channeled digital messages to the proper addresses.) As proof, he contrasted a footnoted item in the Mercury offering prospectus with a copy of an internal accounting document from Cisco Systems, the giant manufacturer of Internet operating equipment. Whereas the prospectus claimed that Mercury had purchased over three million dollars' worth of equipment from Cisco in the last year alone (and even listed the products: the 12000 series Gigabit Switch Router, the 7500 series router, and the MC 3810 multiservice access convertor), Cisco's internal "customer revenue summary" showed cumulative sales to Mercury during the period 1999–2002 totaling just $212,000.

The missive ended with an unusually brazen sign-off.

Shocked, loyal readers? Not as much as the hotshots at Black Jet, I'll bet. Or are they in the know? Here's a quick

*lesson, Mr. Gavallan: No routers, no customers. No customers,
no moolah! Remember, it's never too late to ix-nay the deal,
Jett. You've done it before at the last minute—and for less of a
reason. Will your pride permit you to do it again? Or is the going price for honesty two billion smackers these days? Hey, all
you lowlifes in San Francisco, can you say "due diligence"?
Better yet, can you say "class action"? See you in court, Jett!*

"Class action, my ass," spat Gavallan, chewing the inside of his lip, fighting to control the fount of anger
welling inside him. "I toured their network operations
centers in Kiev, Prague, and St. Petersburg. Their facilities are top of the line. They've got a dozen engineers on
payroll in Geneva laying out plans for the new expansion
grid. He's got it all wr—" Aware that his words were
sounding more like an excuse than an explanation, he cut
himself off. "This is bad, Tony."

Llewellyn-Davies crossed his arms, nodding. "Indeed.
Do we just ignore this too? I mean we can't, can we? This
is the second time in two weeks he's come after us. First
Moscow, now this. Hasn't that chum of yours found him
yet? The Internet detective, what?"

"No, not yet," said Gavallan, wanting to add that he
was hardly a chum. Two days earlier, he'd contacted a
man rumored to be the best in the business at what he
did—namely, track down thieves and criminals who traf-
ficked hidden inside the web—and provided him with
the Private Eye-PO's web address along with instructions that he needed him found within seventy-two
hours. "Found" meant a name, address, and telephone
number. A price was given: a fifty-thousand-dollar retainer to be wired to an account in the Cayman Islands,
and fifty thousand more should the deadline be met.

Llewellyn-Davies printed out the accounting document and handed it over. "Ask me, it looks shoddy
enough to be real. Still, these days you can't tell. Any
two-bit con artist could run up a copy of Cisco letter-
head."

"But why would he?" asked Gavallan, happy to have someone else defending Mercury for once. "Tell me that and I'll tell you if the documents are real or phony."

"Ah! The million-dollar question," declared Llewellyn-Davies. "First answer's obvious: Chap wants to push down demand so he can scoop up some shares himself. Hold 'em or flip 'em, it's all the same. He knows Mercury's a golden goose and he wants to make some dough."

"If it were anyone else, I might agree. But this guy's reputation's too good. He's no pump-and-dump artist. And Mercury's no penny stock. Last few tech IPOs out of the gate he's called to within ten percent of their first day's close. The guy's a sharpshooter."

"The question remains, why is he taking aim at us?" Llewellyn-Davies pursed his lips and put a finger to his chin, and Gavallan noticed that his skin had taken on a peculiar yellowish cast. He couldn't help thinking the man looked even thinner than usual.

"I suggest we call Cisco right away," Llewellyn-Davies went on. "Tell them we're double-checking, engaging in a round of last-minute due diligence." Rising to his feet, he picked up Gavallan's phone and dialed 9 for the main operator. "Let's see if there's anything to this."

An astonished voice bellowed across the room. "Put that fuckin' phone down, Two Names."

Bruce Jay Tustin stormed into Gavallan's office, his cheeks flushed, eyes afire. "What a disaster! I can't believe this son of a bitch. Christ, Jett, what did you do to get this guy so pissed off at us—spill a couple drops on his shoe in the men's room? I mean, this sounds personal. Fuckin' Hatfields and McCoys."

Llewellyn-Davies lowered the phone. "We'll thank you to keep a civil tone, Mr. Tustin."

"Excuse me, your majesty," said Tustin, curtsying before Llewellyn-Davies. "Call Cisco and word will be out before lunch that we're having doubts about our client. I can hear it now. 'The hotshot investment bankers who don't know if the biggest IPO they've ever brought to market is a "scam dog with mucho fleas." ' Jesus, you queens and your dramatics." He put on a terrible English accent and walked mincingly around the room. " *I suggest we call Cisco right away. Just say we're double-checking, what?*' What is it, Tony? Those cocktails you take every day starting to include a little gin?"

"Piss off, Bruce. You're a fucking cretin."

"Excuse me for breathing. When did you get such a thin skin?"

"Cool it, you two," said Gavallan. He was in no mood for Tustin's theatrics or his bullying, but he had enough respect for the man to give his counsel a hard listen. Bruce Jay Tustin was the firm's resident historian, its link to the past. He'd come up on Wall Street in the heyday of greenmail, leveraged buyouts, and insider trading, in an era when news of a twenty-billion-dollar merger shook the world and of a man's taking home five hundred million dollars in salary enraged the masses. At one time or another, Bruce Jay Tustin had worked with all the great names—Henry Kravis, Boone Pickens, Carl Icahn—and some of the not so great ones—Ivan Boesky, Martin Siegel, Mike Milken. He was rude, maladroit, and pathologically disrespectful. He was also savvy as hell, and he wasn't shy about shining his Diogenes lamp on Black Jet's own offerings.

"Bruce has a point," said Gavallan. "Best if we keep our lips sealed for the moment."

Llewellyn-Davies replaced the phone in its cradle, but not before whispering a catty, "Fuck you, Bruce."

Gavallan returned his attention to Tustin. "You think it's personal too? What gives you that idea?"

"Hell, I don't know, but what's all that stuff about pride and 'you lowlifes' and canceling a deal at the last minute 'for less of a reason'? Guy sounds like as much of an asshole as me."

"I won't argue with you there." The truth was that Gavallan had also thought the Private Eye-PO's latest remarks sounded personal. Something in his words rang a bell, and though Gavallan couldn't quite put his finger on it, it disturbed him nonetheless to think that somewhere in the past he'd wronged someone badly enough that the person would seek him out and try to return the favor. "You remember anyone we cut off at the last minute?"

"Last minute?" asked Tustin. "Two years ago we canceled the whole goddamn slate overnight. We had eight companies registered that we had to shelve. I think we ended up saving two of 'em. The others went back for more rounds of funding or got snapped up by bigger fish."

"I'll do some checking," volunteered Tony Llewellyn-Davies. "See how many issues we pulled in the last five or six years."

"What's the word on the street, anyway?" Gavallan asked Tustin. "Anyone buying this guy's shtick?"

"Fidelity's already been on the horn with me, and so has Vanguard. I told both of them the guy was full of shit, but Fidelity cut their order. Said they didn't like the Eastern European exposure. If you ask me they're gonna flip and get out."

Gavallan ran a worried finger across his chin. Fidelity was the nation's largest manager of mutual funds. If it backed out, others would too. "Anyone else call?"

"Scudder and Strong," offered Llewellyn-Davies, giving the names of two more influential funds. "Not to worry. They're still buyers, both of them, and looking to build a big position in a couple of their funds. I'm sure we'll hear from others in the course of the morning."

As it so often did, the market was sending Gavallan

contradictory signals. Someone believed the Private Eye-PO. Someone else thought he was a raving lunatic. It was a constant game of tug-of-war. Gavallan likened it to guessing which way the wind would turn, and felt the only thing to do was to sniff the air and go on your own instincts. He walked to the window and looked down on the city. The streets were glossy and gray and crowded with automobiles.

As if reading his thoughts, Tustin asked, "You're not thinking of postponing the offering?"

"Might not be an unwise move," mused Llewellyn-Davies. "Give us time to sort everything out. Set this Private Eye-PO chap straight."

"It would be a very unwise move, and we all know it," Gavallan replied sharply. "The question is whether we have a choice. Word hits that Fidelity's cutting their order and others might follow suit. It could kill us."

He watched Tustin and Llewellyn-Davies exchange concerned glances. For all their adversarial banter, the two were close friends. A year earlier, when Llewellyn-Davies had suffered a relapse, Tustin had visited him nightly, bringing books and videos and sometimes sneaking in a plate of the Englishman's beloved five-alarm curry from his favorite Indian restaurant.

"I thought we were safe on that one," said Tustin, his swagger conspicuously absent.

"It's spread out," said Gavallan. "Lehman and Merrill took ten apiece, but it's still a handshake deal. Best case, we're left holding thirty million."

"That's a high price to win some business, Jett, old boy."

"Maybe," said Gavallan.

They were talking about the bridge loan he had floated Mercury to win the deal: a short-term, fifty-million-dollar facility to help the company tie up real estate, purchase much-needed hardware, and lease fiber-optic cable. In good times, bridge loans were a wonderful way to leverage the fees a bank could earn on a transaction. You were out the money maybe ninety days. You charged a juicy premium over prime. And you won the loyalty of your client by showing faith and shouldering some of his risk.

But these weren't good times, and right now the bridge to Mercury was looking to be a damned fool thing. First off, it had eaten up the last of the firm's capital. Second, it had left Black Jet reliant on current earnings to meet its cash flow requirements. Maybe Tustin was right. Maybe it was a high price. But it had been necessary. Crucial even. Black Jet needed the Mercury business and the bridge had won it, allowing the smaller upstart to steal the prestigious offering from under the noses of the big guns in New York.

So far, Gavallan had managed to farm out twenty of the fifty million to a few friendly banks—half of what he'd hoped. If the deal went south, Black Jet would be out thirty million dollars. It would be too late for layoffs. He'd be forced to sell his company to the first interested party at a fire-sale price. *If the deal went south . . .*

Gavallan swore to himself it would not.

"We can't just sit still," he said, at once disheartened and energized by the latest development. Like all adrenaline junkies, he functioned best in time of crisis. "Our silence will be regarded as an affirmation of the Private Eye-PO's warnings. The pictures were one thing, but Tony's right—he's gone too far this time. It's as if he were building a case against us." *Against me*, came an unprovoked thought. "Bruce, do me a favor and get Sam and Meg down here, on the double."

Sam Tannenbaum was Black Jet's in-house counsel, Meg Kratzer its head of investment banking.

"Aye, aye," said Tustin, saluting, then turning on a heel and hustling out of the room.

"Stupid git," laughed Llewellyn-Davies, a bit of color returning to his cheeks. "Doesn't even know you're Air Force."

Gavallan laughed too. "You want a coffee? Something to eat while we wait?"

"No thanks. I'm fine as is."

"Sure? I'm thinking of a breakfast burrito. Sausage and egg. Maybe a soda. Didn't teach you to eat like that at Eton, did they?"

"Stone the crows, no. A burrito would probably send me to the heavens." Llewellyn-Davies coughed once, violently. "Pardon," he said, raising a hankie to his mouth.

"You okay, Tony?" Gavallan asked, concerned.

"I'm alive, Jett. That's good enough for me."

"If you need anything . . ."

"Yes, I know. *Ask*." Llewellyn-Davies knitted his brow inquisitively. "Not looking for another ticket to the ball tonight, are you? Hoping I might opt out?"

"No," said Gavallan abashedly. "No, no, no."

"Good, because I have every intention of attending. I can't wait to see you mount the dais and make a bloody fool of yourself. You have to pay good money for that kind of entertainment."

"You bastard!" said Gavallan, laughing in earnest for the first time that morning and clapping his friend and colleague on the back. Sometimes it was hard to hide his admiration for Llewellyn-Davies. It had to be damned tough living your life on a leash, he thought, relying on ten different combinations of six different pills—"cocktails," they were called—to be taken six times a day. He remembered the frail, sallow man who'd showed up for the interview seven years earlier, the thousand-yard stare, the unflinching honesty.

"I'm sick," Llewellyn-Davies had said. "You can see that. But I can work. Have to, actually. Can't go out leaving debts behind me. What would my dad say? An accountant, don't you know?"

His resume read like gold. Oxford, Harvard, a year at a bulge bracket firm before being fired for excessive absences. Gavallan had made some calls beforehand. Smart as a whip, came the unanimous response. Polite. Great sense of humor. Clients love him. But, come on, the coughing, the sweating, all those doctor's appointments. How long's he got, anyway? Six months? A year? Who wants to sit next to a fuckin' cadaver all day long? Besides, you never know. Shit may be contagious that way, too.

"The job's for a trader on our Swiss franc book," Gavallan had said. "Pays fifty thousand a year plus a fifteen percent bonus if you don't lose us too much money. If you have to miss work, get someone to cover for you. If you can't find someone to cover for you, call me. Understood?"

Llewellyn-Davies had nodded, his jaw clenched, eyes welling. "Monday is it, then?" he'd asked, wiping his cheek with the back of his hand.

"You kidding?" Gavallan had exclaimed, standing and walking to the door. "You're starting now. Take off that necktie and come with me."

Gavallan looked at Llewellyn-Davies now, wondering if maybe he was remembering the same moment. Seven years later, Tony wasn't simply alive but a vital component of Black Jet Securities and one of Gavallan's most trusted lieutenants. For a few more seconds, neither man spoke, and the silence that invaded the room was soft and comforting.

"Jett, do you think it might be true?" Llewellyn-Davies asked finally, in his mildest brogue. "You think Kirov's having us on, then?"

"Is it true?" For once, Gavallan didn't have an answer. Shrugging, he was unable even to mouth the requisite denials. The answers, he knew, lay elsewhere. In the past. In his judgment. In his greed.

And instead of looking at the delicate features of Antony Llewellyn-Davies, he was meeting the brooding, religious gaze of Konstantin Romanovich Kirov the night they had first met six months before.

8

"You are Mr. Gavallan, I think."

"Mr. Kirov. It's an honor."

The two were standing in a plush reception hall on the campus of Stanford University. Kirov had been invited to deliver the annual Grousbeck lecture on foreign affairs. As his subject, he had chosen the current state of the Russian legal system, and his performance had been impressive, an impassioned sixty-minute discourse hitting all the buzzwords a liberal California audience was dying to hear. The need for an independent judiciary, ratification of the nation's highest judges by a legislative authority, freedom of the press, the right to free speech. It was the *Federalist Papers* dressed up in an Italian blazer, Cartier links, and Lobb shoes, and topped off with an irresistibly cosmopolitan Russian accent. Kirov was still glowing from the standing ovation he'd received.

"Such a joy to speak to an American audience," he said, patting his brow with a folded handkerchief. "If only my countrymen understood the importance of democratic institutions as well as yours. I must always remind myself that you have two hundred years' experience to put your ideas into practice. Russia has a thousand years of an altogether different experience: oppression, tyranny, poverty. In short, the boot." He balled his hands into fists and stamped his foot dramatically on the wooden floor, but his optimistic grin promised Gavallan and the circle of devotees around him that if Konstantin Kirov had anything to say about it, "the boot" would soon be a thing of the past.

"Shall we find someplace private to speak?" Kirov asked Gavallan, and grasping him amicably by the arm, led him from the crowded reception room into a quiet hallway outside. "There, that is better. Now we can talk. Man to man."

Kirov was a slim, compact man with narrow shoulders and an economical step. Leaving the reception area, Gavallan remarked upon the strict posture and bowed head, the carriage of the arms tucked close to his body, and rushed ahead to open the door, as if ushering a clergyman or someone whose life conveyed a sanctity of purpose greater than the never-ending quest for the almighty dollar. This higher calling was also visible in Kirov's face. It was grave and focused, the skin so pale as to be translucent, the eyes dark, deep-set, and menacing as a witches' hollow. His hair was a raven's black. Cropped close to the skull, it accentuated the sharp cheekbones and drawn jowls. But there was fun in him, too. His mouth was puckish, as if ready to smile given the slightest reason. His eyes could surprise you with their playfulness. And he had a fine, boisterous laugh, louder than one would expect from such a small man. Mostly, though, what Gavallan sensed about the man was a monastic self-control, a zealot's singularity of purpose.

"I've heard much about you, Mr. Gavallan," Kirov went on. "Believe me when I say the honor is all mine. Thank you for making the trip to see me. Since you have come, I take it you are familiar with my company, Mercury Broadband?"

"Naturally," said Gavallan, aware he was being patronized. He sure as hell hadn't driven to Palo Alto to brush up on the principles of American democracy. "You've built an exciting platform for the industry. We're all very impressed."

The mandate to take Mercury public was the hottest ticket on the street. All the big boys wanted in. Credit Suisse, Morgan, Goldman. Gavallan considered it a miracle in itself he'd been able to secure an hour of face time with the Russian tycoon.

"Yes, it is time we offer shares in Mercury to the investing public," said Kirov. "Time to show the world Russia is no longer a second-class country. That Russia is not a land *of* criminals, *for* criminals, and *by* criminals. That rights of ownership, once documented, are respected by rule of law."

"I couldn't agree more," said Gavallan, liking the man: the muted confidence, the palpable determination. Of course, if Mercury Broadband had been solely a Russian company, as Kirov was implying, Gavallan wouldn't have touched it with a ten-foot pole. But with operations in Switzerland, the Czech Republic, and Germany—and even an R&D facility literally just up the road in Palo Alto—Mercury Broadband deserved to be called a multinational, and multinationals were exactly the kind of client Gavallan was looking for. "The timing is ideal. The market's hungry for a first-class international operation like Mercury. I'm confident an offering would be greeted favorably."

"I am of the same opinion," said Kirov.

"Mercury's revenues have demonstrated a pattern of consistent growth. You have a solid record of earnings and a sustainable business model. We've taken a close look at the financial statements you so kindly provided, and my colleagues and I believe an offering in the neighborhood of five hundred million dollars is realistic."

"Five hundred million?" Kirov pursed his lips, his expression puckered with uncertainty.

"For ten percent of the company," Gavallan hastened

to explain. "We'll go out with fifty million shares priced at ten bucks per, then float another ten percent in a year when the market sees what a great job you're doing and values the company accordingly. We don't want to sell Mercury short before you realize your true worth."

Normally, if a company met its revenue forecasts, it could count on floating additional shares within twelve to twenty-four months at a price significantly superior to the original offering. It was important, therefore, that the client not give away too much of itself at a less than maximal price.

"So you believe Mercury deserves a valuation of five billion dollars?"

"No," said Gavallan. "I'd say ten or fifteen billion, but we'll need time to work the market up to that level." It was crucial he offer Kirov a mildly inflated but marginally realistic value for his company. There were others out there chomping at the bit to get the deal, and he could only guess at how high they had valued Mercury Broadband.

The process of winning the mandate for an IPO was called a "bakeoff " or a "beauty contest," and like all mating rituals it had its own strict rules. Bankers strolled down the runway in their scantiest togs, planted themselves suggestively in the prospective client's lap, and immodestly drew attention to their most lubricious assets—namely, where they ranked in the league tables, the number of IPOs their firm had done in a similar space, and the performance of those stocks six, twelve, and twenty-four months after the offerings.

Next, they turned their attention to the client, whispering tantalizing nothings in his ear about the true market value of the company in play, boasting about the size of the offering—bigger was *always* better—and giggling, with eager eyes, about how diligently they would support the stock. *Yessir, we'll keep the price up, up, up.* After a drink or two, it was time for the bankers to drop their negligees and show some skin, letting slip that their analyst, invariably an *Institutional Investor* "first teamer," would start the party off with a bang by issuing a "strong buy" on the stock.

If the client was not yet sufficiently aroused, the banker would trot in the big guns, often the bank's CEO himself, to drive home the firm's overwhelming desire to win the business. With a wantonness that would make even the most jaded harlot blush, the CEO would run his hand through the client's hair, drown him in butterfly kisses, and promise his firmest, longest-lasting, and deepest professional and personal commitment to the stock.

In short, it was a diamond-crusted striptease, and the bank with the nicest tits won.

"I was thinking more in the neighborhood of two billion," Kirov suggested. "We have ambitious plans to expand. When you learn of the full scope of operations, you will be convinced."

"I don't doubt it," conceded Gavallan, not wanting to lose the business before he had it. "Two billion is doable, provided you're willing to part with the extra chunk of your company. I wouldn't advise that at such an early stage."

"Two billion," Kirov repeated, his resolve to be found in the firm set of his jaw, the narrowing of his eyes. "We must have two billion. Now is the time for us to expand. We must strike while the iron is heated."

"Two billion it is. It's big for Nasdaq, but why not."

"I'm afraid that Nasdaq is out of the question," said Kirov, his voice hardly a whisper.

"Oh?" asked Gavallan, knowing that this was how the Russian showed his anger, not with bluster but with discipline, the fist clenching tighter.

"Nasdaq is for new, unproven companies. We are established. We are profitable. A market leader in the East. Perhaps you are not as conversant about our company as you should be. It comes down to a question of face. We, Russians, have a terrible inferiority complex. Several of our nation's larger corporations are already trading on the New York Stock Exchange. We must list Mercury alongside them. It is the New York Stock Exchange or nothing."

Gavallan made the appropriate soothing noises, ego gratification being perhaps the most important job of a chief executive. He'd bring up the listing requirements at a later date—*if there was a later date*. After a promising start, the meeting had embarked on a series of wrong turns. The first order of business was to change the atmosphere. A long, drafty hallway was hardly the place for this conversation.

Gavallan suggested they continue their discussion in the provost's lounge, where they might sit and have a cup of coffee. He had attended business school at Stanford and knew the provost's lounge as the spot where the university president wined and dined the school's more important benefactors. Apparently there was something about oversized club chairs and oil portraits of long-dead scholars that made people free with their checkbooks.

Inside the lounge, the two men sat down, agreeing almost immediately that the chairs were wonderfully comfortable. Settling himself in, Kirov delved into his pocket for a sterling-silver cigarette case. "Sobranie?" Opening it, he offered the case to Gavallan. The cigarettes were long and black, the two-headed Russian eagle stamped boldly above a shiny gold filter. One head faced east, the other west. In Russia, danger had always come from within and without.

"No thank you," said Gavallan. "I don't smoke."

"I know, I know," pleaded Kirov, as he slipped one into his mouth and lit it with a matching silver lighter. "But a man should be allowed one vice." The brows jumped excitedly under the curtain of blue smoke. "After all, we are not saints!"

Kirov drew thoughtfully on the cigarette, inhaling for what seemed an eternity before expelling the smoke in neat flutes through his nose. "I have spoken with a few of your competitors these last days," he said offhandedly. "As you can imagine, a good many are anxious to work with us. Please don't think me rude, but I was hoping you might be able to tell me why I should consider someone outside of New York. Someone so much smaller."

Gavallan made it a point never to discuss his competitors—comparisons conveyed weakness and insecurity. "True, we're a smaller company," he said, launching into a pitch he'd given a thousand times, "but we think our size is one of our advantages. We choose our clients with great care and we like to think they exercise the same scrutiny in choosing us. Our record in the Internet sector is second to none. Of the forty-two companies we've taken public in the last four years, more than fifty percent are trading at significant multiples of their offering price. Not one has gone belly-up. We're selective with whom we work, Mr. Kirov. Black Jet's name on a prospectus has come to indicate a certain quality. We're deeply committed to the companies we offer our investors. The clients for whom we do choose to work receive the complete and dedicated resources of our company."

"So *you* choose your clients?"

"I prefer to think that we choose each other. Hopefully, bringing Mercury public will be the first step in a long relationship between our two groups."

"So you wish to work with Mercury? You are sure?" Kirov's amused tone indicated he hadn't heard this approach before and just might be buying into it.

"It would be a privilege. And I think I can promise that in the current environment, Black Jet could insure that a Mercury offering would be a home run."

Kirov nodded approvingly. If nothing else, he looked to be enjoying the courtship. He questioned Gavallan about Black Jet's ability to manage so large an offering, its relative inexperience in working with international companies, and its commitment to supporting the stock once it began trading. He asked about Black Jet's analyst, inquiring whether he was on *Institutional Investor*'s first team (*he was, at a salary of four million a year!*), and was curious to know if the larger funds would be buyers of the stock, meaning if they would look to build a long-term position in Mercury.

In short, he asked all the right questions. Either he'd been briefed by his chief financial officer or he'd already sat through a dozen of these pitches.

Gavallan addressed each of Kirov's concerns in turn. Knowing he was at a disadvantage to the bulge bracket firms, which could commit a sales force double the size of his own to the IPO and promise a hundred-million-dollar kitty to keep the float active, the stock price above water, he concentrated on Black Jet's strengths: its top-flight research team; its position at the vanguard of the new economy; its close ties to the nation's largest mutual funds. In the end, though, it came down to personality. Everybody on the street was offering the same services, more or less. It was a question of whether Kirov liked Miss August or Miss November.

At the close of Gavallan's comments, Kirov placed his hand atop the American's and gave it several pats. "I have received advice from people close to me—people I trust—that you are good man. That your company may soon be very big, very powerful. Like Mercury, I think." Another pat to let him know they were on good terms. "I like you, Mr. Gavallan. You are young. You are ambitious. I sense you are honest, even if you are arrogant." He laughed quietly. "*You choosing your clients.* Very good. I must remember to use that myself one day. But I must have a reason to explain to my own shareholders why I choose your company. We, Russians, like big names. BMW, Gucci, Rolex. We feel we must carry these brands with us to prove our legitimacy. Again our inferiority complex; excuse us. But if I may speak frankly, Black Jet is not yet such a big name."

"You're right, sir. We have only nine years behind us. I hope many more will follow."

"I am sure of it. Absolutely positive," Kirov declared collegially, but the next moment he was wincing, lowering his eyes. The reassuring hand returned to its owner's armrest. "But so much is at risk. It is a critical moment for my country. For so long, we have been held back, our heads pressed beneath the water. Now that we are free, I fear we are terribly greedy. We want to suck in great mouthfuls of this oxygen we call liberty. We claim democracy as ours. We crave progress. Personal progress. Progress measured on the human scale. A phone for every house. Running water. Showers that function. Toilets that flush. Proper medical care. Hospitals stocked with adequate antibiotics, surgical dressings, and sufficient blood. We demand the latest technology.

"You see, technology is our lifeline to the West. We cannot afford to fall farther behind. The Russian people are smart and curious. They are voracious in their hunger for knowledge. We are not a nation of peasants. We are a nation of Ph.D.'s, of scientists, of doctors, and businessmen. Every new PC brought into an Eastern European household is a soul saved from our autocratic past. Every home that logs on to Red Star has a window into the future. And once they see it, they will not let go." Kirov leaned closer, his eyes sparkling with hope. "In the past, weapons and ignorance kept East and West apart. But the arms race is finished. It is time technology and the quest for knowledge bring us together. The race to advance humankind has begun, and its progress will be measured in computers, not missiles. Over time we will evolve into a single empire, a democratic union of all peoples...." Abruptly, Kirov stopped. He was breathless, and a sheen of perspiration clung to his fore-head. His forgotten cigarette had burned down to his fingertips, a two-inch section of ash drooping precariously toward the carpet.

Gavallan found he was breathless, too. Kirov had spoken into his heart. He had addressed all his unsatisfied selves: the conscientious benefactor, the penitent sinner, the advocate of change happiest when striving. He had touched not only his dreams but his desire to dream, which was even more important. In a world scarred with cynicism, Kirov dared to have ideals.

The Russian fixed him with a challenging gaze. "Do you believe, Mr. Gavallan?"

"Yes," said Gavallan, without hesitation. "I do."

Kirov said nothing for a few seconds, his black eyes burning into Gavallan. He had the gift of silence, of dignifying thought for thought's sake. Just then, he noticed the cigarette and rushed to put it out. He smiled, embarrassed, and the evangelist became once more the man. "I'm sorry to say you have put me in a difficult position," he said. "I have very much enjoyed our chat, but I have a late dinner with the president of one of those big names we Russians so like. He has flown in from New York to see me. I think he will promise me the moon if I ask him."

Gavallan sighed as he scooted toward the edge of the chair. Pitch over. Business lost. Next. Despite himself, he acknowledged a jab of disappointment and had to sit straighter to keep his shoulders from sagging. He knew he had had no right to count on winning the business, but he truly believed that Black Jet could do the best job for Kirov.

"Don't let me keep you," he said. "I'll be in the office tomorrow if we might answer any questions for you. If you have a free hour, I'd enjoy showing you around the firm." He rose. "But, Mr. Kirov, I want you to know one thing."

"Yes?"

"I do believe."

Kirov rose from the chair, but a moment later sank back down into its cushioned folds, motioning Gavallan to sit. "I will make you proposition, Mr. Gavallan. We are close to finishing the buildout of our central Russian operations. Kiev, Minsk. These are large cities; maybe a hundred thousand subscribers each. Unfortunately, we need fifty million dollars to complete the construction."

"Fifty million?"

"I am thinking a loan to be repaid from the proceeds of the IPO. It is uncommon?"

"Not at all," said Gavallan, unable to keep the excitement from his voice. Part of him wanted to jump at the chance, another to take a step back. A fifty-million-dollar loan would exhaust Black Jet's resources and leave it perilously exposed to the market's vagaries. It was a tremendous risk. Yet, the fees the deal would bring promised to be tremendous, more than anything Black Jet had ever earned on a single transaction. Add to that the interest on the loan, and of course the prestige . . . My God, Gavallan said to himself, the prestige alone would do wonders for the company.

He looked at Kirov, doing his best to size him up. The personality contest went both ways. The man was controlling, vain, and at least a little bit of an egomaniac. But his conceit was his strength. How else could he muster the energy, the dedication, the tenacity to build a company like Mercury? Who but the vainest sort of individual would dare talk of aiding his country in such grandiose terms?

Gavallan turned his thoughts to the bigshot flying in from the Big Apple on his big Lear or big Cessna or big Gulfstream. Inside, he smiled. It was a delinquent's smile, an outsider's smile, and it reveled in the pique and fury and disbelief that the overconfident executive would feel when he learned that Black Jet had won the two-billion-dollar mandate to bring Mercury Broadband public. Nothing came easier to a Texas farmboy than spitting in the eye of his betters.

Maybe the Russians weren't the only ones with an inferiority complex.

"Tell you what," said Gavallan. "Cancel that dinner engagement. Let Black Jet take you public and I'll write you a check first thing in the morning for fifty million dollars. Prime plus seven to be repaid out of the proceeds of the IPO." He stuck out his hand.

Konstantin Kirov hesitated, searching Gavallan's eyes. "I can trust you with my baby? It is not just for me, but for my Russia, too."

"Yes, you can trust me."

"Prime plus five and we repay within thirty days."

"No," said Gavallan, tasting the deal, wanting it more than anything, but never so much as to make a poor agreement. "It has to come from the proceeds."

Giving a fateful shrug, Kirov rose laboriously from his chair and grasped Gavallan's hand. "Yes, we shall work together. You are a believer. I see it in your eyes." He laughed richly. "I tell you something. Between us, I never like BMW anyway. But you must promise to call me Konstantin. In Russia, business is family."

Gavallan stood, and though the handshake was awkward and formal, he found himself laughing with his new client, new friend, and new family member, Konstantin Romanovich Kirov.

9

THEY'D MOVED INTO A CONFERENCE ROOM down the hall.
A "working room," they called it, and it was fitted for the
late nights and early mornings that claimed so large a
part of an investment banker's existence. Besides the
glass table and low-backed chairs, there was a refrigerator stocked with Coke, Mountain Dew, Red Bull, and, as
if an afterthought in their caffeinated universe, Evian.
One cupboard held chips, cookies, and candy bars, and
another, rumor had it, fresh fruit—though Gavallan had
never seen anyone munching so much as a grape. Next
door there was a pantry with a microwave oven, a freezer,
and a coffeemaker. A paper plate bearing the remains of
Gavallan's sausage and egg burrito sat half in, half out of
the trash can. A pall of cigarette smoke hovered below
the ceiling. Let mortals worry about ulcers, colitis, and
quadruple bypasses. They weren't subject to daily dead-
lines that could cost a firm tens of millions of dollars and
their own paychecks that extra, all-important zero.

Gavallan leaned back in his chair, balancing on its rear
legs. He'd already gone over the Private Eye-PO's most
recent message and its accusations of misrepresentation
and fraud. Reluctantly, he'd let everyone in on Grafton
Byrnes's secret visit to Moscow and his failure thus far to

report in. He did not, however, feel it necessary to tell them about Byrnes's early checkout.

"Listen, people, our back's up against the wall here," he said. "We need to take a close look at our deal books and see if we can find any holes that correspond to the areas the Private Eye-PO is attacking—namely, the Moscow network operations center and Mercury's hardware purchasing. I don't think we will, but I'm not going to my grave like the captain of the *Titanic* saying, 'She's unsinkable.' No one's leaving this room until we decide just what the heck we're going to do. *Comprende?*"

His eyes moved from face to face, waiting for someone to pick up the baton. Bruce Jay Tustin, Tony Llewellyn-Davies, Sam Tannenbaum—or "Shirley Temple," as Tustin had christened the blond, ponytailed lawyer—and Meg Kratzer. He was waiting for someone to share his outrage, but outrage, he knew, implied responsibility, and the Mercury deal had been his and his alone from the beginning. Finally, Meg Kratzer chimed in—Meg, for whom silence was an accusation of laziness.

"Look," she said. "We handled all customer and managerial questions in-house. If something weren't kosher about Mercury's Moscow operations, we would have heard about it from one of their customers. Financial, accounting, and operational issues were completed by Silber, Goldi, and Grimm in Geneva. If there were a problem with Mercury's physical plant and inventory, they would have found it—guaranteed! I don't know a bigger tight-ass in the business."

"I do," said Tustin, rolling his eyes and lofting a thumb in Meg's direction.

"I appreciate the compliment, Mr. Tustin," she responded. "It's hard to be more thorough than a Swiss with a microscope and a mandate to inspect. Coming from someone who's such a renowned tight-ass himself, that's very high praise indeed. I will thank you, however, to keep that greasy kid stuff in which you drown your last three remaining hairs off my deal books. I needed a whole bottle of Mr. Clean to get it off last time."

"Very funny," retorted Tustin, above the nervous laughter. "Just so you know, it's *pommade*. That's French, for 'classy.' "

Meg Kratzer circled the table, passing out a thick red three-ring notebook to everyone present. She was a vital, animated woman, short, stocky, and neatly attired in an olive Valentino two-piece. Her red hair was pulled back into a severe bun. Her blue eyes glimmered with healthy determination. At age sixty-three, she was a mother of four, a grandmother of ten, and self-appointed godmother to Jett Gavallan. She'd put in twenty-five years at a well-known securities house, only to be told when she turned fifty that her shelf life had expired. The termination letter called her "irascible, opinionated, and obstinate," and said she was "unable to meet the rapidly evolving dictates of the financial arena."

Gavallan saw those same qualities as forceful, experienced, and demanding, and found her as up-to-the-minute on all matters financial as the most arrogant graduate of Harvard Business School. She was also articulate, responsible, and possessed of a wicked sense of humor.

As the firm's head of investment banking, Meg had supervised the due diligence performed on Mercury. Its being an initial public offering, this involved the systematic deconstruction and analysis of the client company. Balance sheets were audited; bank balances verified; company officers interviewed (and often investigated); clients telephoned and questioned about their relationship with said company; corporate strategies parsed; and physical assets inventoried down to the last pencil and paper clip. It was a strip search really. With rubber glove and all.

Gavallan pulled the deal book closer, glancing at the Mercury name and logo that adorned the cover. The notebook had to weigh five pounds, and inside it was all the information Meg and her team had collected as part of their due diligence on Mercury.

"Let's start with clients," he said, flipping the notebook open. "Section one."

Section one contained single-sheet summaries of over 150 telephone conversations conducted with Mercury's clients in the Czech Republic, Ukraine, Germany, and Russia. Leafing through the pages, he kept a sharp eye out for those customers based in Moscow. He thumbed past the Czech Ministry of Communication, the Kiev Education Committee, Alpha Bank (Minsk branch office), the Dresden Youth League. All declared themselves satisfied with Mercury's product and services. Finally, he arrived in Moscow: the Moscow Municipal Transportation Service, the Moscow State University department of telecommunications, NTV (one of Moscow's larger television networks). Again, all were satisfied. There were more: Romanov Bank, the Greater Russian Health and Casualty Insurance Company, Nezhdanov Construction, Imperial Aluminum Smelting and Manufacturing.

It's bullshit, Gavallan thought, perusing the summaries. Everything the Private Eye-PO had said is patently false. Unadulterated garbage. And again, he wondered who the man could be, why he was trying to savage Mercury, and why he was making the issue so personal, repeatedly mentioning Gavallan's pride.

When they'd finished with section one, Meg directed them to section three, titled "Company Infrastructure," which contained questionnaires filled out by Mercury's management. In an expectant silence, Gavallan and the others read one job description after another, all dictated by the eager and capable executives who worked at Mercury Broadband. Finally, he came upon one provided by a man he knew, Václav Panič, Mercury's CTO—chief technical officer—of European operations, a Czech-born doctor of electrical engineering, formerly a professor of computer science at Brno University.

Gavallan had toured Mercury's Prague office in Panič's company. In his mind, he saw the cool marble floors, the legions of busy workers glued to their workstations, the aisles of servers, routers, and switches housed in trim glass cabinetry. One wall in the office's conference room displayed a map of Mercury's European operations and highlighted its expansion plans. Red fairy lamps depicted network operations centers, white lines denoted the cable or satellite connections, blue lights indicated cities with over twenty thousand subscribers, and green lights showed areas where service was to be offered within twenty-four months. Mercury was driving west to Berlin, south to Budapest, north to the Baltic republics, and east to the oil and mining boomtowns of Siberia. Standing there, Gavallan had felt the company's pulse as surely as if it were his own.

"There's not a scrap in here," said Tony Llewellyn-Davies. "Mercury's as clean as a whistle. Bravo, Meg. Well done, Jett. There's absolutely nothing to worry about, at least nothing we could see."

"That doesn't excuse us if we're wrong," cautioned Gavallan. "Our name's still on the prospectus."

"Not my name, Jett," Bruce Jay Tustin pointed out frankly. "She goes south, you're on your own."

"Thank you, Bruce. You're comforting as usual."

"My pleasure," replied Tustin. "Naturally, I do expect to get your office while you're doing your time in the pokey—oh, excuse me, I mean the men's correctional facility. I've always loved the view."

"Please, Bruce," cut in Tony Llewellyn-Davies, his cheeks pink with anger. "You're being exceptionally rude, even for yourself." He offered Gavallan a look of perfect exasperation, then turned back to Tustin. "You know damned well we agreed I was to get the office."

"No, me," said Meg. "The office is mine. Age before beauty, gents."

Everyone laughed, and the tension in the room was cut by half.

"Thanks, fellas. Thanks, lady," said Gavallan. "I appreciate your efforts. Now if we can finish up, I believe we're scheduled to talk to Silber, Goldi, and Grimm."

Meg Kratzer punched some numbers on the phone. "I've got Jean-Jacques Pillonel, their MD, on conference when we're ready"—"MD" in this case meaning "managing director."

Gavallan reached a hand over the notebook and activated the speakerphone. "Jean-Jacques, it's Jett Gavallan. Good morning."

"Bonjour, Jett. Ça va?"

"We've got a minor problem over here. Just a headache, I'm sure. Meg tells me she's gone over it with you. Can you help?"

"Jett, this is nonsense. I read this web page already. Mercury is here in Geneva with us. We spent a week camping in their offices. Certainly there's no question of revenues; we've got the bank statements from UBS and Credit Suisse."

"Jean-Jacques, no one is questioning the revenues. It's a matter of the physical assets." Gavallan leaned over to Meg Kratzer and whispered, "They handled that too, right?" She nodded, and he said into the speakerphone, "Who did the on-site inventory?"

"Mostly, we hired independent specialists," Pillonel replied. "Systems engineers, information technology guys, you know. I supervised the project myself. A favor for my American friends. I know this is a big deal for you."

"Thank you, Jean-Jacques," said Meg, as Gavallan and everyone else at the table rolled their eyes.

"Jett, listen, no worries, my friend. We checked Mercury up and down. We even look in their shorts and count their pubics, you know. Forget this guy on the Net. *Je te dis, ça va.*"

Tustin lobbed an arm across the table and punched the mute button. "*Ça va, ça va.* Same thing the fuckin' frogs said about the Maginot Line. *It ees inveencible!* Look how that turned out."

"He's Swiss, Bruce," Meg pointed out.

Tustin shrugged. "Swiss. French. Whatever. A frog's a frog."

The room tittered nervously and Tustin turned off the mute.

"And Moscow?" asked Gavallan. "Who did you send?"

"I went myself."

"You?" It was odd, not to say completely out of the ordinary, for a senior partner of an internationally prominent accounting firm to hole up in a client's offices and physically inventory its assets. That was a job reserved for "newbies."

"With my associates, of course," Pillonel added quickly. "We have a new office in Moscow, so it was a side trip. Like I say, a favor."

"And you saw all their operations, including the network operations center?"

Suddenly the Swiss adopted a belligerent tone. "Hey, Jett, we put our signature on the offering memorandum. Last time I checked, our name still meant something— or do you pay just *anybody* two hundred fifty thousand dollars for their help?" The voice regained its diplomatic flavor. "You are worried for nothing. How can Mercury earn so much money without having the equipment to do so? You can't harvest wheat without a thresher— know what I mean? Mercury is doing a hell of a good job, I tell you. Look at their metrics: over four million hits a day. You know I have an order with you to buy a lot of shares."

"And we'll see you get filled," said Gavallan. "Thank you, Jean-Jacques. *Au revoir.*"

"Au revoir, tout le monde."

For a moment, there was only silence. The sound of pens tapping the table. Legs crossing. Meg Kratzer lit a cigarette and took pains to direct her smoke toward the ceiling.

There it was, Gavallan told himself. The managing director of Europe's largest accounting firm had just confirmed that Mercury's Moscow operations were up and running. Gavallan asked himself why he hadn't called Jean-Jacques Pillonel in the first place. *Because you can only trust your own*, a cynical voice reminded him. *Because people lie.*

More and more, he was certain the Private Eye-PO had to be someone he knew, someone with a personal ax to grind.

"So, are we back at square one," he asked his colleagues, "or did we just cross the finish line?" Unspoken, but hanging up there near the ceiling with Meg's cigarette smoke and the lingering scent of his half-eaten burrito, were the words "postpone," "shelve," and "cancel."

"Where the hell is Byrnes?" griped Tustin.

"Give him time," said Llewellyn-Davies. "He'll get back to us."

"It's ten o'clock in Moscow. How much time does he need?"

"Relax, Bruce," said Meg. "I'll take Jean-Jacques's word over the Private Eye-PO's anytime. I'm sure Graf will only confirm what we already know."

"Maybe," said Tustin grudgingly. "But I still want to hear from him."

So did Gavallan. Every minute that passed without word from Byrnes fueled his worry over his friend's well-being. Still, he was pleased with the give-and-take of the discussion. If there were any doubts about Mercury, it was best that they surfaced within the confines of the office.

"So, Sam, what's your call?"

"Tough one."

Tannenbaum was the firm's resident bohemian. With his tight jeans, flannel shirt, and flowing blond hair, painstakingly groomed and tied into a ponytail, he looked like a refugee from Big Sur. "We seem to be stuck between believing in ourselves and believing the Private Eye-PO. From what I can gather, Mercury is everything we say it is. You think so. Meg thinks so. Jean-Jacques thinks so. Jupiter Metrix says so. It's a 'go deal.' At the same time, we feel compelled to trust the Private Eye-PO because he's been accurate in the past."

"Jesus, Shirley, you're getting me hard," whined Tustin. "Say what you want to say and let's get on with it."

Tannenbaum shot him a withering look, but refused to be hurried, either by Tustin or by any of the other curious faces staring at him. "Unfortunately, I don't know what to say except that we need to find the Private Eye-PO as quickly as possible and ask him where he's getting his information."

"Only one problem," said Gavallan. "We still don't know who he is."

"Can't we shut him up?" asked Meg. "Slap an injunction on him for false and deprecatory statements? I mean, what he's doing isn't any different from some wiseass issuing a phony earnings warning."

"Sure," said Tannenbaum. "But again, we have to find him first, then we have to get an injunction, and eventually we have to take him to trial. We don't have the time. The balloon is going up in five days."

Gavallan was suddenly restless. Frustration cramped his shoulders and clawed at his neck. Rising from his chair, he walked slowly round the table. All roads kept leading back to the same place. The deal was sound. The Cisco receipts were bullshit. So were the pictures of the Moscow NOC. Some asshole getting his jollies trying to hurt Black Jet or Mercury. It didn't really matter who he was, or why he was doing it. Which left Byrnes. No one knew better than he how important the deal was. Absent his word to the contrary, there was only one way to go.

"Okay, everyone, that's a wrap," Gavallan said. "We all decided on this?" Approaching the table, he extended his hand over its center. "Tony?"

"It's a go, Jett." Llewellyn-Davies laid his hand on top of Gavallan's.

"Bruce?"

"Fuckin' A, bubba. We're going in!" Tustin slapped his hand atop the two others.

"Sam?"

The lawyer looked unsure. "Umm, if you say so. Sure." Another hand joined the pile.

"Meg?"

"Hee-yah!" she shouted, half laughing, throwing her hand on top of the stack. "We're on the road to glory! Two billion or bust!"

Gavallan felt the weight of the four hands on top of his own. For a moment, his eyes passed from one person to the next. Bruce, the congenital loudmouth. Tony, the gutsy survivor. Sam, the reluctant corporate warrior. And Meg, the discarded treasure.

These were more than his friends, more than the closest of colleagues. These were the members of the family he'd chosen for himself. The pillars of the life he had built after his world had crashed in ruins about him. It all came back to people. To teamwork. To mutual accomplishment. He waited a second longer than usual, enjoying the communion of flesh, the union of wills.

"All right then," he said. "We're decided."

Without another word, he pulled his hand from beneath the others and walked out of the conference room.

BACK IN HIS OFFICE, Gavallan stood by the window. Patches of blue peeked through fast-moving clouds. The harbor was alive with mid-morning traffic, tugs and ferries and tankers leaving frothy trails in their wakes. Tired, he pressed a cheek to the glass, enjoying the feel of the cool, slick surface against his skin. "Mercury is solid. Mercury is solid." He repeated the words over and over, a mantra to convince himself and the whole world. But he'd been in the business too long to believe it. Skepticism had become second nature.

Right now only one thing was certain: If what the Private Eye-PO claimed was true and Black Jet Securities went ahead and brought Mercury to market, he, as sole owner of the firm, would be looking at a class action lawsuit of tobaccoesque proportions. Forget recouping the thirty-million-dollar bridge loan. Forget selling the company. Black Jet Securities would be doing a Drexel quicker than he could say "Mike Milken," and he himself would be learning to trade stocks by Touch-Tone phone from the inside of a federal prison.

Returning to his desk, he found the shaman staring at him. He met the squat carving's gaze and stared right back.

"Find him," he ordered the Indian medicine man. "Find him, now!"

10

CHILD'S PLAY.

Jason Vann took a look at the Private Eye-PO's web page and smirked. *An amateur.* He could see it right away. No sidebars. No pull-down menus. No search fields. And certainly no banner advertisements that might earn him a little dough. Just the guy's name written across the top in faggy script, a half dozen hypertexted headlines, and a bunch of charts chronicling the latest goings-on in the exciting world of venture capital financing, tech-related mergers and acquisitions, and initial public offerings.

There were tables showing IPOs coming to market next week, IPOs recently priced, the performance of IPOs just launched, and the year-to-date performances of the Private Eye-PO's personal picks. The symbol for each stock was colored an electric blue, denoting a hyperlink to drive the reader to a related site. Vann double-clicked on a few of the links. As expected, they led to commercial portals that offered free content—Yahoo! Finance, CNBC, Bloomberg. Definitely a one-man show. Best of all, there was an E-mail address at the bottom of the page. PrivateEyePO@hotmail.com. Vann read it, and his smirk took on a decidedly arrogant cast.

This would be the easiest hundred grand he'd ever earned.

The individual whom Jett Gavallan had called "the top man in his field" kept his office in two spartan rooms on the second floor of a modest colonial home in Potomac, Maryland. And the "field" to which Gavallan had been referring was alternately called "cyber-sleuthing," "systems security," or, if you were a black-hat hacker, "betraying the cause."

If you needed to find someone on the Net quickly—friend or foe, cracker, script kiddie, or gray-haired hacker—Vann was your man. The FBI had called him to discover who had hacked into NORAD and raised the entire United States defense establishment to Defcon 2. Since then, he'd lectured regularly at Quantico. The CIA had paid him handsomely to track down a team of cyberterrorists who had defaced Langley's mainframe. They'd thought so highly of his methods that they'd contracted to keep him on permanent retainer. Five thousand dollars a month so the spooks in Virginia could install a direct line to his home.

And Mr. John Gavallan of San Francisco was paying him a hundred thousand bucks to find out the name and home address of some Net loudmouth calling himself the Private Eye-PO.

Child's play.

Vann's offices were small, each room ten by twelve. Windows high on the wall overlooked a green pasture where horses were left to run. Not that Vann spent much time looking. Everything in the world that interested him could be found in this room or the next. Every bare surface was packed with computers and peripheral equipment: PCs, Macs, servers, scanners, printers. At last count he had nine systems up and running, twenty-four seven. He also had some cool *Lord of the Rings* stuff on the shelves, a Lava lamp he'd gotten for Christmas that he couldn't decide whether was lame or not, and a model of the Eiffel Tower he'd gotten at Paris! Paris! on a trip to Las Vegas last year with his parents.

Scrunching his nose, Vann saddled closer to the monitor. Though not entirely necessary—given the parameters of the assignment—he decided to spend a few minutes studying the Private Eye-PO's web page. He backtracked through a month's worth of the man's weekly columns, basically "rants and raves" about new issues coming to market. Finding the attacks on Mercury Broadband, an IPO managed by Black Jet Securities, he understood why Mr. Gavallan was in such a hurry to find out who had written such mean-spirited words. If it had been his stock the Private Eye-PO was attacking, Vann would have killed the guy.

The first thing Vann did was contact a buddy who worked for Hotmail.com and get him into a private room on IRC, the Internet Relay Chat.

Hotmail.com was a free mail service, and anonymous— that is, you could set up an account there without giving your name, address, phone number, or credit card, any of which would have made it way too easy for someone like Jason Vann to find you. You did, however, have to provide a valid E-mail address to retrieve the password you needed to access the system. Unbeknownst to the lay user, the sign-on page contained an "x field" that recorded the IP address—the "Internet protocol" where the mail was sent.

Vann's contact at Hotmail.com was Ralph Viola, who went by the handle "Stallion."

> JV (Jason Vann): My man, I need the 411 on one of your users. Usual terms apply. Here you go: PrivateEye-PO. Whatcha got?
>
> Stallion: Wait a minute while I get the logs.... Okay, got it. Your man's IP=22.154.877.91. Logged on this morning at 7:21 EST. Gaming tonight? We're doing Stalingrad. You can be General von Paulus.

JV: Screw that. Krauts always lose in that one. Too busy, anyway. Who is the ISP?

Stallion: Not so fast, jack. Time to up the scratch. People watching over my shoulder. Five bills'll do the trick.

JV: You're a thief, but since I'm in a hurry, okay. Try it again and I'll brand thee "Highwayman."

Stallion: And thee "Rogue!" The ISP is BlueEarth.com in Palm Beach, Florida. Thanks and aloha, McGarrett!

JV: Aloha!

Since word had gotten out that Vann had joined up with the feds, everyone had started calling him McGarrett. Like Steve McGarrett of *Hawaii Five-O*, which even the biggest dumb-ass knew was the coolest cop show ever on TV. *"Book him, Danno!"*

He looked down at the name of Private Eye-PO's ISP, or Internet service provider. BlueEarth.com. Every time the Private Eye-PO logged on, his modem was connected to one of BlueEarth's servers, and that server had its own unique and permanent Internet protocol address. Stallion had given him the server address where the Private Eye-PO's mail was last sent and the time of transmission. All Vann had to do was contact BlueEarth.com and find out the IP and corresponding phone number that had logged on to that particular server at 7:21 EST this morning.

Child's play.

Vann entered his mail program and pulled up a file containing the names, E-mail addresses, and web handles of people who worked for ISPs. When he'd first gotten hooked on the Net there were maybe a hundred ISPs across the country. Now there were thousands. He guessed BlueEarth was a newcomer, because he couldn't recall ever coming across the name before. No matter; he was sure that somewhere in his files, he'd have something about BlueEarth. Some of the information came from his friends. Some he purchased. Some he procured by more sophisticated means.

Amazingly, the search failed to turn up any associates he might contact at BlueEarth.com, no Ralph "Stallion" Viola he could slip five hundred bucks in exchange for Private Eye-PO's IP and phone number. Vann scratched at his hair, frowning.

Suddenly the screen stuttered, went blank, then colored a sizzling hot pink.

Reset. Fatal exception at F275A-II/7. 13:52:45.

Maybe it wouldn't be the easiest hundred thousand he'd ever made.

A long gulp cleaned out the Dew. He tossed the can in the trash and slid back his chair.

It was a lovely day outside: blue sky, a few clouds, temperature closing in on ninety. The Bullises had their Thoroughbreds roaming free in the pasture. He particularly liked the bay gelding and was certain it would have made an excellent charger. If he ever learned to ride, he might ask the Bullises to allow him to take the bay to the jousting tournament at the annual Renaissance Faire in College Park. He toyed with the idea for a few seconds, then discarded it. He'd never be able to find a decent suit of armor. Besides, before that, he'd have to learn how to drive.

Cracking his knuckles, Vann brought his chair close to his PC. It looked like Mr. Gavallan was going to make him earn his money today. Vann didn't like hacking into an ISP, but sometimes a carefully considered violation of an individual's or enterprise's privacy was necessary. If anyone had a problem with it, they could take it up with the FBI. Agent Fox Mulder would be pleased to assist in the matter. And whistling the theme from *The X-Files*, he began banging code into his computer, working his way, step by laborious step, into BlueEarth.com's innermost sanctum: the customer address files where they guarded the names, phone numbers, and IPs of all their clients.

THREE HOURS LATER, he was still working.

The sun was setting and the small room had grown hot and stuffy, the air as rank and cloying as a high school weight room's. Vann didn't notice. Head bowed, he banged line after line of code into the computer, waiting for the walls to fall. So far, every one of his ploys had failed. He couldn't find a back door. The firewall was impenetrable. And he couldn't keep hacking into the site much longer for fear of being spotted by BlueEarth's security programs.

A voice called from downstairs. "Jason, dinner's ready!"

"Just a second."

Vann tapped at the keys a few moments longer, then threw his hands up. He was beaten and he knew it. "Damn it all!" he muttered, sliding back from his desk and staring at the impotent keyboard.

"Jason!!"

Vann logged off the Net and stalked from his room. There were other ways of finding the Private Eye-PO. It might take a little longer, but in the end, he'd nab him just the same. These "messiah" types were all alike. They craved attention. The anonymous ones were the worst. They couldn't go a day without dropping into some chat room on the web or the IRC to learn what their public thought of them. And next time the Private Eye-PO did that, Jason Vann would be waiting for him. He just hoped it was soon. Vann wanted the fifty-thousand-dollar bonus.

"Coming, Mom," he called.

"And be sure to wash your hands and face."

Vann closed and locked the door behind him. Here he was, thirty-nine years old, and his mother was still telling him to scrub up before dinner. Maybe when he turned forty she would start treating him like an adult.

11

GHOSTS IN A FROZEN MIST, they ran.

Twelve men. Bold apparitions clad in white, doggedly advancing to the same silent cadence, their breath erupting in violent, staccato bursts. Forward. Ever forward. Against the wind. Against the snow. Against themselves.

The cold seeped through their boots, clamping their toes and nipping at their heels with teeth as hungry as a bear trap's. The snow was deep here—two feet, at least—a soupy, devilish mixture of slush and dirt and the spores from the unyielding tundra. And this one week from midsummer's eve. A frantic wind howled around them, clawing at their eyes, scratching their cheeks, slyly slipping beneath the folds of their anoraks and burrowing through their sweaters, their fatigues, and their thermals, biting their skin like ice on fire.

The men's legs were strong, their muscles hard and conditioned, exquisitely calibered pistons willing to carry them over hill and dale hour after hour. Their arms swung by their sides, the dry, rhythmic chafing of the snowsuits sounding like sandpaper scraping velvet. Each man carried a pack, and in that pack a jumble of rocks and stones weighing twenty-five kilograms—fifty-five pounds. They leaned forward as one, their well-toned shoulders and tensed abdomens working in concert to distribute the load. Soon the packs would be filled with a different cargo—timers, fuses, detcord, and plastique, sophisticated devices as far evolved from stones as men were from apes.

The wind died. The icy curtain fell, and for a minute or two the men were permitted a view of the bleached panorama around them. It was a bleak vista, white hills rolling away to the east and west, an endless plain advancing before them. The sky hovered low and gray, a sweeping expanse of nothingness. It was a pale, barren land with no sign of animals, vegetation, or human habitation. Man did not belong here, so far north; his existence counted for nothing. As punishment for their intrusion, the wind picked up so abruptly as to slap the men across the face. They were not welcome here.

Still they ran. Invaders of the Arctic Circle. Five kilometers remained to the halfway point, then back again to base by a different, more difficult route. Another twenty kilometers over uneven, climbing terrain. It was their last training run, a brutal, delirious culmination of four months' preparation. Four months without leave, without a single day's rest, without alcohol, tobacco, or women. Physical conditioning was placed at a premium, but there were mental exercises as well: endless hours mastering English, in particular the American roughneck's slang. Courses in engineering, physics, and the mathematics of high explosives. And, of course, the endless repetition of their tactical objectives. Practicing over and over until every step was memorized and every permutation analyzed, countered, and defeated.

They had been chosen from the best. In other times and other places, similar men had made up the elite forces that had carried names like La Légion Étrangère, the SAS, and the Delta Force. More familiar to them was the Spetsnaz, their own country's vaunted Black Berets. They were called, simply, Team 7. If the name did not carry the same mystique as those of their illustrious antecedents, it was for good reason: Team 7 did not exist. No record could be found anywhere in the administrative logs of the army, navy, or air force testifying to their founding. No roster listed their names, their ranks, the units from which they had been seconded. When they completed the operation, they would disband and flee to the four corners of the globe, sworn never to speak with one another again.

They were all munitions specialists, five drawn from artillery, four from infantry, and three from underwater demolitions. Explosives were their game, and there were no soldiers anywhere who could better their adeptness with plastique, C-4, or gelignite. They had blown bridges in Kunduz and waterworks in Grozny. They had mined highways in the Sudan and mosques in Eritrea.

It was not, however, their skill under fire that recommended them, but the artist's care with which they practiced their craft. Deft fingers shaped the soft, explosive putty as a sculptor handled his clay, and with the same eye for effect. They could blow out a lock and leave the door standing or bring down a ten-story building with a single charge.

Their target lay thousands of miles away, across the roof of the world. The mission would require speed and stealth, but mostly care and concentration. With the smallest of charges, they would wreak the greatest of damage. Nature would have its revenge on man. And man would fall to his knees in apology. *Never again*, he would promise. *Never again*.

The shadows moved into the distance, their steps slower, but still confident, a faint humming now dancing from their lips. It was a song they knew well: the anthem of their birthplace. And as their fatigue grew, they hummed louder. They would rebuild their country. They would make it strong once again. Formidable. A force.

A strong wind lashed across the landscape and they were gone, faded to obscurity inside the umbrella of grit and rain and sleet.

Ghosts who had never been.

Soldiers who never were.

A team that did not exist.

12

"*In nomine Patris, et Filii, et Spiritus Sancti* ..."

Konstantin Kirov was dizzy. He had been standing in the front row of the Church of Christ the Savior for two hours, listening with the rapt attention expected of the guest of honor as Archbishop Nikitin, primate of Moscow, droned on and on, giving thanks for Kirov's gift of a fifteenth-century icon by the master Rublev depicting St. Peter slaying the dragon. The icon rested upon the altar. Only fourteen by seven inches, the portrait was a masterpiece of its kind, watercolors and gold leaf applied to a wood canvas, then glazed with albumen. Peter rode astride his stallion, lance carried high. His face was fevered, yet calm, his fear replaced by a trust in the Almighty. A faint halo crowned his head. The dragon, of course, was unseen. Iconography demanded that full attention be given the subject.

Kirov clamped his jaw as the archbishop passed close to him, swinging the censer and scenting the air with pale, acrid smoke. The columns swirled upward toward the cathedral's vaulted ceiling, the vanishing fingers signifying man's prayers lifting unto the Lord. Kirov followed the smoke along its course, viewing the church's interior with a mixture of piety, awe, and disgust. The acres of stained glass, the armies of tortured sculptures, the fabulous array of frescoes and trompe l'oeils awash in gold leaf: It was the Sistine Chapel times ten, without a trace of its grandeur. But what could one expect? Michelangelo had needed seven years for the chapel's ceiling alone; the entire Church of Christ the Savior was constructed in three. Its religiosity was so overwhelming as to be garish, laughable even, thought Kirov. There was not a better example of the contemporary Russian soul to be found in the entire country.

The Church of Christ the Savior was Moscow's latest miracle and the mayor's crowning achievement. Four inferior onion domes crowned each of the cathedral's transepts and surrounded a fifth and dominant dome whose enormous golden gilt swirls were visible across central Moscow—a candle's flame unto the heavens indeed. The church was a larger replica of the original Church of Christ the Savior that had been built on the same site between 1833 and 1883, designed by the architect Konstantin Toms and inaugurated by Czar Alexander II. Stalin in his good graces had torn the church down, melting the gold leaf for the Communist Party's coffers and using the land to erect one of his "Stalin Skyscrapers," atop which he wished to mount a ten-story statue of Lenin. When the land proved sandy and unstable, Stalin shelved the skyscraper and built instead Europe's largest outdoor swimming pool, which he personally christened "the Lido."

"Konstantin Romanovich Kirov, please step forward."

Awoken from his daydream, Kirov placed one foot in front of the other and advanced toward the ornate altar.

"In the name of the holy church, I commend your generosity of heart and spirit, and thank you for the wondrous gift to our diocese." Archbishop Nikitin grasped Kirov's shoulders and bestowed three kisses upon his cheeks, his long, grizzled beard scratching Kirov's face. The mayor followed, placing a bronze medal around his neck. "The city of Moscow is grateful, Konstantin Romanovich," he whispered. "You have done a great service."

"It is my pleasure." The mayor might reek of vodka, but at least he was clean-shaven.

The choir chanted. An organ played. The congregation was dismissed.

In front of the church, Kirov posed for photographs with the archbishop and mayor. It was a happy union of commerce, church, and state. Come morning, the beaming threesome would be on the front page of the city's newspapers.

"Should you need anything, I insist you call me," the mayor said as the crowd broke up. "We must lunch at the Café Pushkin soon. At my table in the library."

Kirov smiled dutifully. "I look forward to it."

The mayor went on talking about his favorite dishes at the tony restaurant, but Kirov only pretended to listen, for a voice in his earpiece had begun speaking. "Excuse me, sir. Rosen here. We have a small problem."

"Yes?" mumbled Kirov, his chin pushed into his chest. The Russian flag decorating his lapel was, in fact, the microphone of his cellular phone.

"Some news on the Net regarding Mercury. This fellow the Private Eye-PO again. You will not be pleased."

"I'll be there at noon," he said.

The mayor eyed him queerly. "I'm sorry, Konstantin Romanovich, but I am not free at noon. Perhaps next week. And if you can get another icon like that, we'd love to have it in the Novodevichy's chapel. Name your price."

WE MUST FIND HIM," Kirov declared. "I want no expense spared."

"It isn't a question of expense, I'm afraid," replied Janusz Rosen. "He leaves us no name, no address."

The two were standing in Kirov's spacious office on the second floor of Mercury Broadband's Moscow headquarters, located in a newly renovated building one block from the Arbat.

"What do you mean, 'no name, no address.' Look here"—Kirov brushed a hand against the monitor displaying the Private Eye-PO's latest attack on Mercury Broadband—"someone is sending us this page, some server at some ISP. He has even given us his E-mail address. Surely we have contacts at Hotmail, if not at Microsoft."

"I've done my best to track him down. He's sharp. He knows how to make himself invisible. If he wishes to remain anonymous, it will be impossible to find him."

"Nothing is impossible." The admission of defeat crouched within the Pole's words angered Kirov. Ten years ago he was lying on a bunk in Lefortovo Prison, Moscow's main military jail, surviving on hardtack and water; today he was on the verge of a deal that would make him a billionaire. "If the mouse won't come to you, offer him some cheese," he said playfully, advancing on the gangly computer scientist. Then the eyes narrowed and the voice dropped a notch. "Find him, Janusz. Or I'll find someone who can. Someone a little hungrier for shares in our nation's most promising public offering. Remind me, will you ... are there many U.S. dollar millionaires in Gdansk?"

"No, of course not—I mean yes, I'll do my ..." Rosen raised an acquiescent hand, his words drifting off as he scurried down the hallway.

Kirov shut the door quietly and walked in measured paces to his desk. *"Anonymous!"* he scoffed, shooting the monitor a killing glance. Who would wish himself such a terrible fate?

A hunched, dark man in a houndstooth jacket sat in a chair in the far corner, mumbling angrily into a cellular phone. Kirov ignored him. Picking up the phone, he dialed an internal number. "Boris," he said when a male voice answered. "Bring round the cars. We've a meeting with the prosecutor general himself in half an hour, and a little bird whispered in my ear that it would be wise to be punctual."

Hanging up the phone, he collected a sheaf of papers and shoved them into his briefcase. The papers were unimportant, just something to give the case a little heft.

"So?" asked the swarthy guest. He had mournful black eyes and a swirling salt-and-pepper mustache.

"Nothing more than a 'chat,' " said Kirov, not looking up from his briefcase. "Still, one never knows these days." It was an understatement. Political winds were swirling in violent, unfamiliar patterns; the government a clumsy Hydra, with each head acting independently of the other. One day the boys in the Kremlin were doing their best to promote the affairs of the country's more prominent businessmen, the next they were accusing them of every violation in the penal code, littering included.

"Be careful," ordered the man.

Kirov did his best to smile. "As always."

13

WATER, KONSTANTIN ROMANOVICH? You look a bit flushed. Something to eat?"

"A sherry would be nice. Perhaps some foie gras."

"I can offer water and a cracker," said Yuri Baranov.

"Thank you, but no." Folding his hands in his lap, Kirov adjusted his immaculate posture and the smile of infinite goodwill that went with it.

For two hours, he had been seated in the same chair listening to Yuri Baranov, the nation's prosecutor general, rant about the sum of one hundred twenty million dollars missing from the coffers of Novastar Airlines. Theft of government property. Illegal exportation of hard currency. Grand larceny. Fraud. Even treason. The accusations went on and on and Kirov was quickly growing tired of them. How many times could a man say he was sorry, but he had no idea what had happened to the money?

"Let us proceed on a new tack," declared Baranov grimly, selecting a document from one of the bottomless stacks that littered his desk. "May I ask if the name Futura Holding conjures any memories?"

"Futura Holding, you say? I'm sorry, but it is not a name to me."

"So I may take it that if you were listed as a director of the company, it would come as a surprise?"

"I am a businessman. I sit on the board of a great many companies. It's difficult to keep track."

Baranov leaned forward in his seat and offered him the document. He was seventy if a day, a gray, stiff man in an ill-fitting suit with yellowing teeth and a well-worn expression of permanent outrage. A poster boy for the old regime, thought Kirov, hating and fearing him in equal measure.

Baranov was known to every Russian over the age of fifty as the man who had tried the arch-spy Oleg Penkovsky, the GRU colonel and war hero who had fed his nation's secrets to JFK and the Americans over an eighteen-month period in 1961 and 1962. Kirov could still remember the fuzzy black-and-white images of Baranov standing on the steps of the Lubyanka calling for Penkovsky to confess his crimes, name his co-conspirators, and publicly apologize to his countrymen if he wished to receive the Rodina's mercy.

Confess! Collaborate! Apologize! Only then will the Motherland shower her mercy upon you.

"Do you wish then to deny that you are a director of Futura Holding S.A., domiciled in Lausanne, Switzerland?" Baranov asked.

Kirov shook off the memory and concentrated on the document in his hand. He recognized it immediately. The articles of incorporation for said Futura Holding S.A. The paper was dated March 13th of last year. Kirov was listed as 51 percent shareholder in the company; the purpose of the holding noted as "investments in foreign corporations." "So I am a director of Futura. So what?"

"On March 15th, shares in Novastar were auctioned to the private sector. As the winning bidder, you were permitted to purchase forty-nine percent of the company. A month later, the shares were transferred to Futura in Lausanne, Switzerland."

"That's hardly news. Everybody in the country knows I purchased Novastar. About time someone decided to run one of our national airlines properly. Besides, forty-nine percent is hardly a controlling stake. If I recall, the government owns fifty-one percent."

"A formality. Managerial control of the airline was ceded to the private sector as a precondition to the auction. Therefore Futura is responsible for Novastar's day-to-day operations. The government is a silent partner."

"Apparently no longer."

Baranov continued. "On the seventeenth of March, Novastar management sent a directive to all its foreign sales offices ordering all remittances to be wired to an account in an offshore bank." He picked up a new document and read from it. "I quote, 'All proceeds from advance ticket sales, tour bookings, late fees, and penalties are to be paid into the account of Futura S.A. at the Banque Sino-Suez.' The directive is, in itself, an infraction of our legal code. Revenues accruing to the Russian government are to be transferred to Moscow. I could have you thrown in Lefortovo for that alone. What was the purpose of this measure?"

Lefortovo. Stones dripping with damp. Lice-infested beds. Midnight searches of prisoners' cells.

"Ease of accounting. A Swiss firm does all our work."

Baranov dismissed the answer with a sneer. "What concerns me more, however, is that since the time of this directive there has been a shortfall in income of over one hundred million dollars from last year's sales."

"Business has fallen off this year," Kirov explained, his mouth grown parched. "It would help if the government initiated a campaign to bring tourists to the motherland."

For once the pasty lawyer smiled. "Actually, bookings are up fifteen percent over last year."

"Fifteen percent?"

"Fifteen point six to be exact."

Kirov held the attorney's eye, hoping to conceal the tide of unease crashing inside him. First Futura and now mention of Novastar's bookings. Next thing Baranov would say he had the banking records to boot. A word scratched at Kirov's throat, begging to be acknowledged, spoken, screamed. *Spy.* Someone was slipping his organization's most important records out of his offices.

"I don't involve myself in the day-to-day affairs of my companies," he finally said. "I know nothing of the directive, but you have my word it will be discontinued immediately. I'm sure the shortfall in revenues is simply an accounting error."

"One hundred twenty million dollars is more than an accounting error."

"Then the error is surely yours, not mine."

"I think not, Konstantin Romanovich. Don't be surprised to find a government delegation coming to your offices for an early visit one of these days. You know my boys—the ones with ski masks, camouflage utilities, and machine guns. I've been made to understand that you are a demon for order—some might even say obsessive. Who knows what we might find. Perhaps some documents with the Banque Privé de Genève et Lausanne name?"

The Banque Privé de Genève et Lausanne? How the hell had Baranov come up with that name?

Kirov colored, but his voice remained calm and modulated. "Is that a threat?"

"One hundred twenty million dollars is missing," said Baranov solemnly. "Return to the state that which it is due and this inquiry will be terminated."

Confess! Collaborate! Apologize! The iron voice echoed across forty years.

"A raid will not be allowed," protested Kirov. "If you wish to launch a formal investigation into my handling of Novastar's affairs, you're welcome to do so. But use the proper channels."

Baranov slammed an open hand on the table. "The Rodina is in a pitiable condition. Our people need money, not justice. The rule of law must take a backseat to economic necessity. We will no longer stand by as you and your like continue to rape the country, as you strip Mother Russia of her wealth to line your own pockets. You oligarchs are jackals, one and all."

"Never have I robbed the Rodina," said Kirov, his voice silk to Baranov's sandpaper. "I do not sell her minerals on the cheap. I do not smuggle her diamonds or gold out of the country. I do not squander her oil. I am a builder. A creator. Look around you. Half the new buildings in this city are mine. Offices. Apartments. Restaurants. I started a television station from nothing and built it into our city's most popular. A thousand rubles says the radio in your car is tuned to my station. It is I who have upgraded our country's phone lines, I who have brought the Internet to our young people and businesses."

"Yes," said Baranov, all outward calm evaporating. "You have constructed buildings, but at twice the true cost. Your offices charge outlandish rent to your own companies. Advertising billings collected by your television station are booked to offshore companies. Income tax—I don't even dare ask what you pay ... *or don't*. As for Mercury Broadband and your interest in the upgrading of our nation's infrastructure, it is as suspect as the rest of your operations. Be most assured, Konstantin Romanovich, we are aware of your ambitious plans—*all of them*—and we will decide which are acceptable."

Kirov was not blind to the threat. He shuddered to think what might happen to the Mercury Broadband IPO should his offices be raided by government troops. The press would be forewarned. Pictures would be broadcast over Russian television by noon and in America by nightfall. The offering would be postponed, or more likely canceled. Two billion dollars gone. And why? Because Kirov had conducted himself according to standard Russian business practice? Because he'd dared to prosper in perilous times?

He blinked, and despite himself his eyelids stuttered. Whatever else might happen, the IPO had to go through. Too many people were relying on its success. He, to build the first great company of the new millennium and to gild his path through the corridors of power. Others, to advance ambitious plans of their own, plans that would restore luster to the country's sword and shield.

Fathoming for the first time the insidious nature of the forces arrayed against him, he shed his mantle of insecurity and donned his fighting gear. If Baranov expected him to roll over and give up, he was sorely mistaken. Kirov had been fighting intimidation his entire life. As a Jew. As an intellectual. And as a businessman.

"Your threats are reprehensible," he declared in a soft, dangerous voice. "But nothing more than I expected from one of Brezhnev's bullyboys. I remind you we live in a democratic society these days. I've even heard a rumor we have rights."

"Thieves have no rights!" Baranov stood, his chair tumbling behind him. "Return to the state that which is its due and the inquiry will disappear. You have my word."

"*Your word?* Your word is as reliable as the false accusations you've been tossing at me all afternoon." Only his mother's ingrained good manners prevented him from spitting on the floor. Suddenly, he could stand it no longer: the musty room, the weak lightbulbs, the worm-eaten furniture. Any moment, Khrushchev himself would walk through the door and start banging his shoe on the table.

Standing, Kirov buttoned his jacket. "Excuse me," he said politely. "I have a pressing engagement."

Lowering his head, he rushed from the room. There was a spy burrowed inside Mercury, and Konstantin Kirov had to root him out.

14

LOOK, MR. GAVALLAN, it's simply too early to start looking for your friend," said Everett Hudson, a consular officer with the United States Embassy in Moscow. "Twenty-four hours? I don't think they consider a man missing in Russia for a *week*. Until then they just think he's drunk."

Hudson had a squeaky, somewhat unsure voice. A Yalie on his first assignment with the foreign service, guessed Gavallan. Or a baby spy still wet behind the ears. "Mr. Byrnes is not a Russian," he said gravely.

"Of course he isn't," agreed Hudson. "Look, I'll forward the description you gave me to the police, and I'll be more than happy to phone the larger hotels. But I remind you, Moscow is a large city. It covers nine hundred square kilometers and has over ten million inhabitants all included. There's a lot of places to hide."

"Mr. Byrnes isn't hiding. He came to Moscow on extremely urgent business. He is a reliable man. He was due to call me this morning. As he hasn't, I have to assume something ..." Gavallan hesitated, searching for the right word. "Well, that something *bad* has happened to him. He's a former Air Force officer. He's ..." Gavallan didn't bother finishing. He had already offered a nutshell explanation of Byrnes's reason for visiting Moscow; it would serve no purpose to offer any further testimonial to his character. "Something's just wrong, okay?"

"Can I be honest with you, Mr. Gavallan?"

"Please." Gavallan took a sip of Coke and set down the can. The clouds had moved on, leaving the sky a pale-washed blue. Whitecaps and a considerable chop attested to a steady offshore breeze. Feeling tired, frustrated, and more than a little pissed off, he kneaded the top of his knuckles while ordering himself not to explode.

"Moscow is kind of a strange city. I've been here four years, and you wouldn't believe the stuff I've seen. What I mean to say is that sometimes people go a little crazy when they get here."

"Crazy?"

"Well, not crazy, but they tend to let go. Especially men. You see, it's kind of a free city these days. After so long under the thumb, the Muscovites have gone a little wild. Let their hair down, if you know what I mean."

"What is your point, Mr. Hudson?"

"Your friend Mr. Byrnes is forty-four years old, correct?"

We've gone over that.

"Yes."

"And you mentioned he was divorced?"

We've gone over that, too.

"Yes."

"Without wanting to sound rude, there's a lot of trouble a forty-four-year-old man can get into over here. If I called the police right this minute and said I was looking for a man like Byrnes, a well-to-do American, first time to Moscow, staying at the Baltschug, missing twenty-four hours, they'd laugh at me. They think every American is in town for one reason and one reason only: to shack up with their women. And they're not half wrong. Why, last week I had a call from the head of human resources for a major accounting firm in New York. She wanted to know if I might be able to explain why so many of her younger managers refused transfers out of Moscow. What was so special about the town that made them so reticent to leave? She said if she knew maybe she could make people stay in their Cleveland office longer."

"If you're trying to insinuate that Mr. Byrnes is off on some drunken jag through Moscow's fleshpots, you're mistaken."

"I'm suggesting no such thing," he said unconvincingly. "I'm just saying relax. Wait a little longer. Honest, Mr. Gavallan. It is too soon to be worried."

"Let me be the judge of that, Mr. Hudson. I've known my friend for a long time and I know when to worry."

"Really?" Hudson's voice grew contemplative. "It's my experience that you never really know anybody. I mean not really. At least not in Moscow. Here anything's possible." Hudson's voice lost its dreamy cast and Gavallan could almost picture him perking up at his desk, sitting straighter, putting on the consular officer's permanent-press smile. "I'll look for your friend—you have my word. Just don't get your hopes up, okay?"

"Thank you, Mr. Hudson. You have my number."

After he hung up the phone, Gavallan spent a moment wondering if what Hudson said was true—about never really knowing anybody. Naw. It was bullshit. If there was one person he did know, it was Grafton Byrnes. Something had to be very wrong for him not to have called by now. Robbery, kidnap, murder. One by one he turned over the possibilities. There was one, however, he had not yet named. It lurked hidden in shadow in the corner of his mind, but he refused to grace it with serious thought.

"Jett," came Emerald's efficient voice on the speakerphone. "I've got Moscow on the line. Mr. Kirov."

It was Gavallan's turn to sit up straighter. Taking a last

sip of Coke, he threw the empty can in the trash bin on top of three others—Mountain Dew, A&W Root Beer, and Big Red—then slid back his chair and stood. "I'll take it, thank you." He snapped the receiver to his ear. "Konstantin, you're up late."

"I suppose you know all about this. It's a disgrace, really. Why didn't you call with the news?"

Kirov spoke slowly, his voice so quiet as to be a whisper, and immediately Gavallan sensed the control, the ironfisted discipline, that governed his emotions. Danger, he told himself. But for another moment, he didn't respond. He was unsure whether Kirov was referring to Grafton Byrnes's unannounced visit to Moscow or to the Private Eye-PO's latest broadside.

"I was interested in getting your opinion," Gavallan said noncommittally. "Besides, I thought it could wait until tomorrow morning your time."

"My opinion? What do you think my opinion is? I'm incensed. I am as angry as I have ever been in my life. He really is too much. He's gone too far this time. What I want to know is if anybody out there is stupid enough to believe him."

The Private Eye-PO. Kirov had read the lastest posting on the web.

Gavallan let go his breath, fighting his disappointment. He'd been sure Kirov had called to say that Byrnes had contacted him about his visit to Mercury's Moscow NOC. "Unfortunately, a good many do. Fidelity cut their order this morning. Not a good sign."

"And you? Do you believe it?"

"No, I don't. But I'd like you to tell me I'm right."

"Of course you're right."

"And you've purchased exclusively Cisco routing equipment for your Russian IP backbone?"

"I don't know if we've purchased Cisco exclusively. We buy from Alcatel, Sun, and a dozen others. But we do buy from Cisco, and I can prove it. I'm calling to say that

I've asked my chief technical officer in our Geneva office to fax you copies of our purchase receipts from Cisco for the past two years."

"The receipts? Yes, that would be wonderful. Very helpful. Thank you, Konstantin." He swallowed. "Still, if anything is amiss with your platform in Moscow—*anything*—we can shelve the offering and wait a few months. Demand for Mercury is strong enough that we'll be able to reschedule the issue." The words came hard, tumbling out of his mouth like stones.

"Shelve the offering? Out of the question. We have concrete plans for the money, or have you forgotten what is contained in our prospectus? Shelve the offering? Why ever would you even suggest such a thing? You believe him, is that it? You believe what the Private Eye-PO has said?"

"No, Konstantin, I don't. I want the deal to go through as badly as you. But as a licensed securities dealer, it's my duty to make sure everybody's talking from the same page, that's all."

"And we're paying you very generously for that duty. Moscow is up and running. Everything is a hundred percent operational. Have you got the fax yet?"

Just then, Emerald hustled into the room and laid a sheaf of papers on Gavallan's desk.

"I'm looking at it now for the first time. Give me a minute."

Gavallan's eye passed from one page to the next. The receipts detailed the purchase of over a million dollars worth of various routers and switches. The client was Mercury Broadband Geneva. The manufacturer, Cisco Systems.

All at once, a smile broke out on his face, and he had to work very hard not to burst out laughing. The Private Eye-PO was wrong. He was dead wrong. Someone had fed him a load of malarkey.

"They look good," said Gavallan, as the weight lifted

from his shoulders. He read the documents a second time, still not quite believing them. Only one thing bothered him. It was a small detail, but he had spotted it nonetheless. The receipts were dated February 12 of the current year, yet the summary posted by the Private Eye-PO showed sales for the past three years. He dismissed the discrepancy, if it was one. Before his eyes, he had receipts that clearly confirmed Kirov's statement that the Moscow NOC was "up and running."

"They'll make everyone feel a lot better," he said. "I'll post these as a response to the Private Eye-PO on our web page by the end of business today."

"I hope so," said Kirov. "And what about the Private Eye-PO? What do you plan on doing to him? Surely you do not expect us to sit still while our good name is besmirched."

"I have some people on it already. With any luck, we'll have him located by tomorrow, day after at the latest."

"And then? All of us have our part to play to insure Mercury's future. We expect you to take any and all measures to silence this man. Nothing can stand in the way of Mercury Broadband's going public. Nothing."

"And nothing will," said Gavallan. "I'll see to it the Private Eye-PO's mouth is shut—*permanently*, if I have my way. In the meantime, these receipts refute his accusations nicely. I'd say we're back on track."

"Good," said Kirov. "It's time to put an end to this tomfoolery. There's already been enough snooping."

The line went dead. Hanging up, Gavallan failed to experience the sense of victory, the burst of joy, that Kirov's call and the Cisco receipts should have brought. Instead, a bitter, unsavory taste lingered in his mouth, and he was left with a question.

Exactly what snooping had Kirov been talking about?

———

ROY DIGENOVESE STOOD at the window of a vacant office suite on the forty-first floor of the Peabody Building, peering directly into Jett Gavallan's office seventy feet away. The banker was walking back and forth, one hand to his neck. It was clear he was either very pissed off or very worried about something. "Are you getting a good read now?"

"Yeah, wind's died down so I'm right on target. Hold on." Mills Breitenbach, a tech specialist from the San Fran field office, put a hand to his ear while fiddling with some knobs on a metal device camouflaged to look like a Sony minidisc player. At his feet rested a twelve-inch satellite dish, its cone pointed in Gavallan's direction.

"Hurry up, damn it," said DiGenovese. "Don't want to miss what he's saying."

"Give me a sec. I've got to up the amperage on the beam. Here it comes. Showtime! You're on *Candid Camera*."

Breitenbach punched a button, and Jett Gavallan's voice filled the office. "No, Konstantin, I don't. I want the deal to go through as badly as you. But as a licensed securities dealer, it's my duty to make sure everybody's talking from the same page, that's all."

There was silence as the party on the other end of the phone spoke. DiGenovese noted the exact time. "We'll pick up the other end of this when we get the transcripts from the tap tomorrow," he said to Breitenbach.

Again, Gavallan's voice filled the room, sounding eerily close. "I have some people on it already. With any luck, we'll have him located by tomorrow, day after at the latest."

Breitenbach raised the silver casing to his lips and gave it a kiss. "You are the best, baby!"

The device that allowed the men to listen to a conversation being held seventy feet away through two plates of glass each an inch thick was called a unidirectional lasersat. Shooting a sensitive laser at the window of Gavallan's office, the lasersat read the infinitely subtle vibrations in the glass caused by human speech, then matched the vibrations against a sonic database, or "dictionary," and translated them into distinct words. Measuring the tonal frequency of each syllable, the lasersat was able, to a degree, to re-create the speaker's voice.

"I'll see to it the Private Eye-PO's mouth is shut—*permanently*, if I have my way," came Gavallan's voice, tinny and emotionless, but recognizable. "In the meantime, these receipts refute his accusations nicely. I'd say we're back on track."

"You getting a load of this?" asked DiGenovese. "These guys are cozier than a pearl and an oyster. Fuckin' Clemenza and Vito Corleone."

Breitenbach smiled and patted the lasersat, a father proud of his baby. "You got what you need?"

"Oh, yeah," said DiGenovese, dark eyes blazing. "More than that. A lot more."

15

HE CAME TO.

The world was as he had left it, a dark, rank confessional, choked with the smoke of a hundred foul Russian cigarettes. He didn't know how long he'd been out—if after the pain had become too much he'd slept, or if it was just a period of nonexistence, where everything inside you kept ticking but your brain shut itself off. His legs burned. The rope that tied him to the chair cut into his calves, restricting circulation. He had that tingly feeling in his toes you get when your feet fall asleep, but they'd been tingling like that all night, and now the tingling had sharpened, so that even though he hadn't stood for hours, his feet screamed as if he were walking across a field of broken glass. His arms were where he'd left them, too, stretched taut in front of him, hands laid flat on a coarse plank, wrists secured by means of leather lanyards strung through the wood. His face throbbed. The right eye had swollen closed. He tried to open his eyelid, but nothing happened. Engine one, shut down and unresponsive.

Boris had left the left eye alone.

Boris from Metelitsa.

Boris, his unblinking Torquemada.

He was seated across the table, his posture rigid, his pale, soulless gaze alert, appraising, mocking, and finally condemning. The gaze never changed. It was the one constant in his swirling, unending nightmare, the hard blue eyes never leaving him even when the pain had become too much and his vision had gone blurry, and the scream had exploded inside him, and mercifully, oh God, yes, mercifully, he'd left the waking world.

Seeing him stir, Boris sat forward. He looked at him sadly and shook his head, as if saying, "One more hard case."

"You call now?"

The voice was as dead as the eyes. It was not a request, nor a plea, nor a command. Slowly he unrolled the chamois leather case containing his tools.

Pliers.

X-Acto knife.

A vial of rubbing alcohol.

A roll of gauze.

A lamp hung above the table, the bulb weak, stuttering. A relentless, pulsating backbeat seeped through the walls, causing the lamp to sway as if they were at sea rocking on an easy swell. Somewhere above him, people were dancing. He thought of his children, children no longer, then pushed their faces from his mind. They did not belong here. He would not tarnish them with this filthy place.

The cone of light swung right, and he looked at the hand splayed on the coarse plank. It was hard not to think of it as another man's hand. The thumb, raw, exposed, slick with blood, and lying next to it the thumbnail, extracted with a backstairs surgeon's precision, broken into two rough-hewn pieces.

At some point, he'd taken a clinical approach to things. An objective view. The pain was his, no mistaking that: the shaft of fire bolting up his arm, the paralyzing scream starting far down in his belly, the cry desperate to escape, discovering the mouth stuffed with a rubber ball and secured with a length of duct tape. Yes, the pain was all his. But as the pliers dug deeper beneath the nail, as the X-Acto knife sliced away layer upon layer of stubborn connecting tissue, as Boris pulled and yanked and twisted, his apathetic, unshakable gaze never wavering, he'd given up the hand.

The beat from above grew louder. The walls quivered with the thud of the bass and he could make out patches of the music. "West End Boys." Boris half sang a few words. *Vest-ent boyz*. He stopped and stared hard.

"You call?"

Grafton Byrnes listened to the music a moment longer, savoring it, knowing it to be the last taste of a sane universe. In the dark hours of his captivity, he had fashioned a plan, but it required patience. And patience meant more pain.

Eyes burning with defiance, he shook his head.

Boris reached for the pliers.

16

THE INVITATION READ:

A Midsummer Night's Dream,
A Fantasy, A Flirtation
The St. Jude Children's Hospital's 25th Annual Black
and White Charity Ball
8 o'clock PM
Governor's Ballroom,
The Fairmont Hotel

Gavallan stepped from the passenger seat of the Range Rover, adjusting his dinner jacket while his date for the evening circled the car to join him. He had just enough time to admire the fairy lamps strung across the portico, the baby ficuses and swirling cypresses dressed with tinsel and crepe to look like Shakespeare's enchanted forest, before Nina Slenczka rushed to link arms with him and guide them up the maroon welcome carpet.

"Remember to smile, hon," she said, her flack's professional grin splitting her ruby red lips. "This one's for the morning papers."

Nina handled all of Black Jet's PR, and to Gavallan's mind the date was strictly business. Not to say he didn't find her attractive. Twenty-nine years old, blond, petite, and lithe, she had dressed for the evening in a skintight black sheath, spaghetti straps, and just enough fabric to cover her nipples and navel, maybe a little more. Yes, she was attractive. Stunning even. But Gavallan wasn't looking.

Gavallan paused in front of the bank of photographers to allow them a few seconds to rejigger their flashes and pop off a few shots.

"Let everyone see those baby blues," Nina said, keeping a tight clutch on his arm, not letting him even think of moving on until the photographers were done. She might be a prig, but she knew her stuff when it came to corporate PR. She was right about the importance of his projecting a confident image, especially when one of his company's issues was under fire.

It was a classic San Francisco evening. An offshore breeze had cleared out the cloud cover, leaving the sky clear, dusted with stars. Across the street from the Fairmont sat the Mark Hopkins Inter-Continental and down the block the Huntington Hotel and the California Club, a gentleman's conclave so stodgy that only ten years ago it had refused entry to a serving mayor due to her sex.

A hundred years ago, Nob Hill had been home to the Big Four: Collis Huntington, Mark Hopkins, Chester Crocker, and Leland Stanford, the railroad and silver barons who'd built California. Setting foot on their stomping grounds, Gavallan never failed to feel bucked up, as if the tycoons had left behind some of their marauding spirit. Tonight was no exception.

Inside the ballroom, he made a beeline for the bar. It proved a long and arduous journey. Every two steps he was accosted by a friend or business acquaintance. Half were eager to congratulate him on the honor to be bestowed that evening, half to learn how the Mercury deal was likely to fare.

"I need a cassette player," he whispered to Nina, after swallowing half of his vodka rocks. "I only need two answers: 'Thank you' and 'Just fine.' I'll say I'm saving my voice for my speech."

"Come on," said Nina, "they're your friends and they're happy for you. You're the star this evening. They have to pay their respects. It's your duty to smile and play the good host."

"And I shall not disappoint," he said gallantly. Despite his distaste for glad-handing and small talk, he recognized that Nina was right, and that of all his duties, civility and good cheer were the ones he could guarantee were met.

Gavallan had been donating to St. Jude's Children's Hospital for eight years, dedicating ever-larger chunks of his salary to the institution and its programs to battle children's cancer, spina bifida, and infantile paralysis. He was quick to point out that he was hardly an ascetic. He had the house in Pacific Heights with the roomfuls of Kreiss furniture and Pratesi bedding. He wore whatever clothes he liked. Music came via the firm of Bang & Olufsen, stereo makers to the King of Denmark; television courtesy of a sleek Sony Plasma screen. He owned two Remington bronzes; some lithos by Branham Rendlen, a local artist he thought was dynamite; and, of course, the Mercedes.

There were other claims on his money. He saw to his mother's needs, helped out with his sisters' occasional purchases—washing machines here, new pickups there, schooling for their kids if they asked. He kept a fair amount in the bank, a little in stocks and bonds. (Or at least he had until he'd stuffed it all into his company.) He had enough to take care of him and his family in comfort should everything go to hell in a handbasket.

The rest he gave away.

The ballroom was filling up quickly. Elegant couples drifted through the carousel of tables, a monochromatic mélange of tuxedos, cocktail dresses, and ball gowns, laughing, chatting, and, to his eye, having a sincerely good time. San Franciscans enjoyed their liquor, and under the influence of a stiff drink or two their voices began to rise and fill the room with a jolly din.

Gavallan ordered another drink, then asked Nina if she wouldn't mind going to their table. Bruce Jay Tustin and Tony Llewellyn-Davies were already seated, Tustin with his wife, Nadia, Two Names with his partner, Giles, another wayward Brit. Meg sat at the adjoining table with her husband of forty years, Harry.

Gavallan greeted his guests with exaggerated bonhomie. He wanted it clear that the day's problems were behind them. Tonight they could relax and let their hair down. "Don't I know you nice folks?" he called, lending his voice a bit of the old Rio Grande twang.

The table stood as one. To Caesar, his due.

"Look who's here," said Bruce Jay Tustin. "And I thought security was supposed to keep the riffraff out. Do you have a ticket, young man?"

Meg sprang from her chair and wrapped her arms around him. "Congratulations, Jett. We're all so proud. You done good."

And then the others were up, shaking his hand, hugging him, treating him like a returning war hero. It was easy to forget that he'd only left them two hours earlier.

"Seriously, Jett, we're honored to share this evening with you," sounded Tony Llewellyn-Davies. "Believe it or not, we care about you deeply." He held Gavallan at arm's length, then proclaimed, "Oh, what the hell. I'll say it for everyone. We love you and we're overjoyed to be here. And that's the last nice word you'll get from any of us this evening." And with that he gave Gavallan a peck on the cheek.

"Here, here," added Giles, a handsome youth in his

twenties. The two-carat diamond stud in his ear and eighteen-karat gold Cartier on his wrist hinted that his interest in Tony was more pecuniary than personal. Gavallan hoped his friend wasn't being played for the sap.

"The honor is mine, ladies and gents," he said, touched by the outpouring of affection. "It's rare that you get to work with your friends, and for that I feel both privileged and grateful. Now enough of this smarmy nonsense. Let's sit down and enjoy the evening." Raising his glass, he quoted from Bum Phillips, former coach of the Houston Oilers and honorary "good old boy." "Every man have a drink. Every *good* man have two!"

"Hoo-yeah!" shouted Tustin, glass raised high.

Gavallan clinked glasses with Tustin and his wife, Two Names, Giles, Meg, Harry, and Nina. He couldn't help but think of the one man who was missing from their ranks. After everyone quieted, he raised his glass again.

"To Grafton Byrnes. Let's pray for his health and safe return."

IT WAS MIDNIGHT IN POTOMAC, Maryland. Streets in the leafy suburb were so calm as to be deserted. A warm, gusty evening breeze carried the sweet scent of cut grass and the merry sawing of crickets. On Dumbarton Road, the lights in most houses were dimmed, the occupants asleep. But in the Vann residence, a stuttering spectral light glowed from the second-floor dormer windows.

In his bedroom, Jason Vann dashed from computer to computer, pausing long enough to type in a sentence or two, before moving to the next. Beads of perspiration rolled down his forehead. A hunted look shadowed his drawn face. Round and round he went, enraptured by this game of his creation. A game of cat and mouse. Vann was after the Private Eye-PO. He was trying to lure him into the open, and his bait was praise and scorn and disbelief and any number of the hundred emotions that stock enthusiasts routinely express.

At that moment, he was working five characters on the IRC, the Internet Relay Chat, and they were discussing the Mercury Broadband IPO to be brought to market in five days by Black Jet Securities. Mario was a high school student who was president of his stock club. Julie was a middle-class housewife who grew interested in the market after her husband had lost all of their money. Al was a New York know-it-all, a seasoned investor, and a veteran of many (losing) campaigns. Krystof was a programmer of Polish descent who believed that the stock market was every immigrant's way to riches. Heidi was a computer science teacher in Mamaroneck, New York, who had just invested her first five thousand dollars. And they all lived in a twisted corner of Jason Vann's conniving mind.

> Al: The market's gonna gobble up Mercury like a pastrami sandwich. I'm saying double the first day. Think positive.
> Krystof: You are sure? I also think it time for big success again.
> Heidi: Is it safe?
> Mario: I doubled our stock club's fund investing solely in IPOs last year. But be careful. Didn't you see the latest news?
> Julie: Where were you when my husband started trading?
> Al: The Private Eye-PO don't know his ass from his elbow. He's probably a trader pushing his own stocks, knocking down the others. Caution!

Vann rushed from chair to chair, simulating the voices and thoughts of these five would-be investors. He'd spent three hours online introducing them, getting them into a chat room and allowing them to grow comfortable talking in the open. His job was to create a fictitious universe the Private Eye-PO might stumble upon and wish to join. So far he hadn't had a nibble. He was getting discouraged. It was time to up the ante.

> Mario: I disagree. I think he's the only one we can trust. I follow his advice to the letter. If he's a trader, he's a darn good one. Remember what he called Mercury? A scam dog!
>
> Julie: Sounds like you're the Private Eye-PO himself, Mario. Come on, tell us the truth!!
>
> Mario: Ha, ha.
>
> Krystof: Who is this Private Eye-PO? In Poland, you never trust man who does not tell you name. I mean, *his* name. Excuse me.
>
> Al: No way a company like Black Jet is gonna touch Mercury if it's got problems. No way. Be real. I saw Gavallan on CNBC. The guy's a pro. He was a pilot!

Vann had slid back into Mario's chair when a new name popped onto the screen.

> Val: Pros, schmoes. Make up own mind. I buy Mercury and buy big. I have own sources. Nay to Private Eye-PO.

Dismayed, Vann frowned. No way was Val the Private Eye-PO. He sounded like a foreigner. Jumping into Krystof's chair, he tried a ruse.

> Krystof [in Polish]: Hello, new friend. Welcome. You are a fellow Pole, perhaps?
>
> Val [in Polish]: From Gdansk. The great Lech Walesa's home. And you?

"Score!" cried Vann aloud, grabbing a Nerf basketball and stuffing it for a quick two points. Then, collapsing back into Krystof's chair, he typed:

> Krystof [in Polish]: Kraków. I left in '98.

Vann, whose father's real name was Wladisaw Vanniewski, didn't dare add more. His Polish was rusty; anything more than the basics would expose him as a phony. Anxious to keep the dialogue afloat, he moved to Heidi's chair.

> Heidi: A friend of mine is from Warsaw. He made a fortune buying tech stocks. Can they still go up?

There was always at least one total idiot in any chat room.

> Val: They can only go up. Mercury will lead way. To heaven!

Boy, thought Vann. He's a real supporter. As he slid back into Al's chair, another name popped onto the screen.

> Spade: Hey, kids, you want the inside skinny? Talk to me. Your very own celebrity reporter has come to the rescue. Heidi, dear, listen closely to me if you want the *oop-scay* on Mercury. All the rest of you neophytes, *am-scray!*

Vann froze in his chair, eyes wide. "Spade" as in Sam Spade. As in the Private Eye-PO. Could it be? Scooting his chair closer to the computer, he felt his heart pounding like a jackhammer inside his chest. The bait had worked. The fish was on the line.

Wiping his forehead, Jason Vann smiled.

Now he just had to reel him in.

＊

THE FIRST COURSE HAD BEEN CLEARED. Peter Duchin and his orchestra had begun to play an up-tempo version of "Witchcraft," the vocalist doing a very acceptable Sinatra. Couples flocked from their tables to the dance floor. Deciding he'd done enough penance for one evening, Gavallan turned to Nina and asked if he might have the next dance.

"Sorry, Jett, but I've promised Giles. He's dying to cut the rug."

Gavallan smiled understandingly, though he was a little irked. While same-sex partners might be permitted at society functions, their dancing with each other was still touchy. If Tony or Giles wanted to dance, it had to be with a member of the opposing team. Gavallan thought the whole thing ridiculous. He couldn't care less who did what with whom as long as they were happy. Still, Nina was his date and he wanted to dance. "Try and save one for me, will you?"

"Sure thing, hon."

Gavallan watched the happy couple dodge their way to the dance floor, then stood up and set off in the opposite direction. The path to the bar looked mercifully clear of congestion. If he moved swiftly, he might make it scot-free. Fifteen seconds later he was there, leaning against the oak railing and perusing his choices. Whiskey had been his daddy's drink, but Gavallan preferred vodka. Spotting a familiar bottle with yellow script, he decided on one more of the usual. And why not? It wasn't often you put all your chips on red and gave the wheel a spin. After a day like today, a guy deserved to get hammered. It might even add a few laughs to his speech.

"Hey, chief," he called to the bartender. "Let me have an Absolut Citron."

"How would you like it, sir?"

"*Rocks, no twist,*" answered a playful feminine voice behind him. "*And pour it heavy.*"

Gavallan felt a hand brush his shoulder and turned to face a tall dark-haired woman with glossy bangs that fell shy of amused green eyes.

"That's my line," he said.

"And my drink. You stole it."

She had chosen white for the evening, a simple cotton shift that fell to her knees. Her luxuriant hair had been cut short and barely brushed her shoulders. She wore only a trace of makeup—a dash of eyeliner and a shadow of rouge. She'd never liked coming to these fancy dos. She refused to wear high heels and was shy about her shoulders, complaining they were better suited to a lumberjack than a society maiden. She was his tomboy in waiting. His eyes passed over the swell of her breasts, the planes of her belly, the curve of her hips, remembering.

"Hello, Cate," he said. "You look wonderful."

"I wish I could say the same. You look tired. What happened? Some of your clients beating you up over that last IPO? Trivium, wasn't it?"

"Trillium," he corrected her. "And don't be snippy." Trillium Systems was a maker of enhanced circuit boards whose shares had traded down 50 percent the first week of trading. No one batted a thousand. "Just the usual really. Trying to keep the boat afloat. I'll have to have a word with the shaman to help me out."

"You and your shaman." Cate Magnus's hand went to his cheeks. She leaned closer and checked his eyes. "You okay?"

Suddenly he remembered how overwrought she could become. He used to tease her that she'd been programmed with an extra sensitivity chip. "I'm fine. Nothing that a good night's sleep won't cure."

Cate patted his chest lightly, a sign she'd checked him

over and he was in fine fettle. "So is the twenty-million-dollar man ready to entertain the troops? How's the speech? Did you actually write something down or did you plan on winging it?"

Gavallan hadn't given the hospital twenty million dollars outright, but pledged it in annual increments of one million dollars. The third installment was thirty days past due. Not a word had been spoken about the tardy donation.

"You're the writer," he said, sipping at his cocktail. "Me, I just have a couple of drinks and let my silver tongue carry me where it may."

"Silly of me to ask. But be careful, Jett. Too much booze loosens the tongue. You might let a few words slip about all the fires you've been putting out."

"What fires are those?"

"You tell me."

Gavallan registered confusion. "I thought you were a columnist," he complained. "Sounds to me like you're looking for a way to get back on the front page. That why you're here?"

"No," she said. "I slipped by the guards to pay my respects to a pretty neat guy I used to go out with. I think it's great what you've done for the hospital."

"Least I could do, really," he said, searching out her gaze, wanting to stare headlong into her vivid eyes, hoping to find that the connection was still there. But Cate was careful to keep her eyes aloof and darting across the crowd, only briefly engaging his.

"I've been reading that stuff on the web about the deal you've got coming to market," she said. "I hope you're being careful, Jett. I always told you to steer clear of Mercury."

"Come on, let's not start that again."

Cate began to say something, then bit her lip. Offering a noncommittal shrug, she ordered a Stolichnaya straight up, no ice, no chaser. *Her drink.*

Catherine Elizabeth Magnus was a handsome woman, more striking than beautiful. With her angled features, pale complexion, and high cheekbones, she called to mind an exotic strain of royalty. A princess from Liechtenstein, a *Gräfin* from Pomerania, an Italian *contessa*. Her posture was immaculate, her step light, yet directed. When she walked it was for the audience she'd grown used to long ago. And it was the coupling of patrician bearing with her commoner's unpretentious personality that he found so attractive. It didn't take a genius to figure out why. Cate Magnus was the class Jett Gavallan never had.

She'd worked as a reporter at the *Financial Journal* for as long as he'd known her, writing a weekly piece for the paper she called "Gold Rush." Every Friday, she filled twelve column inches on the front page of the *Journal*'s second section with offbeat, funny, and often poignant stories about the ins and outs of surviving in the capitals of the new economy: Silicon Valley, Seattle, Austin, and the few city blocks in Manhattan someone had baptized "Silicon Alley." Her subjects ranged from how the skyrocketing price of real estate was making millionaires out of middle-class home owners to the social etiquette of pink-slip parties to the personal peccadilloes of the new and obscenely rich. The rise and fall of Black Jet Securities would make perfect fodder for her column.

"Speaking of fires, I had an interesting call this afternoon," he said, allowing himself to move a few inches closer to her. "Between you and me, everything the Private Eye-PO has said is bullshit. Complete and utter garbage." He went on to explain about the receipts, his conversation that morning with Jean-Jacques Pillonel, and Konstantin Kirov's personal guarantee that everything was "up and running" in Moscow.

"Kirov himself told you? Well then, I guess you don't have to worry at all."

"Don't start about Kirov. Please, Cate. Not tonight."

"All I said was that you shouldn't trust him. He's an oligarch, for Christ's sake. How do you think he got where he is?"

"He is a businessman, and a damned good one. Neither of us has any idea of the conditions he has to work under over there. I'm not saying he's a saint, but Mercury speaks for itself. It's a gem."

"It sure does."

"What's that supposed to mean?"

"It means he's ruthless and conniving, and maybe even a little more than that. He's a good businessman all right. If that's what you call it."

"Cate!"

Her eyes flashed, and he could feel her straining to rein in her temper. "Okay," she conceded. "You win. Just be careful. Word is you're risking a lot on this deal."

"Whose word is that?"

"Everyone's. No one's. You know how it is. The street's got wind you're putting a lot on the Mercury deal. I just was curious if the rumors are true."

It was Gavallan's turn to shrug. But looking at her, at her lustrous black hair, her keen eyes, her pale, pillowed lips, he had a sudden desire to tell her everything. A need even. Whether she knew it or not, he valued her counsel more than that of any of his colleagues at Black Jet. She was smart. She was well-informed. She was discreet. They'd been together over two years, and though privy to his every insider secret, she'd never once abused his trust.

Cate who was trustworthy.

Cate who was loyal.

Cate who was the most sensuous lover he'd known.

Unable to restrain himself, he ran a hand across her cheek and let it glide through her hair. "I miss you."

"Jett, no," she whispered, her eyes fluttering. It was a plea, a denial, a memory.

"Come on," he said. "Let's dance." And before she

could answer, he grabbed her hand and led her to the parquet floor. Continuing its tribute to "Old Blue Eyes," the orchestra launched into "A Foggy Day." Gavallan drew her closer. In seconds, their hands had found familiar places, their bodies secret havens.

"So what do you want to know?" he asked.

Cate looked taken aback. "You're serious?"

"Have I ever kept anything from you?"

"That was when we were ... That was before," she said.

Before. He hated the word. "You will, however, have to recite the sacred oath."

"Oh, Jett, come on."

"Sorry. You know it's important to me. I am an Eagle Scout, you'll remember. The oath, please."

Cate looked uncertainly to her left and right, then raised her right hand to her shoulder, arranging the fingers in a familiar salute.

> *"On my honor I will do my best*
> *To do my duty to God and my country*
> *and to obey the Scout Law;*
> *To help other people at all times;*
> *To keep myself physically strong,*
> *mentally awake, and morally straight."*

Gavallan nodded his approval. "At least I know your time with me was not completely misspent." He cleared his throat. "Anyway, I guess the first thing you should know is that I'm pretty much tapped out. That much of the rumors is true."

And with that he launched into a recitation of the entire day's events: Byrnes's disappearance, the meeting at Sten Norgren's, his taking out the second mortgage, the particulars of his personal and professional liquidity crunch. He left nothing out.

"So, I guess you had a pretty dull day," she said afterward.

Seeing the mischief in her eyes, he laughed. For the first time since he'd woke, he felt as if things might turn out okay.

17

THEY'D DANCED THREE SONGS IN A ROW. The entree was being served, and suddenly they were the last couple on the floor. Gavallan didn't need to look toward his table to know that Nina was staring daggers into his back. Let her, he thought. I'll take Cate. She can have Giles. Only Tony will be the poorer off.

"So let's get this straight," Cate was saying, "you floated Mercury a fifty-million-dollar bridge loan with no collateral—I mean, other than their stock? Shoot, Jett, I'd be worried, too, about what the Private Eye-PO says."

"Don't be ridiculous," Gavallan countered. "Mercury earned sixty million in profit last year on revenues of three hundred ninety million. No one's disputing that. They couldn't have earned it without the Moscow market. It's one of their biggest."

"I hope you're right, Jett. I really do. Because God forbid that Mercury isn't every inch the company your prospectus says it is, and you bring a fraudulent company public. And in this case I mean 'public' with a capital P. Two billion dollars' worth. Because your life will be over as you know it and everything you hold dear will be taken away from you. Your money. Your company. Everything.

The only good news is that you won't have to worry about that second mortgage anymore. You'll have rent-free accommodations for the next seven years or so. Depends on the judge."

Gavallan listened to her assessment, his worry growing because it was the same one he'd made himself. Earlier, he'd told Tustin and Llewellyn-Davies they had to be true to their client. But Cate's skepticism, coupled with his partner's lingering silence, lent him second thoughts, Cisco receipts and Jean-Jacques Pillonel's word notwithstanding.

"A guy I know is tracking down the Private Eye-PO," he said. "Once we find him, I plan on having a heart-to-heart, just him and me, find out why he's going after Mercury before I have a judge slap an injunction on his ass."

"Why do you think he's going after Mercury?" Cate demanded. "Because he has the goods on them."

"Actually, we were looking into the possibility it might be personal, a grudge or something against Black Jet, or maybe even me."

"Oh, come off it. A grudge? Sometimes you really piss me off." The voice had hardly risen, but her eyes had narrowed and a rigid control had taken hold of her body. Dropping her hands, she turned and walked off the dance floor, weaving through the maze of tables to the hallway outside the ballroom. Gavallan knew she meant for him to follow.

She was waiting outside the ballroom, hands on hips, head cocked defiantly.

"Jett, I want you to listen to something I have to say. And I want you to promise me you won't get mad. You sent Graf to Moscow to check on Mercury's operations there and now you can't find him. Gone from the hotel. Not calling back. Whatever. Point is he's disappeared while he was supposed to be looking into Mercury."

"Yeah?"

"And at the same time the Private Eye-PO issues another warning about Mercury. He's never wrong, that guy. You know it and I know it. Accuracy is his hallmark."

"So?"

Cate's eyes widened. "Do I have to connect the dots? Maybe Graf's disappearance isn't a coincidence. Maybe the Private Eye-PO has the goods on Mercury. Maybe Kirov called you to make sure you were still on board."

"That's enough, Cate. Now you're talking like a fool."

"Am I? Think about it, Jett. Just think about it." The challenge hung between them, the ensuing silence warming her concern from professional to personal. Nearing him, she rested a hand on his jacket and neatly brushed a hair from his lapel, so that for a moment, he dared believe she might still love him.

"So what's your advice?" he asked.

"I'll only tell you if you promise to take it."

"Forget it," he said, turning to go back to the party. "I already know what it is. Drop the deal. I'm not going to do it. I *can't*."

"Postpone the offering," she pleaded. "Let me put you in touch with some of our guys in Moscow. Let them look into it. They're hooked into the whole scene."

Gavallan bit his lip, bitter, confused, wanting to say a million things, not daring to say a word. "The offering is going through, Cate. Like I said, Mercury's a gem. I know it, even if you and the Private Eye-PO don't. Now, if you'll excuse me, I have to go give a speech to three hundred of our city's snootiest before they get too sloshed to understand a word I say."

And opening the door, he walked back into the ballroom.

IN POTOMAC, MARYLAND, and across the ethereal veins of the Internet, the roundtable between Jason Vann's cast of disgruntled characters and the man calling himself Spade was growing more heated.

> Al: Listen to me, kid! You want the inside skinny on Mercury, I'll tell you. You're way off base on this one. My sources tell me Mercury's double the deal you think.
>
> Spade: Whoopee for you! We've all got our sources, honey. And mine is indisputable.
>
> Val: Listen to Al. Where you get silly pictures? I see this and laugh.
>
> Heidi: What picture?
>
> Mario: Go to his website and take a look— www.PrivateEyePO.com. You'll see!
>
> Spade: Thanks, chum. Always nice to know what side your toast is buttered on. As for ye of little faith, the picture cometh straight from the hand of God. Cross my heart and hope to die.

Jason Vann rubbed his hands together, a worried look narrowing his eyes. He was desperate to angle the Private Eye-PO into a private chat room.

> Al: If it's "straight from God" you want, come with me, big mouth, and I'll show you something that'll make you close your yap.
>
> Spade: I go everywhere and nowhere. You got the goods, send them to my address at Hotmail.
>
> Al: You want to keep up that winning percentage, you'd be wise to jump my way. You're not the only one with inside info. I've also got some documents from Mercury. And they tell me the opposite of what they tell you.
>
> Val: I come, too. I also know people at Mercury.
>
> Spade: Who? Give me the name, cutie pie. Don't make me beg.

Val: Janusz Rosen. A Pole like myself. He is programmer. Damn good one, too!

Jason Vann stared at the last sentence, wondering
who the hell "Val" was, why he was so keen on butting
into Mercury's business. If Val was Rosen, then the boys
at Mercury were probably running their own gig to track
down the Private Eye-PO. Surely, "Spade" knew this.

Al and Spade engaged in a few more volleys, the shadowy Val lurking close by, until by sheer force of will Al
broke down Spade's barriers. Immediately, Vann created
a private chat room for Al and Spade to enter, then
slammed the door closed before Val could sneak in. Once
they were inside their cozy, private corner of cyberspace,
Spade relented.

Spade: Your 411 better be white hot, chum. Send
me the stuff to Ponyfan@earthlink.com, and give
your return address. If it's as good as you say, I'll fill
you in on the nitty-gritty with Mercury.

Vann jumped out of his chair, roaring. "Gotcha, you
big m.f. You are so nailed!" Vann had a dozen buddies
at Earthlink. A few calls and he'd have Ponyfan's IP address before he knew it. From there, it would be smooth
sailing. By morning, he'd have all the info he needed to
earn his fifty-thousand-dollar bonus from Mr. John J.
Gavallan: the Private Eye-PO's name, home address,
and phone number.

Child's play!

THE LINE FOR THE VALET CAR PARK stretched from the
curb to the lobby. Gavallan stood near its head, Nina at
his side. She'd barely said a word since he'd returned
from his extended tête-à-tête with Cate. At least he

wouldn't have to worry about how to avoid a good night kiss. Giles was dutifully back with Tony. Meg and her husband, Harry, stood arm in arm, mooning at each other like love-struck teenagers. A cell phone chirped, and every man, woman, and valet froze, listening to hear if it was theirs. Gavallan answered. "Yeah?"

"Jett? That you?"

"*Graf?*" he asked, the relief spontaneous, bringing a wide smile to his face. "Graf, where the hell are you?" He laughed out loud, thinking it was wonderful. Byrnes was okay. He was safe. The fucking shaman had answered his prayers.

"Where do you think? The heart of the evil empire: Moscow. Back in the USSR."

Gavallan turned his back on the crowd and walked a short distance up the sidewalk. "You were supposed to call this morning, you prick. You had us all worried."

"Sorry. Had to double-check on a few things before I got back to you. Didn't want to give you any information until I knew for sure. Look, I've scoped out Mercury's operations. I made it out to the network operations center. Place is in Timbuktu, I don't mind saying. I've seen their offices in town. It's all like we thought it was. The Private Eye-PO is full of shit. Mercury's up and running."

"So the deal's a go?"

"Green light all the way."

"Fantastic," said Gavallan, controlling his urge to holler. Turning his head, he saw the others locked in a group stare in his direction. He waved a hand and gave a big thumbs-up.

"You there?" asked Byrnes.

"Hell, yes. I'm definitely here."

"I knew you'd be happy. Listen, Jett, everything's co-pacetic over here. Copy?"

"Yeah, I copy, pard. Thanks for the great news. I'll get that champagne all iced up; you bring back the caviar.

Two billion, man. Our biggest fish ever. Can you believe it? Just let me know when you're getting back."

And then the words sunk in and Gavallan held his breath while the hairs on his arms and neck stood on end.

Everything's copacetic.

"I'm going to stay the weekend if you don't mind," Byrnes went on. "Moscow's a hell of an interesting place. Thought I might check out some of the sights tomorrow. Saturday, Kirov's invited me out to his summer house in the country. An honest-to-God dacha—can't miss that. By the way, he sends his regards. He's delighted that we decided to take a look for ourselves. Says we're welcome anytime."

"Tell him thank you." It was another man speaking Gavallan's words. "So he wasn't upset when he found out you'd flown over to check out Mercury without letting him know beforehand?"

"I told you he wouldn't be," said Byrnes. "He wanted me to tell you that Mercury must be as transparent as any of its counterparts in the West."

"Did he?"

"Yes, he did. Anyway, I thought I'd fly into New York and meet you for the launch party."

"Sure thing," said Gavallan, searching for words, stumbling. He felt hollow, shaky. A rod of pain, searing and white-hot, fired inside his skull. Wincing, he touched at his forehead. "Um ... yeah, sounds good, see you Monday. Oh, and call Emerald and give her your flight details. We'll send a limo to pick you up at JFK. When you see Kirov, ask him if he's free for dinner."

Gavallan waited for a response, but the line was broken and only static answered his words. Besides, it didn't really matter. Grafton Byrnes had told him everything he needed to know.

Everything's copacetic.

18

GAVALLAN WAS WALKING THE WARD.

His pace was slow, his steps measured. The click of his heels against the linoleum floor sounded to his anguished ears like the final ticks of a time bomb. With every step, he was tempted to draw a last breath, to squeeze tight his eyelids in anticipation of the blast to come. But what would it destroy? he wondered. What was left that hadn't already been torn apart by his own merciless conscience? What might it damage that hadn't been shredded eleven years ago?

The clock on the wall read 2:15. The room was extremely bright and extremely quiet, a fluorescent universe of hushed sounds. His ear seized each in turn—the rise and fall of a neonatal respirator, the gasp of a fragile patient, the sibilant bleed of oxygen—then he continued his all-night vigil.

He was back at the Zoo, doing tours of the Quad for having missed his second curfew in a month. He was pacing the ready room before his first flight into combat. He was the star witness at his own trial. All that was left to decide was the penalty. The verdict had already been given. Guilty on all counts.

"Everything's copacetic," Byrnes had said, a footnote

from their shared history to let Gavallan know he was testifying under duress.

Hardly, mused Gavallan acidly.

A skeleton staff presided at this late hour: a few nurses, orderlies, and cleaners. Through the glass partition, he kept track of a janitor polishing the corridor, his green-clad back bowed and sober, his worn mop eating up miles of hallway with a methodical, unerring rhythm that was a science unto itself.

Gavallan glanced down at the child in his arms, a frail boy swaddled in a sky blue blanket. He'd been awarded the provisional name of Henry, and the name would stick until his mother could come to long enough to provide him a more permanent one. He'd been born one week before, full term, 4 pounds 2 ounces, 14 inches long. To look at him, he was a healthy child. His features were well-formed. Broad nose. Full lips. Dignified chin. His eyes were closed, and a cap of curly black hair crowned his brown skin. But the experienced eye knew differently and ticked off the indicators of the infant's affliction with weary ease. The bluish, trembling lips. The drawn cheeks. The eyes twitching beneath the lids and the head that every minute or so jerked along with them. Ataxic aphasia, they called it, a condition prevalent among children born to crack-addicted mothers.

A tap on the window drew Gavallan's attention.

"Coffee?" asked Rosie Chiu, the head duty nurse, pointing at her own mug. If she was surprised to see a man wearing a dinner jacket beneath his operating gown in the pediatric intensive care ward, she didn't show it. He'd been coming too long for that. Always at night. Always alone.

Gavallan shook his head and said no.

He'd first visited St. Jude's eight years earlier on a Friday evening benefactors' tour. The donors were lectured about the miracle of magnetic resonance imaging, the latest advances in open-heart surgery, and the newest cures in the war against children's leukemia. But it wasn't until Gavallan made it out of the neonatal intensive care unit that he grew angry. His neck grew hot, his suit two sizes too small. Like little Henry, he'd become twitchy all over. He wasn't sure why, but suddenly, he was mad—white-hot, steaming mad. Maybe it was the relentless sunniness of the place—the yellow walls decorated with dancing murals, the cheery nurses, the upbeat smiles—contrasted against the bleak reality of the situation. Even if these kids survived, what did they face? A life lived in medical institutions, state-run homes, or at best foster families. These kids with underdeveloped lungs and diseased eyes, with hair-trigger emotions and chronic aphasia. They had no right to their expectations, he'd railed silently.

But ten minutes later, when Nurse Chiu finished her talk about the hospital's need for volunteers willing to come and walk the infants—to help them grow comfortable with the touch of another human being, to teach them to accept the gaze of another set of eyes, and, yes, just to keep the noisy little gremlins quiet—he'd found himself alone agreeing to return. And he wondered whose expectations he was challenging. His or the kids'?

Gavallan shut his eyes. He couldn't handle another body laid at his feet. Oh no. Byrnes's call had freed him of illusions. Konstantin Kirov was just as Cate had described him—"ruthless and conniving, and maybe even more." This time Gavallan could not look elsewhere for excuses. This time he couldn't fall back on bungled intelligence or fumbled orders. This time it was up to him.

"Don't know if I can handle this one, chief," he whispered to Henry's sleeping brown face. "Think you can give me a hand?"

And he marveled in disbelief at how once upon a time he'd been a warrior.

The whine in his ear built slowly, as it had in the

plane itself. A steady high-pitched cry that signaled the powering-up of the aircraft's avionics package. He was going back to the Gulf. To Saudi Arabia. To Iraq. To Desert Storm. To the night the infrared cameras on the underside of *Darling Lil* recorded the tape that sat even now in his flight locker. The tape titled *Day 40—Abu Ghurayb Presidential Complex*. He was going to his own private little corner of hell, and his familiarity with the territory did little to lessen his terror over the trip.

"Thunder three-six. Red one. How do you read?"

"Roger, Red one. This is Thunder three-six. Ready to copy words. Which way to Wonderland?"

Gavallan is sitting in the cockpit of *Darling Lil*, far out on runway two-niner at King Khalid Air Force Base deep in the Saudi Arabian desert. It is 01:15 Continental European Time, the morning of February 25, 1991. Day 40 of Desert Storm. Ground operations had begun twenty-four hours earlier and the vaunted Republican Guard is surrendering en masse. Morale is high. But Gavallan is ever cautious. When will Saddam unleash his biological weapons? Is he waiting until the last minute to launch a nuke at Israel? What exactly is the Iraqi dictator keeping up his sleeve?

Despite the cockpit's airtight seal, the desert air seeps in and surrounds him. It smells of jet fuel and sweat and a million square miles of superheated sand. Gavallan loves the scent. Inside its arid folds, he can taste his country's victory.

Darling Lil is fully loaded for her night's work. Two GBU-27s sit inside the weapons bay. Each a two-thousand-pound package of high explosives capped with a delayed detonation fuse and a laser guidance system to guarantee hand delivery to the target.

"Thunder three-six. You are clear for takeoff."

"Thunder thirty-six copies all. Salaam Aleik'hum."

Gavallan wraps the fingers of his left hand lightly

around the throttle and guides it forward. For a moment, the plane rocks, as if a boat in a chop, then he releases the brake and the Black Jet begins its shot down the runway. At 180 knots, he rotates the aircraft up and the wheels lift off the ground. He loves this moment, when the aircraft leaves the earth and he feels as if he too has been freed from his temporal moorings. The first climb is brief. At fifty feet, he levels off the aircraft and allows it to build speed to three hundred knots, then pushes up the nose and begins his ascent to his cruising altitude of twenty-four thousand feet.

Outside the cockpit, the sky is cloudy. Few stars are visible. Gavallan's eyes are trained on his instruments: altimeter, flight speed, fuel. Tonight's flight plan is typical of the twenty-two missions he has logged to date. Takeoff to be followed by a rendezvous with a KC-135 to top off the tanks. After the completion of midair refueling, he will cross the Iraqi border and hit two targets, an IOC, or intercept operations center, at Ash Shamiyah, and an SOC, or sector operations center, at Ali Al Salem, one hundred miles to the south. Time to target is two hours forty-seven minutes.

Gavallan runs a hand over his pistol, flight harness, and G suit, fingers probing for the search and rescue map wedged into his leg pocket and the cloth "blood chit" on top of it. The blood chit is to be used in case of forced landing or ejection and carries four "tickets" offering a reward to its holder for helping shepherd the downed airman to safety. The 9mm pistol is in case the ragheads need more convincing.

Suppression of enemy air defenses has been ruled 98 percent successful, but someone has forgotten to inform the Iraqis of the fact. The flak that has greeted Gavallan on his most recent sorties is as hot and heavy as on the first night over Baghdad. Sooner or later, he will be hit. It is a law, not a probability.

He completes refueling without incident. Routine, he says, working to quell his apprehension, feeling restless in the green-glow midnight of the Black Jet's cockpit. He stays on the KC-135's wing for ninety minutes, then "stealths up" and turns east, driving *Darling Lil* into Iraq. As he kills the primary radio, he glides his thumb over the CD player in his flight suit and hits the play button. Axl Rose screams, "Welcome to the jungle."

Ash Shamiyah goes off without a hitch. A grown man's video game. Bomb armed. Systems check good. Target acquired: a gray rectangle dead center in his infrared display. Bombs away. The long downward ride, his thumb steering death on its unerring path. Thirty seconds later the screen whites out—a desert flower blossoming on his IR display. The IOC is a rectangle no more.

Gavallan pushes the stick left, banking the plane hard into a four G roll. Gut tight, head in a hammerlock, he turns to a heading of 210 degrees, driving *Darling Lil* to the night's second target. Five minutes later, static tickles his ear. The steely guitars of Guns N' Roses abruptly cut out.

"Thunder three-six. We have a code red, change of target."

Gavallan stiffens. The primary rule of Stealth flight has been broken. Radio contact on the newly installed EML—emergency transmission link.

"Proceed to target designation 'Alpha Golf.' This is a Priority One, Ring One engagement. Do you copy?"

Priority One. Ring One.

Unconsciously, Gavallan leans forward, a tiger who has caught scent of his prey. Ring One refers to "command control communications centers," or C3s, the highest-priority target on the modern battlefield. Priority One denotes that the commander of the C3 may be present at the target. In Iraq there is only one man who carries the moniker Priority One, and one of his many palaces is located in Abu Ghurayb—target designation Alpha Golf.

"Thunder three-six. Copy."

"Okay, Tex, this is your chance for the big time. Don't fuck it up."

It is his flight controller, Rob Gettels, and for once Gavallan can't think of a witty response. Suddenly his throat is dry, his stomach jittery. He's a rookie all over again and he's taking the plane up for his first flight. But a second later, the nerves calm, the hand steadies, and the breathing slows. He programs the onboard navigational system and banks the plane north. He is on his way. Priority One. Ring One. The Abu Ghurayb Presidential Complex.

Twenty minutes later, the radio crackles to life.

"Thunder three-six, green light on target Alpha Golf."

"Copy."

Gavallan lowers his seat an inch or two so that he can no longer see out of the cockpit. His world shrinks to the cocoon of instruments surrounding him. The stick between his legs. The throttle and weapons guidance joystick to his left. The infrared display that looks like a six-inch black-and-white television screen. The heads-up display above it.

He is at bombing altitude. A finger toggles the "master-arm" switch. The bomb is primed. Eyes forward on the IR display. Target spotted. A pale stable of buildings silhouetted against the gray desert floor. He has studied the target before, as he has studied all of Hussein's palaces, and he knows the main suite of bedrooms to be in the eastern wing, a slim outcropping from the principal complex of buildings. His middle finger slews the crosshairs back and forth across the palace until he decides he has found the wing. Then, as if a mechanism itself, the thumb locks down. Jett Gavallan does not miss his target. Distance five kilometers. A yellow light flashes. Laser acquisition engaged. Red letters fire on the heads-up display. Target in range. Gavallan hits the "pickle," a red button on top of the stick, and the weapons bay doors open. *Darling Lil* shudders. Still no ack-ack. No SAMs corkscrewing their way through the night sky. No 57mm shells bursting like flashbulbs on his old Kodak Instamatic. Gavallan does not question. He does not hesitate. He attacks. He is the spearhead of his country's arsenal.

Gavallan depresses the pickle again and the bomb falls from the aircraft. Suddenly lighter, *Darling Lil* jerks upward, and as his harness strap cuts into his shoulder, he grunts with a secret pleasure. His eyes lock onto the IR screen and the delicate crosshairs positioned over the east wing of the Abu Ghurayb Presidential Complex. All external stimuli disappear. He is in a tunnel. At the far end rests his target. The crosshairs do not move. Thirty seconds to impact. Twenty.

Too easy, a voice whispers. *Where are the SAMs? Where's the flak parade?* It is the voice that will haunt him for the rest of his life. He sees plumes of exhaust approaching the palace. He counts one, two, three vehicles. Tanks? Jeeps? Trucks? Ours? Theirs? Someone running away? Someone arriving?

Ten seconds.

The crosshairs do not move.

The radio screams. "Thunder three-six. Abort run. Copy?"

The bomb appears on the screen. A dark dot skimming across the ground at an impossible speed. Above the screen, a red light blinks. Fuel warning. Tanks low.

Five seconds.

"I repeat. Abort run. Friendlies in area. We have friendlies on-site."

The words fire in Gavallan's ear as a warning bell sounds in the cockpit. The fuel light is dim. Above it, another light blinks in time to the urgent keening of the warning bell. The Allied Forces Locator. He has engaged friendly forces. His eyes dart between the lights, hesitating. Events blur.

Two seconds.

Only then does the finger dodge right, the crosshairs leave the palace and land in the desert. Or did it go earlier? Before the command? It does not matter. The bomb does not listen. She has been too long on her downward trajectory and it is as if she is too stubborn to alter her course.

"Abort run! Confirm, Thunder three-six!"

One second.

The desert flower blossoms. The screen blanches. A blizzard of white noise. The palace reappears. The east wing is no more, a bonfire of angles fallen in on itself. The heat signatures have disappeared, too, replaced by the blotchy, pulsing quasars that indicate fire.

Ours? Theirs? Coming? Going?

Jett Gavallan does not miss his target.

"Friendlies hit! Friendlies down!" It is Gettels, his operational calm obliterated. "Christ, Tex, I said abort!"

Gavallan blinks his eyes and catapults through space, through time, through the firestorm of his emotions to the present. He is walking. In his sleep, the baby named Henry twitches and is still.

Ten Marines dead. Two in wheelchairs for the rest of their lives. Forward elements of Task Force Ripper, he was to learn later. Scouts who got too far ahead of themselves. Gavallan knows their names to a man. He has sent the families checks for years. But their financial support is skimpy fare for a ravenous conscience. Everywhere he looks he sees pleas for help. Ask me, he begs the unfortunate. Order me. But his appetite for atonement is insatiable. Guilt, he discovers, is a desire, not an emotion. It can be slaked, but never extinguished.

And Saddam? Was he within one hundred miles of

the palace? Not likely. News reports showed him touring Baghdad the next day, his beleaguered people showering him with praise.

As for the postscript, well, it went as he had imagined. The immediate transfer out of the theater of operations. The flight stateside. The firm and not so polite request that he resign his commission and never speak of the incident again. More he never learned. Who'd gathered the intelligence? Who gave the order for the raid? Why had the abort command come so late? Was the fuel light faulty? Was the allied locator on the fritz? What did it matter? No amount of rationalizing could scrub the blood off his boots. He had committed the cardinal sin: He had killed his own.

Now, if he didn't watch out, he'd have another name to add to the list. Not a heat signature in desert fatigues, but his best friend in the world. The man who'd stood by his side at weddings, christenings, and funerals. The man he'd worked alongside twelve hours a day, week in, week out, for seven years. The man he'd sailed with to Hawaii, ate steaks with at Alfred's, got drunk with at the Chaya. The only man he knew who gave a good goddamn about John J. Gavallan from Brownsville, Texas.

"Hey, Graf," Gavallan called silently across the miles. "Hang on, bud, I'm coming to get you. Don't ask me how or when, but I'm coming."

Hundred-hour war, the world had called it. *Piece of cake.*

Gavallan looked down at Henry. The boy looked like he was smiling.

Piece of cake, kid.

19

KER-THUMP!

Cate Magnus woke from a sound sleep, stirred by the jarring thud. The noise had come from downstairs. The den, she thought at first, still fuzzy. No, the study, she decided a second later, pinpointing the sound as having come from the room directly beneath her. Sitting up in bed, she trained an ear to the silence. The house was still and part of her wondered if she'd heard anything at all, or if the noise had simply been the slamming of a car door down the block.

It was early morning, and a predawn mist cloaked the bedroom in a grainy light. After a few seconds passed, she was able to make out the ottoman at the foot of the bed and the pile of magazines stacked on top of it. The *Economist*, *Vogue Italia*, *Harvard Business Review*, and, God help her, the *National Enquirer*. Throw them out, she ordered herself. All of them, before they become a fire hazard. Her eyes flitted to the hand-carved walnut desk under the window where she worked on her precious journals, black-speckled notebooks stuffed with daily musings, ideas for the column, personal promises, resolutions and dreams, press clippings of current events, photographs, drawings, and caricatures—a thirty-year-old's running commentary on the world and her place in it.

In the corner stood her rotting, half-drunk armoire, teetering to one side on its bum leg. Beside the armoire rested her easel, her vase and brushes, and the fisherman's bait box that held her oils and acrylics. With the painting I've done lately, I ought to throw those away too, she thought. The guarantee date on her precocious talent had expired ten years ago. But for her treasured possessions, she found no comfort in the familiarity of her surroundings. After a two-year absence, the room remained unfamiliar, foreign, more a hotel room in a distant city than the home for which she'd scrimped and saved for so long.

Ker-thump!

The low-pitched noise came again, confident, brazen. Cate could feel the floorboards shiver, as if the house had been punched in the gut. The noise came from the study. Sure of it now, she acknowledged the first intimation of fear. Her stomach knotted itself into a ball and, holding her breath, she sat very, very still. She was not by nature easily frightened, but of late she'd been on edge. She was, she realized, a woman alone in a three-story house in a part of town that might be called "lovingly frayed." Or less generously, "down at its heel."

The workers!

It came to her in a shower of relief. At once, her body slackened and her lungs opened for business again. As quickly as her fear had come, it vanished.

For the last twenty days, her home had been a hive of activity as laborers from every guild assembled beneath her roof to help with the pouring of a new concrete slab beneath the existing structure. She'd learned quickly that tradesmen were no respecters of the eight-hour day. Electricians were as likely to show up at seven at night as seven in the morning. Carpenters were happy to stay until you kicked them out.

It's Howie, she told herself, the long-haired foreman who looked as if he couldn't lift a hammer. He's come to check on the job's progress and bum his morning espresso. Caffeine freaks seemed to find one another, and neither Cate nor Howie could start the day without their Lavazza double espressos.

Or maybe it was Gustavo, the drop-dead-gorgeous Basque bricklayer who didn't go a day without asking her for a date. "Meez Magnus, we go deen-er together. You like ke-bab? I show you perfect good time, *non*?" Ten rejections, and still no sign of giving up.

Three weeks into the project, the cost had skyrocketed from eighteen to thirty thousand dollars, and there was no end in sight. Each day brought a new complication: faulty wiring, rusted pipes, asbestos. *Yes, asbestos!* Yesterday, she'd learned the hundred-year-old Victorian fixer-upper suffered from a healthy case of softwood termite infestation. Once the slab was completed, the house would have to be tented and fumigated. Cost: seven thousand dollars. Where she'd get the money to pay for it seemed to be no one's concern but hers, and the cause of one hangnail, a persistent headache, and very soon, if she wasn't careful, an ulcer.

Cate had no choice in the matter. The work was obligatory. The building code demanded it, and The Code's will be done. It had all started because of a faulty outlet. First her toaster blew, then her rice steamer. She called in the electrician, who traced the problem to a frayed circuit box beneath the kitchen floorboards. But the circuit box wasn't the real problem, he'd informed her while writing out his bill. The house, it turned out, had been built half on a wooden foundation, half on bare earth. It was a code violation of mythic proportions. By law, he was required to inform the building inspector. She asked him how the house had managed to remain standing through a century of earthquakes, including, if she wasn't mistaken, a couple of doozies in 1906 and in 1989. The electrician didn't know. He only knew that a bare-earth foundation was against code.

Code!

She'd learned to hate the word and had reserved a place for it in her personal lexicon alongside "fascist," "fibber," and "philanderer," three hall-of-fame baddies.

Even with her name in bold print beneath a weekly column, she barely earned sixty thousand dollars a year. Take away taxes, utilities, car payments, and her mortgage, and she was left with a disposable income of eight hundred dollars a month. Enough for one martini and a cowboy rib eye at Harris's, a couple of movies, a pair of tickets to a Giants game, and maybe a pair of shoes—all depending on how she filled the fridge. Every time she heard a politician say she was "affluent," she wanted to brain him.

Ka-lunk!

The sound was louder this time, as if someone had dropped a bowling ball onto her precious stained-pine floor. Cate cocked her head, no longer so confident it was the workers. The problem was the thump itself: The quality of the noise, its pitch and timbre, was unfamiliar. She did not recognize it.

Over the last month she'd become fluent in the buzzes, bangs, and squawks of a construction site. She could rattle off any of a dozen different tasks simply by listening to the frequency of the saw blade or the whine of the drill bit. The thump was not a sledgehammer. It certainly wasn't a pick. No, the sound coming from the study was that of a large object being dropped upon the floor.

The thump was a stranger, and it scared her.

Only then did Cate pick up her watch from the nightstand and look at the time. It was 4:06. The streetlights reflecting off the dense fog had lent the sky an eerie luminescence, feigning sunrise and providing a false dawn.

4:06.

Cate stared at the dial, anger and fear welling up in her in equal parts. No workman showed up at a job site at 4:06. Even Bob Vila didn't go to *This Old House* until six-thirty at the earliest! Suddenly, she was wide awake, her senses honed, her radar on full alert. She could smell the oil from the cement mixer parked out front. She could hear the ticking of her watch, the hum of the PC on her desk. The screensaver ran on a loop reading, "John Galt is dead. John Galt is dead." Her capitalist manifesto.

Someone she did not know was inside the house. There was an intruder in her study. *Call the police.* She reached for the phone, but froze halfway there, paralyzed by an older and more wrenching fear. There were worse things than physical peril.

Retrieving her hand, she slid her back against the headboard and waited for a footfall on the landing, for the door to her bedroom to be flung open. For a few moments, the house was silent, and Cate decided it was better for you to go get them than for them to come get you. Gathering her courage, she placed her feet on the ground and stood. For once, she'd make impatience her strong suit. She took one step and stopped, but only for a moment—just long enough to double-check if her sanity was in its proper place, tucked between her aversion to cigarettes and her love of Vermeer—then padded across the room to the bedroom door. The wood planks were cold to the touch and groaned at her meekest step.

Slowly, she ordered herself, concentrating on rolling her feet from heel to toe. You're a Shaolin priest walking on rice paper, she said, quoting from the bible of late-afternoon TV. Calmly, Grasshopper. But to her revved-up ears, she sounded like a newly shoed colt crossing the smithy's floor.

Cracking open the door, she peered to her right and left. The landing was empty, dusted with a sheen of plaster that glowed in the dark like some phosphorescent algae. There were no lights on in the house. Advancing on the staircase, she began to get the motion right, heel to toe, rolling her foot, and her tread fell as delicately as a doe's.

But if her steps were controlled, her mind was running full tilt. She remembered that she hated living alone and cursed herself for moving out of Jett's four-thousand-square-foot home in Pacific Heights. At the same time, she reminded herself she'd had no choice, even though leaving had been the hardest thing she'd ever done.

Continuing her spate of recriminations, she turned to the alarm system—or more specifically, to her practiced nonchalance about turning it on at night. What was the point? With so many workmen traipsing in and out of the house at all hours, it was better to keep an open door. Besides, it was hardly as if there was much to steal: a ten-year-old TV, a few silver candelabra, a stereo she had yet to hook up since her return to singledom.

Her neighborhood on the fringes of Haight-Ashbury wore its poverty like a genteel curse. Rusted VW vans, twice-repainted Olds 98s, SS Camaros with fat racing stripes running across their hoods, lined the curb, their bumper stickers badges of membership to a bygone era. "Drop in, Turn on, Tune out," "Age of Aquarius," and her favorite, "Keep on Truckin'," with the magnificent Crumb icon strolling along flashing the peace sign. On a sunny Saturday afternoon you couldn't pass two houses without hearing Mason Williams's "Classical Gas" or catching the scent of Colombian Gold wafting from an open window.

But you didn't put in the alarm to protect your possessions, a wise voice reminded her. *You installed it to protect your-self. You always knew they would come. You should have known it would be now.*

Laying a hand on the banister, she began her descent. There were fourteen steps to the first floor, the lower six sick with termites. With every step, she craned her neck farther over the rail, curiosity winning over fright as to what or whom she might discover.

Ka-thunk!

Cate stopped cold, frozen so still she might have been geologically petrified. Silhouetted against the ivory wall, her figure was slender, well-proportioned, and if ten pounds heavier than she would have liked, the more fit for it. She ran three times a week, made it to Pilates every Saturday morning, and ate enough Cherry Garcia to make it all for naught. She liked to think of herself as strong and capable, but alone in her house at 4 A.M. the opinion seemed boastful and ridiculous. Refusing to budge, she asked herself who it could be banging away in her study so contemptuously, who the interested party was who was practically daring her to come down and ask what the hell was going on.

Again she entertained the notion that it was a burglar, but she knew better. Nor could she bring herself to believe it was a rapist, a psychopath, a deviant, even a garden-variety lunatic trying to lure her downstairs to have his way with her. It was none of them. Or anyone else, for that matter, who might have randomly chosen her home to break into on this damp, foggy night.

She knew why there was someone in her house and she knew what they were looking for. She had known for some time that her existence could no longer be accepted with a tolerant grunt or dismissed with a paternal wave. Not with events moving as quickly as they were. It amused her that some people might think her dangerous. Cate Magnus, graduate of the East Coast establishment: Choate, Georgetown, Wharton. She, the failed painter, exiled executive, sucker for beat-up Jeeps and obscure French films. The reporter with a dozen great ideas for books and never the tenacity to complete an outline, the lifelong fugitive from romantic misadventures. Why should anyone be afraid of her? She was someone whose fingers felt more comfortable teasing the keys of a computer than the trigger of a gun.

Cate stared at the pistol in her hand, dull, gray, and bluntly menacing. For the life of her, she could not remember fishing it from the cache on the side of her bed. She noticed, too, that she was wearing her panties and nothing else. Great. Get the gun, but forget your clothes. Show 'em your boobs, then shoot.

No, countered the wise voice again. *You're still fooling yourself. You're a searcher, a collector, a seeker of the truth. You are a woman with a vendetta and the means to exercise it. In fact, you're very dangerous. Never more than now, and you know that, too. As for the gun, don't be coy. You trained five nights a week for a year so that you could hit a nickel at twenty paces. Why did you steal it from your boyfriend's house if not to use it?*

The thud came again. *Ka-thump.*

Suddenly, she knew what they were doing. There were two of them. There were always two. They were trying to get into her safe, the little fireproof model she'd picked up at Home Depot to protect her zip drives and her journals against fire. They were lifting it and dropping it or banging something on top of it in some brutish attempt to pry it open.

Cate reached the first-floor foyer. At the end of the hall, the door to the study was shut, a light burning beneath the crack. She advanced a step, holding the gun in front of her. They really were insolent, she thought, praying anger would fuel her courage.

Something warm and feathery brushed against her leg, and Cate nearly jumped out of her skin. She wanted to scream, but found her heart already lodged in her throat. She looked down and stifled a shrill note of terror.

It was Toby, her gray Angora. Toby, the meowing mauler of Menlo Park, whom she'd threatened to get rid of a hundred times because the damned kitty never shut his mouth. "Shh, Toby." She reached down to pet him, but he was already gone, bounding upstairs to doze in the folds of her duvet. "Coward," she hushed after him.

And straightening her body, she summoned the will to open the study door. *I'm a dangerous woman*, she thought proudly, taking another step. *I can plug a nickel at twenty paces. I can—*

She didn't hear him coming. Not a footstep or a whisper or even a breath of wind. One second she was alone, the next a large, sweaty hand had clamped itself over her mouth. Cate struggled to turn, to drive an elbow back and into his ribs as she'd learned in self-defense class, but the man was upon her, pulling her into his body, his free hand locking onto her wrist, wrenching the gun loose with one furious twist.

"We're in the library," he said. "We've been waiting for you to join us."

Cate stopped squirming and allowed the man to guide her into her study.

Two men stood by the safe. They'd managed to open it, God knows how. One was perusing her journals, the other tearing through her desk. She knew their type, if not their names. The crew cuts, the aggressive eyes, the pumped-up shoulders and size-twenty necks.

"What are you looking for?" she said when he'd removed his hand.

"You know what," replied the man holding her. "Why are you talking to the police?"

"I'm not." Her fear had vanished, cowering before her mammoth indignation. "You're wasting your time."

"We'll see."

He let her go and spun her around, and for a moment she thought that was it, he was moving to the rough stuff right away. She had no illusions about her ability to guard her secrets. If they beat her, she would talk. Instead, the man brushed by her and devoted himself to a tour of her bookshelves. She remained where she was, quiet, suddenly embarrased by her nudity, covering herself.

After a few minutes, the man gave up his perfunctory search. "Anything?" he asked, turning to his colleagues.

Shrugs were their only response.

He approached Cate, taking her face in his meaty hands and bringing it close to his. He was older, with pitted cheeks, black eyes, and a slit for a mouth. "Keep your mouth closed," he whispered. "Understand?"

When Cate didn't answer, an angry expression contorted his face. "Understand?" he said again, squeezing her cheeks and twisting her jaw.

"Yes," she managed to grunt. "I understand."

A minute later they were gone, leaving the front door open behind them. Cate walked to the door and shut it. As an afterthought, she turned on the alarm. But as she climbed the stairs to her bedroom, a smile of bitter satisfaction played on her lips.

She had them on the run.

20

STOP IT THERE!" shouted Howell Dodson, deputy assistant director of the FBI, slapping a palm onto his desk. "I want to hear the last part again."

Roy DiGenovese reset the digital recorder, punching the play button when he'd gone back exactly thirty-one seconds. A tinny voice began to speak, the Eastern European accent faintly noticeable.

"And what about the Private Eye-PO?" asked Konstantin Kirov. *"What do you plan on doing to him? Surely you do not expect us to sit still while our good name is besmirched."*

"I have some people on it already," answered Jett Gavallan. *"With any luck, we'll have him located by tomorrow, day after at the latest."*

"And then? All of us have our part to play to insure Mercury's future. We expect you to take any and all measures to silence this man. Nothing can stand in the way of Mercury Broadband's going public. Nothing."

"And nothing will. I'll see to it the Private Eye-PO's mouth is shut—permanently, if I have my way. In the meantime, these receipts refute his accusations nicely. I'd say we're back on track."

"Good," said Kirov. *"It's time to put an end to this tomfoolery. There's already been enough snooping."*

The recording ended, and DiGenovese turned the machine off.

It was eleven-thirty in Washington, D.C., and outside the temperature registered a sweltering ninety-two degrees. From his office on the second floor of the J. Edgar Hoover Building, Howell Dodson, chairman of the Joint Russo-American Task Force on Organized Crime, could see the early lunch crowd making their way to the mall in hopes of staking out shaded benches or dipping their big toes in the Reflecting Pool. It wasn't much of a view. The prime offices were on the opposite side of the building, facing south and offering a panoramic vista of the Capitol, the Washington Monument, and Mr. Thomas Jefferson, fellow Son of Virginia. One day he hoped to gaze out at the Lord of Monticello, but good views required good politicking, and good politicking required a cunning he did not possess.

"What do you say, Roy?" Dodson asked in a slow Williamsburg drawl, his voice the texture of cured tobacco. "Mr. Gavallan talking prudent business practice or did we just hear collusion among conspirators?"

"That depends on Mercury, sir. If the business is legit, I'd say we listened to a bunch of execs who want to stop someone from bad-mouthing their stock. If not, we just tuned in to a group of criminals discussing murder. Me, I opt for the latter. I think we caught some crooks red-handed."

"So the Private Eye-PO is correct? Mercury's nothing but 'a scam dog with mucho fleas'? That what you're saying, Roy?"

"We're getting the same information from our informant in Moscow. Why shouldn't we believe it?"

Dodson couldn't help but chuckle. Three years in the Bureau and Mr. DiGenovese still considered an informant's cant the holy scripture. The boy was a greenhorn. Yes sir. Nothing but a big-city hick. Dodson himself wasn't so much interested in whether what the Private

Eye-PO said was correct as in how he came to be in possession of the information. And for that matter, just who in the hell he was. "What's the latest on finding this boy? Mr. Chupik have any luck?"

Lyle Chupik was the Bureau's in-house webhead and the man who'd been charged with tracking down the Private Eye-PO.

"Nothing yet, sir," said DiGenovese. "Says he's close to nabbing him, though."

"Close?" Dodson lifted a thumb beneath his suspenders and let them slap on his chest. "Close don't count but for horseshoes and hand grenades. Isn't that right, Mr. DiGenovese? Mr. Gavallan seems to think he'll have him located today. That leaves us one step behind. And I don't like stomping through another horse's droppings," he whispered, with just a smattering of menace. "Follow?"

"Likewise, sir."

"Good boy. It's time we considered using an outside source. Find me the name of that odd fella does some consulting for us. If I'm not mistaken, he doesn't live too far away. Get him in here this afternoon and put him to work. Here's a dollar. Go buy Mr. Chupik a couple of those chocolate Yoo-Hoos he's so fond of, and tell him better luck next time."

Howell Ames Dodson IV was a Son of the South and ever proud of it. He was tall and lanky, with a shock of brown hair that fell boyishly into devilish blue eyes that teased the world from behind a scholar's half-moon glasses. He favored poplin suits in the summer, worsted gabardine in the fall, and the finest manners all year round. He liked smartly striped shirts, exuberant ties, snazzy cuff links, and pocket squares. He was foppish and a bit of a dandy, and if anyone cared to say a word about it, he'd point them to his unmatched arrest-to-conviction ratio, the commendations he'd received from

onthly retainer, all of which came from Howell
's operational budget.

I'd like to bring in Gavallan immediately," sug-
DiGenovese. "Rustle his feathers a little, question
out his dealings with Kirov."

he point being?" asked Dodson, with a little pep-
Only thing you'd get out of him is an invitation to
with his lawyer. No, son, we'll bring in Gavallan if
hen we charge him with a crime. Right now, let's
the focus on Mr. Kirov, where it belongs."

ut, sir—"

odson cut him short with an icy glare. Like every
aget who worked for the FBI, he thought twice these
days about whom he did and did not arrest. After
Whitewater and the special prosecutor's spending forty
million dollars of the public's money for little more than
a cum-stained dress and a couple of iffy convictions, the
government had become more demanding before allowing its lawyers to get involved. These days, the powers
that be were asking for a 90 percent probability of conviction before they'd even look at a case. Law enforcement had become a business. Guys like Howell Dodson
had to demonstrate a good ROA if they wanted to move
up the ranks, "ROA" meaning "return on *attorneys*,"
no sets. And that "return" was convictions.

ouble with you, Roy, is that you've got too much
pis d vinegar running through your veins. This isn't
on unday afternoon raid in downtown Mogadishu.
We onducting a sound and systematic investigation
alleged wrongdoings of some very sophisticated
ies. Time we slow down, examine the evi-

"

men," sang Dodson. "Finally, we agree
And he offered his subordinate an
him know there were no hard fe

the President of the United States, and a certain article
in the *Washington Post* he kept tucked away in his desk for
just such occasions.

The article described the shooting of four Georgian
mafiosi by an unnamed FBI agent in a sting gone sour
in the city of Tbilisi late last summer. The article was
sketchy in parts. It failed to mention that the agent
had shot the men after escaping from their custody or
that he'd pulled off the feat fifteen minutes after having two fingers on his left hand severed with a carpet
knife.

Sliding the digital recorder toward himself, Dodson
listened to the pirated conversation again. "So, Roy," he
said when the recording ended. "Think our boy isn't
content with a little innocent fraud? That why you asked
for this crash meeting? According to you, Mr. Gavallan's
joining the big leagues. Premeditated murder is moving
up the ladder p.d.q., wouldn't you say?"

"Sir, the Mercury offering is for two billion dollars,"
answered DiGenovese, leaning across the desk. "Leagues
don't get much bigger than that."

"No, son, they do not," said Dodson, rocking in his
chair, tapping a pencil on his weathered shipwright's
desk, a nineteenth-century antique on loan from the
Dodson Family Collection. "Just wish that damned recording didn't make them all sound like robots. Hard to
tell if Gavallan's joking or if he's serious."

"Sir, with all due respect, when an associate of a
known criminal talks about permanently getting rid of
someone, I think that qualifies as serious. Our job is to
take a man at his word, not to guess his intentions."

Such fire, mused Dodson, looking at the lean, vital
young man seated across the desk. Such drive. His hair
was ruffled, his suit wrinkled and in need of a press,
but his black eyes were awake and dancing with a mean-
spirited ambition. DiGenovese was the kind of agent

who wanted to arrest the whole damned world to keep it safe for the police.

"Come now, Roy, we both know that conversation doesn't amount to a hill of beans," he said kindly. "It wouldn't hold a drop in any court in the land. Between you and me, I doubt it would even garner an indictment from so docile a beast as a sitting grand jury. I will grant you one thing, though: It does appear that Mr. Gavallan and Mr. Kirov are closer friends than any of us thought."

Dodson could have added that contrary to DiGenovese's opinion, Kirov was hardly a known criminal, but he didn't want to dampen the boy's enthusiasm. DiGenovese's killer instinct was about all the task force had going for it these days. Truth was, Kirov hadn't ever been charged with a crime, let alone convicted. Not that Dodson didn't think Kirov was dirty. It was just that these days you could label any businessman worth his salt in Russia a suspected criminal. What with all the bribery, extortion, and strong-arming that went on to make the wheels of everyday commerce go round, if you looked closely enough just about anybody was guilty of one infraction or another.

"Now do tell, Roy, what did your team find in Mr. Gavallan's private chambers? Love notes between him and Mr. Kirov? Written promises about how they're going to split the booty? Plans to overthrow the President?"

"No sir," DiGenovese answered without a hint of regret, going on to explain that they hadn't found any documents of an incriminating nature, not with regard to Mercury, Novastar Airlines, or anything else. The bugs were clean too. Only thing they learned was that Gavallan liked to listen to country music. Before going to the ball last night, he'd sat in the bath for half an hour singing along to Bob Wills and the Texas Playboys.

"Bob Wills, eh?" asked Dodson, cleaning his bifocals with a hankie. "At least Mr. Gavallan has himself some

taste. Still, it is a shame. Goir[...] nothing. A damned shame indeed[...] displayed no irritation, he was, [...] Howell Dodson wanted Kirov mor[...] Mr. DiGenovese or Mr. Baranov [...] ambition but realism that told him t[...] career depended on it.

Konstantin Kirov had popped onto the[...] half a year back, when Yuri Baranov had lau[...] vestigation into allegations Kirov was embe[...] Novastar Airlines, the country's recently priva[...] tional carrier. Three months into the case, the [...] authorities had managed to slip an informant into [...] head office. Since that time, all he'd unearthed we[...] few documents relating to some shell companies [...] Switzerland and Kirov's connection with the Dashamirov[...] brothers, a trio of Chechen warlords-cum-businessmen[...] with whom he held interests in some aluminum smelting[...] factories in Perm and a chain of used-car dealerships. As[...] for Novastar, they hadn't managed to find a thing linking[...] Kirov to the missing $125 million, and Dodson had his[...] doubts as to whether the Russian was involved at all—o[...] to be honest, whether the money was missing in the fi[...] place.

The link to Gavallan came as an adjunct[...] Novastar inquiry. Baranov's informant had [...] that Mercury Broadband was being used to [...] funds Kirov had skimmed from Novast[...] surveillance on Gavallan. Hence the "[...] monitored every E-mail going into a[...] securities. So far, the Russian sto[...] a shred of evidence to back up h[...] had taken to wondering if th[...] Moscow operations cente[...] ad[...]ate routers and swi[...] jus[...]ersions to justify th[...]

[torn fragments, partially visible:]
dollar m[...]
Dodson[...]
"Sir[...]
gested[...]
him a[...]
"T[...]
in[...]
pe[...]
de[...]
some[...]
ing n[...]le[...]

Dodson had come to the Bureau late in life, abandoning a promising career as a CPA with an international accounting firm to help balance the scales of justice. Taxes were his bag, but sometime after his thirtieth birthday he'd undergone a conversion. The private sector wasn't for him, he decided. Helping one bigwig after another whittle down their tax exposure brought scant satisfaction. He certainly didn't need the money. The Dodsons were comfortable, thank you very much, Southern planters who'd moved from corn to tobacco to semiconductors without a backward glance. So on a whim, he quit, joined the FBI, and became a thirty-one-year-old neophyte loping over the O-course at Quantico, acing his criminal justice exams, and taking target practice with an H&K 9mm. Time of his life.

As chairman of the Joint Russo-American Task Force on Organized Crime—or the "ratfuckers," as some wiseacre in forensics had nicknamed it—Howell Dodson's mandate was to corral acts of racketeering associated with business endeavors aimed toward the West. In sixty months of operations they'd jailed crooked oil salesmen, murderous rug merchants, and every type of illegal operator in between.

Of late, however, pickings had been lean. Nine months had passed since the last arrest was made, and talk had surfaced about shuttering the task force, assigning its members to more productive areas of the Bureau. Feelers were put out to Dodson about taking a posting to Mexico City as the Bureau's liaison to the *Federales*. It was a lateral move in title, but came with a higher pay-grade salary and a diplomatic allowance. Dodson read it as recompense for his two fingers and wanted none of it. Margaritas, mariachis, and menudo, he summed it up, cringing at the prospect. *No, gracias.*

Mr. John J. Gavallan hadn't been the only man cheering when Kirov entered his life.

"Roy, I want you to humor me," said Dodson, easing back in his chair. "If you're so sure Gavallan's in cahoots with Kirov, start from the get-go and make your case against him. It'll be good for you to polish those argumentative skills. But make it quick. The missus is due in any minute."

Dodson had recently become a father for the second time. At the age of forty-two, he'd been presented with twin baby boys to go along with his sixteen-year-old daughter. Every day at noon, Mrs. Dodson stopped by to leave her boisterous infants with their father while she whipped by Lord & Taylor and Britches of Georgetown to pick up a few household necessities.

"I'll do my best," said DiGenovese, rising from his chair and striding to a bookshelf. Between legal tomes and hefty accounting manuals, room had been cleared for a changing pad, a stack of diapers, and wipes.

"Gavallan's company has hit the skids," he began, pacing slowly, using his hands effectively. "Three years ago, he was on his way to joining the big boys; now he's treading water while guys are passing him left and right. In the last nine months, he's made three infusions of cash into the company to counter quarterly losses and keep his underwriting status with the SEC. Around twenty million and change if I'm not mistaken. The banking records we subpoenaed show he hasn't taken any salary in six months. Bottom line: The guy's hurting and he needs a savior."

"If I might interject. Black Jet was hardly the only company interested in Mercury. All the big-name firms were courting Kirov. Any of them would have jumped at the chance to take his company public."

"And loan him the fifty million to boot?"

"It *is* a bank's business last time I checked," said Dodson.

DiGenovese grinned madly, the cat who'd swallowed the canary. "Thank you, sir. You just made my case. If anyone would have loaned Kirov the dough, why did Kirov choose Black Jet over so many larger, more prestigious firms—the Merrills and Lehmans of this world? Gavallan's never done a deal in Russia. He's never done an IPO valued at more than a billion dollars. Now, all of a sudden he's taking a Russian company public for two billion. By what stroke of good fortune did Kirov fall into his lap? Let me tell you. Because Gavallan's the only one desperate enough to overlook all of Mercury's shortcomings. Because he and Kirov are thick as thieves in this thing. Because both of them are dying to pull this deal off."

"Dear me, you are drawing a picture of a very cold man. Not exactly the type I'd bet on to donate twenty million to a children's hospital."

"Window dressing," declared DiGenovese. He'd unbuttoned his jacket and was stalking the room like a wolf in his den. "So far he's given two mil, and he's a month late on this year's pledge. Five'll get you ten he never delivers." Abruptly, he stopped his pacing and thrust his hands on Dodson's desk, his peasant's jaw jutting forward. "Mercury's a phony, sir. Kirov's got it dolled up to look like AOL when it's really CompuServe. Gavallan's in bed with him, and together they're going to pull the wool over investors' eyes and pocket the takings. You see what he's pulling down on fees for this deal? Something like seventy million dollars? Seventy *million*!"

"My, my, Roy," drawled Dodson appreciatively. "That would make Mr. Gavallan even more ambitious than you. Isn't that a scary thought? One thing is for certain: Mr. Gavallan's not in this alone. In the first place, Black Jet didn't even do all of the due diligence on this thing. I don't know how many lawyers and accountants and consultants he had signing off on Mercury, but believe me it was a lot. You saying they're part of this, too?"

"Never know."

Dodson nudged his glasses to the end of his nose.

"Quite a conspiracy you're cooking up, Roy. Seen any Kennedys flitting around out there in never-never land? Or just Peter Pan and Jett Gavallan?"

Rummaging in his ashtray for a rubber band or two, he wrapped them around his index and middle fingers and, kicking his feet up onto the desk, began to spin the bands forward and back. He liked the bent of the argument, if he wasn't convinced of its veracity. He thought of the transfer to Mexico City, the traffic, the bad water, the horrid food—*enchiladas*, Heaven forbid—and came to a quick and rational decision that the American angle was just what they needed to drum some new life into the investigation.

A billion-dollar fraud involving a Russian oligarch, a former fighter pilot, and that holy of all holies, the New York Stock Exchange. It was practically treason. He caught himself thinking that the press would have a field day and the man who put Jett Gavallan behind bars would be instantly famous. He stopped himself there. All the infighting, posturing, and backbiting were getting to him. Still, for a last second he couldn't help but imagine that the man who put Gavallan behind bars would have a south-facing office and the promotion to assistant director that came with it.

Rising from his desk, Howell Dodson strode to the window. The harsh glare showed off wrinkles near the eyes normally unseen, a determined cast to the jaw, and a nasty downturn of his pale, fleshy lips. Suddenly, he didn't look so boyish anymore, not every inch the amiable Southern gentleman he pretended to be. Get close enough to any man, he would say, and you could glimpse his true nature. And underneath his easygoing drawl and unflappable smile, Howell Dodson was a nasty sumbitch who did not like to get beaten.

Just then, the cries of his two baby boys exploded from down the hallway. A moment later, a trim, very blond woman bustled through the door, a wailing infant in each arm. Rushing to greet his wife and sons, Dodson softened his expression into a broad smile.

"Hello, Jefferson. Hello, Davis. And how are my two little generals this mornin'?"

21

A MOMENTARY LULL HAD DESCENDED on the trading floor at Black Jet Securities. Phones had stopped ringing—or blinking, as has become their convention—conversation had fallen to a whisper, the shuttle of chairs to and fro between desks had come to a halt. "A rest between rounds," Gavallan liked to call it on good days. Or "the calm before the storm" on bad ones.

Incisex stock had begun trading on Nasdaq—the National Association of Securities Dealers' Automated Quotation System—thirty minutes earlier at 6:55. Ticker symbol CSXI—pronounced "sexy"—Incisex was a pioneer in the field of nanotechnology, the branch of science concerned with building sophisticated engineering devices—engines, motors, valves—on a submicron scale. The company's breakthrough product was a battery-powered valve no bigger than the head of a needle that when surgically implanted into a coronary artery restored proper blood flow to the heart. For men and women suffering from arteriosclerosis or any vasocirculatory problems (and for their cardiologists), it was a godsend. The IPO would net Incisex seventy-five million dollars, funds it would use to move into larger facilities and to upgrade its research and development efforts. Black Jet's fee was the standard 7 percent of the offering.

"Seventeen bid, seventeen and a quarter ask," announced Bruce Jay Tustin from his post behind a dozen color screens and monitors. "We're going up, up, up!"

The issue had been priced at $14 a share and after thirty minutes of trading, demand had lifted the shares 20-odd percent to $17. Checking a screen above Tustin's shoulder, Gavallan saw that buyers outnumbered sellers three to one. It was a far cry from the bonanza days when one new issue after another would double or triple on its first day of trading, but Gavallan wasn't complaining. In a rational world, a first day's gain of 20 percent qualified Incisex stock as "popping" all the same.

"I think we can open the champagne now," he said to an assembly of four men and two women standing to one side of the room. "Mr. Kwok, would you do the honors?"

On cue, Wing Wu Kwok, a newly hatched associate who had accompanied the Incisex brain trust on their two-week road show across America, uncorked a bottle of Moët & Chandon, filled a half dozen flutes, and offered round a silver tray bearing beluga caviar, toast points, and china dishes brimming with chopped egg white and diced onion.

Gavallan accepted a glass of bubbly and raised it high. "To Incisex and that rarest of all marriages—profit and the public good. Cheers!"

There were huzzahs all around. Hugs and handshakes followed the clinking of glasses.

"May the sun be ever in your eyes," Tustin chimed in, "and the wind at your ass."

"Here, here." Gavallan managed a smile, but just barely. Two hours' sleep had left him exhausted and haggard. With Grafton Byrnes's predicament increasingly weighing on him, it was difficult to maintain a cheerful façade. If no one had remarked upon the dark circles beneath his eyes, it was only because he was the boss.

For a few minutes, he mingled with the executives from Incisex, taking refuge from his worry in the cloak of chief executive. He slapped some backs, he partook of the caviar, he extolled his clients' rosy future. But even as half his mind concentrated on projecting a carefree exterior, the other half remained fraught with doubt. Two words from his best friend had turned Cate Magnus's hotly worded suspicions about Kirov and Mercury into Gavallan's worst nightmare.

"Everything's copacetic."

Gavallan had to imagine the rest. Grafton Byrnes was being held against his will somewhere in Russia and would never return. He knew too much. He was sure to be killed, if he wasn't dead already. It was all that simple. That terrible.

Pondering his conclusions, a new thought dawned on Gavallan, one that his trusting mind decided was more frightening than the rest. If Kirov felt so secure that the Mercury offering would come to market that he would risk kidnapping Byrnes, he had to have someone in place at Black Jet to push through the offering despite the chairman's opposition, someone highly enough placed in the company that he might persuade Jett that Byrnes's disappearance was a coincidence, nothing more.

As quickly as it had come, the lull on the trading floor abated. Lights began flashing on the checkerboard consoles that connected Black Jet to over a hundred banks, brokerages, and financial institutions around the world. Voices boomed as traders greeted their clients with news of the strong offering. Casters groaned as the bankers recommenced their daylong jitterbug.

The trading room of Black Jet occupied the entire western length of the fortieth floor. Desks ran perpendicular to floor-to-ceiling windows, twelve carrier decks bisected by a flight tower constructed from the newest in flat-screen monitors. Currencies were to the left of the room, followed by bonds, options, and finally, equities, both domestic and international. Chairs were situated at four-foot intervals and nearly every post was occupied by a man or woman, standing, seated, or in some pose in between. One hundred forty traders in all, and when things heated up, the place took on the frenetic currents of a Middle Eastern bazaar. It was the Casbah gone California, Evian and Odwallah replacing hookahs and hashish.

Gavallan leaned a hand on Tustin's desk, marveling at his ability to goad the price of the stock ever higher. Picking up a receiver, he patched himself into Tustin's call.

"Hey, Brucie, what d'ya got for me on Incisex?" The voice belonged to Frank MacMurray, a trader at Merrill Lynch.

"Her name's 'sexy' and I can give you a block of ten thousand at 18."

"Eighteen? Last bid's 17½. Gimme a break."

"Got ten other johns lined up right behind you, Frankie," Tustin said. "But listen, pal, since you're cute, I'll cut it to 17⅞. Buy or fly."

"Done, and get me ten more at the same price."

"You're filled."

Tustin aimed a finger at another flashing button, this one connecting him with Fidelity Investments, the nation's largest manager of mutual funds. "Yallo, Charlie, what are you looking for?"

Gavallan knew from reading the "book" that Fidelity was a buyer of Incisex. They'd loved the stock's story and planned to build a position in it in one of their biotech funds. Accordingly, they'd given an indication they'd take 10 percent of the issue. No one firm would be allotted a full 10 percent of the offering—in this case over five hundred thousand shares. As it was important that Incisex had a broad and liquid market, Black Jet had a duty to sell shares to a great many customers, some of whom were retail brokerages—Merrill Lynch, Paine Webber, Bear Stearns and the like—that would in turn pass on their allotments to their own clients. To say you wanted 10 percent was equivalent to requesting as much of the new issue as Black Jet might give you. Powerhouses like Fidelity, Strong, Janus, and Vanguard couldn't waste time following small positions in hundreds of stocks. When they committed to a new stock, they expected the issue manager to help them acquire a meaningful stake in the company, somewhere upward of 2 percent of the offering. All through the day, Fidelity would be phoning to buy more shares—especially as the price continued to rise.

"Yo, Brucie, give me everything you got at 18."

Tustin checked his screens for available shares. Many of Black Jet's clients had bought the stock not to buy, but to "flip"—that is, to sell after an hour or two with the expectation of making a small, risk-free profit.

"Got you five grand at 18 and another five at 18 and a teeny," said Tustin. A teeny was a sixteenth of a point. It was Tustin's job to mark up the stock each time he made a sale as a commission to Black Jet. The amount of his markup depended a lot on how good the client was. In the case of Fidelity, one of the firm's best clients, he would slap on a sixteenth at most. "And this just in: a block of twenty thousand at 18⅜. You a buyer?"

"Send 'em over," said Charlie. "We're buying and we're buying big. We're starting to feel good about this baby."

Tustin put down the phone, grinning like a madman. "Five days from now, it'll be Mercury's turn. Two billion dollars. Oh yeah, we're hitting the big time!"

"Yeah, Mercury," said Gavallan, the words stale in his mouth. "Great."

Tustin stared at him oddly. "You okay, Jett? You look kind of like shit. You go out after the ball last night? It was that Nina, I bet. She looked like a goer. Wearing anything less, they'd have arrested her. You always get the sexy ones. But then, you're the boss."

If Tustin was cheeky, it was no more than his usual self. Everyone was in a grand mood since Byrnes had resurfaced; Incisex's successful launch had capped it. Instinct told Gavallan not to reveal his suspicions about Byrnes's situation. He'd explained that Graf was remaining in Moscow for the weekend and would be accompanying Konstantin Kirov to New York come Monday. The words "prisoner" or "hostage" never entered the discussion.

"I'll tell you what Graf's really doing," Tustin went on. "He's shacked up with some Russian babe. I've heard they're lookers over there. Yeah, that's it. Graf's getting himself some commie cooze. Probably got a dozen of them in bed with him."

"Can it, Bruce!" Gavallan barely reined in his outraged voice, infuriated by the insinuation of illicit sex.

But Tustin insisted on going on, his compact figure bouncing up and down in his chair like a jack-in-the-box. "I can see that old fart now. Probably got a club sandwich going, laying there between a blond and a redhead like the filling in an Oreo. Got some pussy in his face and some chick gnawing on his hog. Hoo-yeah! Go, Air Force!"

"I said shut up, Bruce. Now!" Gavallan felt his shoulder tense, his fist bunch up, and he knew that if he didn't leave this second, he'd either pick up Tustin and chuck him across the room or belt him a good one right in the jaw.

"What crawled up *your* ass and died?" asked Tustin. "Ah, you're jealous, that's it. Maybe Nina *didn't* take such good care of you. No, no, no. I got it. It's Cate you were after all along. I saw you two, cheek to cheek. You want some of *that* poontang, that it? I'm a sucker for black bush myself. Drives me cra—"

A cord snapped inside Gavallan and he slugged Tustin, a lightning-fast jab to that oh-so-loud mouth. The trader tumbled into his chair, gasping, raising a hand to his bleeding lip. Thankfully, the Incisex crew had moved down a few aisles and were talking to Mr. Kwok about a listing on foreign exchanges; only the traders in the vicinity saw what happened. For a few seconds, they froze, no one speaking or moving a muscle. Just as quickly, they discounted the act and continued with their work. The expressions on their faces said Tustin had been due a spanking.

"Sorry, man," squealed Tustin, dabbing at his swollen lip. "I was just joking. Really, Jett. No offense, man."

"Damn you, Bruce," whispered Gavallan, sitting down, lowering his head next to Tustin's. "Why can't you just learn to shut up once in a while? Shit. I'm the one who's sorry. I apologize. I was out of line."

And looking into Tustin's pained eyes, he asked himself, *Is it you, Bruce? Has Kirov got his hooks in you?*

Just then, Tustin's private line rang. Gavallan grabbed the phone. "Hello ... Yeah, Emerald."

"Jett, I've got a caller who says he has to speak to you right away. He says his name is Jason. He won't give me his last name, but he insists you know him and that it's urgent. Should I send the call down or do you want me to take a message?"

"Tell him I'll be right up. Pass it through to my office." Gavallan handed the phone back to Tustin, a surge of adrenaline making his feet antsy. "Make my goodbyes for me. I've got to run. . . . I'm sorry, man."

Two minutes later, he was upstairs, standing beside his desk. Spotting the shaman, he offered the crude, powerful statue a hopeful nod before picking up the phone.

"Jason, that you?"

"Guess what," said Jason Vann. "Good news. Got a pen handy?"

"Shoot." Gavallan scribbled furiously as Jason Vann rattled off the name, address, phone number, and E-mail of the Private Eye-PO. Gavallan read the name a second time and smirked. "You sure this is the guy?"

"I'm sure that the web page dissing your company originated from his home address. Maybe he's got a kid who's doing it, but I doubt it."

"Why's that?"

"Umm, you're still going to wire me the other fifty thousand dollars, aren't you?"

"Deal's a deal, Jason. I always keep my word."

"Well," said Vann. "It just seems like something this guy might do. You see, I found out a little more about him than you asked. Sometimes I get a little too interested in my work. Occupational hazard."

"Do you now?" Gavallan doubted that Vann knew more about the Private Eye-PO than he did.

"First off, this guy's no dummy. He went to college at M.I.T., then worked for Synertel in Milpitas. He was a big shot. The CTO. But that's not the good stuff. You see, your guy has himself a criminal record. When the company flamed out, he lost it and beat the crap out of the chief executive, before trying to burn down the building. He did nine months in Soledad Medium Security Correctional Facility for Men in California. I guess that explains why he didn't tell anyone his name."

"Guess so," said Gavallan, amazed at all you could find out in the space of twenty-two hours if you knew how and where to look.

"I'm sorry I couldn't get his picture for you," said Jason Vann. "The Department of Motor Vehicles' mainframe has a decent security system. Not that I couldn't have hacked it, but you sounded rushed so I thought I'd stick with the basics."

"No need," said Gavallan. He had a pretty good recollection of what the Private Eye-PO looked like. "Got anything else up your sleeve?"

"Uh, there is one more thing. I hope you don't think me out of place, but I thought I might be able to do you a favor."

"A favor? What do you have in mind?"

"Well, I kind of found out you were in the Air Force and that things didn't go so well for you. You sound like a nice guy—I mean you paid me quicker than anybody else has before—so I just wanted to say that if you ever wanted me to upgrade your discharge, you know, to an honorable one, I can."

"You can?"

"Yeah. Free of charge. Hacking the Pentagon's a piece of cake."

"Good-bye, Jason. I'll wire the remainder of your fee this morning."

Gavallan hung up the phone and turned his attention to the name and address written on the notepaper: *Raymond J. Luca. 1133 Somera Road, Delray Beach, Florida.*

"Ray Luca of Synertel," Gavallan murmured. "Who'd have figured?"

Synertel was a high-flying manufacturer of optical switches that Black Jet had been set to take public for north of five hundred million dollars. Two weeks before the IPO was set to go, the company's primary product was trumped by a competitor, rendering it obsolete before it had even been introduced. Gavallan canceled the IPO on the spot. Three months later, Synertel went bust.

Luca's being the Private Eye-PO explained the pissy note to his warnings. It did not, however, discount the veracity of his statements. Luca might have a bone to pick, but he was telling the truth about Mercury, or at least hinting at it.

Gavallan punched a button on the speakerphone. "Emerald," he began. "Book me a—" He stopped dead, deciding it might be wiser for him to make his own travel arrangements. "Emerald," he started anew. "I've got to run out for a while. Actually, I'm feeling pretty lousy. Forward any calls to me at home. Thanks."

Replacing the receiver, he picked up his jacket and satchel, turned off the lights to his office, and shut the door behind him.

From here on out, Gavallan was on his own.

22

WE'RE USING THE SAME GUY," announced Roy DiGenovese when he stuck his head into Howell Dodson's office at four-thirty in the afternoon. "Gavallan's paying the same fella we got on contract to the Bureau. Vann. Jason Vann."

Lifting his feet off the desk, Dodson slid his chair forward and afforded DiGenovese his fullest attention. "Do tell, dear boy. I smell progress."

Dodson had been reviewing the casework on Kirov and Mercury, trying to figure out what Gavallan's role in the whole thing was and whether or not it might be wise to alert his friends in the SEC or the Treasury Department about it. It was a thorny issue. The Bureau didn't need any multibillion-dollar lawsuits accusing its very own Howell Ames Dodson IV of maligning, defaming, tarnishing, or slandering a wholly legitimate enterprise. Every request he'd made to Baranov to send some of his investigators over to Mercury's Moscow operations center had been met with deafening silence. The man hadn't lifted so much as a finger. He cared only about Novastar. Mercury was the Americans' problem.

Dodson had the tape from Mercury Broadband USA,

the allegations of a paid informant, and that was it. The skeptic inside him refused to follow in DiGenovese's rabid footsteps. When it came to fashioning a winning indictment, they were no better off than they were four weeks ago. Effectively, the decision had been made for him. He didn't dare open his mouth to another federal agency about his concerns over Mercury Broadband. For now, they would remain an in-house matter.

"Vann found the Private Eye-PO," DiGenovese continued, taking a seat opposite Dodson. "His name is Raymond Luca. He's a resident of Delray Beach. M.I.T. grad, and get this . . . an ex-con."

"And what does Mr. Luca do, pray tell, when he's not playing the Private Eye-PO?"

"No idea. Just got a name and an address. Vann said he could find out more, but he's already run over his hourly commitment and it would run us another few thousand dollars."

"Very well," said Dodson. "Run Mr. Luca's social security number through the IRS, do a thorough credit check on the man, contact M.I.T.'s alumni relations board. Someone can tell us how he earns his daily bread." He shifted in his seat, unsatisfied. "What else did Mr. Vann have to tell us?"

"Nada. Just gave me the same info he gave Gavallan."

"And how much did Mr. Gavallan pay our Mr. Vann?"

"Didn't ask."

"Next time ask," ordered Dodson, wondering if Vann might be holding something back. "And find out where Vann likes his funds wired. I don't take to people double-timing the Bureau—goes against my sense of patriotism. While you're talking to our colleagues at the IRS, why don't you have them take a peek at Mr. Vann's latest 1040s. Might be nice to have some leverage in the future."

DiGenovese had been writing all this down on a

notepad he carried in his left hand. Finished, he looked up. "Next flight down to Miami's at seven-fifteen. I booked us two seats."

"Pardon me?"

"You heard Gavallan," DiGenovese said, in a tone as surprised as his superior's. "He wants to permanently shut Luca's mouth."

"And do we have any evidence that Mr. Gavallan's going anywhere near Florida these next few days?"

"Well, no. I mean, not yet. We don't get transcripts of the wiretaps until twenty-four hours after they're picked up. I thought it would be a good idea to have a talk with Luca, let him know that he might be in some danger."

Dodson shot DiGenovese a stern glance as if to say he'd been silly even to think of flying to Florida that evening. In fact, his reluctance to leave so quickly was rooted in his domestic situation. His wife, Clara, was a woman of the times, and would raise holy hell if he popped down to Florida without advance warning. She didn't stand for unannounced departures, late nights at the office, or working more than a half day on weekends unless absolutely necessary—and "necessary" meant that an agent's blood had been spilled.

"Calm down, Roy. If you're so worried about Mr. Luca, give him a call on the telephone. Tell him to lock his front door. I would, on the other hand, enjoy speaking with Mr. Luca about where in God's name he's been getting our confidential information. Book us first thing in the morning."

"You don't think he needs protection?"

"No, Roy, I do not. Now off you go. Book us those seats for tomorrow."

DiGenovese shifted in his chair, and Dodson could see he was using all that Ranger discipline of his to keep from arguing. The Army's fine training won out over DiGenovese's impetuous Sicilian blood, and after a few seconds he complied. "Yes sir. I'll get back to you about the times."

"Good man," said Dodson, beaming. "What's that you always say when things are going well?"

"Drive on, Airborne."

"Yes, yes. Well then, 'Drive on, Airborne.' "

23

CATE MAGNUS HELD THE NOKIA CELL PHONE close to her ear, clicking the volume higher so she could hear the man's voice over the earsplitting whine of a jacksaw.

"It's just not what we want this week," Jimmy Murphy was saying. "Metrics are so dry. Your readers don't give a fiddler's fart whether Yahoo! gets two million hits a day or two billion. And they care even less what exactly constitutes 'a hit' on a website. This isn't a scientific review here. You're supposed to liven up the rag, not dull it down."

"It's not the methodology I'm interested in, Jimmy," she retorted, pacing the length of her bedroom. "It's the way you can cheat on these things. Use one method and it looks like five hundred users a day are logging onto your site; use another and it's more like five thousand. The whole thing stinks. I mean, who are you supposed to trust?"

"Good question, Cate. Tell you what: Let's leave that question until next month. Give me something lively, something dishy."

Cate lowered the phone from her ear and mouthed a very nasty word in Mr. Jimmy Murphy's general direction. Murphy was the features editor at the *Financial*

Journal, a rail-thin, choleric Kansan who took it as part of his job description to be permanently dissatisfied with his writers' offerings. More and more, he was pushing the column away from the serious fare she favored—namely, an examination of the personal and societal ramifications wrought by a once-in-a-century upheaval in technology—toward dishy, prurient pieces on the lifestyles of the sick and famous. It was partly her mistake. A year ago, she'd written a piece on young women who worked for a certain gentlemen's club in San Mateo that catered to the wild and wildly expensive whims of the valley's glitterati, such as they were. One of the girls she'd interviewed had talked about the habits of one of her regulars, a nationally known Internet exec who liked to do weird things with whipped cream, motherboards, and electrodes on his nipples.

Or there was the time Murphy had sent her to Bangalore, India, to check out the booming match-making market for up-and-coming high-tech wizards. It was the Indian women who paid for introductions to men, and the depth of questioning they had to endure approached the ridiculous. "How would you propose to cure your husband's impotence?" "What family remedies can you offer for baldness?" "Would you object to your husband's taking a mistress? Two mistresses?" and her favorite, "What is the proper serving temperature of chicken tika-tika? In Celsius *and* Fahrenheit, please."

It wasn't lost on her that 90 percent of the *Journal*'s readers were men.

This week's "Gold Rush" dealt with a more serious topic: the internecine warfare going on among competing firms in the field of metrics. "Metrics," as related to the Internet, involved defining precise methodologies to measure usage of the World Wide Web, or more important these days, providing objective information as to exactly how many visitors clicked onto specific websites.

Now that the bloom was off the rose and the new

economy was looking a little long in the tooth, metrics had assumed a new importance. Acquisition had replaced IPOs as the prevalent exit strategy for start-ups, and the price a company could demand was directly correlated to the number of hits its website received. Each company in the metrics game claimed to offer the sole, incontrovertible means of measuring a site's popularity. The only hard part for the client was finding the boys who'd put you at the top of the list, and Cate was sure that a little extra vig would better your final score.

"Look, Jimmy," she started again, wincing at the syrupy sound of her voice. "Maybe the piece is a little heavy on the number crunching. Let me talk to rewrite; I'll soften it up, give it a little more color."

Cate was frustrated. She'd finally come up with a story that allowed her to put into practice some of the financial carpentry she'd picked up at Wharton, and no one gave a damn.

"You're not listening to me," carped Murphy. "Where are those personal items we so loved? Remember last year when you followed a Range Rover into and out of a shop six times in three months? We had letters for a year wondering what happened to that lemon—some nut even wanted to buy it. Hey, hey, here's an idea! Hot off the wire. Why not give me something about the house. How does a savvy reporter knee-deep in tech hoopla deal with the down-and-dirty world of home renovation? Give me a thousand words on pouring a new slab. How do they do that, anyway, without having to tear down the house?"

"Noisily," Cate answered, putting a finger to her ear to drown out an eager jackhammer. "Very noisily. Listen, Jimmy, I want you to run my piece as is. Give me metrics this week and I'll give you whatever you want next Friday. Come on, Murph. A favor."

"A favor?" Jimmy Murphy's voice cracked, and she could picture him at his desk, hurriedly figuring the angles. No doubt he was wearing one of his bright red dress shirts with a collar two sizes too big for his scrawny neck. "Deal," he said, finally. "I'll get back to you on a subject. Maybe we can find out what Jim Clark's doing these days. Whatever happened to that boat of his? Maybe you could track it down, go for a sail."

Cate sighed. That was someone else's story. A real writer. Someone who possessed the wherewithal to write a book. "Sure thing, Jimmy. See you."

Collapsing onto her unmade bed, Cate put down the phone while shaking her head. Thank goodness, she'd convinced him to run the column. Time was precious. Even the smallest skirmishes counted as battles. She was mustering her troops, marshaling her evidence for the final assault. Rolling over onto her stomach, she pulled the top sheet off her bed, then the fitted cover. Slipping a hand down the side of the mattress, she found a horizontal indentation, and dug her hand into it until her fingers touched a sheaf of papers. Still there, she confirmed, awarding herself a contented smile. Not the most imaginative of hiding places, but for a girl who'd passed up spy school, not bad.

After replacing the sheets, she made the bed. The room looked better now, friendlier. Her armoire wasn't drunk, just a little tipsy. The desk Jett Gavallan had built for her beamed with memories of their time together. The furniture was a little too "shabby-chic" for her taste, but it would have to do. The furniture, the bedroom, the house, all of it was cover. A mask she'd put on eight years ago.

Her eyes drifted back to the desk, and she thought of Jett. Jett, her erstwhile love. Jett, her weathered Boy Scout. Jett, her pigheaded ex who refused to blink his eyes at the lights of an oncoming train.

Until seeing him last night, she'd thought her loyalties decided upon, her duties sworn. But five minutes in his presence had weakened her resolve. She wondered how much more she could tell him about Mercury before he'd finally accept her words as the truth. How much before she revealed too much about herself.

Rising, Cate turned on the radio and headed to her closet. The raucous jangle of The Clash's "Rock the Casbah" hit her ears, and immediately she felt better. She loved Western music. The hard guitars, the irreverent edge, the joyous mocking of authority.

> *Sharif don't like it*
> *Rock the Casbah, rock the Casbah!*

She was still shaken from her early-morning visit. That she hadn't been harmed was small consolation, runner-up only to the fact that the men hadn't found what they'd been looking for. Their haphazard rummaging of the house made it clear that no one had any proof she was behind the attacks. They had come to frighten her. They had come to let her know she was being watched and that she could be controlled. They had come to signal that her life as she knew and loved it could come to an end anytime they wanted it to.

They had come to tug at the mask.

Sliding back the door, she chose a pair of faded jeans, a bold blue and white striped dress shirt, and a cowboy's leather belt Jett had given her on a trip to his ranch in Montana. Cate chose her clothing carefully, rarely buying trendy items or accessories that might be out of style the next season. She knew how to read a stitch and checked a garment's cut and the quality of its material before making a purchase. She'd worn enough cheap clothes to know the difference between good and bad. Her only extravagance was a pair of Todd's driving shoes, fire engine red and buffed to a gloss.

Moving to the mirror, she applied her makeup in quick, deft movements. Two strokes apiece for the eyelashes, nothing for the brows—they were too dark as it was, too arched for her liking. A hint of eyeliner. Nothing for the lips. The lips would do on their own, she thought, pressing them together. The lips were her best feature, wide and sensual, full without being grotesque. Yes, she'd keep the lips.

Finished, she took a step back, checking for any sign of the fear she felt bubbling inside of her. Her eyes were clear and registered their usual nonchalance. Her smile was in place, and she was glad to see it still conveyed the promise of mischief, a hint of merriment. She found her face too serious as a whole. The high cheekbones, the narrow nose, the widely spaced eyes—all conspired to lend her a haughty, insolent regard that she felt was the opposite of her true personality.

No, she concluded, giving herself a final looking-over, there was scant sign of fear. And she was cheered by her mastery of her emotions.

Strolling from the bathroom, Cate stopped at the dresser and picked up her handbag. She spent a moment checking the contents—recorder, notepad, digital camera, phone, pager, wallet, hairbrush, Tic Tacs. All present and accounted for.

Just then, her pager buzzed. She picked it up and checked the digital readout. "Urgent information about our mutual friend. Let me know when to send." Excitedly, Cate set down her purse and keyed in a response, then dashed downstairs and stood by the fax machine. A minute later, the phone rang and the fax began to stutter.

The writing on the paper was Cyrillic, the stationery that of the "Prosecutor General of the Russian Republic," but the message was written in English. Dated May 31, the transmission was a copy of a memorandum from Yuri Baranov to "Deputy Assistant Director Howell Dodson of the FBI, Chairman, Joint Russo-American Task Force on Organized Crime."

Cate held her breath, reading the body of the text.

"Pursuant our inquiry re: subject Kirov, Konstantin

R., evidence forwarded my offices regarding Novastar Airlines graded sufficient to obtain warrant. Issuing date 7 June. Details of operation to follow. Suggested timetable: Week 23."

Operation? She wondered what they had in mind. Week twenty-three had begun Monday of this week. Damn it, she cursed, why was she always behind the curve?

Cate reread the fax. While there was nothing on the page mentioning Mercury by name, it was a damning document nonetheless. Investors would shy away from an offering for a foreign corporation whose chairman was being investigated on charges of corruption and money laundering by his own government.

Moving to her PC, Cate scanned the document into her hard drive. For all her effort, she was still unsure of the good it would bring. She was sowing doubt, when she needed to be bringing evidence. The article on metrics would help, even if it didn't mention Mercury. More certain was the pain her efforts would cause Jett. He'd lose the deal and his bridge loan to Kirov. He might even have to part with his company. Wouldn't it simply be easier to call Jett up and have a heart-to-heart?

About what? the steely voice inside her demanded. *He's been warned. There's nothing more you can do.*

Cate ignored the voice. One look at Jett Gavallan last night had brought back all her strenuously suppressed feelings. Lowering her eyes, she remembered the touch of his fingers, the defiant glance when she told him to drop the deal, the tide of blood in his eyes. She told herself it wasn't fair for any woman to demand so much of herself.

The hard voice laughed. *Fair? What's fair?* She only had to call to mind her own past—her struggles, her denials, her battle to rebuild a career from scratch, to carve a new identity for herself—to know that "fair" was not a promise life often kept. But there was more to it than that. There were some things she could never say, no matter how much her heart demanded.

Cate regarded the fax, and her sentiment fled. "Too bad," she whispered, hardening herself to the task. Jett was a big boy. He'd been warned. From here on out he would have to take care of himself. She'd done enough already, even if he didn't know it.

Straightening her back, she accessed her E-mail program and uploaded the fax. After addressing it to her friend in Florida, she hit the send key, confident that he would know how to make proper use of it.

24

THE RAIDING PARTY ASSEMBLED quietly and with precision. In all they were twenty-two men, divided among three vans and two BMWs from the prosecutor general's office. Crack troops from OMON—the special militia created by Mikhail Gorbachev and now attached to the Ministry of the Interior—the men were dressed in black utilities with matching bullet-proof vests and Kevlar helmets. Nazis for the new millennium. Flash grenades were pinned to their waists and machine pistols dangled from their hands.

The assembly point was Mayakovskya Square, a kilometer from Mercury Broadband's offices. Yuri Baranov moved among the militiamen, offering grunts of encouragement, pats on the back, the occasional grim smile.

"On no account are you to fire a shot," he repeated time and again, until his gruff, tobacco-wearied voice grew sore. "We are all sons of the Rodina, the motherland, even if some of us have lost our way."

He felt old and stiff and spent among such young men. He knew their simmering blood lust, their jacked-up bravado, and it left him uneasy and sad. He'd seen enough suffering in his lifetime to know what those emotions inevitably wrought.

"Move quickly. We must rush the entrance and force the door. We've come to gather evidence—nothing more. Treat the civilians with respect."

On Baranov's signal, the convoy moved out, advancing in tight formation through the serpentine alleys that combed the Moscow cityscape like fissures in a crumbling wall. The prosecutor general rode in the front seat of the lead BMW. His posture was forced, his back barely touching the leather bucket seats. Opulence, even in an automobile, made him uncomfortable. Checking his watch, he leaned forward further, so that his hands clutched the dashboard. The informant had alerted them that Kirov made his banking transfers each day between eleven and twelve o'clock—nine and ten in Switzerland, where the banks had just opened. It was Baranov's goal that warm afternoon to obtain hard-copy proof of Kirov's theft from Novastar Airlines.

One hundred meters from their destination, Baranov turned on the siren. A few seconds later, the sedan screeched to a halt. He jumped out. "Police," he shouted, storming the building's front stairs. "I possess a warrant to search the premises. You are to provide every cooperation."

Jump boots slapped the ground as the troops rushed to his side. Baranov had pulled open the door and taken a step into the building when three hulking men picked him up and carried him back into the street. At once, the thugs were overwhelmed by the onrush of OMON troops and thrown spread-eagle onto the pavement.

Squirming free, Baranov saw a blue metal curtain falling in front of the door. "Quick!" he yelled. "Someone. Inside."

Several of his men struggled to hold down Kirov's security guards, searching them for weapons and giving them a few sharp kicks. The rest were blocked by the confusion at the door. No one could enter the building.

Without making a conscious decision to do so, Baranov

charged up the stairs a second time. A single thought galvanized him. He had come for Kirov's banking records, and God help him, he would get them. The barricade was three feet from the ground and falling quickly. Crouching to one knee, then to his hands, he threw himself beneath the metal curtain and tried to crawl inside. The steel curtain struck his back, driving him to the ground.

"Ah," he cried out, feeling old and brittle, hating himself for his weakness. He was half inside, half outside the building, his cheek pressed to a white marble floor. "You will raise the barricade and open the door at once," he called to a team of black-suited bodyguards running at him from across the reception area. "I have a warrant to search the premises."

They were on him in a flash, hands grasping his shoulders, his head, shoving and pushing him back under the curtain. "Out, old man. You have no business here."

"In!" yelled Baranov over his shoulder. "Push me in!"

From beyond the steel curtain, friendly but no less forceful hands took hold of his legs and waist and muscled him forward. He moved an inch one way, then two inches the other. Ferociously angered by such disrespect—for his age, his circumstance, and his office—Baranov gave a mighty grunt and pulled himself forward. The barricade crashed down behind him. He was inside.

"Bring me Kirov," he shouted, climbing to his feet and setting off across the wide reception area. "Tell him he has a visitor!"

SEATED IN HIS CUSTOMARY CHAIR in the far corner of Konstantin Kirov's second-floor office, wearing his favorite houndstooth jacket, was a wiry, olive-skinned man with close-cropped black hair, a long, crooked nose, and a black mustache thick enough to sweep the floor. But one did not dwell long on the man's features or his dress. What captured one's attention were the eyes. They were dark and deep-set, twin orbs of unblinking obsidian framed by unusually long, luxuriant lashes. They were the eyes of a zealot.

To meet Aslan Dashamirov's stare was to look into the abyss, to see death and life and know that they were separated only by the razor's edge of his will.

"I understand we have a problem," Dashamirov was saying. "Someone in our organization talking more than he should, being a bit too free with his opinions, taking papers from the workplace that are better left at his desk."

Kirov did not know how Dashamirov had discovered the details of his sit-down with Yuri Baranov the day before, but he knew better than to be surprised. "Yes," he replied. "Some confidential papers have found their way into the prosecutor general's hands. Nothing to worry about in and of itself. What concerns me is how the papers slipped out of the office."

"Any idea who the culprit is?"

"We've narrowed it down to someone in legal or administration. Unfortunately, our staff has doubled in the past year. Don't worry—we'll put our finger on him."

"And is it the same one who has leaked the information regarding Mercury?"

"I certainly hope so."

"And the American?"

"At the dacha. You may have him when he's no longer needed."

Dashamirov bowed his eyes, which was as close as he ever came to saying thank you.

Chechen by birth, a Muscovite by upbringing, Aslan Dashamirov was fifty-two years old, the same age as Konstantin Kirov, and the two had been in business since Kirov had first moved to Moscow—or "the Center," as it was called—from Petersburg. Dashamirov had no pretensions of civility. He was a criminal born and bred, a *Vory v zakone*—a thief of thieves—a man sworn to conduct his life outside the pale of law and order. Still, he carried a title in the contemporary Russian business world, a position that was acknowledged by none, yet respected by all. Aslan Dashamirov was a *krysha*—or "roof"—and every businessman engaged in the pursuit of profit somewhere in the Republic kept a man like him on his payroll, whether by choice or not.

A *krysha* performed a variety of functions. He obtained permits, persuaded politicians, sweet-talked creditors, and harried debtors. He offered protection against racketeers, bargained with corrupt law enforcement officials, secured banking privileges at friendly financial institutions, and helped negotiate the treacherous corridors of the judicial system. His methods were crude but effective, and ranged from bribery and extortion to torture, kidnapping, and murder.

The fee for his services was 15 percent off the top of all Konstantin Kirov's businesses.

"So you're confident the deal will be a success?" he asked.

"Absolutely," declared Kirov. "Absolutely."

"I believed you the first time," said Dashamirov. "Not the second. What is Baranov after?"

"Novastar," volunteered Kirov. "He believes a hundred twenty million is missing from the company's accounts. I told him he was crazy."

"Dollars or rubles?"

"Dollars."

Technically Novastar counted as one of Kirov's private investments. As a long-running enterprise until recently 100 percent controlled by the state, it had never required any of Dashamirov's subtle legerdemain. No scrupulous customs men to brain with a lead pipe. No stubborn inspectors to "bribe" with a blackjack and brass knuckles. No defiant board members to convince with the help of a slender glass mixing rod and a hammer.

"I'm certain Baranov is mistaken about the missing money," Dashamirov said at length. "I know you would never skim a little cream from Novastar without sharing your rewards. We are brothers, nah? Such behavior among kin is unthinkable." He scratched at his mustache, crumpling his brow as if pained. "Still, we cannot allow problems with one business to interfere with another, certainly not at such a delicate moment in our company's history. That is why you hired me. To look after your interests, nah?"

"Why else?" agreed Kirov.

"First we will find our rat," announced Dashamirov. "Then we shall ask him where he got the idea that someone is siphoning a little money from Novastar, and why he wishes to share such silly notions with the government."

At that instant, a siren wailed, the keening so close, so loud, so unexpected, as to make Kirov bunch his shoulders and duck involuntarily. Another siren joined in. Tires screeched. Doors slammed. An entire Army corps was assembling on the pavement beneath his window.

"A raid," Kirov said calmly, remembering Yuri Baranov's veiled threat. And to himself, *He will pay. This will not go unpunished.*

Dashamirov remained immobile as Kirov moved in three directions at once. One hand depressed the internal alarm while the other found the phone. Dialing a number, he strode to the window and looked outside. Two sedans and three vans were parked by the entry. Soldiers were charging up the stairs.

"There's a corridor beneath the building that will take you to the Arbat."

Without a word, Aslan Dashamirov scurried out of the office.

Placing the phone to his ear, Kirov waited for an answer. The number he had dialed connected him to a modern office complex hidden in the forest just north of Moscow, a suburb known as Yasenevo. The sleek gray buildings housed the offices of the FIS, or Foreign Intelligence Service, one of the successors to the KGB, or Committee for State Security. An officious voice answered. *"Da?"*

"Leonid, listen and do not say a word. Yuri Baranov and his men are outside my offices. He's come with his OMON brutes and they're making a show of gaining entry. Send over some of your people immediately, a dozen young men with a little fire in their blood."

Ten years his elder, Major General Leonid Kirov was the ranking officer of FAPSI, the Federal Agency for Government Communication and Information, an offshoot of the former KGB's Eighth Chief Directorate.

"Calm yourself, Konstantin Romanovich. Tell me again what is happening?"

Kirov bit back an epithet, detesting his brother's propensity to give orders and his own to follow them. "It's a business matter," he explained. "The prosecutor general has exhibited more independence than I gave him credit for. All we need is for him to bring in a tank and try to blast his way in. That would make the evening news, don't you think? Where would that leave us?"

The mention of television and its promise of mass and biased dissemination of information sparked in Leonid Kirov a combustible fury. "I imagine that would leave us in the shithouse. Back to Lefortovo for you, retirement on a government pension for me. I don't know which is worse. OMON troops, you say? How many?"

"Twenty, twenty-five. All dolled up in riot gear. If you'd be so kind, Leonid, I would appreciate your doing as I asked. Need I remind you we are five days from immortality? Once the offering is completed, they'll be modeling a bust of you to put in Red Square. Right next to your old boss Andropov and Iron Feliks himself."

Kirov pictured Leonid seated in his brightly lit office, desk immaculate, books and papers aligned at right angles to each other, the large color portrait of the new president hanging in pride of place opposite the door. Leonid would be wearing the navy suit he ironed himself each night, his white dress shirt spotless, silver necktie held in place by the tie clasp Chairman Andropov had awarded him on his twenty-fifth anniversary in the service. His white hair would be brushed and parted just so, his proud chin kept at permanent attention. A single cigarette would be burning in the ashtray, a filthy Belamor Kanal, the brand Stalin had enjoyed, and every minute or two he would allow himself a long, generous puff, then replace it fastidiously.

"Older brother, a response would be welcome."

"Hold the fort," ordered Leonid. "I'll send some men over right away. Whatever you do, keep the press away. It might get messy."

Kirov hung up the phone, only to hear it ring again almost immediately. "Yes."

"Baranov is in the building." It was Boris, and he sounded shaken. "I am sorry, sir. He managed to crawl in under the barricade. What shall I do? He is demanding we raise the barricade and let his deputies enter."

Baranov. Of course he *crawled* in. The man was a worm. "Do as he asks. Open the door. Give me two minutes, then escort him upstairs."

Flinging down the phone, Kirov fled his office. A minute later he reached the data center. "How long until the files are erased?"

An unshaven tech in a red Adidas T-shirt barked his reply. "Ten minutes, sir."

Ten minutes. An eternity. He imagined the documents Baranov would find if he got into the data center before then. The government would see everything. "And we downloaded a backup last night?"

"Yes sir. At 1900 to our data recovery center in Geneva."

"Very good. Go back to your work. Pay the siren no heed."

Continuing down the hall to finance and administration, he found a dozen secretaries and accountants at their desks, diligently stuffing page after page of bank statements, revenue records, and payroll stubs into their shredders with a military efficiency. On the wall a red strobe light flashed in two-second bursts.

"Hurry up," he said. "There, there, you're almost done." Watching them, pride warred with disbelief that one of them might be Baranov's spy.

"Kirov! Where are you?" echoed a familiar voice outside in the hallway. "I have a warrant. I demand you open the doors at once."

"Calm down, Yuri Ivanovich. We have nothing to hide." Closing the door behind him, Konstantin Kirov came face-to-face with the prosecutor general. Behind him stood two of his deputies, breathing hard, pink-cheeked, and Boris. Discreetly, Kirov glanced at his watch. Eight minutes remained until the files were erased. He noticed his jacket jitter ever so slightly with the beating of his heart. "You don't mind if I have a look at the warrant."

"Afterward," said Baranov heatedly. "Move aside. I wish to enter this room."

"No need really. It's only a—"

Brusquely, Baranov and his deputies pushed past Kirov and entered the accounting office. Seeing the men and women shredding documents, Baranov shouted, "Stop. You know who I am. Stop at once. Anyone who does not obey will be placed under arrest."

Several clerks stopped shredding, but most continued. Baranov's cheeks flamed red. "Anyone who does not stop immediately will spend the night in the Lubyanka. With your families. Your children, too."

The shredding ceased at once. Baranov passed from desk to desk, picking up random papers, studying them. He dashed off instructions to one of his deputies, who immediately began gathering all the papers together.

Baranov had found a receipt that interested him. "And what business do you have with the Banque Privé de Genève et Lausanne?" he asked, holding the paper in his hand with a victorious smile.

"A private matter. Nothing to concern so august an office as your own."

"We shall see."

Baranov spent another minute or two examining the shredders, digging his hands into the basket and coming up with wads of slivered paper. "We will take this, too. I know some people who can reconstruct these documents."

"All yours," said Kirov munificently. He was beginning to sweat. He could only pray that the most secret of his documents had already been shredded. Reconstructing them would take a year's time. *A year!* Anything could happen by then.

"Now, I wish to go to your IT center," said Baranov.

"Do you mind if I ask what it is exactly you want?"

"You know damned well what I want. Now let's go. I believe it's on this floor, just down the corridor."

"If you know your way around so well, I'll allow you to find it yourself." Kirov had no intention of helping Baranov do his job. He had opened the barricade when requested. He had greeted the man cordially. No charges could be brought for obstructing justice. The rest the prosecutor could do on his own. Fuck him!

Baranov left one of his deputies behind in the accounting office and hurried into the long, airy corridor. Kirov followed. A few offices were open, windows raised to let in the warm afternoon breeze. From outside came the sound of car doors slamming, voices shouting, and footsteps entering the building.

Finally!

Kirov hastened to a window. A delegation of ten young spies from the FIS had confronted the OMON troops outside. Their leader was a handsome blond man in business attire. His deputies were similarly dressed, but were less handsome and had exchanged neckties in favor of Kalashnikov assault rifles. Shoving broke out between the two groups. One FIS man fell to the ground, pistol-whipped. Then it was the OMON's turn, losing a storm trooper to more conventional means: a well-aimed kick to the balls. Voices rose, then fell.

"Good boy, Leonid," said Kirov softly.

"What is it?" demanded Baranov, bustling alongside.

"See for yourself."

Baranov looked down at the sparking confrontation. "Leave them," he called to his men. "There is to be no fighting. We are all comrades. Let them be." He stormed out of the office, looking this way and that before getting his bearings. He arrived at the entry to the data center as the delegation from Yasenevo poured out from the elevator nearby. Trying the handle, he found it locked. "Konstantin Romanovich, I demand you open the door."

Kirov checked his watch. Fifteen seconds until the files were deleted. He took a breath, rummaging in his pockets for a key. "Ah, here it is." He managed another delay fitting the key into the lock. "There."

Kirov opened the door.

The tech in the red Adidas shirt sat at his desk, studying a manual. "Ah, Mr. Kirov. I have bad news," he said, springing to his feet, his clever eyes taking in Baranov and his deputies. "Terrible, really."

"What?"

"A bug has hit our computers. I'm afraid we have lost all our data."

Baranov stared first at Kirov, then at the technician, and then at Kirov again. Without a word, he turned and left the room.

KIROV FOUND JANUSZ ROSEN waiting for him in his office.

"Yes, Janusz, what is it?"

"Good news, sir. Great news, even. I found him."

After standing by impotently as Yuri Baranov had carted off two dozen boxes full of Mercury Broadband's financial records, Kirov needed some good news. "Who?"

" 'Who?' " Rosen registered a look of gross disappointment, his glasses falling to the tip of his nose. "Why … *him*."

"Him," of course, was the Private Eye-PO. "About time. What is his name? Where does he live?"

"His name is Raymond J. Luca. An American, naturally. A resident of Delray Beach, Florida. I found him trawling the web early this morning. Another investor invited him into a private chat room and I was able to sneak in."

"Don't look so proud of yourself," said Kirov. "That's what I pay you for, remember?"

MINUTES LATER, Kirov stood alone in his office, phone to his ear. He had banished Rosen with a handshake and the promise of more shares in the Mercury IPO. He had told his secretary to hold all calls. The room was silent, a quiet compounded by the absence of sirens and army boots.

"Damn it, girl, answer."

Five rings. Six.

"*Da?* Allo."

"Tatiana, you don't know how happy I am to hear your voice. I hope you haven't any pressing plans for the evening."

"Konstantin? Is this you? I am tired. I have had a long day. What is it, please?"

Rude, wasn't she? Sometimes he found it hard to believe she was a convent girl. Then again, he hadn't hired her for her good manners.

"Tatiana, I have a trip in mind for you. A junket abroad, actually. Tell me, my little bird, how do you feel about Florida?"

25

RAY LUCA WAS IN THE ZONE.

Perched on the edge of his secondhand office chair inside his four-by-four-foot cubicle on the floor of Cornerstone Trading in downtown Delray Beach, Luca was a model of concentration. All of him—his eyes, his ears, his mind, his square, compact hands with the nicely buffed fingernails, even the downy black hairs on the back of his neck—was dialed into the cascade of information spewing from the twin columns stacked on the desk in front of him.

Ten inches from his all-seeing brown eyes, the wall of color super-VGA displays broadcast a blinking, stuttering, ever-changing array of graphs, bar charts, and streaming price quotations advertising real-time fluctuations of the twenty-seven stocks he was currently following. The setup was called a Level II quotation system, and it allowed him not only to see markets being made in each of these stocks but to directly place a buy or sell an order via an electronic communications network, or ECN. One hour after he'd glued his bottom to the chair, he was finally where he needed to be: deep in "the zone," the Zen-like fusion of focus, mental agility, and intuition necessary to master the godless art of day trading.

It was in this church of unbiased information that Raymond J. Luca, five-foot-five-inch native of Worcester, Massachusetts, and Florida transplant, one-hundred-forty-pound washout from the United States Marine Corps and the Catholic faith, chronic sufferer of duodenal ulcers and incurable myopic, divorced father of three wonderful daughters and Ph.D. from M.I.T., ex–altar boy, ex-tycoon, ex-con, and soon to be ex–day trader, also known as the Private Eye-PO, took his daily communion, a high mass beginning at 9:30 A.M. Eastern Daylight Time and ending at 4 in the afternoon, every day of the year save weekends, holidays, and the running of the Flamingo Stakes at Hialeah.

Luca had five open positions at the moment, all buys: Nokia, Solectron, Merck, Juniper, and Amgen. He didn't care what they marketed, manufactured, or sold, who ran them or whether they had a chance in hell of making a decent return over the long run. It didn't matter where they traded—Nasdaq, Amex, or the Big Board—only that they were high-volume stocks that bounced around like a kid on a pogo stick. Volatility was the name of the game.

At the moment he was concentrating on Solectron (symbol SLR), a box maker that after years of double-digit growth and the accompanying rise in share price had suffered a violent tumble to earth. He'd bought eight thousand shares of the stock a few minutes earlier, just after it had made a "double bottom," meaning that twice in the last thirty minutes it had tested its lows and rebounded. Classically, a stock exhibiting this behavior goes on to break through its earlier intraday high. Watching the market makers enter their orders, he noted a couple of things: One, buyers were pouring into the market (also reacting to the double bottom). And two, sellers were few and far between. The stock was set to pop.

Sellers inched into the market, eager to accept the

quickly appreciating bids. Luca held on as the stock advanced an eighth, a quarter, a half. An eye flicked to the volume chart and a sixth sense told him the stock was running out of steam. Spotting a bid for eighty round lots, or eight thousand shares, that would lock in his half-point profit, he dashed off an order to sell. Bingo! Four grand in the plus column. In and out in twenty minutes.

"Trade, don't invest." The diligent day trader's motto.

Luca turned his attention to his position in Merck as a gaggle of male voices burst out shouting down the aisle. One raucous laugh stood apart from the others. It was Mazursky—or "the Wizard of Warsaw," as he called himself—and he was crowing about taking down three points on a position inside an hour.

"Thirty grand, baby. Thirty fuggin' large! Oh, yeah! The beers are on me tonight, fellas. And whoever wants to buy me the first shot of Jagermeister will be the recipient of my daily tip. Ooh-yeah!"

Luca shuddered at the Pole's shameless bragging. He didn't need to look to know that Mazursky was doing his victory dance, the revolting little number where he clasped his hands behind his head and rotated his hips and potbelly in ever-widening circles.

Luca felt himself being dragged from the zone, his cerebral connection to the ether evaporating. Annoyed, he leaned even closer to his precious screens, clenching his jaw and grinding his molars in a desperate attempt to lock out the distraction. But it was too late. His connection was severed. He was free-falling back to earth and his place among mortals. Ducking a head outside the cubicle, he saw the regulars crowded around Mazursky's hangout—Krumins, Nevins, Gregorio—all giggling like teenagers.

"Hey, Ray, that goes for you, too," said Mazursky, spotting him and waving him over. "First beer's on me."

Surprised, Luca smiled. It wasn't like Mazursky to

count him in. Ray Luca wasn't one of the guys. He didn't share tips on what stocks were about to pop. He didn't discuss his trades or offer advice on how others could make as much money as he did. Part of the reason was that he was naturally a timid person who never did well in groups. People often mistook his shyness for aloofness. Another part was that, well, they were right: He did operate on a different level than these ham-and-eggers did. He was a theorist, an inventor, an evangelist. He was the father of the Synertel fiber-optic switch, a cutting-edge technology that almost—*almost*—revolutionized the web. If he shared a work space with them it was only a temporary measure, a fluke in the cosmic plane.

Standing, he tucked an errant shirttail into his trousers and ventured a wave. As long as he was out of the zone, why not try to socialize a bit? Truth was it got lonely being a theorist and an inventor. "Hey, Maz," he said. "Beer sounds good. Where you guys heading?"

"What? A word from his highness?" cackled Mazursky. "We serfs are touched."

"Come on, Maz," said Luca. "You guys going to El Torito or what?" Luca felt all eyes on him. Don't look away, he told himself as he jammed both hands into his pockets. Keep your chin up. But already he was fighting for the gray, neutral comfort of the carpet, his chin bobbing up and down, the blinking going haywire. "Umm, what time?"

"I'll be happy to tell you," said Mazursky, "just as soon as you put your stuck-up wop nose up my hairy ass and tell me what I had for dinner last night."

The teenagers burst out laughing and the victory dance began. Round went the hips. Jiggle went the belly. *Ooh-yeah.*

Luca dropped like a stone into his chair, his cheeks afire with humiliation. Instinctually, his eyes began trawling the bank of computer screens, checking stock prices, volume charts, news alerts—anything to lessen the pain of rejection, his shame at wanting to fit in, his anger at himself for not knowing better.

Mazursky, you jerk, he cursed silently. Just you wait. Another month and everything will be different. You'll be begging to buy me a drink, to spend even a minute in the presence of the owner and editor of *The Private Eye-PO*, the nation's hottest investment newsletter.

And with that he went back to work.

For the past three years, Ray Luca's life had been divided into two halves. Nine to five, he was another "hard-timer" trying to put together a decent grubstake trading the market. It wasn't easy. With alimony claiming six grand a month off his paycheck and child support another three on top of that, he had to make a killing just to keep his head above water. In a good month, he cleared thirty grand. Nine went to his ex-wife, seven to the IRS, and five to settle his penalty to the federal government's Department of Corrections. Living expenses ate up another two grand. Small wonder he was never able to put together a decent capital base.

But every evening he devoted himself to a systematic and thorough dissection of the market for initial public offerings. He educated himself about particular businesses going public. He researched their viability and analyzed their business plans. He compared each upcoming offering against past issues in similar market segments. If the market for IPOs had cooled down, it was to his benefit. Ray Luca was a dyed-in-the-wool contrarian, and he didn't frequent pastures where the grass had been chewed to the roots. Working alone, he was unable to analyze more than two offerings a week. The current market conditions suited him fine. As long as three or four solid new issues hit the street each month, he was on track. His goal was to build a reputation as the nation's foremost prognosticator of IPOs, and on this sunny summer day he could say with equal degrees of modesty and certainty that he had succeeded. Forty thousand hits a day on his website qualified what some might label "hubris" as a mere statement of fact.

Luca sighed, thinking it was a long way from Sand Hill Road in Palo Alto to Cornerstone Trading in Delray Beach. Unlike other casualties of the boom that went bust—the dot-wronged and the dot-bombed—he had no one to blame but himself. He'd been positioned at the right time at the right place with the right technology. Synertel was bulging from two hundred million in VC funding. A white-hot investment bank was set to take the company public. Market capitalization was projected to be eleven billion, leaving Luca's 5 percent stake worth a little more than five hundred million dollars ... *and that was before the issue hit the market.*

The bad news had come one week before the IPO was set to begin trading. Luca was in Milwaukee on the fourteenth day of a sixteen-day road trip. He'd just emerged from his thirty-third face-to-face investor meeting, talking up Synertel and its position as a vanguard in Internet transmission technologies. The fund manager evinced interest and promised to put in for 10 percent of the offering. There was talk of Synertel's stock tripling the first day. In Luca's mind, his five-hundred-million stake had already grown to over a billion dollars. His days as a lab rat were near their end, his years of sixteen-hour days, forgone vacations, and forgotten family about to pay off. Ray Luca was as good as a billionaire, and as such qualified to call himself a visionary, a creator, *an evangelist of tomorrow.*

And then it was gone.

Out of nowhere a team from Lucent bettered the speed of Luca's fiber-optic dynametric switch by two gigaseconds. *Two fuckin' gigs!* Less time than an atom took to circle a molecule, but an eternity in the world of high-speed Internet transmissions.

Black Jet Securities shelved the offering, Jett Gavallan, its CEO, publicly calling for a reevaluation of Synertel's technology. Investor interest evaporated faster than rain in the Mojave. Luca was fired. His wife, doomed to another go-round as a start-up spouse, said "Screw this" and took the girls to live with her mother in Boston. In the space of seventy-two hours, Ray Luca went from billionaire-to-be to bum-in-training. Unemployed, unwanted, and unloved, dismissed by everyone and everything that had meant something to him, he was as instantly obsolete as his very own fiber-optic switch.

Taking in the agro-fluorescent lights, the soda-stained carpeting, and the chest-high cubicles, he wheezed dejectedly. It was time to get out of this jail.

The thought of escape drew his eyes to the battered Samsonite at his feet. Dropping a hand, he unlatched the silver briefcase and gingerly removed the fax he'd received this morning. Simply holding it made his fingers tingle, his stomach swoon. It was his pass to the big time. His golden E-ticket. His invitation to the major leagues. He reread it for the hundredth time, his eyes tripping over the mention of "Prosecutor General," "Joint Russo-American Task Force on Organized Crime," and "FBI." He planned on spending the entire night calling sources in Europe—reporters for the *Financial Times*, the *Wall Street Journal*, and the *Washington Post*—asking if they'd heard anything about Kirov's being arrested or a raid on his offices.

He considered calling Cate Magnus, too. She'd sent him the fax; maybe she could shed some light on what was going on in Russia. He discarded the idea immediately. The rules were clear. Only she was allowed to initiate contact.

"Hi, I'm Cate Magnus," she'd said when he'd picked up the phone at his home on a sultry spring evening hardly four weeks before. "Jerry Brucker at the paper told me it would be worthwhile for us to have a little talk."

"Oh?" He recognized her name, and Brucker was an old pal from M.I.T.

"I've got an interesting piece of news that could do you some good. Mercury Broadband," she whispered. "Take a closer look. I think you'll find something the Private Eye-PO might like to share with his readers."

The next day he'd received an envelope containing the photographs of Mercury's Moscow downlink facility. If her claims sounded sketchy, the Cyrillic letters and twin-headed eagle of the Russian crest stamped on the backs of the photographs did not. A friend had translated the words as "property of the Prosecutor General's office," and Luca had shivered. Next came proof of Mercury's phony purchases from Cisco, then just this morning news of Kirov's impending arrest. If everything Cate Magnus said was true, Mercury wasn't just a scam dog—it was a monumental fraud. An international incident waiting to happen.

Envisioning the Black Jet name on the prospectus, he knew it was meant to be.

"Come on, Jett, just give us some time," he'd pleaded with Gavallan at their last meeting. "Don't cancel the offering. Six months and another round of financing and we'll be in the clear. We'll dust those losers from Lucent."

"Sorry, Ray. I don't think the VC guys would go for it. Six months is a lifetime, you know that. It's tragic. We're all disappointed for you. But unfortunately, this kind of stuff happens."

"Four months," Ray had pleaded, grabbing at Gavallan's sleeve, pawing at him. "I'll double the speed.... Come on, Jett. You gotta believe. Synertel can do it."

"So will Lucent, Ray. It's not the speed. You need a new technology."

A new technology. The words had defeated Luca. Four years later, they still did.

Luca put the fax away. He could only hope that when the raid mentioned in the memo took place, he would learn about it. Picking winning stocks, while worthy of admiration, was one thing. Revealing fraud and corruption on an international scale was quite another, and it turned Luca's role from profiteer to patriot. He was defending his country against a new Red Peril. Any aspersions about his past would be bleached clean by the mantle of "Nation's Defender."

On a personal note, it would be Ray Luca's pleasure to cancel Mr. Jett Gavallan's largest IPO. There was a symmetry to the affair that pleased Luca's mathematical mind.

One thing was certain: It would be a helluva way to launch the Private Eye-PO's investment newsletter.

Refocusing his eyes on the collage of screens, Luca felt a new energy plucking him up. He might not ever become a billionaire, but from where he stood in his beat-up Docksiders and floral-print shirt, "millionaire" sounded damned impressive. He'd done the math a thousand times. By multiplying the number of daily hits on his website by the standard browser-to-buyer conversion rate of 2 percent, he'd arrived at the figure of three thousand wise men and women willing to fork over five hundred dollars a year to receive the Private Eye-PO's twice-monthly newsletter. A cool one and a half million in revenues for a start.

Luca felt giddy at the prospect. If nothing else, at least he'd have the money to win visitation rights with his daughters.

It was then that he remembered his sell order for Merck. In the ten minutes he'd been daydreaming, the market had moved against him. Merck was trading at

38½ and falling fast. He sent in his order and was filled at 38⅛. Instead of making five hundred bucks, he'd lost almost two thousand.

Luca dropped his head into his hands. It was time his luck changed.

26

GAVALLAN ARRIVED AT THE RITZ-CARLTON in Palm Beach
a few minutes before midnight. Once in his room, he set
down his bags, opened the windows, and stepped onto
the balcony. The smell of gardenias and the sound of the
sea washing onto the beach greeted him. He always forgot how far south Florida sat, how tropical it could feel.
It was hard to believe he was still in the States and not in
some island paradise. A second later the first mosquito
buzzed his ear and landed on his cheek. So much for
paradise. He slapped at it, then went to the bedside
phone and checked for messages left at his home. The
first was from Tony Llewellyn-Davies.

"Jett, where the hell have you been all day? Thought
you were sick in bed, laid up with a summer flu. Anyway,
Jett, if you're not in bed now, go there immediately. I've
got a piece of bad news. Jack Stuyvesant called from
Lehman about the bridge loan to Mercury. Seems his
board gave it the thumbs-down. They won't accept the
ten-million-dollar tranche to Mercury. Meg told him
that Graf had called and said that everything was hunky-
dory. She tried to get him to take a smaller piece instead,
five million, even three, but Stuyvesant said Lehman
wouldn't lend Kirov twenty bucks if it was guaranteed by

the full faith and credit of the U.S. government. That's not all, I'm afraid. Barron Bleriaut at Merrill is out, too. Same reasons. At least he was polite about it. Said if we got all the news sorted out about Mercury, he'd be back in. So that's it. Looks like us poor sods are left holding the bag. Fifty million of our best Yankee greenbacks in Mr. Kirov's pocket. 'Course, it will be all to our favor once we get Mercury public, that much more change in *our* pockets. You might want to call Jack or Barron if you get a chance. A word from the lord of the manor might be in order. Cheers."

Gavallan slumped onto the bed, the phone dangling from his hand. Lehman was out. Merrill was out. Black Jet was left holding the entire fifty-million-dollar bridge loan to Kirov. But maybe it was just as well, he figured. Save an extra lawsuit or two down the road. Running a hand through his hair, Gavallan wasn't sure he could believe the string of bad luck. His right eye twitched, then twitched again, and he realized he'd developed a tic. Maybe this was what it felt like to be shell-shocked.

Fifty million of our best Yankee greenbacks in Mr. Kirov's pocket.

That's it, Gavallan said to himself. That's the death knell. He could almost hear the bells pealing.

Unless somehow he could turn the company . . . No, Gavallan admonished himself, discarding the idea as quickly as it had come. It's foolish to keep hoping.

With great effort, he took off his clothes and climbed under the sheets. Sometime later, he fell asleep.

FROM HER SEAT in the executive jet bound from New York to Miami, Tatiana stared transfixed at the limitless plain of water spreading below her in every direction. She had never seen the ocean, and it made her feel small in a way she never had before. Not forgotten or useless or empty, which was how she felt when she had driven across the endless Russian countryside traveling from her convent school near Novosibirsk to Moscow. But small in a way that left her comfortable and secure, feeling part of something large and wondrous, and maybe even magical.

The ocean, she decided, made her feel happy. It was an odd sensation.

Next to her, Boris Nemov yawned, then looked at his watch. "Eight o'clock. Good. We will land in thirty minutes. Did you get any sleep?"

Tatiana said yes, lying. She was much too agitated to sleep. She could not get Konstantin Kirov's words out of her head. She had never heard him so angry.

"This man is trying to harm us. Not just me, Tatiana, but you, too, and Boris, and everyone in our family at Mercury. He is spreading lies about the company. It is because of him that the American came to Moscow. You know, my sweet bird, that I abhor violence as much as you do, but sometimes . . ." His voice had trailed off, and she could feel his hurt, his fear, his apprehension.

"Boris will tell you what you must do," he'd gone on. "It will be quick, but messy, and for that I am sorry. Get in. Do the job. Get out. The Americans will think it was one of their own. This type of thing happens every day there. 'Running amok,' they call it."

Tatiana glanced at Boris, who had his nose buried in an American newspaper. "What do you find so amusing in the paper?" she asked.

"Amusing?" Boris cast her a sidelong glance. "Why, nothing. This is the *Wall Street Journal*. Business news. Nothing amusing at all." He began to read the newspaper again, but stopped after a moment, lowering it to his lap. "I am not going to stay with Konstantin Romanovich forever, you know."

"Oh?" Tatiana was surprised at the admission. Herself,

she never intended on leaving Kirov. One of his TV crews had found her in a Petersburg brothel, a twelve-year-old runaway doing ten tricks a day. Incensed, Kirov had seen the house shut down and taken her in as his private ward. He gave her lodging, clothing, food. He was kind. (Which meant he'd never tried to sleep with her.) He was important, and she greatly enjoyed being in the employ of someone who commanded so much respect. No, she reassured herself, she would never leave. "What will you do?"

"A few more years and I am going to start my own company," he confided in an excited whisper. "Security, I think. For Westerners doing business in the Rodina. Maybe insurance. Our people will need insurance one day. I am not certain yet." Giving her arm a friendly punch, he smiled. "Maybe we work together. I give you a job."

"Maybe."

"Not what you are doing now. You cannot continue with your work forever. I think you should move into public relations. You are young. You are pretty. How many languages do you have?"

"Four, maybe five, if you count Baku."

"There, you see. If nothing else you can be a translator."

Tatiana smiled, wanting to convey a measure of interest. In truth, the prospect sounded appallingly dull. *Business. Public relations. A translator.* Her world possessed a more pungent vocabulary. *Slut. Thief. Whore.* Words that had been tattooed across her soul long ago. And more recently, *killer.*

She made a show of returning her magazines to her carry-on bag, then leaned back her head and closed her eyes. Enough talk of the future. Of dreams that might never come true. It was time for work. Time to begin steeling her mind to the task ahead.

Killing came easily. All she had to do was imagine a

man's body on top of hers, his brow knit in concentration, his mouth open, dripping with lust, his eyes swallowing her whole as if her beauty was his for the taking. She would feel his pounding, taste his sweat. Her vision would grow hazy, the periphery dissolving into a grainy white cloud. Only her target would remain in focus. At the final moment, she would drift outside of herself and watch as another woman pulled the trigger.

Boris had told her it was rage, because she was upset about her time in the convent. She wasn't to blame, he said; anyone who had spent twelve years in a state-run orphanage would feel the same. She recalled the bowls of kasha, twice a day, every day, the haircut every six months, the dull scissors shearing her hair to the scalp, the bar of lye that came next to burn away the lice, taking two layers of skin for good measure.

She remembered the sacred sisters' midnight ministrations. The awkward touches under her gown, the cold raw hands, the bony fingers and ragged nails probing her private places, the sour breath smelling of cabbage and wine and whispering for her to stay quiet, that she was doing God's work, and all the while the chafing of their bristly mounds against her leg, punctuated by the staccato, irreligious grunts.

Tatiana swam through the smells, the sensations, the images, pleased they no longer frightened her or moved her in any way. Yes, she agreed, anyone would feel the same as she. But it was not rage they would feel, or anger. They would simply feel nothing.

Killing was easy if you were not alive.

GAVALLAN ROSE AT SEVEN. After a long run on the beach, he showered, then breakfasted on the veranda. The effects of the exercise and the lush surroundings left him feeling restored. Hardly himself, but not the shell who'd crawled into bed the night before. He put in a call to Emerald, explaining he'd be back that night, then left word for Tony or Meg to call him pronto.

At nine sharp, he knocked on the front door of 1133 Somera Road, the residence of Raymond J. Luca. He decided to play it straight from the get-go, explain that he too had learned that something was amiss with Mercury and ask where Luca had gotten his information. But the door never opened. In Gavallan's new world, nothing went as planned.

Returning to his car, he spotted a neighbor walking a pair of toy poodles. He was an older man with gray hair, glasses, and a wary eye behind the welcoming smile. Gavallan asked him if he knew Ray Luca, and if so, where Luca worked.

"You a friend of his?" the man asked.

"You might say that. We were at M.I.T. together." Gavallan thanked his stars for Jason Vann's inquisitiveness.

"Another egghead, eh?" The older man chuckled. "Don't know what I'd do without Ray. Helps me with my taxes. Saves me a couple hundred bucks each year. And the kid won't take a dime. It's not right, I tell him."

"That's Ray. He's a sweetheart. Say, I went by his house, but he's not home. Know where he works?"

Gavallan didn't want to come on like the authorities and made sure not to press too hard. Soon enough, the older man, who'd introduced himself as Ralph O'Mara, gave up the information.

"You can find him at Cornerstone. 714 Atlantic. He's a whiz, that boy. All we talk about is the market."

"Got any recommendations?" Gavallan asked before heading to his car.

"No, just one to stay away from."

Gavallan said good-bye before O'Mara could give him the name. He already knew what it was going to be anyway.

THE DELTA AIRLINES 727 inched forward on the runway. Out the window, Howell Dodson counted seven jets lined up in front of him, waiting to take off. Friday morning gridlock at Ronald Reagan National Airport.

"Rush hour—my, my," he said to DiGenovese. "Who'd have thought it? Least we've left the gate. Won't be but fifteen, twenty minutes till we take off. We'll be on the ground by nine, you'll see. Do some of that New York City driving, you can have us in Delray Beach in an hour's time."

Dodson had decided not to alert the Dade field office to their arrival. Protocol demanded that an assistant deputy director be met by the office's ranking agent. He'd have to explain why he was in the area. That meant going into the flimsy case on Kirov and the even flimsier reason for looking up Mr. Raymond Luca. Breathe one word of premeditated murder and someone would suggest setting up surveillance on Luca's house.

No thank you, said Dodson to himself. He didn't care to waste the Bureau's resources on snipe hunts. DiGenovese's hypothesis about Gavallan's murdering ways left him unconvinced.

"Roy," he said, "I think I'm going to avail myself of the free time to catch up on some rest. Twins never did get to sleep last night. Tell you, it's danged tough being a new father at my advanced age." And tucking a pillow under his head, Dodson settled in for a little shut-eye.

DiGenovese sat in the seat next to him, glowering.

UPON LANDING, Boris and Tatiana rented a car and the two drove the sixty miles north to Delray Beach. The morning was hot and muggy. The sun sat high in a hazy blue sky. The heat made Boris uncomfortable, and Tatiana wondered if it was too much for him. Every two minutes he had to wipe his brow and take a swig of the bottled water. Tatiana, though, was too taken by her new surroundings to notice the heat. From her first step inside the airport, she was mesmerized. Everything was so clean, the floors waxed a brilliant white and free of cigarette butts, gum wrappers, newspapers. Everyone appeared tanned, fit, and prosperous. And so many smiles. Not a worried brow among them.

They stopped once at a sporting goods store in Fort Lauderdale, where a man was waiting for them in the parking lot. He introduced himself as Andrei and spoke with a Georgian accent. Later Andrei explained he worked with the American branch of the Solnetsevo Brotherhood, the business group that controlled Moscow's northern neighborhoods.

Andrei led them to his car, opened the trunk, and handed Boris a green training bag. Inside was a map of Delray Beach, with instructions on how to find Mr. Raymond Luca and a layout of the building where he worked. He was a "day trader," Boris had explained with some envy, a man who made his living trading the stocks of important companies. Tucked in the bottom of the bag were two 9mm pistols and several boxes of ammunition.

Back in the car, Tatiana took a nail file from her purse and carved an x into the nose of each bullet to make it flatten on impact. Then she fed the bullets into the clip. She enjoyed the crisp click each emitted upon entry. Finished, she used her palm to drive the clip into the pistol.

"I'm sorry, my little bird," Kirov had said, "but on one point we must be clear. There can be no survivors. No witnesses. It is for the best. For your safety and mine."

With the help of Andrei's map and the rental car's onboard navigation system, they found the offices of Cornerstone Trading. Parking the car a block away, Boris told Tatiana to wait while he entered the building and checked if Raymond Luca was in. She watched him cross the street, thinking he did not look so bad dressed like an American in blue jeans, a white button-down shirt, and high-top tennis shoes. It was nice to see him in something other than a black suit.

She was dressed in nearly the same attire, except that her shirt was a blue and white chalk stripe and her tennis shoes were white and dainty.

Boris returned five minutes later.

"He is there. Fourth cubicle to the right."

"What is a 'cubicle'?" Tatiana asked.

"Like a little jail cell. Four walls that rise to your chest and a chair inside. He is seated working at his computer. He wears a baseball cap. Yankees of New York, I think." Though his face was grave, his eyes were bright, over-excited. "You are ready, little sister?"

Tatiana nodded her head. Somewhere back up the road, her tourist's fascination had faded, replaced by a professional's icy detachment. She did not wish to speak. The pistol tucked into her pants, she simply nodded.

"I will be in the alley in back of the building," Boris continued. "Once you enter, you have one hundred twenty seconds. Eight men downstairs. Two upstairs—the managers. Shoot, then move. Shoot, then move. Do you understand?"

Again, Tatiana nodded. Shifting in her seat, she adjusted the bandages that flattened her breasts, then pulled the baseball cap lower on her head. Boris took her hand and kissed it. "Go now."

Tatiana opened the door without a backward glance.

Eight downstairs. Two upstairs. Shoot, then move. Shoot, then move.

One hundred twenty seconds.

Go.

27

YESTERDAY WAS THE ZONE. Today was multitasking.

Ray Luca backhanded a glob of ketchup from his mouth and planted his double chili cheeseburger on the only available sliver of free desk. Chewing contentedly, he flicked his eyes from monitor to monitor and screen to screen, from the market being made for Intel to the closed-circuit feed of Thoroughbreds taking their morning run at Hialeah, to the "Money Honey" on CNBC reporting live from the floor of the Exchange and back again. At the same time, he sipped at his coffee, tapped out a series of buy orders, and managed to hum a little ditty.

Let the good times roll. Yeah baby, let the good times roll.

The market was up strongly. The sky was as blue as a Tiffany gift box, and on his lap was a completed copy of the Private Eye-PO's latest editorial concerning the Mercury Broadband offering. He particularly liked the title. "Mercury in Mayhem."

Another bite of the double chili cheese, a gulp of coffee, then a moment's glance to reread and edit.

Private sources report an explosive confrontation Thursday afternoon outside Mercury Broadband's Moscow offices *on Kropotkin Ploshad between OMON militia troops led by Russian prosecutor general Yuri Baranov and members of the FIS (read KGB) loyal to Konstantin Kirov. Armed with a search warrant, Baranov had hoped to seize financial records incriminating Kirov in the theft of $125 million from the coffers of Novastar Airlines. Kirov, law-abiding citizen that he is, denied the OMON troops entry, preferring to let his legion of house-trained espiocrats do his talking for him. No doubt he'll call Baranov's visit just another case of political harassment motivated by his advocacy of free speech and a free press.*

The question Luca had yet to answer was what members of the state security apparatus were doing at Kirov's offices and why they had stood to his defense. It was akin to the CIA's defending Ted Turner on American soil.

Whatever Kirov may say, the Private Eye-PO continued, *there can be little doubt, dear hearts, that not only he, but Mercury Broadband as well, is skating on very thin ice. Do tell . . . if he didn't steal the $125 million, who did? Maybe we should ask Jett Gavallan for the answer? After all, if he's Kirov's banker, who better to point us to the missing loot?*

Stay tuned, campers, for more news from the Russian Kleptocracy.

Luca put down the pages, pleased but tired. It had all started just after eleven last night, when Jack Andrew, a correspondent for the *Financial Times* in Moscow, had called him in a furor to demand how he had known beforehand about the raid on Kirov's offices. Luca dodged the question, instead pounding Andrew for every detail imaginable about the encounter. Afterward, like any solid journalist, he double-checked his source. He phoned his contacts at the *Post*, the *Wall Street Journal*, and the *Moscow Times*. All of them said they'd heard whispers about the raid, but as yet could get neither Kirov nor the prosecutor general to confirm or deny.

Adding a few comments here and there, Luca folded up the article and put it back into his briefcase. He'd meant to get it onto his server and uploaded to his web page this morning, but he'd overslept, and his cardinal rule was never to miss an opening. Good thing, too. The market was riding an updraft the likes of which he hadn't seen in a year. Fifteen minutes after the opening the Nasdaq was up 80 points and the Dow up 100.

In a parallel universe, Mazursky and his crew were yelling loud enough to rouse the Miracle Mets. Let 'em, thought Luca. With the news about Kirov, he'd be out of there inside a month. The newsletter would do better than he'd ever imagined. Forget three thousand subscribers. Why not four thousand? Five thousand? Ten, even? Luca would buy a little house and a Boston Whaler he'd had his eye on. He'd arrange a weeklong trip to Disney World for the girls. Maybe, just maybe, he could convince his wife to come back to him.

Enraptured by this rosy vision of the future, he found it difficult to breathe. It could happen, he told himself. It really could. The family back together again. Ray and his four girls. It was all he had ever really wanted.

Minutes passed and the market continued higher, headed straight for the stratosphere. Volume. Tick. S&P futures. All were rocketing up, up, up. One after another he put on a buy, not bothering even to take profits on his earlier positions. At ten o'clock, the Nasdaq was up 150 and the Dow the same. A quick tally showed him ahead twenty-five grand.

Once in a while Luca looked down at the briefcase. Part of him said to close his positions, take his profits, and get home to post his newest article—the sooner the better. But Luca ignored the voice. He wasn't leaving today. Today he was a trader. He could be the Private Eye-PO tomorrow, and for the rest of his life.

HELLO, RAY."

Luca jolted in his chair as if he'd seen a ghost. "Jett Gavallan. What a surprise. What brings you round these parts?"

"I'm sure you can guess. You've been doing some good work—or should I say your sources have. Looks like I was wrong about Mercury."

Luca eyed him warily. "You're going to cancel the deal?"

"Postpone it. The company isn't all bad. Maybe it isn't everything we billed it to be, but there's some decent stuff there. It's Kirov I'm worried about."

"So you heard?" Luca's eyes flashed triumphantly.

"Heard what?"

"Yesterday there was a ..." Luca sat back, rubbing at his chin as a mean-spirited grin darkened his features. "Sorry, Jett, you'll have to wait and see."

Gavallan lowered himself onto his haunches so he could look Luca in the eye. "Ray, this isn't about Synertel. I'm sorry about what happened. It was a lousy turn of events. I can imagine it was a letdown."

"A 'letdown,' was it? Is that what you call losing a billion dollars? Having your wife throw you out on the street? Watching your children shy away from you because they're too embarrassed to give you a hug? A 'letdown'?"

"Like I said, I'm sorry it turned out that way. It was a tough break."

"What the hell do you know about 'tough'? You, sitting up there in your luxury penthouse, driving your snazzy car? You bankers are all bloodsuckers. Best friends when times are good, out of there like lightning when things get rough. Payback, Gavallan. This one's on me."

"I did what I had to do. You would have done the same thing if you were in my place. Look at me, Ray. You know it's true. Now, listen, I need your help. I have to know where you got your information about Mercury. I'm trying to work back up the chain, figure out who pulled the wool over our eyes."

Luca laughed, a little wildly. "You're not serious? You don't just expect me to tell you." Shifting his gaze away from Gavallan, he spent a moment tapping an order into his computer. "Tell me, what do I-bankers earn these days? An hourly rate will be fine."

"This is a lot more important than what I earn."

"Two hundred an hour?" Luca cut in. "Or am I out of date? Three hundred? Four?"

"It's not just about Mercury and Black Jet. You're in this too, Ray ... or the Private Eye-PO is. We need to talk. You could be in a lot of danger."

"Danger? Ooh, I'm shivering. Can't you see me shaking in my boots?" He tried on another smile, but Gavallan's grim expression stole his mirth. "What kind of danger?" he asked after a moment.

"I'm not sure exactly. But if I can find you, so can Konstantin Kirov. After all the crap you've been spreading on the Net about his company, I don't think he'll be in a charitable mood."

Something in Gavallan's tone reached Luca. The angry cast to his eye softened and the tension left his shoulders. "Okay, okay," muttered Luca. "But I can't leave now. Take a look at the market. I got to make some money."

"Take a break."

"Got too many open positions. Tell you what, though. I'll stop at noon for fifteen minutes. Believe me, that's all we'll need. Meet me next door at Alberto's. We'll have a cup of coffee."

"Deal," said Gavallan, rising to go, happy to get out of the rancid confines. "See you at twelve. Alberto's, right?"

Luca nodded. "And, Jett? Order yourself a drink

beforehand. Something strong. You're going to need it."

Leaving the building, Gavallan turned left and headed down the sidewalk to his car. He didn't see the slender young man in the baseball cap enter the building less than a minute after he left.

28

LUCA HARDLY HEARD THE FIRST SHOT.

A door slamming, he thought, keeping his eyes on the screens, but then came the moaning, the fevered imprecations not to shoot, followed by another bang. This time the noise was unmistakable. Achingly loud. Frightening. His ears rang, and then he caught a whiff of smoke and his nose began to burn. Cordite, he thought. Yet for all the sensory data, it came to him slowly. A gun. A very, very big gun.

At first, he thought it had to be Mazursky, some kind of joke he was playing, but a glance down the aisle told him he was wrong on that score. The Wizard of Warsaw lay twenty feet away, his jaw opening and closing like that of a fish out of water, eyes wide open, a pitch-black crater on his forehead starting to leak blood.

And for a split second, Luca thought, Jesus, it took a bullet to shut that loudmouth up.

But by then Krumins was yelling and running toward the front door. Halfway there he seemed to leap out of his shoes and slam against the wall, and when he slid to the ground there was a wide, bloody red swath tracing his path.

Gregorio stood up in his cubicle, and his blond head

seemed all at once to vaporize in a cloud of red mist. Nevins crawled past Luca down the aisle. The gun roared, and he went flat and stopped moving, without even a grunt.

"Ray?"

Four feet away stood the shooter. The voice gave her away as a woman and foreign, though it was hard to tell by how she was dressed.

"Ray Luca?" she asked again.

"Yes?" he said, frozen, confused, very, very scared. Kirov, he thought. Kirov sent you. "What do you want?"

But she didn't answer. Striking with the speed of a cobra, she wrapped an arm around his neck, brought him to her chest, and laid the pistol against his temple. Paralyzed, he tried to scream, but the words lodged in his throat.

No, no, it can't be. We're going to Disney World. My wife and daughters, we're going to—

29

ALONG ATLANTIC AVENUE in Delray Beach, traffic slowed to a crawl. Jett Gavallan braked, trying to see ahead and determine what might have caused a traffic jam at eleven-fifteen in the morning. He caught a slew of flashing lights, bright metal, and the rush of uniformed men and women to and fro. A pair of police cruisers, strobes spinning, barred the street a block ahead. An auto accident, he surmised. And a bad one at that.

"Tony, Bruce, I want you both to listen to me," Gavallan was saying into his cell phone. "No more calls to farm out the bridge loan. It's time we show some confidence in the client. If Lehman wants out, fine. Ditto for Merrill. We'll keep all fifty on our books. End of story. I don't want the market to see us sweat."

"It's not a question of seeing us sweat," replied Llewellyn-Davies. "Just simple financial prudence. If I can unload twenty million of our exposure to Kirov, I'm damned well going to."

"No, you're damn well not," barked Gavallan right back.

"He's right, Jett," chimed in Tustin. "Deal goes south, you'll be thanking us, kid."

"And when it goes through you going to fund me the eight hundred grand we passed up?"

"*Youfugginkidddinme?*" bawled Tustin. "I'm just an employee, bwana."

"Reconsider, Jett," said Llewellyn-Davies. "That's a right decent chunk of risk you're willing to shoulder for eight hundred thousand dollars."

Gavallan shook his head at their tenacity. Not now, fellas; this is not the time. It was imperative everything continue as before, that he not give the slightest hint he was going to scupper the deal before it hit the street, or that he had an inkling that Grafton Byrnes was in a world of trouble.

"The decision has been made," he declared. "No more calls."

He hung up.

It was a picture-postcard day, lacy clouds scudding across a pale blue sky, trade winds blowing up from the Caribbean, tangy with sea salt and suntan oil. Close your eyes and you might hear some marimbas and steel drums, catch a scent of jerk pork roasting on the spit. A day to relax, he decided. Play a little golf, take the boat out for a sail, drink a six-pack on the back stoop. A cynical voice laughed at his middle-class musings. In nine years, he'd never taken a day off except when sick. His longest vacation had lasted all of four days, cut short by the minicrash of '98 and the demise of Long Term Capital.

"When you work, work. When you play, play," Graf Byrnes was fond of saying. "But goddamn it, don't think the world is going to stop if you don't show up for work one day. The graveyard is filled with indispensable managers."

Gavallan took the words to heart, deciding that when this thing was over, when he had Graf Byrnes safe and sound back in his office in San Francisco, he'd do some serious playing. A month in Maui. The safari in Kenya he'd promised himself. Maybe he'd charter a yacht, do a little island-hopping near the Bahamas.

"*Alone?*" a cynical voice asked, and the glow of his dream vacation lost its luster.

"Come on, come on. I'm in a hurry here."

Rapping his palm against the steering wheel, Gavallan urged the column of cars to advance. Yard by yard, the cars edged forward, past the color-coordinated strip malls painted the same gay shade of coral, the casual cafes, the brokerage offices, and the cruise ships offering two-day jaunts to the Bahamas for $99. Delray Beach had the look of a theme park for seniors, with cappuccino and conch fritters replacing cotton candy and corn dogs.

The car in front of him turned onto a side street, offering Gavallan full view of the street ahead. Four patrol cars sat behind the cruisers blocking the road. Parked at odd angles to one another, they looked as if they'd hit a patch of ice and spun to a stop. Two had their noses half to the curb, a third his rear tires on the sidewalk. The last was frozen in the center of his lane, a track of spent rubber thirty feet long attesting to the urgency of his arrival. He sniffed the air. Burnt rubber mixed uneasily with the bloom of summer gardenias and the scent of freshly cut grass.

In the blink of an eye, his curiosity turned to apprehension.

Sliding a knee onto the seat, he lifted himself up and peered over the convertible's windshield. Emergency vehicles jammed the street: three ambulances, rear doors flung open, gurneys absent; a fire truck; a trio of identical navy Crown Vics that screamed federal law enforcement; and bringing up the rear, a TV van, horn blaring, advancing foot by foot. For all the activity, Gavallan had no way of figuring out what exactly had happened. He knew only one thing: This was no auto accident.

A swarm of uniformed men and women buzzed back

and forth across the street, running into and out of a building in the center of the block. Two cops carrying spools of yellow and black tape began to walk toward the building, and the words "crime scene" flashed through his head. A gurney emerged from the building and rattled along the sidewalk, shepherded toward an ambulance by three determined paramedics. Their sober pace didn't give Gavallan much hope for the patient. Neither did the woman following them, a middle-aged peroxide blond, hands to her face, sobbing. Another gurney rolled out, this one in a hurry. Above the din, he heard a voice. Strident. Losing its calm. "Move it. We got one alive. I need four units of ..."

The words were drowned out by a chopper flying in low overhead, a Bell Ranger hovering a hundred feet in the air. Police? No. More TV.

It was then he recognized the building: the mint green plantation shutters, the barrel tile roof, the Mediterranean arches. Cornerstone Trading.

"All right, sir, let's get a move on," said a tan young traffic cop, patting a hand on the hood of Gavallan's rental car. "Nothing here for you to see. Detour to your right and be on your way."

"Any idea what happened, officer?" Beneath the tourist's smile, Gavallan was aware of his breath coming fast and shallow. He had to fight not to wipe the sweat from his lip.

"Nothing to concern you," answered the policeman. "Just move along. I'm sure you'll be able to read about it tomorrow."

"Looks bad," Gavallan persisted. "Anyone hurt?"

"Move along, buddy. Now!"

Giving a curt wave, Gavallan activated his turn signal and drove the Mustang rental up the block. After finding a place to park two blocks up, Gavallan ran back to the crime scene. By now a sizable crowd had gathered. He threaded his way through the onlookers, stopping on the sidewalk opposite the entry to Cornerstone Trading. He'd hardly had time to gather his breath before a young man standing next to him began to fill him in.

"Guy just lost it, man. Went in and capped his crew, then did himself. Got every one of them. Ten dudes, all dead." He was a handsome Hispanic kid, maybe fifteen, with spiked hair dyed henna, a golden nose stud, and cargo pants cut to the knee. "I heard it, man," he went on. "I work at the Orange Julius next store. It was like this, check it out: *bang, bang, bang, bang.* Shit was loud, and quick, like maybe two seconds between shots."

"You think you ought to tell that to the police?" asked Gavallan.

"The police? Heck, no. I don't need that hassle." Suddenly, the kid jumped back a step, his brown eyes skittish. "You ain't the man, are you?"

"No," said Gavallan. "I ain't the man." He beckoned the boy closer. "You said, 'The guy just lost it.' You know who did it?"

"Nah, man, no one knows. But I know one of the dudes was in there. My man, Ray. 'Fact I made him a burger this morning—his favorite, a double chili cheese with jalapeños. Calls it his 'victory burger.' Dude came in real happy, see, smiling even, and that's something. My man Ray is one serious dude."

A victory burger, Gavallan said to himself, remembering Luca's cocky grin, the mention of having some dirt on Kirov.

"When did it happen?" asked Gavallan.

"When did what happen?"

All at once, Gavallan's patience left him, evaporated under the tropical heat, worn away by the endless string of setbacks, one more trading loss in Black Jet's column, who knew? Grabbing the Hispanic youngster by the arm, he shook him once, hard enough to frighten him. "The shooting," said Gavallan. "The murder. Whatever went on inside of that building."

"Yo, man, chill," the kid said, eyes bugging. "Like an hour ago." He flicked a wrist to check his watch. "Ten, ten-fifteen. Ten-twenty. Round there. We cool now?"

"Yeah, we're cool." Gavallan patted the kid's arm and moved off toward his car. A glance behind told him he'd already been forgotten. The Latino was busy offering his story to the next bystander who'd happened along.

Gavallan wiped the sweat from his forehead.

This was not how the day was supposed to have gone.

THE BODIES LAY where they had fallen. Some sat slumped at their computers, too surprised, too frightened, to have reacted. Others had run, though none had made it more than a few feet from his or her desk. The mess was terrible and overwhelming, gore spackled onto the walls and cubicles in chaotic, Technicolor blotches. Ponds of blood stained the carpet, clotted now, hard as ice. Black Ice.

Dumdums, thought Howell Dodson as he walked slowly down the center aisle of the trading room at Cornerstone Trading. Bullets modified to flatten on impact. Small hole going in; big hole coming out. He passed a victim, his face missing below the hairline, a gaping mask of blood, bone, and gristle.

Despite himself, he gasped. He'd seen men killed, women too. He'd witnessed death many times over in all its inglorious pageantry. He'd sat at a wooden table, arms and legs bound, and watched as the pinky and ring finger of his left hand were severed with a carpet layer's dulled blade. The smell of blood and the scent of fear were familiar companions.

But this was different, he thought, stepping carefully over another corpse. These were the innocent, the unknowing, the unsuspecting. Death didn't belong in these stained, shabby, ordinary corridors.

"Ten bullets, ten bodies," explained Lieutenant Luis

Amoro of the Delray Beach Police Department, a beefy Cubano of fifty who looked about two sizes too big for his khaki rayon uniform. "Guy started at the entrance, went seat by seat taking out each of his buddies, then ran upstairs, got the managers. We figure he came back down afterward, looked around, made sure no one was still alive, everything wrapped up nice and neat, then did himself."

"Some shooting." It was the only thing Dodson's normally glib tongue could manage. For all his time on the job, for all the wanton and terrible things he'd seen and experienced, he was having a tough go with this one. The question "Why?" kept jabbing away at his mind, and he had no answer.

Since entering the building, he'd been overwhelmed by a desperate and irrational fear for his sons' welfare. Though the infants were over a thousand miles away in McLean, Virginia, safe in their Talbots sweaters and Eddie Bauer strollers, he wanted nothing more than to hold them in his arms and guarantee their safety. "Christ our savior," he whispered.

Leading the way to the end of the aisle, Amoro knelt beside one of the bodies and pointed to a neat round hole inside the man's hairline by the temple. "We figure he's the doer. Everyone else got theirs from a foot or more, usually in the back of the head."

Dodson eyed the inert form. "Mr. Luca leave any note? Any message for his loved ones?"

"Not a word. Looks like he came in, worked for a little while. Around ten, something must have gotten him pissed. He got up, took out his haymaker, and went about his business." Amoro did a double take. "Hey, how'd you know his name?"

Dodson ignored the question. His eyes were glued to the banks of monitors, the blinking screens of blue and yellow and green. "Wouldn't figure a man to be so upset on such a good day," he said, pointing at the ticker for the Dow Jones Industrial Average. "Market's up three hundred points. I'd say that's cause for celebration. Guess there's just no pleasing some people."

A large, dull gray pistol lay near Luca's outstretched hand.

"A Glock," said Amoro, kneeling down, pointing at the weapon with a pencil. He spoke with a docent's tone, as if the men were touring a museum, not a charnel house. "Serial numbers are filed off, but if you use an acetate wash you can usually bring them back up."

Dodson stooped to get a better look at the weapon. "Where do you suppose Mr. Luca got himself a toy like that?"

"I imagine the same place he got his bullets. We took one out of the wall. He wasn't messing around. These things can penetrate a Kevlar vest. Cop killers, we call 'em. Not a good policy to be on the receiving end of one of these."

Dodson nodded amiably. "I'll take that under advisement, Lieutenant Amoro. Thank you."

"Our boys are checking for prints. We'll do a residue analysis on Luca's hands once we get him to the morgue, just to tie everything up."

"Good idea. Never can be too thorough." Dodson's eyes flitted across the crime scene. While murder was a matter handled by local or state police, the day trading angle and the use of the Internet raised questions of interstate commerce and securities fraud, both crimes squarely in the federal purview. Amoro might know a thing or two about dragging up filed-off serial numbers, but he was far too lax in securing a crime scene.

Laying a hand on the officer's shoulder, Dodson guided him to a quiet corner. "It may interest you to know that Mr. Luca here was the subject of a Daisy tap and a participant in an international investigation involving the Russian *mafiya*. I'm afraid that I'll have to declare this crime scene under federal jurisdiction. I'd like you and your men's fullest cooperation."

Amoro answered with surprising civility. "You want it, it's yours. Worst crime we've had this year is grand theft auto and a rape up on the county line. Between you and me, it's why I transferred out of Miami. It's nice to be able to say that murder's beyond your reach." He added skeptically, "The Russian mafia in Delray Beach? Come on."

"World's a small place," said Dodson. "Now if you'd be so kind, tell your men not to touch a thing. I've called in some of my colleagues from the Miami Dade office. They should be getting here any minute."

He meant the members of the violent crimes unit, sixteen strong. DiGenovese had wanted to alert them yesterday and ask that they put a twenty-four hour watch on Ray Luca. Dodson had said no. The decision would haunt him the rest of his life.

Feeling a tug at his elbow, he turned to see Roy DiGenovese sliding several 8-by-12 photographs from a manila envelope. "Crowd pics from the crime scene an hour after the murders took place," he explained. "Take a look. Second row. Good-looking guy, sunglasses, blond hair."

Dodson slipped his bifocals out of his jacket pocket and looked hard at the face. "Couldn't be," he said. "Must be a resemblance."

"Who else stayed in room 420 of the Ritz-Carlton in Palm Beach last night?"

Dodson was impressed. "My, my, Roy, well done. Seems I taught you well. Anything else up your sleeve?"

"Gavallan got in yesterday night at eleven. He's booked back today at three. American out of Miami. He's driving a Mustang convertible, gold."

"All well and good, Roy. I am a tad curious,

however, how Mr. Gavallan slipped past your boys in San Francisco?"

"We were soft," replied DiGenovese unapologetically. "And we were strung too thin. We'd grown used to following him in his car. With two men on duty, it was tough to cover him on foot. Like you said, he must have slipped by."

"Must have. Now let me take another look at these pictures." Dodson brought a photo close to his eyes, shaking his head incredulously. "Come now, Roy, cooking the books with Mr. Kirov is one thing; this is major wetwork. You think he has the *cojones* for this kind of thing?"

"You heard the tape, sir. Gavallan said if he had his way he'd shut the Private Eye-PO up forever. I don't think it's a coincidence that Gavallan's here. The man has the means, the motive, and the opportunity. I think you taught me that, too."

Dodson didn't believe it was coincidence either, but he couldn't get his arms around pinning Jett Gavallan, a wealthy, law-abiding citizen, a philanthropist, and an ex–Air Force officer, as a mass murderer. You didn't put a square peg in a round hole.

"I'll agree with you that it wasn't poor Mr. Luca here who made such a mess," he said. "My guess is gangland. One of Kirov's American cousins. Let's get on to surveillance in New York. See if any of the shooters in Little Odessa have taken a holiday of late."

"Yes sir. But would you let me bring him in now? Get a B-4 for the records. I'd say we have probable cause."

"All right, Roy, you can bring him in. Have the police issue an APB in the area, put some of our men on his house in San Francisco, get some agents into his office. We want him to know this is for real."

DiGenovese nodded, unable to hide a malicious grin. "I'll take real nice care of him, don't you worry, sir."

"But no arrest warrant until we collect some evidence, and I mean something that will stick in court. His lawyers come charging in now and we'll never get a conviction."

DiGenovese frowned, hanging his shoulders. "What about a fugitive flight alert?"

Again Dodson's instincts told him no. If Gavallan was hanging around the murder scene, he didn't appear to be in any hurry to leave the country or to fear being captured by the police. The acrid scent of burnt powder tickled his nose, making his eyes water. Standing there, feeling his assistant's gaze burrowing into him, appraising him, exhorting him, damning him, Dodson wondered if his hesitancy to act more boldly was really prudence, or just a neatly disguised fear of failing. He forced himself to stare at the bodies, one by one. Each was a member of a family, a loved one who would be missed and mourned and grieved over for years to come. Fathers, brothers, uncles, friends, neighbors. The admission of guilt clutched him by the neck, and he found it difficult to swallow. He tried to argue that he wasn't at fault, that he couldn't have prevented this, but his words rang hollow. He'd let professional hubris and personal comfort interfere with sound police work. He might as well have pulled the trigger himself.

"Put his passport on the watch list," said Dodson. "Get some men to the airport. Send a team of agents to his hotel. And get me his cell number. Guy like that's got to have at least one phone on him at all times."

Excusing himself, he made his way outside and hurried round the corner of the building. There on a neat patch of grass, Howell Dodson fell to his knees and vomited.

Never again, he swore to himself. *Never again*.

GAVALLAN DROVE THE MUSTANG SLOWLY, keeping his speed under the limit as he listened to news of the shooting on the radio. The announcer put the final tally at ten dead—eight males, two women. The Latino kid had been right: There were no survivors. The poor joe on the gurney hadn't made it. Police speculated the killer was a disgruntled trader working out of Cornerstone, but had not yet identified him. The announcer spoke of another grim American tragedy. A lonely man. A failed career. A last desperate act.

Gavallan knew better. Ray Luca was the target, even if he'd been made to look like the killer. If Konstantin Kirov hadn't pulled the trigger himself, he was responsible. By now the pattern was clear. Ask a question, risk Kirov's wrath.

He reached the end of Biscayne Boulevard and stopped the car at a red light. Staring out over the placid blue water, he felt a sea change come over him. He was done being the victim. Done feeling guilty. He'd never been well-suited to playing the patsy anyway. A new emotion took hold of him—maybe a whole cocktail of them. Anger. Vengeance. The will to act, not react. He'd come a fair distance in his life, but not so far as to forget his roots, or the struggle he'd waged to get where he was today. He wasn't about to let a smooth-talking Russian take it all away.

The light turned green. A left would take him to his hotel, where he could pick up his belongings. If he hurried, he could make his three o'clock flight home. He gazed up the road, at the seaside hotels and neat bike path. An elderly couple walked hand in hand along the sidewalk.

Gavallan looked to the right. The road offered the same amusements, but led in another direction altogether, to the uncharted places on ancient maps decorated with serpents and dragons.

Gavallan turned right.

30

DAMN IT!" muttered Gavallan as he turned the doorknob and found it locked.

He was standing at the back door of Ray Luca's house, a run-down clapboard cottage with dormer windows, a weather vane, and paint peeling by the bucketload. Bougainvillea, ferns, and frangipani grew untended on three sides of the small home, enough vines and vegetation to qualify the place as a jungle. Frustrated, he took a step back, looking for spots where Luca might have hidden a key. He ran a hand along the door frame; his only rewards a splinter and a dead beetle. A few potted plants dangled from exposed rafters. His fingers probed the moist dirt, again without success. Behind him, a redbrick patio stretched twenty feet in either direction. A hot tub occupied one corner, a rusted hibachi and a flimsy set of lawn chairs the other. He walked to the hibachi and removed the lid. Fired charcoal briquettes dusted the interior. He replaced the lid carefully, his grasp that much tighter because of the sweat rolling down his forearms. The heat and humidity, coupled with his anxiety, made him feel plugged in, electric. He held out his hand and it trembled slightly, not so much with fear as with adrenaline.

He had parked two blocks up the road and walked boldly to Luca's front door, calling out his name to show the world he was a friend. He'd decided that noise was less suspicious than silence, and that an innocent visitor wouldn't think to camouflage his arrival. The neighborhood was sleepy bordering on comatose, with quaint cracker box houses spaced twenty to thirty yards apart and a scarred macadam road shaded by a palm canopy. Though he hadn't seen a soul, he could be sure someone had laid eyes on him. He figured he had fifteen minutes before his window of safety closed. After that he had no idea who might come—police, the FBI, a nosy neighbor.

His anxiety growing as the seconds ticked by, Gavallan returned his gaze to the rear of the house. A watering jar, a can of insecticide, and a terra-cotta pot holding a spade and a trowel sat a few feet from the door. Taking out his handkerchief, he wiped his forehead and dried his palms. *Eeny-meeny-miney-mo.* He chose the watering jar. Wrong again.

The key was under the insecticide.

INSIDE THE KITCHEN, Gavallan stood with his back pressed to the door, listening. He heard the tick of the oven clock, the whir of the ice machine, the deafening static of abandonment. Mostly, though, he heard the draw of his own shallow breathing and the *boom-boom-boom* of blood thumping in his ears.

Satisfied the home was deserted, he made his way through the dining room, past the front door, and into the den, or what his daddy would have called "the parlor." A sky blue La-Z-Boy recliner occupied pride of place, four feet from a big-screen television. Luca hadn't watched TV; he'd bathed in it.

Blinking, Gavallan remembered his father's recliner, an olive velour "EZ-cliner" from Sears, armrests threadbare but spotless after fifteen years. The Captain's Chair, his daddy had called it, though it was strictly for enlisted men. He saw, too, the fifteen-inch black-and-white television, the creatively mangled wire hanger that served as its antenna, and the TV's cinder-block perch, prettied up with a pink pillowcase and a shiny glass jar filled with freshly picked daisies. Cleanliness alone had rescued the Gavallans from poverty.

A curtain fluttered and a faint breath cooled the room, but instead of catching a hint of jasmine and wisteria, he tasted the day-old scent of red beans and rice and the wet, ambition-robbing heat of a Texas summer.

Keep moving, he told himself.

Luca's bedroom lay at the end of a narrow corridor. The queen-size bed was neatly made, colorful stitched pillows strewn over a white bedspread. Poster prints of Monet's water lilies tacked to the wall supplied the culture. Gavallan spotted a few photos of three young girls he presumed to be Luca's daughters—skinny little things with pigtails and overalls, around four, six, and ten. A personal computer sat on a long desk that took up one wall. A screensaver flashed a field of racehorses with the header "254 days until the Flamingo Stakes."

Ray liked the ponies, mused Gavallan. And his "victory burger" with jalapeños.

Six piles of neatly stacked paper were laid out to the left of the computer. Technical charts. Analysts' reports from bulge bracket firms. Typewritten notes. His eye stuck on a page with strangely familiar script. Craning his neck, he looked closer. The header was written in Cyrillic and the body of the text in English. The fax was dated two days earlier, and addressed to Assistant Deputy Director Agent Howell Dodson, Chairman, Joint Russo-American Task Force on Organized Crime.

As he dropped a hand to pick it up, something creaked in another part of the house. It was a distinct sound, high-pitched and whiny, lasting a second or more. It was the kind of noise that made you shiver. A door closing? A footstep?

Ten seconds passed. Fifteen. Gavallan held his breath, his ear tuned to any vibration that might indicate the presence of another. He wasn't feeling so electric anymore. Not so plugged in. Jittery was more like it, the adrenaline long gone. He was breaking and entering into the home of a man shot and killed barely two hours earlier. If the police found him, he could count on a one-way trip to jail with bail an impossibility for days.

The house held its breath and was silent. Using his handkerchief, Gavallan pulled the chair out from under the desk and sat down. He had no intention of leaving any fingerprints. As far as he or anyone else was concerned, he was never here. Picking up the fax, he read about the proposed raid on Kirov's headquarters. A second go-through and he'd memorized the cast's names—Baranov, Skulpin, Dodson of the FBI. He knew the star personally: Kirov, Konstantin R. Replacing the fax on the desk, he recalled an old saw about playing cards: If you can't spot the sucker, it's probably you. A disgusted smile burned his lips.

But if Gavallan thought he'd found his trophy, the souvenir of his secret visit, he was mistaken. A marked-up copy of the newest article for the Private Eye-PO's web page lay crumpled in the trash can by his feet. "Mercury in Mayhem," it was titled, and it offered a blow-by-blow account of Prosecutor General Baranov's failed raid on the offices of Mercury Broadband.

That would have done it, thought Gavallan, reading intently. Word that Kirov was under investigation would have proved the straw that broke the camel's back. And so the victory burger!

"Ah, Ray, you were so close."

Finished reading, he laid the paper to one side. He had no time to digest, just to collect. Still using the handkerchief, he clicked on the mouse and watched as the parade of galloping Thoroughbreds was replaced by a copy of the same article. Closing the file, he thought of burrowing into the computer's directory and deleting it. He decided against it. Mercury was what it was. He'd never planned on abetting a fraud. He wouldn't start by erasing a dead man's last words.

A bedside clock showed the time as 12:08. His window of safety would close in seven minutes. Abruptly, he rose. Collecting the Russian fax, he laid it on top of Luca's last article, then folded the papers in half, as was his habit, script side up. That was when he saw it: ten little numbers printed across the top of the page, indicating the phone number of the sending fax machine. Area code 415 for San Francisco, 472—and he knew the rest by heart.

Leave, a voice told him. *You can be sick outside.*

He had stepped into the corridor outside the bedroom when a door opened and closed. This time there was no mistaking the noise. Footsteps crossed the kitchen floor, squeaking on the checkerboard linoleum. He made out voices. Murmured. Controlled. Guilty.

Gavallan ducked back into the bedroom, eyes desperately seeking a hiding place. Under the bed? Too narrow. Behind the door? Too easy to find. In the closet? He didn't have time to find anything better. The sliding doors were half open. Five steps and he was inside. Edging into the tight space, he moved as far as he could to one side, maneuvering between neatly hung pants and shirts, jostling a golf bag. Laying his fingertips on the sliding doors, he eased them together, leaving a slim crack through which he could see the room.

The man came in first, big as a linebacker, hair cut to a jarhead's exacting specifications—high and tight with plenty of whitewalls showing. Military, Gavallan thought, spotting the caged stance, the disciplined posture. The intruder scoped the room, moving immediately to the computer.

"Tatiana," he called, then issued instructions in what Gavallan took to be Russian.

A young blond girl dashed into the room, her stride as taut as a feline's. A lioness, to be sure. What else would you call a svelte knockout wielding an automatic with a marksman's ease?

"*Da*, Boris," she answered.

A flash of platinum blond, the wink of gunmetal, and she was gone.

The man named Boris busied himself at Luca's desk, gathering the day trader's papers and shoving them into a plastic duffel he'd produced from his pocket, then sitting down and tapping a blizzard of instructions into Luca's PC. From his hiding place, Gavallan could just about read the windows popping onto the screen, asking Boris if he was sure he wanted to erase the files. A voice inside of him railed and grew frantic. *That's your proof he's destroying. Your evidence that Kirov manipulated the offering from the beginning, that you weren't part of the whole damned scheme.*

Gavallan found the golf clubs. Sliding a hand from the clubhead to the grip, he selected what he thought was a five-iron and deftly withdrew it from the bag. He was no longer thinking, but acting. Rationality had left him when he'd entered the house. Inching the closet door open, he found his vision framed by a fizzing red tide.

You killed Luca and nine others.

You kidnapped Graf Byrnes.

You're going to kill him too, if you haven't already.

Then he was out of the closet, closing the gap between himself and soldier Boris. An eye darted to the door. He could hear Tatiana rummaging through another part of the house. Cocking his wrists, he drew the golf club back, his strength coiling in his arms, his shoulders.

"Hey, Boris."

"*Da?*"

He swung as the man swiveled toward him, involuntarily holding back a fraction as the iron connected. The club struck a glancing blow, toppling Boris from the chair. Gavallan ran to the doorway, ready to deliver a like blow to the girl. Behind him, Boris was already rising, a feral groan escaping his bloodied mouth. No way, muttered Gavallan, retreating a step. Hands slick on the leather Fairway grip, he brought the club back for a second shot. Tatiana appeared in the doorway. Her gun was rising, her laser blue eyes focused on Gavallan's.

"*Nyet*, Tanya," called Boris, waving her off. He rushed a few words in Russian that Gavallan took as a caution.

Tatiana inched toward the closet. Boris, a hand assaying his bruised jaw, held his ground next to the desk. Gavallan shifted his eyes from one side of the room to the other, from the lithe blond to the hulking thug. He felt tingly and alert and unafraid.

"You, be calm, okay?" said Boris.

"I'm fine. Why don't you two just turn around and leave. This is not your home. You shouldn't be here." His hands tightened on the club. "Just go. . . . I wouldn't want to hurt you."

"You, hurt us?" Boris wiped at the blood and drool leaking from his mouth. The bastard was smiling.

And then, the telephone rang, an old-fashioned jangle that in the tense silence practically blew the roof right off the house. Boris's eyes shot to the phone. Tanya shifted her head. And in that instant, Gavallan moved. Jumping forward, he drove the iron hard into the soldier's ribs.

"Boris!" screamed the girl as the flat top collapsed to a knee.

Gavallan kept the iron in motion. It rose into the air, then dove in a silver arc, the shaft striking Tanya's hands, sending the pistol pinwheeling across the carpet. The girl registered no disappointment. Planting her feet, she came out swinging. One fist darted at his head, another at his gut. Gavallan sidestepped the blows, and as the girl's momentum carried her by him, he dropped the club and drove an elbow into her back. When she rose from the floor, Gavallan had the automatic in his grasp— a Glock 9mm, he now recognized.

"Freeze," he said, one eye scanning the room for Boris. "Don't move a mus—"

The blow hit him low in the back, a kidney punch delivered with ferocious verve. He wanted to cry, but no sound escaped him. His body was paralyzed. The cords of his neck flexed, his shoulders bowed, his lips bared over screaming teeth. The whole of his being grimaced with a pain it had never known. He collapsed, first to his knees, then to his chest, his arms and hands ignoring his every reflex to cushion his fall.

HE WASN'T SURE HOW LONG he was unconscious. A minute. Maybe two. Boris stood by the desk, dumping the last of Ray Luca's papers into his duffel. The computer had been turned off. Tatiana kneeled close by, smelling pleasantly of lilacs and rosewater, the gun once again in her possession. Her head was tilted, and seeing his eyes open, she smiled. "Allo, Mr. Jett."

Hearing Tatiana speak, Boris abandoned his duties. "I'm sorry, sir, but we will kill you now," he said, turning toward Gavallan. "Mr. Kirov, he insists. He says to tell you, it is business only."

"You mean, 'It's only business,' " said Gavallan.

Boris shrugged. "My English is not so good as should be."

Gavallan lifted his head. Watching the blond cock the hammer and level the barrel at his forehead, he felt like a spectator to his own death. He wasn't frightened; he was too groggy for that, too fatigued by pain. He felt only disappointment, a terrible sense of letting Graf Byrnes down, of sentencing his company to an unknown fate, of allowing life to get the better of him.

"Ray? Ray, you home? What's going on back there?"

The voice came from inside the house. Boris whispered something to Tanya and she moved toward Gavallan.

"Ray? That you?"

Gavallan opened his mouth to cry out, but at the same instant, Tatiana brought the butt of the gun crashing onto his head. The last thought to pass through his mind, even as he drifted into darkness, was that he knew the voice.

Cate.

What the hell are you doing here?

31

GENERAL KIROV, some mail."

Major General Leonid Kirov glanced up from his work to see Levchenko, the department's newest probationer, advancing across his office, a small parcel wrapped in brown wax paper in one hand.

"From Belgium," Levchenko announced. He was whey-faced and chubby, more boy than man, and he was wearing the kind of sharp blue Italian suit that passed for a uniform these days among rising members of the service.

"Belgium, eh?" Kirov covered the timetables, bus schedules, and flight itineraries he had been studying, then stood and accepted the package. "What could it be, then? Chocolate? Some Flemish lace?"

He, too, was wearing a blue suit, but its boxy cut, worn serge, and frayed sleeves identified it as a trophy of Soviet tailoring. Still, the creases were razor-sharp and the jacket spotless and wrinkle-free, the result of habit, discipline, and his grandmother's three-kilo iron.

Turning the package over, he checked the franking. The postmark revealed it to have been mailed from Amsterdam the first of May, six weeks earlier. Amsterdam was, of course, in Holland, not Belgium, but he didn't feel like burdening Levchenko with the information. The caliber of probationers being what it was, Kirov supposed he should be grateful the fool hadn't thought Amsterdam in Africa.

"Sign here, General."

As Leonid Kirov scribbled his signature on the clipboard, he could not help but feel bitter and shortchanged. Twenty years earlier, the nation's top graduates had clamored to join the KGB. To say one worked for the *komitet* gave one a prestige no amount of money could buy. No more. Enterprise, not espionage, had become the career of choice among tomorrow's leaders. Money was what mattered. The crème de la crème of Moscow University and its brethren was not impressed by a starting salary of $150 a month. Waiters at the Marriott Grand Hotel on Tverskaya Ulitsa earned more.

A last look at the deliveries prompted a sigh of disgust. Only two other names were listed on the delivery sheet. One was his own, dated two weeks earlier, signifying receipt of a reconditioned toner cartridge he'd purchased with his own money. Handing back the clipboard, he grunted his thanks. "You may go."

Levchenko gave a flaccid salute and exited the office, slamming the door behind him. Instead of firing off a rebuke, Kirov merely sighed with disgust. Very soon all this would change. Men like Levchenko would be shown the door. Fresh toner cartridges would be found in every laser printer. The Service would cast off its dusty veils and reclaim its proud birthright. And in his new mood of cautious optimism, Leonid Kirov decided the Service wasn't dead. It was just sleeping.

With a few crisp strokes, he gathered the paperwork for his upcoming trip, slipped it into his briefcase, then tucked the briefcase under his desk. Then he patted his breast pocket. The plane ticket was there. Sunday, 11 A.M. Novastar Flight 44. Moscow to Perm. A top-secret trip to the Arctic Circle.

Only then did Kirov's eyes return to the glossy brown parcel.

"*Lapis,*" he whispered. Finally!

Lapis was the work name of an agent he had inserted into Philips, the Dutch electronics behemoth, three years earlier. In early May, Lapis had called in a state of high excitement. He had managed to photograph documents relating to a new eavesdropping technology Philips was developing for the Dutch Intelligence Service. Within Philips, the project was graded "eyes only," and its timely exploitation would allow his department to hack into the Dutch spy service's mainframe and read its take as if it were their own. Six weeks later, the film had arrived. Kirov couldn't help but shake his head. Gone were the days of the diplomatic pouch and emergency couriers. There was no cash in the budget for private jets or even economy-class tickets on KLM. As for commercial courier service, Federal Express had canceled its account two years back on grounds of nonpayment. These days, the Service sent and received its mail through the Russian post, like anyone else.

Six weeks!

A gentle shake of the package caused a small hard object to carom inside its folds. It was the film, no question. And despite his dismay, he felt a current of excitement rattle his bones. This was work, he told himself. This was the Service. Running an agent instead of worrying about copiers and toner cartridges.

Leonid Kirov had spent his entire career with the *komitet*. His postings had ranged from Brazil in the sixties to Hong Kong in the seventies, and finally to Washington, D.C., in the last tumultuous years of the regime. His specialty, then as now, was industrial espionage, and in his position as chief of FAPSI he oversaw all espionage measures implemented to advance the country's scientific and technological capabilities.

Outside, a warm sun shone down on the white birch

forest that surrounded the office complex. Kirov had always enjoyed the view, finding calm and serenity in the leafy environs. Unfortunately, he could no longer see many of the trees. Dirt an inch thick coated the windows. The window washers had left with Gorbachev. Closing the blinds, he stretched on tiptoes to turn on the electric fan. He would have preferred to open the window, but that was not an option. The "empire at Yasenevo," as some of the intelligence service's detractors called the twin office blocks situated on the outskirts of Moscow, had been constructed in the late 1970s, a prefabricated concrete jigsaw puzzle once a marvel of the Brezhnev era. Soon after its completion, the foundation had mysteriously settled, leaving Kirov's tower "whiff skew," warping the steel superstructure and rendering the windows impossible to open.

Kirov benignly dismissed the shortcomings. He would gladly trade the second-rate power unable to pay its own postage for the fiercesome Soviet State responsible for the frozen windows.

Opening the top drawer, he rummaged for a letter opener. The sound of the tape's being ripped off the wax paper was like a scream in an abandoned church. He upended the package, and a neat black cartridge tumbled onto his desk. Pinching the cartridge between his fingers, he read the ASA number, and below it, written in Lapis's neat script, the actual film speed used in taking the photographs. He scribbled both figures on the corner of the newspaper. Post-its, notepads, and unruled paper were rationed commodities. A moment later he was out of his office, attacking the hallway with the no-nonsense gait of a man half his age.

At seven o'clock on a Friday evening, the building was deserted. Spying had become a nine-to-five job. Walking through the fusty corridors was like touring a ghost town. Doors to many of the offices were open. A glance inside revealed chairs tipped forward onto desks, as per regulations, carpets rolled up, occupants long gone. Some had been let go. Most had fled to the private sector, modern-day defectors.

Four flights of stairs took him to the eighth floor and photo processing. Elevators were out of service over the weekend. Power was supplied by the department's own generators, and the lifts consumed too much electricity. The chief was quick to point out that oil was priced for export and paid for in dollars.

Ah, oil, he mused. In the end, everything always comes back to oil.

He thought of the detailed model of the pump station locked in the old briefing room. He would permit himself a last look while the film was drying.

The lab was open and, like the rest of the building, unoccupied. Kirov flicked on the lights and set to work developing Lapis's film. He was happy to find the necessary chemicals in abundant supply, less so to discover only two pieces of photo paper remaining. He would use one as a proof sheet, the second for any "gems" Lapis might have turned up. There was no use being upset, he decided, reminding himself that a year ago the lab had been out of paper for three months. This was simply the result of democratization—proof positive that unfettered capitalism had no place in modern Russia.

Over the past ten years, the KGB had withered like a rose starved of water. Thirty foreign residences had been closed, staff cut by 80 percent. Typically, a foreign residency could count on a minimum of sixteen officers. Officers were assigned a particular duty, a specific "line" to manage. The PR Line officer was responsible for political, economic, and military affairs. The KR Line officer oversaw counterintelligence. The Line X officer was in charge of collecting scientific intelligence. Other officers took care of signals intelligence, harassed Soviet émigrés in the area, and kept a watchful eye on the local Soviet colony. These days a foreign residency could count itself lucky to have two officers to fulfill all these functions.

Not only had the KGB shrunk, but it had been divided into four separate and self-governing entities. The SBP, or Presidential Security Service, handled the protection of the president. The Border Guards manned the frontiers. The FSB, or Federal Security Service, made up of branches of the *komitet* that had once repressed internal political dissent, dealt exclusively with domestic police matters. And the FIS, or Foreign Intelligence Service, carried on the job of the First Chief Directorate—namely, the gathering of intelligence designed to further Soviet foreign policy goals and the implementation of a broad range of "active measures," such as disinformation, murder, and the support of international terrorism with the goal of destabilizing the country's enemies.

Kirov could not say with any precision how large the KGB's budget had been in its glory days. Twenty billion dollars? Thirty billion? Fifty? At its height, the KGB and its operatives had numbered in the millions. He knew, however, the size of the *komitet*'s current fiscal operating budget to the penny: $33 million. Less than the combined annual salaries of a Formula 1 race car driver and a top-flight American baseball player.

Kirov bit back a covetous smile. In a matter of hours, the figure would multiply thirtyfold.

IT HAD BEEN HIS IDEA.

A way to get the monkey off your back, he'd told Konstantin three months earlier. A way to be free of the state's meddling. The writing was on the wall. The oligarchs were no longer to be tolerated. Look at Gusinsky and Berezovsky and all the others. Forced to trade their assets for their freedom. The favor of the state was capricious, he'd argued. It could be withdrawn as easily as it could be given.

Now it was Konstantin's turn in the hot seat. Everyone knew he'd been stealing from Novastar. Thievery was the oligarchs' acknowledged modus operandi. How long did he think he could keep Baranov at bay?

"What can I do?" Konstantin had asked over lunch at his lavish offices on the Novy Arbat on a squalid March day.

"Same as you've done before. Buy your way out."

"Impossible. Baranov's beyond reproach. Besides, I don't have the money."

"But you will."

"You're talking about Mercury?" Konstantin asked warily. "Impossible. The money's spoken for. We've got to upgrade our systems, build out the infrastructure to handle our future customer load. Routers, switches, servers, firewalls. We're almost there. I'm not the jackal you all think I am. Mercury's for real."

"Of course it is," Leonid soothed. "No one doubts your ambitions or your skills. Selling a piece of your television network to Murdoch was a coup. They still speak of it at the office. Still, younger brother, the offering *is* for two billion dollars."

"Two billion. Hardly buys you a laptop and a modem these days."

"You're exaggerating. Spend it the right way and two billion could buy you much, much more. You'll have plenty of time to 'upgrade Mercury's infrastructure' later. Right now, I'd be more worried about my freedom. Difficult to upgrade anything from Lefortovo. No DSL there."

Konstantin's hand began to shake. "Is there something you know? Something you're not telling me?"

Leonid hesitated for precisely the right amount of

time. "Of course not. I'm only talking common sense. You are not invulnerable. A contribution to our well-being—to our *rebirth*, if you will—could not be ignored."

"And you can guarantee this?" Konstantin pushed away his plate and thrust his monk's head across the table. "How?"

"The Service is not without friends. Some in very high places, I needn't remind you."

"How much?"

"Half."

"Half?" Kirov uttered the word with utter contempt. "Half? You're crazy. And you call me the greedy one."

"The first billion is ours," said Leonid, firmly, as if the decision had already been made. "The second is yours to use as you see fit. Who couldn't call you a patriot?"

"And you could guarantee that my operations remain untouched?"

When Leonid nodded, Konstantin withdrew into himself, eyes glowering at everything and nothing, one hand folded on top of the other in a pose of practiced contemplation. Finally, his head rose and he fixed Leonid with his intense, steadfast gaze.

"It's a deal," he said. "The first billion is yours."

TWO KEYS EXISTED to the briefing room. Kirov kept one. The other resided in a certain office in the Kremlin. Unlocking the door, he moved inside and turned on the lights. A halogen spot illuminated an angular white mountain atop a table in the center of the room. Kirov approached reverently, a pilgrim to his shrine. Slowly, with due respect, he removed the sheet, folded it, and laid it on a chair.

As always, the first sight took his breath away. The attention to detail was spectacular. The green and yellow decals with the BP logo; the small diamond-shaped warning signs reading "Danger: Flammable." Every valve turned. The miniature doors really opened. The engineers had taken an industrial complex half a mile long and a quarter of a mile wide and shrunk it down so it fit inside a conference room. It was all there: the oil reservoirs—paint chipped, metal rusting; the power plant; the pump station; the dormitories and administration buildings.

Even the terrain was accurately reproduced, noted Kirov as he circled the table. The target rested on a wide, flat expanse of concrete in the midst of a verdant meadow. Drifts of snow ranged from five to fifty feet in height, depending on the time of year. They'd built a life-size mock-up of it in Severnaya, on the southern rim of the Arctic Circle.

They were there now, training, practicing, awaiting the green light. Team 7 from Department R of the First Directorate. Former Spetsnaz men trained to fight in all weathers. He imagined them clad in white, moving over the rough terrain—white anoraks, white snowsuits, white balaclavas.

Kirov thought of the audacious plan. Soon everything would be different. Seventy-two hours until Mercury went public in New York. Seventy-two hours until the FIS—*oh, fuck it*, he would call it what it was—until the KGB received a billion dollars into its private account. Seventy-two hours until the planes took off from Severnaya, heading east over the top of the world.

Imagining what was to come, Leonid Kirov shuddered. His brother was right: They would reserve a place for his bust in Red Square, next to Andropov and Iron Feliks. Nothing less would do for the next director of the KGB.

HE REENTERED THE DARK ROOM a few minutes later. The timer sounded, and he anxiously moved to the ropes of dangling film to check the negatives. Every frame was a blank, a pearly white slate, overexposed due to heat, low doses of radioactivity ... there might be a hundred reasons why. Kirov chucked the worthless film into the trash bin and scowled. He'd had enough of rinsing mercury off his hands.

32

GAVALLAN WOKE IN THE BACKSEAT of a large car. His head was splitting, his mouth bone-dry. With a grunt, he tried to sit up. His back screamed as if gouged by a hundred razor blades. "Shit," he grunted, and fell back.

"Jett, are you all right? Does your head hurt dreadfully? Let me look at you."

Squinting at the bold sun, he made out Cate's form seated behind the wheel. He'd do it, if only to show her. One hand found an armrest, the other the ridge of the rear seat. Teeth gritted, he hauled himself to an upright position.

They were driving north toward Palm Beach along A1A, a two-lane blacktop shaded by gnarled banyans, Norfolk pines, and giant clumps of frangipani. To the right, peeking between the ornate mansions that made up the communities of Gulfstream, Oceanridge, and Manalapan, lay the Atlantic Ocean. To the left were golf courses, more homes, and the intracoastal waterway.

"Jett, who did this to you?" Cate asked, reaching a hand back, laying it to his cheek. "Did you see them?"

Gavallan brushed away her fingers. "You mean you didn't?" Despite her role as savior, she was the enemy. Someone to be distrusted, kept at arm's length.

"I found you alone in the house, lying on the floor. The bedroom window was open. I suppose they left that way."

"*They?* How did you know there was more than one person?"

"I didn't. They . . . he . . . I was just . . ." She pulled up short, her features crunched into an offended grimace. "I don't suppose thanks are in order."

Gavallan eyed her suspiciously. As usual, she was dressed as if she'd been born to the place: khaki shorts, navy polo shirt, a pair of Ray-Bans hiding her eyes. Two nights ago she'd been the princess of Nob Hill. Today she was a soccer mom. He'd been quick to pick up on her chameleon's gift of adaptability, her ability to look at home in places she'd never set foot in before, to make new acquaintances feel as though they were old friends. She could talk XML with the code pounders from Sun, deliver an address on the future of the Net to an auditorium of grade-schoolers, or bandy about internal rates of return with Meg and Tony, all with equal aplomb. It was her journalist's secret weapon, and when they were dating, he'd often found himself amazed at her social dexterity. Today it made him nervous. He wasn't certain who it was driving the car.

"Thanks." He uttered the words without an ounce of gratitude.

The windows were open, and a stiff, cooling breeze swept through his hair and across his face. Closing his eyes, he inhaled deeply and was reinvigorated by the fresh, salty drafts. The throbbing of his head subsided. The rhythmic stabbing deep inside his belly eased. The pain became bearable. But the deception remained, and he decided it was far worse a companion.

"Stop the car," he said.

"What?"

"I said, 'Stop the car.' "

Cate signaled and guided the car onto the grassy shoulder. Gavallan pushed open the door and lowered himself gingerly to the ground. He had to move, to be free of their faux walnut and Naugahyde confinement. Cate came round and offered a hand, but again, he waved it away.

"Talk, damn it," he said. "Don't just stand there playing nursemaid. Talk to me. What are you doing here? You're in this every bit as deeply as I am—even more, from the looks of things. Your fax number is all over Ray Luca's correspondence. You've been feeding the Private Eye-PO his information. Why, Cate? I want to know what in the world is going on. And then I want to know why you didn't tell me before."

"I wanted to ... I was worried ... I don't ..." She started and stopped a dozen times, groping for a place to begin. Gavallan had never seen her so flustered. All part of the act, he decided.

"Just the truth, Cate. That's all. It's not so hard."

Her features hardened as though she'd been slapped in the face. "If you saw the fax, then you know," she said. "It's about Kirov. He's a criminal—not just a man who cuts a few corners, but a gangster. He's as bad as Al Capone or John Gotti. He's been under investigation by the police for six months now. The Russian prosecutor general and the FBI are all over him. The focus of their inquiries is Novastar Airlines. Kirov took over the company for half of what it was worth and is milking it of every cent, sending its foreign revenues to his private offshore accounts."

"What about Mercury? Is the FBI looking at that too?"

"No one's looking too closely yet, but with Kirov everything's rotten. You've seen the proof. It's hardly a model of propriety."

"You mean the pictures of Mercury's Moscow

Operations Center? The Cisco receipts? If the cops aren't concerned about Mercury, why are you trying to pull it down?"

"To get Kirov."

"To get Kirov?" Gavallan smirked, drunk with disbelief. "What the hell does a reporter covering the mating habits of yetis in San Francisco have to do with a Russian billionaire ten thousand miles away? Sick of being a social gadfly? Is that it, Cate? Is this your bid for the big time? Looking for a promotion to hard news? Maybe a Pulitzer? Or is sinking Black Jet what you're after? Dumping me wasn't good enough."

Cate's eyes flared. "You bastard!" She took a step toward Gavallan, raising an opened palm, then stopped, her fury reined in. "You have no idea what you're saying, how your words hurt."

But Gavallan could match neither her emotional nor her physical control. Rushing forward, he pinned her to the car, squaring his face an inch from hers. "Kirov, eh? Bullshit! You don't even know the man. What in the hell could he have done to get you on the warpath?"

"Stop it!"

Gavallan grabbed her by the arms and shook her. "Tell me."

Cate raised a defiant chin, freezing him with her eyes. "He killed a friend."

"Who?" Gavallan fired back with equal vitriol.

"Alexei," she answered, the heat draining from her voice. "He killed Alexei."

"Alexei who?"

"Alexei Kalugin. I loved him."

"Tell me about it." For the moment, he couldn't believe anything she said. *Cate the deceiver.*

"It was so long ago. Another life." She gathered herself for a moment, and when she saw that Gavallan was waiting for her to go on, she drew a deep breath. "His name was Alexei Kalugin. We met at business school.

When we graduated, we both took jobs at the K Bank in Moscow. It was our big adventure; our chance to see the world. Alexei started on the trading floor. I worked in international credits, handling the American correspondent banks. After about a month it became clear to both of us that the K Bank wasn't on the up-and-up. Kirov was insisting we grant loans to companies that had no collateral, no creditworthiness whatsoever. It was crazy."

"I'll bet," said Gavallan.

Cate took off her sunglasses and tucked a strand of hair behind her ear. Her motions were clumsy, and he could sense her reticence, her confidence gone AWOL. Vulnerability was a new color for Miss Catherine Elizabeth Magnus, and to his dismay, it rendered her in a flattering light.

"After a couple of weeks, Alexei grew tight with the locals," she went on. "The traders took him under their wing. They treated him as if he were one of their own. Then, it just happened."

"What happened?" asked Gavallan.

"Alexei learned that Kirov and his crew were manipulating the market for aluminum futures. Kirov was buying the stuff from the country's smelters at something like five cents a pound and selling it on the international market at forty-five cents. We're talking major piracy."

"I'd say a markup of nine hundred percent qualifies."

"Alexei showed me what he'd found and I told him he had to go to the police. He didn't want to. He knew it would be dangerous. It was '96, remember. The oligarchs were at war with each other. Anyone who said a bad word about them ended up dead. Every day there were bodies on the street. He just wanted to quit and go back to the States. But I insisted. I held his hand, and together we went to the district attorney, or whatever you call that post in Russian. The next day, Alexei disappeared. We took the Metro to work together. He went to the first floor. I went to the fifth. We had our usual lunch date, but he never showed. They found his body on the banks of the Moskva River a week after that. He had a bullet in his head. His tongue had been cut out. I left the country the same day."

Gavallan kicked at the grass, doing his best to take it all in. He felt aghast and betrayed. Mostly he just felt enraged. Ten people had died this morning, ten precious lives that might have been saved had Cate not withheld her secret history from him. He didn't think it necessary to offer his condolences for one more person he'd never met. Stepping closer, he pointed a finger at her heart. "You worked for Kirov? You knew he's a murderer? Why didn't you tell me?"

Cate shook her head disconsolately. "What's there to say? Yes, I worked for Konstantin Kirov. Yes, I got my boyfriend killed. It's not something I care to remember. Don't be mad, Jett. I told you: It was another life."

"No!" cried Gavallan, slamming his hand against the roof. "It was *our* life! I told you everything. The best and the worst of it. I gave you *my other life*. What makes you so special you couldn't give me yours?"

"I tried a thousand times. You weren't listening."

"The hell you say. You think if I knew that Kirov killed your boyfriend I'd have gone ahead with the deal? That if the FBI and the Russian government were checking him out, I'd have kept Mercury on the calendar? I'm sorry, ma'am, if you hold so low an opinion of me."

"Don't you be self-righteous with me. The deal's had warning signs on it since day one. You and the rest of the market were so hungry for a winner you never stopped long enough to check them out."

"Bullshit."

"It's true and you know it."

The barb pierced Gavallan, its sting all the sharper because she was right. "You want true?" he railed. "Ray Luca is dead. Nine innocent men and women are dead. None of them will be going home to their families tonight or tomorrow or ever again. All because I've continued pushing Mercury, when you knew I shouldn't have. Oh, and there's something else you ought to know: Graf Byrnes is alive. He called me after you ran out of the ball the other night. He told me the deal was good, that we could go ahead, but he made it clear Kirov had put him up to it. That's where he is right now, I imagine—locked up somewhere in Russia with a gun to his head. For all I know, he could be dead by now. Since you know Kirov so well, honey, why don't you tell me what Graf's chances are."

"Damn you," she shouted, her lips trembling, a solitary tear streaking her cheek. "You've got no right."

"Lady, I have every right. Mercury was my deal. Like it or not, I'm just as responsible as Kirov for those ten people who died today."

"I'm so sorry." The sobs came in huge waves, tremulous currents that racked her shoulders and sent shudders down her spine. Part of Gavallan demanded he comfort her, and almost instinctively, he stepped forward. But, reaching an arm toward her, he caught himself and pulled back. No, he told himself. She deserves this.

"Okay, I should have told you," she said finally. "I see it now. I didn't and I should have and I'm sorry."

"Damn right you should have," he boomed, his anger bursting like a thunderclap around them.

"I said I'm sorry. What more do you want?"

Gavallan said nothing. He felt estranged from her. He decided he'd been right—he didn't know her. Maybe he never had. And that was what hurt most.

"I didn't want to put you at risk," she said, wiping at her tears, fighting to control her breath. "I just wanted to pull down the IPO. I thought if I could stop the Mercury offering, that would be enough to get at Kirov. A man like him only cares about money."

"And Ray Luca was your helper?"

Cate nodded. "A friend at the *Journal* went to school with him, knew about his playing the Private Eye-PO."

Gavallan turned his back and walked away a few steps. He was working the angles, trying to sift what was left of Mercury from the cinders of Cate's emotional firestorm. He kept revisiting his tour of Mercury's offices in Geneva and Kiev and Prague, seeing room after room of routing equipment, offices humming with motivated employees. Mercury had the vibe of a successful, efficiently run company, and that was something you just couldn't fake. "I saw the fax in Luca's bedroom—the one from the prosecutor general's office. It'd been sent from your home. Where did you get all your information, anyway?"

"One of the detectives who investigated Alexei's murder was part of the task force looking into Kirov's affairs. Detective Skulpin is his name. Vassily Skulpin. We both knew Kirov was behind Alexei's death, but Detective Skulpin could never gather any proof. Over the years we kept in contact, and when Skulpin's task force began to move against Kirov he let me know. Detective Skulpin was the one who told me Kirov had faked the due diligence."

Gavallan winced as if he'd been slapped. "He told you that?"

"He has an informant inside Mercury. The informant said that someone who works for Kirov was covering up its faults, painting a prettier picture than reality allowed. The only proof was the photos. And then the receipts."

Of course Kirov had faked the due diligence. If Luca's claims were true, there was no other way to have slipped it by. *Kirov faked the due diligence.*

"Look," he said. "Let's get to the hotel. I've got to pick up my things. If we hurry we can still make the three o'clock flight back home."

Cate slid behind the wheel and started the engine. They drove in silence for a minute or two, then Gavallan shot her a sidelong glance. "The hotel's just up the road, north side of Manalapan." He brought a hand to his forehead. "Oh, shit, my rental car. I left it a block away from Luca's."

"We'll pick it up later," said Cate. "Right now, let's go get your bags. The Ritz-Carlton, right?"

Gavallan rolled his eyes without humor. "Remind me to have a word with Hortensia about keeping my travel plans quiet," he said, referring to his housekeeper.

"Don't be mad at her, Jett. I called your office to apologize for my behavior at the ball. When they said you were home ill, I spoke to Hortensia. It's not fair to ask her to keep secrets from your friends."

"Yeah. Not like some people I know."

Gavallan's cell phone rang. "Hello." He listened to the man on the other end of the line rant for fifteen seconds, then covered the mouthpiece and shot Cate a sinking glance. "It's Tony. We've got problems."

33

JETT, ARE YOU POSSIBLY IN FLORIDA?" Tony Llewellyn-Davies was saying. "Bruce, Meg, and I have some unannounced guests who very much would like to speak with you. The gentlemen appear to be from the FBI, and they're asking some very nasty questions about you."

Gavallan's eyes darted to Cate, then back at the road. An hour ago, the news that federal agents had invaded his office would have shocked him. Now, he took it in stride. "Tell your friends they're bang on. Say I came down here to have a word with Ray Luca and find out why he was bad-mouthing our offering. Just be sure to let them know that someone beat me to him."

"I'll relay the message, Jett." A moment passed and Llewellyn-Davies asked if he might put him on the speakerphone. Gavallan said fine. There was another pause and he pictured his friends standing around his desk, the Transamerica Tower and Golden Gate Bridge looming in the background.

"Mr. Gavallan, Special Agent Vernon McNamee of the Federal Bureau of Investigation speaking. Good day, sir."

Against his every reflex, Gavallan found himself saying "Good day" back.

McNamee said, "Sir, we'd like to speak with you about the murder of Mr. Raymond Luca and nine other individuals this morning in Delray Beach, Florida."

"Here I am. Speak."

"We'd prefer to conduct the interview in our offices. We'll be happy to explain everything to you when we meet. The field office nearest to you is in Miami. The federal building on Northwest Second Avenue."

"You want to arrest me for Ray Luca's murder? Is that it?"

"No sir," said McNamee. "I said no such thing. We'd simply like to ask you a few questions. I'm sure it will just be a formality."

"A formality?" Gavallan wondered if the team of FBI agents shaking down his office in San Francisco was also just a formality. "Agent McNamee, let me make something clear. I did not kill Ray Luca. I'll be happy to point you in the right direction, however. The man you are looking for is—" Gavallan stopped himself short. He wanted to say that Konstantin Kirov was the man responsible for Luca's and the others' deaths, and to offer a detailed description of the individuals he believed committed the crime. The first was a six-foot-four-inch male the size of a Sub-Zero refrigerator, approximately thirty-five years of age, blond hair, blue eyes, with a nose that had seen more than a few fistfights. Went by the name of Boris. The other was a woman, platinum hair, blue eyes, maybe nineteen, skinny, and feisty as a cornered bobcat. Tatiana was her name. Russians, both of them, in case McNamee hadn't caught it.

"Do you have a name you'd like to give us?" the FBI agent inquired.

"No, I'm afraid not." For the time being, Gavallan would have to keep his knowledge of Kirov's role in Luca's death, as well as his intention to cancel the Mercury deal, to himself.

"Well, then, sir, it's my duty to inform you that unless

you turn yourself into local law enforcement authorities within two hours' time, we will have no option but to issue an arrest warrant on your behalf."

Gavallan drew a breath. Not good. The last place he wanted to be was locked inside a six-by-eight jail cell. "You guys still there? Listen, I want you to get on the horn to Kirov and tell him everything's copacetic with the offering. We're going ahead as planned. Understood?"

"You're sure, Jett?" It was Meg Kratzer. "Maybe it would be wiser to postpone the deal. We can reschedule it six months from now. Put Mercury on the calendar as the first big IPO of the new year."

Gavallan answered for his audience, his script penned by Konstantin Kirov's hand. "No way, Meg. Mercury's a gem. I told you what Graf said. This whole thing with the Private Eye-PO is just a terrible, terrible coincidence. Nothing more. Now, keep your chin up. Come Monday, we'll all be sitting in the Peninsula in New York drinking some bubbly and laughing about the whole thing. Except for Bruce, that is."

"What do you mean, except for me?" Tustin crowed.

"Sorry, Brucie, no children allowed in the bar. We'll be sure to send up some chocolate milk to your room."

Gavallan heard some chuckles and knew he'd won back his team's confidence.

A firm tap on the leg directed his attention to Cate. "What's going on?" she demanded. "What did Bruce say? Are the police looking for you? You didn't mean what you said about Mercury. Go on, now. Tell them what you told me. About Boris and the girl. Tell them who killed Ray."

"Shh," he said to Cate. "Give me a second." Then to McNamee: "Tell you what. You want to talk, get me one of your bosses on the phone. A Mr. Howell Dodson. He runs your task force on Russian organized crime. Name ring a bell? Find him and we can talk till we're blue in the face."

McNamee hesitated, and Gavallan could hear some discussion in the background. After ten seconds, the agent returned. "If you'll give me a minute, I'll patch him in."

"Tell him to call this number." Gavallan rattled off Cate's mobile, hoping he was making it more difficult for anyone to track him down, then hung up. In less time than it took for Cate to fire up her journalist's interrogation, her phone chirped. Gavallan slid it from her bag. "Mr. Dodson, I presume."

"Hello, Mr. Gavallan," replied a smoky Southern voice. "I'm sorry to disturb your vacation. Or is it a working holiday like our other famous Texan is so fond of taking?"

"Neither, actually," replied Gavallan flatly. "I came here to speak with Ray Luca. When I learned he was the Private Eye-PO, I wanted to talk to him face-to-face and ask him why he was so intent on discrediting one of our upcoming IPOs."

"That would be Mercury Broadband, would it not?"

"That's correct." Gavallan added, "I take it you're acquainted with Mr. Kirov."

"Not as well as I'd like to be. Perhaps you could introduce us someday."

"I would enjoy meeting you, though, Mr. Gavallan. A little sit-down, just the two of us. How 'bout in an hour's time at your hotel? You're staying at the Ritz-Carlton, I believe. I'm sure you're not too far away."

About a hundred yards if you really want to know, answered Gavallan silently.

Cate had turned the Explorer down a narrow lane leading to the hotel. A pink pastel palace beckoned at the end of a manicured drive. Emerald lawns as smooth as velvet rolled from either side of the road. An imposing portico welcomed guests. Two police cars were parked beneath it, their front doors open. A few uniformed officers mingled with some stiff types whose short haircuts and inviolate posture identified them as members of the law enforcement community.

"Keep driving," Gavallan said coolly, one hand covering the phone. "We're a couple of tourists having a look around. Whatever you do, don't stop. And if they come after us, floor it."

"You're scaring me. What did Dodson say?"

"Just keep driving."

Gavallan froze in his seat, eyes to the fore, phone at his ear. But Cate handled herself as if born to a life of crime. Passing the quartet of police officers, she waved a hand and offered a cool smile, circling the portico at the same steady speed. The officers looked from Cate to Jett to Cate again, somber in their khaki rayon uniforms and Smokey the Bear hats. Tourists didn't rate a second glance, and in a moment the four were talking amongst themselves. There was a fifth man nearby, standing at once among and apart from the police officers. He was a tall, professorial man with neat brown hair and a pair of half-moon bifocals. He was wearing Clarence Darrow's seersucker suit and suede bucks, and he held a phone to his ear.

Howell Dodson. *Had to be.*

A moment later, Cate and Gavallan were through. Gavallan didn't dare look behind him for fear of what he might see. "We clear?" he asked.

Cate's eyes jumped to the rearview mirror and back, and he could see now that her smile was superglued to her teeth and that she was frightened. "We're clear," she said.

"Mr. Gavallan, you still with me?" Dodson was saying.

"I'll take a rain check, if you don't mind," said Gavallan. "For now, why don't you just call off the hounds. Sending your storm troopers into my offices really is a little much."

"I'd say it made the appropriate point. Come now,

Mr. Gavallan, let's sit down like a couple of good ole boys and have ourselves a little chat. I'm sure that in no time, we'll have everything all cleared up."

Gavallan chewed on the idea. Dodson was a charming son of a bitch who sounded like he'd be at home as Robert E. Lee's aide-de-camp. The question remained, however, as to whether he would listen to good sense. Gavallan rejected the idea as too risky. Once inside a cell, there would be no way out until Monday morning. Grafton Byrnes could not wait that long.

"Let's just say I know more than I can divulge at the moment," he said. "We can call it a gentlemen's agreement. I'll tell you just as soon as I'm able. Tuesday latest."

Dodson's voice tightened. "You can do better than that. I've got ten bodies that deserve an answer, Mr. Gavallan. Now. Not Tuesday."

Cate patted Gavallan's arm. "Jett!"

"Just a second," Gavallan whispered. Then, "I'm sorry, Mr. Dodson, but that's the best I can do."

"I am trying to be civilized about this. Make no mistake, I have a nasty side. If you choose not to cooperate, I'll slap a warrant on your behind faster than you can say Strom Thurmond and we can conduct our powwow from a federal detention facility instead of a beautiful hotel."

"Believe me, I am sorry. If there were any way I could share with you what I know, I would, sir. For now, I can only say I had nothing to do with Ray Luca's murder. I saw what happened on the news and I'm as shocked by the events as you."

"Two hours, Gavallan. That's what you got to come into our Miami offices. Then we come looking for you. And I mean all of us. The United States government."

"Don't waste your time, Howell. We both know you're looking in the wrong direction. Turn ninety degrees until you're facing due east. Right out over the ocean. That's where you want to go. Catch my drift?"

"Jett!" This time Gavallan could not ignore Cate's plea. "What?" he asked, peeved.

Cate gave her head a slight nudge, behind them. Gavallan eyes fell to the side-view mirror, where a white and blue Palm Beach police cruiser had taken up position on his tail. Behind the car, he could make out a lanky figure beneath the portico charging up the stairs into the hotel.

"Just drive," he said, ending the call.

34

FIVE MINUTES LATER, the police car was still riding their tail.

They were doing the tourist trail, thirty miles an hour along Ocean Boulevard, past Mar-a-Lago, the old Meriwether Post estate Donald Trump purchased in 1990 and renovated to its jazz age glory, past Bethesda-by-the-Sea, the Kennedys' chapel of choice during long-ago winter visits, past the Flagler estate, Worth Avenue, and Green's Pharmacy and Luncheonette. A few billowy clouds hovered low over the ocean—"puffy white fuckers," they'd called them when he was flying.

"Jett, what do I do?" Cate's voice was pitched high, her features frozen in a brittle mask.

"Just keep going," Gavallan advised. "If he hasn't pulled us over yet, he isn't going to."

"I'm not very good at this."

"At what?"

"Running."

"We're not running. Once you see a siren and I tell you to floor it, then we'll be running."

"The police only want to talk with you," she said. "We'll give them the evidence we've gathered about Mercury and tell them the truth."

"I can't do that."

"But you're innocent."

Gavallan gave a quick, bitter laugh. "You know that and I know that. But right now, Howell Dodson isn't looking for the truth. He's looking for a suspect ... *any* suspect." He turned in his seat, wanting to engage her fully. "By eight o'clock tonight, pictures of Cornerstone and the horror of what happened there will be burned into the memories of every man, woman, and child in this country. This is the biggest case the FBI has going. They're not looking for the murderer, they're looking for meat. They need to utter the magic words, 'Suspect in custody.'"

"Dodson said he just wanted to talk," Cate persisted. "You can help them."

"Are you listening to me?" Gavallan retorted. "Haven't you heard a single word that's been said? Dodson threatened to put out an arrest warrant on me. Frankly, I can't say I blame him. You don't need to be Perry Mason to see that I've got 'prime suspect' written all over me." He counted on his fingers. "One: Seventy million dollars in fees that hinge on the successful completion of the Mercury IPO. Absent that, the fifty-million-dollar bridge loan we'll lose if the deal goes south. That's a hundred-twenty-million-dollar swing. Two: Back there in Ray Luca's house, I put my hands all over a snazzy Glock nine-millimeter that for all I know was the murder weapon. And three: I'm here, aren't I? You don't need any more than that for a conviction."

Cutting his gaze to the side-view mirror, he noted that the police car had edged closer, sniffing at their rear like a horny dog. A brown Chrysler hung behind it, and Gavallan wondered for a moment whether he had two cops on his tail. He looked at Cate. She was sitting too straight in her seat. The color had left her cheeks and a sheen of sweat clung to her forehead.

"Just cancel the deal," she said. "Tell the FBI you're

pulling Mercury from the market. What more proof do they need than that? Why would you kill Luca if you were going to shutter the IPO?"

"And Graf? What about him? You may not give a good goddamn about what happens to other people, but I do."

Cate started in her seat, turning her head, raising a hand in protest. She stopped halfway there. Mouthing a silent obsenity, she sank back in her seat and locked her gaze straight ahead of them.

"It's like this," Gavallan explained in an even tone, knowing he'd gone too far. "I can't turn myself in, and I can't inform the FBI—or for that matter the SEC, the New York Stock Exchange, or anyone else—that Black Jet is going to cancel the Mercury offering. Kirov has to believe I'm playing ball. He has to think I want the deal to go through as badly as he does. That's why I told Tony to call him and tell him I was standing behind the IPO a hundred percent. That's why I said that stuff about Mercury being a gem and Ray Luca's death a bad coincidence. I'm sending Kirov a message we're on the same team. Maybe it'll keep Graf alive until I can figure out a way to get him home."

"I get it," Cate said. "I'm not sure I like it, but I get it."

"Good," said Gavallan. "Glad to hear you're with the program."

Cate crossed her arms, shooting him a stern glance. "I was always with the program. Now, instead of riding me so hard, why don't you figure out a way to get us off this island."

"I'm working on it. I'm working on it."

Gavallan looked to his left and right, exhaling loudly. He was doing his best to think clearly, to come up with a plan that would get him out from under the FBI's thumb. Sometime during the last two days, his world had been turned upside down, and he was still trying to right it. Graf Byrnes's midnight call, Ray Luca's murder, Cate's miraculous last-second appearance, and a couple of sucker punches to boot—it had all left him feeling as beat-up as a secondhand catcher's mitt.

At two o'clock on a Friday afternoon, eyes glued to the rearview mirror, his stomach in knots that at any moment the police car on his tail would hit the siren and pull him over, Jett Gavallan's emotional reserves had run dry. Grief, hope, worry—all were tapped out, and the only thing he was capable of feeling now was dread. For Graf. For himself and his company. For the whole damned world.

Inclining his head out the window, he caught a glance of himself in the mirror. He looked tired, a lined veteran of too many corporate campaigns. Thirty-eight going on sixty. Yet it wasn't the fatigue that surprised him, but the hunted look in his eyes. He appeared weak. Defeated. Once a warrior, he had been softened by a decade behind a desk, where nerve was a cocktail of figures and formulas, and risk measured in dollars, not lives.

And Graf? a fighting voice asked him. How's he faring right about now? He wouldn't be too thrilled to learn you're feeling a little long in the tooth. Get this through your head: You don't have a choice whether you're tired or not, whether you think you're up to it. Someone else is depending on you. You have an obligation. *A duty.*

The word galvanized him as no other could have, and he remembered a saying that Graf Byrnes had taught him at the Academy, words rich with sacrifice and the blood of history.

"A man can never do more than his duty. He should never wish to do less."

They had left the commercial center of Palm Beach and ventured into the northern residential district, where homes lay hidden behind twenty-foot stands of eugenias and gardeners needed cherry pickers to prune the trees. Parked along the curb, battered pickups loaded with lawn mowers and leaf blowers kept company with polished Rolls-Royces whose signature winged hood ornaments had been removed lest they inspire thieving minds. Gavallan wanted to make a U-turn and head for one of the bridges that led to the mainland, but he was fearful any move might be viewed as flight and make the cop want to pull him over.

"Jett!"

The police cruiser had turned on its strobes and hit them twice with its high beams. A moment later, the siren's shrill attack pierced the air.

Gavallan laid a hand on Cate's arm, swiveling in his seat to look over his shoulder. The police officer was waving them to the side. Running was out of the question. Palm Beach was an island. Three bridges linked it to the mainland and there would be a roadblock on every one before they could make it halfway across.

"Pull over," he said. "Up ahead by those hedges."

Cate edged the car to the side of the road, but a few seconds later she still hadn't slowed. He saw her looking at him uncertainly, her lips half moving; then suddenly, she spat out, "Jett, I have a gun in the car."

"What?"

"In the glove compartment. It was for protection. I was afraid of Kirov."

Opening the glove box, he lifted the pistol—a snub-nosed .38 police special—and took out the rental papers. "My God," he said, swallowing hard. "You mean business, don't you." Once the police found the gun, no amount of smooth talking would set them free. "Same goes as before. Pull over. We cooperate. 'Yes sir. No sir.' Whatever you do, don't tell them who I am. There's no way they can have a picture of me by now. We're tourists from California and we'll wing the rest. Somehow, we'll talk our way out of this."

He didn't believe it for a second.

Cate steered the Explorer off the road, braking gently as she brought the car to a halt beneath a cluster of co-conut palms. But as her tires sunk into the sandy shoulder, a strange and wonderful thing happened. Instead of following them onto the embankment, the police car pulled into the center of the road and shot past, its V-8 engine growling magnificently. In a moment all that was visible was a pair of taillights flashing back and forth like the blinking eyes of a railroad crossing guard back home in the Rio Grande Valley.

Cate looked at Jett, and he looked right back at her. He was staring into her eyes, marveling at their depth, wondering, as he often had, if he would ever really know her. He continued to her nose, her lips, the swell of her neck.

I loved you, he said to her silently.

A cicada's electric crescendo filled the car. It died down, and then there was only the surf rushing onto the white sand beach and the melancholy drone of a single-engine plane flying high above.

"We're free," she said, in a whisper.

"For now." Gavallan dropped his eyes, uncomfortable with his feelings for her, wanting to trust her, to lower his guard, knowing it wasn't possible. "Let's not press our luck. Let's get off this island. Better yet, let's get out of this state." He looked at his watch. "If Dodson makes good on his offer, the FBI will be checking outgoing flights up and down the coast within the hour; they probably already are. If they know I'm in Florida, we can count on their knowing how I got here and how I planned to go home."

Cate fished in the side compartment for a map. "There's an executive airport in Boca Raton," she said, spreading a multicolor canvas on her lap. "I flew in once with the guys from Redmond to cover one of Microsoft's confabs. It's got a runway long enough for business jets and a few hangars. Think we can charter a plane?"

" 'We'? Where do you think *you're* going?"

"With you."

"But I'm not going home. And I'm not going to be responsible for you."

"No one's asking you to be. I'm thirty, Jett. Last time I checked that qualified as an adult. Correct me if I'm wrong, but wasn't it you who needed looking after about an hour ago?"

Gavallan knew it was more than a question of responsibility. It was a question of trust. Cate had become an unknown commodity. Yes, she had saved his life. Even so, her presence made him antsy, aware that he was in the middle of something bigger than himself, something gray and menacing whose borders he might never discover.

"Look, you've won," he said. "Mercury's not going to come to market. Go home. And thanks. Thanks for saving my butt back there. I mean it. But that's it. This is where it ends."

"And Graf?"

"He's my problem."

"Your problem? You think you can sit there and call me uncaring, brand me with the responsibility of ten people's deaths and expect me just to forget it? I know Grafton Byrnes too. Remember? I'm proud to say that I count him as a friend. You want to be responsible for him? Fine. But you didn't know Ray Luca. And you didn't know Alexei Kalugin. Those two are mine, whether I like it or not. No matter what might happen to Kirov, I have to live with the fact that I was responsible—at least in some way—for getting them killed. You can't just pawn me off. You said it yourself: I'm in this even deeper than you are. Longer, anyway." She spent a moment studying the map. A quizzical expression skirted her features. "By the way, what do you have in mind—I mean if you're not going home, that is? Are you planning on chartering a jet to Moscow, driving up to Kirov's house, banging on his door, and asking him to give you Graf back? Do you have any idea how well-protected a man like Kirov is? He's an oligarch, for Christ's sake. The man has his own private army. The second they know you're in Moscow, they'll whisk you off the streets and stuff you in the same hole where they've put Graf. If they don't just shoot you on sight, that is. Right about now, I'd say you rank number one on Kirov's 'Most Wanted' list."

For a moment, Gavallan didn't answer. He knew well enough that he couldn't just traipse up to Kirov's door and demand his friend's return. In truth, he had no intention of going to Moscow. Securing Graf's return would require a none-too-subtle gambit of barter and blackmail, along with a fair dose of luck. He had only the rudiments of a plan, and they involved his visiting another city on the European continent. Geneva. He needed chips to sit at Kirov's table. What better place was there to get bankrolled than Switzerland?

"If your friend Skulpin's right, Kirov couldn't have faked the due diligence without the help of Silber, Goldi, and Grimm," he said. "They're the ones who visited Kirov's operations. They hired the experts to verify that Mercury's operating platform was up to snuff. They signed off that everything was a hundred percent as advertised. If something was amiss, they'd have to have seen it."

"You told me the other night you'd spoken with Jean-Jacques Pillonel and that he swore the whole thing was good as gold."

"He did."

"Okay then. At least we know where to look."

Gavallan knew the tone of voice too well. Smug, confident, unimpeachable. He couldn't deny her claims on Kirov. On a strictly practical note, it would be safer traveling in her company. The FBI was looking for a lone murderer, not a vacationing couple.

If for Graf's sake alone, he would allow her to come to Geneva with him.

Taking the map from Cate's lap, he spread it across his own. The Boca Raton airport looked to be an hour's drive. His knowledge of private airports taught him they ran the gamut from dirt landing strips with a Coke machine and a gas pump to state-of-the-art facilities equipped to assist their pilots to fly anywhere short of the moon. He was quick to assume that the Boca Raton airport, with its proximity to Palm Beach, Fort Lauderdale, and other monied suburbs of south Florida, ran to the latter variety. On the one hand, it would definitely have several planes available for charter. On the other, it'd be first in line to cooperate with the authorities should questions be asked about flight plans filed that afternoon by a certain investment banker.

Further study revealed several other private airports in the region, but Gavallan liked what Cate had said about a long runway. If they were going to Geneva, they'd require a decent-size jet: a Cessna Citation, an upper-end Lear, a Gulfstream III.

"Boca it is," he said. "Let's get moving. We've got a few stops to make before we get to the airport."

JETT GAVALLAN ROLLED ACROSS the tarmac of the Boca Raton Executive Airport, a bent old man pushed along in a shiny wheelchair by a rather too attractive companion. One stop at the nearest mall had taken care of their requirements. A windbreaker, a broad-visored sun hat, and some dark glasses hid Gavallan's features. The blanket was Cate's idea. Old people got cold, she said, even when the thermometer topped eighty-eight degrees Fahrenheit and humidity was 90 percent plus. The disguise wasn't much, but it might keep the Feds off his trail if they were as eager to find him as they said.

He'd taken other precautions as well. He'd chartered

the plane under a fictitious name and paid via E-cash, transferring the fees directly from his bank account to the aircraft leasing company—all before setting foot on airport grounds. He wanted as few people as possible to remember seeing them. In this at least he was successful. Their total time in transit from parking lot to tarmac was ten minutes.

Ahead lay their chariot: a white Gulfstream III with a sporty blue pinstripe running the length of the fuselage. A team of mechanics swarmed around the engines. The pilot and copilot circled the tail, completing their preflight walk-around. A fuel truck lumbered alongside, and a hose was extended to the plane's wing. The sight of the gleaming aircraft did wonders for Gavallan's bruised morale. Airplanes, of every size and vintage, never ceased to thrill him.

"She's a beaut," he said.

"She is," said Cate. "You thinking of getting behind the controls yourself? Give me a show of the Air Force's greatest talent?"

"No," he said coldly. "That part of my life's over. These days I ride just like any other paying customer."

"Maybe someday," suggested Cate.

"Maybe." Gavallan pulled down the brim of his hat to shadow his features.

They'd spent the hour's ride to the airport discussing what to do once they reached Geneva, how to approach Kirov if they were able to extract a confession from Jean-Jacques Pillonel or if by God's grace they got their hands on some material evidence of Silber, Goldi, and Grimm's fraud.

But their conversation hadn't ended there. Sometime during the drive the focus had shifted from freeing Grafton Byrnes to making Kirov pay for his crimes.

"Canceling the Mercury offering might hurt Kirov," Cate had said, "but it's not nearly enough. Not anymore.

I want the man to pay. I want him to suffer for the people he's killed."

And for stealing Black Jet, Gavallan added silently.

Canceling the Mercury IPO would deal his company a swift and severe blow. He could forget about the seventy million in fees. He'd have to write off the bridge loan to Kirov, worth another fifty million. And that would be that.

Two choices would be left him. He could embark on a wholesale restructuring of the firm that would require firing a few hundred employees and shuttering his London and Chicago operations. Or he could sell. He and his top executives would pocket large sums, but they would hardly be compensated for the business's true worth. And the prospect of working for another firm left him cold. Were he to leave, his core team of executives would follow, willingly or not. Neither Tony, Bruce, nor Meg fit the mold corporate behemoths demanded these days. Meg was too old. Tony's illness branded him unreliable. And Bruce ... well, simply put, Bruce was an asshole. It wouldn't be a week before he'd have called the new managing director a bootlicker or an ass-kisser or God knows what, and that would be the end of Bruce.

"The only way to hurt Kirov is to put him in prison," Cate said. "Rob him of his power, his money, his position."

"Easier said than done," said Gavallan, unable to cloak his pessimism. "He's a Russian citizen. He'll never stand before an American judge to answer for Mercury—if, that is, we can even prove he meddled."

"Oh, he meddled all right. Just like he meddled with Novastar. What we need to do is nail him for stealing the hundred twenty-five million from his own country. Put him in the gulag where he belongs."

"One thing at a time, Cate. I'd say our plates are full as it is."

"I can dream, can't I?"

Cate wheeled the chair to the foot of the stairwell and helped Gavallan board the plane. It wasn't hard to adopt the gait of an older man. His lower back had stiffened and the throbbing in his head had returned with a vengeance. Still, it was impossible to deny the rush of excitement he felt as he entered the fuselage.

"So, you old codger," she said. "Where you headed?"

"Geneva. I hear there are a lot of crooks in those parts. Guess you're coming too?"

Cate stared at him over the top of her sunglasses, but when she spoke the smile had left her voice. "Wouldn't miss it for the world."

35

GRAFTON BYRNES ROSE at the sound of the approaching engine and shuffled to the wall. It was late afternoon. The sky was cloudy, the air growing cooler. He was sick with fever and painfully hungry. The engine meant dinner, if that was what you called a mess tin half filled with weak broth and a few skimpy vegetables. Twice a day, an old, dented truck lumbered into the clearing, delivering the same meal. Twice a day he both cursed and rejoiced. He'd never imagined how famished a man could grow in two days. How terribly, desperately hungry. The stomach did not accept maltreatment complacently. It howled, it stabbed, it cramped.

Glancing up, Byrnes noticed dark clouds gathering overhead. A drop of rain dodged what was left of the roof and caught him on the cheek. Days tended to be warm, but when the sun fell, the temperature plummeted to freezing, the wind picked up, and his teeth chattered like marble on ice. Wiping away the raindrop, he tried to imagine another night lying huddled like an animal in the corner of the shed, toes dug into the dirt, bandaged hands clenched, tucked close to his chest, left with only his trousers and Ascot Chang's finest Egyptian cotton dress shirt to fend off the cold. He began to shiver.

He knew men who'd toughed out eight years in the Hanoi Hilton. He told himself he could stand a couple of days at the Moscow Marriott, or as Konstantin Kirov had eloquently christened the place, "the dacha." Either way, it would be over soon, his freedom granted in one form or another.

He looked down at his bare feet, at the toenails clogged with dirt, at the white, defenseless flesh. "Bastards," he muttered, the shivering growing worse now. "You could have left me my socks."

The shed measured six feet by six feet and had been constructed from the slim, round corpus of birch trees. The walls rose eight feet in height. A padlock secured the door. There were no windows, but by peering through the gaps that separated one log from the next, he had a fine view of the compound. A three-room log cabin with a stone chimney and large picture windows stood a hundred feet to his right. Two smaller structures stood farther away, visible among the towering pines. One was a rotted cabin with a rickety antenna attached to its roof, the other a stone sump house with a redbrick smokestack. In his time at the dacha, Byrnes had yet to see a soul anywhere, save the grizzled man who served as his jailer.

To his left, maybe sixty feet, was another shed like his own: a storage shack, if the shards of coal and wood embedded in the dirt floor were anything to go by. A double fence surrounded the compound, twelve feet high, topped with a run of razor wire. Again he wondered why there were no guards. He stared at the fence. He guessed it was electrified. There was no better guard than twenty thousand volts of raw current.

It would be difficult to get out, Byrnes knew. Difficult, but not impossible. The real question was where he'd go once he was free. He had no money, no shoes. His clothes were tattered and bloody, his face a mess. In his

present condition, he could hardly expect to walk back to
Moscow.

Difficult ... but there was a way.

A few rotting signposts stood inside the fences, and
Byrnes recognized the place as a military camp of some
kind. Though blindfolded during the drive out from
Moscow, he'd felt the rise in elevation, especially on the
last stretch of road. He could tell by the sun they'd
driven north. If he had to guess, he'd say he was in an observation post, something Stalin had built in the paranoid years after the war when the Russians thought every
American hiccup presaged a full-scale invasion.

The sound of the approaching motor grew louder.
Byrnes's trained ear was quick to notice the smoother,
richer growl of the engine. It wasn't the run-down
pickup that brought him his meals every day. This was
a new-model vehicle with a sturdy V-8. He listened
closer. Two trucks, one engine pitched lower than the
other.

Pressing his cheek to the coarse wood, he found it
suddenly very hard to breathe. He'd warned himself
it would happen. It was the natural course of events.
He'd signaled Jett the deal was rotten. Jett had canceled
the IPO. Kirov had sent his men to make good on his
promise.

Newton's Third Law, barked a strict voice from a long-
ago classroom. *For every action, there is an equal and
opposite reaction.* Or as the modern world had cynically
paraphrased it: *No good deed goes unpunished.*

Byrnes stepped away from the wall and brushed the
sprinkling of dirt and pine needles from his clothing. He
stood a little straighter. This is how they would find him,
he decided. With his pride and dignity intact.

A black Chevrolet Suburban pulled into the clearing
in front of the main cabin. Doors opened and two of
Kirov's troopers got out, dressed in dark suits, shirts open

at the collar. Byrnes wondered whether they minted men like that in a factory. Six-feet-something, two hundred pounds of bone and muscle. The first was stocky, with a Marine's crew cut and a Slav's dark scowl. The second, who was taller and had blond hair pulled back into a ponytail, hesitated by the passenger door, then barked out a series of instructions. A moment later, he leaned into the cabin and pulled from it a thin, belligerent man, whom he chucked onto the ground kicking and screaming as if he didn't weigh anything at all. Not finished, the blond giant leaned right back in and came out with a woman, whom he threw over a shoulder and dumped a few steps away, where she lay among the pine needles, silently gathering herself.

Byrnes slid his eyes to the second SUV, of which only the hood was visible. His worry had shifted from himself to the poor wretches fifty feet away. Above the pained whimpering, he heard more voices—economical, cultured, at ease.

Konstantin Kirov appeared, dressed in a charcoal suit, a topcoat tossed over his shoulders in the manner of an Italian aristocrat to ward off the coming rain. Beside him walked a slim, dark-skinned man sporting a traffic cop's mustache and wearing a grimy houndstooth jacket. Byrnes caught the eyes—the steady, soulless gaze— and recognized the type if not the man. He was the muscle.

Kirov and his colleague took up position fifteen yards in front of Byrnes, their backs turned toward him. They stood that way for a minute or so, taut, motionless, two general officers waiting for their troops to pass in review. Another man stumbled into sight, clothes torn, nose bloodied, followed by the big-boned clone who'd shoved him.

Kirov addressed the three unfortunates in a formal voice, and Byrnes was able to pick out a phrase here and there. *"Sorry to have disturbed you." "Over quickly." "Tell the truth. You have nothing to fear."* And finally, an absurdly polite, *"Spaseeba bolshoi."* Thank you very much. As if these people hadn't been dragged from their homes or offices and driven to a deserted army outpost two hours outside of Moscow to answer to Kirov for their offenses, real or alleged.

Kirov ambled out of sight, and his partner took over. Immediately, the atmosphere changed, and Byrnes knew the exaggerated politeness had been for show. He had a feeling something terrible was about to happen. It was as if nature knew it, too. The soft breeze had stopped altogether. The birds ceased their incessant chatter. An uneasy stillness reigned.

"You!" shouted Kirov's friend. Byrnes pegged him as an ethnic tribesman, the kind of tough, battle-hardened man you saw on television fighting for his country against the Iraqis or the Slavs or the Russians. From his coloring, Byrnes guessed he was a Chechen.

"Name," he called.

The first man in line said, "Vyasovsky. Rem Vyasovsky."

"You are a thief?"

"No."

"A spy?"

Again, "No."

"You steal papers and give them to the police?"

The man pulled his jacket tight around him. "Of course not," he answered defiantly. "I am a clerk. This is a misunderstanding. If you want my job, you can have it. Fifty dollars a week is not enough for—"

The Chechen advanced three paces and clubbed the man viciously in the head with a ball-peen hammer. The man collapsed without a sound. The woman next to him screamed, and kept on screaming as the Chechen fell to a knee and hit him again and again with the hammer.

"Christ Almighty," murmured Byrnes, something inside him twisting in grief and bewilderment. Somehow he guessed what it was all about, that this was a show for his behalf. Slumping to the ground, he buried his face in the crook of his knees, covering his ears with his hands. Yet, he had to listen. To bear witness. To accord Kirov's victims a last measure of respect.

"Name."

"Ludmilla Kovacs."

"Position?"

"I am a secretary at Mercury Broadband. I work in the finance department for Mr. Kropotkin."

"Do you know Detective Vassily Skulpin?"

"I do not."

"Are you stealing papers from Mercury to give to Prosecutor General Baranov?"

"No." The screams were gone. In their place came crisp emotionless answers. The dialogue went on for some time, and it seemed like the Chechen was pleased with her, that she would not suffer her fellow worker's fate. Then came the horrible thud, the rushed outflow of breath, the slack, undignified thump of the body as it fell to the ground. The blows continued, merciless and mundane, and Byrnes could hear the Chechen's labored, rhythmic breathing above them, greedy, excited, ambitious.

"A ghastly business."

Byrnes jumped at the voice. Looking up, he saw Konstantin Kirov standing at the back of the shed. He was smoking one of his black cigarettes, and he looked pale and unsteady.

"A legal matter," Kirov explained. "Someone has been slipping information out of our offices, giving them to individuals unfriendly to the cause. We're adjudicating the matter in-house."

"Your questioning methods are very efficient."

"They are hardly my methods, but, yes, they are

efficient. We can't be certain which of the three stole the information, only that it was one of them. People are so adept at lying these days."

"So you kill them all," said Byrnes without irony. "Clever."

Kirov paid the remark no heed and went on smoking. "Would it surprise you to know that I was once in a position similar to yours? Mr. Dashamirov recruited me in the same manner. More roughly, actually. He put a bullet in my best friend's head, then asked if I wanted the same."

"Is that why I'm here? For recruitment?"

"We're long past recruitment. 'Retirement' might be a more appropriate word."

Again, Byrnes was left to wonder why the deal hadn't been canceled. He was certain Jett had understood his message. He'd heard it in his voice. It came to him that Gavallan had to have a reason not to have canceled the deal, and that he, Grafton Byrnes, might be it. He looked over his shoulder. The woman, Kovacs, lay motionless in the dirt, her blond hair matted with blood. He knew what lay in store, if not today, then soon.

"Doing business in this country's so damned difficult," Kirov complained, dropping his cigarette to the ground, grinding it with the tip of his shoe. "You think I *want* to be Mr. Dashamirov's partner? I have no choice. What do you think would happen if I gave up? Would Mercury exist? No. Two million legitimate subscribers would lose their connection to the world. Thousands of intelligent men and women would be out of a job. And Russia? What about it? Have you thought what might happen to my country if I threw in the towel just because of Mr. Dashamirov's unsavory methods? Would my country have independent television? Unbiased journalism? The answer is no. It is a question of priorities. Of recognizing what is achievable and doing the necessary to see it through. Of rolling up your sleeves and getting a little dirty in the kitchen."

"Of the greater good?" Byrnes offered.

"Yes, damn it, the greater ..." Kirov stopped mid-sentence. His eyes burned with a fervor, an inner fire Byrnes had never seen. More than ever he looked like a crazed monk. "It is too bad you will not see it come to pass."

The whip-crack explosion of three heavy-caliber bullets fired in close succession snapped Byrnes to attention. Glancing over his shoulder, he made out Dashamirov holstering a pistol as he stepped over the corpses. The coup de grace had been administered. Kirov's spy was no longer.

Grafton Byrnes watched Kirov rejoin his partner. After a few words, the two disappeared from sight. An engine fired and one of the vehicles departed. Sickened, Byrnes wondered why he was still alive. The answer came at once. *He still needs you.*

Time passed in strange fits and spurts, and Byrnes knew his fever was worsening. He sat and watched as one after another the corpses were picked up and carried to the stone sump house across the compound. After a time, he heard the muted, regular fall of an ax. Smoke began to course from the chimney. The scent reached him, and he retched.

Sometime later, the second Suburban drove away.

IT WAS NIGHT when the van carrying his food arrived. A steady rain pattered the roof, sliding with ease between the irregular birch boughs and making the floor a muddy hell.

Curled into a ball, Byrnes lay in a corner, moaning. As his jailer opened the door, Byrnes moaned louder. "Doctor," he said several times. The jailer set the mess tin on the ground and relocked the padlock with nary a second's hesitation. But Byrnes was sure he'd heard the words, sure he'd noticed him. In the morning when he returned, he would find the prisoner in a similar position. And the next evening, too.

By then, Byrnes would be ready.

36

HOWELL DODSON WAS NOT HAPPY to be in Florida at six o'clock on a Friday evening. His daughter Renee's soft-ball game had begun a half hour ago, and at this very moment he'd hoped to be seated in the bleachers next to his wife, chomping on popcorn, swilling a Coke, and yelling his lungs out for his little girl to belt one over the left field fence. He'd promised her he wouldn't miss the game, and each day this week before he went to work, she'd reminded him of his obligation. *Friday night at seven-thirty, Daddy. It's the league playoffs. You have to come.* In fact, he hadn't just promised to come—he'd sworn it. Cross his heart and hope to die. This was one game the Bureau would not interfere with. And goddamn it, until ten o'clock that morning, he'd had every intention of attending. Until a cold-blooded killer had stormed into Cornerstone Trading in Delray Beach, Florida, and massacred ten innocent people, Howell Dodson would have broken legs to see the game.

"It's all right, Dad," Renee had said when he'd called earlier to tell her he would not be able to make the game. "I know you wanted to come. That's what's important."

"Hit a homer for me, will ya, slugger?"

"Sure thing. I'll try for two even."

Hanging up the phone, Dodson struggled to come to grips with her newfound maturity. When had his little girl grown up on him? When had she become possessed of such poise and understanding? When had she stopped needing him to cheer for her?

Dodson's temporary office was located in a small room in the basement of the Miami-Dade Federal Building. There was a metal desk, a clerk's rolling chair, and a sagging love seat done in transparent plastic slipcovers. The sole artwork came from the U.S. Government Printing Office: a copy of the most recent "Ten Most Wanted" circular.

Standing, Dodson moved to the door, smoothing his blue and white seersucker suit, appraising the knot of his yellow paisley necktie, as if checking that his uniform was presentable for inspection. He looked onto a large, open linoleum floor that might have welcomed the smaller, less prestigious variety of convention. Chiropractors, roofers, or morticians. Desks and chairs were being set up on the double. A man passed carrying a chalkboard. Another labored beneath a half-dozen cases of Coke. Behind him followed a woman with grocery bags full of juice, cookies, and tissues. In an hour or two, the first of the victims' relatives would arrive for questioning. Pinching the bridge of his nose, Dodson sighed. It would be a long and painful night.

From afar, he spotted Roy DiGenovese storming across the floor, dodging a pushcart loaded with potted plants. His eyes were bright, his olive cheeks flushed with excitement. Since Dodson's appointment as director of the Cornerstone investigation, DiGenovese had been more gung ho than usual, almost dangerously so.

"What is it, Roy?" called Dodson. "You look about ready to burst."

"We got Gavallan's prints from the Pentagon. There's a ninety percent probability they match the partials we took from the golf club in Luca's bedroom, as well as the smudges on the closet door. The lab's still comparing them against the prints found at Cornerstone. Nothing yet."

"Lucky for us he's a vet. Always handy to have a suspect's prints on file. Has the Air Force sent us over a copy of his records yet?"

"Due in twenty-four hours."

"Good news." Dodson motioned the younger agent into his office and shut the door behind them. "What about the blood in the house?"

DiGenovese pulled a spiral notepad from his jacket pocket, flipping back a couple of pages. "Gavallan's O-positive. The stuff on the floor is AB-negative."

"How recent?"

"Very. The samples were hardly dry when they collected it. Three hours tops."

"And Luca's blood type?"

"O-positive, too."

"Got sex?"

"Still checking. Preliminary DNA's due by nine."

"What about the acetate test on the murder weapon?"

As Lieutenant Amoro of the Delray Beach P.D. had been so kind to point out, it was nearly impossible to completely erase a weapon's serial number. While the numbers could be filed down so that the human eye could not see them, an overnight's bath in a sodium acetate wash often brought out the latent stamping sufficiently to be identified by an infrared scan.

"Started an hour ago," said DiGenovese. "But I got something better." He was bouncing on his toes, the muscles in his jaw flexing. Yes sir, young Roy was worked up over something.

"Better? Working your magic again, Agent DiGenovese?"

"J45198890," said DiGenovese, reading from his notebook.

"What's that? My tax ID number? The IRS looking for me again?"

"No sir. It's the serial number of Gavallan's Glock."

"The wh—" The words plummeted from Dodson's mouth, a sudden and debilitating disorientation coming over him. "Mr. Gavallan owns a Glock?"

"A Glock 17; a nine millimeter with an extrawide stock to hold seventeen rounds."

Circling the desk, Dodson collapsed in his clerk's chair. "Would I be correct in guessing that's the same model and type of weapon we've got in the lab right now?"

"You would be correct indeed, sir."

Dodson smiled weakly. He knew he was being made fun of, but he didn't feel like sharing in the humor. DiGenovese's revelation didn't just startle him, it forced him to see the case in an entirely new light, to reblock his compass and find a new true north.

Cornerstone had all the hallmarks of a professional job: the marksmanship, the blind entry and exit (meaning no witnesses saw anyone enter or leave the building at the time of the shooting), the speed with which the job was done. The whole thing was too neat. The powder tests on Luca's hand had come back inconclusive. There was residue on his fingers, but not enough for him to have fired the weapon ten times. No one was taking it for a suicide rampage, a day trader run amok. It was bigger than that, a premeditated homicide to be sure.

But Gavallan?

Simply put, the man did not fit the profile of a professional killer. The very idea that he possessed the training, the sangfroid, to enter a building and methodically shoot ten innocent people was absurd. A panorama of the bloodshed inside Cornerstone played out in Dodson's mind, and he shuddered. Only a monster could commit that kind of atrocity.

Yet there was Gavallan at the scene of the crime not forty-eight hours after he'd proclaimed himself interested in shutting up the Private Eye-PO forever. And there he was again at Ray Luca's house, leaving behind another man or woman's blood. And now, it turned out he owned a gun identical to that used in the crime.

"Sir, I don't make it my business to try to piece together everything that happened," said DiGenovese, sliding forward on his seat, eyes narrowing. "All I know is that everywhere we look we find Gavallan hiding. He's working in close association with an oligarch, a guy he's gotta know is a gangster. It's a matter of professional life or death if the Mercury deal goes through. I mean, come on, do you think he paid Jason Vann a hundred grand to track down the Private Eye-PO just to talk to him? No sir. Gavallan shelled out that kind of dough because he wanted Luca's mouth closed. And pronto. He wanted the Private Eye-PO dead. Even if he didn't pull the trigger himself, he made it happen. And now he's running."

At some point in his short speech, DiGenovese's tone had shifted from exposition to accusation . . . and it was Howell Dodson he was accusing.

"That he is, Roy. Full points on that one. And don't you worry, we're going to find him. The question remains whether he's running because he's innocent or because he's guilty."

Dodson had known plenty of innocent men and women who'd refused to cooperate with the authorities for one reason or another. Weak nerves, ingrained distrust of authority, fear of the police, the advice of their friends . . . the list went on and on. Of course, there was a difference between merely being tight-lipped and going on the lam. The former was not a reliable indicator of guilt. The latter was.

"Roy, I want you on a plane to San Francisco tonight. First thing in the morning, I want you inside Gavallan's house looking for that gun. Don't you worry about breaking and entering—I'll get you a warrant in plenty of time. If you can't get a commercial flight, we'll fire up one of the Bureau's Lears for you. This is key, Roy. You search that house from top to bottom, ya hear? If that gun is there, you find it. Now, shoo! Get on out of here."

AFTER DIGENOVESE HAD LEFT, Dodson slid the phone nearer and stared at the Post-it bearing two ten-digit phone numbers that lay next to it. Plucking free the paper, he dialed first one, then the other number. Each time a recorded message informed him the desired subscriber could not be reached. Typical, thought Dodson, for a banker to carry two numbers and answer neither.

Fishing a rubber band out of a side drawer, Dodson began twirling it around his fingers. Forward and back. Forward and back. He asked himself where he would run if he were Gavallan. Home to San Francisco? New York? Overseas? The man had offices in Chicago, London, and Hong Kong, or had he gone to ground in Florida instead? Dodson had the firm impression Gavallan was on the move, that he had an agenda of his own that called for more than eluding the authorities. Whatever it was, Dodson had to give Gavallan one thing: He was a slippery fish.

As of five that afternoon, Dodson and his men had the state of Florida sewn up tight. Partnering with the Florida State Bureau of Investigation, the Coast Guard, municipal police departments, and county sheriffs, Dodson had contacted every airport, harbor, marina, bus station, and train terminal in the state. Faxes were sent to hotels up and down the coast. When agents could not visit a site themselves, a description of the suspect was faxed and a phone call made to get across the urgency of the request.

The phone rang and Dodson answered. "Well, well, Mr. Chupik," he said, recognizing the cocksure voice.

Lyle Chupik was the three-hundred-pound, ponytailed, Yoo-Hoo–swilling techie who ran the FBI's computer surveillance lab. "What a surprise."

"I got a track on one of those phone numbers you gave me this afternoon," said Chupik. "A call was placed at two-thirty to a Coastal Aviation in Fort Lauderdale."

"I see you're atoning for your sins."

"If that's atoning, what I'm about to give you ought to send me straight to heaven, and I mean directly to St. Peter. The front of the line."

"Do tell."

"The number we got a nibble on didn't belong to Gavallan."

"It didn't?" Dodson examined the phone numbers. Both had a 415 area code, and the prefixes that followed them were similar. He'd assumed they belonged to Gavallan. "Go on."

"The number belongs to another one of our Daisy taps. A Ms. Catherine Elizabeth Magnus. Ring a bell?"

"I confess I hear a wee tinkling," said Dodson, as a deadly voice inside intoned, *Enter the third murderer*.

"Anyway, that number's connected to a pretty decent phone," Chupik continued. "Kind of a hot rod. It's a WAP device—a wireless assisted protocol. Third-generation equipment. It can send and receive E-mail, as well as download pages from the web. I had the NSA send over the latest Daisy downloads attributed to that phone number. Usually, they sift it for the keywords we give them before sending it over, but I got it raw. This is what I found. At two thirty-two Eastern Daylight Time, the number logged onto a cash transfer site on the Net. Quickpay.com. At two thirty-five, the user ordered sixty-five thousand dollars transferred from an account at the Bank of America in San Francisco to an account at Florida Commerce Bank. The beneficiary was Coastal Aviation."

"And the sender?"

"Drumroll, please. . . . Mr. John J. Gavallan."

Dodson's stomach tumbled. "Bless your soul, Mr. Chupik. I'll mention your name to St. Peter tonight in my prayers."

"Actually, I'd prefer if you'd mention it to my supervisor. I'm kind of sick of being a GS-15. Time I moved up a notch. You wouldn't want to lose me to the private sector."

"Rather to Satan himself."

IT TOOK ANOTHER HOUR for Dodson to put the rest of the pieces together.

While his assistants confirmed that Catherine Magnus had indeed arrived in West Palm Beach that morning—via an American Airlines red-eye, making stops in Las Vegas and Chicago—Dodson contacted Coastal Aviation. They were quick to report that they had, in fact, set up a private charter that afternoon, but neither the names Gavallan nor Magnus appeared on their manifest. The plane in question, a Gulfstream III, was chartered by an elderly man and his nurse. The flight plan called for a leg to Teterboro, New Jersey, then a transcontinental leg to Los Angeles.

"I'm sorry if my knowledge of business jets isn't as up to date as it should be," Dodson had said politely to the desk man at Coastal Aviation. "What is the range of a Gulfstream III?"

"About four thousand miles. But this one's got an extra fuel tank. It can go six thousand easy."

"Pray tell, did the elderly gentleman in question—"

"His name's Dodson, just like you."

Dodson bit back an expletive. He did not abide smart alecks. "Did *Mr. Dodson* request that the plane be fully fueled?"

"Sure did. Said he was picking up his son in Jersey and didn't want to hang around very long. Funny thing is, he's already half an hour overdue."

"He is?"

"Plane took off at three-fifteen sharp, should have landed at seven latest. This Dodson fella's not a relative of yours, is he?"

"No," said the real Mr. Dodson. "You can rest assured he is not."

THE MAP WAS ANCIENT, circa 1989, a moth-riven relic five feet wide and four feet tall dug up from a closet in the research library on the third floor. Politically, it was obsolete. Myanmar was called Burma. Germany was still two countries. And the Soviet Union was a single rose-colored mass spanning eleven time zones. But Howell Dodson couldn't care less about what belonged to whom, whether Ingushetia was shown as independent or if the Panama Canal was denoted as American territory. All that mattered to his fevered brain was that the map be geographically accurate, and it was.

Leaning over the map, Dodson spread a yardstick in a line from Fort Lauderdale, seeing just how far his six thousand miles would take him. He fanned the yardstick from north to south and east to west, from Alaska to South Africa. Six thousand miles was a long distance, he discovered, and gave a man plenty of places in which to hide.

"By God, he's gone AWOL on us," Dodson whispered to the team of stern, clean-cut agents who had been assigned his acolytes. "Mr. Gavallan's taken a flier on the FBI. I understand if he didn't want to meet me at his hotel. I can see how he wouldn't want to come into our offices right away. I'm not an unreasonable man. But damn it, when a United States citizen flees the country while being sought for questioning in connection with a multiple homicide, that's just wrong. Get me Pierre Dupuis at Interpol. Then get me Yuri Baranov in Russia." Something inside Dodson cracked, and he felt a flash of anger, as white and hot as lightning. "Oh, fuck, get me Crawford at Langley, as well. I suppose they should know about it too." He looked at the eager faces staring at him. "It's time we run along and see the judge upstairs about issuing that arrest warrant."

Howell Dodson would teach Mr. John J. Gavallan not to toy with the United States government.

37

FLORIDA HAD DISAPPEARED HOURS AGO, a tobacco brown smudge swallowed by an azure sea. Distance, darkness, and the pleasant hum of a pressurized cabin relegated Gavallan's worries to another world. Ray Luca wasn't dead. Boris and his blond girlfriend were figments of his imagination. And Howell Dodson and baying hounds were no longer nipping at his heels. Not for the moment, anyway. Flying north by northeast at a speed of 500 knots and an altitude of 42,000 feet, Gavallan's greatest threat lay five feet away, tucked beneath the sheets of a foldout bed.

Why are you here? he asked Cate's sleeping countenance. *Why did you follow me to Florida when you could have phoned just as easily? What else is there you're not telling me about your other life?* And finally: *Who are you really?*

Rising, he stepped across the cabin and adjusted the powder blue blanket so that it covered her shoulders. Cate stirred, turning onto her side and bringing her knees closer to her chest. A comma of blue black hair fell across a cheek. Her pale, generous lips parted. The cabin lights were dimmed, the door to the cockpit shut. They were in the otherworld of flight, and the sandpaper silence granted her an immunity he was not willing to extend himself.

God, how he wanted to draw back the sheets and crawl into bed next to her, to run his hands up the hard ridges of her back, to slide them around and cup her breast, to kiss that neck, that wonderfully warm and silk-soft neck, to feel her nipple harden beneath his thumb.

But she doesn't love you anymore. Maybe she never did.

After years of his not feeling a thing, she'd awoken the dead part of him. She'd made his nerves tingle and his heart dance. She'd made him smile at odd moments. Mostly, she'd given him hope.

And then she'd taken it all away. Like that. In the snap of a finger.

THEY'D MET THREE YEARS EARLIER at an I-bankers' conference one of the big firms had sponsored at the Four Seasons on Maui, this one to chart the Internet's boundless future. It was a lavish shindig. Suites for the big shots, ocean views for everyone else. Unlimited cocktails at the hotel's numerous bars. Breakfast buffets, whale-watching sails, excursions to the neighboring isles of Molokai and Lanai. Thrown in for respectability's sake were a few lectures by industry specialists on topics of burning import, all to be concluded by 11 A.M. sharp lest someone miss his or her tee time at Kapalua or the jitney into Lahaina.

The conference wasn't his style: all the glad-handing, everyone so buddy-buddy, patting each other on the back when the day before they'd been vowing to rip out the other guy's guts. It was an exercise in ass-kissing, all expenses paid. Like it or not, though, it was a great way to build the name, to fly the firm's banner where all the big shots could see it.

Gavallan had come to give a talk on the banker's role

in preparing start-ups for their IPO. The few stalwarts who caught his 9 A.M. speech managed to laugh in the right places, even if it did cause their booze-soaked noggins to ring like the Liberty Bell. Cate was there to deliver a speech on the social ramifications of the Internet, and you can bet not one of the attendees missed her early-morning presentation. She strode to the dais wearing a flowered Hawaiian halter atop a blood red sarong, a white gardenia tucked behind one ear. Her feet were as bare as her midriff. And yes, she'd dared to wear her navel ring.

Today, Gavallan reflected, the outfit would have caused an uproar. Too sexy, too provocative, too disrespectful by half. But this was before the correction. The Nasdaq was making new highs every day. The Dow was puffing like the eighty-year-old geezer it was to keep up. Funding was flowing from venture capitalists like champagne from an excited bottle. This was a celebration of the new economy. A toast to the little engine that could. Graham and Dodd were dead and good riddance to the old blowhards! In short, it was as close to pure bacchanal as Wall Street was ever going to get, in this or any other lifetime.

He'd spotted her by the beach bar the afternoon after she'd given her speech. She'd exchanged her halter and sarong for a black string bikini, and ditched the gardenia in favor of a cycling cap advertising Cinzano. He'd come out of the surf after a mile swim and was still dripping.

"Liked your talk this morning," he'd said, leaning against the bar and asking for a beer. "You're a real believer."

"In the Net, absolutely. In these prices, I'm not so sure. What's your take on things? Is the market really going to keep going up, up, up?"

"For now," he said, seeking out her eyes. "Lot of money on the sidelines waiting to join the parade."

Turning toward him, Cate propped her elbows on the

bar and leaned back. "A hundred fifty times earnings is pretty hard to support in the long run, don't you think?"

"Shh!" he said, bringing a finger to his lips. "Trying to upset the apple cart or what?"

"Just saying that reality always catches up to speculation." Cate stole the wedge of lime from Gavallan's beer and bit it between her teeth.

"Not too soon, let's hope. Besides, I didn't hear you mention anything about speculation up there on the podium. 'The Internet is going to radically redefine human existence.' Aren't those your words?"

"Wow. A listener. I'm impressed. You must have been the only guy who wasn't staring at my boobs."

Gavallan choked on his beer, laughing while stumbling back a few steps. "Not necessarily."

"Oh?" Her voice sounded distressed, but her smile confessed her pleasure.

"Just remember, Miss Magnus, when you make money, it's called investing. When you lose it, it's speculation."

"I'll keep that in mind, Mr. Gavallan. At least you don't have to worry as much as the others. You're not a gold digger. Not yet, anyway."

"What's that supposed to mean?"

"It means you've got some common sense." She grinned. "You want the B-school verdict?"

"Why not?"

Cate drew a deep breath. "It means that you alone among your peers have demonstrated prescience and restraint in selecting and bringing to market only those companies whose products not only have a sustainable competitive advantage but whose business models promise long-term profitability." She wagged a finger for him to come closer and, when he did, whispered in his ear. "You know how to separate the pyrite from the gold."

Gavallan backed away, his expression bemused yet

appreciative. "Sorry if I'm staring. I didn't know Michael Porter had such a nice ass."

"I pay Professor Porter royalties."

"Can I buy you a drink?"

"Sure. But that means you'll have to take me away from this slum," she said. "At the hotel, everything's comped. I know a decent place in Kahului. A hole in the wall where the windsurfers hang out. You eat meat, don't you? They have great burgers."

Gavallan took the question as an affront to his dignity. "Where I come from in Texas, them's fighting words."

"I know," she winked. "I read the article in *Fortune*. Meet me in the lobby at seven."

THEY FEASTED ON CHEESEBURGERS and mai tais and promised not to say one word about the market. They talked about diving and sailing and designer tequila, consciously steering away from the other's past or anything more frothy than their horoscopes—he was a Scorpio, she a Leo—and their favorite movies—his was *Bridge on the River Kwai*, hers *Anastasia*. He stuck fifty cents in the jukebox to hear Junior Brown "a-pickin' and a-grinnin'," and she protested, saying that they didn't have any of Pearl Jam's greatest hits. He said that if he hadn't gone into finance, he would have chosen forestry. She lied as adeptly, saying that greeting cards were her secret passion and that journalism just paid the bills.

Before long, they'd broken their promises and she was telling him about her teenage years—high school at Choate, college at Georgetown, business school at Wharton. Her father was in international business, her mother had passed away years ago. He told her about school in Brownsville, about being one of twenty-four Anglos in a graduating class of eight hundred, about thinking he was Mexican until he was six and went home crying to his mother and demanding to know why his hair wasn't black like everyone else's.

Afterward, the two climbed into Gavallan's Jeep for a drive up the Hana Road. She wasn't the only one who knew their way around Maui. Half an hour later, he pulled into a drive-by just past Hoolawa Bridge.

"Come here," he said, running round the Jeep and offering a hand down. "Five minutes to the most beautiful spot on God's green earth."

Cate regarded the trail before them. A dense tropical canopy obscured the path ten yards in. " 'And they were never found again,' " she said, shaking her hand free and setting off into the jungle.

The path led up a steep hill, following the course of a tumbling stream. Cate's pace soon slowed and Gavallan took the lead, careful to point out the exposed banyan roots and moss-covered stones that one could trip or stumble on. Though the night was cool, both were soon covered in a light sweat.

"I thought you said five minutes?" Cate asked, stopping and placing her hands on her hips, her breath coming hard.

"Okay, maybe ten. But we're almost there. Fifty yards max." Gavallan brushed back a smattering of low-hanging vines, praying he was on the right trail and that he could find the way back to the Jeep. No sooner had he rounded the next bend than he came upon it: a wide pool fed by a crescent-shaped waterfall that dropped from a cliff twenty feet above. A half moon shone high in the sky, and its reflection was caught in the pool's obsidian calm.

"It's beautiful." Cate stood at the edge of the water, her arms wrapped around herself. "Should we go in?"

"If a little mountain water doesn't scare a city girl, why not?" Gavallan bent low and stuck a hand in the water. *Fur-eezing!* The stream was fed from the summit of Haleakala, elevation 10,500 feet. Him and his big mouth. "It's great," he said, even as he suppressed a shiver. "Not bad at all."

Cate stepped closer to him, her hands rising to her neck to untie her dress. Suddenly, she stopped and fixed him with a wary grin. "You didn't bring me up here to seduce me, did you? I mean, you don't really think I'd sleep with you on our first date?"

"Of course not ... er, um, uh ... well, I am an optimist."

"I like optimists," she said, dropping her hand from her dress and running it along his chest. "Tell you what: Think positive and I'll let you buy me dinner tomorrow, too. Deal?"

"Deal."

Then, kicking off a zori, she dipped a toe into the pond. "Not too bad at all. Enjoy yourself."

And before he could ask what she meant, she pushed him into the pond, shorts, T-shirt, Top-Siders, and all.

GAVALLAN STARED DOWN at her sleeping form, remembering the moment. *Three years.*

Just then, Cate opened her eyes. "Hello," she said sleepily.

"You never told me why you said no."

"Sorry?"

"You never gave me a reason."

She sat up stiffly. "I didn't know I had to."

"You don't," he said. "But I'm asking you to. It's time we were honest with each other."

Cate threw him a suspicious look. Pulling off the sheets, she rose and walked past him to the bulkhead counter where the first officer had set up an urn of coffee and laid out some cellophane-wrapped sandwiches. "Tuna ... chicken salad—what do you feel like?"

Gavallan padded across the cabin, taking up position at her shoulder. "Cate."

She turned to face him. "It just wasn't right."

"What wasn't right? We didn't get along? We weren't okay in bed? We didn't like the same movies? You liked Chinese, I liked Indian? *What* exactly?"

Cate started to say something, but caught herself. Frowning, she shook her head as if to say, "No, no, I'm not playing this game," then brushed past him.

"Cate, I'm talking to you."

"Excuse me?" she asked, snapping her head. "I don't recall being one of your employees. You can't order me to talk back. Just leave it, okay?"

And shooting him a dismissive glance, she continued to her seat, making a derisive noise on the way, a frustrated exhalation that sounded like a tire bleeding air.

It was the look that did it—the condescending way she had of averting her eyes, of showing him the back of her hand as if warding off an autograph seeker. Until then, he had kept his cool. It had been a difficult day—the hardest he'd known since the war. Neither of them needed another spate of accusations, rebukes, or recriminations. Then she gave him that look, and his calm was a thing of the past. Lost like a candy wrapper out the window of a speeding car. His heart pounded. Blood raged in his ears. Grabbing Cate by the shoulder, he spun her around and looked her straight in the face.

"Stop ducking the question. It's been three months. You think a day goes by without my wondering what happened? What I might have done wrong? I mean, one night you're lying in my arms talking about what's-his-name at the *Journal*, your editor, and what you're going to write for your next column, the next you're gone. The house is empty. Closets bare. Bathroom deserted. Not a sign you'd ever been there. You even took that chunk of wheatgrass out of the refrigerator. We're not talking a civilized separation here. We're talking a 'scorched earth' retreat. You're damned right I want to know. It's the least I deserve. What happened, Cate? Did you meet someone? Is that it? Just tell me. At least then I'd understand."

"No," she replied coolly. "I didn't meet anyone. It's not that, Jett."

"Then what?"

"It just wasn't going to work. Maybe I could see something you couldn't. It was too painful for me to hang around, so I left."

"That's no answer."

"Oh, Jett, grow up. Stop thinking you're so goddamned special that a girl wouldn't ever dare walk away from you. It didn't work and I left. That's it. Just leave it, okay?"

"No, I won't. I'm sick of leaving things. I'm past closing my eyes and pretending it didn't happen. I need an answer. Do you understand that? *I need it*." He touched a hand to his chest. "In here. For me."

Cate stared at him for several seconds without answering. He'd surprised her. He could see it. Maybe she didn't want to see how much she'd torn him up, but that was all part of it. He was through hiding his feelings. Abandoning her hostile stance, she leaned forward and put a firm, unemotional hand on his arm. "Jett, we had three good years. Three *great* years. But they're over. We both have to go on. It's as simple as that."

Gavallan covered her hand with his. "But they're not supposed to be over. We were supposed to be with each other for the rest of our lives."

Her composure left her in stages, like ice slowly melting. She lowered her eyes, and he could see her lip trembling. She began to shake her head. She looked up once, trying to say something. She got out one word— "damn"—and that was it. The tears broke, and after a second she put her head on Gavallan's chest and let them come.

"Just leave it, Jett," she whispered throatily, catching her breath. "Please, just leave it. For me."

Gavallan put his arms around her and hugged her. Okay. He would leave it. For now. *For her.* He hoped that someday she would tell him. But with sadness, he realized it would have to be on her own time, and of her own will.

He helped Cate to her seat, then kneeled and looked out the window. An orange scythe slit the horizon. He checked his watch. It was midnight Eastern Daylight Time, or 6 A.M. in Geneva. Their flight plan had taken them northeast from Boca Raton over the Atlantic, past Bermuda, then east toward the European continent where the sun was already rising. In an hour they'd cross the southernmost tip of Ireland, then continue over England and France, entering Swiss airspace from the northwest.

"You think he'll be there?" she asked, eyes glued to the wondrous sight of dawn's approach.

"Pillonel? Yeah, I think so. He's got a place outside of town where he grows his own grapes. Each year he sends over a case of his wine as a Christmas present. Not bad stuff. Anyway, he's always going on about coming out to visit his winery. I figure if it's decent weather, odds are he'll be playing the grand vintner."

"What makes you think he'll talk to us?"

"I can be persuasive when I have to be. Besides, we've got plenty of help. Luca's last letter and that fax to the FBI won't hurt. A guy like Pillonel's got a heck of a lot to lose if he gets caught. He's got to be feeling a little nervous already."

"And you'll play on his guilty conscience?"

"Yeah. And if that doesn't work, I'll beat the living tar out of him."

"Ah, a diplomat."

Gavallan bridled at her dismissive tone. In case she'd forgotten, they'd passed diplomacy a ways back, somewhere after Graf Byrnes had been kidnapped and before Ray Luca had taken a bullet in the head. "Whatever works."

"You sound like Alexei."

"Ah, the mysterious Alexei."

"You're mad I never told you?"

"Shouldn't I be?"

Cate glanced up, her eyes red and swollen. "You can be mad, but don't be unkind. I don't want to cry again for a month."

"I'm sorry."

Cate dropped her eyes to the floor, hiding her hands in the ends of her sweater. "I had to identify his body. Seeing him like that, so damaged, I wanted to die myself. I had urged him to go to the police. I'd hugged him and told him he would be a hero for exposing Kirov. It was my fault. Alexei wasn't a fighter. When he heard me talk about Kirov stealing from his country, breaking the laws that men like him had just made, he adopted my anger as if it were his. He joined my armchair rebellion. It was his way of showing that he loved me."

Still on his knees, Gavallan reached out a hand and touched her cheek. "You can't hold yourself responsible for someone else's actions. Maybe you asked him to go to the police, but he made that decision himself."

"Maybe, but still . . ." Cate shuddered. "I never realized how bad I might feel. Even now." She reached for his hand, intertwining her fingers with his. "I see now I should have told you. I'm sorry, Jett. Forgive me?"

He nodded, filled with affection for her. Not a sexual yearning, but a stronger, deeper emotion, an encompassing happiness simply that he was there with her.

The cockpit door opened and the pilot stepped into the cabin. "We're an hour out," he said. "Weather looks fine in Geneva—a few clouds, otherwise it should be a sunny day in Switzerland. Mr. Dodson, you have any idea when you'll want us to be ready to take off again? We'd be appreciative if you could give us some idea of our destination ahead of time. We're required to file a flight plan, even if we don't stick to it."

The relationship was strictly business, mercenary all the way. Once they were airborne, Gavallan had bribed him with ten crisp hundred-dollar bills. Ask no questions and he'd tell no tales.

"Be fueled up and ready to go by four. I'll give you a call later this morning to let you know where we're headed."

"That's fine. Couple hours are all we need."

The pilot left. Gavallan took off his watch and reset it for Geneva time. "An hour to go," he said. "Think this bird's got a decent shower?"

Cate pointed to the rear of the aircraft. "Give it a shot. Might as well get your money's worth."

He headed to the shower, but pulled up suddenly, hoping she might be getting out of her seat to join him. "Cate . . ." he started, but she was still seated, her eyes not on him but glued to the window, staring into the orange dawn.

He could only wonder what she was thinking.

38

You are happy, my friend?" asked Aslan Dashamirov.

"Relieved," Konstantin Kirov replied. "I slept better knowing there was no longer a risk of someone slipping our papers to the police. It was a difficult business. I'm glad we've solved the matter."

It was a cold, rainy Saturday morning. The two men walked arm in arm across the muddy field outside of Moscow where Dashamirov had set up one of his used-car lots. A row of crapped-out automobiles ran next to them. Fiats. Ladas. Simcas. None with less than a hundred thousand miles on them, though the odometers showed no more than a quarter of that. Scruffy pennants dangled from a line strung overhead. A ways back, tucked conveniently amongst a copse of baby pines, stood a blue and white striped tent where prices were negotiated and payments made, often in tender as suspect as the cars themselves: televisions, refrigerators, stereos, cigarettes, narcotics, women.

"I'm not so sure," said Dashamirov.

"Oh?"

"No one talked. Not one of them admitted to working with Baranov or with Skulpin. Only the innocent are so brave."

"You didn't give them the chance." Kirov hated himself for playing up to the Chechen. He was a brigand, really, an uneducated hood.

Dashamirov looked at him as if he were a wart on his finger. "I am thinking we did not find the right person."

So that was why his *krysha* had called the meeting, thought Kirov. He should have known the man wouldn't be so easily put off. Of course, Dashamirov was right. He was always right. This time, though, Kirov had beaten him to the punch.

He'd put his finger on the traitor, a young securities lawyer working in-house on the Mercury deal, and had taken care of the problem himself. Quickly. Neatly. Quietly. A single bullet to the man's brain delivered in the comfort of the traitor's own flat. None of this barbaric business with a hammer. Imagining the fierce blow against the skull, Kirov shivered, a spike of fear running right through him to the pit of his belly.

He stared at Dashamirov. The mustache, the crooked mouth, the eyes at once dead, yet so magnificently alive. The man was a beast. But a smart beast. He was correct in his assumptions. Only the innocent *were* so brave. The lawyer had spilled his guts after a few threats and a bloody nose. Had Dashamirov pressed him for details about the money missing from Novastar, it would have been Kirov getting the hammer yesterday morning.

The hammer.

He ground his teeth.

"What's important," said Kirov, "is that Mercury will go forward without any further problems. For that I have you to thank."

"I was thinking rather about Novastar," said Dashamirov, dropping his arm to his side, quickening his pace as the rain picked up. "The question of the missing funds haunts me, my friend. Where there is one rat, there may be more. Perhaps someone in your organization is stealing the money from the airline. A hundred twenty-five million dollars is too large a sum to take lightly."

"Perhaps," replied Kirov thoughtfully, "though that would be difficult. I alone have signature power over the airline's bank accounts."

"Yes. You are right. Perhaps it would be wise to study the books." He opened his slim, spidery hands in a gesture of conciliation. "If, of course, you do not mind."

It was not a request, and both men knew it. Kirov looked around. A dozen of Dashamirov's clansmen loitered among the cars. *Vor v Zakone.* Thieves of thieves. God knew they were wealthy, but look at them. Standing around in the pouring rain, hair wet, clothing as sodden as the omnipresent cigarettes that dangled from their lips. In four days' time, Dashamirov stood to take home 15 percent of Kirov's billion—a neat $150 million dollars. The next day he would be here, or at one of the other fifty lots he ran in the northern suburbs of Moscow, standing in the rain, drinking filthy coffee, smoking.

"I will speak to my accountant immediately," said Kirov. "He is in Switzerland. It may take some time."

"By all means." The courteous reply was accompanied by a damning smile. "There is no hurry. Have the latest quarterly report for Novastar, as well as the most recent banking statements for our Swiss holding companies, Andara and Futura, in my office by Monday."

"I am in New York Monday," said Kirov, puffing out his chest, trying to muster some authority. "We will price the Mercury offering that afternoon. We can sit down together when I get back in the country on Friday."

"Monday," repeated Dashamirov, less courteously. "By four o'clock. Or else I will begin looking somewhere else for the thief within your company. Somewhere closer to the top."

A bead of sweat broke high on Kirov's back and rolled the length of his spine.

"Monday," he said, knowing it would be impossible.

39

THE JET BANKED HARD TO THE RIGHT and drifted lower. From her window, Cate stared as the city of Geneva rushed up to greet her, as if she were looking at a postcard from her teenage past. The city looked no different than it had when she'd last seen it, ten years before. The *jet d'eau* shot a geyser of water two hundred feet into a young blue sky. A flotilla of boats bobbed lazily on the lake's scalloped surface. The prim row of banks and hotels that lined the Quai Guisan nodded a courteous "Welcome back."

Beyond the cityscape, the Saleve rose vertically from a buckle of forest, a brooding granite soldier guarding the town's southern flank. The only Calvinist remaining in a city gone to the devil. But the familiar sights brought forth no haze of nostalgia, neither a wish for the past nor a desire to recall her youth. They promised only trouble. This was her other life. Her secret self. The history she'd sworn to keep hidden. Stealing a glance at Jett, her stomach tightened. In fear. In sorrow. In anticipation. And as the plane touched down, the wheels bouncing once before embracing the runway, she shivered with a premonition of loss. She was certain that everything she'd spent her adult life working toward was about to come undone.

A WHITE VOLVO with the orange and blue markings of the airport police waited on the tarmac beside their assigned parking spot. Two policemen, submachine guns tucked under their arms, approached the aircraft.

"Let me handle this," said Cate.

"Be my guest." Gavallan handed her his passport and stepped aside. She didn't know how he could stand there so calmly with a pistol tucked into his waistband.

Customs and immigration were conducted "*sur place.*" The policemen examined their passports. One climbed into the cargo hold to inspect their luggage while the other checked the flight log.

Keeping to English, Cate explained they had nothing to declare and were, in fact, only staying in Geneva for the day. A little sight-seeing. Lunch at the Lion D'Or. A run up to the UN. Would either care to join them? They needed a guide, she said, her itchy nerves fueling the giddy repartee. Someone who knew the language and could provide some local color. Could they tell her where Audrey Hepburn was buried? Wasn't it near Crissier? And didn't Phil Collins live nearby?

Suddenly, the policemen were all smiles. Beneath the blue berets, neither was more than twenty. "*Pheel Collins? Oui, oui, il habite tout près.*" He lives nearby. But neither could come up with the town. As for guides, they were unable to help. "*Désolé, Madame,*" they replied. They were in the midst of their annual military service and their next scheduled leave was not until the following Friday.

Thirty minutes later, she was driving a rented Mercedes sedan along the highway. Jett sat beside her, a map spread upon his lap. "Keep your eye out for the Aubonne exit," he said. "Looks like it's about twenty klicks down the road. Just up from the lake."

Cate shot him an apprehensive glance, frightened by his retreat into military vernacular. He'd been brooding since they'd crossed over the continent, speaking less and less, avoiding her gaze.

This is the Jett Gavallan I don't know, she mused. The Air Force Academy grad who never whispers a word about his time in uniform. The jet jock who clams up at the first mention of the war he fought. He's going back, she realized. He's suiting up for battle.

"Klicks being what?" she asked. "Kilometers?"

He nodded without looking at her.

"Just don't let me miss the turnoff," she said, though she knew the way to Aubonne as well as to her own home.

"I won't."

Jean-Jacques Pillonel did not live in Aubonne, but in Lussy-sur-Morges, a quaint village situated high on the vine-covered slopes of Lac Leman (she would never call it Lake Geneva) about halfway to Lausanne. She knew the spot only because one of her art teachers had lived there, a man named Luc Caprez with whom at the age of eighteen she'd had her first affair. Luc and his briar pipe, who spoke of the courage to live a dangerous life, dangerous meaning to brave the landscape of your ideals, to pursue your dreams no matter where they led. Luc, who lectured her even while making love.

She kept her foot firmly on the gas, taking the car to 160 kilometers per hour as she passed the exits for Nyon, Gland, and finally, Rolle, where she'd gone to school for four years at Le Rosey. She glimpsed the campus to her left. The schoolhouses were done up as old villas and sat on a plateau cut into the hill. She took in the steep mansard roofs, the limestone façades, and the window boxes heavy with purple and red geraniums.

But it wasn't the sights so much as the smells that lent

her a melancholy feeling and sent a current of doubt rustling across her belly. It was the smell of sun-warmed soil carried by an easy lake breeze; of Saturday afternoons trawling the back alleys of Geneva; of Sunday mornings saddling horses at the stable.

It was, she realized, the long-absent smell of her youth.

Cate caught sight of her eyes in the mirror and was frightened at their intensity. When had she adopted the mantle of crusader? she wondered. Had she finally embarked upon the "dangerous life" she'd promised herself she would one day lead? Or was she just tagging along with Jett for the ride?

Until now, she'd been content to fight through others. At the K Bank, she'd transferred her dissatisfaction to Alexei and let him do the dirty work. As a reporter, she hid behind the banner of the paper, relying on its influence and reputation to forward her watered-down causes. In her bid to derail Mercury, she'd recruited Ray Luca to fire her broadsides. As always, she preferred to remain one step removed, a gray eminence sheathed in fear.

But overnight things had changed. The battle had landed on her doorstep with a thud, a personal invitation stained with the blood of innocents. RSVP Konstantin Kirov, Moscow. There was no more escaping, no more hiding behind another.

This was the dangerous life.

Yet it was not guilt that had led to her decision. It was you, she said to Gavallan's silent profile, seeing in his strained, concentrated features the determination that had brought him so much success, the confidence that had led him to the brink of disaster, and the generosity of spirit that had captured her heart. I came because of you. Because I can't let you go on with all you don't know. Because your foolish confidence isn't enough to save you. Because I love you and you're all I have left.

As she settled into her seat, Cate's eyes once more found the sparkling asphalt. Grimly, she saw the days ahead playing out. All paths led in the same direction, ended at the same destination. What would happen when he found out? How could she explain? Above all, Jett was an honest man. He detested liars. She was sure she detected a new coolness between them since she'd brought up Alexei. And that was just the tip of the iceberg. How could he ever love a woman whose entire life was a lie? Sooner or later, he would discover the truth. And she would never have a chance to win him back.

"There it is," said Jett. "Aubonne. A thousand meters."

Cate signaled and guided the Mercedes off the highway. "Which way now?" she asked, sliding into the left lane.

"A left under the bridge, then bear to your left again."

I know, she wanted to say. *I used to live here.*

She was struck by a desire to touch him. She reached out a hand, only to pull it right back. Let him go, she told herself silently. He looked at her and she tried to smile. "I'm glad I'm here," she said.

For a moment, Jett's eyes softened, and a question danced beneath his lips. As quickly, it was gone.

"Turn here," he said, spotting a sign with the name of Pillonel's village. "Morges is at the top of this road. Pillonel's house is at 14 Rue de Crecy."

"*Roo-duh-Cray-cee,*" she repeated, correcting him, her schoolgirl's accent still perfect.

Gavallan eyed her remotely. "You never told me you spoke French."

Cate shook her head, laughing sadly. What the hell? Sooner or later, he was going to find out everything anyway.

40

JEAN-JACQUES PILLONEL'S WEEKEND HOME rested at the end of a short gravel drive, a majestic chalet nestled among the vines with an unobstructed view of the lake. Twin Jags were parked in front of a detached garage. Away to one side sat a barn coupled with two smaller outbuildings. Stacks of crates leaned against one of them, faded pictures of grapes stenciled on the splintered wood. Gavallan figured it must be where he kept the press and bottled the local tipple. All in all, impressive. More the residence of a country squire than the managing director of an accounting firm.

"Jett, but what a surprise," called Pillonel as Gavallan climbed from the car. "And is that Cate I see? You two are together again? *Mais tant mieux.* Come in. Come in. The door is open."

The squire was easy to spot. He stood on the first-floor balcony, clad in khaki work pants and a denim shirt, the nobleman's obligatory sweater tied around his neck. One hand was raised in polite greeting, though Gavallan knew he had to have been wondering who the hell was doing something so decidedly un-Swiss as dropping by without an invitation.

Waving hello, Gavallan allowed Cate to precede him

up a groomed path framed by a rose garden in full bloom. She was his calm, the antidote to the rage that had been building in him since they'd landed and that had taken firm grip of his every muscle. Left to himself, he would have run up the path, broken down the door, and wrung Pillonel's neck until he confessed his every last crime, guilty or not.

Detective Skulpin was right, he said to himself. *It had to be you. You handled the on-site inspections. You sounded the all-clear. You toyed with the pictures.*

"Really, I am surprised," Pillonel announced from the head of the stairs. "You are here on vacation? Why didn't you phone me in advance? You're both very naughty."

He was a handsome man, tall, slim, with a bit of the dandy about him. He had a full head of hair that was a shade too black for a fifty-five-year-old and gray eyes that sparkled a little too brightly. He liked to wear ascots when they dined out at night, Gavallan remembered, and he smoked Silk Cuts with an ivory cigarette holder.

"Unfortunately, we're here on business," said Gavallan, climbing the stairs, doing his best to return the hearty handshake. "Mercury."

"Ah. I see," said Pillonel, light as a feather. "The big deal. Cate, may I take your jacket?"

"No thank you," she answered, nearly wincing as he kissed her cheeks in greeting.

"Come along. I was just finishing breakfast." Extending an arm, Pillonel showed them to the balcony. A table littered with croissants, jams, napkins, and a pot of coffee sat near the railing. The lake lay a mile away, a shimmering blue crescent stretching as far as the eye could see in either direction. Beyond it, through a mid-morning haze, rose the snowcapped peaks of the French Haute Savoie. The good life, thought Gavallan.

"Claire will return shortly," said Pillonel. "She's out with the dogs. You remember my wife?"

"Of course," said Gavallan, calling to mind a slightly built, argumentative woman with prematurely gray hair and skin the color of alabaster. He walked to the edge of the balcony and made a show of surveying the surrounding vineyards. "So this is where the Pillonel wine comes from?"

"Yes, the famed Chateau Vauxrien." Pillonel pointed out the boundaries of his estate. "We have only ten hectares. It's a modest parcel, but if the sun shines through September and we don't have too much rain, we can make some good grapes. You would like a glass? I have some open just inside. Last year's vintage. A bit young, but nice. Jett? Cate?"

"No thanks," they both said.

Gavallan turned his back on the vineyard and, crossing his arms, fixed Pillonel with a grave stare. "We've got some major problems with the Mercury deal. I spoke with Graf Byrnes on Wednesday night. He was in Moscow checking out whether the rumors we'd been reading on the Net were true."

"I told you—it's rubbish. Nothing to worry about."

"Graf doesn't agree. He let me know in no uncertain terms that the deal was bad. Unfortunately, circumstances didn't permit him to tell me how bad or what exactly was wrong. Before I cancel it, why don't you tell me what you really know about the company."

"What I *really* know? Why, we discussed it on the phone the other day. The Private Eye-PO's accusations are ridiculous—frankly, laughable. You can't be serious about canceling the IPO?"

"Oh, you bet I'm serious. The deal's over." Gavallan took a step closer to Pillonel, eyes wandering over every inch of his face, searching out where he kept his guilt hidden. "What do you think Graf could have found,

Jean-Jacques? I mean, you promised me on Wednesday everything was hunky-dory. What could it have been? Everything's 'up and running,' right?"

A brisk shake of the head. "I don't know." Swiftly, he added, "Yes, everything is up and running. You said Graf was not able to tell you what was wrong. Why not?"

"I'll tell you in a minute. Let's stay where we are for the time being. The photos? You're certain they're fakes?"

"Positively. They're rubbish. I've seen the facilities myself. You're making much too much of the Private Eye-PO's words. He's a pest. If I were you, I wouldn't even bother."

"Oh, someone bothered, I can tell you that."

He really is a pretty decent actor, Gavallan was thinking. And marveling at the man's practiced deceit, he felt his anger rustle and loosen a notch. A hand dropped to the pocket of his windbreaker. Through the fabric, he let his fingers brush the butt of Cate's pistol. He added, "The Private Eye-PO was killed yesterday. His name was Ray Luca. A gunman entered his workplace and shot him, along with nine other men and women. It was a bloodbath. Didn't you read the papers this morning?"

Pillonel's eyes widened in astonishment. "This is the rampage in Florida I read about. This is the Private Eye-PO? They say a man went crazy. That he killed all his friends, then himself. How horrid."

"He didn't go crazy," said Gavallan flatly. "Take my word for it. It was a professional job."

"You're sure the killer was not Luca? The police sounded like they knew precisely what happened."

"Yes, I'm sure. Who do you think would kill nine in-nocent people just to get at one man?"

"I have no idea."

"You're lying," said Cate. "You know damn well who

might want the Private Eye-PO dead. Who *needed* him dead. We all know. Ray Luca was a friend. He died with nine innocent men and women because what he said about Mercury was true. You had to know it. You told us yourself you visited the Moscow Operations Center."

"Cate, please, you're mistaken," said Pillonel, retreating, his eyes begging Gavallan for an explanation. "*Je vous en pris....* Please, Jett, you must have a word with her. I don't know what she is saying.... My God, this is all so crazy."

"You're the one who's mistaken," retorted Cate. "If you think you can jump into bed with Konstantin Kirov and walk away from this untouched, you're a fool. How much is he paying you? A million? Two million? Ten? Or did he promise you shares in the deal? Tell him, Jett. Tell him about Ray Luca. Tell him about Graf."

The mention of money, its hint of bribery and collusion and all things criminal, sparked a radical change in Pillonel. In an instant, his apologetic stance vanished, replaced by one of undisciplined outrage. "That is enough now," he declared, pulling the sweater a little tighter around his neck. "I hope you haven't traveled all the way from the States just to insult me like this, making these fantastical accusations. This is crazy what you say. Really crazy. You are badly mistaken if you think I am involved in some type of illegal affair with Mr. Kirov. I've said it time and time again: Mercury is fine. It's your conduct that is criminal. I'd like you to leave. Now."

But Gavallan did not move. He remained standing at his place near the balcony, stiller than he'd ever been in his life. If he lifted a finger, if he blinked an eye, if he let out his breath, he'd lose control over the animal rage that was clawing at his neck. All too clearly, he imagined himself hitting Pillonel with his fists, pummeling the man until his features were broken, his face a bloody pulp. He felt the gun heavy in his pocket, full of promise. The muscles in his jaw flinched, and a second later the vision passed.

"After six years, Jett, I thought we had a relationship," Pillonel droned on angrily, self-righteously, a man wronged in his own house. "That maybe we were even friends. I see I was wrong. Now, go. Both of you. Take your accusations and make them to the police. Maybe I'll call them myself."

"Friends?" Gavallan asked, cocking his head. "Did I hear you say you thought we were friends?" He advanced on Pillonel. Something inside was stretching, growing taut, moaning like the hull of a submarine down past its depth limits.

Pillonel took another step back, palms raised as if he were calming an angry dog. "Come now, Jett. You stop there or I call the police."

Gavallan grabbed the phone from a side table and thrust it at Pillonel. "Go ahead. Call them. Or do you have the balls?" He threw the phone on the table. Another step. "We know what you've been up to, and it's not what friends do to each other."

Cate said, "Jett, please ..."

Gavallan did not remove his eyes from Pillonel. "We know you faked the due diligence reports. Your men scoped out Mercury's assets. Your men signed off on its physical plant and inventory. It couldn't have been anybody else."

"This has gone far enough," said Pillonel, stopping, crossing his arms. "I've had quite enough of your bullying. You will go. Now. I demand it."

But it was Gavallan who had had enough. Later, he wasn't sure what finally made him break: the insistence of Pillonel's denials, the man's elegant ignorance, or just that he was sick of being lied to and didn't know any other way of making Pillonel admit his sins.

Drawing the pistol out of his pocket, he grabbed

Pillonel by the collar, yanked him close, and laid the snub-nosed muzzle against his head. "How's that, you fuckin' prick? You want bullying? This is bullying. And I'll tell you something. We aren't going anywhere until you start telling the truth."

"Jett, put it away," pleaded Cate, rushing to his side. "Stop it."

"Don't worry," said Gavallan, cocking the hammer, pressing the barrel harder into Pillonel's forehead. "We're friends. We're just playing. Right, Jean-Jacques? Just palling around?" When Pillonel didn't answer, he said, "Yesterday, two of Kirov's creeps put a bigger gun than this one on my forehead, right there in the same place. Do you know what they said to me, Jean-Jacques? Do you? They said, 'Sorry, Mr. Jett. Mr. Kirov says you have to die. He says it's business only.' "

Gavallan shoved Pillonel across the balcony. The Swiss stumbled over a chair and collapsed on his behind.

"Ten people are dead because of Mercury. *'For business only.'* As for Graf, I can only hope he's okay. The reason he couldn't let me know the exact details of what he'd found out about Mercury was because he's with Kirov. A prisoner, I guess, if Kirov hasn't already had him killed. If nothing else, you're going to tell me the truth for him— for Graf Byrnes—so that maybe I might have a chance to get my friend back. Understand?"

Pillonel got to his feet. Righting the upended chair, he brought it to the table and sat down. His tan face had gone gray. *"Mais non,"* he said. *"Ce n'est pas possible."*

Cate wandered closer. *"Si,"* she replied. *"C'est bien possible. En fait, c'est la vérité."* It's the truth.

Gavallan slipped the gun back into his pocket and sat down in a chair next to Pillonel. Just looking at the man made him weary. Accountants had no business being criminals. They lived in a cloistered world of financial reports and P&L statements, of interminable client meetings and rushed lunches. Of clipped fingernails and polished shoes. They had no business consorting with murderers and gangsters.

"Our friend in Moscow is nervous," Gavallan said. "His empire's falling apart. Mercury. Novastar Airlines. So now he's tidying up. Covering his tracks. I'd be scared if I were you. Geneva's a helluva lot closer to Moscow than Florida."

Cate opened her handbag and gave Pillonel the Private Eye-PO's last report, the document titled, "Mercury in Mayhem." When the Swiss executive had read the whole thing, she slipped him Yuri Baranov's fax to the FBI calling for a raid on Kirov's headquarters.

"Call Baranov," Cate suggested. "His number's on the fax. He'll be glad to tell you all about it. His offices have provided us the evidence about Mercury. They have an informant inside the company."

"But this has nothing to do with Mercury," protested Pillonel. "I know nothing about a raid. It is of no concern to me." He made an effort to stand, but Gavallan waved him down. "Sit down. *Now.*"

Pillonel shrugged and sat. Affecting a pensive pose, he averted his gaze from his guests. "You know you can see Évian from here?" A tremulous hand pointed to the French side of the lake. "They have a marvelous casino. Right out of the thirties. I go sometimes with Claire. We put on our evening clothes, take the steamer from Ouchy. Maybe we all go, the four of us? Take the waters. Do a little gambling."

When neither Jett nor Cate responded, he shifted in his chair, drawing a breath as he faced his accusers. His color had returned, and he looked remarkably composed. He made a little gesture with his shoulders, a timid shrug that was at once ashamed and contrite. "I'm no murderer. Maybe foolish with the girls. Maybe, I gamble sometimes. But murder? No. That's not me." He sighed. "*Alors*, how long have you known?"

Gavallan looked down as the anger bled from him. "Since yesterday. Why, Jean-Jacques? What made you do it?"

"Why?" Cate repeated.

Pillonel answered without hesitation. "Money, of course."

Cate shook her head. "You pig."

Pillonel shrugged. Dusting off his shirt, he sipped from his coffee and began to explain.

Seven months ago, Kirov had come to him with a plan to take Mercury public. The thirst for broadband services was unquenchable and Kirov claimed to be in a perfect position to exploit it. Mercury had been growing rapidly for four years. He was already the number two Internet service provider in Russia. Business conditions were stable and the country was increasingly prosperous. It was the time to offer shares. There was only one problem, Kirov confided: Mercury wasn't quite where it should be, the infrastructure not exactly as advertised. Moscow was a problem and so was St. Petersburg. But it was nothing to be concerned about, he promised. The problems would be rectified once Mercury received the infusion of capital an IPO would bring.

"I asked him about his revenues," Pillonel said. " 'How is Mercury making so much money if not through offering broadband services, Internet connectivity?' "

Gavallan raised a hand for him to stop. "What did you know about his revenues?"

"Earlier in the year we'd taken a participation in the German accounting firm that did Mercury's work. When we integrated operations, we took over all their back office operations. We saw the funds coming into Mercury's accounts. In fact, we hold copies of all the financial transfers the company has made over the past three years."

"You're saying you were Mercury's accountants before

I farmed out the due diligence to you? That's conflict of interest. You had no right to accept the assignment."

"Of course, you're right," said Pillonel in a dull voice, as if that were the least of his misdeeds. "I asked Kirov where the money was coming from, if not from Mercury. When he just stared at me, saying nothing, looking through me with that charlatan's smile, I knew he had me. We'd been signing off on the books of a thief."

But Gavallan was more interested in something Pillonel had said earlier than in the accountant's belated discovery that Kirov was a thief. "He came to you about the IPO seven months ago?"

"Maybe longer. It was November. I remember, because we were about to take our holiday. Claire and I go every year to the Seychelles. It is beautiful there, and one must get away from the *brouillard*—you know, the fog."

"How did he know you would be doing the due diligence for us?"

"I've been doing Black Jet's European work for years."

November, repeated Gavallan to himself. But Black Jet hadn't officially won the deal until January.

A few seconds passed. Pillonel offered another of his Gallic shrugs, then rose and said, "Stay here. I'll be right back. I've got something that may interest you." He returned a minute later carrying a raft of notebooks. "Here is the report," he said, handing a green binder to Gavallan. "You'll find the experts' testimony inside. The Moscow station was run-down, but they've fixed it up since. The company's a year behind on its infrastructure. Maybe you burn the papers and close your eyes. Go forward with the offering. The company's really very strong. Kirov just needs time to build up his customer base and modernize his network."

Gavallan read through the notebook, skimming from page to page. It was all there, just as Pillonel had said.

Mercury's operations checked out in eight of ten of its major markets. The problems lay in Moscow and St. Petersburg. Mercury had purchased insufficient servers, routers, multiplexers, and the like to handle the number of customers it claimed to have.

As Gavallan absorbed the information, he found himself as impressed with the company as he had been when Kirov first told him about it. Mercury was solid. It possessed excellent market share, capable personnel, and a sound business plan. Maybe the offering wasn't worth two billion dollars, but depending on the true value of its revenues it could be worth eight hundred million, a billion, easy.

"You said you saw the exact flows on money coming into and out of Mercury?"

"Yes. The bank sends us copies of all the account's activity: deposits, transfers, monthly statements."

Gavallan closed the notebooks. At least he'd be able to figure out what Mercury was really worth. He would still cancel the offering; he had to. But that didn't mean his involvement with the company had to end there. There was another way to spin the deal. And imagining the possibilities, Gavallan felt the first glimmerings of hope. For himself. For Black Jet. And for Mercury.

Putting aside the notebooks, he felt a small weight lift from his shoulders. He had his proof that he hadn't been involved in faking the due diligence. Now he would take Pillonel to his offices and recover some of the copies of the funds transfers into and out of Mercury's accounts. If Kirov had done what he suspected, Gavallan would have the chips he needed to sit face-to-face across from the Russian oligarch.

He might just have a chance to win back Byrnes.

"It is enough?"

Looking up, he found Pillonel gazing at him. "Excuse me?"

"It is enough?" the Swiss repeated.

"The report. Yes, it'll do nicely, thank—" Gavallan cut himself short, seeing an unsatisfied look in Pillonel's eye. A moment passed, and he felt his stomach tighten. "You mean there's more?"

"What I've shown you is to protect yourself," said Jean-Jacques Pillonel. "To protect Black Jet. Now I give you something to protect me."

41

THE FAX FROM INTERPOL arrived on the desk of Detective
Sergeant Silvio Panetti of the Geneva Police Department at 9:15 A.M. It was a fugitive arrest warrant for an
American citizen sought in connection with the murder
a day earlier of ten persons in Florida. The FBI had reason to believe he had fled the United States, the fax indicated, and gave the tail number of a private aircraft in
which he was said to be traveling. A bold "Urgent" headed
the message and it was followed by the instructions that
any information was to be forwarded to Assistant Deputy
Director Howell Dodson in Washington, D.C., or to the
consular officer of the local U.S. embassy.

Panetti yawned and lit his third cigarette of the shift.
Urgent, eh? He was impressed. Too often, American law
enforcement was interested in tax evaders, money laun-
derers, or other equally bloodthirsty types. Reading the
message a second time, his eye tripped over the words
"murder" and "ten victims" and "extremely dangerous."
A hushed *"Ma foi"* escaped his mouth. Would someone mind telling him why the fugitive might be headed
to Switzerland? And Geneva in particular? The two
countries had extradition treaties in place with regard
to capital crimes, and lately, no one could argue that

Switzerland had been anything but the model of cooperation.

Picking up the fax, he strolled into his boss's office. It was empty, as he'd expected. Saturday was the chief's day for sailing. With this weather, you could bet he was already halfway down the lake to Montreux. Panetti looked up and down the corridor. Seeing no one, he blew a cloud of smoke into the office. A little present for the chief. *Pauvre mec* had quit smoking the week before and was having a tough go of it. Half the *département* puffed like chimneys, and the only place in the whole building the chief could get away from the smoke was his own office. Chuckling, Panetti checked that the windows were closed and shut the door behind him, but not before slipping a couple of packets of Gauloise Bleus onto the chief's desk. *Bonne chance, mon lieutenant.*

Returning to his desk, Panetti paused long enough to pick up his lighter, his phone, and his pistol—in that order of importance—then left the office. He wasn't much to look at. Middle-aged, of medium height and medium build, he was one of the Lord's weary travelers. He owned a sad, pouchy face and deep black eyes that guarded a sparkle of mischief. He hadn't shaved this morning, and the two-day stubble combined with yesterday's outfit gave him a shabby charm. Panetti shrugged. At least no one would mistake him for a banker.

Descending the staircase to the parking garage, he called Cointrin to ask for flight operations.

"Claude, I need a favor. Got a list of incoming traffic? Private, not commercial. A jet. Yeah, I'll wait, thanks."

Traffic was light, and he was over the Pont Guisan when he got the answer.

"She's a nice bird," said Claude Metayer, flight operations chief of Geneva International Airport and, to Panetti's everlasting dismay, his brother-in-law.

"You mean the plane is here?" Panetti felt his heart give a rat-a-tat-tat.

"A G-3. Came in an hour ago. Passengers are gone, but if you want to talk to the pilots, I'll tell them you are coming."

"Keep them there," ordered Panetti. "Be there in ten."

"Where are you now?"

"Passing the Hotel President. Why?"

"I'm hungry. Be a pal and get me a brioche. Uh, hold on a sec. And grab a half dozen *pain-au-chocs* for the boys."

"Eh, Claude?" said Panetti, ramming his foot against the accelerator and throwing the siren onto the roof. "Fuck your *pain-au-chocs*."

THERE SHE IS."

Claude Metayer pointed at a white Gulfstream parked two hundred meters across the tarmac from the control tower. "N278721. That your bird?"

Panetti checked the numbers against those written on the fax. "Yep. That's it. See anyone get out? A man and woman, maybe?"

"No," said Metayer. "But I wasn't looking."

Panetti studied the plane through a set of binoculars. *Mince*, but she was a beauty. His first thought was "expensive." Whoever owned that plane had to be very wealthy. The words "filthy rich" crossed his mind, and instinctively he sucked in his gut and stood a little straighter. A second later he relaxed. Sometimes he hated being Swiss.

"Where are the pilots?" he asked.

"Downstairs," answered Panetti's brother-in-law. "But go easy. I don't want any blood like last time."

PANETTI HAD THE INFORMATION he needed in sixty seconds. No blood. No threats. Not even a raised voice, thank you very much. The suspect, John J. Gavallan, and his accomplice, Catherine Elizabeth Magnus, had rented a car from Hertz. They were expected back at the plane sometime that afternoon. The pilots had instructions to be refueled and ready to take off at 4 P.M. More than that, they said they didn't know, and Panetti believed them. A five-minute stroll took him to the Hertz desk. He flashed his badge and asked for the make, model, and license number of the car the Americans had rented. The answer came immediately. A black Mercedes 420S, Vaud license 276 997 V.

Panetti thanked the employees for their help. He was lighting cigarette number seven of the shift when the manager appeared from his office, waving a fey hand to get his attention.

"*Attendez. Attendez.* Officer, thank goodness you're here."

"Oh?" asked Panetti through a blue haze.

"You are interested in the Americans?"

"*Banh oui.*" Panetti raised a brow, curious as to what the Americans might have done to so disturb this fat old poof.

"*Ils sont terribles, les Amis.* Come, I show you." The manager led Panetti to a bank of phone booths, pointing archly at the third in line. "There. Look. See for yourself."

Panetti sauntered over to the booth. He picked up the receiver and put it to his ear. The dial tone sounded as innocuous as ever. He flicked the coin return. A-OK. "What's wrong?"

"*Non, non, les annuaires,*" puffed the manager breathlessly. The phone books. And pushing Panetti aside, he pulled open the registry for the canton Vaud. "They stole a page. They ripped it right out. I saw them."

"A page? The whole thing? And you didn't call right away? Next time, I'll have to arrest you for not reporting the incident."

The manager curled his face into a sour smirk. "Very funny."

"Okay. Off you go. Your poodle is waiting."

"I don't own a ..." The manager hoomphed, then spun on his heel and hurried back to his office.

When he was out of sight, Panetti sat down on the stool and laid the phone book on his lap. He flipped through the directory several times until he spotted the frayed pennants of the missing page. He had no idea whom Mr. Gavallan might be looking for, but the missing page might indicate where that person—or business, for that matter—might be. Swiss directories were divided alphabetically by city or town, with the locale's name printed on the top outside corner of each page.

Panetti was in luck. The same town was listed at the top of the preceding and succeeding pages.

Lussy-sur-Morges.

He had the local police on the line within fifteen seconds. And Mr. Howell Dodson of the FBI a minute after that.

42

You're saying you work for Novastar, too?" Gavallan asked Jean-Jacques Pillonel on the way to Silber, Goldi, and Grimm's headquarters in downtown Geneva.

"As their accountants, we do all of their book-keeping," replied Pillonel. "As their *fiduciare*, we counsel them on setting up offshore accounts, shell companies, the usual song and dance to help our customers avoid paying too much tax."

"And how much is that?" asked Cate from her post in the backseat.

"Why, *any*, of course," answered Pillonel, who was driving. "When Mr. Kirov purchased Novastar Airlines last year, he came to me to set up a holding company outside of Russia where he could deposit the shares."

"Why would he want to deposit Novastar's shares outside of Russia?" asked Gavallan.

Pillonel smirked, but didn't take his eyes off the road. "You'll see soon enough."

SILBER, GOLDI, AND GRIMM'S HEADQUARTERS were located on the Rue du Rhône, one block from the lake.

The newly remodeled building was a symphony of brushed steel and exposed girders. The lines were spare, the profile vibrant and supremely confident. One moment Gavallan thought he was looking at the Beaubourg in Paris; the next, the Hong Kong and Shanghai Bank on Hong Kong Island. Modernism had trumped tradition. Prudence had been declared a four-letter word. So had conservatism, stability, and any other trait that implied the slightest resistance to change.

Once on the third floor, Pillonel guided them along a dim corridor. Stopping in front of an anonymous doorway, he placed an eye to a retinal scanner. The lock disengaged and the door swung open.

"The funny thing is I knew this would happen," he said, allowing Cate and Gavallan to pass and enter the storage room. "I did it anyway, and I'm still not sure why. Foolish, wasn't it?" He looked at Cate. "You wanted to know how much Kirov was paying me? Fifteen million."

"Dollars, I hope."

"No. Francs."

Cate gave him a sad look. "Was it worth it?"

Even now, Pillonel's venal nature demanded he think on the answer. "*Alors, non.*"

THE FIRST ROADBLOCK was set up one hundred meters north of Silber, Goldi, and Grimm's office at the intersection of Rue du Rhône and Place les Halles. The second was erected fifty meters south, at an intersection not visible from the silver and steel office building. Plainclothes policemen filtered down the busy streets, quietly demanding pedestrians to leave the area, in a few cases forcibly escorting them off the streets. A crisis headquarters was established in the shopping gallery below the Confederation Centre, the office complex that housed the Geneva Stock Exchange. Two armored personnel carriers painted a royal blue arrived. The back doors opened. Twenty-four policemen from the elite *Division D'Intervention Rapide*, or DIR, of the Geneva Police Department, clad in full battle gear, jumped to the ground, forming into two squads and moving out toward their target. Snipers scrambled up stairwells in adjacent buildings and established shooting platforms with a clear line of sight of Silber, Goldi, and Grimm's lobby.

Watching the activity unfurl around him, Detective Sergeant Silvio Panetti stroked his mustache. *"Mince,"* he whispered to himself. *"C'est sérieux."*

It had been simple to track down Mr. John J. Gavallan. Lussy-sur-Morges had but two hundred twenty residents. One by one he had read their names to Mr. Howell Dodson of the FBI. Dodson recognized Jean-Jacques Pillonel's name immediately. A team was sent to the man's chalet. Pillonel's wife did not know where her husband had gone. Ten minutes later, a patrol car spotted Gavallan's rental on the Rue du Confédération, a block from Silber, Goldi, and Grimm. The rest Panetti figured out for himself.

A walkie-talkie near him crackled. "In place," said a crisp voice.

"Entendu," replied Captain Henri L'Hunold, commander of the DIR. "Await my signal."

STEPPING INTO THE DOCUMENT STORAGE ROOM, Jean-Jacques Pillonel took up his tale where he had left off in the car ten minutes earlier.

"As I said, it is part of our job as fiduciaries to keep a permanent record of our customers' accounts. This means keeping copies of the bank confirmations showing all monies that flow into and out of them: every deposit, every wire transfer, every cash withdrawal."

"But you're not a bank yourself?" asked Cate.

"Good Lord, no. But as their accountants we require

the confirmations to perform the audits of our customers' accounts. We scan them immediately and transfer them to hard drive. Every month, we download the
new confirmations onto our customers' private CDs."

The three were snaking through aisles of chest-high
filing cabinets colored a wan yellow. Pillonel was their
leader, and he moved like an automaton through the
metallic maze, drawing first one CD, then another, his
destinations memorized long ago.

"What was Kirov's game?" Gavallan asked. "Didn't
he want to pay the tax man his due?"

"Forget the tax man," said Cate. "Kirov didn't even
plan on giving the money to Novastar. As far as he was
concerned, Novastar's revenues were his, and he made
sure they didn't turn up anywhere on the company's
ledgers."

"It's a bit more complicated than that," cautioned
Pillonel. "Once Kirov won the auction for Novastar, he
transferred the company's headquarters from Moscow
to Geneva. Moscow was too parochial, he said; an international airline needed an international presence. He
asked me to set up a holding company for his forty-
nine percent stake in the airline. We were happy to
oblige. The company is called Futura. It is domiciled in
Lausanne."

"Is Kirov the sole shareholder?" Cate demanded.

"No. There is a second man. His name is Dashamirov.
Aslan Dashamirov. You know him?"

Gavallan and Cate said they didn't.

"He is trouble, this man." Pillonel offered a secret
smile. "He is Chechen. Not so polished as Mr. Kirov.
From the bandit country. Anyway, at the same time as we
opened Futura for Mr. Kirov, he asked us to set up a second company, this one offshore in the Dutch Antilles—
Curaçao, I believe. That company is named Andara.
Now of course we all know why he did this, but I was surprised at his audacity. First, he instructs all of Novastar's

foreign offices to transfer their revenues to Futura, instead of to the company's old accounts in Moscow. This means all the money Novastar earns from sales of plane tickets made in Los Angeles or Rio or Hong Kong come to Switzerland."

"I have a feeling we're getting to the good part," said Gavallan, giving Cate a fateful glance.

"If you mean the part that concerns Mercury, you are right," said Pillonel. "From Futura, Kirov would transfer the money into Mercury's accounts here in Geneva. But only at certain times during the year, and just briefly—one day in, the next day out. He timed it so that Mercury's quarterly bank statements showed the effect of the transfer. Usually, the inflows increased Mercury's revenues by around thirty percent."

"Thirty percent? Not kidding around, was he." It was Gavallan's policy to involve himself in the due diligence being done on Black Jet's larger deals, and he remembered poring over Mercury's banking statements, corroborating the balance held at the bank with the sum shown on Mercury's books. In one day, out the next. Clever, but you could only get away with it with the complicity of your accountant.

Then again, fifteen million francs bought a lot of complicity.

Cate said, "So once Mercury booked the funds as revenues, they wired the money back to Futura?"

"Only about ten percent, actually. The rest was always transferred to Andara, the company in Curaçao, for the personal benefit of Mr. Kirov and Mr. Dashamirov."

"That explains why Baranov and the Russian government are so pissed off," Cate said. "The revenues from the foreign rep offices never made it to Moscow. The government privatized Novastar to increase its profitability and bring it up to Western business standards. They expected the fifty-one percent they retained to earn them a decent chunk of hard currency."

Pillonel had completed his rounds of the filing cabinets and was heading toward the back wall, where a long desk divided by partitions into carrels offered a dozen personal computers and printers for everyday use. Next to the desk stood a row of IBM mainframes, their blinking red and green pinlights the only indication they were in service. Sitting down at a carrel, he selected a CD and slipped it into the PC's disc drive. "It's all here. See for yourself."

Gavallan watched from behind Pillonel's shoulder as copies of Novastar's transfers to Futura flashed onto the screen. Two hundred thousand dollars from New York. Three million French francs from Paris. Four hundred thousand deutsche marks from Frankfurt. All the money headed for Switzerland. Pillonel flipped through the transfers, taking the three of them on a paper trail across the globe. Shanghai, Mexico City, Toronto, Chicago, Paris again. Around the world in eighty seconds.

"Like I say, it's all here." Suddenly, Pillonel laughed, a high-pitched, hysterical whinny. "I don't know who is going to be madder—the Swiss because I break the secrecy law, or Kirov because I violated his trust."

Oh, I can tell you the answer to that one, buddy, declaimed Gavallan silently: Kirov by a long shot.

Pillonel switched discs, and a new set of transfers scrolled onto the screen. "Here are the transfers you are most interested in, Jett: the funds injected into Mercury." The amounts were larger, the transfers less frequent. It would be an easy task to back out the amounts Kirov had transferred into Mercury's accounts and arrive at a true reckoning of Mercury's revenues, and thus its market value.

Pillonel switched discs again, and the screen was filled with transfer after transfer out of Mercury and into Andara, Kirov's private strongbox. The sums were staggering. Ten million dollars. Thirty-two million. Six million.

It's the gold seam, thought Gavallan. A hard copy trail showing Konstantin Kirov's meticulously executed efforts to divert Novastar's revenues to his personal account. A how-to manual on stealing from Mother Russia. He found Cate's hand and gave it a squeeze. "I don't suppose Mr. Kirov will be too keen for Baranov to get his hands on these."

"Forget Baranov," said Pillonel acidly. "He's powerless. Kirov will flee the country if any charges are filed against him. He'll set up shop in Marbella with the other Russian expats. They've got a whole little community down there. Like I said, forget Baranov ... he's a paper tiger. You want to hurt Kirov, I'll show you something that hurts him."

Pillonel slipped the third compact disc into the e-drive. Once again, the screen was filled with scanned copies of bank transfers. Gavallan leaned closer. It took his middle-aged eyes a few seconds before he could read the names and numbers on the screen. He recognized the account number of Andara, the Curaçao holding company, but the beneficiary was an anonymous numbered account at the Banque Privé de Genève et Lausanne.

"Isn't that your brother's bank?" Gavallan asked. Pierre Pillonel was Jean-Jacques's fraternal twin. One had chosen banking, the other accounting. What more could a Swiss mother desire?

"Yes. Pierre is managing partner for two years now."

Cate put a finger to the screen. "And to whom may I ask does account number 667.984Z belong?"

"Who do you think?" Pillonel scalded her with a reproving glance. "Mr. Kirov, he trusted no one—not even his partner, Mr. Dashamirov. After the Chechen left our meeting, Kirov asked me to open a private account for him here in Switzerland. This man is not content simply to steal from the Russian government—he wants to steal from his partner, too. If I were Kirov, I wouldn't be afraid of the prosecutor general, Mr. Baranov. Baranov can only put him in jail. Me, I am afraid of Mr. Dashamirov. Mr. Dashamirov catches Kirov stealing, he will kill him."

Cate lowered herself to her knees and spun Pillonel in his chair so that he faced her. "You're saying that these transfers show Kirov siphoning off money from Andara to his own private account?"

"*Exactement.*" Suddenly, he stood, forcing his way past her, the compact discs clutched between the fingers of one extended hand. "Take them. Take them all. They're yours. Use them quickly. As I said, I'm not doing this for you—it's for me. I am only safe once Kirov is in jail, or if he is dead. I ask you only one favor. You give me time."

"Time for what?" Gavallan accepted the discs and passed them to Cate, who slipped them into her purse.

"I am not sure yet. If I am a coward, I go to Brazil. Maybe Kirov finds me. Maybe he doesn't. One more man in jail, what does it change? Who's the better off? I've played the game the way I was supposed to. I helped you, my friend. Save your company. Save your friend. I've earned a chance to save myself."

Gavallan realized he didn't have much choice in the matter. Having Pillonel arrested would only alert Kirov to the fact that he was intent on canceling the IPO. He couldn't tell Pillonel to stay home and wait for the police until Tuesday or whenever he was able to find Grafton Byrnes. It boiled down to this: Pillonel was a free man until Gavallan was ready to turn over his evidence to the authorities.

Even then, he couldn't be sure whether the Swiss would arrest him. Though Mercury was technically a Swiss company, the fraud had taken place in conjunction with a listing on the New York Stock Exchange. That was a lot of borders to cross. Borders meant red tape and red tape meant delay.

"Go home," said Gavallan, frustrated. "Go to Brazil. I don't care. But whatever you do, take my advice and keep a low profile. And stay clear of Kirov."

Grabbing one of his arms, Gavallan half pushed Pillonel down the corridor to the elevator. They rode in silence to the lobby, then the elevator opened and Gavallan stepped out. "Cate," he said, looking over his shoulder. "How far to the airport?"

"*Police! Arrêtez!*"

A black-clad figure hit him low in the knees, throwing him to the ground. Gavallan felt the air rush from his lungs, his vision blur, then steady. Iron hands gripped his shoulders, pressing them to the concrete. A knee drilled into his chest. A second later, he was staring into the yawning muzzle of a large-bore pistol.

"Police!" shouted the aggressor. "Do not move!"

43

"You're sure he's here?" Konstantin Kirov asked his brother Leonid as they entered the murky staff auditorium on the ground floor of the Foreign Intelligence Service's headquarters at Yasenevo. The room was at once enormous and stifling. Worn maroon carpeting ran beneath Kirov's feet. Wood-paneled walls hovered over him. The time was 2 P.M., but imprisoned in the eternal dusk, he had to remind himself that outside the clouds had cleared to usher in a warm summer's afternoon.

"Oh, he's here," replied Leonid. "I spoke with him ten minutes ago. He was upstairs checking on some old friends."

"But there are no cars," Kirov protested, "No sign of his security detail. He's the president, for God's sake. He's not a ghost."

"He's also one of us. He likes to use his tradecraft now and then. Keep himself fit. In practice."

"*Nimble,*" came a voice from the darkened recesses of the auditorium. "*Like a cat.*" A familiar figure strode onto the stage at the far end of the room. "I can't tell you how advantageous it is being able to get away on occasion. To disappear. It keeps everyone on their toes. Friends. Enemies. Everyone."

The president of the Russian Republic jumped off the stage and advanced on Kirov, fixing him with an odd gaze. He was a slender man with sloped shoulders and a retiring manner. All the same, he demanded the room's focus. There was an unpredictability about him, a hidden strength crouched in his rolling walk, a shy ruthlessness in his eyes. Kirov shook his hand and, from somewhere deep in his Russian blood, obeyed the command to bow his head.

"Seventy-two hours," said the president. "All is in order, I trust?"

"Interest is strong," answered Kirov. "Our bankers report heavy demand for Mercury on all fronts, both institutional and private. A 'bellwether,' some are even calling it."

"And why shouldn't they?" asked the president. "Oil prices remain high. Our GDP is growing at eight percent. Unemployment is falling like a stone and the ruble is stronger than it has been anytime since the new era began. You say demand for Mercury is strong, I say not strong enough."

"I couldn't agree more," said Kirov. "And so does the investing public."

The president ran a hand up and down Kirov's lapel. "I don't want to hear about any of your shenanigans on this one."

"I beg your pardon?" asked Kirov, casting an eye to his brother for backup. Leonid remained silent, his chin dug into his chest.

"I'm talking about Novastar," said the president in a hushed voice. "Not happy with the fortune you're taking out of our aluminum industry, so you're stealing from our airlines, too?"

"A lie," said Kirov. "The airline needs to be restructured, that is all. A few new routes, a little less staff."

"I have your word?"

Kirov nodded, and felt the curse of the damned fall

upon him. It took every fiber of his being to keep his eyes locked on the president's. "In fact, I welcome Baranov's investigation."

The president patted Kirov's arm, his brow lifted skeptically. "Don't go too far, Konstantin Romanovich," he whispered. "It's me, Volodya. Remember? The mayor's bagman from Petersburg. If I'm not mistaken, I had the pleasure of ferrying some of your donations to Mayor Sobchak before his untimely passing. You and I know you're robbing Novastar blind. Just keep it quiet. And if you can't, then quiet Baranov." His hand found Kirov's neck, and gave it a squeeze. "Don't worry. You've become much too valuable to your country to put in jail. For the moment, at least."

Quiet Baranov? Had he heard correctly? Kirov mumbled some words, thanking the president.

"You are a good Russian." The president took Kirov's head in his hands and kissed him three times upon the cheek. Releasing him, he walked back toward the stage. "A billion dollars," he said. "Not bad for a new beginning. Do you hear that, comrade Lenin? Or should I say *Mister* Ulyanov? We've been relegated to stealing scraps from the capitalists' doorstep." Turning his gaze, he stared up at the wall behind him. It was barren, save for the shadow of a familiar profile where a memorial sculpture had once hung. "Without Lenin, who are we? A country of bumbling democrats and corrupt capitalists? A band of impoverished states linked only by the tragedy of our common history?" The president was gathering steam as he spoke. He was giving a speech to convince, even if he was the only one who needed convincing. "We are Russians," he declared. "We did not stop being a superpower when we ceased to be communists. We did not cast off our ideological fetters only to lose our national identity."

If communism didn't work, neither would democracy, Volodya went on. Both were too extreme. He would steer a middle course, but the hand on the tiller would be a firm one. The press would be reined in, the media made an organ of the state once more. As another had said some seventy years before, "the trains would be made to run on time." Some might call it fascism, others benevolent despotism. He saw it differently. Two thousand years of history had made the Russian a serf at heart. He did not simply respect authority—he craved it. And in return for his subjects' obedience, he, Volodya, the fifty-year-old president of Russia, would act as Lord and rebuild their country. He would make sure they ate, see to their education, and care for their sick.

"Most importantly, we will give them something to be proud of," he said. "Nothing less than the country's future is riding on this offering. The state is grateful, Konstantin Romanovich." And here the president's voice turned to ice. "But be sure of one thing: Should anything go wrong, I shall hold you personally responsible. You and you alone."

44

THE CELL WAS TWELVE FEET BY EIGHT, by Gavallan's measure, curdled cement painted a blinding nautical white floor to ceiling. One wall offered the comforts of a fold-down metal cot—no mattress; no blanket; no pillow—another a stainless steel toilet and matching sink. The door was battleship gray, a solid steel curtain with a rectangular spy hole cut into it. They'd taken his wallet and passport, his belt, his shoes, and his watch. The gun had earned him a kick in the ribs. Cuffed in the backseat of the police car, he'd looked on as a search of the rental car had turned up the authentic due diligence reports Pillonel had cached in his chalet. It went without saying they'd uncovered the compact discs, too. Isolated and alone, Gavallan was back at square one.

Metal groaned, a latch fell, and the viewing slat slid back to reveal a pair of pouchy brown eyes.

"I want to speak to the U.S. Embassy," Gavallan shouted, springing to his feet and rushing the door. "I'm an American citizen. I'd like to know why I am being held."

"Relax," grunted a put-upon voice. "You are thirsty? Want a Coke? A Fanta?"

"I want to call my embassy. I get a call, don't I?"

"Sure you do. In a couple of days. Perhaps a week."

"A week? You've got to be kidding."

"Next thing you'll be asking for a lawyer."

"Damn straight I want a lawyer," said Gavallan. "Ever heard of innocent until proven guilty?"

An amused chuckle trickled through the slat. "Yeah, but not around here. We suspect someone's guilty, we put him in jail, *then* we collect the proof. Sometimes it takes a month. Sometimes a year. It depends. I wouldn't worry, *mon ami:* It's not us who wants you. It's your friends in America. The longest you'll be here is two months. They'll extradite you before then ... unless, of course, you fight it. Now sit down and relax. I bring you a Coke, anyway."

"Just give me a phone."

The slat banged shut, and Gavallan slammed his fist against the door. Calm down, he urged himself. No one's going to find you guilty of a murder you didn't commit. Five minutes in front of a judge and you'll be free.

But he wasn't worried about himself so much as Grafton Byrnes. It was the fear of being trapped that rattled him, of being powerless to affect his friend's destiny. It was the stock dream of being chased down a street, your pursuers getting closer and closer while your flailing legs carried you nowhere. It was the terror of the silent scream.

In a little more than sixty hours, Mercury Broadband was set to go public. Kirov would get his two billion dollars. And Grafton Byrnes would have outlived his usefulness.

All Jett Gavallan could do was sit quietly and lament it.

IT WAS A PERFECT DAY FOR GOLF. At 5 P.M. in Zurich, the sky remained a regal blue, not a cloud to be seen. The temperature had crested at a lovely 75 degrees. The air smelled of pine and grass, and occasionally of the lake a few miles below them. Hay, freshly cut and rolled, sat ready for pickup in the fields nearby.

On the fourteenth green at the Golf & Country Club Zurich, located in the quaint township of Zumikon in the hills above his country's banking capital, Hans-Uli Brunner, Swiss minister of justice, spent a second longer studying the line of his putt. Ten feet for a birdie. Taking a breath, he approached the ball, settling his feet a shoulder's width apart. He looked at the hole, then at the ball, then at the hole again. *A birdie.* On a two-handicap hole, no less, where he already got a stroke. Sink this one and the match was his.

He steadied his head.

He drew back the blade of the putter.

As he stroked the putter toward the ball, an ominous tune chimed from within his golf bag. The first bars of "Beethoven's Fifth." The blade met the ball askew and it sailed three feet past the cup.

"Damn it!"

Stalking to the fringe of the green, he unzipped his bag and answered the call. "Brunner," he said gruffly.

"Is that any way to greet an old friend? And all this time I thought the Swiss were so polite. A nation of innkeepers?"

Brunner looked back toward the pin, where his playing partners were scowling openly at him. "Excuse me," he called, a gloved hand cupped to his mouth. "An emergency."

Though friends of thirty years, the three players did not disguise their displeasure. It was against club rules to carry a cell phone on the golf course, though in Brunner's case, a grudging exception had been made.

Zumikon, as the course was referred to, counted itself the most elite golfing establishment in Switzerland. Accordingly, the rules of golf were worshiped with a sanctity accorded the Ten Commandments. No better proof could be found than the Englishman brought over each April on a seven-month work permit to serve as club manager, normally a retired military man with long golfing experience. Only an Englishman would do. He was their mantle of legitimacy, their direct link to the "ancient cradle of golf."

Brunner hurried a few yards down the fairway until he was out of earshot of his fellow golfers.

"Good afternoon, my dear fellow," he said with a smile, the frustration of his missed putt eons away. He'd recognized the voice immediately, and knew it might promise many good things. "What a pleasant surprise. How have you been?"

"In truth, better, Herr Minister. I'm calling on a matter of some delicacy."

"Go ahead."

And for two minutes, His Honor, Bundesrat Hans-Ulrich Brunner, member in high esteem of the seven-man council that served as Switzerland's executive branch, listened as his "close friend" outlined his problem and how he wanted it resolved.

"Geneva, you say. He's wanted for murder? Yes, yes, I can understand that you want to deal with this on your own. Get him back into your neck of the woods. Good idea. As it happens, I have some close friends in the canton. It will be difficult, but I may be able to arrange things."

"I hope the usual arrangements are acceptable?"

Brunner glanced back at the green. He thought of the missed putt, the heated expressions, the apologies owed. Surely he would have to buy the foursome drinks, maybe even dinner. *A call on the fourteenth green.* They would talk about it for days. "The usual" was hardly adequate.

"It is the weekend," Brunner explained, "and we are talking about Geneva." His apology was pained and heartfelt. "*Alors, la Suisse Romande.* These Calvinists ... I'm sorry to say they are notoriously difficult to convince."

"Will a million francs suffice?"

Brunner looked at the three golfers glaring in his direction. One raised his arms as if to say "What the hell is going on?" Brunner waved them onward. He would pick up his ball and return to the clubhouse at once. It was a sin not to finish a round, especially when he had a chance to take them all, and on such a beautiful day ... but alas, duty called.

"You're too generous," Brunner responded at once. "Now, as to the account details ..."

IT WAS 8 A.M. PACIFIC DAYLIGHT TIME, and in San Francisco the fog had returned. It hugged the streets, curling through alleys and climbing the city's steep hills like a fibrous, undulant snake. Approaching the end of Broadway in Pacific Heights, Roy DiGenovese pulled his car into the driveway and killed the engine. He took a moment to finish his double espresso, then wiped his mouth and climbed from the car. He was tired. The flight from Miami had been long and bumpy. A guy six-foot-two just didn't fit in the back of a commercial airliner—at least not in seat 32J he didn't, sandwiched between an Hispanic *Hindenburg* and the rapper DMX's biggest fan. Maybe someday he'd warrant business-class travel. Maybe someday he'd get to ride in that Lear Mr. Dodson had been going on about. And maybe someday he'd be a Supreme Court justice. DiGenovese laughed at himself. It wasn't so bad being an optimist, he thought. Just keep it real.

Two cars had parked behind him, and their occupants met him on the sidewalk. This morning, they had no need to hide, no call to sneak in the back way. Leading his team of five special agents, DiGenovese knocked on the front door.

An Hispanic woman opened up a few seconds later. "Good morning," she said. She was older, dressed in blue slacks and a 49ers sweatshirt. Her eyes were cautious, scared.

"I'm sorry to bother you so early, ma'am," said DiGenovese, smiling and showing his badge. "We've come to take a look through Mr. Gavallan's belongings. It shouldn't take too long, an hour or two at most. We hold a warrant from a United States Federal Magistrate giving us a right to search the premises. Here's my card. If you'd like, you can call my supervisor. His name is Mr. Dodson. He's at the number written right there on the back."

"Mr. Gavallan, he is okay?"

"He's fine, ma'am."

DiGenovese made it a point to be polite. His mother had spent her working life cleaning homes and offices, and as a child he'd accompanied her on her rounds. He would never forget the dismissive glances, the rude comments, the smug ill will of the moneyed classes.

The woman studied the card for a moment before shrugging and yielding the door. "Okay. You can go."

"Thank you. We'll try to leave things as we found them."

DiGenovese set off through the house, directing his men to take the bigger rooms first: living room, den, guest bedroom, office. He wanted the master bedroom for himself. Gavallan was a former military man. If he kept a gun, odds were it was nearby, either in a night table or a closet.

The house was open and casual, with just the right amount of furniture, not cluttered like the homes of a lot of rich people. The floors were mostly wood, the décor kind of Spanish, giving the place a hacienda-like feel. By the time he reached the bedroom, DiGenovese had decided it was just his style. If, that is, he were to ever become a multimillionaire.

Inside the bedroom, he made straight for the night tables. He pulled out each drawer in turn, finding a few books, a handkerchief, a box of allergy medicine. He moved to the opposite side of the king-size bed. That night table was empty, not even a used Kleenex. Lifting the mattress, he ducked his head and checked for a gun. Nothing.

To the closet. Shelves to the left. A hanging bar to the right. He ruffled through the stacks of shirts and sweaters, at first setting them neatly on the floor and then, growing frustrated, flipping them onto the ground. No bullets. No holster. Nada.

DiGenovese paused, catching sight of himself in the mirror, seeing the furrowed brow, the look of stormy determination. Actually, he didn't want to find the gun. But not finding it drove him crazy just the same. Go figure.

He moved into the bathroom.

Drawers. Nil. Medicine cabinet. Nil. Beneath the sink. Nil.

"Roy!"

The call came from Gavallan's office. DiGenovese hurried to the oak-paneled study, collaring his excitement. "What do you got?"

"Check it out," said Rosemary Duffy. She was a short, stocky woman, thirty, with cherubic cheeks and sparkling blue eyes. "Gavallan's holster. Minus the piece."

DiGenovese rushed forward and examined the leather. It was creased and worn from long years of cradling a pistol. He rubbed a finger inside it, and it came away oily. "What do you think? A long time since the pistol's been removed?"

Duffy smelled the holster. "A week. A month. Hard to tell."

Within minutes the study became a charnel house of wild, barely disciplined activity. Books were pulled off the shelves. Pillows pulled from the sofa and gutted. The stereo yanked from its tethers. This time it was DiGenovese who got lucky. Pulling a well-thumbed copy of the Bible from the shelves, he spotted a hidden compartment in the wall. "Rosie," he called. "Get over here. Do your stuff."

Within a minute, Duffy had opened the compartment. Reaching in her hand, she came out with a cardboard carton six inches long, three inches wide and three inches high. The word "Remington" was neatly printed on each side of the box.

DiGenovese opened the carton of 9mm shells.

Half the shells were missing.

"Sonuvabitch!"

HOWELL DODSON PUT DOWN THE PHONE. He felt light-headed, bewildered, and ashamed. How could he have been so wrong about someone? Why hadn't he listened more closely to Roy DiGenovese's warnings earlier? Why, even after the murders in Delray Beach, had he been so slow to warm to Gavallan as the prime suspect?

A holster with no gun, DiGenovese had told him.

A half-empty box of bullets.

And now this.

Dodson stared at the manila envelope that had arrived a few minutes earlier stamped "Department of the Air Force: Confidential" and the sheaf of papers that comprised Captain John J. Gavallan's service record lying neatly on the desk beside it. Pushing his bifocals onto the bridge of his nose, he began to read the papers again. Once was not enough. His conscience was as obdurate as his investigative instinct and it demanded he be presented with the error of his ways a second time.

He stopped a few pages in, his index finger frozen halfway down. The entry was innocuous enough: "Summer Semester 1985 / USAF SOC / Grade: Pass." And below it, in capital letters, signifying a commendation: "HONOR GRADUATE."

Translated, the entry stated that during the summer between his junior and senior year at the Air Force Academy, Jett Gavallan had attended the Air Force equivalent of Army Ranger training—the Special Operations Air Command course—and graduated at the top of his class.

When Dodson asked DiGenovese about the Air Force commandos, his assistant whistled long and low. "They're hard-asses, sir. Mostly trained for rescue ops, but rescue ops in hot situations. Lot of gunplay, hand-to-hand combat, that kind of thing. Mean muthas, if you get my drift. Best thing I could say is I'd let them back me up any day. They're pros."

A little probing got Dodson the following: Special Operations Air Commandos were trained to scuba dive and parachute, to support themselves off the land for periods of up to three months, and to master land navigation and map reading. That wasn't all. They were also taught to be experts in small arms and had to qualify as sharpshooters with an M16.

Jett Gavallan wasn't just a pilot. He'd trained as a commando. To use sophisticated weapons. To kill with his hands.

Gavallan was their man, plain and simple.

Dodson read a little further. Even with the glasses, he had to squint to make out the letters. Though he tried to focus on the words, all he could see were bodies. Bodies pitched onto their desks. Bodies strewn across the floor. Bodies slumped in the corner. A tear slid down Dodson's cheek and fell to the paper.

Removing his bifocals, Howell Dodson rubbed at his eyes.

It was time he got a new prescription.

45

In the clearing, the pickup's engine grumbled, then died.

Grafton Byrnes lay in the corner of the shed, curled into a fetal position, his face half bathed in mud. A steady rain fell. His clothes were sopping wet, as if he had just emerged from a swimming pool. His hair was matted and dripping. The sky was darkening, choked with clouds. He had no idea what time it was, only that it was evening.

A little longer, he told himself. *You're almost there.*

An eerie wind whistled through the pines as rain blew through the cracks in the wall, peppering him like sand on a windy day at the beach. He was cold. He shivered in waves, violent spasms that racked his body, the tremors beginning in his lower back, then traveling up his spine with icy, muscular fingers that wrapped themselves around his ribs and squeezed mercilessly, provoking terrible, wrenching grunts.

The truck's door opened and closed. Byrnes clamped his jaw. By force of will, he stopped shivering. He lay still. Absolutely still.

Boots trudged through the mud, slurping and sucking.

Keys jangled. Metal scratched metal and the padlock to the shed opened.

Byrnes gripped the stone close to his chest, the stabbing of his wounded thumb stoking his resolve to act. This was his chance. He was sick and getting sicker. His throat was raw, and he had begun coughing. He was starved and feverish. Another night in the open and he'd be too weak to stand, let alone escape.

A boot landed near his head. The mess tin holding his ration of tepid soup dropped into the mud, spilling half its contents. He made no move toward it. That morning, like the night before, he'd played the dying wretch, murmuring "Doctor" over and over again. Now he was silent. He sensed his jailer's presence, could smell the pig shit on his boots. He urged him closer. He wanted to feel his breath, to look into his eyes. Then he would strike.

The jailer hawked and spat on Byrnes's back, then he muttered a word and laughed.

The boots moved away. One step. Two.

No! screamed Byrnes in private torment. *You cannot leave.* He gripped the stone harder. It was blunt and heavy. Trying to dig his way under the wall, he'd found it beneath six inches of topsoil and clay. Great treasures had been more easily won.

The jailer stopped, and Byrnes heard his breathing, the jagged wheeze of a lifelong smoker. He sensed the man's indecision. There came a new sound—the rustle of clothing—followed by a distinctive two-tiered *click*. The rain seemed to amplify it, and Byrnes knew it was a firing pin being cocked. He clenched his body, willing himself not to move.

Lie still. Lie absolutely still.

The gun fired, a deafening explosion inside the shed. The bullet impacted the ground an inch from Byrnes's eyes, blasting him with mud and stone.

Lie still.

Seconds passed.

The boots approached and prodded his ribs. First gently. Then less gently. Byrnes scrunched his face, biting back the pain. A labored groan as the jailer knelt on his haunches and slid his hands beneath the prisoner. Another grunt as he turned him over.

Byrnes opened his eyes. And in the moment before he smashed the rock against the Russian's cheek, he met his jailer's gaze.

"Bastard, go spit on someone else."

"Chto?"

The rock crushed the man's face, toppling him to the earth, leaving him sitting upright, stunned and immobile. A jagged gash on his cheek leaked blood.

Rushing to his feet, Byrnes brought the stone above his head. He was slow and awkward, and by the time he'd clamored to his feet, the jailer was up too, a mean, dumb grin on his face. A hand fell to his belt, and dropping his gaze from Byrnes, he searched for his pistol. Byrnes charged, ramming the Russian with his head, driving him against the wall. It was then he knew that his jailer was drunk. It wasn't the smell so much as the man's general lassitude, the confused coordination.

Throwing his left arm high and pinioning the man's neck, Byrnes scrabbled for the pistol, his infected thumb screaming at every contact. "Stop it," he yelled, retreating a second later, the pistol held in his right hand. He was irate, crazed, divinely pissed off. "You think you can lock a man up, barely feed him, leave him to die slow? Do you? Answer me!"

The Russian was leering crazily, teetering on his feet. He wasn't drunk—he was absolutely shit-faced. Three sheets to the fuckin' wind. "You ready? *Eh, Amerikanski?*"

"Don't," said Byrnes, his anger seeping from him. *"Nyet.* You stay there."

Muttering, the Russian took a step forward, spreading

his arms as if entering the wrestlers' circle. "Come. You want fight?"

"Stay there."

The pistol was an old .22 long barrel. A peashooter. The cylinder held six slugs. Holding it proved difficult, but Byrnes managed by using both his hands, the palm of his left hand pressing the butt firmly into his right. "Stay right there," he said again. He had no desire to kill a man.

Then everything happened quickly, but in distinct steps, so that afterward Byrnes was able to dissect them in minute detail.

The Russian leaped forward, growling like a bear. Byrnes fired the pistol into his gut. A meek geyser of blood spouted forth, then died. The Russian swatted at it as if it were a fly, nothing more, and kept coming. Byrnes raised the gun. At a distance of two feet and closing, he fired into the man's chest. It was a bull's-eye. The jailer collapsed at the knees and fell face forward to the ground without uttering so much as a whisper.

Byrnes looked down at the body, the acrid scent of the spent cordite sickening his stomach. His ears rang from the shots, dizzying him. "Stupid fool," he said, half out loud, kicking the corpse lightly.

Kneeling, he turned the Russian over and began unbuttoning his coat. He started at the neck and worked his way down, helping the buttons through the eyelets with his index fingers, not daring to let his thumbs do the work. Even so, the pain was nearly too much. Several times, he drew his hands away and swore viciously.

Trouble arrived with the third button. It was stuck. He tried everything to get it undone but it would not advance through the eyelet. "Sonuvabitch," he said, taking a deep breath, looking toward the door. He needed the jacket. He needed something dry, something warm. Oh Jesus, he needed it.

"Slowly," he urged himself.

Moving closer to the body, he leaned over the Russian's chest. There was surprisingly little blood and the coat was not as dirty as he'd expected. With iron discipline he commanded his fingers to move. His left index and middle fingers carefully spread the eyelet wide. With his right index finger, he maneuvered the drab gray button through it. A smile creased his face. "Gotcha!"

"*Nyet!*" screamed the Russian, sitting up, wrapping his hands around Byrnes's neck, squeezing with all his might, sharp uncut nails digging into his flesh. "*Nyet, Amerikanski.*"

In a moment, the jailer was on top of him, straddling his chest, the man's weight full on his neck, strangling him. Byrnes fought at the hands, but could not grip them. The gun. Where was the gun? Byrnes groped around in the dirt. He was oblivious to the pain, to the daggers flaying his arms. Then he had it. Grasping the barrel, he bought the handle in a wide arc and struck the Russian across the bridge of the nose. Once. Twice. Blood gushed from both nostrils, but still the hands kept their grip, still those mad, leering eyes bored into him.

Byrnes felt the life ebbing from him, his vision dimming. Lowering the gun to the dirt, he turned it quickly and took hold of it by the grip. With a single fluid motion, he brought it up, laid the barrel against the jailer's temple, and pulled the trigger. Gunpowder exploded and a spigot of blood blew out the opposite side of the jailer's head. The death grip on Byrnes's neck lessened. The light went out in the Russian's eyes. Slumping, he collapsed on top of Byrnes, stone dead.

THE ENGINE RUMBLED ROUGHLY while the heater blasted him like a wind from hell. Behind the wheel of the pickup, Grafton Byrnes sat staring at the fence. The sliding ten-foot gates granting one entry and exit to Konstantin Kirov's "dacha" were closed. Next to him on the seat was a remote-control device with a nine-digit keypad. He picked it up, held it in his right hand, using the fingers of his left to peck out a couple of tries. It was hopeless. He didn't even know how many digits the code required. Three? Four? Five?

"Fuckin' useless," he muttered, dropping it on the seat.

Byrnes was wearing his jailer's jacket, as well as his socks and boots. The gun was back in the shed with the dead Russian. It turned out it was loaded with five bullets, not six, and between them, they'd fired them all. He had drunk his soup and found a chunk of bread in the pickup. He was alive and relatively well and had a few hundred rubles, a pocketknife, and a pack of cigarettes to get him to the U.S. Embassy in Moscow.

If, that is, he could get through the double fences.

He stared at them awhile longer, wondering what twenty thousand volts would do to a car. If he drove over the metal, would it short out? Would the rubber tires ground the charge? Or would the touch of the fender conduct the electricity through the chassis and fry him like an egg on a griddle?

There was only one way to find out.

Byrnes put the truck into reverse and backed up about a hundred feet. Finding neutral, he gunned the engine a few times. He was a hot rod driver on a Saturday night. "Big Daddy" Don Garlits waiting for the green light. He imagined the Christmas tree counting down. The lights blinking red, red, red, and finally green.

Ramming the gearshift into first, Byrnes floored the truck. He passed the main cabin, the radio shack, the crematorium. And as he hit the fence, he loosed a savage howl.

Metal buckled, wire bent and moaned, the engine roared, and then he was clear, hurtling down the rutted dirt road at sixty kilometers an hour.

It was only then that Byrnes looked at the fuel gauge. The needle hovered on empty.

46

GAVALLAN WATCHED THE LAKE SLIDE BY, a moss green mirror shattered into myriad shards by the sun's piercing rays. It was eight o'clock in the evening. After twenty-seven hours in custody, he'd been released with hardly a word, escorted from the rear of the police station, and ordered into the backseat of an unmarked Audi. Every time he asked a question the plainclothes officer next to him would mutter *"Ça va,"* and give him a smile like he was the dumbest fuck on the planet Earth.

"Where are you taking me?"

"Ça va."

"Where is Miss Magnus?"

"Ça va."

"Is Mr. Pillonel in jail?" *Or was the rat ever taken there in the first place?*

"Ça va."

They played stop and go through a succession of traffic signals, turning left on the Guisan Bridge and crossing over the lake. Angry gray clouds spilled over the mountains on the French side a few miles up, gathering low above the surface and advancing toward them. A flash of lightning exploded from the sky. They were in for a gully washer.

The car slowed and came to a halt at the center of the bridge. Reflexively, he dropped a hand to the door and let his fingers toy with the handle. He had no illusions about his status. He might have been relieved of his cuffs, but he was hardly a free man. The car's doors were locked, the windows rolled up. One glance at his taciturn companion with the sinewy forearms assured Gavallan he was still a prisoner. The only question was where he was headed.

With a jerk, the car took off, zero to fifty in five seconds flat. The storm clouds were moving quickly toward them, a sheet of black rain dicing the water. The driver continued along the Rue du Mont Blanc, past the tourist shops selling cuckoo clocks, Swatches, and chocolate bars, veering left through a tunnel that took them under and around the train station. A sign ahead showed Annecy and Lyons to the left, Lausanne, Montreux, and Genève Aeroport to the right. The Audi shunted right.

Two minutes later they were out of the city, accelerating down an open stretch of highway. Green fields stretched to their left and right. Bales of hay sat rolled and wrapped in opaque plastic, ready for pickup and transport to the farmer's loft. The driver lowered his window an inch. Immediately the rich, loamy scent of ground under cultivation flooded the car. He shook loose a cigarette and, half turning, offered it to Gavallan. "Smoke?"

"No thanks."

A whistling roar built in the air around them and suddenly an MD-11 passed directly over their heads, its pale metal belly close enough to touch. Strobing yellow landing lights beckoned to Gavallan's right, and beyond them the crenellated façade of the landing terminal.

The airport.

He was going home.

He didn't like the idea, but there was no use fighting it.

It wasn't until the car passed through a sentry gate and drove onto the tarmac that he started questioning the mechanics of his release. Didn't extradition require weeks, if not months, of legal wrangling? Shouldn't he have been asked if he wished to fight the order? If he hadn't been charged, by what authority were the Swiss loading him onto a plane to send him back to America? And why the hell were they letting him climb back aboard the chartered G-3?

He could see the plane crouched on the apron a few hundred yards away, landing lights on, turbines spinning lazily, an iridescent stream of exhaust escaping the engines. He had to wonder who was waiting at the other end. Dodson and his crew from the Joint Russo-American Task Force? Or would representatives of the Florida police comprise his handpicked welcoming committee? And why was he being smuggled out of the country like a plague bacillus?

Another Audi was parked next to the plane. He saw a door open and Cate's figure emerge. She seemed to hesitate, not wanting to board the plane. Two policemen bracketed her and began walking her to the aircraft. It was then that Gavallan sat up straighter, his nose pressed against the window. The plane was too big. It had too many windows. It wasn't a G-3 but a G-5; no mistaking it. The detailing was different too. A red pinstripe that hadn't been there before ran the length of the fuselage just below the windows. It wasn't the chartered jet at all.

And then he spotted the flag painted high on the tail, and he shivered.

The white, blue, and red tricolor of Russia.

HE CAUGHT UP TO CATE as she was about to mount the stairs.

"You okay? Did they keep you locked up this whole time?"

Cate lifted her shoulders, giving a fatigued nod. Her eyes were red, her hair being blown about her by a whipping wind.

Two familiar faces waited at the top of the stairs. Boris and Tatiana. A few hours behind in their forty-million-dollar jet, but no less vigilant.

"Hello, Mr. Jett," said Boris, as if they were old acquaintances from the club. His jaw was blue, swollen like a grapefruit, but his eyes said "No hard feelings." "You come now. We hurry. Storm will be here fast."

Gavallan glanced behind him. The Swiss police had formed themselves into a phalanx, and their stolid expressions said there was no going back. Offering Cate his hand, he guided her up the stairs. She mounted the first step, then stopped. Turning, she grabbed his shoulders and kissed him. "Tell me you'll understand."

Gavallan searched her eyes for an explanation, but saw only confusion and hurt. "What?"

Fighting the wind, Cate drew back the hair from her face and wiped away a tear. She opened her mouth to speak, then shook her head as if the thought were not worth mentioning. With a silken touch, her hand slipped from his. As quickly, she was herself again. The eyes cleared, the jaw firmed.

She mounted the steps rapidly, nodding perfunctorily to Boris as she entered the cabin. Over the wind, Gavallan was only just able to hear what he said to her.

"Good evening, Miss Kirov. Your father sends his regards."

47

THE TWELVE MEMBERS OF TEAM 7 crouched low on the riverbank, knees dug into the sandy moraine, watching, waiting. Fifty yards away, inside the compound, a man left the administration building and headed toward the pump house. He walked slowly, taking time to stretch and light a cigarette.

"Mark?" whispered Team Leader Abel. Each member of Team 7 was known only by his operational name. Personal details were not to be shared.

"Mullen. Jonathan D. Shift supervisor," responded Baker, his second in command. He did not add that Mullen was thirty-four years of age, an engineer who had received his degree at Purdue University in the state of Indiana. They had long ago memorized the faces and vital statistics of the crew who worked here. Mullen was easy. He never went without a Yankees windbreaker.

The American stopped a few feet from the pump house, flicked his cigarette to the ground, then opened the door and disappeared from sight.

To a man, Team 7 focused their eyes on the industrial landscape that lay beyond the fence, a dull metallic carcass sprawled beneath the half light of the midnight sun. Pump Station 2 of the Trans-Alaska Pipeline, or TAPS, lay at the foot of the Endicott Range on the border of the Arctic National Refuge. Its job was to guarantee that crude oil flowed smoothly through a sixty-five-mile section of pipe along the environmentally sensitive south fork of the Koyukuk River. The pipeline began two hundred miles to the north at Prudhoe Bay and cut south in a zigzagging pattern to Valdez, the southernmost Alaskan port that remained free of ice year-round. There, the oil was loaded through one of four primary pumping berths onto the giant supertankers that carried it to points south in America, Europe, and Asia. Over a million barrels of oil arrived at Valdez each day, and at any time some nine million barrels filled the length of the pipeline.

Pump Station 2 was built on a flat rectangle of land five hundred yards long and two hundred yards wide that had been razed from surrounding grasslands and forest. Three oil storage reservoirs stood in a row on the western side of the station, mint green lozenges two stories high and a hundred feet in diameter capable of holding 420,000 barrels of oil. Due to the breakdown of two of the Valdez Marine Terminal's four pumping berths, the reservoirs were topped out.

In the center of the facility, a power plant had been constructed capable of generating four megawatts of electricity daily. It took fuel to make energy and energy to move fuel. The power plant stood gleaming in the dusky night, an elaborate steel Tinkertoy with blue and red lights blinking from catwalks and stairways and metal mesh terraces.

Dormitories, administrative offices, and the pumping station itself occupied the grounds on the eastern side of the compound. Staffing ran between ten and twenty-five persons, depending on whether maintenance was being performed. Current manpower stood at eleven. The exclusively male complement worked twelve-hour shifts,

seven days on, seven off. In five minutes, at the designated strike time of 2 A.M., a skeleton staff was set to be
on duty: a foreman and a technician. Others were asleep,
catching up on some precious rack time before suiting
up for their grueling shifts at 6 A.M. Six days into their
shift, the lot could be counted on to be tired, irascible,
and unobservant.

The pipeline entered the complex from the north, a
giant stainless steel tube forty-eight inches in diameter
lifted three feet above the ground by a series of vertical
support members, or VSMs, located every sixty feet.
From afar, the pipeline looked as if it had been built
yesterday. But Team 7 knew different.

The Trans-Alaska Pipeline was a disaster waiting to
happen. Defective berthing pumps at one end. Rusted
and corroding pipeline in between. Hazardous drilling
practices on the North Slope. Over 50 percent of all
shutoff valves—valves strategically placed to isolate sec-
tions of the pipe and minimize the volume of spills—
were inoperative. The earthquake monitoring system
designed to cut flow through the pipeline no longer
functioned. A year earlier, a temblor measuring 5.7 on
the Richter scale had shaken the residents of Central
Alaska out of their beds. The monitor hadn't given a
peep. Oil had continued to flow as normal. Not a single
valve closed automatically, not one pump station shut itself down. It was a miracle the pipeline had not snapped
clean in two.

Completed in 1977, the TAPS was an aging, brittle
dinosaur, one slip from an ecological disaster of heart-
rending proportions.

Team 7 had arrived to give it the push.

Ghosts no longer, the members of Team 7 had exchanged their anoraks, fatigues, and combat boots for the
casual attire favored by American blue-collar workers.
They wore blue jeans and corduroys, denim jackets and

parkas, work boots and baseball caps. In place of rank, they boasted the insignia of western apparel: North Face, Nike, and Levi's. The uniform of the enemy.

They had buried their parachutes, jumpsuits, and altimeters two miles away in holes four feet deep, now filled and covered with stones and moss and the natural vegetation of the region. Each wore a compact backpack no different from one a college student might be likely to carry. In it they hefted eight 125-gram sticks of C-4 explosives, a length of det cord, three electronic fuses, and a model TA9 remote detonator no larger than a transistor radio. All traces of the C-4 would theoretically vanish in the blaze following the explosion. If, however, investigators were to discover a trace of the plastique and to analyze its chemical signature, they would learn it belonged to a shipment stolen from an American armory two years earlier.

No one carried a weapon. Ghosts did not leave behind corpses.

From somewhere in the wilderness, a foghorn sounded. One bleat, rude and ominous, then silence.

The members of Team 7 scattered.

They were divided into three squads of four persons each, designated, in American military vernacular, as "Alpha," "Bravo," and "Charlie." Alpha and Bravo Squads climbed from the protective cornice of the riverbank and ran at a crouch to the fence surrounding the enclosure. The fence stood only six feet high. It was designed to keep animals away, not to deter intruders. Coldfoot was the nearest town and it was seventy miles away. Springing over the fence, they landed softly on the balls of their feet, eyes peeled for oil workers.

Alpha Squad moved to the right, toward the giant reservoirs filled to capacity with North Slope crude, oil from the mammoth field at Prudhoe Bay. Skirting the rear of the reservoirs, they kept out of sight of the supervisor's office (located some two hundred feet across an open concrete field) until they reached the fat, white intake pipes that fed oil into the tanks. Team Leader Abel slung his pack to the ground and removed two sticks of the green C-4, several fuses, and a length of det cord. He gave Baker one stick. One stick he kept for himself.

Immediately, Baker began to roll the stick between his palms to soften the putty. As the C-4 grew malleable, he broke the explosive in two, affixing a slim strip to joints in the pipe that had recently been welded together.

At the same time, Abel ran up the metal staircase attached to the side of the reservoir. He stopped halfway to the top where a blunt valve extended from the side of the wall. The valve allowed for the manual release of oil from the reservoir. After softening the explosives, he fashioned a long tubular section and wrapped it around the valve. With his fingers, he worked the putty into the crease at the base of the valve, as if stanching a leak. Plastique was a forgiving mistress, he thought as he pressed the putty against the cold metal; hit it with a hammer, burn it, shoot it even, and still it would not ignite.

Between his fingers, he held an electronic fuse, two inches in length, one half inch in diameter. From his pocket, he withdrew the det cord and plugged it into the electronic timer. Next he stabbed the det cord deep inside the putty. Det cord was simply a thin plastic cord filled with PETN, a fast-burning explosive. With a glance over the stairs, he snapped his fingers and dropped the cord to the ground where Baker picked it up, similarly attached it to the electronic fuse, and inserted it into the C-4.

From the corner of his eye, Abel spotted the other two members of his squad doing a like job on the next reservoir in line. He checked his watch. They were ahead of schedule.

Bravo Squad had split in two. Two men were now at the north end of the complex, lying on their backs beneath the pipeline itself. They worked quickly and efficiently, molding the plastique to the joints of the pipe, where one forty-foot section was welded to another. Det cord was produced, electronic fuses primed and inserted.

The other two men of Bravo Squad moved to the pump station itself. Sliding against the wall, they lifted their eyes over the windowsill and glanced inside. They saw no one. As expected, the staffers on duty were huddled inside the supervisory shed, where they would remain unless an equipment failure or breakdown summoned them to one part or another of the compound.

Turning the corner of the building, they opened the door and entered. Inside, they moved to the control panel, a wall of dials and gauges, none younger than twenty years old. Screwdrivers were produced. Wirecutters. Needle-nose pliers and a miniature battery. Their work required five minutes' time. The sensitive gauges that comprised the leak detection system and monitored the pressure of oil flowing through the pipeline had all been "adjusted." Even when all oil had ceased coursing through Pump Station 2, it would relay flow as "normal" to the other ten stations up and down the line.

A half mile north of Pump Station 2, Charlie Squad swarmed on top of and around a remote gate valve. The valve looked like the conning tower of a submarine. A red pennant flew from its uppermost walkway, crackling in the wind. Ninety-five such valves were placed up and down the length of the Trans-Alaska Pipeline, eighty-six of them remote-controlled to close in event of a rupture or spill. Plastique was carefully formed to the joists and the undercarriage of the 78,000-pound valve. The charge used was minimal, enough to rupture the pipeline cleanly without igniting the oil inside.

Tasks accomplished, Alpha, Bravo, and Charlie Squads met up at their assembly point, one hundred yards from the periphery of Pump Station 2. No one spoke a word. All took a knee as Abel activated the TA9 transmitter. Three white pinlights came to life, indicating that the electronic fuses were primed and a signal established. Moving his thumb to the ignition switch, Abel paused and, in the second before he depressed the button, imagined the horror of what he was about to unleash.

The charges placed on the reservoirs would simulate a "sparking" incident that occurred when rusting, corroded pipes brushed against each other. The oil would ignite. The reservoirs would blow. The ensuing explosion would shoot hundreds of thousands of gallons of flaming oil hundred of yards in every direction, scorching the sensitive landscape, fouling the air, and incinerating the crew of Pump Station 2. Seventy miles distant from the nearest habitation, the explosion would go unnoticed until the next day when Pump Station 2 did not respond to its routine morning calls.

The charges placed a half mile north of the station would rupture the pipe and allow the crude oil to flow freely onto the Alaskan plain. Oil would spill at the rate of forty thousand barrels per hour. As each barrel held forty-seven gallons of oil, nearly a million gallons of North Slope crude would foul the pristine meadows of the Arctic National Refuge each hour. The oil would form first a pond, then a lake, and soon it would spread into a black viscous ocean. The oil would seep into the ground and foul the water table. It would leak into the streams and the nearby Yukon River. Entire colonies of steelhead trout and chinook, chum, and coho salmon would be destroyed, their pristine habitats forever fouled.

As the oil spread across the rolling plain, it would take with it rookeries of Canada geese. It would tar the nests of the sandhill crane. It would permanently spoil thousands of acres of feeding area for caribou, elk, moose, and Roosevelt elk. By the time the spill had been stopped, somewhere between three and seven million gallons of oil would have blackened the Alaskan landscape.

Abel pressed the button once, firmly. Clouds of green smoke burst from the oil reservoirs and, farther away, from the remote gate valve. But there were no explosions, no fireworks, no hellish cataclysm to light the early-morning sky.

The Klaxon sounded again, this time longer, a full three seconds.

The only explosion, if indeed it was one, came from the sky, where a hundred feet above the ground, rafts of fluorescent lights flickered to life. The lights hung from the ceiling of an enormous hangar, eight hundred yards by a thousand.

Alaska had come to Severnaya high on the Siberian Plain.

A digital clock hanging from the observation tower at the far side of the hangar stood frozen at 8:23:51. The soldiers cheered, if briefly. On this last dry run, they had bettered their time by twenty-two seconds.

Their cheer died down, replaced by a grim determination, a silent resolve. One man after the other met his comrades' eyes. The time for training was past. After four months, the operation was at hand.

Clapping one another on the back, they moved off at a jog to return to their barracks. It was time to write the letter. In a month or two, their parents, girlfriends, loved ones (none were married or had children), would receive the short note explaining simply that Jan, or Ivan, or Sergei had decided to leave the country to seek a new life outside of Russia. He didn't know where or how long he might be gone, only that his absence would be a long one and that they should move on with their lives without him.

One meal remained, one night's sleep. Tomorrow, they would board planes to take them east across the top of the world.

To their destiny.

To America.

48

THEY TOOK OFF INTO THE STORM, the last plane out before
the clouds enveloped the airport, and Gavallan wondered if the pilot had disobeyed the control tower and
said, "To hell with it, I'm taking off whether you like it or
not." The sky was black, absolutely black, the plane jolt-
ing up and down and every which way with sudden, violent tremors.

"I want to talk to Cate," he said to Boris. "Excuse me,
I mean Miss Kirov. Your boss's daughter."

The two men were seated facing each other at the rear
of the roomy cabin. Cate was up front with the sofas and
conference tables, Tatiana her assigned guardian.

"Sorry, Mr. Jett. You are not to talk to her." Sweat
coursed from his forehead and his complexion had gone
sallow. "Right now, you stay in seat."

"Just give me five minutes," Gavallan persisted, undoing his safety belt, standing. "It's important. I'll be right
back."

Despite his sickly mien, Boris was up in a flash, thrust-
ing an open palm against Gavallan's chest. "You sit.
Understand? You talk to Kirova when you get to Moscow.
Okay?"

Gavallan knocked away the offending hand. "Yeah, I understand."

Sitting down, he refastened his seat belt. Boris waited a moment, glowering above him. The plane hit an air pocket, fell for a second, then pancaked, shoving Boris into his seat. His hands scrambled for his seat belt. His mouth was open, breath coming fast and hard.

"You *should* be scared, buddy," Gavallan whispered.

He knew he should be scared, too, but right now anger was kicking fear's ass in the emotional war raging inside him. Leaning his head to the right, he caught sight of Cate, seated forward in a separate grouping of sofa and lounge chairs closer to the cockpit. Even now, she looked as if she had things under control. Eyes closed, hands laid calmly on the armrests, head back, she looked as though she was taking a nap. He knew she had to be frightened to death. Why didn't she just show it like anybody else?

Suddenly, it was painful even to look at her.

He stared out the window. The wings were torquing something awful. The pilot had flown them directly into the maw of a thunderstorm. Either he was one crazy mother or he was under instructions to get his new passengers to Moscow as quickly as possible. Either way, he was reckless—the pilot's cardinal sin—and Gavallan hated him for it.

A bolt of lightning struck the aircraft, a hellishly bright flashbulb that bathed the cabin in pure, electric luminescence. Then came the thunder, a rollicking, tumultuous clap that seemed to explode inside the cabin itself. The plane rolled into a thirty-degree bank, the nose going down, down, down. Skeins of Saint Elmo's fire flitted around the bulkhead, a freakish blue and white light emanating from every piece of exposed metal. The port engine whined furiously, the turbine seeking purchase somewhere in the maelstrom of conflicting air currents.

The fuselage shuddered as if God had taken the plane in his hand and was shaking it to within an inch of its life.

Gavallan looked around. Soldier Boris's eyes were closed, his chest pumping up and down, hyperventilating. Fore, Tanya had gone whiter than the dead. Her diamond blue eyes were wider than they'd ever been, the cords of her neck stretched to breaking. Her mouth was parted, and over the rattle and hum he could hear her moaning. Anytime now, he figured, she'd either break out into hysterics or throw up all over herself.

He caught Cate's eye. She was scared all right, and despite his distrust of her, his unremitting fury that she had deceived him not once but time and time again, he wanted to be next to her.

The shaking worsened. The starboard overhead luggage bin fell open. A handheld fire extinguisher tore loose from its clasps and crashed onto Boris's head. Oxygen masks dangled from the ceiling. In the galley, plates tumbled from their shelves, shattering. A chaotic choreography danced to the nerve-jangling accompaniment of Tatiana's grating scream.

Then, just as suddenly, there was calm. The plane righted itself. The nose came up and they resumed a steady climb. The engines purred. Sunlight flooded the cabin.

Unbuckling himself, Gavallan crossed to the Russian. Boris was shaken, and a gash on his forehead was seeping blood. Bastard, thought Gavallan, too bad it didn't break your neck. Finding his handkerchief, he pressed it to the cut. "Keep pressure on it."

"*Spaseeba*," said the Russian, removing the compress, seeing the blood and swearing. "You want to talk, you go now," he said, jutting a thumb over his shoulder toward Cate. "Maybe you don't have so much chance later. I take Tatiana to the bathroom. Clean her up. Go. I owe you favor."

Gavallan waited until Boris passed him, an arm around Tatiana's shoulder en route to the lavatory, then walked fore and took a seat facing Cate. He wanted to make light of the bumpy ride, to offer her his pilot's confident smile and say, "That was nothing," but the words caught in his throat. He'd left his store of niceties back on the tarmac, along with his willful naïveté. One question needed to be asked.

"Did he know about us?"

Cate looked at him for a moment, not saying anything, her flashing eyes boring into him with unsettling frankness. "Who? Father?" She gave a tired laugh. "Yes, Jett, he knew."

Gavallan glanced out the window. They had climbed above the clouds and were soaring across an azure sea. Sporadic lightning flashed below in a downy gray quilt, smothered eruptions that reminded him of distant gunfire.

"Well, that explains a lot," he said. "You both had me going, I'll say that. Jett, the consummate dealmaker. Mr. Big Shot wangling Mercury away from Goldman and Merrill and every other big swinging dick on the street. Hell, those suckers didn't have a chance. At least I know how Pillonel learned that Black Jet was getting the deal a month before I did."

"What do you mean?"

"Didn't you hear him this morning? Your father recruited him in November to do his dirty work. You know, to fake the due diligence and say that Mercury was more than the sum of its parts. The funny thing is, Black Jet didn't win the deal until January. Remember? You refused to toast the occasion. I drank the entire bottle of DP myself."

"Yes, I remember."

"I paid your father fifty million dollars of my firm's money to win a deal he had every intention of giving me anyway. This is enormous, Cate. I handed a man fifty million bucks to give me the royal screwing of the century. I sank my company for no reason whatsoever."

"Jett, don't do this to yourself."

"And you knew the whole time that it was rotten. The story just gets better and better."

"My father was involved. It couldn't be legitimate. It's that simple." Her tone was apologetic, conciliatory. "I tried saying everything I could to put you off the deal: 'Kirov's a crook.' 'You can't trust an oligarch.' I reminded you he'd gone bankrupt twice before."

"Yeah, yeah, yeah," said Gavallan. "We've already had this conversation."

"What else did you want me to say?"

"How about the truth?"

"I already told you. If you'd done your job, you would never have touched the deal to begin with."

"If you'd told me he was your father, if you'd told me about what happened to Alexei, I would have pulled the plug in a New York minute." He looked at the floor for a moment, then back at Cate. "Why?" he asked again.

She hesitated, her emotions close to the surface. "I couldn't. I just couldn't."

"Of course you could! Ten people, Cate. Ten people are dead. Graf ... the company ..." He shook his head, and then the anger, the frustration, the deception, grew too much for him to bear. Balling his hand into a fist, he pounded on the armrest once, twice, three times, with all his might. "He's my friend. My best friend. He's got kids. He doesn't deserve this."

"I didn't know what would happen," Cate shot back. "None of us did. You can't blame me. You have no right, no right at all. You don't know what I've been through, why I'm even here."

"Then tell me. But this time, I'd appreciate the truth, *Miss Kirov.*"

Cate sat straighter, and when she spoke the apology that had cracked her voice had fled. Anger, disdain, conviction, seeped in, bonding the fissures. "Five years ago, I swore that Konstantin Kirov would never be a part of my life again. I vowed to myself that my father would never touch me again in any way. I moved back to the States. I changed my name. I found a job as a journalist. I built myself a new life from scratch. I became Cate Magnus and I stopped being Konstantin Kirov's daughter. I tried to pretend my father no longer existed, but it was impossible. For me, he will always exist, his birthright like a disease." She took a breath. "Did you know I skated, Jett? That I was an alternate to the Russian Olympic team in 1988 when I was only fifteen? The day I left Moscow, I quit. Did you know that my favorite writer is Chekhov? Or that I adore Tchaikovsky? That I cry every time I hear the Violin Concerto in D Minor? Since coming back to the States, I haven't read a page of Chekhov or listened to a single piece of Tchaikovsky. I can't, because *he* gave me those things. He gave me his love of literature, of art, of music, and I will have nothing to do with him. Nothing! It's like having dirt all over your body that you can't get off. No matter how much I wash, how hard I scrub, I can't clean his blood out of my veins or his name from my soul. Inside, I will always be Katya Kirov. And I will always hate being her. At least on the outside I can be someone I like. Someone other people might like, too."

"You could have told me. I would have understood."

"I don't want you to understand! That's the whole point." Cate squirmed in her seat, and he could sense the frustration that was consuming her. "For me, he does not exist. Or do you think I should have given up everything I'd built, all I had become, to help you avoid a bad business deal?" She stopped, staring hard into his eyes. "Besides, Jett, I did tell you. You just weren't listening."

"I didn't listen? To what?" And then it hit him. He exhaled grimly, stunned. "You said no because he was your father."

Cate nodded. "When I saw that no matter what I said you wouldn't back away from the deal, I had no choice. If we stayed together, I knew it was inevitable you'd find out the truth, my secret history. I couldn't allow that. No matter how happy we might have been together"—she grabbed Jett's hands and squeezed them lovingly—"I would have been terrified of that day. I can see now that you would have understood ... that it's me who's the problem ... but I don't care. Even now, I despise you seeing me as his daughter. I hate you knowing. I'm not like him, Jett. Not at all."

"Of course you're not," said Gavallan after a moment. But he was unable to bring himself to sit next to her.

SO, IS CATE YOUR REAL NAME?" he asked. The door to the lavatory was open and he could see Boris wiping a washcloth across Tatiana's face. "I mean, if your last name's Kirov, maybe the rest is different, too."

"Actually, it's Ekaterina Konstantinovna Elisabeth. My mother was a quarter English. Her grandmother married an English soldier who'd come to fight alongside the Whites in 1920."

"Where'd you come up with Magnus?" But even as he asked, the answer came to him. "Oh, I get it. 'Magnus' as in great ... as in 'Catherine the Great.' Clever."

A modest shrug. "I had to come up with something."

All you had to do was look and you'd have known, Gavallan scolded himself. The high cheekbones, the Slavic eyes. It was all in front of you the whole time. He remembered how their conversations had always turned awkward when he'd made even the slightest mention of her father, the moderately successful international trader. Never a picture. Never a word.

"And what you said about Kirov—er ... your father—it's true?"

"You mean about killing Alexei? Yes. It's true. Pretty awful, huh?"

"It's beyond that."

"All in a day's work for Mr. Kirov," she said, her jaw riding high, eyes to the fore, the soldier bearing up under her ungodly burden. He could tell she was fighting to keep it together, doing whatever jig or two-step she danced to prevent all those jagged edges rustling around inside her from ripping her to bits.

"What hurt most was the betrayal," she went on, the hurt ripe in her voice eight years later. "Learning that your father wasn't the man he'd built himself up to be. He meant everything to me. Mommy was dead. I had no brothers or sisters. He was the world."

"I can imagine."

"Did you know that originally he was a curator at the Hermitage? Icons were his specialty. He was one of the world's leading authorities on religious subjects. When the winters grew cold and the heating in our apartment building gave out, we'd spend whole weekends inside the museum just to keep warm. He would take me through the workshops below the palace and show me how the paintings were renovated—so much paint, so much albumen, so much shellac. You should have heard him preach. 'Art was honest. Art was untainted. Art was the truth. Everything we could be, if only we tried.' This was in '85 or '86. 'Perestroika' was the word of the day. Glasnost was in full bloom. Suddenly, it was okay to admit how worm-eaten the regime was. Art was his way of proving that even in a lousy world, light still shines. Or at least that's what he had me believe. All the while he was smuggling icons from the museum's stock out of the country, building up a fortune on the side."

"What about Choate? What about growing up in Connecticut?"

"Don't worry, Jett, I'm not a total phony. I'm still a Choatie. My father had me thinking that one of his rich American friends was paying my tuition. When he was arrested and the checks suddenly stopped coming, I was able to convince the headmaster to let me finish up my classes and graduate. One semester without tuition, he could let slide. He couldn't kick out the valedictorian, could he?"

"I guess not," said Gavallan.

"Anyway, soon Kirov was back in business. No more skulking through dark alleys. Now he could conduct his affairs in the open. The K Bank, he called it. Finally, he was the businessman he'd always aspired to be. Everything aboveboard. On the straight and narrow. I forgave him. Worse, I believed in him again. 'Katya, we are making Russia great again!' he would say. 'Come join me. Work at my side.' You know how persuasive he can be."

Gavallan nodded. Yes, he knew. He had believed Kirov too. Every word.

"I took a plane to Moscow the same day I finished my exams at Wharton," she continued. "I couldn't wait to get to work. To help make Russia great again. To rebuild my country. The Rodina, we call it. The motherland. And then..."

Behind them the lavatory opened, and Cate clipped her words. The sound of running water mixed with weary sobs drifted into the cabin. Checking over his shoulder, he saw Boris's muscled shoulders easing into the gangway. Cate tapped his knee, and he said, "What?"

When he turned back, he saw that she'd opened her purse and was handing him her pink compact. "What should I do with these?" she asked, a thumb flicking her makeup kit open. Tucked inside were the minidiscs Pillonel had given them from Silber, Goldi, and Grimm.

"Jesus, you still have those?"

Cate nodded eagerly, her eyes darting over his shoulder. "Take them. Quickly."

Gavallan recalled the painstakingly correct and intimate strip search to which he'd been subjected in Geneva. He'd assumed Cate, as a fellow prisoner, had suffered like treatment. "No. They're better with you," he said, glancing over his shoulder. "If anything happens, get them to Dodson."

"But—"

"Cate. Keep them. Use them if you get a chance." He held her eyes, signaling he had no illusions about what awaited him when they landed.

Rising, he headed aft, loitering in the cramped gangway long enough to allow her to conceal the financial records that were their only proof against Konstantin Kirov and the key to the salvation of Black Jet Securities.

49

WHAT DO YOU MEAN he's not in your booking facility?"
Howell Dodson demanded, the phone to his ear. He was
very angry. His cheeks had points of red in them, and he
jabbed at his distant interlocutor with the arm of his bifocals. "You only got him yesterday. Would you be so
kind as to tell me what goes on in the Swiss penal system
between Saturday night and Sunday afternoon?"

"He was released on order from the government," responded the unnamed party who had fielded Dodson's
call. "I am sorry."

"*Released? To whom? When?* I'm the government who
wants him. Do you mean to tell me some other country
has issued a warrant for Gavallan's arrest?"

"*Non, non.* You misunderstand," the polite French-
accented voice chirped. "Our government ordered his
release. The *Swiss* government, Monsieur Dodson."

Dodson chewed on his eyeglasses, fighting a rear-
guard action against fury, guilt, and incredulity. Gavallan
was gone? It couldn't be. Lord help him, it just couldn't
be. He looked toward the matching strollers parked in a
corner of his office. The boys were having their morning
nap, bless their souls, while their mother attended a
Baptist service in Georgetown. Outside, a cloudy sky

promised rain. At nine-thirty on a Sunday morning, the streets of the nation's capital were asleep.

"Who signed for his release?" Dodson asked, in a calmer voice to avoid disturbing his two dozing generals.

"*Un instant, je vous en prie.* One moment."

Waiting, Dodson walked across the room and gazed down at Jefferson and Davis bundled up in their powder blue blankets. It was hard not to lean over and give each a kiss on the cheek. Gone barely two days and he had missed them like the dickens.

Learning that Gavallan had been detained and incarcerated by the Swiss gendarmes, Dodson had returned to Washington the night before. It had turned out Gavallan was their man after all. He owned a gun similar to that used in the Cornerstone shooting. The gun was missing—ergo, he had taken it with him. He'd received training as an elite commando. And of course, he had every reason to want Luca dead. Though as yet circumstantial, the evidence was overwhelming.

In Geneva, the slippery voice returned to the phone. "A lawyer named Merlotti signed for Mr. Gavallan."

"And he's with the government?" Dodson asked.

"*Non, non.* You misunderstand. He's a private citizen, of course. A prominent attorney, actually."

"But you said Mr. Gavallan was released to the government."

"*Non, non.* You misunderstand," the man said again in his singsong voice. "I say that the government permitted Mr. Gavallan to be released to Mr. Merlotti."

"And for whom does Mr. Merlotti work?"

"That I do not know."

Of course not, Dodson grumbled inwardly. No doubt it would constitute a violation of your canons of secrecy, confidentiality, and inbred chicanery. "I'm sorry, sir, but I didn't get your name yet?"

"LeClerc. Georges LeClerc."

"Well, Mr. LeClerc," Dodson said, "if I cannot speak

with Mr. Gavallan, would you be so kind as to connect me with your own Detective Sergeant Panetti?"

"That is not possible. Sergeant Panetti is on holiday."

"Will he be back tomorrow?"

"*Non, non.* You misunderstand. He is on *summer* holiday. He will return in three weeks."

If Howell Dodson "misunderstood" one more time, he vowed to himself, he was going to catch the next plane to Geneva and beat LeClerc over the head with the phone until he *under*stood that the FBI meant business. Then the words sunk in.

"Three weeks!" Dodson shouted, losing his cool, then checking his voice and darting a glance at the twins. Jefferson stirred and began to cry. "You've got to be—"

The light went on in his head, and he stopped arguing. It was a put-up job. LeClerc was running interference for some very powerful, very nasty shit who'd pulled some strings high up in the Swiss government to have Jett Gavallan released. Some VVIP who did not want anyone knowing his identity.

"And that's it?" Dodson picked up the wailing infant and held him to his shoulder. Patting his boy on the back, bouncing lightly as he walked the room, he wondered if this officious Swiss prick actually expected the United States Federal Bureau of Investigation, the goddamned finest law enforcement outfit on Earth, to give up searching for a fugitive wanted for capital murder as easy as that. The mere suggestion infuriated him.

"I'm afraid we cannot help. Mr. Gavallan is no longer in the country."

"Isn't he?" asked Dodson. For once they were getting somewhere. "Has he returned to America?"

"I'm afraid I cannot say where he has gone."

Of course not. "Just one last thing," said Dodson, as Davis began to stir in his carriage. "The girl who was with him? Miss Magnus? Where is she?"

"They leave together," LeClerc replied promptly,

eager to be free of his responsibilities to international justice.

"That's what I thought," said Dodson. "*Au revoir.*"

Asshole, he added silently, in a most ungentlemanly tone.

THEY CANNOT DO THAT," declared Roy DiGenovese unequivocally. "If a suspect is detained on the basis of an international warrant, he may be released only to the custody of the government that issued the warrant, and then only if he's waived his right to fight extradition. It's a mistake. Has to be. He must have been transferred to a different jail, maybe to a federal prison. There's one near Bern. It makes sense. He'd be nearer our embassy."

DiGenovese had rushed back from San Francisco, arriving at six that morning. Still glowing from his triumph, he was dressed in a sports shirt and blazer, his black hair neatly combed. Dutifully, he held young Jefferson in his arms, cradling him back and forth.

"That's what I aim to find out," Dodson stated. "I'm as appalled as you are."

The phone rang and he picked it up. It was the international operator with the private number of a Mr. Silvio Panetti. Jotting down the phone number on his blotter, he thanked the operator, then called Panetti.

The detective answered on the third ring. Dodson introduced himself and asked what in the world was going on with Gavallan.

"Business as usual," answered Panetti, sounding half in the bag. "We pick up your Mr. Gavallan Saturday afternoon. A formal arrest on the Interpol mandate cannot be filed until Monday. Through their contacts, Mr. Gavallan's lawyers were able to secure his release before the charges were ever filed. Officially, Gavallan was never apprehended. It is a triumph of technicalities."

Dodson thought it was a crock of shit, pardon his

French, and he planned on filing a formal complaint. "Any idea where he went, Detective Sergeant?"

"You know, Monsieur Dodson, I am on vacation," Panetti protested perfunctorily. "I am not supposed to discuss official police business. On the other hand, I was not planning on taking this vacation, so what the hell, I tell you. After leaving the station, Gavallan drive directly to the *aeroport*. Please understand, I did not see him, not with my eyes, but my friend say he climb on a private jet."

"Was Miss Magnus with him?"

"Yes. She go, too."

"Any destination?"

"*Je ne sais pas*. I don't know and I don't ask. I am already too much involved, I think. I am smart, Mr. Dodson, not brave. You want to know where Gavallan go? You find out for yourself."

"Surely you can phone the airport...."

"Surely you can, too. *Au revoir, Monsieur. Bonne chance*."

Dodson hung up the phone.

"Where is he?" asked DiGenovese. "Is he headed back this way?"

"Gone," said Dodson, taking Jefferson from his assistant and laying him on his shoulder. "Vanished into the night."

50

THE PLANE TOUCHED DOWN at Moscow Sheremetyevo Airport just after midnight. A light rain fell, collecting into greasy puddles on the tarmac. The air smelled stubbornly of smoke and exhaust. Deplaning, they were led to a convoy of black Chevrolet Suburbans. A corps of rugged, sloe-eyed men in navy tracksuits lined the path. One waved his hand at Gavallan, pointing the way to an opened door. A funeral cortege, thought Gavallan as he slid into the backseat. A day or two and the same cars will be taking me to the cemetery.

The ride into the city took forty minutes. Cate sat up front, sandwiched between the driver and Boris. Tatiana slouched next to Gavallan, sullen and listless after the flight. The driver turned on the radio and a mishmash of wailing voices, discordant guitars, and arrhythmic tambourines filled the car. Top 40 from the Muslim republics to the south, Gavallan thought. It was brash, unsettling, and foreign, and it made him feel alone and abandoned. Stretching an arm forward, he found Cate's shoulder. A moment later, she took his hand, intertwining her fingers with his.

For a time they drove dead straight along a quiet four-lane highway. Billboards advertising a variety of products kept them company. Samsung. Volvo. Fisherman's Friend. Cate asked the driver a question and he answered politely, as if she were a guest, not a prisoner. She'd picked up two languages in a day: French, now Russian. Waiting for her translation, he thought, *This is the real Cate, and I don't know her at all.*

"We're going to my father's clubhouse in Sparrow Hills," she said, turning and meeting his eye. "Across the river where all the *nomenklatura* used to live. Brezhnev, Chernenko, Andropov."

"Just like Pacific Heights, huh?" Gavallan said icily.

They were in the city now, and it looked like the other parts of Russia he'd visited, only larger, more impressive, more desolate. The highway had been swallowed by a boulevard eight lanes across and they continued without regard for traffic signals. Green meant "go"; red meant "go faster." The grand avenues craved a dignified audience—skyscrapers of steel and glass, noble town houses, even a decent minimall. Instead, they were awarded stooped stone apartments and crumbling office buildings weeping soot and grime, all wedged together, all the same height, all devoid of personality. And then Gavallan remembered why: Personalities were allowed only inside the Kremlin. Or maybe these days in Sparrow Hills.

Suddenly everyone was sitting straighter, stiffly even. The driver turned off the music. Cate's shoulders left the seat. Even Tanya lifted her head from the glass to look. The motorcade descended a long slope, and ahead he could make out a bridge and, running beneath it, the choppy, evanescent surface of a broad, fast-moving river. To his left, the night sky softened, lit with a warm chiffon glow.

And then he saw it too. Bathed in the arc of a hundred discreet spotlights, a tall, curving fortress wall ran the length of the riverbank. The wall was painted an imperial yellow, with stone battlements rising every fifty feet, and behind it, silhouetted against the blue black sky, soared the swirling onion domes and proud towers that housed the seat of the Russian government.

The Kremlin.

He was in the heart of Mother Russia, and to his eye, it still looked every bit the evil empire.

JETT, MY FRIEND. How nice to see you again."

"Cut the bullshit, Konstantin," said Gavallan, walking past the man, ignoring the outstretched hand, the offer to play it as if the events of the past five days were nothing more than a difference of opinion. "We're not friends now. We never were."

"I suppose we weren't," replied Kirov. He looked fatigued. His pallor was funereal, his eyes pouchy and rimmed with wine black circles. "Come and sit. I'll be brief, then we can go to bed."

"I'd rather stand."

The two men faced each other in a stark, glacial space the size of an emperor's ballroom. The floor was a sea of pale travertine, the walls painted a glossy white. A sleek Italian couch and matching chair, both an incongruous orange, sat in the center of the room, a low-slung coffee table showing too much chrome between them. The only other furniture was an antique cocktail cabinet miles away at the far end of the room. If they seemed alone, it was an illusion. A brace of security guards stood outside the door, ready to enter at a moment's notice.

Cate had been shown to a study across the foyer. "I haven't seen my father in six years," she'd said. "I'll happily wait a few more minutes."

"A drink?" asked Kirov. "I heard you had a rough flight in. Something to calm your stomach? Cognac? Brandy? A Fernet, perhaps?" He strode to the liquor cabinet and poured two snifters of brandy from a cut-glass decanter. Even at one in the morning, he was his usual elegant self, dressed in a tailored navy suit and solid maroon tie.

"No," said Gavallan. "I want to talk to Graf Byrnes."

"I'm afraid that isn't possible. He's spending a few days at my dacha in the country. It's quite remote. No electricity. No phones. But don't worry: I'll make sure you two see each other tomorrow."

"That won't do. I want to speak to him now. You and I have nothing to discuss until I know he's alive and well."

"Oh, he's alive. You have my word. As for 'well,' that's a different matter altogether. I'd like to say his condition rests squarely upon you. What you do. What you don't do."

"News flash, Kirov: Mercury isn't going near the market until either Graf or I say so. Without our go-ahead, the deal will be pulled. Enough controversy has surrounded it already. My disappearance will be the last straw."

"Will it?" Kirov sneered, lifting the snifter to his lips and taking a generous draft. "There seems to be some concern that you've gone a little crazy. Hitting Mr. Tustin on the trading floor. Flying to Florida without alerting your staff. Fleeing the FBI. I have it on good authority that the offering will go forward as planned without your go-ahead."

"Whose authority is that?"

"Now, now, Jett. You don't expect me to show you all my cards, do you? Suffice it to say it's someone who can run the show perfectly well in your absence. Besides, you shouldn't be too angry if your friends decide not to follow your orders."

Seething, Gavallan circled the grouping of furniture. Who did Kirov have his hooks into? Bruce? Tony? Meg? Had the words not come from Kirov's mouth, Gavallan never would have thought it possible. Despite his fury, his heart beat slowly. His hands were cool and dry. His vision had sharpened. It had been eleven years since he'd felt this way. It was his calm in the face of a coming storm. "Battle-bright," they called it.

"And just what do you think is going to happen down the road?" he asked. "Mercury won't last two weeks once it goes public. You'll have analysts crawling over your operations like flies on shit. They're a tough group—nosy, ambitious, eager to make their reputation at your expense. They'll suss out the company's problems in no time."

"I'm not worried. With proceeds from the offering, we'll quickly shore up any remaining operational deficiencies."

"The money Mercury receives from the offering is slated for acquisitions that will insure you meet your forecast growth rate. That's cash to move forward, not to come up to speed. Miss one quarter's estimates and the stock will fall into the cellar. Miss two and it's all over. The price will dip below a dollar and you'll be delisted from the Exchange."

"I can assure you we have no intention of missing our estimates," said Kirov. "As per your own instructions, we have a few surprises in the pipeline. 'Unexpected' good news that will increase our earnings and allow us to beat our own optimistic expectations. What did you call it, Jett? 'Sandbagging'?"

"Sandbagging" was a common enough practice, a simple trick designed to goose the price of new issues six months out. The idea was to keep a little good news in your back pocket: a juicy contract about to be signed, word of another cable route about to be granted, a new and unforeseen use for a company's proprietary technology—anything that would augment your revenue stream and boost your earnings. Six months down the road, when the time came to issue your first earnings report, you peeled away the blinds and announced that "due to the dramatic customer response" to your new software or router or "fill-in-the-blank," your earnings had beat forecasted estimates by a nickel. The stock jumped 10 percent and everyone was smiling. Bankers. Customers. The investing public.

"Sandbagging's one thing," retorted Gavallan. "Lying about your customers and your revenues is another. What are you going to say about your problems with Novastar? Having the prosecutor general riding your tail doesn't quite fit with your investment scenario. It's my experience that investors prefer to see CEOs of newly listed companies in the boardroom, not in jail."

Kirov laughed softly, but his irritation was beginning to show. He was blinking incessantly, his fingers appraising the knot of his tie. "I agree that jail isn't part of our 'investment scenario.' If you're talking about Mr. Luca's article, I read it, too. 'Mercury in Mayhem,' I believe it was titled. A shame no one else will have the pleasure. Boris is very thorough. He promises me he erased the story from Mr. Luca's computer and that he confiscated every copy in the apartment."

"Wrong again," said Gavallan. "Even Boris couldn't stop Luca from E-mailing the article to his friends before he was killed. It's a matter of time until it turns up on the Net."

"So what?" spat Kirov. "One more rumor floated by a dead lunatic. One more piece of jetsam drifting over the ether. The public will pay it no mind. As for Yuri Baranov, I don't think he's going to be holding office much longer. I have it from a reliable source that the president is dissatisfied with his performance. Let me be the first to proclaim the investigation into Novastar Airlines closed."

Gavallan stared into Kirov's eyes, catching a glint of

real malice. He wasn't sure what Kirov was hinting at—Baranov's impending firing or his murder. He knew only that he was dealing with a killer, a man utterly without morals for whom murder was a legitimate business tool.

"I think there's been a little misunderstanding between us," he said, walking up to the oligarch, standing close to him to emphasize the difference in their heights, in the beams of their shoulders. "I'm the guy's got you by the short and curlies, not the other way around."

"Is that right?" Kirov kept his eyes locked on Gavallan's, neither man giving an inch.

"Before I visited Silber, Goldi, and Grimm's offices this morning, I took a few precautions to cover my ass, just in case something like this happened. You see, I'm pretty thorough, too. First thing I did was make a copy of Pillonel's original due diligence report and send it to my lawyer. We spoke, and I filled him in on everything that's gone on over the past couple of days. I told him that if I didn't get in touch by Tuesday morning at the opening, he should contact the stock exchange and the SEC's enforcement division. I gave him instructions to hand over the real due diligence report and to inform them that Black Jet was pulling the Mercury IPO."

"You're lying."

"Am I?" Gavallan picked up the brandy and downed it in a gulp. Fuck it. He needed a drink even if the poison came from a scoundrel like Kirov. "Pillonel was a big help too. Sang like a canary, Jean-Jacques did, right into my attorney's tape recorder. I wouldn't say the confession was entirely of his own free will, but so what—it'll do in the short run."

"You're lying." Kirov broke off his stare and retreated behind the sofa. "You didn't have time to make a copy."

"We had plenty of time."

"No, no. It's not possible. It simply isn't." The words were high-pitched, almost hysterical. Kirov's mouth twitched and his eyes furrowed in thought. "Why should you have bothered taping a confession? Was it not your intention to turn Pillonel over to the police? No. No. You're lying." And as he reasoned through Gavallan's actions, his voice calmed, the steady confidence returning. "You couldn't have known you were being followed. You had every intention of flying back to the States with your precious evidence. Maybe even with Pillonel. There was no reason to take precautions at that point. I wouldn't have. You're lying. I know it."

Gavallan shook his head, his iron gaze letting Kirov know he was not. Putting down the snifter, he pointed a blunt finger at his host, his jailer, his willing executioner. "Here's the deal: Tomorrow morning, you will wire me the fifty million dollars you borrowed from Black Jet. With interest. Graf, Cate, and I climb on board a commercial airliner and fly back to the States. And you will issue a statement that due to unforeseen market conditions, you've decided to postpone the offering to a later date." Gavallan thought about Ray Luca and the others at Cornerstone, enraged that no one would ever be brought to trial for the crimes. "Believe me, you're getting off easy."

Kirov's eyes seemed to bulge from their sockets, to expand with boiling hatred. "So now you're issuing ultimatums? Look around you—you're hardly in the right place. If you like ultimatums, however, I'll be happy to give you one of my own: The Mercury offering will go through. It will be a bigger success than any of us dares imagine. We shall earn our two billion and then some. And you, dear friend, will help see to it. Do you know why? Do you? Because if you don't, Mr. Grafton Byrnes will die. Slowly. Terribly. Very, very painfully. And you will be on hand to watch it."

"Fuck you, Konstantin. You've got the wrong guy. I don't respond well to extortion."

Kirov laughed, an ugly derisory snort. "We'll see very

shortly what you do or do not respond to. Personally I think your story about Pillonel is utter shit. But not to worry: One way or another we'll ferret out the truth. Either Jean-Jacques Pillonel will tell me or you will." He smiled invitingly. "I guarantee it."

51

THIS WAS WHERE ALL PATHS LED.

To Russia.

To Moscow.

To her father.

Cate waited alone in the wood-paneled den off the entry hall. The lights were dim, and the room smelled of new carpet and worn leather. Through the heating vents, murmurs of a violent conversation drifted to her ears. Jett and her father were arguing, and it made her afraid. She'd spent her last teenage years here. Something about the Edwardian house seemed to goad its inhabitants into perfectly dreadful behavior. She used to lie with her ear to the floor, listening to every word of her parents' fights, wincing, crying, silently ordering them to stop and make up.

The past.

Everywhere she looked it was crowding in on her, suffocating her with nightmares and obligations.

Moving to the window, she drew a curtain and peeked outside. If she lifted her eyes, she could make out the top floors of Moscow State University, towering above a stand of trees. Well past midnight, the building's lights were ablaze. Built in the late 1940s as one of seven

"Stalin Skyscrapers" meant to showcase Soviet prowess in architecture and engineering, the university was ever the brilliant trophy. The stern spires and bold, conformist tower were masterpieces of their kind and stirred in her pangs of nostalgia so strong as to be painful. It was not the first time this evening she'd been overcome with sentiment.

Passing St. Basil's, the Novodevichy Monastery, the Kremlin, even the most mundane of office buildings, she'd found her throat choked with emotion. These were the landmarks not only of the city but of a childhood she'd willed dead and buried, and each in turn provoked a cascade of memories. Cate and her mother pausing for a tea in one of the unsmiling cafes that dotted the upper levels of the GUM department store. Cate skating for the first time on an impromptu ice rink in the courtyard of their apartment building, the result of a broken main that had spewed water into the air for two weeks running. A reverent Cate, barely thirteen, passing through Lenin's tomb for the first time, frightened for the life of her to stare down at the great man's embalmed face, her teacher stopping her and forcing her to look, berating her in the sacrosanct hall to open her eyes and gaze upon the motherland's savior. She'd obeyed and fainted straightaway.

But the stirring went deeper than nostalgia. It went to her heart. To her blood. It was her history awakening inside her. The past beckoning her to return. She was no longer Catherine Elizabeth Magnus, but *Ekaterina Konstantinovna Elisabeth Kirova*, a Russian woman born in Leningrad to a Catholic mother and a Jewish father thirty years ago. There was nothing her devotion to the West could do about it. Nothing her love for Ayn Rand or her addiction to Bruce Springsteen could do to rectify the error of her birth. All were accessories she'd acquired to paper over her true colors. Garments designed to deceive, to camouflage, to lie. The intended victim, of course, being none other than Katya Kirov herself.

Too wound up to sit, she dropped the curtain and made a tour of the room. The walls were covered with photographs, cartoons, framed articles, and here and there a diploma or honorary citation. Their common link was Konstantin Kirov. There was her father with Boris Yeltsin. Her father with Gorbachev. A photo with Bush the Elder. Oh, how he loved mingling with the big names, if only so he might position himself as champion of the free media. If, that is, one's definition of "free media" meant using your television stations, your newspapers, your radio networks, to trumpet your own pet causes. If "free media" meant decrying taxes on aluminum production in order to favor your smelters in Krasnoyarsk. Or savaging the academic who had issued a report claiming that oligarchs exerted a drag on the economy equal to two percentage points of GNP. If so, then Kirov was your man.

Cate stared at her nails and stupidly wished she'd had a manicure before coming. She felt dirtied by her time in a jail cell. Catching a glimpse of her reflection, she flicked a strand of hair from her face, then rushed to her purse to apply some lipstick, only to throw the makeup back inside before she'd finished. Why did she give a damn about pleasing her father? She hated him and everything he stood for. He was a thief, a plunderer, a murderer. The epithets grew stale on her tongue, and pausing for breath, she was left with her original question: Why did she give a damn?

Unhappy sitting, she returned to the window and looked outside. A stream of headlights rolled up and down Kutuzovsky Prospekt. Marshal Mikhail Kutuzov, hero of Borodino, who had defeated Napoleon not on the battlefield but off it, by withdrawing his troops from Moscow and burning the city in his wake. There was something about his methods, something about sacrificing one's children for personal glory, be it a nation's or a businessman's, that rang a bell with her.

And taking a breath, she found the answer to her question. It had been lying in front of her for days, months, years even. She gave a damn simply because he was her father. Her blood. And she would never be free of her ties to him.

Worse still, he had defeated her once again. For all her actions to halt Mercury, her promises to avenge Alexei's death, her desire to help Jett, she'd come up short. She still had no way to punish her father for his sins. She was ever the little girl powerless in her father's presence. And she hated herself because of it.

HELLO, FATHER. It's been a long ti—"

Konstantin Kirov crossed the study in three quick steps, slapping her hard across the face before she could finish her words. "Shut up, whore."

Cate fell back onto the couch. Her hand dabbed at her mouth and came away red with blood. She struggled for something to say, but the onrush of emotions, hot and angry and prideful, cluttered her throat, leaving her defenseless and speechless.

Kirov gazed down at her, shaking his head. He looked older, smaller, ascetic even, but he had the same energy, the same conviction.

"How dare you even look me in the eye?" he went on. "Look away. Look at the ground. Out the window. Just don't set your eyes on me." He stalked to the window, threw back the curtains, then turned on her again. "Here is my darling daughter returned from America with her new name and new boyfriend. Have you any idea the shame you bring to my house? The disgust I feel showing you to the men who work for me? I brought you into this world. I cared for you in difficult times. I gave you an education worthy of a princess. And how do you repay it? First by sending your weak-spined boyfriend to the police with some ludicrous accusations that I was fixing the market for aluminum. I'll never forget that boy. That Kalugin. He lasted five minutes before spilling his guts, sobbing that you put him up to it. You should thank me for relieving you of his company. It was a favor, believe me."

Aghast, Cate stared at her father. He was no longer just a corrupt businessman, no longer merely a killer even. He'd become a monster. Inhuman. A beast. "Stop it," she said, her voice a whisper.

But Kirov went right on, trampling over her words as he had always trampled over her wishes, her desires, her opinions. "And now," he said, "after I allow you to make a new start, you dare to use all your resources to destroy the greatest professional achievement of my life. You conspire with the prosecutor general's office, you feed that sick-minded day trader rumors, you turn my partner against me—"

"Stop it!" she shouted. "Stop your lying! You can lie to Jett. You can lie to Baranov, to your adoring public. But you will not lie to me. I am your daughter, though the word scalds my tongue. With me you will speak the truth." Cate stood and pushed her way past him.

"The truth?" Kirov spun, following her, his expression saying he found her suggestion murderously amusing. "Oh, it's the truth you want, is it? You are a big girl now. A grown woman. I suppose I can tell you the truth. The truth is simple: We are building a new country. We are raising a phoenix from the ashes. What you may consider extreme is in fact mundane."

"I'm all for building a new country," she said through tears. "But legitimately."

"Legitimately?" Kirov jumped on the term. "The word is not in the Russian vocabulary. How can there be legitimacy when no one knows how to define it? You think everything must be done the American way. It is easy for them. They draw upon a tradition of common law dating back a thousand years. A thousand years ago Moscow was a swamp. Huns, Goths, Tatars ... we had them all at one time or another, riding pell-mell across our territories. Law was whoever had the faster horse, the sharper sword. 'Kleptocracy' is hardly a recent term. Only this time it's the businessmen doing the heavy lifting, not the government. Have you any idea what it took to bring Mercury this far? What it costs to bribe the Czech communications minister? The going rate to secure cable construction permits in Kiev? Do you? So what if we're not up to Western standards of transparency? We're starting from so far back it's a miracle we've gotten this far. If we'd kept to the letter of the law, Mercury would consist of two cans and a string. Be reasonable, my love. We are only asking for a chance."

"But you cheat. You lie. You kill. Ten people, Father. Why? Just to disguise the murder of one?"

"What are the lives of ten people to insure the prosperity, the education, the livelihood, of thousands? I would have killed a hundred if necessary. A thousand, if the Rodina demanded it."

"Another lie. You didn't kill Ray Luca and the others for the Rodina. You killed them to help yourself. To take Mercury public. To steal your billion dollars and make yourself rich."

Kirov approached her slowly, reaching out and taking her face in his hands. "But, Katya, don't you see? I had no other choice. As Mercury goes, so goes the country. I *am* the Rodina."

Cate grasped her father's wrists and took his hands from her face. She felt sickened, her soul nauseated. "No," she said. "You are not the Rodina. You are one man. You are greedy and desperate and you will fail. Oh, Father, you will fail. You cannot build a country on evil. If anyone should know it, it is we Russians. Hasn't our history taught you anything?"

"Yes," he said, suddenly thoughtful, sliding his hands into his pockets, pursing his lips. "It has taught me that perhaps we weren't ruthless enough. I, for one, will not repeat the mistake."

"You won't succeed. We won't allow you to. Not I, and not Jett."

Kirov laughed softly. "The defiant ones. A pity, really."

Cate looked at her father, wondering for the thousandth time how she could share his blood, carry his genes. "I'm the one who is ashamed. I am not your daughter. Not anymore."

Kirov's smile disappeared, and an ugly resolve settled about his face. "Be thankful you are, Katya. Be thankful you are."

His eyes said the rest.

Or you would be dead, too.

52

TWO VEHICLES APPROACHED from across the valley, their xenon headlights cutting an electric blue swath before them.

Christ, they're driving like hell, thought Grafton Byrnes, squinting at the harsh beams. As they neared, he yanked at the wheel, steering the truck onto the shoulder of the narrow road. The cars flew past in a flash, but a flash was all the time Byrnes needed to recognize them. Twin black Suburbans. Outland sentinels from the Kirov fleet.

Byrnes rammed his foot impotently against the accelerator. The engine did not respond. The pickup continued its downhill run, the gearshift parked in neutral, speedometer showing seventy kilometers per hour. He had run out of gas two miles from the dacha. Somehow he'd babied the truck to the edge of the slow grade that led from the hilltop observation post to the sweeping flatlands below. He'd been coasting for a while now. It was hard to tell how long. Five minutes. Maybe ten. He checked the rearview. The taillights were already specks, Satan's fireflies receding into the distance. They would be back. And when they came they wouldn't be coasting at a leisurely fifty miles an hour. They'd be hauling ass at a hundred easy, looking for the truck they'd passed five minutes earlier.

Despite his anxiety, a wave of exhaustion swept over him, and Byrnes gripped the wheel more tightly. His vision blurred. His jaw fell to his chest. Just as quickly the exhaustion passed, the band of cold sweat dampening his forehead its only reminder. He took a breath, steadying himself. Had he really expected to get away? He was feverish and half starved. His body was struggling to fight off the infection raging in his hands. He couldn't touch the steering wheel without wincing. How could he have thought himself in any condition to make it to Moscow?

Because he had been trained as an officer and an officer's duty was to escape.

Because Jett Gavallan would have done the same damned thing.

Because there was no other choice.

The slope began to flatten. The needle on the speedometer eased to the left—65 . . . 60 . . . 55. The rain had stopped. A half moon played hide-and-seek behind fast-moving clouds, its slow-blinking light casting a silver shadow across an endless vista of waist-high grass. Desperately, Byrnes scanned the horizon, looking for some sign of a village, a service station, an all-night 7-Eleven, where he could pop in, buy a coffee, and make a lifesaving call to the embassy in Moscow. The plain was infinite and dark, sheaths of grass waving back and forth in a whispering wind.

The speed continued to bleed—45 . . . 40 . . . 35. Byrnes guided the pickup off the road, letting it cut a path across the grass for a few hundred yards, hoping he might find a gully, a hollow, where he could hide the truck. No such luck. The truck hobbled to an arthritic halt on flat ground. Byrnes got out and looked back. He was close enough to the road to see the pavement. The roof of the pickup shimmered in the moonlight. Where to go? Where to hide? He didn't think about his chances. He had none.

He began to run. South. Toward Moscow.

The ground was hard and even. The grass fell effortlessly before him. He crossed back over the highway, hoping to confuse the pursuers he knew would soon come. His step acquired an ugly, pounding rhythm. Once he'd routinely run three miles in eighteen minutes. He'd cranked out a hundred sit-ups in a hundred twenty seconds and dropped from the bar after twenty-two pull-ups. Once he'd eaten nails for breakfast, spat fire, and drove his country's hottest jets.

Once . . .

Byrnes laughed bitterly at himself. He was forty-four years old. He drank a half bottle of wine every night with dinner. In the twenty-odd years since he'd graduated from college, he'd added thirty pounds to his runner's frame. The last time he'd run any kind of distance was a year ago on vacation in Hawaii with his fifteen-year-old boy, Jeff. After a lousy half a mile, old Dad had veered off the white sand beach and ditched at sea, crashing his well-marbled bulk into the delightful ocean water.

Byrnes thought of Jeff now, and of his daughter, Kirsten. He saw their faces in front of him. He ran to them. He ran to the warm saltwater oasis. His breath came hard. He was sweating, really sweating, beads of perspiration rolling off his forehead, stinging his eyes. The boots were small, tight in the toe. A blister was coming up on the heel. Another hour and his feet would be bleeding.

Still, he ran.

He ran because he was scared. Scared of going back to the dacha, scared of being caught, scared of what they would do to him. He didn't have the strength to go through another session with Boris.

"No," he whimpered aloud at the thought, fear beginning to grip him.

Mostly, he was scared he might betray his friend and the company they'd built together.

And for a minute his steps lengthened, his gait quickened, and he swore that he would not allow himself to be used by Kirov.

He thought of the pistol, of the cylinder that held five bullets instead of six. It was an old rancher's trick. You always left the barrel that was in the firing position empty. That way there were never any accidents. To advance the cylinder, you had to pull the trigger.

He wanted the gun.

He wanted the bullet. One bullet.

Mr. Kipling knew what to do in such an instance. Mr. Kipling, every soldier's favorite.

When you're wounded and left on Afghanistan's plains,
And the women come out to cut up what remains,
Jest roll to your rifle and blow out your brains
An' go to your Gawd like a soldier.

Panting, he recited the quatrain aloud. Again and again. Until he had no more breath left to talk with. His stride slowed. His legs grew heavy. His chest burned.

An' go to your Gawd like a soldier.

He heard the roar of a motor and looked behind him. Xenon beams swept over the grass; the murderous engine growled. He ran harder, dodging to the left, shooting quick glances over his shoulder.

"No," he said aloud, sucking in short, dry breaths. "God, no."

The lights dodged left, too.

Byrnes ran.

53

HE HIT ME. Six years and not even a hello. Just a slap across the face."

Cate walked into the bedroom, a hand to her mouth. She looked gray, pale, her eyes drifting here and there. Gavallan was at her side in an instant. Taking hold of her hand, he pulled it from her mouth and examined the wound. A nasty cut marred her lower lip. It had stopped bleeding, but without a stitch might open again. Closing the door behind her, he ventured a quick look into the hallway. A shadow sunk back into the doorway of the next room. One of Kirov's security boys. So far he'd counted nine of them patrolling the corridors.

"Come in," he said, leading her to the bathroom. "Let's get that cleaned up."

"Kind of you, Mr. Gavallan. It's not often a disloyal, disgraceful slut gets any TLC, especially at two o'clock in the morning."

He moistened a washcloth and dabbed at her lip. He had no words for her, no way to assuage her tortured feelings. Abruptly, she pushed him away and stormed into the bedroom.

"I'm leaving," she said. "Damned if he can keep me here." She spotted her travel bag and scooped it up.

"After all, I'm a traitor to his blood. An unrealistic dreamer who's getting back at her father for simply protecting his own interests. He shouldn't want anything to do with me." She reached the door and turned the knob. Locked. She tried again and again, finally slamming her fist against the wood-grained panels. "Let me out," she cried. "I'm going home. *My real home.* My name isn't Kirov. It's Magnus. Do you hear? I'm an American now."

Gavallan laid his hands on her shoulders, turning her slowly, taking her in his arms. "Sit down. Have a glass of water. It's going to be all right."

"No, it's not. It's not going to be all right. He's going to kill us. Like he killed Luca. Like he killed Alexei. Like he kills anyone who's in his way."

"No, Cate, he's not going to kill us. He just wants to frighten us a little."

She turned, staring at the walls, knowing as well as Gavallan that the room was wired for sound, and probably for pictures, too. "You win, Daddy," she said. "I'm scared. I'm scared as hell."

Gavallan got her to the bed and gave her some water. After a few minutes she recovered her calm. Her eyes cleared and her breathing eased. "Shit, that hurts," she said, touching her lip. "The little prick."

She caught Gavallan's eye, and they laughed. After a minute he walked to the television and turned it on. He flicked through the channels looking for something loud or raucous enough to allow them to talk or at least whisper freely. He stopped at Channel 33, a smile flitting across his face. A basketball game was under way, Lakers versus the Knicks. Game three of the finals. Turning up the volume, he retook his place on the bed next to Cate. "Tell me what your father had to say."

"He's rebuilding the country and we're stopping him. Mercury's his greatest professional achievement and we're letting a few minor details sour our view of the whole enterprise. We don't see the big picture. I'm the criminal, not him. I'm the one guilty of treason. Of harming the Rodina. He's gone insane, Jett. I swear it. 'L'état, c'est moi.' He practically uttered the words himself."

"What about tomorrow? Do you know where he's taking us?"

"No. He didn't say. We didn't end the conversation on an up note. He implied I should be glad not to be in Ray Luca's shoes with all I've done. What about Graf? Oh, Jett, I'd forgotten him for a moment. How is he?"

"Alive, from what I gather. More than that your father didn't say, except that we'll be seeing Graf tomorrow."

"Thank God," said Cate. "What else did you say to him? I hope you didn't threaten him."

"Only with the truth." Gavallan nodded subtly for her to go along. "I told him about Pillonel's confession and that my attorney in the States will turn over the due diligence reports if he doesn't hear from us. I told him I wanted the fifty million back from the bridge loan and that we had all better be on a plane to the States tomorrow. Graf included."

Kobe Bryant swished a three-point bomb and the crowd at the Staples Center went crazy.

Cate cast her head to one side. "Did he agree?"

Gavallan heard the hope in her voice. "No. He's convinced I'm lying. Says he'll find out for himself tomorrow whether I'm telling the truth."

"What does that mean?" Cate looked away, and when her eyes returned to him they carried the dreadful intent of her father's words. "No, Jett, he can't. You've got to—"

"Shh." Gavallan nodded reassuringly. "I'll be all right. He still needs me. I have the feeling he can't walk away from this deal."

"So do I," said Cate. "There's more to this than just Mercury's continued success as a company. It's much more than a mere business matter—Mercury's grown larger than just an initial public offering."

Gavallan rose and walked to the window, drawing back the curtain and peeking outside. The view gave onto an interior courtyard where two of Kirov's Suburbans were parked. A trio of guards were busy giving the SUVs the chauffeur's professional polish, leaning their butts against the chassis, talking furtively, and smoking cigarettes. Each cradled an Uzi beneath his arm. Gavallan tried to open the window but found it locked. The frame had been nailed to the sill.

Releasing the curtain, he took a second look at his carpeted prison cell. The room was large and luxuriously decorated in shades of brown and ochre, with a wooden four-poster bed, a sofa, a desk, a wet bar, a plasma-screen television hanging from one wall, and what looked like an authentic Matisse hanging from another. Welcome to the Stalag Four Seasons.

"Looks like we're here for the duration."

"The duration?"

"Of the night." He refused to think about the next day, about Kirov's keen desire to find out exactly what he did or did not know about the Russian's operations.

"I know you wanted to get me alone," said Cate, "but isn't this a bit much?"

"Hey, you know what we Boy Scouts say: 'Take it where you can get it.' "

"Very romantic."

Gavallan slid his arm around her waist and drew her near him so that their shoulders were rubbing against each other. Turning toward her, he lifted her jaw with the tip of his finger. He looked at her eyes, serious, compassionate, and defiant, and the faint circles beneath them; at her cheeks wiped clean of blush; at her broken lip stern, uncompromising, slightly aquiver. "You don't look so bad all rough-and-tumble, Miss Magnus."

"It's Kirov. Better get used to it."

"Okay, Miss Kirov. But not for long."

"Is that a promise?"

He answered with a kiss, gentle as a candle's breath.

"Oww," she moaned, smiling. She stood. "Stay here a second." Opening her night bag, she went round the room and covered the Matisse with a skirt, the mirror with a pair of pants, and the triptych of Moscow by night with her blouse. "I don't care if my father hears me," she said, "but I'll be damned if I let him see me."

HE ALWAYS BEGAN WITH HER SHOULDERS. The skin there was a shade darker, more luminous, an intimation of her mysterious self. Gently, he pulled her shirt away and kissed her, breathing deeply to get the scent of her, enjoying the firm response of her flesh, feeling the muscles quiver at his touch. He kissed her neck, the cusp of her jaw, and then, unable to wait any longer, he lay her down on the bed. She threw her arms above her head and narrowed her eyes. It was a temporary capitulation, a tactical maneuver to lure him helter-skelter into her ambush. She moaned, and he could feel himself falling into her, a boundless, head-over-heels plunge into a warm, velvety abyss.

Somewhere within him he found the power to stop, if only for a second. He raised himself on an elbow to look at her. He saw not just her beauty but the sum of her self staring back at him: her strength, her courage, her will. Her humor, her obstinance, her frailty, her fear. She met his gaze, and her frank ardor roused in him a heady sensation, a cocktail equal parts respect, desire, honor, and lust that he had come to recognize as love.

"Jett."

Her voice was husky, ripe, unfulfilled. Raising a hand to the back of his head, she ran her lithe fingers through his hair and pulled him to her.

He surrendered.

IN ANOTHER BEDROOM, in a less surveilled wing of the house, Konstantin Kirov lay awake, unable to sleep. Through a drizzly haze he was visited by a revolving medley of faces—Baranov, Volodya, Leonid, Dashamirov— each taking a turn to lambaste and curse and threaten him. Scariest of all was the father of modern Russia himself, Lenin, all too alive, rising from his dank tomb and waving an angry fist at him. "Mercury must go through!" he shouted as if addressing a band of discontented dockworkers in Petersburg. But instead of bread and peace, he was extolling the benefits of free market economics, of unfettered capitalism. "The offering is essential for the well-being of the nation. The president demands it. Your brother demands it. The future of the Rodina depends on it. On you, Konstantin Romanovich. *On you.*"

Sitting up, he pushed back his sheets and rubbed his eyes. He didn't know why he was worrying so. He had Gavallan. He had Byrnes. The Private Eye-PO was no more. True, he had a few loose ends to tie up, but soon those would be eliminated as well. He'd tracked Jean-Jacques Pillonel and his wife to a hotel near the Zurich airport where they were spending the night awaiting a 9 A.M. departure to Mahé in the Seychelles. With a sly smile, Kirov silently advised all bettors not to wager on the Pillonels making the flight. Seats 2A and 2B would remain unoccupied, their occupants last-minute no-shows.

And then there was Baranov. Yuri Ivanovich Baranov, the prosecutor general who didn't know when enough was enough. In the morning, Kirov would have a word with him, too, and that would be another problem taken care of once and for all. Mercury would go through exactly as everyone demanded, Lenin included!

Instead of lamenting his fate, Kirov urged himself to celebrate it.

One thing still bothered him: Katya. His beloved and unloving Katya. Sadly, he recalled the sting of his hand across her cheek. I'm sorry, my love, he apologized, seeing the blood curling from her lip, her eyes wide with shock and pain and fury.

Oh, Ekaterina Konstantinovna, why can you not understand your father? Why can you not see the sacrifices that must be made to insure our people's welfare? And our family's? Is it wrong to desire a nice station in this life? To earn enough to provide a few luxuries to brighten our short days? Can you not see that I am a visionary, a leader, and, as will be evident in a few short hours, a patriot, too?

Floundering for an answer, Kirov scowled, then rose from the bed. Crossing the room, he sat down in front of a bank of small video monitors, twelve in all, discreetly hidden behind a false wall of books. His daughter's room was dark. She had covered several of the cameras, but not those embedded in the crown molding. Playing with the controls, he was able to zoom in on the bed. Faintly, he made out her sleeping form, and next to her, Gavallan. It really was a pity about their not marrying. He could have used an investment banker in the family. He had little hope of Katya—or *Cate*, as she called herself these days—falling for the next director of Black Jet Securities.

Turning up the volume, he heard only steady breathing.

"Sleep, Katya, sleep," he whispered, kissing a finger and touching it to the monitor.

Kirov returned to bed and soon fell into an uneasy slumber. The dream came as he knew it would, the walls closing in on him, the ceiling falling toward the bed. He could smell the damp, taste the rot of centuries.

Somewhere deep inside a voice promised him he would never go free.

Lefortovo.

GAVALLAN ROSE FROM THE BED and padded to the bathroom. Darkness his cloak, he found the sink, lowered himself to a knee, and set to work. The first screw came off easily, the second cost his fingertips a layer of skin. Careful to make as little noise as possible, he jostled free the capton—a slim rectangular piece of metal that controlled the vertical motion of the drain—and laid it beside him. So much for the grip. Now he needed a blade. His hands ran from the U-shaped PVC drainage pipe to the smaller bore fishnet cables that supplied the water. A long slim rod, smooth and round as a screwdriver, ran between them, a bolt attaching it on either end. Only brute strength would free it. Sliding himself farther under the sink, Gavallan fastened his hand around the rod, counted to three, and yanked it furiously downward. The rod broke off cleanly, with hardly a snap.

Suddenly, he smiled. There was a time when his parents would have been glad if he'd said he wanted to be a plumber, or a carpenter, or just about anything else that would have stopped him from walking around town with his fists in front of him looking for a brawl to get into. With a bolt of clarity, he remembered how he felt in those days. The wild yearnings that would well up inside him, the unheroic desire to slug another man in the face—always someone bigger, someone imposing—to see the blood gush from his nose, maybe even hear the crunch of bone. For the life of him, he'd never understood why he was such a mean little bastard.

Now, these twenty-five years later, he had the answer. Divinity. God, nature, the force—whatever you wanted to call it—had provided him with some early on-the-job training for what was to come later in life.

For what was to come tomorrow.

Gathering the rod and capton, he slid from beneath the sink. A length of curtain wire would bind the two together; padding from beneath the carpet would serve as a grip.

He only needed something to sharpen the rod into a killing blade.

54

"You want Kirov, I can help. Meet me at Pushkinskaya Metro, southwest exit, at seven o'clock. And make sure to bring a briefcase. You won't believe the shit I have on him."

A coarse laugh, and the call ended.

Yuri Baranov, prosecutor general of the Russian Republic, put down the phone. Eyes rimmed with sleep, he checked his watch. It was six o'clock. Through the curtains, a hazy sun filtered in. It took him a few moments to clear the cobwebs from his head and evaluate whether the call was legitimate or a crank. Since the investigation into Novastar had begun, his office had been inundated with complaints against Konstantin Kirov. Everything from an employee's griping about her unfair dismissal to anonymous promises to obtain Novastar's offshore banking records. Baranov thought the call a ten-to-one shot, but decided to go anyway.

Rising, he ducked beneath the clothesline that bisected his one-room apartment, picking off a shirt, some clean underwear, and a pair of socks, then shuffled to the window. There was a carton of milk on the sill, along with a jar of pickles, some plums, and a plate of smoked herring left over from last night's dinner. He owned a refrigerator, but it was broken and he couldn't afford to repair it, never mind the electricity to run it. Opening the window, he brought the food inside and performed a hurried ballet, dressing and eating at the same time. A strip of herring while he buttoned his shirt. A plum while he threaded his belt. A last sip of milk as he knotted his tie.

Four days after seizing some eight hundred fifty-three pages of documents from Kirov's headquarters, his investigators had yet to find the evidence they needed to link Kirov to the millions of dollars stolen from Novastar Airlines. Oh, they'd dug up false receipts, double billings to clients, all manner of petty schemes to launder money and avoid paying income taxes. The practices were illegal. The state would file suit. But they'd come across no smoking gun that Baranov could set before a magistrate. The few documents he had found from the Banque Privé de Genève et Lausanne had led nowhere. The Swiss bank would not even confirm that Kirov was the holder of the numbered account.

Finished dressing, he considered taking some of the precautions that had become second nature to any government official working to put a crimp in an oligarch's style. He thought about calling his deputy, Ivanov, and asking him to come along. No, he decided; Ivanov deserved to eat breakfast with his family. Better to request a police escort. Baranov dismissed that idea, too. The police would never show up on time, even if they had a car parked in Pushkin Square. Besides, he wasn't so old that he couldn't meet an informant on his own. He was hardly meeting a gang of thugs in a dark alley at midnight. This was Pushkin Square. Early on a Monday morning there would be throngs of passersby.

Dressed in yesterday's trousers, his scuffed briefcase strangely light in his hand, he headed down the stairs and walked the fifty meters to the subway. The morning air was crisp and clean, not yet fouled by the legions of automobiles that had taken Moscow hostage these last years. Street signs advertised the latest American films. One showed four grotesquely obese Negroes seated on a couch, smiling like idiots. Baranov had no doubt but that the picture was an unquestionable masterwork, something Eisenstein himself might have directed. Giant billboards demanded he drink Coke and enjoy it. Part of him bristled at this relentless onslaught of Western imperialism, this secret invasion of the Rodina that was occurring can by can, frame by frame, ad by ad.

Relax, Yuri, he told himself in a voice that belonged to the new millennium. *Let the people enjoy themselves. Life is hard enough as it is. Besides, Coke beats the hell out of Baikal any day.*

He arrived at Mayakovskaya station at six forty-five. Descending the escalator to the Circle line, he ran his impromptu caller's words over and over in his mind. *You want Kirov, I can help*, the man had said. Baranov tried to put a face to the voice. Was it an older man or a younger one? A Muscovite or someone from Petersburg? He decided the voice was familiar. Was it someone in his own office? Or someone they'd interrogated from Kirov's? A Mercury insider, perhaps? Vexed at his inability to come up with an answer, he caught himself breathing harder and gnashing his teeth.

He had forgotten just how much he hated Konstantin Kirov.

JEAN-JACQUES PILLONEL was having a terrible dream.

He saw himself from afar, a tired, bent man dressed in prisoner's garb, gray dungarees, a matching work shirt, his feet carrying the heavy boots one saw on the rougher sort of motorcyclist. The man, who was at once him and not him, was marching in a circle around a dusty yard.

There were no walls, but a voice told him he was in prison and that he was not free to go anywhere else. He continued his rounds, but with each circuit his steps grew heavier, his body denser, his mass harder to move. He began to sweat. He was not frightened by his plight as a prisoner so much as by the impending impossibility of mere locomotion. He realized that his burden was not one of extraneous weight but of conscience, and that he would never be rid of this load. A current of anxiety seized him, threatening to paralyze his every muscle.

The scene shifted and he was looking in the mirror at this man who was and was not himself. He was gaunt, poorly shaven. His eyes were lost, forlorn. This isn't right, he was telling the familiar visage in the mirror. The reward for honesty must be greater, the relief more fulfilling, certainly longer lasting. The anxiety grew stronger, arcing up his spine, bowing his shoulders. Sensing he had no more time, he raised a fist and drove it into the mirror. The looking glass shattered. Everywhere shards of green and silver glass fell to the floor.

Struggling to the surface of consciousness, he felt a rustling in the bed next to him. A kick in the legs. He heard a shout, but it was muffled, distant.

"*Claire?*"

He opened his eyes.

His wife of thirty-two years stood across the room, held in the arms of a black-clad intruder. He had her by the neck, one hand over her mouth, the other pinning a knife to her throat.

"Claire!" he yelled, sitting up. A half second later a coarse, powerful hand cupped his mouth and forced him back down onto his bed.

"Silence!" The voice belonged to a stocky figure clad entirely in black. Black trousers. Black sweater. A black stocking snubbing the nose, rendering the lips flat, grotesque. The intruder wore plastic gloves and in one of his hands he held the knife. It was a monster, the blade twelve inches long, partly serrated, curling upward to a hungry tip.

"You've been a naughty boy," he said in accented French. "You don't know how to keep secrets."

"*Non,*" Pillonel argued. "I can. I can."

The flattened lips drew back into a smile. "We shall see, Monsieur Pillonel."

THE SUBWAY PULLED INTO PUSHKIN SQUARE at six fifty-seven. The timing was perfect, thought Yuri Baranov while riding the wooden escalators up to the mezzanine level. And as he entered the tunnel that passed beneath Tverskaya Ulitsa to the Metro's southwest exit, his gait assumed a triumphant rhythm. Something told him this was the real thing. That Kirov's goose was finally cooked. His step faltered only once, when he wondered whether the informant might wish some quid pro quo. Immunity for his own crimes, perhaps, which Baranov could grant. Or money, which he couldn't. Marching past the babushkas hawking their flowers and the Chechens their pirated videos, he decided he wanted Kirov so badly he'd be tempted to dish out a little of his own savings if it might help secure the villain's conviction.

A humble table stood at the end of the tunnel, covered with an embroidered muslin cloth and decorated with twenty or so candles of varying colors and heights, all burning. The candles served as a memorial to the innocent victims killed at the spot a few years back by a Chechen guerrilla's bomb. Some had whispered it was a ploy by the president to drum up support for the never-ending war against the insurgent republic. Baranov didn't believe a word of it. Volodya was an honorable man. Who else would give him free rein to pull in thieves like Kirov?

It was with a subdued smile that Yuri Baranov mounted

the stairs to the southwest exit of the Pushkinskaya Metro station. He did not notice the phalanx of young, crew-cut males who quickly erected a chain of sawhorses to block the tunnel behind him. Nor did he pay attention to the scaffolding at the head of the stairs, or the seesaw pounding of a jackhammer nearby. Construction was an omnipresent hazard in modern Moscow and the century-old subway stations were in constant need of repair.

The first shot took him high in the leg. He hadn't heard a thing and had it not been for the spout of blood that erupted from his pant leg, he would have thought it a bee sting at worst. One hand grasped the railing for support, while the other fell to his thigh. "This is absurd," he heard himself saying, and then somewhat irrationally, "It's Monday morning, for Christ's sake," as if murder were not a state-approved way to begin the workweek. His eyes darted around, but he saw nothing. A sense of desperation seized him. Frantically, he tried to continue up the stairs. He took one step and fell to the pavement, writhing in pain.

"Get up, Baranov. It's unseemly for government officials to grovel. Especially honest ones."

It was the voice from the telephone. The voice he couldn't quite place. Only now, he knew exactly to whom it belonged. Grimacing, Baranov lifted his head and squinted to make out the figure at the top of the stairs. "You," he said.

"Who else?"

Konstantin Kirov stood in a black suit with a black tie, hands on his hips, offering a gaze as morbid as his attire. "I have a message from the president. He asked me to deliver it personally." Kirov snapped his fingers, and someone tossed him a large rifle. A Kalashnikov. With a halting, unsteady motion, Kirov cleared the chamber and brought the weapon to his shoulder. The gun looked ridiculously large in the small man's hands.

"He said, 'Be quiet,' " Kirov finished.

Baranov raised himself to his feet. He felt neither fear nor lament, but a pervasive contempt for this pitiable excuse for a human being.

"Liar!" he shouted.

A hail of bullets riddled his body in time to the jackhammer's renewed assault.

TELL ME THE TRUTH," said Konstantin Kirov.

"Yes, I promise."

"What did he want?"

Pillonel hesitated, and the knife dug in. "Mercury," he said. "They knew I had faked the due diligence. They wanted proof."

"And you gave it to them. Without so much as a call to a lawyer or the local police, you gave it to them."

"They knew," said Pillonel. "They already knew, goddamn it. Gavallan said he was going to the SEC with or without my help. He was going to report me to the Swiss authorities." The intruder had tied his hands and feet to the bedposts with elastic cord and was kneeling beside the bed. In one hand, the man held the knife delicately, as if ready to fillet a fish, the point inserted meanly between Pillonel's ribs. In the other, he had a cell phone, which he pressed to Pillonel's ear. Pillonel had an urge to explain everything at once. "Gavallan had a gun. He put it to my head. I thought he would kill me. I had no choice. Of course I gave them the real books."

"I can understand your anxiety at being confronted with your misdeeds. But why did you take them to your offices?"

"Gavallan demanded I show him Mercury's exact financial condition—how much money the company had really been earning, its revenues, its expenses, its profits."

"And you showed him. How kind of you to be so helpful." The voice was more ominous because of its even tone, the complete absence of aggression, irony, or anger. "Did you ever once consider telling him he was mistaken, to leave you alone?"

"I couldn't. I told you, he had a gun. He said you had killed the man on the Internet, that you would kill me next."

"I never knew you for such a gullible sort." Kirov laughed, then resumed his unhurried interrogation. "And after Mercury, what did you show them? Did Gavallan have any idea he was so close to the crown jewels?"

"Nothing. I gave them nothing."

"Novastar?"

"It did not come up."

"Not even a mention? What about Futura and Andara? Baranov knew well enough about them. Didn't Miss Magnus have any questions about them? You didn't show them the holding company's banking records?"

Pillonel lay still, the lie poised above him like the blade of a guillotine. "I'm no fool. The records would take me down too."

"If you gave them Mercury, you were already going down. If I were you, I might have taken the opportunity to win over the authorities, show them the error of my ways, maybe even try to offer up something to protect myself. I'm sorry I must be so thorough in this matter, but I'm sure you can understand that it is of the utmost importance I learn exactly what materials you gave Mr. Gavallan and Miss Magnus."

Pillonel looked at his wife, his eyes begging her forgiveness. "I gave them nothing," he whimpered. "Only Mercury. Novastar did not come up."

"Ah, Jean-Jacques, you are a poor liar. Calm yourself now. You have nothing to worry about. I have them both with me—Cate and Mr. Gavallan. No more harm can be done. You don't have to worry. I think you know what will happen if you decide to go to the authorities."

"Yes, absolutely. Not a word."

"Now tell me the truth and you'll be on your way to Mahé before you know it. What evidence did you give Gavallan?"

Mahé. Sanctuary. A new life.

Pillonel grasped at the words, seeking solace and safety. His hands came away scratched and empty. *Kirov was also a poor liar.* "Nothing."

"Good. I'm happy for it. As for the confession, you know that they don't hold up in court when made under duress. Don't be too hard on yourself. I wouldn't be surprised if Gavallan's lawyer throws the thing away."

"What confession is that?" he blurted.

Pillonel heard Kirov murmur something like "I knew it" under his breath. Then he heard a harsher "Damn him," and he realized he'd said something wrong. Something very, very wrong.

"Well," scoffed Kirov, "at least this conversation wasn't a *total* waste of time. Give the phone to Sergei."

Sergei took back the phone and after a moment hung up.

"Well?" said Pillonel, eyes paralyzed with hope.

"Good news and bad news. The bad news is you're both to die. The good news is you go first." And even as the words left his mouth, he slid the razor-sharp blade between Pillonel's ribs, puncturing his heart and killing him instantly.

55

WHEN WILL YOU PUT SOME FURNITURE in this place?" asked Leonid Kirov, throwing open the door to his younger brother's study. "Every time I walk in I'm sure I've come to the wrong address. A museum or a mausoleum, I don't know which."

"I need space to think, Leonid. To imagine. To dream." Konstantin Kirov crossed the floor with a statesmanlike gait, extending a hand in welcome. "It is from rooms like this that our country will be reborn."

He was in an exuberant mood. Baranov was dead. Pillonel, too, but not before exposing Gavallan as one more paper tiger, his ruse about the taped confession a last, desperate ploy. All obstacles had vanished. Only time separated Konstantin Romanovich Kirov from reaping his billion-dollar reward.

He'd decided he'd had enough of Dashamirov, too. Fifteen percent was too much to dole out for a little protection now and then. Besides, he had a new *krysha:* the *komitet.* A few words to Leonid's colleagues in domestic security and the vile Chechen would be a memory. A billion dollars bought that kind of service.

"Come sit down. Have some breakfast. Not often we get a chance to catch up on things, just the two of us."

Leonid took his place at a table that had been set up for the two of them. Fastidiously attaching his napkin to his collar, spreading it across his chest, he appraised the bounteous meal. Broiled kippers, poached eggs, sausages, melon, bacon, and hashed brown potatoes. A grunt signaled his satisfaction. Lifting his knife and fork, he met his brother's eyes. "It's all over the radio this morning. You can't change the station without hearing it. A return to the days of yore. The gangsters are back. Nothing like a little fear to keep the naysayers in line. Well done. The president is pleased."

"Honesty was his only vice," said Kirov. "He was admirable in his way. Just outdated. Obsolete."

"Baranov?" scoffed Leonid. "He was a pain in the ass. Always has been. Even during the old regime, we called him 'our conscience.' That was not a compliment, I can promise you. God, but you made it bloody enough. How many times did you shoot him?"

"A full clip. I thought he was worth it."

"What do you mean, *you* thought? Don't tell me you got your hands dirty, younger brother?"

"I discovered I had a rather emotional attachment to the prosecutor general. I decided he merited my personal attentions. A hell of a way to relieve some stress, I can tell you that."

Leonid said nothing, but there was no denying the look of admiration. Younger brother had finally done something worthwhile. "Witnesses?"

"A few. We took their names."

"Give them to me. We don't want any trouble."

Kirov shivered, for the first time feeling the power of the state in his hands. No longer was he beholden to the likes of Baranov or Dashamirov. From this day forward, Konstantin Kirov was a partner of the state. An equal of Mother Russia.

He was *the Rodina*.

"And you?" Kirov asked. "All goes well? Where are you going with those boots? Perm?"

"Severnaya, if you want to know."

"Severnaya? Good God, that's the Arctic Circle. What gives you reason to go up there?"

Leonid gave a look at his boots. It was a proud look, Kirov noticed. A look of deep satisfaction. "Oil, if you must know."

"Have we discovered a new field? Wonderful news." Immediately, Kirov began to scheme how he could get in on things—leasing drilling equipment, securing a contract for the construction of the new pipeline, arranging a turnkey operation; there were a hundred ways to make a fortune when one was the first to learn of such news.

"Not exactly, younger brother. There is a new field, but it is not ours. These days it's not a question of too little oil, but too much. The world is drowning in the stuff. If OPEC ever opens the spigots we'll be back at fourteen dollars a barrel and that will be the end of us. If our country is to continue growing, oil prices must remain high. Twenty-seven dollars a barrel at least. Only then can we earn enough to keep our GDP growing at eight percent a year. Continue at this rate and in ten years we'll be a superpower again. One decade. It's not really so long, is it?"

"Not long at all. Then why the trip to Severnaya? It's awfully far to travel if there's no oil there."

"An exercise in prevention, younger brother. While we may wish for higher prices, others abhor the idea. One in particular has taken to the notion of self-sufficiency. Unfortunately, they have the resources. It would be devastating to our country should they exploit them. We must see to it they do not consider the option." Leonid finished chewing a bite of sausage, then asked offhandedly, "Speaking of America, you do have Mr. Gavallan here, don't you?"

Kirov felt himself jolt, his stomach rebel.

"Don't look so surprised," Leonid continued. "Just because the *komitet*'s stinking bankrupt doesn't mean we don't do our job. Is he here or out at the field observation post with the other one? Excuse me, I mean your 'dacha.'"

"Mr. Gavallan is here. He'll be joining his colleague at the dacha."

"And Katya?"

"As well."

Leonid set down his cutlery, pulling the napkin from his neck and wiping his mouth clean with one stroke. His plate was spotless. "They are dangerous. Either of them can compromise the operation."

Kirov wanted to disagree. Never would he allow Cate or Gavallan to interfere with Mercury. Then, he realized Leonid wasn't talking only about Mercury. He was talking about Severnaya, the preemptive exercise he had cooking on the cusp of the Arctic Circle. Somehow the two had become hopelessly intertwined.

"Gavallan, of course," he added, a bit uncertainly. "I had no intention of continuing our working relationship. But Katya ... Naturally, she'll remain in Moscow under my supervision."

"Cut the crap, Konstantin. You know what has to be done." He leaned across the table, his square gray head looming foremost in Kirov's vision. "No one can compromise the *komitet*, younger brother. Our name may have changed, but our principles haven't. I'm sorry, but that's that. After all, this is the second time the little missy has tried to put you away. You should be happy to have an excuse to be rid of her."

"Come now, Leonid, let's be realistic. Gavallan is one thing, but family ... Katya is my only daughter. She's strong-willed, of course, but nothing more—"

"No buts, younger brother. Remember where you

live. The only family you have is the state." Leonid stood, buttoning his jacket. "So I can tell him you'll take care of matters? Clean things up? We don't like to leave a mess. That hasn't changed either."

Kirov swallowed hard, the taste of his bile acidic, repellent. He felt tricked, massively deceived. A victim. "Yes. Tell the president to have no worries."

"He'll be most grateful. Good luck, and remember, you are representing the country. The president will be watching on television. Oh, I almost forgot." Leonid reached into his jacket and handed his brother a small blue velvet box.

Opening it, Kirov saw a colonel's polished golden oak leaves. "What's this?"

"Message from the president. You work for us now."

SHE HEARD IT ALL. Not every word, but snippets here and there. Enough to piece the conversation together. Enough to grow as frightened as she'd ever been in her life.

"He's going to kill us," she repeated silently, as if repetition would make the certainty less ghastly. In her panic, she reverted to her journalist's guise. There's a word for it, she told herself. When a father kills his child . . . there's a word for it. But her distress was such that she couldn't remember what it was. Plain old "murder" fit the bill, and that was bad enough.

Kneeling inside the den, Cate kept her head tilted toward the heating vents. She had come downstairs ten minutes earlier, Boris her escort. Her father wished to speak with her, she'd been informed. Alone. But as Boris locked her in, she caught the back of her uncle Leonid charging into the living room. He was unmistakable. The blue suit. The stiff shoulders. The iron gray hair.

Her father and uncle had been estranged during her

childhood. Curious as to what common bond had brought them together, she'd pressed her ear to the grate. Listening, she had forced herself not to cry out at the tales of barbarity bandied about by the two men.

The doors to the den opened.

"He is ready to see you," said Boris, motioning to follow him across the foyer.

"Of course."

It was moving day in Sparrow Hills. At nine o'clock, the clubhouse was a picture of commotion. The twin front doors stood open wide, the muscular growl of a supercharged V-8 flooding the entry. The snout of a black SUV pulled into view. Car doors opened and slammed. Boots slapped the pavement. A steady stream of her father's bullies entered and exited the house, at least half sporting Uzis slung over their shoulders. Luggage was brought downstairs. Another Suburban arrived.

At last, her father emerged from the living room.

"Good morning, then," he said, with an affable smile. "I apologize for my behavior last night. I was distraught. I hope at least that you slept well."

It was an act. A murderous masquerade. "Fine. And you? Sleep of the innocent?"

"Always," he replied in his soft, deathly courteous tone. "I wanted to have a last word with you before you set off."

"I thought we covered everything last night."

Her father stepped closer, patting her arms understandingly. "Katya, there's so much you don't know. So much I want to explain to you. I'm sending you with Jett to my dacha for a few days. When I return from New York, we will sit and talk. I'm not the ogre you think. I will listen to what you have to—"

"What is there to talk about? Mercury is a lie, but you're going ahead with the deal anyway. You hold your daughter as if she were a prisoner." She shook off his hands. "We have nothing to talk about. Not now. Not ever."

Kirov retreated a step, a blithe smile on his lips. "I can see you're upset. It is understandable. When I return, we can speak again. If you'll excuse me, I must hurry. The pricing is set for four P.M. this afternoon in Manhattan. Bye-bye, Katya."

She fixed him with an unloving stare. "Don't you mean *adieu*, Father?"

56

THE GLOVES WERE OFF, the last semblance of civility fading as quickly as the Moscow skyline behind them. They rode in separate cars, Gavallan in the lead vehicle with Boris and two guards, Cate bringing up the rear with Tatiana and another two guards of her own. A glance over his shoulder earned him a twisted smile and a view of an Uzi pointed directly at his back, a taut finger laid across the trigger.

They lumbered across the Moskva River, then joined the Outer Ring Road, leaving the city along the path they'd taken the night before. Instead of turning off at Sheremetyevo, they continued north toward St. Petersburg. After that he was lost. The road markers were in Cyrillic and he couldn't decipher a word. The highway narrowed to two lanes and all signs of the city tapered off. Potato fields spread to their left and right, bordered by elevated dirt berms—half levee, half road. Occasionally, he caught sign of a town away in the distance and wondered how, without any marked exits, one was supposed to reach them. Birch forests came and went as if moved en bloc.

Gavallan shifted in his seat, laying an arm across the backrest. It was hard to sit still. Tucked into the waistband of his undershorts was the shank he'd fashioned the night before. He had no idea how he'd use it, or even if he'd be given a chance. Pitted against an Uzi with a full clip, a handmade dagger didn't amount to much. Whatever happened, he wouldn't go easy.

HER NAME WAS KATYA, once again, and as she drove, a gothic fantasy played in her head. She was the Czarina en route to Ekaterinburg. Anastasia, of course, on her last journey. Her fate was sealed, but she was too proud to acknowledge it. How many nights until the brigade of toughs stormed the lodge and forced her to the cellar? How long until her father's eager band of revolutionaries signed their name to her short history?

The first intimations of disaster came at 11:06 by the digital clock on the dashboard. The driver left the highway at an exit marked "Svertloe" and took up a new course on a single-lane macadam road leading intrepidly across a meadow-grass plain. Once the preserve of boyars, or nobles, and the wealthy bourgeoisie, dachas tended to be rustic cottages located in pine forests or near lakes or mountains. Most served as weekend retreats and could be found within thirty miles of the city. But one look at this stale landscape told her that no right-thinking man would build a dacha within a hundred miles of this place.

The road began a steady climb uphill toward a pine forest. The macadam quit, replaced by hard-packed dirt. She glimpsed silver. Straining her eyes, she made out a fence. She leaned forward, knowing it was her destination. One fence became two, each ten feet high and topped with curls of barbed wire. The gate, though, was in ruins, bent and mangled, lying to one side. They entered the compound, and she looked around. There were a few log cabins, nothing quaint or rustic about them. *The dacha*, indeed. One more of her father's sick jokes. The car pulled up in front of the largest building. She saw the windows and gasped. They were decorated with stout iron bars placed three inches apart.

This was where all roads led.

To Russia.

To her father.

To her death.

GAVALLAN SPOTTED THE RUINED FENCE and knew it was Graf. He was alive. He had escaped. He had crashed through the fence. Right now he was in Moscow alerting the embassy. It was a matter of time before they sent out their delegates in the company of the Russian militia. His blood stirred and he grew giddy with a desperate joy.

Then he saw the battered truck parked behind the main building, and his spirits crashed to earth. The pickup's fender was dented, the windshield cracked. Whoever had driven through the fence hadn't gotten far.

The SUV lumbered to a halt in front of a large cabin. Gavallan spotted the bars and knew he would have to act fast. Once inside, they'd be locked up and then he'd have no chance for surprise. He imagined that the day's agenda called for interrogation and torture, followed sometime in the afternoon by death. Call it the Russian trinity. He'd have to hit someone before he got locked up. He swallowed hard, steeling himself to the task. He'd never killed anyone, not with his hands. He was a pilot. Tell him to drop a couple bombs from twenty thousand feet and he was your man. Ask him to shove a three-inch blade into a man's belly and he'd say, "No thanks, that's the next guy's job." Except today there wasn't a next guy. Today there was him and Cate and five Russian thugs with at least two Uzis and a couple of handguns between them. He looked at the driver and at Boris. Who would be first? It didn't matter so long as he had one of the machine guns. That's what he needed. From then on out it would be a crapshoot.

"We are arrived," said Boris.

Gavallan descended slowly, pushing his stomach out to keep pressure on the shank, make sure it remained inside his waistband. The air was dry and dusty, hinting of resin and mint. He looked around, his eyes making a desperate survey of the compound. Besides the main building, there were three smaller cabins, shacks, really. Two stood to his left, fifty yards away. A third was closer, more a shed, constructed from pale birch wood. Gavallan thought he saw something move inside it. He looked closer. He could see the fingers of two hands extended through gaps in the wall, grasping the wood.

Graf.

His heart beat with a violent resolve.

The second Suburban pulled into the clearing and stopped. Tatiana jumped from the car, and a moment later Cate appeared. Behind them, Boris's cronies had formed a small welcoming committee. The Uzis were out, and not just for show.

Gavallan walked over to Cate. "It's gonna be okay," he said, taking her hand.

"No, Jett," she said. "It's not."

57

THEY STOOD IN THE CLEARING in front of the cabin waiting for Boris to open the door, a vacation party anxious to get into their summer rental. Gavallan held Cate's hand, every bit as much for his comfort as hers.

"You okay?" he asked.

Cate nodded, shifting her head toward him. "We have to talk."

The blunt nose of an Uzi jabbed Gavallan's back before he could reply. "Quiet. No speak."

"Take it easy, bud," said Gavallan. Irritated, he turned to face his newly appointed guardian angel, all two hundred and forty pounds of him. He wanted to shove the guy, gun or no gun. "We're not going anywhere. Give us a break."

"Fuck you." The guard had white blond hair done in a burr cut, dull blue eyes, and pitted cheeks that had fought a losing battle against teenage acne. He feinted with the Uzi and Gavallan jumped back, drawing a bored chortle from the spectators.

The drivers lolled against the doors of their Suburbans, arms crossed, smoking and chatting up Tatiana, who was dressed like a California teenager in Levi's, cowboy boots, and a black tank top. Her shoulder holster and pearl-handled .357 Magnum were strictly adult fare, though, and christened her the flat tops' dream date. She responded to their catcalls desultorily, her voice flat, her eyes glued to the cabin, to Gavallan and Cate.

She was a pro, Gavallan decided. She was trouble.

Shifting his eyes around the clearing, he took in the trees that stood stiff as sentries, the furrowed track that had brought them here, the twin fences, and the ruined gate. The entry to a storm cellar could be seen a ways off, next to a depleted woodpile. In the same direction were two smaller cabins, one with an antenna, the other a crude smokestack. But Gavallan's interest was first and foremost on the shed. He took a step toward it, pointing. "Is Mr. Byrnes in there?"

No one answered.

"Boris, is Mr. Byrnes in there?" The Uzi stabbed his back and Gavallan spun rapidly, knocking it away. "Hit me again with that thing and I'll ram it sideways up your ass."

Finished unlocking the cabin, Boris hurried back toward Gavallan. "Why you no shut up? We ask you once, twice. Still, you talk."

"You can't just—"

Boris fired a fist into his jaw, knocking Gavallan to a knee. "Shut up. *Ponimayu?*"

"Jett!" Cate jumped to his side and Boris picked her up kicking and struggling and carried her back a step or two. Setting her down, he rattled off a barrage of words at her. Cate relaxed again. She stood rock-still, her eyes glued to Boris. She was playing the obedient schoolgirl, and Gavallan was glad for it.

A little longer, my girl. Play along a little longer.

Slowly, Gavallan found his way to his legs. He hadn't been hit like that in a long time. It didn't hurt so much as make him want to give Boris one right back. Brushing the pine needles off his pants, he checked for the butt of his shank. It was still in place. I owe you one, buddy, he promised himself, meeting Boris's eye. Payback. And it's coming sooner than you think.

"My father forbids you to talk," Cate explained a moment later. "To me or to anyone. Graf is in the shed. He says if you want the same punishment as him, all you have to do is keep speaking."

"*Ponimayu?*" Boris repeated, firing two fingers into his chest. "You understand now?"

"Loud and clear."

Boris jumped onto the porch and waved his arm for them to follow. "Inside."

The Uzi nipped at Gavallan's back and he took a step forward, bending to help Cate with her bag. "I'll get it," he said. He needed the bag every bit as much as the shank that was cutting into his waist. The bag was his decoy. A prop to buy him time.

"Thanks," she whispered, her smile a present.

Gavallan crossed the threshold and looked around. The floor was wooden, swept clean and covered with a sisal throw rug. Four battered desk chairs were scattered about the place. A trestle table took up one wall. On it was a propane-fueled heating ring, a few dishes, and a tray of cutlery. A portable Honda generator sat in a corner, along with a space heater and two jerry cans he presumed were filled with gasoline. A pile of dirty magazines littered another corner. Man's fundamental needs had been reduced to heat, food, and jerking off.

"Nice place," said Gavallan. "Tell me, is it a time-share or do you own it outright?"

"You will only stay a few days," said Boris.

"We shouldn't be staying here at all. You know your boss is in trouble. Come on, Boris, it's time to call it quits. Let's all get back into the cars and go back to Moscow. I'll buy you a drink at the Kempinski."

Gavallan waited for him to say "Shut up," to throw another punch. But this time Boris merely laughed. "You think I should quit? And do what?"

"You've got a good head for the market. Use it. With your knowledge, I bet you could find a job as a broker in no time."

"With you? With Black Jet?"

"Why not? It's better than staying with Kirov. Where do you want to start? San Francisco? New York? Let's get Mr. Byrnes and head back to town."

"New York, eh?" Boris hummed a few bars of "On Broadway." *Un Brod-vey*. Abruptly, his gaze darkened. "Mr. Kirov is not in trouble. You are in trouble, Mr. Jett. Go with Ivan. He show you to your room."

"Boris, listen to me—"

"Shut up, Mr. Jett."

All trace of the Russian's former good nature had vanished. Gavallan knew why: He was steeling himself for the job ahead. Putting on his armor. As Ivan led the way down the hall, Gavallan grabbed Cate's hand. "Hang in there," he said.

The first room offered a cot, a table, and a wooden bucket. The second was less accommodating. A peek inside revealed a sturdy wooden chair with broad, flat armrests and a stiff back bolted to a concrete floor. He'd seen chairs like it before, but usually they had straps for your arms and legs and came with a metal bowl and a few electrodes to clamp on your freshly shaven head. The floor was stained black and sloped toward a drain in its center.

"Jett ... oh, Jesus, no." Cate's gait faltered, and Gavallan rushed to support her. "Go," he said, propelling her forward. Sensing he had a moment, he put his mouth to her ear. "Hit the floor when I tell you."

"What?" Cate asked, brow knitted.

Seeing Ivan's eyes on them, Gavallan backed off and didn't answer.

Ivan opened the door to the room at the far end of the corridor. "Come," he said, motioning them closer.

Cate ventured a look behind her and Gavallan nodded for her to go on, his eyes gifting her with the confidence he was lacking. She stepped into the room and, moving to the left, disappeared from Gavallan's sight. A last check over his shoulder showed Boris hovering near the front door, distracted, barking instructions to Tatiana and her suitors.

There were two cots placed against opposite walls with a window in between them. Cate stood to his left, arms crossed over her chest. She was nervous, her sea green eyes flicking this way and that.

"Which one is mine?" Gavallan asked, pointing at the beds. His body had gone rigid; his hands itched for action. His jaw still tingled from Boris's punch, and fighting blood stirred inside him. Ivan stood in front of him, the Uzi pushed back to his side, his forearm resting on top of it.

"Ex-cuze me, I no—" he began to answer, his fractured English bringing an ugly grin to his lips.

But by then Gavallan was already moving.

Shoving Cate's overnight bag into Ivan's stomach, he drove the white-haired Russian into the far wall. While one hand blocked the Uzi's rise, the other dropped the bag and freed the shank from his pants. With curt, vicious thrusts, he rammed the blade into Ivan's neck, once, twice, then brought his arm around in a windmill and stabbed the Russian in the back. His actions were savage, feral, unthinking. Ivan fought to push his attacker away, to bring up the Uzi, but his efforts were divided, unfocused. Hugging him close, Gavallan shoved home the shank. The Russian's back arched in spasm. His fingers left Gavallan and grasped at his ruined throat, but the only sound he could produce was the clotted cough of a man choking to death on his own blood. His body shuddered, then was still.

"*Ivan!*"

Boris's strident voice echoed through the cabin as his footsteps pounded down the hallway. Gavallan freed the submachine gun from Ivan's shoulder and let the corpse fall to the floor. "Down," he yelled to Cate as he darted to the doorway and his thumb kicked off the safety. He ducked a head into the corridor and a chunk of wood exploded from the door frame, accompanied by the ear-numbing blast of a large-bore handgun.

Blindly, Gavallan stuck the Uzi into the corridor and fired. Three short bursts. Left. Right. Then left again. He could hear the bullets strike Boris, three fastballs thudding into a catcher's mitt. His steps slowed violently and the Russian collapsed to the floor.

Gavallan peered into the hall. Boris was on his stomach, one hand patting the ground as if he were a wrestler signaling his surrender. The pistol lay a few inches away. Gavallan fired a quick burst and Boris's skull disintegrated, freckling the walls with gore.

"The others are coming," Cate shouted. "Hurry!"

"Get the gun and stay here," Gavallan instructed her.

With a leap, he cleared Boris and made for the open front door. Running, he glanced out the window. The two drivers were rushing the cabin. Tatiana was nowhere to be seen. Stopping short, he fired through the glass in a wide arc. His goal wasn't to kill but to halt Kirov's soldiers' advance. Both men dived headlong to the ground and, as if trained for this exact scenario, began crawling in different directions. The nearer sought refuge in the lee of the landing. The other skidded backward on his hands and knees toward the automobiles.

You can only get one, a voice whispered in Gavallan's head.

Steadying himself, he took aim and fired. A short burst, five bullets max. The black suit approaching the cabin stopped moving. Gavallan fired again. Filaments from the man's jacket flittered into the air where the bullets struck.

"Cate," he yelled, "get on your hands and knees and crawl to me."

Gavallan had slammed the front door and was running

from window to window, scouring the woods for sign of Tatiana's platinum hair, her blue jeans running among the trees. He didn't see her anywhere. Fire broke out from the front of the house. Bullets thudded into the cabin, then found the windows. Glass shattered and tinkled to the floor, sending him tumbling to the floor. Lifting his head above the windowsill, he saw their driver firing his Uzi over the Suburban's hood. It's a feint, Gavallan decided. He's keeping us pinned down for the girl. For Tatiana.

"Take the Uzi," he said to Cate, trading her the machine gun for Boris's .44 automag. "If he tries to leave the car, fire." He showed her how to hold the gun at arm's length and helped fashion her finger around the trigger. "Just short bursts. Fire; let go. Fire; let go. You don't have many bullets left."

Cate accepted the weapon, tried to get a feel of its heft. "Short bursts," she said, her eyes keen.

"Yeah, and keep looking every now and again. He may try to rush you."

"And you?"

Gavallan had remembered the woodpile twenty five feet from the cabin and the boarded-up entry to the storm cellar next to it. He'd already located the stairs to the cabin's cellar. The only question was whether there was a passageway leading between the two. Given the severity of Russian winters, he was counting on it. "I've got to check on something. I'll be right back."

Mindful that speed was a factor, he moved off before she could protest. The automag leading the charge, he crashed down the stairs to the cellar. The room was dank and dark. He scurried along the walls, his hand checking the concrete for a door. He found nothing. He took a step backward, puzzled, and a hollow thud greeted his footfall. He was standing on a trapdoor.

Falling to his knee, he slipped two fingers into the

rusty pull ring and yanked open the door. Stairs led to an abyss. Slowly, he descended them, one by one, and when he reached the bottom, he stopped. The room was pitch dark. He waved a hand in front of his face. Nothing. He listened. Nothing.

But what did you expect to hear over the hobnailed beating of your own heart? a voice chided him.

Hurry, he commanded himself. Cate is alone. And then, more frighteningly: You could be wrong. Tatiana may know another way into the house.

Groping the wall, he set out, holding the gun in front of him as he would have a flashlight. He calculated that twenty paces would take him to the storm cellar. Water dripped from the ceiling. Instinctively, he lowered his head. Something damp and sticky danced across his face. Grimacing, he swiped it away.

Ten paces.

"Jett! Come here! Now!"

Gavallan spun his head in the direction of her voice. He retreated a step. It was the driver. He'd gotten bored and was mounting his own lonely charge. Just then, the door to the storm cellar opened and sunshine flooded the passage. Gavallan froze, squinting to adjust to the light. A black cowboy boot landed on the stairs forty feet in front of him.

"Jett!" Cate's voice came again.

Gavallan slid backward, his head turning one way, then the other. On the stairwell, the boots became blue jeans, and the blue jeans were joined by a pale hand holding the pearl-handled .357 Magnum. Gavallan dug his feet into the dirt floor. There was no going back. Bringing his left hand up to the grip of the .44 automag, he assumed the Stableford stance: left foot forward, right arm extended, left hand supporting his shooting wrist. He waited until he saw her face—the diamond blue eyes, the pouting lips. "Stop," he yelled.

Tatiana's only reaction was to raise the gun as quickly as she could. Gavallan hesitated, but only for a fraction of a second.

Then he fired three times.

HE FOUND CATE standing in the center of the front room.

"I killed him," she said.

"So I see." The driver had, after all, decided to mount a charge—a very ill-advised one. His body lay twisted and prone a few feet from the Suburban. "Good shot."

Cate shrugged, laying the Uzi on the table with a professional's ease.

"Sure you never fired one of those before?" he asked.

"I never said that."

"I just assumed . . ."

Cate gave a crisp shake of the head. "Don't assume too much. Remember, you didn't even know my real name until yesterday."

Gavallan knew she meant it as a joke, but he could not laugh. He was upset, jittery, waiting for the adrenaline to run down, for the electric colors to fade. "Come on. There's someone here who's very anxious to see us."

"Oh, Jesus, I almost for—" Cate bolted out the door, jumping off the porch and making toward the shed. "Graf!" she called. "We're coming, Graf!"

58

MIND EXPLAINING THIS?"

Gavallan rested on a knee next to Grafton Byrnes, fingering the frayed bullet hole in his friend's jacket.

Pale, unshaven, dark circles denting his eyes, Byrnes sat on the bare earth outside the shed, legs spread, sipping from a cup of water. His lower lip was cracked and swollen. A minute earlier, he'd smiled to show Cate and Gavallan the incisor he'd lost after he'd been recaptured the night before and returned to the camp.

"All you need to know is I wasn't wearing it when it happened," he said.

"I hope the guy that was got what he deserved."

Byrnes looked away, his voice as distant as his gaze. "Oh yeah."

"All right then," said Gavallan, seeking to rouse the fighting spirit in Byrnes. He knew their freedom was an illusion, a temporary gift that might be yanked away at any time. It was a long trek to the border and he needed Byrnes at his side, not lagging behind.

Gavallan's eyes kept coming back to his friend's hands. The bandages covering his thumbs were torn, the gauze stained black with dirt and blood. His palms were colored rust, dried blood tattooing the flesh. "You okay, pard?"

Byrnes caught his glance. "Six months," he said, raising his right hand, turning it over in the sunlight. "That's how long I've heard nails take to grow back. Tell you one thing. I'm not ever getting another fucking manicure in my life."

"Amen to that," said Gavallan, patting him on the shoulder. He knew he could never appreciate the barbarity his friend had suffered. A glance at the bandages, at the wounded eyes, told him enough.

A breeze came up, rustling the trees, scattering pine needles across the dirt, and freighting the air with the scent of turned earth, loam, and, somewhere distant, burning leaves. It was a melancholy scent, and Gavallan was overcome with sorrow and sadness and a sense of failed responsibility.

"You ready?" he asked, getting to his feet. "Time to saddle up."

"I thought you'd never ask."

Byrnes stood shakily, throwing an arm to Gavallan's shoulder for support. He took a few steps toward the clearing to better see the shot-up cabin, the bullet-riddled Suburban, the corpses sprawled pell-mell in the dirt. He stopped. Turning, he fixed Gavallan with a stunned, disquieted gaze, almost as if looking through him. Then he rushed forward and wrapped his arms around his friend, hugging him tightly. "Thank you," he said, pushing his cheek into Gavallan's hair, and Gavallan knew he was crying. "Thank you for coming to get me."

Gavallan returned the hug. He tried to say, "Anytime— that's what brothers do for each other," but something was blocking his throat and he couldn't trust himself to speak.

THE SECOND SUBURBAN had survived the shoot-out intact. Not a dent in its black armor, nor a streak of dirt marring the high-gloss finish. Gavallan and Byrnes walked toward it, Cate following a step behind.

"Why didn't you just cancel the deal after I left you the message?" Byrnes asked.

"What message was that?"

"About the network operations center."

"It's a wreck. We know that. Just like the Private Eye-PO said."

"No," protested Byrnes, stopping short, waiting for Cate and Gavallan to face him. "It's not a wreck at all. On the contrary. That's what I called to tell you. It's a state-of-the-art facility. The NOC is Kirov's beard. Don't you see? It's his disguise. It's what fooled us."

"Fooled us?" asked Gavallan. "How?"

Byrnes described the vast room filled with row upon row of personal computers logging on and off Red Star, Mercury's wholly owned and operated Internet portal. "There were a thousand in there, maybe two thousand. I couldn't count them all. Each logs onto Red Star, then visits a site or two—Amazon, Expedia, the high-traffic sites. Some make a purchase, then they log off. A minute later, they dial Red Star back up again. Over and over, ad infinitum. All running off some master program."

"Metrics," explained Cate, pushing a comma of hair off her forehead. "Has to be."

"I was thinking the same thing," said Byrnes.

"You knew?" Gavallan demanded.

"God, no. But it makes sense. I just wrote about the same kind of shenanigans for the paper. You know ... how websites use metrics to manipulate the tally of monthly visitors. It's a gag to fool the firms that measure Red Star's traffic. Make them think Mercury has more customers than it really does. Jett, when you were doing your due diligence on Mercury, didn't you talk to a metrics firm to validate Kirov's claims about Red Star's size?"

"Jupiter in San Jose. Their report tallied perfectly

with Mercury's figures. Two hundred thousand subscribers in Moscow alone."

"Of course it did," said Cate. "He knew Jupiter or someone like them would be called in to check how many hits Red Star got every day. He couldn't risk there being a discrepancy. He needed two hundred thousand subscribers to justify his sky-high revenues, and two hundred thousand he got. Only his customers weren't customers at all. They were straw men, or maybe I should say 'straw machines.'" Cate took a breath. "Don't you see? It's a twenty-first-century Potemkin village."

"You're saying he set up shop out here and created a cybercommunity of Red Star fanatics?" asked Gavallan.

Cate nodded disgustedly. "Kirov had it worked out to a fault so you wouldn't question how rapidly the company's revenues were increasing. He knew from the beginning the kind of revenues Mercury had to post to max out its IPO. He could get the money easy. He stole it from Novastar. The subscribers were the hard part. That's what required the creative thinking."

"My God," muttered Gavallan, shaken. "He played us like a fiddle."

"More like a Stradivarius," said Cate. "But his performance is over. And there will be no encore, thank you very much."

Grafton Byrnes signaled his incomprehension. "Hold on, I'm missing something here. What's Novastar Airlines got to do with this?"

Cate explained to him about her dealings with Ray Luca and what had happened in Delray Beach, about the trip to Geneva and Jean-Jacques Pillonel's complicity with Konstantin Kirov to hide transfers from Novastar Airlines to Mercury Broadband and then to Kirov's personal accounts.

"But what put you onto Kirov's case in the first place?"

"Don't ask," said Gavallan, and Cate elbowed him.

"Actually, he's my father," she answered.

Byrnes's eyes registered shock. "You said 'father.' You don't mean ...?"

Cate nodded.

"Can't say I see a resemblance."

"Thank God for that." She went on with her explanation: "I don't think we'll ever learn who Detective Skulpin's informant was, but whoever it was that had the guts to go up against my father, I'd like to thank him."

"I think you can forget about that," said Byrnes reticently. "On Friday, Kirov—er, your father—showed up here with a nasty piece of work named Dashamirov. They had three employees of Mercury with them. Dashamirov went to work on them...." The words trailed off. "Anyway, you can figure it out."

Cate Magnus shut her eyes, and a chill seemed to pass through her. "I'm sorry, Graf. I'm sorry about my father. About everything that's happened to you."

"Don't be," Byrnes said. "You didn't have a damned thing to do with this. You're a good egg—I can't imagine the guts it must have taken to come back and face him. The hardest thing a kid can do is step outside the shadow of a parent, especially a father. And then if he happens to be a rogue like Kirov, well ..." Byrnes shook his head, then leaned forward and kissed her on the cheek. "Thank you for coming, too."

Cate shrugged forlornly. "Tell me I'm forgiven?"

Byrnes brought her to his chest. "You're forgiven, kid. Big time."

THE SPEEDOMETER ROSE STEADILY. 180 ... 190 ... 200 kilometers per hour. Hands clutched to the steering wheel, Gavallan kept his heel hard against the accelerator and sent the Suburban hurtling across the green Russian plains. They'd left the dacha an hour ago and were headed back to Moscow.

A cell phone lying on the front seat between Cate and Gavallan chirped. She picked it up and read the digital readout. "Him again."

For the last thirty minutes the phones they'd taken off Boris, Tanya, and the two drivers had rung more and more frequently. The digital readout indicated that it was the same caller every time—no doubt Kirov calling from his private jet, eager to know how the interrogation of "Mr. Jett" was proceeding.

"Jett, we've got to answer. He'll know something's wrong if we don't."

"No," said Gavallan. "Not yet he won't. When you're forty thousand feet up it's a crapshoot if your call will go through. Besides, what are you going to say—'Hi, Dad. Having a great time. Wish you were here'?"

"He's right," said Grafton Byrnes. "It'll buy us some time."

Cate cut off the call. "Have it your way."

"Look, he's still at least four hours outside of New York," said Gavallan. "Believe me, he'll put it off to atmospherics. Now get on with your story. How can you be so sure you heard right?"

"I was there. Right next to the study. Everyone was going every which way. The front door was open. I got almost every word." Cate pinched her voice and added her father's nasal timbre. " 'I thought he deserved my personal attention. I gave him the full clip.' Animal," she added angrily, pounding the sideboard with her fist.

"And your uncle Leonid said the president was pleased?"

"It sounded as if Father was doing him a favor. Like the president wanted Baranov out of the way too."

"Of course he did," said Byrnes from his post in the backseat. "The president made his career as a spy. He's just looking out for his cronies who are still in the trade. It's the old boy network, Volga style. If Kirov's promised him some money from the offering, you can bet the president will do what he can to help him."

" 'An exercise in prevention,' Uncle Leonid said," Cate informed them. "Something to keep oil prices high and stop America from developing its own resources."

"What do you think it is?" wondered Gavallan aloud. "The only major resources we have are in Texas and Alaska, and I'd scratch off Texas from the git-go—most of those are old wells with a only few good years left in them. Alaska's our treasure trove. If we ever get around to developing it."

Byrnes laughed bitterly. "Hell, I can think of a dozen ways to stop us from opening the land up there to drilling. All Kirov has to do is hire himself a few good lobbyists. That'll tie up Congress for a couple years right there."

Cate didn't share in the humor. "But Leonid was going to Siberia. They're going to do something!"

"Prevention, huh?" said Gavallan. "Only way to prevent us from exploiting our reserves is to keep us from drilling in the Arctic National Refuge. I mean, what other new resources do we want to exploit? Sons of bitches. If they try anything to ruin that land …"

Gavallan didn't know if he should laugh, cry, or scream bloody murder. He shouldn't have worried about the bush-league charges of defrauding his investors. Dodson's accusations of murder didn't amount to anything. No, he'd really hit the jackpot this time. He'd moved up to the big time—the bulge bracket all the way. Black Jet Securities was underwriting the KGB in its efforts to economically sabotage the United States, however they intended to do it. He had set his company on a line to commit a crime that was tantamount to treason. Willingly or not, he was abetting his nation's oldest, and still its most formidable, enemy. A country that until recently spied on its citizens as a matter of course, that tortured, imprisoned, and executed men and women without trial or benefit of counsel, that believed human freedoms were secondary to the will of the state. A country that even now was on the slippery slope to fascism.

Cate handed Gavallan the cell phone. "Call your office, Jett. Tell them they've got to cancel the offering."

It was 4 A.M. in San Fran. The office was just coming to life. A voice answered, "Black Jet," and Gavallan hung up. "Graf," he said urgently, looking over his shoulder, "when did you leave me that message?"

"Same day I got into Moscow. I got spooked by Tatiana at a dinner club and decided to check out the NOC for myself, then and there. I was sure you'd gotten it."

"Well, I didn't." Gavallan paused, thinking of Kirov's spy. He recalled the first intimations in San Francisco that someone had to be slipping Kirov information, then the Russian's gloating confirmation last night that he'd lured one of Gavallan's lieutenants to his side. "Who took the call?"

Byrnes fixed him with a cynical glance. "Who's always loitering around your office the last six months waiting to have an urgent word? Who'd we catch looking in your drawers before Memorial Day? Who's the one attending all of Mercury's due diligence meetings when they never had before?"

"Jesus," said Gavallan as a face came to mind. Family. One of the inner circle. A small part of him died, and he swore revenge. "Never said a word."

"Fucking ingrate," murmured Byrnes.

"Call back," Cate implored. "Cancel the offering. Tell them all—Bruce, Tony, Meg. Call the SEC, too. And the stock exchange. If you won't, I will."

"And then what?" asked Gavallan, throwing the cell phone onto the seat between them. "What happens to Kirov after we cancel the offering? You think that's going to put an end to him? Hell, it won't even put a crimp in his style."

He could see the events of the following days unspooling like clips from the evening news. Kirov being detained in Manhattan, then handed over to the Russian authorities. Kirov being set free as Russian prosecutors bemoaned a lack of hard evidence. Kirov appearing triumphant a year later, trumpeting his latest highflyer. There would follow an IPO in Paris or Frankfurt. A private placement in London. The world was full of believers. Gavallan knew it for a fact, firsthand.

"We have the Novastar evidence," said Cate. "The proof he stole from the country. That ought to land him in jail."

"And we're going to keep it," declared Gavallan. "We're going to use it for ourselves."

"But we have to give it to the prosecutor general," Cate protested.

"Baranov's dead with the president's consent," Gavallan said in disgust. "If his successor has any sense, he'll give your father and Novastar Airlines a wide berth."

Cate shook her head, fashioning an answer, but the words died on her tongue.

"Remember what you said to me back in Florida when we were boarding the plane?" Gavallan asked. "You said canceling the offering wasn't enough. You said that you wanted your father to pay for Ray Luca, for the others at Cornerstone, for Alexei and Graf. Well, now you can add the three that Graf saw killed too. And the others to come."

Byrnes leaned forward to be nearer to Gavallan and Cate. "What are you saying, Jett? That you're not going to cancel the deal?"

"Of course we'll cancel it. We have to. Just not now."

"But when? Look around you, buddy. We're a hundred miles from Moscow. It's three o'clock in the afternoon. I hope you don't plan on delivering the message in person. Given what you told me about Kirov and his family relationship with the KGB, I don't think it's going to be a wise idea to line up at the Aeroflot counter and purchase three first-class tickets to New York—if, that is, there's even a flight leaving tonight."

"I've got until nine-thirty tomorrow morning New York time."

"You're pushing it, Jett. This is way outside the envelope."

The envelope? They'd broken through the envelope days ago. All he wanted was a return to earth. A chance to get back to where he was before all the madness had begun.

Cate laid her hand on Gavallan's, and when she spoke her voice had acquired the edge of dangerous dissatisfaction that he himself felt. "What do you have in mind?"

Gavallan looked at her, and saw she was game. "Plenty."

59

JUST BECAUSE THE KOMITET WAS BANKRUPT did not mean they stopped doing their job....

The car was a black four-door Chaika, property of the FSB, the division of the directorate concerned with internal security. The binoculars had been lifted from Directorate 6, the Border Guard, but the men seated sternly behind the dashboard, Lieutenant Dmitri Mnuchin and Major Oleg Orlov, were from FAPSI of the Eighth Chief Directorate, and as such, Major General Leonid Kirov's own.

Mnuchin and Orlov were old hands at this sort of thing—the sitting and waiting, the long idle hours, the marathon sessions of chai and chewing gum. You would not know it, however, from their looks. Both were lean, athletic, and possessed of an alert, aggressive gaze. Both spent their free time in the gym and on the soccer field. They were the new breed: the smart young men who would reinvigorate the *komitet*.

From their vantage point three miles to the west of Army Forward Observation Post 18—recently ceded to Konstantin Kirov and renamed, according to secret transcripts of Kirov's conversations "the dacha"—Mnuchin and Orlov had an unobstructed view of the wooded hilltop. Their assignment was to maintain Level 1 surveillance on Kirov's men—that is, to keep track of their whereabouts, but not to worry about their specific activities. It was an undemanding job, nothing like their usual work involving the installation and monitoring of sensitive eavesdropping apparatus. Both held doctorates from Moscow State in electrical engineering. Today all that was required were a pair of binoculars and a logbook to note the time and nature of their targets' movements.

"A hundred rubles he doesn't do it," Mnuchin said, a loving hand appraising the stubble of his new crew cut.

"You're on. Konstantin Romanovich is every bit as cold as the General. If he were here, I wouldn't be surprised if he did the job himself."

"Never. No man can kill his own daughter. Frankly, I think he's sick. I would have told the General to fuck off."

"The hell you say," Orlov said with a smirk. "You would cut your dick off with a butter knife if General Kirov told you to."

Shrugging his agreement, Mnuchin picked up the binoculars. "Anything for Mother Russia." A moment later, his posture stiffened and the grin dropped from his face. "They're leaving."

"Already? Impossible. They've been there hardly thirty minutes." Orlov picked up the logbook and noted the time: 12:47. Laying the journal by his side, he drew on his seat belt, taking care that it did not interfere with the pistol he wore beneath his left arm, and checked that the mirrors were adjusted properly.

"False alarm," called out Mnuchin. "Only one vehicle."

"You get the signal?"

"Not yet."

The *komitet* had its own man inside Kirov's organization. He had promised to signal when the executions had been carried out: Two flashes of his high beams would mean that the American and Kirov's daughter were dead.

The Suburban rushed past, its midnight-tinted windows making it difficult to get a clear look into the interior.

"Give the plates to dispatch," said Mnuchin, settling back into his seat. "If they want, they can assign a team."

Orlov called in the license plates and advised central dispatch of the events. The report would be forwarded to their superior officer, who would either contact General Kirov with the news or make a decision for himself. Either way, it meant another few hours of sitting in the car. "You think we should call up there? See what's going on?"

Mnuchin trained his binoculars on the dacha. All he could see were the broken fence and the tail end of the second Suburban. "Why? We wouldn't want to interrupt their fun."

THE CELL PHONE RANG AGAIN.

Cate checked her watch. It was nearly four o'clock. They were driving south on the M4 motorway, nearing the Moscow city limits. For miles they would see no one, then traffic would come to a halt as they came upon a convoy of ten or twelve broken-down trucks, tailpipes spewing exhaust, tires wobbling precariously, lumbering down the center of the road. Jett would steer the Suburban onto the shoulder, negotiate the borderland of waist-deep potholes and basketball-size rocks, until once past the trucks he could reclaim his position on the pavement.

"Leave it," said Gavallan.

Cate stared at the phone as if it were a bomb. She knew her father. She knew his impatience. He was not a man who allowed "atmospherics" to stand in his way. "No," she said brusquely, surprised at the force of her reply. "I won't."

And before Jett could make a move, she picked up the phone and put it to her ear.

"*Da.*" It was another woman's voice, rougher, more unpolished than her own. If it didn't sound exactly like Tatiana, it didn't sound like Katya Kirov either.

"Give me Boris," ordered her father.

"He is busy," Cate responded.

"Is Gavallan talking?"

"Not yet."

"Tell Boris to hurry up."

"Sure."

"And my daughter . . ."

"What about her?" Cate stared out the window, willing her soul to become as desolate as the passing countryside.

"Please make it as painless as possible. Surprise her if you can. It is better if she does not know it is coming. As her father, it would please me. It is the least I can do."

"You are too kind."

A long silence followed. As Jett stared daggers at her, Cate wondered if she had gone too far, if she'd tipped her hand. Then her father's voice came back, as focused and self-centered as before. "Have Boris call me as soon as he's done. I've been having a terrible time getting through. The pilot says it's the aurora borealis acting up this time of year. If there is a problem, have him try me at my hotel. He has the number."

Cate hung up.

"What did he say?" Gavallan asked.

Cate met his eyes. "He wants Boris to call him when we're dead."

MOSCOW.

Rush hour in the Center. Ten minutes inside the city limits and Gavallan decided it was every third world hellhole he'd ever known. Jakarta. Bangkok. São Paulo. Traffic was snarled. Militiamen stood impotent amid the blaring horns and packed metal, smoking cigarettes.

The pollution was choking and oppressive. Inside the narrow urban canyons, the sky was bleached a puke yellow, a swirling sea of grit, garbage, and carbon monoxide. The heat was oppressive. Combined with the noxious smells, the jangling din, the stop-and-go traffic, it left Gavallan off balance and wary.

"There's the embassy," said Cate, pointing ahead of them at a large traditional yellow and cream colored building on the right-hand side of the road. "That's the main building there. But the consular offices are around the corner."

"Where do I park?"

"You don't. Just pull over."

A tall concrete wall painted white surrounded the complex. Entrance was gained through a reinforced gate guarded by two Marine sentries and untold plainclothes security guards. Spotting the Stars and Stripes flying behind the wall, Gavallan pulled into the right lane and cut his speed.

"You ready, pard?" he asked, catching Byrnes's eyes in the rearview mirror. "When I stop, you skedaddle. Don't let anyone stop you from getting inside those four walls. They touch you, scream bloody murder."

"Don't worry about me. That there is sovereign territory of the United States of America. I'm as good as home."

Gavallan shifted his gaze to the side-view mirror and the gray Chaika sedan that had been on his tail, precisely three cars behind him, for the last thirty minutes. He looked at the two men inside the car—dark suits, dark glasses, short haircuts, chilling caricatures of the once and future totalitarian state. He looked back at Byrnes, not betraying a thing.

"Yeah, well, don't get too comfortable. I want you out of there tomorrow morning."

"Swissair flight 1915 to Geneva," Byrnes recited. "Departs at nine-fifteen; arrives ten-fifteen local time."

They'd gone over the formalities several times already. Byrnes was to ask to see Everett Hudson, the consular officer with whom Gavallan had spoken when he was in San Francisco. He was to explain that he had been kidnapped and to ask for immediate medical attention. Any requests to have him speak with the local police were to be politely but vigorously turned down. The embassy would supply clothing and a place to sleep.

"If they give you any trouble about issuing a new passport overnight, tell them to call the senator." Gavallan figured his contributions to the winning side had been hefty enough to guarantee him at least one favor. Besides, the senator was a former mayor of San Francisco. It was the least she could do for one of the city's own.

Byrnes leaned against the door, his fingers gripping the release. "You're sure about what you're doing?"

"Yeah, I'm sure. It's the only way." Then a lick of pragmatism tempered his confidence and he added in a subdued voice, "You might want to have a word with the defense attaché. Give him some advance warning. I'll have the other side warmed up and waiting."

"Just keep it low and slow. Even if we are all buddy-buddy now, remember, you're not flying the friendly skies of United. And watch out near the Polish border—they scramble on a heartbeat these days."

"You know, some people might think you're still my CO."

Byrnes didn't smile. His eyes did not flicker. "Good luck."

Gavallan stopped the car directly in front of the embassy, but only for a second. "Go. Get the hell out of here."

The passenger door opened and Byrnes was gone, running across the sidewalk to the Marine security guards. Gavallan accelerated. In his rearview mirror, he watched his close friend pass into the compound and disappear from view. It was only then that he voiced his newest suspicions to Cate. "Bad news."

"Oh?"

Discreetly, he poked a thumb behind him. "We've got company."

60

MR. KIROV, it is an honor to welcome you to New York and to Black Jet Securities," boomed Bruce Jay Tustin as he greeted Konstantin Kirov outside the main entrance of 11 Madison Avenue.

"The honor is mine," said Kirov, climbing from the limousine. Shaking Tustin's hand, he glanced up at the building, a noble façade of steel and glass. "It's a privilege to be here."

"If you don't mind, let's get upstairs. We're in a bit of a hurry. We've got a lot of people waiting for the big event."

"Do I have time to button my jacket?" He was always taken aback by the American ability to be overly polite and unbearably rude at the same time. He followed Tustin through the swinging doors and into the lobby, where Tustin pinned a badge on his jacket and shepherded him past the security desk.

At three-thirty in the afternoon, the lobby was pleasantly busy. A steady stream of men and women churned past Kirov. White, black, mulatto, Asian, Hispanic—as many ethnic mixes as in the former Soviet Union. There was an eagerness to their faces, an alacrity to their step, a forthrightness in their demeanor, that both amazed and frightened him. Such confidence in the world. Such faith that the system would not disappoint. He was sure every one of them held a valid claim on dreams of expensive cars and luxury apartments and vacations in Paris. No doubt they already possessed color televisions, PCs, cellular telephones, digital cameras, Japanese stereos, and closets full of fine clothing, most of which they never wore. They owned refrigerators choked with fresh vegetables, eggs, milk, cheese, leftover Chinese food, soda, and foreign mineral water. Still, they ate out twice a week. They had bank accounts and ATM cards and Swiss watches and cable TV. Many owned automobiles. In short, they had everything. And look at them. Hungry as wolves for more. Bravo!

Kirov was a student of the American brand of greed, a fan of the excess that capitalism bred. He had always been curious as to how the old barons of the Kremlin, all dead and buried (and, he hoped, rotting in hell), could have believed that dogma and political creed could suffocate the competitive drive of the human soul, could stifle man's innate desire to exploit his talents to the best of his abilities, to toil and be compensated accordingly. What hubris! What arrogance! What barbarity!

I am the first of the new breed, Kirov told himself with the same ambitious cynicism he read painted on the faces around him. *I am a pioneer sent to show my countrymen the path to success. To midwife Russia's transition to a modern economy.*

A few bold Americans had lit the way a century earlier. Men who had overseen the growth of the railroads, the introduction of oil, the mass manufacture of steel. Some called them "robber barons," but Kirov thought differently. They were men of vision, builders, creators, founders of a new empire. The riches they amassed were small compensation for the legacy they left behind.

He was no different. Bold? Yes. Aggressive? Always. Immoral? Unethical? Unscrupulous? Let the next generation judge. He was a modern-day Gould. A twenty-first-century Vanderbilt, if not quite a Rockefeller.

They entered a waiting elevator and Tustin pressed the button for the twelfth floor. "Tired, sir?"

Kirov breathed deeply, suddenly feeling quite at home. "On the contrary, invigorated."

He looked closely at Tustin, standing with his arms behind his back like a latter-day Napoleon. The banker was dressed in a bold gray pinstripe, a pink broadcloth shirt, and a blaring red necktie that could be heard back in Petersburg. His hair was slicked back with enough pomade to fill a lake. There was a slight bruise on his lip where Gavallan had punched him, but Kirov decided not to mention it. He was playing it by the book, pretending to be a client just like any other.

"Any word from Mr. Gavallan?" he asked.

"None, but I'm sure he'll check in shortly."

"I'm sure he will too. Still, it is disturbing."

Tustin simply lowered his eyes, and Kirov thought, *Here is a man who cares less for Gavallan than I.* "I see the markets are up today," he said.

"The Dow's up one twenty, the Nasdaq about the same. Sentiment is very positive lately. Maybe you're bringing us luck. After all, you brought us some blue skies. For the last couple of days, the city has had nothing but rain."

"You know the old saying. 'When angels travel, the heavens smile.' And what about the pricing?"

"I'm sure you'll be pleasantly surprised. There are a couple of formalities we like to engage in before we make an official announcement. We've got a conference room reserved. Like I said, a few people will be joining us."

"Very good," said Kirov, keeping the smile pasted to his face. Inside, however, he was worried. *Formalities? What formalities could remain at this eleventh hour?*

The doors slid back and Tustin requested that Kirov follow him. They walked past the elevator bank and onto the trading floor, threading their way through aisle upon aisle of men and women seated in front of a myriad screens. And as they walked, something strange and marvelous happened. The room grew hushed. The incessant chatter died down. At first Kirov heard one pair of hands begin clapping, then another. He looked around, eager to spot the source of the applause, wondering in his vain yet insecure mind if it was mocking or adulatory. The next thing he knew every person in the room had risen and was pounding his or her hands together. Respectfully. Enthusiastically. Lovingly. Every living soul on the trading floor of Black Jet Securities was saluting his arrival.

Slowing his gait, Kirov raised a hand to acknowledge the applause. He selected an expression of imperious solemnity to greet the masses. He was Alexander riding into Macedon. Caesar returning to Rome. Chuikov arriving in Red Square after taking Berlin.

"It is too much, really," he said, bowing to speak into Tustin's ear.

"Nonsense."

And then Kirov heard the music and he stopped walking altogether. The strains of "The International," the majestic Russian national anthem, played from hidden loudspeakers. The applause died and all eyes fell on him. Kirov was stunned, and for a few seconds he didn't know what expression to choose. The music grew louder, and his skin shivered with goose bumps. Emotion plucked at his eyes, and Kirov was damned if he wasn't crying, this man born to peasant stock, this servant of free speech, this disciple of technology. This son of Russia.

Tustin patted his shoulder, nodding as if to say it was all right to shed a tear, that his pride was well-deserved, and for a moment Kirov loved him, too, as he loved everyone else in the room. This handsome, well-attired, overtly intelligent assemblage of financial professionals.

The anthem came to an end and the applause again started up, but only briefly. Kirov offered the victor's smile expected of him, gave a final wave, then followed Tustin to a conference room that took up a corner of the floor. Twenty or thirty people were milling about the glassed-in room, drinking champagne, munching on canapés, and making small talk.

"Janusz, Václav, Ed, hello. So glad you could make it." One by one he greeted his underlings from Mercury, then the others who had shepherded the Mercury offering through the offering process. Lawyers, bankers, accountants. And there was old man Silber himself—gray, bent, and exceedingly ugly, a Swiss gnome indeed. Kirov shook his hand. Apparently, the dinosaur hadn't yet gotten the word about the fate of his in-house tout, Pillonel.

"Welcome to Black Jet," said Antony Llewellyn-Davies, tapping him on the shoulder and handing him a glass of champagne. "We're delighted you were able to make it on time. One never knows with those small jets."

"What is small about a G-5?"

"Oh, nothing, I just ..."

"Thank you." Kirov accepted the champagne, averting his gaze. The Englishman always left him feeling nervous and inadequate, with his soft eyes and snobby manner.

A spoon clinked a glass and the room fell silent. Bruce Jay Tustin cleared his throat, and those around him stepped back to clear a small space. "Ladies and gentlemen, if I might have your attention, please. It's time for us to conduct some important business...."

DON'T LOOK BEHIND YOU," Gavallan instructed Cate, laying a hand on her leg. "They've been there since we got into the city. Maybe before, but I didn't pick them up."

"How can you be sure?"

"I got the first two numbers of their license plates. I'm sure."

"It could be routine," said Cate. "The traffic militia getting ready to shake us down for a little bribe."

Gavallan eyed her doubtfully. "We both know better than that."

"But why didn't they stop Graf?"

"I can't say. Probably they didn't have orders to. All I know is that we stick out like a sore thumb in this car. We've got to ditch it in a hurry."

They had crossed the river and were driving south on Kutuzovsky Prospekt, a broad boulevard eight lanes across. Traffic was heavy, but moving. Stone apartment buildings five stories high, each a block long, lined the street. Gavallan maneuvered the large SUV into the center lane, checking the rearview mirror. A few seconds later, the Chaika followed, a hearse amid a carpet of colorful Fiats, Fords, and Opels.

They're obvious about it, that's for sure, thought Gavallan.

"You know where we are?" he asked.

"Of course."

"It's time to abandon ship. Find us a good place around here for us to get away from those goons."

"Ahead is a factory district. There are a lot of side streets, alleys really, that separate the different warehouses and manufacturing plants. It used to be kind of run-down. You wouldn't want to go there at night, I'll tell you that."

"Sounds good."

"You really want to just leave the car?"

"They won't be expecting us to. It'll give us a head start at least."

Gavallan kept the Suburban in the center lane, pointing out to Cate their best possible path. Approaching the next stoplight, he slowed to insure he would be the last car across as it turned red. The light turned from green to yellow. He waited, watching the cars nose in aggressively from his left. The light turned red. At the last instant, he gunned the engine, making it through the intersection amid a barrage of horns and obscene gestures as a wave of cars closed off the street and left the Chaika behind him, marooned.

He drove twenty yards farther and then, blocked by the grid of automobiles in front of him, stopped. "Get out."

He and Cate opened their doors and ran across the three lanes of traffic. Reaching the sidewalk, Gavallan glanced behind him. "Holy shit."

Heads were popping out of several of the cars stuck in traffic ahead of them. Two men appeared from a yellow Fiat. Another two from a white Simca. A lone man from a Mercedes. All left their vehicles and began threading through the gridlock toward them. Swallowing hard, Gavallan looked back. The goons from the Chaika were out too, rushing through the intersection as if fording a stream, brandishing pistols for cars to stop.

"Move! Move! Move!" Gavallan yelled.

Cate led the way, running up the sidewalk to the first side street and dashing right. Fifty yards up she crossed the pavement, took another left, then ducked into an alley that ran between two apartment buildings. Her strides were long, her arms pumping, her eyes aimed to the fore. Gavallan stayed at her heel, daring a glance behind them every ten or fifteen steps. He counted seven men running after them. They looked to be bunched in groups: three a hundred yards back, another three seventy yards away, and a lone man fifty yards and closing.

Coming to the end of the alley, Cate darted to the right. They were confronted by two crumbling roads that led at odd angles toward low, decrepit wooden warehouses set in fields of uncut grass. Cate continued to the right. They passed through the field, Gavallan stumbling in a pothole and catching sight of the lone runner, nearer now, a gun in his right hand.

"We've got to get off the road," he panted, catching up to Cate. "There's one guy back there we're not going to shake."

Cate nodded, her lips drawn taut. At the far side of the warehouse, they came to another street. Apartments on both sides. All of them newer, almost modern—the pre-fab monstrosities the press used to mock: paper-thin walls, plumbing that leaked from the ceiling like rain, air currents that rushed between the crevices that separated one unit from the other. They found another alley. Cate ducked left and after ten steps halted.

"What?" asked Gavallan.

"Come on. Hustle." She was already crawling through an open window into a ground-floor apartment. Gavallan followed, slamming the window behind him, ripping the curtains closed. He was in a bedroom. It was neat. A nicely made-up single bed covered with a red top sheet. Posters of Los Angeles and Mexico City on the walls. A crib. A dresser with mirrored drawers.

Into the hallway. A shout. Gavallan found Cate in the front room, speaking feverishly to a young dark-haired woman cradling a baby on her lap. The woman stared at Gavallan with intense, frightened eyes. Smells of soup and burnt toast. Another instant and they were out the front door, walking briskly down a dim corridor.

Up the stairs. One flight. Two. Gavallan followed, too winded to ask any questions, happy to have someone else take the lead. After four stories, they reached the rooftop. The door was locked. Gavallan stepped past Cate, raised his leg, and kicked viciously at the handle. Wood splintered. The door flung open, rebounding on its hinges. Sunlight flooded the stairwell.

Cate ran to the edge of the roof and peeked her head over. Raising her arm, she signaled Gavallan back. He dropped to a crouch and eased himself toward the parapet. The seven men were gathered in the street. Arms gesticulated wildly. Raised voices drifted up to them. Then there was a screech of tires. A silver sedan rounded the corner, shuddering to a halt, disgorging four men.

"We can't wait here," said Gavallan, mopping the sweat from his eyes. "They're mustering an army down there."

Cate backed away from the precipice. Setting her hands on her hips, she looked first left, then right. "These apartments are built one next to the other. We can work our way along the roof. At the end of the block, we'll go downstairs and come out on the next street over."

They jogged across the rooftops, easily jumping the gaps between buildings, until they'd reached the end of the street. Lowering himself to his belly, Gavallan ventured a glance below. The men, now eleven in number, stood a hundred yards away, still congregated in the center of the street. An automobile approached from the other direction and made the mistake of honking at them. Immediately, one of the men broke off from the group and pounded savagely on the intruder's hood. A head came out the window. Words were exchanged. Several more of the secret policemen approached. In a moment, they had the driver out of the car and on the ground, and began kicking him.

"Now's our chance," said Cate. "Let's get down to the street."

"But we don't have a car."

"Don't worry," she answered, already moving toward the stairwell. "I'll get us one."

IT'S BEEN A WHILE since we've had an occasion to use this room," Bruce Jay Tustin began. "There's no need to mention that it's been a rough year, but boy, *it's been a rough year!* I guess it was natural, then, for the Mercury Broadband offering to pose some problems of its own. It wasn't the easiest deal to put together, but it's a testament to our professionals and to Mercury's solid management team that we were able to stay focused and surmount those obstacles, so that we're able to stand here among one another today."

"Here, here," murmured the assembly.

Tustin affected a modest stance, his pugilist's chin tucked into his collar. "Let me say that I'm not the one who should be giving this speech. That privilege belongs to another man, someone who for very grave reasons cannot be here today. For those of you who just flew in, I'd like to say that I don't know any more about Jett's whereabouts or his status than you do. I think it best that we offer him our prayers and keep the faith. I'm sure everything will turn out for the best."

Silence reigned as John J. Gavallan, the firm's founder, majority shareholder, and guiding spirit, was sent their prayers. But only for five seconds—then the voices began to swell again. Standing at once among and apart from the assembly, Kirov felt a violent tick in his brain. Enough of the preliminaries. It was time to get to the main event. What had they priced the damn security at?

Finally, Tustin clinked his glass one more time.

"They say 'All's well that ends well,' " he intoned. "And, ladies and gentlemen, I stand before you this evening with news that the Mercury Broadband deal will end very well indeed!" Pulling a note card from his jacket, he slipped on a pair of bifocals. "I don't need these, but I hear they make me look sexy," he said, to a chorus of groans. Then he read: "After a three-week road show that took our executives from Shanghai to Stockholm, from Pittsburgh to Peoria, and after a total of seventy-four investor meetings, I am happy to offer the following comments: The Mercury order book stands at forty times oversubscribed. We have an unprecedented thirty ten-percent orders. And on one-to-one meetings, we scored a cumulative hit ratio of ninety-two percent."

Translated, Tustin's words meant that they had orders for forty times as many shares as they would allocate. Thirty of their clients had asked to take as much of the offering as Black Jet would give them. And 92 percent of the firms with whom Mercury executives had met to pitch the offering had put in orders. By any measure, it was an extraordinary success.

So much for the Private Eye-PO, scoffed Kirov silently. So much for Baranov and Gavallan and even Katya. There would be no mourning any of them. They had brought their fates upon themselves. No one ever said empire building was without pain.

Tustin continued over the sustained hollering and applause. "I guess there's only one piece of information left to give you guys. For that, let me turn the floor over to Tony." He walked over to Llewellyn-Davies and gave him a big bear hug. "Two Names, you done good."

"But seriously, folks, we have had some difficulties with Mercury," Llewellyn-Davies declared as his smile faded and his cheeks grew taut. "Like it or not, though, the time has come for us to put a price on this thing. So here goes. Based on the market's appetite for Mercury stock and using some valuation models of businesses in similar spaces, we've finally come up with something." He shot Meg Kratzer a glance. "This is going out on the hoot and holler, isn't it?"

Meg held up the speaker box. "You're going out live, Tony."

"Great," he said. "Super. So anyway, where was I? Oh yeah, *pricing*. Ladies and gentlemen … Mr. Kirov … tomorrow morning at nine-thirty, shares of Mercury Broadband—ticker symbol MBB—will be issued at thirty dollars a share. *Three dollars above our highest estimate!*"

Llewellyn-Davies crossed the room and placed himself in front of Kirov.

"Mr. Kirov," he said formally, as if asking him to swear in court. "As chairman and majority shareholder of Mercury Broadband, do you accept the price?"

Kirov had already done the math. Thirty dollars a share brought the total offering to 2.2 billion dollars. Deducting Leonid's share and the underwriting expenses, he would still pocket over a billion dollars. And that was just for the 33 percent of the company that was being offered to the public. Were he to value a hundred percent of the shares, Mercury had a theoretical worth of nearly seven billion dollars.

"Thank you, Mr. Llewellyn-Davies, Mr. Tustin," he said. "On behalf of all my employees and colleagues at Mercury, I accept."

Applause erupted. Whistles and catcalls.

And taking a sip of champagne, Kirov thought, *Screw Vanderbilt. Fuck Mr. Gould. I'm a Rockefeller now.*

61

SORRY, SORRY. It is too late. We are closed today. You go home to Moscow. Come here tomorrow."

He was tall and mustachioed and the name tag on his washed-out flight suit read "Grushkin, Colonel Pyotr R." His English was outstanding, if not his grammar. Bending to check a register on his desk, he scratched at his generous crop of iron gray hair and said, "No, come Wednesday instead. Tomorrow, I am booked. Mr. Hamada from Tokyo."

Gavallan and Cate were standing inside the cluttered operations office of the Grushkin Flight Academy, formerly known as Hulskvoe Air Force Base. The room smelled of sweat, cottonseed oil, and the lingering exhaust of high-octane jet fuel. One step inside had turned Gavallan's stomach to water. He was back where he'd never wanted to be again in his life.

Through the open door behind them, they could see the blue Toyota Cressida that Cate had flagged down to bring them here, its driver counting his $120 fare, and behind him, parked not ten feet away, a Mig-25 Foxbat dressed for combat in khaki camouflage war paint. With its swept-back wings, boxy fuselage, and sharp, angular nose, the Mig recalled the old F-111 Starfighter, only bigger, heavier, and, from what he'd been taught, slower to turn. A few airmen tended to the bird, throwing chocks under its wheels, climbing a ladder to the cockpit to check on the instruments, leading a hose out for refueling.

Guards had left Hulskvoe ten years ago, when budgetary constraints had shuttered the base along with seventy-one of its brethren across the Russian landmass. Since then it had been put to more profitable uses. Budding aviators, flight enthusiasts, and any other individuals interested in piloting some of the world's most sophisticated fighter aircraft came to Hulskvoe to attend any of the day- or weeklong courses that were offered. Prices began at $2,000 a day and went from there.

"We're not interested in going for a ride," said Cate. "Not exactly."

"No?" asked Grushkin playfully. "Who are you? Media, I suppose? You want free ride in my plane and you promise to show my school on television? Look, I need the press, but flights aren't free. Fuel, upkeep." He rubbed his fingers together to show how expensive it was to care for a state-of-the-art fighter. "Listen, we make deal. I give you discount. Fifty percent off. A thousand cash. Dollars, not lira, eh? But you don't get to take home a flight suit."

"I think you've got things a little mixed up," said Cate. "We're not press and we don't want you to give us a ride in your plane."

"No?" Grushkin's manner turned from solicitous to suspicious on a dime.

"We'd like to make you an offer," she said.

"An offer?" Grushkin stepped around the desk, arms crossed over his chest. "What is it exactly you want?"

Gavallan told him, and Grushkin laughed boisterously. "You got to be kidding."

Gavallan pulled out his wallet and laid his American Express Platinum Card on the table. "On the contrary.

I've never been more serious. How does a million sound? Dollars, not lira."

THE OFFICES OF AMERICAN EXPRESS Travel Related Services–European Division occupied the top four floors of a Victorian building on the Bahnhofstrasse, one block from the Zurich main station. From his window, Benno Notzli, chief of Centurion and Platinum Card Services, had a pleasant view of Johannes Pestalozzi's statue and the manicured square in which it stood. Pestalozzi, as all Swiss children were taught, was the sixteenth-century schoolteacher recognized as the father of modern pedagogy, and the statue showed him merrily helping a child to walk. A McDonald's restaurant bordered the south side of the park, the luxury department store Globus the west side. The time was 6:49, and Notzli had paused in packing his briefcase for his 7 P.M. departure to listen to a band of Peruvian musicians who'd taken up station below his window. He didn't particularly care for Peruvians or any of the ambling bands of musicians who turned up across Switzerland during the summer like fleas on a dog. To begin with, they were impecunious. Secondly, they were foreigners. Lastly, they were not clients of American Express. He did, however, enjoy their haunting mountain melodies. Especially those played with the pan flute.

The phone on his desk began to ring. Seeing it was his private line, he hurried to answer. "Notzli."

"*Herr Direktor*, we have a rather interesting call from Russia. You'd better have a look at the file. I'm sending it up immediately."

"Not again." Notzli sat down with a thump, giving his briefcase a longing glance. So much for a timely departure. *Russians!* He was well-acquainted with the country and its newly affluent citizens. Every weekend another group of Russian businessmen accompanied by their wives, mistresses, nannies, and children flitted their way up and down the Bahnhofstrasse, buying everything that wasn't nailed down. Fifty thousand francs at Bucherer. A hundred thousand at Chanel. Twenty thousand at Bally. Rolexes, furs, diamonds, ostrich shoes, cashmere top-coats, and couture, couture, couture. Shopping sprees of orgiastic dimension.

Notzli knew that most of the merchandise went to government officials flown to Zurich for the weekend to pocket "soft payments" from their counterparts in the private sector for services rendered—past, present, and future. Not that it was his business. It was Notzli's job to review the client's credit and make spot decisions authorizing or denying such purchases.

"What is it?" he asked.

"An odd request from an airport. The Grushkin Flight Academy."

"An airport? Just give me the customer and the amount."

"Mr. John J. Gavallan. An American. The amount is one million dollars."

"*One million dollars!*" Notzli coughed, coming to attention in his chair.

By now the purchase request and client record was flashing on his monitor. The record showed the client's complete credit history, his average monthly expenditures, days payable, and most recent purchases. It also listed the client's estimated personal net worth, his annual income, and any known assets. Finally, it assigned the entire package a letter grade denoting the client's overall creditworthiness.

Last year, Mr. Gavallan had spent $214,987.15. He paid his bills promptly, averaging fifteen days and his stated annual income was $3.5 million. His overall grade was an A+.

Mr. Gavallan was the real thing.

"Do you have the customer on the line?" Notzli asked.

"Yes sir, I'll transfer him immediately."

Adjusting his tie and smoothing his hair, Notzli introduced himself, then gave his title. "So, Mr. Gavallan, sir, I understand you would like to make a rather large purchase. Please bear in mind, it is necessary for us to take some precautions. I hope you don't mind my asking a few questions to verify your identity."

"Not at all. Shoot."

Notzli asked for Mr. Gavallan's social security number, his date of birth, and his mother's maiden name. Gavallan replied correctly. Then Notzli asked for the small four-digit number printed on the right-hand side of the card. Again, Gavallan supplied the correct response.

"I hope you don't find my questions too intrusive. It's just that your request is coming from an odd location. Normally, significant purchase requests come from jewelry stores, art galleries, even auction houses. You, sir, are at an airport in the region south of Moscow."

"That's right," said Gavallan. "The town is called Hulskvoe, if you're interested."

"May I be so bold as to inquire, sir, what you wish to purchase for one million dollars?"

"A plane. A Mig-25 Foxbat. I'm a pilot myself, and I thought it would be neat to have one to tool around with on weekends."

"Is that right?" Notzli didn't know a Mig Foxbat from a jumbo jet. He was a train man, himself. Antique miniatures. Double-A gauge. "And you're certain this aircraft is worth one million dollars?"

"Actually, it's worth a lot more than that. Production price is around twenty-eight million a copy, but they're having a fire sale."

"You're serious?"

"Yes, I'm serious. I must have this plane."

Benno Notzli stared at the screen, evaluating the man's impeccable credit history and the reasonable voice on the other end of the phone. It was his job to see to it his clients were satisfied, that they were able to purchase the baubles, bangles, trinkets, and, well ... *planes* that they simply "must have." One look at the annual salary and credit grade made the decision a snap. If the man wanted to fork over a million dollars for a Mig-25 Foxbat, he could be Notzli's guest. AmEx would be happy to pocket its customary 2 percent fee on the transaction.

"There should be no problem, Mr. Gavallan. I'll be happy to authorize the purchase."

"Thank you, Mr. Notzli."

"And fly safely."

"I intend to," said Gavallan.

All in all, a most pleasant man, decided Notzli, already halfway out the door. If he hurried, he just might make the 7:13.

CATE MAGNUS TOOK A SEAT at Colonel Pyotr Grushkin's desk. Pulling the phone toward her, she dialed information and asked for the number of the headquarters of the Federal Bureau of Investigation in Washington, D.C. The mere act made her jumpy. The thought of asking a Russian operator for the phone number of the Main Adversary's vaunted internal police was hard to fathom.

Waiting, she watched Jett and Grushkin walk around the Mig, Grushkin pointing out the flaps and ailerons beneath the wing, stooping to inspect the landing gear. Jett looked nervous—fidgeting, nodding frequently, wringing his hands, then brushing them off. Well, she thought, that makes two of us.

The operator returned with the number. She hung up and dialed. It took her two disconnections and a string of

"Would you please hold"s before she was connected with her intended party.

"This is Dodson."

"Mr. Dodson, this is Catherine Magnus. I'm sure you know who I am."

"Yes, Miss Magnus. I hope you don't mind my saying I'm a bit surprised to hear from you. How can I be of service?"

"How can you be of service?" If she snapped at him, it was because she was still incensed at his role in her predicament. Were it not for Dodson, she would be safely in the States as she spoke. There would be no question of Mercury's opening for trading tomorrow morning and she could still look at herself in the mirror. "I'll tell you how. First, you can revoke the warrant for Jett Gavallan's arrest. He didn't kill Ray Luca. I was there too—I mean in Florida. Yes, he was looking for Luca, but not to kill him. He wanted to know why Luca was trying to spoil the Mercury Broadband IPO Mr. Gavallan's company was underwriting. Unfortunately, he got there late—we both did, actually. The same people who killed Mr. Luca nearly killed Jett."

"Miss Magnus—"

"If you want to know where to find Luca's killers, I'll be happy to tell you. Drive north from Moscow on the Petersburg road. Take a turnoff for a place called Svertloe and go east another—"

"Miss Magnus, please—"

"You'll find them near a dirty cabin in a small pine forest. They're dead, I'm afraid. We had to kill them. Do you understand, Mr. Dodson? We had to do your job for you!"

"*Miss Magnus, please calm yourself. If you'd like my cooperation, you'll need to compose yourself. Please, ma'am.*"

But Cate had no more words. She was crying, her breath coming in great big drafts, as if she'd been drowning and needed air. She'd killed someone. She'd ended a life. It didn't matter that the man was trying to kill her. Even now, after everything, she could not summon any enmity toward him. She saw him dodging round the nose of the Suburban, running at the house, his eyes so ambitious, focused, blazing with mission. She had aimed the gun and pulled the trigger and he had fallen dead without uttering so much as a whimper. She could feel her finger tight against the trigger, the gentle, even pleasant bucking of the gun, the dull fireworks as the casings ejected and tinkled onto the cabin floor. The bullets struck him in the chest, in a neat diagonal from spleen to shoulder, and down he went. She was expecting more drama, more blood, a shout, the acknowledgment of his wounds . . . something to punctuate the loss of a life. But he just fell and stopped moving and his eyes were still open and that was it.

"It was Kirov," she said, gathering herself. "He sent two of his killers to do the job. Check the flights in and out of Florida. You must have the tail number of his plane somewhere. Look for a late Thursday or early Friday arrival and a Friday evening departure." Cate mentioned Boris and Tatiana and offered descriptions of them.

"Konstantin Kirov? You mean Mr. Gavallan's partner?"

"No, I mean Konstantin Kirov, the man that tried to kill us and is hoping to defraud the investing public out of two billion dollars."

"Let me get this straight. Are you saying that Jett Gavallan does not want the Mercury deal to happen?"

"Of course he doesn't want it to come to market. What Ray Luca was saying about Mercury was true, more or less. Jett looked into it and discovered some serious accounting discrepancies. He would never represent a company that wasn't exactly as advertised. Contrary to your screwed-up line of thought, he is not a dishonest man."

Dodson cleared his throat. "I appreciate the information, Miss Magnus. You can be sure we'll look into it. But if you'd like any cooperation from our side, I'm afraid you'll have to come back to the United States. I take it you are in Moscow now?"

"South of it. Hulskvoe. It's a former Red Air Force base." Drumming her nails on the desktop, she managed to slow her breathing and get a grip on herself. "Actually, Mr. Dodson, *I* want to help *you*."

"You do?"

"Yes. That is, if you're still interested in jailing Konstantin Kirov for skimming two hundred million dollars from Novastar Airlines?"

"Oh yes, ma'am, we're still very interested in Mr. Kirov. But I think you're mistaken on your figures. Kirov stole a hundred twenty-five million from Novastar."

"No, Mr. Dodson, it's you who are mistaken. I have in my possession Novastar's banking records for the past three years. Every transfer into and out of the company. They're all there. I also have the complete banking history of a company called Andara, and one called Futura. I even have a couple of numbered accounts nobody's ever heard of. I guarantee you, it's enough evidence to see Konstantin Kirov convicted in any court in the world."

"And you're willing to turn this over to the government?"

"I am."

A palm muffled the mouthpiece and Cate could hear Dodson's heated voice summoning someone named Roy. Waiting, she watched Jett climb into the Mig's cockpit and Grushkin take his place next to him. Jett looked more comfortable now, and she found her own nerves settling too. Then she reminded herself that in a little while she would have to take Grushkin's place, and her hard-won repose vanished. Suddenly, the Mig looked very big and very dangerous.

"Miss Magnus, you've piqued my interest," she heard Dodson's voice say. "What is it you want?"

"Just a little help getting home."

"Oh?"

Cate outlined Jett's plan for the next twenty-four hours and how the FBI could help.

"Anything else?" Dodson asked. "Dinner with the President? An audience with the Pope?"

"No, thank you," Cate replied, all business. "That's all." Her sense of humor had deserted her sometime back, probably in a dusky pine clearing in the plains north of Moscow. "Is that a yes?"

It took Dodson a long time to answer.

SHE HAD ONE CALL YET TO MAKE. As usual, she'd saved the hardest for last. Half a dozen times already, she'd picked up the handset only to slam it right back down. Grushkin had brought her a flight suit and draped it over the door. A helmet with a dark sunshield sat on the desk in front of her, and she could see her reflection in it. She asked herself who she really was, Cate Magnus or Katya Kirov. And who, after all was said and done, she would choose to remain. The answers came more easily than she expected. As Jett said, there was only one direction: straight ahead.

Picking up the phone, she dialed the nine-digit number that she recognized as belonging to the north side of Moscow. It was a hard part of town, and the voice that answered the phone matched it perfectly. *"Da?"*

Catherine Elizabeth Magnus did not hang up.

YOU READY?" Gavallan asked Cate.

"Yeah," she said, then more certainly, "Yes, I'm ready. Jesus, Jett, what am I supposed to say—hee-hah, let's git? I'm scared, that's what I am. Are you?"

Glancing to his right, he caught sight of her beneath the Perspex bubble next to him. Wearing the oversized helmet, she looked thin and vulnerable. He could see that she was trying to smile and having a hard time of it. Shifting his eyes to the fore, he gazed down the slim strip of asphalt rolling to the horizon. He waited for his heart to beat faster, for the prickly fingers to scratch at the back of his neck, but his heart was calm, and so was his psyche. In the final analysis, he was just flying a plane. Besides, it wasn't takeoffs that frightened him. It was what he'd find up there.

"Am I what?" he asked, a half second later.

"Are you ready?"

"Absolutely," he said, fingering the throttle, inching it ever so slightly forward. Immediately, the engine roared. The aircraft begin to rumble. "Let's go to Germany."

COLONEL PYOTR GRUSHKIN WATCHED his beloved Mig taxi to the end of the runway, turn slowly, then barrel down the asphalt and take off over the golden fields of wheat swaying in the warm evening breeze. Wings sweeping back toward the fuselage, the aircraft climbed higher and higher into the azure sky. The American rocked the fighter port and starboard, a gentleman's good-bye, and Grushkin's heart went with it.

When the Mig was barely a speck in the sky, he walked into his office and made a phone call.

"Jerzy, this is Pyotr. Listen, I have a student taking the jet out for a long run toward the border. Nothing to worry about—just a training exercise. But in case anything funny happens, maybe you could keep your eyes closed."

"What do you mean, 'keep my eyes closed'?" Jerzy asked.

"Take a short break. Forget you saw anything. If any tough guys ask, say everything's quiet as the grave."

"This is a serious matter you are talking about, Colonel. A question of the motherland's security."

"I think it is more a question of a thousand American dollars, *nyet*?" There was a pause, and Grushkin pictured his old crew chief seated at his obsolete radar array, a cigarette burning between his fingers, a tepid cup of coffee on his desk. "Please, Jerzy. A favor."

"It is a very quiet evening. I would be surprised if anything of interest appeared on our screens. Good-bye, Pyotr."

When Grushkin returned to the hangar, he was confronted by a pageant of disappointed faces. He stared back, then slowly allowed a broad, shit-eating grin to crack his stoic face.

"Hey, don't look so glum, you dirty bastards," he shouted. "Somebody break out the vodka! We're fucking millionaires!"

62

THE SAFE COURSE was to keep the plane low, respect a two-hundred-foot ceiling, bleed the speed to five hundred miles per hour, well under supersonic, and take the Mig for a sunset cruise over the rooftops of Eastern Europe. A check of the instruments showed what Gavallan thought of the safe course. Speed: 650 knots. Altitude: 30,000 feet and climbing. Screw the safe course. It was long gone anyway. He'd thrown safety to the wind when he'd busted into Ray Luca's home in Delray Beach Friday afternoon. No, he decided, he'd chucked it earlier than that. He even had the date: January 10, somewhere around three o'clock, when after a boozy lunch at Alfred's in the financial district, he'd signed Konstantin Kirov as a client and pledged Black Jet Securities' every effort to make the Mercury offering a grand slam.

Rolling his shoulders, Gavallan tried to get comfortable in the scooped-out seat. One hand fought the stick. He was holding it too rigidly, nudging the aircraft left every few seconds to compensate for a slight oversteer. The other hand rested on the throttle like a leaden weight, keeping his airspeed steady.

A click of his thumb activated the intercom. "How ya doin'?"

Cate sat beside him in her own self-enclosed turret, his airsick RIO, or radar intercept officer, in her sky blue flight suit and pearl white helmet. "Alive," she whispered. "Just barely."

"We're about eleven hundred miles out," he said. "Another two hours and we'll be on friendly soil."

"Just hurry, Jett."

Cate had greeted the initial rush of speed with an exhilarated "Wow!" and then, a few seconds later, as they'd slowed dramatically, a less enthusiastic "Uh-oh." She'd used two of Grushkin's doggy bags, and Gavallan didn't think there was anything left in her tummy for a third.

"I am," he said. "You can count on it."

Gavallan released his thumb and turned his eyes back to the bank of instruments. He'd expected it to be easier than this. He'd expected it all to come right back, as if sliding into the cockpit after an eleven-year break were the same thing as slipping on an old jacket and finding that it still fit. Instead, the seat felt tight on his bottom. The cockpit was much too small, the stick unresponsive. It wasn't a question of whether he could still fly. He could. The Mig was not especially challenging in that regard. The cockpit configuration was similar to that of the A-10 he'd piloted prior to going into the Stealth program. Aircraft design dictated that form follow function and the throttle, stick, and navigation systems were all in similar places. The gauges and the heads-up display, or HUD, with their Cyrillic lettering might be difficult to read and the airspeed indicator was in kilometers, not knots per hour, but when it came down to it, the Mig was just another jet. All the same, he was flying poorly, stiffly, with no grace, no feel for the aircraft. Even the familiar tightness of the G suit around his thighs and across his stomach, the shoulder harness's stiff bite, failed to comfort him.

Relax, he told himself. You were born to do this. *Born to fly*.

The words set him on a slingshot journey back through time in which he reviewed his every accomplishment as a pilot. Baghdad. Tonopah. Colorado Springs. The images shot past his mind's eye with increasing speed, faster and faster, one on top of the other, blurred, ill-focused, until just as quickly they froze and he saw himself at age fifteen, lying on the hood of his father's Chevy on a hot summer night in Texas. The car was a hot rod, a fire engine red '68 Camaro with a 454 engine, twin chrome exhausts, and a white racing stripe painted down the hood. After spending all afternoon washing and waxing it, he'd driven twenty miles outside of town and parked in the middle of the open plain where alone in the gathering dusk, he could watch the jets from Beeville Air Station, fifty miles to the north, screech across the sky. He would lie there for an hour, looking up at their gleaming silver bodies, listening to their engines shake the very pillars of the sky, dreaming upon the white contrails they left behind. He was born to fly. It had come to him with a certainty that was raw and cold and frightening. Shivering in the ninety-nine-degree dusk, he'd known he belonged up there.

So, fly, he told himself now. *Relax and fly, goddamn it.*

He gazed at the countryside below. The sun had fallen below the horizon, and its waning rays burnt the Earth's cusp a flaming ochre. The sky above was dark and supple and inviting.

Gavallan's eyes fell to the radar array, a square black screen six inches by six inches located on the instrument console. The screen was dark except for his own orange blip and a flashing triangle that was a passenger jet ninety miles to the north. He'd been flying for an hour, and so far he had detected no sign of Russian air patrols. Either Grushkin was a man of his word or Russian air defenses were perilously lax.

Checking his coordinates on the heads-up satellite

navigation system, he put the plane into a seventy-degree roll and brought his heading to west-southwest. Doing some quick math, he figured he'd put the bird down at Ramstein Air Force Base outside of Frankfurt at around 10 P.M. local time. From then on, they'd be living on the good graces of others.

Five minutes passed. Gavallan checked his coordinates against a map on his knee and decided he was somewhere just south of Kraców, Poland, safely out of Russian airspace. "We're going to start looking mighty suspicious to our flyboys anytime now," he said to Cate. "Time to call ahead and give the boys in blue our arrival time." He checked his radio log and dialed in Ramstein Air Force Base, home to the 86th Airlift Wing. As he keyed the mike a second time, a steady howl sounded outside his earphones. At the same time, a red square blinked on his console. *Fire.* Starboard engine. His eyes kicked right. The gauge showing the exhaust gas temperature was maxed out, full in the red. He pulled the handle to activate the fire extinguisher and cut fuel flow to the engine. At the same time, he cut back on the throttle, shut down the engine, and put the plane into a steep dive. A check over his shoulder revealed nothing. But the gauge didn't lie.

The plane shuddered, as if hit from the side.

"Jett!"

"Hold on, sweetheart, just a little problem."

"What is it?"

Gavallan's heart was racing; a lump lodged high in his throat. The stick was bucking in his hand. He jerked it to the right, but there was no response. A high-pitched buzz saw whined in his earphones. He was losing control of the aircraft.

This isn't my plane, he protested silently. I haven't trained in a Mig. A second check over his shoulder showed flames licking the wing. Immediately he hit the auxiliary extinguisher, and a gust of white puffed from beneath the wing. The flames flickered, then disappeared.

And then the world turned upside down on him. The Mig rolled over and went nose down, spinning in a slow roll.

"Jett, help us. Stop this. Oh, God . . . no, no!"

Gavallan looked at Cate, her eyes wide with terror, her helmet pinned to the canopy.

A voice inside him whispered, *You were born to fly. So, relax and fly.*

"Just a little glitch," he said, in the voice Grafton Byrnes had taught him that hot and sunny day in Alamagordo. "Not to worry."

Still inverted, he pulled back on the stick, depressed the ailerons to stop the spin, and pulled the nose through. Gently he goosed the port engine. The single turbine hummed confidently. It was working. The plane was responding to his touch. He was guiding the aircraft instead of allowing it to guide him. A well of confidence grew in his chest, warm and reassuring. It was the pilot's bravado coming back. The certainty he could do anything, if by sheer force of will alone.

And there, as he plummeted toward the earth at four hundred miles an hour, a dam burst in his mind. A clarity of thought, of memory, of action, came to him that he had not possessed for years.

Priority One. Ring One.

The words struck him like a lightning bolt.

The attack on Abu Ghurayb. Saddam's Presidential palace.

He saw himself in the cockpit of the F-117—*no, damn it, he is there* . . . the stick between his legs, the joystick to his left, the infrared display screens. *He is there.* Inside *Darling Lil*, ten thousand feet above the Iraqi desert.

He is at bombing altitude. A finger toggles a switch. Bomb armed. Eyes forward on the IR display. Target spotted. A stable of buildings silhouetted against the gray desert floor. His finger slews the crosshairs back and forth across the palace until he decides he has found the wing. Then, as if a mechanism itself, the thumb locks down. A yellow light flashes. Laser acquisition engaged. Red lights fire on the heads-up display. Target in range. Gavallan hits the pickle and the weapons bay door opens. Darling Lil *shudders. He depresses the pickle again and the bomb falls from the aircraft. He feels the aircraft jerk upward, as if freed from its moorings.*

As the bomb falls, his eyes lock onto the IR screen and the delicate crosshairs positioned over the east wing of the Presidential palace. All external stimuli disappear. He is in a tunnel. At the far end rests his target. Thumb locked. The crosshairs do not move.

"Thunder three-six. Red Leader One. Copy?"

The bomb appears on the screen. A lethal black dot skimming across the ground at an impossible speed. A red light blinks. A fuel warning. Tanks low. Gavallan pays it no mind. It will wait.

"Roger Red One. Come in."

"Friendlies in the area. We have friendlies on-site. Abort run. I repeat: Abort run."

At the sound of the word "friendlies," Gavallan's finger is already moving, skewing the crosshairs away from the palace, guiding the "smart bomb" away from the American troops.

On the console, a second light blinks—yellow, urgent. It is the Allied Forces Locator warning him he has engaged friendly forces.

"Abort run! Confirm, Thunder three-six!"

But the pilot's instincts have beaten the verbal command by a second, maybe two. An eternity in the electronic world that can be translated into two hundred fifty feet of fall time.

Gavallan keeps his thumb pressed to the right, ordering the bomb to follow his instructions. But the bomb does not listen. She has been on her downward trajectory too long and it is as if she is too stubborn to alter her course.

The desert flower blossoms. The IR screen blanches. A blizzard of white noise. The palace reappears. The east wing is no more, a bonfire of angles fallen in on itself. The heat signatures have disappeared, too, replaced by the blotchy, pulsing quasars that indicate fire.

Inside the Mig, Gavallan lets the images fade away. He has seen enough. In an instant, the past has vanished. But it is a different past than the one he has known. A different reality than the one he has lived with these eleven years. No longer will he question his response, second-guess his reflexes. He knows now that he did everything he could, more even, to prevent the bomb from injuring American Marines. Governed by his instincts, he ordered the bomb off its course even before he himself had fully received the command. If his actions were not sufficient to save the lives of ten men, to prevent two others from being robbed of their ability to live full and decent lives, they were still all he could demand of himself. He was an accessory, yes, and for that he would always feel horror and revulsion. But he would no longer feel the guilt, the shame, the dishonor, no longer believe that it was his own poor reactions that had caused those tragic events.

He would never be free of that night, but he was no longer its prisoner.

Slowly, the nose righted itself and the wings found the horizon. The plane shuddered again and was still. They were gliding on a lake of ice.

"Just a little engine problem," he said to Cate. "All taken care of. Sit tight. I'll have us down in a jif."

"Hurry, Jett . . . thank you . . . but hurry."

"Roger that."

Bringing the airspeed down to 250 miles an hour, Gavallan let go a long breath. The Mig flew straight on its course, a black eagle skipping across the European sky.

RAMSTEIN TOWER, this is United States Air Force Captain John Gavallan, retired. Serial number 276-99-7200. I've got a Russian Mig under my butt that I'd like to put down at your place. You should have word about our arrival. Copy?"

"Copy, Captain Gavallan. Sorry, but we have no word of your status. You are negative for a landing. Please exit secure airspace immediately." There was a pause, and the communications link crackled with white noise. A new voice sounded in Gavallan's earphones. "Captain Gavallan, this is Major Tompkins. You are roger for a landing. Please proceed to vector two seven four, descend to fifteen thousand feet. Welcome back to the Air Force."

"Roger that," said Gavallan. Same old. Same old.

AT 10:07 LOCAL TIME, Gavallan brought the Mig to a perfect three-point touchdown on runway two-niner at Ramstein Air Force Base, thirty miles south of Frankfurt, Germany. A jeep waited at the end of the runway, blue siren flashing, to guide them to their parking spot. Gavallan followed at a distance, keeping his ground speed to a minimum. Finding his spot, he killed the engines. Airmen dashed beneath the Mig and threw blocks under his tires. Gavallan waited until they reappeared, flashing him the "thumbs-up," before opening his canopy and unbuckling his seat harness.

The twin, rounded hooks of a flight ladder coupled onto the fuselage and, reluctantly, he climbed out of the cockpit. He stopped at the bottom rung, not wanting his foot to touch the ground. The crackle of avionics still echoed in his ear. The "by the seat of your pants" rush that came with flying a jet lingered inside him like a melancholy phantom. For a few seconds he listened to the cry of the turbine engines winding down and sniffed at the burnt rubber and let the wind brush his cheek.

Technically, he owned the plane, but he had no plans to fly it again. Jets belonged to his past, and he knew well enough not to look back.

Jumping to the ground, he jogged around the nose of the aircraft to help Cate out of the cockpit. "Never again," she said. "And you did that for a living?"

"It's not so bad once you get the hang of it."

A major in neatly pressed blues approached. "Captain Gavallan? I'm Calvin Tompkins, executive officer in charge of field security. Welcome to Ramstein."

Gavallan accepted the outstretched hand. "This is Miss Magnus."

"Evening, ma'am," Tompkins said, offering a crisp nod of the head. "I understand you two are headed stateside."

"We need some transportation. The Mig's got a lousy range—fifteen hundred miles max."

"If you'll follow me, I'm sure we can accommodate you. We've got a Lear fueling up as we speak, courtesy of Mr. Howell Dodson of the FBI. I'm afraid it doesn't have such wonderful range either. You'll have to stop in Shannon, Ireland, to refuel, but it'll have you to New York by morning. We had you scheduled for ten forty-five, but I'm afraid we've hit a bit of a glitch."

"A glitch?" asked Cate, her voice taut.

"Just a solenoid that needs replacing," said Tompkins. "Should have it changed out any sec."

Gavallan knew his luck had been too good. "So what's the new departure time?"

"Right now, we're looking at a midnight ETD."

"Midnight?"

"And you shouldn't have to dally in Shannon long. An hour tops."

Gavallan scratched the back of his neck, rejiggering his math. Takeoff at midnight. Hit Shannon by two-thirty. Takeoff from Ireland at three-thirty. Setting the whole operation to New York time, they'd land at JFK around six o'clock. Enough time should everything go according to schedule.

"Just one question, Captain Gavallan."

"Yeah?"

Tompkins pointed to the Mig behind them. "What exactly do you want us to do with your plane?"

63

IT WAS PAST MIDNIGHT, and in room 818 of the Peninsula Hotel in New York City, Konstantin Kirov was sleeping. The telephone rang. Instantly, he was awake, knocking back the sheets, fumbling for the handset. "*Da?* Kirov."

"Wake up, younger brother. Trouble."

"What do you mean? I thought you were in Siberia."

"I am. But I had a few of my men keep tabs on the dacha. Gavallan has escaped. He took Katya and the other American with him."

"Impossible," said Kirov, sitting up, grabbing at his wristwatch, squinting to read the time. "I assigned my best man to look after them. There were four guards with him."

"All dead," said Leonid. "We found five bodies including Tatiana and, I imagine, your 'best man.' From what we pieced together, Gavallan had a dagger of sorts and used it to kill one of the guards and take his weapon. From there it's anybody's guess."

Kirov tried to imagine Boris and Tatiana and the others dead. A quick rage ignited inside him. He knew why Leonid was watching the dacha. He had posted his men there to make sure Kirov did not spare his daughter's life.

"If you were watching, why the hell did you let them drive away?"

"An oversight on our part." There was a pause. "We were able to track Gavallan to Moscow," said Leonid finally. "I'm sorry to say we were unable to keep in contact with him afterward."

"You lost him?"

"Regrettably," said Leonid. "Have you heard anything from your contact at Black Jet?"

"Not a word. I finished dinner with them an hour ago. The deal is going ahead as planned. As far as they are concerned Gavallan is missing in action. Some think he may be involved with the murders in Miami. Others don't dare to think anything. The deal is simply too important for their company."

"Most probably he is still in Moscow with your daughter. Nonetheless, you may see fit to take precautions."

"Precautions?"

"To eliminate any threats should they become localized. After all, Gavallan holds no concrete proof to stop the deal, does he?"

"Concrete? No. But from what I understand he doesn't need any. A call to the right parties will suffice."

"Perhaps we can assume Mr. Gavallan has decided to join with our side in this matter. From everything you've told me, he needs the deal as much as you."

"And if he does not?"

"There is no going back, Konstantin Romanovich," came Leonid's icy response. "Neither for you nor I. We will not embarrass the president. We will not disappoint the state. We will have our money."

Leonid hung up.

Rubbing a hand over his face, Kirov wondered what else could go wrong. He knew he should be worried, but his sheer lack of options left him emboldened instead.

He told himself that if Gavallan had wanted to cancel the deal he would have done it already. There had to be a reason he hadn't contacted his partners, and that reason was that he wanted the deal to go through. He wanted his seventy million in fees. He wanted to keep control of his company. Kirov had always pegged him as a greedy one. Smooth, yes, silky smooth, but greedy, too. He was, after all, a banker.

There was no going back.

Repeating Leonid's words, Kirov felt a steely resolve firm up inside him. Rising, he crossed to the desk and retrieved his electronic address book from his briefcase. He found the name he needed quickly. He dialed a Manhattan number and a Russian voice answered.

"This is Kirov," he said. "Get your boss on the line. Now."

Gavallan might be in Russia, but Kirov was not going to take any chances. If he could get away from Boris, he might be capable of any number of things. The American was more resourceful than he had anticipated.

A familiar Russian voice came on the telephone and Kirov explained what he wanted. After haggling a few minutes they settled on a price. Satisfied, Kirov hung up, then punched the console for a new line. The hotel operator answered immediately.

"Room 544," he said.

The phone rang three times, four. Finally, a groggy voice answered. "Yes?"

"Some news concerning Mr. Gavallan. It seems he is no longer with my people in Moscow. Are you sure you haven't had any word from him?"

"Lord no. Not a whisper. You're certain he's gone?"

"Still in Russia, no doubt, but out of my control."

"Damn it, Konstantin . . ."

"Shut up. I'm calling to tell you to be prepared, that's all. The offering will go through. Do you understand?"

"Yes."

Hanging up the phone, Kirov turned off the lights and went back to bed. It wouldn't do to look haggard on the most important day of his life. Sleep came easier than expected. It helped immensely to know that when he visited the New York Stock Exchange in the morning, he would have plenty of friends with him.

GAVALLAN PACED THE TARMAC at Shannon International Airport, tired, frustrated, and impatient. Salt and brine from the ocean laced the air, giving the predawn sky a welcome bite. He told himself he should be asleep in the plane like Cate, gathering his energy for the coming day. Lord knew, he was tired. But he was too keyed up to sleep.

Delays. Delays.

They had landed at two o'clock local time to top off their tanks before crossing the Atlantic. Three hours later, they were still there. A bulb in the starboard fuel gauge had burned out and the pilot had refused to take off until it had been replaced. Gavallan had tried to bribe him, but such was military operating procedure that the pilot would not consider the proposal for all the money in the world. The future tottered on the availability of a lousy ten-cent part. Gavallan wanted to scream.

A mist was building over the grass that bordered the runways. Soon it would turn to fog and the airport would be socked in. He looked up briefly, catching the blinking lights of another plane flying high overhead. He couldn't know it, but inside the plane a short, wiry man slept, a blanket pulled to his neck. He was traveling to America for the first time. In fact, it was the first time he had ever traveled anywhere outside of his country. A matter of some importance had forced a hasty and unplanned departure. A business arrangement that needed squaring.

In his sleep, he was dreaming of the old country. Of the rough mountains where he had grown up. Of the rocky soil and rushing streams. Of the impoverished villages and the indomitable people who inhabited them. Some called it the "bandit country," and in truth it was a land that robbed its people of much. But out of nature's cruelty, they had learned to rely on themselves. To count on one another. In these mountains, a man's word was his most valuable asset. He gave it sparingly and with his fullest commitment. While nature was capricious, man had an obligation to be steadfast. To break one's word, then, was to break with his fellow man. Nature could not be punished for its whimsy, but a man could. And the punishment would be awful.

The man dreamt of such punishment.

In his sleep, he smiled.

Gavallan lowered his eyes from the sky. The twin beams of an airport jeep cut through the light fog, advancing rapidly on him. It was the pilot, and as he passed he held up a small cardboard box for his passenger's inspection. "Five minutes and we're out of here."

Finally, thought Gavallan, jogging toward the plane.

64

GRAFTON BYRNES PASSED THROUGH the revolving doors
of the Banque Privé de Genève et Lausanne on the Quai
Guisan in Geneva at precisely 10 A.M. Tuesday morning.
Announcing himself to the receptionist, he was shown to
a conference room on the fourth floor. The picture window offered a splendid view of Lake Geneva. Byrnes
ticked off the sights, running left to right. The Wilson
House, where the League of Nations had first met in
1919; the enormous gray stone monuments that housed
the European seat of the United Nations; and farther on,
past copses of oak trees and manicured lawns, the building where GATT, the General Agreement on Tariffs and
Trade, was overseen.

There was a soft knock on the door, and a hunched,
portly figure clutching a pad of paper in one hand and a
cup of coffee in the other hurried into the room. "Hello,
Mr. Byrnes. I am Pierre Pillonel. Welcome to our bank."
He stared at his visitor through thick, owlish spectacles.
His hair was mussed and his cheeks flushed and red-
veined. If his demeanor was timid, his voice was anything but—a rolling, confident baritone that a politician
would kill for. Setting down the paper and coffee, he

extended a hand, pulling it back at the last moment. "Excuse me, I see you are injured."

"It's nothing," said Byrnes, turning his hand this way and that to show he was in no way hindered. "A mishap with my car. I find I'm getting clumsier with age. Thank you for seeing me on such short notice."

"A friend of my brother's is a friend of mine. Excuse me if I'm not quite myself. I'm still reeling from the news."

"I'm afraid I don't ..." It was then that Byrnes noted the beleaguered cast to Pillonel's eyes. They were red and puffy. His nose was runny, his cheeks not flushed, but inflamed.

"You have not heard? Jean-Jacques is dead. He was in Zurich on his way to a short vacation. A robber surprised him and Claire in their hotel. They were both killed. It's terrible. I shudder." The baritone cracked and a tear rolled down Pillonel's cheek. He tried to keep a brave front, but a moment later a sob racked his chest, his stern mouth quivered, and he began to cry in earnest. "I'm sorry," he said, wiping at his eyes. "I don't know why I came to work. My wife told me to stay home. She said I was a fool to come."

"My condolences," said Byrnes, without sympathy. He wasn't surprised Pillonel was dead. The news hadn't hurried his pulse a beat. If anything, he experienced a brief and satisfying surge of justice done, even if it was cruel on his part. Jean-Jacques Pillonel was as responsible for his ruined thumbs as Boris. He deserved partial credit for the deaths in Florida, and if things didn't turn around quickly, they could stick him with the dismantling of Black Jet Securities, too.

Cautiously returning his gaze to his host, Byrnes caught a passing glimpse of his own reflection in the window. Dressed in a charcoal Brooks Brothers suit, hair neatly combed, thumbs discreetly bandaged, he actually looked presentable. A short discussion with the embassy's legal attaché, a man Byrnes pegged as the local CIA resident, had produced a diplomatic passport, an interest-free loan in the amount of a thousand dollars, and a ticket to Geneva the next morning with an onward connection to New York (including an armed escort onto the plane). A hot meal, a soft bed, and ten hours' sleep had done the rest. Moscow, Boris, and the dacha were quickly fading into a corner of his memory he hoped to rarely visit.

"There, I am better," Pierre Pillonel said after a minute, taking a last swipe at his nose. "Please excuse me."

The two men sat at a lacquered maple conference table, taking their time to unbutton their jackets and nap their slacks, uncap their pens, and take a sip of the mineral water that had been poured for them prior to their arrival.

"So?" said Pillonel, a false, professional smile pulling at his cheeks. "How may I be of assistance to you?"

"As you may know, Black Jet Securities is set to take Mercury Broadband public later today on the New York Stock Exchange," Byrnes began. "It's a large deal. A two-billion-dollar equity offering."

"I've read about it. Should I be asking to buy some shares?"

"I'm afraid that wouldn't be such a good idea."

"*Non?* Why not?"

"Sadly, we've come into possession of evidence showing that Mercury is not exactly the company we sold our investors. Konstantin Kirov, Mercury's chairman, has been siphoning large sums of money from another of his investments, Novastar Airlines, and using the funds to inflate Mercury's balance sheet."

"When you say a large sum, you mean how much exactly?"

"Hundreds of millions of dollars."

"Dieu," Pillonel said under his breath.

Byrnes nodded in agreement. At least they were talking the same language. "Naturally we're canceling the offering. This morning before the opening bell, we'll announce that the IPO has been shelved indefinitely. It will be an embarrassment to Black Jet and a setback to Mercury Broadband, which we feel is still a vibrant, attractive company. We're quite upset at the development. As Mercury's bankers, we feel we should have spotted the problem earlier. If we'd chosen our partners more wisely this wouldn't have happened."

Byrnes let the words hang there, checking for a response from Pillonel—a sympathetic shrug, a world-weary sigh, an admission that "Yes, this could happen to any of us"—but the Swiss banker remained unmoved, his gaze not giving away a thing.

"Black Jet Securities has an obligation to shelter Mercury from Kirov's misdeeds," Byrnes continued. "We want to do everything possible to insure that Mercury's future as a viable enterprise does not suffer because of its chairman's bad behavior. I like to think the Russian government has a right to the money stolen from Novastar."

The mention of money lit a fire behind Pillonel's eyes. Abruptly, he sat straighter, lifting his chin from his neck. "But of course you are right. One cannot condone such behavior. These oligarchs are too much. They think the entire country is their own private fief. They steal a little from here, a little from there. Their conduct is deplorable." He took a sip of water and shrugged fatalistically. "But how do you hope to convince Mr. Kirov to give back the money?"

"I don't. He's a crook and a murderer. He'd never give it back. But I can convince you."

"Me?"

Byrnes delved into his jacket pocket for a translucent envelope and flipped the minidisc onto the table. "Jean-Jacques was working in cahoots with Mr. Kirov to help

Mercury defraud Black Jet and the investing public. They cooked the books together and Kirov paid Jean-Jacques to falsify the due diligence Silber, Goldi, and Grimm performed on Mercury. When Mr. Gavallan presented Jean-Jacques with the evidence this past Saturday, your brother broke down and revealed what he'd done. Somehow Konstantin Kirov got word of his duplicity. Your brother wasn't going on vacation. He was getting the hell out of the country. You don't really think Jean-Jacques was killed by a thief, do you?"

Byrnes stared at Pierre Pillonel. It was hard to believe he and Jean-Jacques were twins. One was the model of continental sophistication, the other its opposite. "If you look at the disc, you'll find that Kirov transferred the money he stole from Novastar to your bank."

"To the Banque Privé?" Pillonel slid the disc back to Byrnes. "I'm sure I wouldn't know. I am not his account manager. Many of our clients hold numbered accounts. I don't have to tell you of our secrecy requirements."

Lies. Lies. Everywhere lies, rued Byrnes. Since when had dishonesty become the currency of discretion? He waited a moment, taking a deep breath. He felt depressed. Deeply and achingly depressed. Leaning across the table, he whispered, "Cut the bullshit, Pierre. You know Konstantin Kirov is a client of yours. Your brother sent him to you nine months ago to open an account and I wouldn't doubt it if the three of you went out and broke bread together and told each other how you were going to screw the world."

Pillonel shook his head and lifted a finger. His mouth even moved, but he couldn't bring himself to protest.

"You are a partner at the bank, correct?"

"Yes," said Pillonel. "Managing partner, in fact."

"And as such you are liable for the firm's debts and grievances, *non*?"

"It is a private bank," said Pillonel. "I am a partner. Therefore I am liable. It is the law."

"Then let me make this clear," Byrnes went on, his voice as cold and hard as a diamond. "If you don't wire every cent of the money Konstantin Kirov stole from Novastar Airlines back to the airline itself, I will make sure that you are shown to have been involved in Kirov's scheme from the very beginning. Whether you really were or not, I don't know and I don't care. But if you don't cooperate, I will do my best to link your brother's fraudulent behavior with your own and tie all three of you together into one great big daisy chain. Family being family, and twins being especially close ..." Byrnes shook his head, letting the threat of a public trial, the front-page articles, the two-minute reports on the evening news finish the sentence for him. "Don't answer now. Check the disc. It's all there."

Without another word, Pillonel left the conference room. Byrnes stood and looked out at the lake, calm and glassy, promising a hundred summer idylls. He was wondering where Gavallan was, if he'd made it to New York, and even then, if he could pull off his plan. Or more precisely, if Cate would allow him to.

And after that? Byrnes asked himself. What are you going to do? Go back to work? Sit back down at your desk as if the last seven days hadn't happened? He wasn't sure. He knew he wanted to see his kids. He thought about making amends with his wife and chucked the idea posthaste. That part of his life, at least, was over. He decided Pierre Pillonel hadn't been so wrong to venture to his office while in mourning for his brother. There comes a point in life when your work and your self—your own idea of who you really are—grow so intertwined as to be inseparable. Byrnes realized he'd reached that point a long time ago. When you spend twelve hours a day, day in and day out for seven years, you pretty much become the job. *And so, where to?* Home, thought Byrnes. To San Francisco. To Black Jet. If Jett could succeed in saving the company, he wanted to be there at his side to help.

Five minutes later, Pillonel returned, accompanied by a dour, rail-thin man whom he introduced as Monsieur Buffet, the bank's in-house counsel. The attorney shook Byrnes's hand once, as if sealing a bargain. He had dark, depthless eyes, and as he spoke they remained drilled on Byrnes. "You realize that the bank abhors criminal behavior in every shape and form. That we do not as a matter of highest principle deal with persons of anything but the most sterling character. And that we knew nothing— *I repeat, nothing*—about Mr. Kirov's activities vis-à-vis Novastar Airlines."

"Yes, I realize all that," said Byrnes. See no evil, hear no evil, speak no evil.

"And should the bank agree to your request, that should in no way be construed as demonstrating either our knowledge of or our complicity in Mr. Kirov's affairs."

Again, Byrnes nodded.

"A terrible business," said Pierre Pillonel, waving his attorney into a far chair. "Black days. So hard to know who to trust, who not to."

"I can imagine."

"Naturally, we are prepared at this instant to wire the funds to the account you mention . . . or to *any other account* you may wish for us to help you set up." Pillonel paused, but only for the shortest of moments. "A numbered account with our affiliate in the Bahamas, perhaps?"

Byrnes kept a mirthless smile to himself. What did the French say? *Plus ça change, plus c'est la même chose.* "No thank you. Novastar's account at the Moscow Narodny Bank will be fine." He handed Pillonel a piece of stationery bearing the account numbers. "By three-thirty today, gentlemen."

65

IT WAS THE QUIET TIME.

The time for reflection. The time to put your personal thoughts in order, separate the good from the bad and take a measure of your life. The time to settle things. The last free moments before the operation went tactical, because once it went tactical and you were doing what you'd trained these last four months to be doing, the only things you thought about were the mission, your part in it, and maybe, if you had the courage, whether you'd get out of it on the other end alive.

The members of Team 7 sat at the edge of the landing strip, using parachutes for seats, twelve castaways eating their rations of Pop-Tarts, Fritos, and protein bars, drinking their Gatorades and Diet Cokes. They were Americans, all of them—the baseball caps and work boots, the insouciant smiles, the two-day beards. Or so you'd swear until looking closer. And then, as you examined each one by one, you would shake your head. Here, the cheekbones too high, the eyes vaguely Asiatic. There, the blond hair a shade too blond. This one's gaze too dark, mirroring a fatalism bred over centuries. That one's face too gaunt, hunted, fearful.

They were born of the East. Mother Russia's children.

A stiff wind snapped at the waist-high grass that bordered the strip. Behind them, the Bering Sea lapped at a beach even more desolate than the deserted airfield. The water was calm and glassy, a dark, dark green that went on forever. If you stood on your tiptoes and the air was clear enough, which it wasn't so late in the evening, and you had the right frame of mind, the proper imagination, you might just see the Alaskan coast forty miles away.

But none of the men looked. No one stood. It was the quiet time.

It had been a long journey to the abandoned airfield on the very edge of the Chukchi Peninsula. Seventeen hours without sleep and the mission had not yet begun. From Severnaya they had traveled to Nordvik by a rusting Tupolev transport, and from Nordvik to Anadyr by a snazzy Air Force Ilyushin. The last hundred miles had been traveled in the rear of a Kam truck that smelled as if it had been routinely used to haul sheep to the slaughterhouse. Each leg of the mission was cut off from the next. Compartmentalized. No one asked where they came from or where they were going.

They were spirits.

Ghosts that never were.

A team that did not exist.

Somewhere in the wind danced the drone of a faraway engine. The team rose to their feet and looked to the sky. The drone grew into a silhouette and the silhouette into a silver form. A minute passed and the Beechcraft 18 came into sight. It was a vintage 1960s floatplane that had earned its stripes ferrying fishermen to and from the Canadian wilds. Its new incarnation called for a more hazardous duty, and the oversized radial engines had been souped up accordingly. Pontoon floats grew from the bottom of the plane, and as the Beech hovered low over the airfield they looked like twin torpedoes, primed and ready to drop. Wheels bobbed from the floats, and the plane struck the landing strip with a military finesse.

Barely had it stopped before the commandos had pulled themselves aboard. Webbing had replaced seats in the stripped-down fuselage. Blankets would do for heating. The men took their places, throwing their chutes on the floor between their feet. Their packs, and the sensitive cargo they contained, they held in their laps.

The Beechcraft turned and roared down the runway, lifting gracefully into the gray-tinged sky. The forecast was good, notwithstanding the gusting northerlies. This high in the latitudes, the wind was a constant, and if not your friend, an enemy to be made peace with.

Inside the fuselage, the men checked their equipment a final time, then closed their eyes. They did not sleep. They rehearsed. They concentrated. They willed themselves to their highest level.

The quiet time was over.

66

IN NEW YORK CITY, on this third Tuesday in June, the sun rose at 5:24. The dawn promised a flawless day. Wisps of cumulonimbus raked a hazy blue sky. A freshening breeze kept the temperature in the low sixties, dousing Wall Street with the honest, vital scent of the East River. Outside the New York Stock Exchange workers draped an enormous banner emblazoned with Mercury Broadband's logo across the building's proud Doric columns. Measuring fifty feet by thirty-five, the banner was decorated with a stylized drawing of Mercury's helmet—the disclike headplate garlanded with two lightning bolts—and the company name, painted gold against a royal blue background.

Inside the building, television crews set up for what promised to be a hectic day. Twelve networks had constructed production facilities on the mezzanine level ringing the Exchange's principal trading floor. Making the circuit, one passed cramped, brightly lit ministudios for CNN, CNBC, the BBC, Deutsch Fernsehen, Nippon Television.... Journalists could be glimpsed applying their makeup, brushing their hair, and practicing their "good morning smiles."

By 7 A.M., the first reports were going out live to audiences around the world. The talk today centered on one subject: the Mercury Broadband IPO. What would be the first day pop? Would the stock keep its head? Was Mercury an exception to a moribund market or the pioneer of a long-awaited rally in technology stocks?

KONSTANTIN KIROV ROSE AT SEVEN-FIFTEEN, showered, shaved, and dressed in a sober gray suit and maroon tie. Despite last night's warnings, he'd slept remarkably well. What will be, will be, he told himself. He'd taken every precaution. He was convinced that once the stock began trading, no one would have the nerve to stop it. If Gavallan were going to make a move, he would have done it long before now. What was the American saying? "No news is good news."

Giving himself a final once-over in the mirror, he asked himself if he was being too confident, too cocksure. Up came his hand with a last spritz of cologne. No, he decided, just realistic.

Picking up his briefcase, Kirov left his suite and took the elevator to the first floor, where he was joined for breakfast in the main dining room by Václav Panič, the CTO of Mercury's European operations, and Janusz Rosen. The bankers were absent, no doubt putting in an appearance at the office before making their promised rendezvous at the Broad Street entrance to the stock exchange at nine o'clock. Kirov ordered a large breakfast, then picked at it. His appetite had deserted him.

At eight-thirty, he and his colleagues decamped to a black stretch limousine berthed in front of the hotel. Kirov settled into the backseat for the drive downtown. The chauffeur announced that due to congestion on the FDR Drive, they would be taking the West Side Highway. Traffic was moderate and they made good time, passing the Javits Center, the USS *Intrepid*—a mothballed aircraft carrier used for various charity functions—and the reconstructed World Financial Center.

The limousine turned onto Broad Street, and through the windows Kirov stared at an imposing neoclassical building at the far end of the street. A steep flight of stairs led to the building, and even he could recognize the statue of George Washington at the top of the steps. The chauffeur explained that the building was Federal Hall, the seat of the United States government from 1776 to 1791. Across from Federal Hall stood the old headquarters of J. P. Morgan & Co., from whose offices the legendary financier had built his empire and dictated the course of the American economy.

To Kirov's left rose the New York Stock Exchange itself. It could have been a temple on Mount Athos, so perfect was its architecture: the soaring Doric columns, the broad plinth, the bas-relief sculpture running lengthwise beneath the roof.

The limousine pulled to a stop. Kirov got out of the car without waiting for the door to be opened. Staring up at the Mercury Broadband banner that hung in front of the fabled Exchange, he gasped.

My God, he thought, I've done it.

THE WHEELS OF THE LEARJET touched down at John F. Kennedy International Airport at 8:47 A.M. Eastern Daylight Time. The eight-passenger aircraft performed an abbreviated rollout, braking sharply and making a quick starboard turn off the runway. The doors to the flight deck opened, the engines revved, and the plane began an easy ride to its parking slot. Unbuckling his safety belt, Gavallan leaned forward, rocking slightly. Through the cockpit windscreen, he watched the impressive girth of a China Airlines jumbo jet cross their path. Inexplicably, the plane came to a halt directly in front of them.

"What's keeping the guy?" Gavallan shouted to the flight deck.

"Waiting for an inbound jet. It'll just be a couple of minutes."

"A couple minutes?" Gavallan wiped a hand across his face, looking to Cate for reassurance. Her only response was to bite her lip and go back to patting her foot nervously.

After an eternity—three minutes by his watch—the Lear arrived at its designated parking slot. The engine died and the plane rocked forward as the brakes were applied and stopped. Rushing to the door, Gavallan leaned hard on the exit lever. The door opened inward, sunlight flooded the cabin, and he went down the stairwell.

A small entourage waited. Three agents of the federal government left the comforts of their four-wheel mount and hurried to the plane. Gavallan recognized the tall, lanky man with the shock of brown hair, the seersucker suit, and the pair of bifocals perched on his forehead as Dodson. Four days earlier he'd seen him talking on the phone beneath the portico of the Ritz-Carlton.

"Mr. Gavallan, Howell Dodson. It's a pleasure, sir," the FBI man said, extending a hand. "Nice flight?" But if his voice was politeness itself, his posture was stiff, his face a mask of tension.

"We're here, that's what counts."

"Miss Magnus, I presume." Dodson gave her his hand and with a cock of the head shepherded them toward the waiting car. "We've got a helicopter standing by to ferry us to Manhattan."

"Tell me the rotors are turning," said Gavallan.

"The rotors are turning, Mr. Gavallan," said Dodson. "Are you sure we can't call ahead? Pull in Kirov as soon as he shows up? We do have resources available."

"No, thank you. That's not part of the deal." This was something Gavallan had to do himself. The FBI was there in a supporting role only, even if the Bureau didn't know it yet. Reaching the sedan, Gavallan tried to open the door, only to find Dodson's hand placed firmly against the window. "Just a second there. You can see that I've kept up my end of the bargain. I wouldn't want to go any further without seeing some good faith from your side."

"You don't trust us?" asked Cate, stepping forward.

"I'm not in the trust business." The smile was gone, the eyes direct, demanding.

Opening her purse, Cate drew out her pink compact, clicked it open, and handed Dodson a slightly dusted minidisc. "I'm not sure what program was used to store the information on the disc. You'll have to do your best with it."

"All that counts is that the data's there. Three years' of banking records, correct?"

"Oh, it's there all right," said Cate. "And then some."

"Thank you kindly." Dodson handed the disc to a fat, unattractive young man chafing in a catalogue-ordered blue twill suit. "Here you are, Mr. Chupik. I don't mean to rush you, but you have eight minutes to let me know what's on this disc."

"Piece of cake," said Chupik, sliding into the front seat and feeding the disc into his laptop computer. "I'll do it in five."

THE JUMP LIGHT BURNED RED.

The members of Team 7 stood as one, affixing their static lines to the jump cable. Team Leader Abel shuffled forward through the bare fuselage and opened the main cabin door. With a mighty rush, a chill midnight wind swept through the airplane. The biting cold stung his cheeks and brought tears to his eyes. Grasping either side of the door, he looked outside. A pine forest rushed beneath them, a dense lush carpet close enough to touch. They'd been crossing it for thirty minutes and still it ran on, measurelessly.

Stepping back, Abel checked his watch and signaled "Five" with his fingers.

All eyes were on him, yet no one responded. There was no need. All tactical contingencies had been dissected, analyzed, solved, and solved again. The time for words had passed. The time for deeds had arrived.

The Beechcraft 18 began a slow ascent. The altimeter rose from 250 feet to 300, then 350, the magnificent radial engines sawing the air with demonic fervor. Several modifications had been made to prepare the plane for its current purpose. All passenger seats had been stripped, all carpet and insulation torn out until the interior cabin was an aluminum and iron husk. Auxiliary fuel tanks were installed in the rear of the fuselage, gifting the plane with a two-thousand-mile range. A sophisticated satellite navigation system had been installed to insure that the men located their target. And unbeknownst to all—even the pilot—a remote-controlled detonation system was attached to the starboard fuel tank: three pounds of plastique governed by a long-distance radio signal.

The Beechcraft leveled off at 400 feet. The pilot slowed the aircraft's speed to 250 knots. From this height and at this speed, the soldiers of Team 7 would jump. It was a standard LALO jump: low altitude, low opening. Once outside the aircraft, they would fall fifty feet before the static line deployed their chutes. Five seconds later they would impact the ground at three times the usual landing velocity.

The forest vanished with a silent white clap. The tundra ran before them, a pale wilderness advancing to the edge of the world.

And then he saw it. Pump Station 2. A necklace of orange lights glimmering far on the horizon. A wisp of smoke rose from the power plant. No homing signal could have been better. Despite his training, Team Leader Abel's throat swelled and grew tight.

He raised three fingers.

PASSING THROUGH THE DOORS at 18 Broad Street, Gavallan received his visitor's badge, walked through the metal detector, then slid through the turnstiles that governed admittance to the Exchange. He'd been on the floor a dozen times over the years, yet he never entered the building without getting a certain buzz in the hollow of his stomach. It was no different this morning, except that coiled among his normal feelings of awe and respect was the unmistakable frisson of danger.

Dodson followed him closely, showing his badge, and Roy DiGenovese entered next. Mr. Chupik had stayed in the car. He'd needed only three minutes to open Pillonel's files. Scrolling page by page, transfer by transfer, deposit by deposit, through Novastar's banking history, Dodson had looked on with a reverent gaze, saying the same words over and over again: "Well, ain't that sweet."

"Miss Magnus doesn't care to join us?" Dodson asked once the three men had assembled in the small foyer just inside the entryway.

"I think she'd prefer to wait outside. She's seen enough." Gavallan didn't add that Kirov was her father, or that she had plenty to do on her own outside the building. Some things the FBI didn't need to know.

"A rough few days, Mr. Gavallan?"

"You can say that."

"I know you had wished to speak with Mr. Kirov alone. Fine by us. Still, I'm sure you'll be happy to know we've taken some steps to see that Mr. Kirov does not flee the premises. If you'll just follow me for a moment."

Dodson led the way down a short corridor, stopping at an unmarked door and knocking once. An African-American agent wearing a navy windbreaker with the yellow letters FBI stenciled on its breast poked his head out the door and said, "Kirov's here. We got him on the closed circuit. He's just leaving the specialist's booth. Did you get what you wanted?"

Dodson grinned while patting the man's shoulder. "You have no idea, Agent Haynes." The grin disappeared, and Dodson found his no-nonsense self. "Our operation is a go. Alert building security that we will be making an arrest. It might be wise to trade your windbreakers for some trading jackets. And bring along a few of your men. Calm, brisk, and orderly, Agent Haynes. Am I clear? We keep our weapons concealed at all times."

As the agents conferred, Gavallan peeked into the waiting room. Eight men and women dressed in the same navy windbreakers stood around drinking coffee, shooting the shit, and checking the pumps on their street-sweeper shotguns. It was the FBI's Tuesday morning coffee klatch.

"They're going to stay in here, right?" he asked.

"Strictly backup. I'm sure we won't have the slightest need for them."

"All right then," said Gavallan. "Let's go."

67

CATE WAITED IN FRONT of the visitors' entrance to the Exchange, pacing back and forth, craving a cigarette, though she'd never smoked in her life. The morning air was cool and invigorating, the sidewalk bathed in the shadow of the surrounding skyscrapers. Still, she was sweating. Every minute or so, she checked her watch. *Where was he?*

She searched the parade of faces, men and women walking purposefully up and down the street. Businessmen in three-piece suits, tourists in shorts and T-shirts, artists carrying sketchbooks and easels. At the corner of Wall Street and Broad, street vendors were selling black-and-white photos of Manhattan, magazines, financial texts. The pavement pulsated with the vibrant human cargo. Hugging her arms around herself, Cate wondered if she was doing the right thing. She knew very well the consequences of her actions. Once taken, there would be no going back.

"He'll serve two or three years, tops. And there's no guarantee of that," Pillonel had scoffed in the archives of Silber, Goldi, and Grimm's headquarters. "Besides, it's not the government he should be afraid of, it's his partner."

She thought of the nasty little dacha north of Moscow, the crude torture chamber with its floor stained black by blood. She remembered Alexei and Ray Luca. She forced herself to imagine the countless others who had suffered or died at Kirov's hands, and the countless more who would surely follow. The blood ties to her father, frayed and fragile, unraveled yet further and finally broke, taking with them her doubt. Someone had to stop her father. At last, she had a way.

A tented canopy had been erected on the sidewalk. Beneath it, two long tables were stacked high with caps and T-shirts bearing the Mercury logo. Handsome young men and women were giving the merchandise to passersby, along with brochures describing the company. Cate looked on, disgusted. It was a fraud, a farce, a fairy tale with a very unhappy ending.

She stopped her pacing long enough to check her watch and compare the time against that of the clock on Federal Hall. Both read 9:20. Her heart raced. Where was he?

"Ekaterina Kirova?"

"Da?" Cate spun. A wiry, dark-haired man attired in a neat houndstooth jacket stood in front of her. She'd never met him before, but she knew him intimately: the soulless eyes, the distrustful smile, the shadow of a beard pushing up an hour after shaving. "Dangerous," Pillonel had said of her father's partner. His *krysha.* "From the bandit country."

"You have something for me?" he asked.

Retrieving the compact from her purse, she removed the last disc and told him what he would find. "Hurry," she said.

But in contrast to her anxious demeanor, the Chechen was all too relaxed. He held the disc between his fingers, examining it this way and that as if deciding whether or not to purchase an expensive piece of jewelry. "No need. Everything is already taken care of."

"What will you do?"

The man from the bandit country met her gaze, and she felt a chill pass through her. Saying nothing, he slipped the disc into his pocket, bowed ever so slightly, and walked off.

THE PARTY OF THREE HAD GROWN TO SIX. Dodson and Gavallan led the way. DiGenovese, Haynes, and the muscle came behind. Haynes and his two agents had donned the shapeless jackets favored by specialists on the floor. Strung out along the corridor that ran parallel to the floor, weaving in and out of the milling throngs of traders, brokers, and specialists, the group managed to avoid looking like the war party it was.

Dodson pulled up at one of the double doors leading onto the floor. "All right, Mr. Gavallan. Here we are. You heard Agent Haynes. Kirov just left the specialist's booth and is on his way up to the podium. Lead on. And remember—calm, brisk, and orderly. We find Kirov and we take him into custody."

The New York Stock Exchange was divided into four trading rooms: the Main Room, the Garage, the Blue Room, and 30 Broad Street. There was no hierarchy among them. The Exchange's seventeen trading posts, scattered across the floor like giant bumpers on a billiard table, were divided evenly between them. Wide passageways lead from one room to the next. But when people thought of the Big Board, it was the Main Room they envisaged. It was here that trading was inaugurated from an elevated podium every morning at nine-thirty, and here that was halted every afternoon at four.

Gavallan led the way into the Main Room. It was large and airy as a convention hall, two hundred by two hundred feet. The ceiling stood several stories above a century-old plank floor. American flags of every size and shape dominated the décor, sprouting from every trading post and hanging on every wall. Brokers' booths ringed the floor's perimeter. Ninety percent of orders to buy and sell shares traveled electronically through the "superdot" computer system directly to the specialists' booths, where they were automatically mated, buyer with seller, at an agreed upon price. This 90 percent, however, accounted for only half the share volume that traded each day. The remaining 10 percent of trades accounted for the other 50 percent of the volume, and these large, or "block," trades required the human attention of both broker and specialist.

Lowering his shoulder, Gavallan nudged his way through a knot of brokers talking last night's hoops and walked onto the floor of the New York Stock Exchange. Keeping a driven pace, he wound his way across the floor, passing the trading posts where IBM, 3M, Freddie Mac, and AIG were traded. The posts bristled with television monitors, flat screen displays, computer keyboards. Eleven minutes from the opening—9:18:25, by the digital clocks hanging high on every wall—each was surrounded by clumps of specialists balancing their orders prior to the start of trading. It was difficult to see more than fifteen feet ahead.

Gavallan reached the post that housed the electronic offices of Spalding, Havelock, and Ellis, the specialist firm assigned to trade Mercury's stock. The booth was a hive of activity. Twenty or thirty brokers crowded around Deak Spalding, the firm's top trader, shouting to be heard. It was a scene that played out whenever there was strong demand for a stock, or strong pressure to sell it.

Gavallan glanced toward the podium. A Mercury Broadband banner was draped across the balcony below it. Another larger one hung on the wall behind it, just below the gargantuan American flag that daily paid tribute to the United States of America and the free market it fostered.

"Well, look who's here," said Deak Spalding. "The devil himself, back from the dead. Hey, guy, how are you? I had old man Grasso himself here not two minutes ago, with your buddy Kirov and some of your troops. Gonna be a big opening. Gotta love it."

Spalding was a broad, florid man with an Irishman's ruddy nose and gift for gab. A pink carnation adorned his lapel.

"Doing good, Deak, thanks. Which way'd he—?" A soft hand fell on Gavallan's shoulder and he spun to see to whom it belonged. "Hello, Tony."

"Jett. You're back. Thank God, you're all right."

"You weren't expecting me?"

"Frankly, none of us were," said Tony Llewellyn-Davies. "Not a word from you since Friday. The FBI saying you're a murderer. We didn't know where you'd gone or what you'd been up to."

He was dressed nattily in a double-breasted blue blazer with his requisite gray flannel slacks and club-striped tie. His cheeks were flushed, his blue eyes excited.

"I find that a little hard to believe," said Gavallan. "You if anybody should have been able to tell them. After all, if you're such good friends with Konstantin Kirov you ought to have known."

Llewellyn-Davies bit back his surprise, his Adam's apple bobbing visibly. "We're hardly 'friends.' I'm sure I hardly know him any better than you do."

"Cut the crap, Tony. I've spoken to Graf. He told me about the call . . . the one you conveniently forgot to relay to me. You knew firsthand Mercury was rotten a week ago. Actually, I guess you knew it a long time before that. Anyway, it stops here. We're pulling the plug on the deal. It's over. I just want to have a quick word with Kirov before I let everyone else know."

"Jett, no . . . you're mistaken. You're talking nonsense. Really, you are."

"How could you? We built something. We did it to-gether. Seven years, Tony. Christ, you're on the board as it is. What was it? More money? A spot at the top? What he offer you?"

Looking at his associate, Gavallan felt betrayed, ashamed, and naive. Part of him still thought it couldn't be. Not Tony, of all people.

"I don't know. Respect. A chance." Llewellyn-Davies sobbed, a single pathetic cry, and lowered his head. "I'm sorry, Jett. Give me a minute to explain. Not here— come into the booth. It's already embarrassing enough as it is." He tried to smile, and a tear ran down his cheek. "The floor doesn't need to see a pooftah having a good cry."

"I haven't got the time. Tell it to your next employer."

Llewellyn-Davies grabbed at Gavallan's sleeve. "No, Jett. Please. I can make it right. You've got to believe me. Don't be a stupid git. It's just me ... *Tony.* Come on."

The official clock read 9:20:51. Gavallan found Dodson and asked him to stay right where he was and, no matter what, to prevent Spalding from initiating trading in the stock. "Give me two minutes. I'll be right back."

"Two minutes, Mr. Gavallan. Then we get Mr. Kirov ourselves."

But Gavallan was already moving, and Dodson's words were drowned by a chorus of babbling voices. Gavallan and Llewellyn-Davies walked the short dis-tance to the Black Jet Securities booth. Curious faces greeted them along the way, along with cries of "Jett, great to see you," "Hey, boss," and "We got a kicker today!"

Llewellyn-Davies opened the door to the manager's office and showed Gavallan in.

It was more a shoe box than a place of business. Two desks pushed against each other crowded one wall. Next to them stood a waist-high server, a monitor, and a printer. There was a refrigerator and a microwave oven, a Bridge data monitor, and another desk covered by telephones. The walls were papered with notices from the Exchange. Like any other essentially blue-collar workplace, there were the obligatory topless photos. Tastelessly, someone had glued a picture of Meg Kratzer's face onto the torso of a black woman with enormous breasts. A second door led to the corridor outside the floor.

"Out, both of you," Llewellyn-Davies said to a pair of clerks. "On the double."

Gavallan nodded at them and they left.

Llewellyn-Davies shut the door, then turned, leaning his back against it. "What a mess, eh?"

"You've got a minute, Tony. Get going."

"Oh, fuck a minute. Come to your senses. Seventy million dollars. The firm's future, for Christ's sake. Let it go."

"It's done, Tony. The deal's canceled."

Llewellyn-Davies stared at him, his pinched, patrician features clamped into a mask of hate. "I'm sorry, Jett, but that's out of the question. Too much work. Too much sweat." The tears had vanished. His eyes were clear, burning with an inner purpose, a rage that Gavallan had never seen in him before. "We need this. You, me, all of us. It's our bloody savior. Can't have you taking us all down as a matter of pride or principle. I don't want to hear about rules. Sod all the rules. Made to be broken, what?"

"Mercury's revenues are a sham. Kirov's going to jail. The FBI's got information tying him to the theft of a couple hundred million dollars from one of the companies he controls. The Russian government is all over him. Now come on. Let's go outside and talk to Deak Spalding."

"Kirov assured me he's remedied the shortfalls in

infrastructure. It's only a question of months until his revenues are up to snuff. It's time to close an eye. For everyone's good."

What was he trying to do? Gavallan wondered. Intimidate him? Threaten him? Did Llewellyn-Davies actually for a moment think he might change his mind? Gavallan stepped closer to the man he'd been so god-awful stupid to trust. "Move, Tony. I have to go."

"Afraid not, chum."

It was then that Gavallan saw the gun. It was a strange gray pistol with a silencer. Plastic, he thought. The bullets would be too. No metal detector in the world could have sniffed it out.

"Some fancy hardware, Tony. A present from Kirov?"

"You damn fool, Jett," said Llewellyn-Davies, shaking his head, his voice tightening. "Don't you see, it's your fault. All of this. Mercury's a gem, just like you said. We've got to see it to market."

"Out of the way." Gavallan stepped forward, and the Englishman fired a round into the floor.

"Christ," shouted Gavallan, freezing, raising a hand. "Have you lost your mind? Put it down."

Llewellyn-Davies held the gun out in front of him, grasping the butt with both hands to control the palsied shaking. "Sorry, Jett. No can do. It's not that I'm not grateful for everything you've done for me. I am, believe me. It's just that it's time I did something for myself. Think ahead. What do you think happens to me if the deal goes sour? Do you think we don't all know how strung-out the firm is? How long do you think the new owners of Black Jet will keep me on? One look at my health records and they'll pack me off with a nice little check and a pat on the back. 'One less liability.' 'Start with a clean sheet.' All that utter crap. I won't have it. I've worked too bloody hard for too bloody long to start over again somewhere else—Christ, if there's someone else who'll even have me."

"It's over, Tony. We'll all make out okay. Put away the gun. What are you going to do? Shoot me? Here, in the Exchange? And then what? The FBI's right outside. Where are you going to run?"

"Yes, I bloody well am going to shoot you. Don't have much choice, do I?"

Someone banged on the door to the office. "Hey, open up. Jett, you in there?" There was no mistaking Bruce Tustin's obnoxious voice. "Gavallan, you there? I saw you crossing the floor. You can hide from your girl-friends, but not from your uncle Bruce ... Jett?"

Gavallan nodded toward the door. "Your move, Tony."

Llewellyn-Davies extended his arm, eyes wincing, head turning slightly away. A moment later, his hand dropped. He began crying. "Oh, damn it all. Damn you ..."

Gavallan walked up to his former friend, gently prying the gun from his hand. "Go on now. Get out of here. I never want to see you again."

68

KONSTANTIN KIROV MOUNTED THE STAIRS to the balcony slowly, a valedictory climb to his new orbit high in the capitalist universe. Reaching the top, he crossed the narrow landing. There was room for fifteen people, maybe a few more. Advancing on the podium, he let his eyes wander over the trading floor. He had expected to play to an audience, but the preoccupied traders were going about their business as if he were not there. One by one his colleagues joined him, and he greeted each with a firm handshake.

The clock directly across the room read 9:28:45. The swell of voices rose as Richard Grasso, president of the Exchange, showed Kirov how to ring the bell, jocularly begging him to wait until the appointed moment. Kirov only half listened. His eyes were scouring the floor for sign of Antony Llewellyn-Davies, the sly Englishman who three months before had agreed to be his spy inside of Black Jet Securities. Minutes ago, Llewellyn-Davies had rushed off, worried he'd seen Gavallan. Kirov was left to wonder whether in fact he had, and if so, whether the Englishman had done as he'd been told.

A crew from Russian Channel One gathered on the floor below, camera pointed in his direction, a red light indicating film was rolling. Reflexively, Kirov stood a little straighter. He was aware that at that very instant his image was being broadcast across the Russian continent. To Moscow. To Leningrad. To Kiev and Minsk. To Odessa, Alma-Ata, Ulan Bator, and Vladivostok. Across eleven time zones, the picture of Konstantin Kirov, Russia's "first Western businessman," the "patron saint of the second Russian perestroika," was gazing down upon the country's citizens. He forgot about Gavallan and Llewellyn-Davies. His heart fluttered madly.

Grasso nudged his shoulder. "Thirty seconds, Mr. Kirov."

The clock read 9:29:30.

Meg Kratzer rubbed his back. "Congratulations," she said. "We're all so happy for you. Just thrilled."

Kirov mouthed a thank-you, wishing he could have arranged for a prettier woman to be at his side.

"*Kirov!*"

The voice came from below. Nervously, he looked to the left and right.

"*Kirov!*"

Good Christ, it was Gavallan. He had climbed on top of the trading post nearest the podium and was shouting at *him*.

"The offering is canceled. Mercury's over. The specialists are closing their books. The FBI is in the building. Come down right now. We want to talk to you."

Richard Grasso looked appalled. "Jett, mind telling me what is going on here?"

"Just hold on to Kirov. Keep him there. We're coming to arrest him."

"Yes, yes, of course." Grasso nodded his head vigorously, but when he checked over his shoulder all he saw was Kirov's narrow shoulders retreating down the stairs.

———

IT HAD BEEN A STRESSFUL DAY for the president.

New uprisings in Grozny threatened the fragile Chechen peace. A group of demonstrators from Greenpeace had camped in front of St. Basil's protesting the country's use of mammals, dolphins in particular, as instruments of war. And an independent newspaper in the south had uncovered decade-old evidence of a bribe he'd carried for Mayor Sobchak back in his days in Leningrad. The travails of politics. Sometimes he didn't think it worth it.

Pouring himself a glass of mineral water, Volodya settled into his chair and turned on the television. Quickly, he found Channel One. The screen filled with the picture of Konstantin Kirov standing on the podium of the New York Stock Exchange. Finally, some good news. He didn't care for the man, but as a representative of Russian business he was acceptable. His English was colloquial and flawless, his dress impeccable. And there was no doubting the man's resourcefulness. Given the proper training, he might have made a decent spy.

The president turned up the volume. An American stock analyst was calling for Mercury stock to rise dramatically the first day, touting the inauguration of Russia into the club of Western nations. Henceforward, the commentator intoned, one could expect a flood of Russian multinationals to be quoted on the world's major exchanges.

The president smiled.

He looked closer. There was a commotion brewing. Konstantin Kirov's face had taken on a decidedly worried cast, and he was looking this way and that. The president leaned forward, eyes glued to the television. The camera panned lower, focusing on a wild man who had climbed atop one of the trading posts on the floor of the Exchange. The commentator stopped speaking, and one could hear with astonishing clarity what the man was shouting. "Kirov. The offering is canceled.

Mercury's over." And then, to the president's horror, "The FBI's in the building."

The camera panned back up and Kirov could be seen fleeing the balcony, leaving his colleagues and advisers questioning one another.

Lifting the remote control, the president turned off the television. He felt sick to his stomach. Kirov had despoiled his country's reputation in front of millions of viewers. Tomorrow, the story would be front-page news. One more Russian thief. Another doomed enterprise. Worse, the man had failed the Service. There would be no money. No money at all.

The president reached for a phone. One fiasco he might be able to explain away; two would reek of conspiracy. There could be no more embarrassments, not even the hint of intrigue. His budding relations with America and the economic favors they promised were too valuable to risk.

His assistant answered, and Volodya roared, "Find me Major General Kirov. Immediately!"

KONSTANTIN KIROV RUSHED DOWN THE STAIRS from the podium, eager to be free of the building. To be free of the city. Of the whole damned country. Four of his men were waiting on the ground floor. They were new faces, dark, sullen, part of the New York crew he'd summoned the night before.

"Get me to the car," he said. "Yours, not mine. A bit of trouble. We must move quickly."

"Follow me," answered one of the men, his accent southern, unfriendly.

Kirov eyed the man, not liking his swarthy features, his dead eyes. But what choice did he have? They set off down the hallway at a dignified clip. Off the floor, the building was quiet and well-lit, and for a few seconds Kirov maintained the illusion that he would be able to waltz scot-free from the building. He soothed himself with the notion that he could still salvage Mercury. He would put his own money into the firm. He would upgrade the infrastructure. He would create the company he had sold to all of Wall Street. If he didn't take the company public today, who cared? He would be back in six months or a year with something even better. Forget Black Jet. Forget Gavallan. He would go to the big boys this time. Bulge bracket only. Salomon. First Boston. Lehman. They'd fight over themselves for the deal.

Fifty feet ahead, twin sets of brass-framed double doors led to the street. A black sedan lolled at the curb, its back door opened. Kirov saw daylight and thought, *Freedom*.

Then he heard the strident voice coming from behind him.

"Mr. Kirov, this is the FBI. Please stop where you are. You are under arrest, sir."

Turning, he saw a tall brown-haired man in a summer suit walking toward him, his gun drawn and hanging at his side. Gavallan was next to him. Two more men whom Kirov took to be law enforcement agents followed close behind. "You're under arrest, Mr. Kirov. Lie down on the floor, sir. Tell your men to do the same."

"Come on, Konstantin," said Gavallan. "Do as you're told. Don't make this tougher than it has to be."

Kirov looked back toward the exit. At the end of the hallway, a pair of the Exchange's security guards, clad in dove gray uniforms, their hands drifting toward their holsters, walked slowly, uneasily, toward him and his bodyguards. Passersby hugged the walls, sensing trouble.

Kirov took another look at Gavallan, then darted toward the exit. At the same time, his bodyguards moved in the opposite direction. They had no guns. They made no move to appear menacing. They simply walked rapidly toward the federal agents, obstructing their line of sight.

Passing the gray-clad security guards, Kirov murmured to his men, "Hold them here. I just need a minute."

Both men, soldiers belonging to the New York side of the Solnetsevo Brotherhood, nodded and took up position in the center of the hallway.

Kirov ran, not daring to look behind, as if he were being chased by the ghosts of his own conscience. He heard the sounds of a scuffle, Gavallan's voice calling after him. Strangely, he sounded more perfunctory than upset. The life seemed to have gone out of the man. Funny—he hadn't pegged Gavallan as a quitter. Passing through one door, then the next, Kirov emerged on the sidewalk. Twenty feet away a car door stood open, and a man inside was gesturing for him to hurry. He caught the words "Hurry, damn you. Run!" Kirov slowed only to lower his head and threw himself into the backseat.

"Thank God," he whispered, his cheek touching the cool black upholstery. "Get me out of here. Fast!"

ONE MOMENT THE BEECHCRAFT was flying straight on its course, its speed a comfortable 250 knots, altitude 400 feet. It had lined up perfectly on its inbound azimuth. The landing site, a circle of knee-high heather sprouting from the snow, was visible. The pilot had opened the cockpit door. Leaning out of his seat, he offered a thumbs-up to the valiant warriors. "Godspeed," he said, though with the tumult of the air invading the fuselage and the propeller engines buzzing so close it was doubtful anyone heard him.

The next moment the plane was no longer there.

Three pounds of plastique ignited the four hundred gallons of jet fuel in the starboard wing, which in turn ignited the auxiliary tanks housed at the rear of the fuselage and then the fuel tanks in the port wing. Expanding at 7,800 meters per second, an enormous, wickedly powerful fireball engulfed the plane. Joint tore from joint, bolt from superstructure. In one-hundredth of a second, the elemental explosion shattered the plane and everyone inside of it into ten thousand pieces, showering the pristine Alaskan tundra with a black and silver rain.

Some attributed the melted tire and grotesquely twisted propeller that landed squarely in the infield of Pump Station 2's summer baseball diamond to a practical joke played by some local miners. Others offered no explanation at all, content to merely scratch their heads. No planes had been reported in the area. The explosion was heard only faintly and seen by no one. Alaska was nothing if not mysterious.

In Severnaya, Leonid Kirov removed his hand from the transmitter. He had tried and he had failed. There would be no bust in Red Square. No promotion waiting upon his return. The president had made his disappointment abundantly clear. The penalty for failure was as severe as the reward for success was generous.

Such it had been in Russia, and such it would always be.

His hand fell to his jacket, hanging on the chair behind him. His fingers probed the jacket's pocket. It was there, as he knew it would be. He felt the cool metal, the smooth expanse of the grip, the curled menace of the trigger. Slowly, he drew the pistol out and laid it on the table. He lit a cigarette, but the smoke tasted harsh, unwelcome.

Standing, he put on his jacket and straightened his tie. He spent a moment adjusting the tie clasp, his gift from Andropov, then drew himself to attention. And raising the pistol, he was careful to keep his chin raised just so, his eyes to the fore. The gun touched his temple, and as he pulled the trigger he made sure to lean his head sideways into the barrel.

SETTLED INTO THE TOWN CAR'S BACKSEAT, Konstantin Kirov expelled a sigh of relief. He was hardly home free, but with a little luck, he'd make it to Teterboro and be airborne and en route to his private hideaway in the Exumas before the authorities could track him down. A man did not make it to his position in life without taking a few precautions, without setting aside a few dollars for a rainy day or establishing a place to keep his head down if the waters grew too rough. He'd lie low for a few years, cultivate his relations with the country's entrepreneurs, work on his memoirs. A return to Moscow was out of the question, at least until a new president took office. As for Mercury, that too would be put on hold. His plan to bring the company public had dissolved the moment he'd heard the words "FBI" and "under arrest."

Looking over his shoulder, he caught sight of Gavallan running down the stairs of the Exchange, pulling up in the middle of the street, arms raised high in exasperation.

"*Yeb vas,*" he muttered. Fuck you.

He truly hoped he'd never see the man again in his life.

Suddenly, he was very thirsty. "Do you have something to drink? Some water, perhaps? Perrier? Evian?"

Two men sat in the front.

"Of course," said the one in the passenger seat. He turned and looked at Kirov. "Anything for my partner," said Aslan Dashamirov.

"But—why—how?" Kirov choked on his own confusion.

"You've been a naughty boy, Konstantin Romanovich," said Dashamirov, waving a slim silver disc between his fingers. "Have you never heard of honor among thieves?"

Kirov threw a hand to the door, fingers clawing for the release. He would make a deal with the FBI. He would show them the inner workings of the Russian underworld. He would forfeit his entire fortune.

With a sturdy thump, the doors locked, and Dashamirov laughed.

Konstantin Kirov cast a last look behind him. Katya had joined Gavallan, and the two stood in the center of Wall Street. He thought he saw his daughter raise a hand and wave, but he couldn't be sure. Tears had blurred his vision.

Epilogue

THE GAVEL SLAMMED WITH FINALITY and a short, exultant cry went up from the executives gathered on the podium. Jett Gavallan shook hands with the Russian president, and then it was everyone else's turn, Meg's and Bruce's and Graf's. Each received the same firm grip, the same swift shake, the same sober nod. The president turned to Cate and kissed her on the cheek three times in the Russian custom. He had been learning English, and Gavallan overheard a few words.

"We are grateful to you both for saving our airline. I only hope the public will treat it as fairly."

"I'm certain it will," answered Cate graciously.

Novastar Airlines had begun the day trading on the New York Stock Exchange at $14 a share and had closed at $15.25. As thanks for returning to Novastar the money that Kirov had stolen, the president had awarded Gavallan the mandate to bring the company public a year later. Black Jet Securities had brought the $500 million offering to market at the upper end of its price range. A first day's jump of nearly 10 percent wasn't too bad for a Russian company, all things considered.

The president clapped a hand on Gavallan's arm. "Now we must talk about our aluminum industry. It is not in good condition. When can you come again to Moscow?"

"Not for a while, I'm afraid. This is our last trip until the big day. Cate can't fly much longer and I don't want to be away when the moment arrives."

"A boy or a girl?"

Gavallan looked at Cate. Her cheeks wore a slight flush, but at seven months pregnant, she'd never looked more beautiful. "It will be a surprise," he said. "But Mr. Byrnes will be happy to travel to Moscow—say in a week? He has some business with another company we're helping to sell."

"Mercury, yes?" asked the president.

"Yes," said Gavallan. "Mercury's being purchased by Bluephone, an Anglo-French telecom company."

"What is the price?"

"One billion."

"Rubles or dollars?"

Gavallan smiled. They both knew the answer to that one.

Cate wrapped an arm through his and gave him a squeeze. Actually, if you added the 50 percent stake in Novastar Cate had inherited from her father and her 85 percent ownership of Mercury, they would be nigh on billionaires. But they had decided not to keep the money, feeling that it didn't really belong to them. The shares in Novastar and her proceeds from the Mercury sale were to be placed in a philanthropic foundation Cate would chair.

With a final handshake, the president left with his entourage. Graf Byrnes headed down the stairs a moment later, with Bruce Jay Tustin and Meg Kratzer in tow. Gavallan stood at the podium, looking over the paper-strewn floor, the blinking monitors, the bold American flags. Ten minutes after the end of trading, the floor of the New York Stock Exchange was quiet, though not deserted. Traders had returned to their posts to tally their books. Brokers were on the phone with their head offices. Over a billion shares had exchanged hands. The cogs of capitalism never stopped turning, Gavallan mused.

Slipping his hand into his wife's, their fingers intertwining, he walked with her down the stairs and across the floor. "See you at seven," he said. "You thinking dinner out?"

"How 'bout room service?"

"You got it."

They walked outside the building. A fierce summer sun cut through the latticework of skyscrapers, warming their cheeks. Ahead, Graf Byrnes was climbing into the rear of a limousine that would take them to Black Jet's midtown offices. "You coming?" he shouted.

"Be right there."

Gavallan kissed his wife on the cheek. "Seven o'clock," he said. "It's a date." Then he brought her close and whispered, "Hey, we did it."

Cate didn't answer. He saw a memory dance in her eyes, a tear well up, then die.

Acknowledgments

I acknowledge with gratitude the help of Andrea O'Connell, Wyc Grousbeck, Richard Pops, Henrique M. L. Gregorio, and Barron Emile Eyraud, who gave willingly of their time and made the calls that set the ball rolling. In San Francisco, Mitch Whiteford, Michael Graham, David Golden, and Cristina Morgan showed me the inside of the tech banking world. In New York, I owe a debt of thanks to Jeffrey Zorek, Richard Cunningham, Paul Meeks, David Ballard, Kevin Keys, Christine Walton, and Derek Reisfield. Murray Teitelbaum shepherded me around the New York Stock Exchange and had an answer to every question. In Moscow, Alexander Poudov was a guide *par excellence*. Andrew Jack of the *Financial Times* gave me a cup of hot tea and steered me through the treacherous alleys of the Russian oligarchy. As always, I can't thank my wife, Sue, enough for her patience and interest in my work. Bill Massey, my brilliant editor at Bantam Dell, hounded me tirelessly and the book is the better for it. Thank you, Bill. My thanks also to Martin Fletcher at Headline in London for his support and unwavering good taste. Irwyn Applebaum and Nita Taublib oversaw every aspect of the work from beginning to end. It is a privilege to work with such talented and energetic professionals. I am lucky to have one of the finest literary agents in the business and his colleagues working on my behalf. My heartfelt appreciation goes out to Richard Pine, Sarah Piel, and Lori Andiman at Arthur Pine Associates.

Lastly, I would like to thank my brother, Bill, who is always there with a kind word, solid advice, and a ready ear. You're one in a billion.

If you enjoyed
THE FIRST BILLION,
get ready for the next pulse-pounding
suspense novel from

Christopher Reich . . .

THE
DEVIL'S
BANKER

COMING FROM DELACORTE PRESS
IN SEPTEMBER 2003!

CHRISTOPHER REICH

AUTHOR OF THE *NEW YORK TIMES* BESTSELLER
NUMBERED ACCOUNT

THE DEVIL'S BANKER

The Devil's Banker

On sale September 2003

1

IT IS DIFFICULT TO WALK casually with five hundred thousand dollars taped to your belly. More difficult still when any of the men brushing past you would gladly slit your throat were they to suspect the king's ransom you carried.

The man who had chosen the warrior's name Abu Sayeed snaked through the alleys of the smugglers' bazaar, careful to check his impatient step. He was close now, but he could not hurry. To hurry invited attention. And attention meant trouble he could not afford.

Around him, shopkeepers leaned in open doorways, smoking cigarettes and sipping cups of tea. He could sense their eyes upon him as they studied his bearing, gauging its strength, deciding whether he was a predator or prey. Instinctively, he stood straighter and thrust his chin forward. But all the while he kept his pace relaxed, his face slack, even as the claws dug into him.

The money was divided into fifty packets, each containing ten thousand dollars, each wrapped and waterproofed in transparent plastic. The packets had sharp, cruel corners that chafed and cut his flesh. He had been traveling for thirty-six hours. His chest and back were flayed as if scored by a cat-o'-nine-tails. Only by thinking of the operation was he able to continue. The prospect of the infidels' death invigorated him with the strength of the Pharaoh's army.

At four P.M., the summer sun was at its fiercest. Dust devils arose on the dusty road, swirled lazily, then spun themselves out. After a brief siesta, the bazaar was rousing itself to life. Beneath fluorescent lights, shelves sagged with cartons of Dunhill cigarettes, Toshiba laptops, and Paco Rabanne cologne, all brought overland from Afghanistan to avoid duty and tax. Other windows displayed less mundane goods: Kalashnikov rifles, Colt pistols, and Claymore mines. Hashish, heroin, even human chattel could be found at the right address. If there was a free market on Earth, mused Sayeed, it was here on the western outskirts of Peshawar, the gateway to the Khyber Pass.

Stopping to purchase a cube of diced sugar cane, he cast his gaze behind him. His depthless black eyes scoured the street, checking for the misplaced face, the averted gaze, the anxious dawdler. So close, he must keep his senses keen. He did not believe that the crusaders knew his identity. Still, he must be cautious. Members of the American Special Forces infested Peshawar as lice infest a beast. Most were easy to spot, with their Oakley sunglasses, Casio watches, and desert boots. A few even dared enter the bazaar, where foreigners were not welcome and Pakistani law held no sway.

The thought of the Americans brought a contemptuous smile to his lips. Soon they would learn that they could not run. The fire was coming. It would burn them in their heartland. It would scald them from within.

And, for a moment, the claws loosened their grip. The pain subsided, and he basked in the glow of destruction.

Satisfied his trail was clean, Sayeed spat out the sinewy cane and crossed the narrow road. To look at, he was no different from any of the thousands of souls who eked out an existence trafficking the porous border that separated Pakistan from Afghanistan. His *shalwar kameez*, the baggy shirt and trousers that made up the local dress, was filthy and stiff with dried sweat; his black headdress smothered with red alkali dust. His beard belonged to the most fervent of believers, as did the AK-47 he carried slung over a shoulder and the bejeweled dagger strapped to his calf.

But Sayeed was not Pakistani, nor was he a Pashtun

from the southern provinces of Afghanistan or an Uzbek from the north. Born Michael Christian Montgomery in London, England, Sayeed was the bastard offspring of a cancerous British officer and a teenage Egyptian whore. His father had died while he was a boy, leaving him a polished accent and not much more. Unable to care for him, his mother returned to Cairo and gave him over to the *madrassas*, the religious schools that gifted him with an Islamic education. His childhood was brutish and short. It was a natural progression to the camps where he learned the creed of the gun, memorized the verse of violence, and worshiped at the altar of rebellion. And from there to the killing fields of Palestine, Chechnya, and Serbia.

At twenty, the Scorpion found him.

At twenty-one, Michael Christian Montgomery ceased to exist. It was Abu Mohammed Sayeed who swore the oath, accepted the mark, and joined *Hijira*.

Skirting a convoy of carts piled high with Korean fabrics, Tibetan rugs, and Panasonic televisions still in their factory packaging, he reached the Tikram mosque. The doors were open, and inside the shadowy hall, a few men lay on prayer rugs, prostrate in worship. His eyes returned to the street. Scanning the intersection ahead, he felt a new pain lash his back. This time, however, it was not the jagged belt that provoked his discomfort. It was fear. He could not see the store. Somehow, he had taken a wrong turn. He was lost.

Frantically, Sayeed turned his head this way and that. It could not be. He was at the Tikram mosque. He had seen the photographs. He had studied the maps. Despair washed over him. Others were waiting. The countdown had begun. Seven days. The thought of failure turned his bowels to water.

Terrified, he wandered into the street. A horn blared in his ear, loud, very loud, but from another universe altogether. Sayeed jumped back a step and a jitney lumbered past, passengers hanging from the doors, clinging to the luggage rack. In its wake, a cloud of rank exhaust choked the already oppressive air. He could not go on. He could not go back. Truly, he was damned.

The exhaust dissipated and he saw it. The gold letters

emblazoned on a black field. BHATIA'S GOLD AND PRECIOUS JEWELRY. His despair vanished. In its place came joy. The light of a thousand suns.

"Inshallah, God is great," he whispered, a bolt of piety swelling his heart.

Guards stood on either side of the doorway, Kalashnikovs to their chest, fingers tickling the trigger guard. Sayeed passed them without a glance. They were not there to protect jewelry, but cash, primarily U.S. dollars, and gold ingots. Bhatia's reputation as a jeweler might be suspect, but his trustworthiness as a *hawaladar*, or money broker, was unquestioned. Faisan Bhatia had long served the local smuggling community as its agent of choice. He was the only broker in the region able to handle the large sums that Abu Sayeed required.

In Arabic, *hawala* means *to change*. And in Hindu, *trust*. Put simply, it was the *hawala* broker's job to affect transfers of cash from one city to another. Some of his clients were traders eager to repatriate their earnings after selling their haul in the bazaar. Others, simple folk wishing to send money home to loved ones in Karachi, Delhi, or Dubai. Both groups shared a distrust of the bureaucracy and paperwork demanded by the country's less-than-solvent banks. For them, *hawala* was a welcome alternative. A system built on trust, hidden from intrusive eyes. A system that had been in place when Arab traders plied the Silk Road hundreds of years ago.

Bhatia, a fat Indian with a streak of gray in his hair, stood imperiously behind the counter. As Sayeed approached, he eyed the customer's caked clothing and unwashed face with undisguised contempt.

"I would like to make a transfer," Abu Sayeed whispered when he was close enough to taste the man's breath. "It is a matter of some urgency."

The Indian did not move.

"The Scorpion sent me."

Faisan Bhatia's eyes flickered, but only for an instant. "Come this way."

2

IT WAS THE MOST GODAWFUL frightening place she had ever been. Some parts of Jakarta came close. Jakarta with its garish slums, oppressive pollution, and packs of teenage muggers giggling with hostile intent. Macao had a few dark corners where you didn't dare venture. And everyone knew about Rio, the gorgeous bad boys on motorbikes, streaking past with their razors at the ready. But here . . . the unremitting heat, the hostile stares, and, worst of all, the *burqa* draped over her head and shoulders, baking her like a ruddy Christmas goose . . . this topped it all.

Her name was Sarah Churchill, operational designation: EMERALD, and through her black gauze veil, she watched the target advance across the intersection. She could see that he was in distress, trying not to limp, compensating by standing too straight and puffing out his chest. Two days she'd been tracking him, up and down the mountain passes, a distance of sixty miles. She was hurting, too, but she'd be damned if she'd show it. Her feet were raw and blistered in their leather sandals, her legs fatigued beyond measure. A little while ago, her lower lip had cracked and she could feel a trickle of blood, salty and strangely reassuring, on her tongue.

A trio of Indian women clad in red and orange saris scurried across her path, and she mimicked their gait. The "second-class shuffle," she called it—head bent, shoulders hunched, eyes fixed to the ground like a dog that's been beaten too much.

Drawing in her shoulders, Sarah made herself shrink beneath the full-length garment. Her horizons seemed to shrink before her and she bridled at her training. *Blend in with your environment:* the first rule of tradecraft taught at Fort Monckton, where all good little English boys and girls go to learn to be spies. Ever the prize pupil, she kept her back hunched and continued to hug the inside of the street.

She was too tall. That was the problem. You didn't see many Pakistani women who stood five feet nine inches in stocking feet. Her height came from her father, a six foot four inch Welshman. Her hair, a raven's black and cut to her shoulders, was her mother's gift, as were her sierra brown eyes.

Her attitude, though, was all her own, and not subject to amendment or revision. She was plucky, outspoken, and a sucker for a smile. Five years ago at IONEC, the Intelligence Officer's New Entrant's Course, she'd set the women's mark for the fifty-mile hike, but when, at her graduation ceremony, her instructors called her their toughest recruit, she'd broken down and cried like a baby.

Her earpiece crackled with static. "Primary still visual?"

"He's gone into the store," she whispered. "Bhatia's Gold and Jewelry." She spelled the name slowly, enunciating each letter just as Matron had taught her at Roedean. "It's the bloody *hawala*, all right. Time to call in the reinforcements."

"Give us a GPS read."

"Coming up." She found the global positioning device on her belt and hit the locate/transmit button. Within a second, the stationary satellites that comprised the Central Intelligence Agency's proprietary GPS had established her exact latitude and longitude to within six inches of where she actually stood, and her altitude above sea level to within four. She'd been transmitting her location every hundred meters since she'd entered the bazaar. Taken together, the coordinates constituted a route marker for the cavalry, or in more dire circumstances, a path to get her the hell out of Dodge.

"EMERALD, you are mapped. An A-team is moving in to clean up. ETA is twelve minutes."

"*Twelve minutes?* He could be out the back and halfway back to Pesh by then. Dammit, tell them to hurry."

Located on the western outskirts of Peshawar, the smugglers' bazaar encompassed an area as big as the City of London, with half again as many alleys, roads, and lanes. Few of the roads were marked, if they even possessed a name. There were certainly no addresses.

The bazaar had sprung up as an informal "gray market," trading in goods stolen across the Afghani border. Carts had given way to shacks, and now most of the stores were housed in sturdy concrete bungalows. A patchwork of dubious signs advertised the wares. Marks and Spencer. Maytag. Pringle of Scotland. Sony. And her absolute favorite: Sacks Fifth Avenue. Though wholly within Pakistan's borders, the bazaar was treated as its own autonomous region. Crime was rampant. Thieves, pickpockets, and worse roamed freely, practicing their trade on the weak and unsuspecting. It was up to the victim to catch the criminal. Once he did, the punishment was up to him too. If there was any rule at all, it was the harsh tribal custom of the Pathan tribesmen who made it their home.

"Maintain visual," snapped the voice.

"How's the picture?" she asked. "Getting what you need?"

"Reception's a little fuzzy. Keep still for a second. I need to reset the color balance."

Sarah held still, staring out at the bustling street. It was hard to imagine that seven thousand miles away a technician was deciding whether the picture was too red or too green. The Sony microdigital camera embedded in her sunglasses was a gift from the boys in Langley. She liked to think of it as a "welcome to our side of the pond" present given upon her secondment from MI6. The Yanks always had the neater toys. The camera's images ran to a transmitter in her belt that relayed both audio and visual signals to a spot station nearby. The spot station, in turn, sent the signals on to Langley. The boys at Langley had also given her a machine pistol, three spare clips of ammo, and a tab of cyanide tucked inside a neat little compartment where her wisdom tooth used to be.

"Give us a slow scan left to right."

Sarah turned her head as directed, the camera capturing the same exotic imagery as her eyes: the mosque and its beautifully carved doors, the merchant stringing fresh offal in his front window, the gunsmith tooling a rifle barrel on the sidewalk, and finally, Bhatia's Gold and Jewelry, where she could make out a tall, lean figure standing at the far counter. Abu Muhammed Sayeed, nicknamed OMAR, for operational purposes.

But they couldn't get the smell. The acrid whiff of long-tended fires; the spiced scent of lamb on a spit; the eye-watering odor of men who toiled and sweated in the one-hundred-degree heat and had not bathed in weeks.

"Close enough? Or would you gents like me to stick my head inside the store and say hello?"

"Negative. Just give me a walk-by. Nice and brisk. We can slow down the pictures on this side."

Sarah crossed the street, dodging a howling Vespa, doing her best to keep to a walk. She was sure that somewhere in the Koran there was a *hadith* banning "righteous women" from running, just as the holy lessons banned them from everything else except catering to the whims and desires of "righteous man folk."

Stepping onto the raised walkway, she continued past the jewelry store, letting her gaze fall on the array of gold chains in the window. The doorway gaped beside her. Two guards with AK's stood at attention inside. Surveillance cameras stared down from the corners. A portly Indian was talking to Sayeed. There were no other customers.

"Confirmed. OMAR on premises. Looks like he's got some muscle in there" came the voice in her earpiece. "Keep it moving."

For a quarter second longer she watched, then continued her promenade. At that very moment, however, there was a flurry of movement inside the store, and she stopped. It was a clumsy, jerky halt, a dead giveaway. And there she stood for one second . . . two . . . a perfect silhouette frozen in the doorway.

"He's going in the back," Sarah whispered. "I mean the two are going together. So is one of the guards. Where are the bully boys?" she asked, desperation crowding inside her.

"ETA nine minutes. Do not jeopardize your cover. Proceed to the Tikram mosque and continue surveillance from there."

"Nine min—" Her rigid training cut short her protest. In her mind, however, she howled with frustration.

At the end of the walkway, Sarah stepped off the curb and stopped. The courtyard to her right was filled with automobile tires. Hundreds and hundreds of brand-new tires, stacked neatly upon one another, row after row, rising thirty feet in the air. Turning, she peered across the intersection toward the mosque. It would be safer to watch from there. An A-team was inbound. She knew what that meant: bullets and lots of them. Abu Sayeed was not the type to turn himself over to the authorities and say, "Okay, Officer. I'll come along quietly."

"EMERALD, this is Ranger." A new voice sounded in her ear, calm, authoritative. *Ranger.* The DO himself. The Director of Operations. "Go on into the store. Take a look around."

"Go in?"

"We wouldn't want him to sneak out on us, would we? Not before the party starts. It's a jewelry store," he went on. "Have a look at a necklace. Buy whatever you like. Call it my treat. You can put it on my expense account."

Her mouth had grown dry, her tongue parched and swollen.

"I don't think they take American Express," she answered blithely, knowing that the banter was to relax her, to deceive her about the peril of his command. And make no mistake, it *was* an order. He was asking her to flit by her lonesome into a shop with the biggest underworld financier on the northwest frontier, and a hardened terrorist associated with a group so secret, so rife with all manner of rumor, that no one even dared whisper its name—if it even had one—because until now no one had wanted to acknowledge its existence. One supreme evil commander was enough for the world these days.

Across the street a fierce-looking man was staring

daggers at her. He wore a black headdress and a black *dish-dasha* and his beard hadn't been cut in a decade. The poster boy for Islamic Ignorance refused to avert his gaze, lips trembling, eyes afire, his entire being a vessel of hate. Through the veil, she met his accusing glare, and from his obduracy, his anger, his bewildering disrespect of the superior sex, she drew the courage she herself lacked.

"Roger last," she said. "I think I'll have a look at some of Bhatia's tat."

"Good girl," said Ranger. And Sarah thought that if he ever called her that again, she'd slug him in the jaw. But by then it didn't matter. She was moving, not thinking. She dodged the curtain of sparks sent up from the gunsmith's forge. She grimaced in her private netherworld as she passed the coils of lamb intestines dangling from the butcher's hook. And then she was inside the store, admiring Mr. Bhatia's mediocre wares as if they were the Crown Jewels.

THE MONEY SAT IN A PILE on a table in Bhatia's private office. With a barber's straight-edged razor, the Indian opened each packet, then handed the bills to an associate to count. When he was finished, he grunted. "Five hundred thousand dollars, as you claimed."

"The Scorpion does not lie," said Abu Sayeed. A bountiful rain had doubled the poppy harvest. One ton of raw opium was Allah's gift to Hijira: his benediction upon the holocaust to come.

"It is not easy to move such a sum," said Bhatia. "How quickly do you need it?"

"Immediately."

"Today?"

"Now."

Bhatia's grave features registered concern. "Where is the money to be sent?"

"Paris."

"Hmm." Bhatia's eyes narrowed, and he mumbled a few words to himself, shaking his head. Sayeed knew it a ruse, the Indian figuring how large a fee he might get away with. "It can be done. However, the cost for such a transaction is two percent."

"One percent."

"Impossible. No one keeps such cash on the premises. A bank will have to be involved. There will be borrowing costs. Overnight at least. Maybe longer. It cannot be avoided. And of course the risk. One and a half."

Sayeed disliked negotiation, but in some cases, it was necessary. Five thousand dollars was a small fee to insure swift delivery of money to Paris. Small, indeed, compared to the damage it would wreak. "One," he repeated. He had his orders. "The Scorpion will show his appreciation."

"How?"

Abu Mohammed Sayeed clamped his hand over the Indian's. "He will not sting you."

FOUR HUNDRED AND SEVENTY MILES above the Indian Ocean, an Intruder Geosynchronous SIGINT (signals intelligence) satellite tasked by the National Reconnaissance Agency to monitor mobile communications in the Pakistan–Northern India–Afghanistan triangle responded to an emergency override command. In the freezing infinity of space, guidance boosters fired for a half second. Rectangular electromagnetic-phased array panels minutely altered their attitude. In an instant, the satellite's field of surveillance or "footprint" shifted forty miles to the north and twenty-two miles to the east, and centered on codename EMERALD's last relayed GPS coordinates.

Several minutes later, the satellite intercepted an open-air cellular transmission based in Peshawar with a respondent in Paris. Along with two thousand three hundred and twenty-nine other calls it had concurrently captured, the satellite's transponders relayed the signal to a ground-based listening station at Diego Garcia, maintained by the U.S. Air Force's 20th Space Satellite Group. In real time, the listening station directed the signals to the National Security Agency in Fort Meade, Maryland, where the conversation was analyzed by a team of parallel-linked IBM supercomputers for any of a thousand "keywords" in one hundred languages and dialects. In .025 of a second, the supercomputer determined the call was of "strategic or military" value, coded it "urgent," and forwarded a digital copy of the conversation to an analyst at the Central Intelligence Agency's headquarters in Langley, Virginia.

The analyst, realizing he was in possession of "real time intelligence," or information of an immediate strategic concern, phoned the Deputy Director of Operations and requested a crash meeting.

"Third Floor. CTCC," said Admiral Owen Glendenning. "Get up here on the double and bring me a copy of the call."

"So," TRUMPETED FAISAN BHATIA, reentering the office after a fifteen-minute absence. "Everything is arranged. The money can be picked up at Royal Joailliers. It is located at the Place Vendôme in Paris. Do you wish their address?"

"Of course." Abu Sayeed smiled secretly. The Scorpion had informed him that Bhatia would use Royal Joailliers. Royal called itself an "haute joaillier," meaning that nothing in its satin-lined showcases sold for less than ten thousand dollars. The cartels were their best clients—Colombians, Mexicans, Russians—and it was their practice to keep unconscionable sums of cash on the premises. When Sayeed had written down the address, Bhatia inquired if he would like to provide him with the recipient's name. "That is not necessary," said Sayeed.

"Very well. The recipient must use a password to identify himself. In this case, a dollar bill will do nicely." Bhatia slid a worn U.S. banknote across the table. "You will take it with you. As soon as possible, I advise you to transmit the serial numbers on the lower left-hand side of the bill to the recipient. When he presents himself to Royal Joailliers, he must give them the identical numbers in sequence. Only then will he be given the money. There can be no mistakes. It is agreed?"

Sayeed knew the rules of *hawala* well. The Scorpion had made use of the informal banking system for years to funnel funds to his operatives. "It is agreed," he said.

"May I offer the use of my telephone?"

"I have my own."

"Very good, then. You will join me for something to eat. If I may say, you look rather done in." Bhatia clapped his hands, barking an order to an unseen consort. A moment later, his wife entered carrying a tray with two porcelain cups and a china teapot. A younger woman followed, bearing a goat's head upon a silver platter. In the cloying ninety-degree heat, flies swarmed the tray, attacking the staring, gelatinous eyes.

"Please," said Bhatia, extending a hand toward the Pakistani delicacy.

But Sayeed was not interested in food. Glancing at the monitor that broadcast the interior of Bhatia's showroom, he watched as a woman clad in a full-length *burqa* examined a tray of jewelry. She had been there the entire time he had been with Bhatia. The picture grew fuzzy, as if losing reception, then snapped back into focus. A tinge of unease soured his stomach. The clock read 4:45. It would be 12:45 in Paris. He wanted to leave. He wanted to make the call. His brother would be waiting.

Without a further word, he stood.

Bhatia set his cup of tea on the table and sprang to his feet. "It was an honor to serve the Scorpion," he intoned gravely, leading the way to the beaded curtains. "You will pass on my regards?"

"The monitor," said Sayeed, lifting his finger toward the screen, "it is a closed circuit system?"

"No," answered Bhatia proudly. "Wireless. New from Japan."

Sayeed stalked from the office without another word.

3

ADMIRAL OWEN GLENDENNING stood at the rear of the Counterterrorism Command Center on the sixth floor of the Agency's headquarters in Langley, Virginia, digesting the latest information. It was too soon to hope, yet he could neither stifle nor ignore the first flush of optimism that reddened the back of his neck and had him curling his toes. Keep on him a little longer, girl, and we're there. Just a little longer.

Projected onto a seven-foot screen, a live feed from Pakistan offered him Sarah Churchill's point of view as she examined a selection of gold chains. She raised her head and Glendenning was faced with a close-up of a frantic jewelry salesman blabbing the usual nonsense about high quality and best price. A simultaneous English translation ran across the bottom of the screen.

A second screen broadcast the footprint of the Central Intelligence Agency's spy satellites on a political map of the globe. Each satellite's footprint was indicated by a shadowed area. Some shadows remained stationary; others crept across the map with the turning of the Earth.

The seal of the CIA highlighted against a navy blue background lit up a third screen, currently unused.

At four A.M., the Counterterrorism Command Center was fully staffed and humming. Three rows of analysts occupied the front position of the auditorium-sized command room. All enjoyed brand-new workstations, the latest flat-panel displays, and state-of-the-art ergonomic chairs that had cost twelve hundred dollars a pop. Glendenning thought it looked like a scene from a movie—the way Hollywood dreamed the espionage community operated. It had been a long time since the Company had access to funds like this, but with the war on terrorism running full bore, the spigots were open wide.

Glendenning was a small, slightly built man with thinning gray hair and an unremarkable face. Dressed in his usual uniform of khaki trousers, white short-sleeved button-down shirt complete with pen protector, and Rockport deck shoes, he looked more like a NASA engineer than a seasoned spymaster. He saved his dress whites and the six rows of ribbons he had accumulated during thirty years of service for his appearances before the permanent Senate subcommittee on intelligence. Briefings that had once been little more than secret check-writing ceremonies had lately taken an adversarial turn. "Where were the results Glendenning had promised?" the more daring senators demanded. A few hundred million dollars in confiscated accounts was fine and dandy, but what about the terrorists behind it? Warm bodies, not frozen assets, were the order of the day.

Picking up a phone, he dialed the Foreign Terrorist Asset Tracking Center (FTAT) two floors below. "Get me Halsey."

Strictly speaking, FTAT was a Treasury operation. Treasury funded it. Treasury supervised it. But when the scope of the investigation into worldwide terrorist financing had become clear, all involved had decided to move FTAT's operations to Langley.

There was a time not too far back that the very idea of the CIA contacting Treasury to share information was practically a jailable offense. There was law enforcement and there was intelligence and never the twain shall meet. But the events of September 11, 2001, had changed all that. With the passage of the Patriot Act, communication between the United States' varied and multiple law enforcement and intelligence agencies was not only permitted, it was encouraged. The old concept of "stovepiping," or keeping information inside the particular agency, or, as was the case with the FBI, inside the individual department that had discovered it, was thrown out the door. Concerns about infractions on civil liberties and personal privacy were quickly dismissed. The threat beyond the country's borders took preeminence, and was, Glendenning knew, far greater than anyone could be told.

"This is Halsey," answered a deep, gravelly voice.

"Don't you have a home either?"

Allan Halsey, chief of the Foreign Terrorist Asset Tracking Center, gave a shallow laugh. "Not according to my wife."

"We nabbed the call," said Glendenning. "The money's being moved as we speak. Come on up and we'll run it from here."

"How much?"

"We're guessing five hundred grand or five million. Either way it's the real deal."

"I don't like it," said Halsey. "Risky to move so much."

"I couldn't agree more. Something's about to pop. Who's running your team in Paris?"

"Chapel, Adam."

"Don't know him. A new guy?"

"Treasury pulled him in after the WTC."

"Military?"

"God no," said Halsey. "A Quant jock all the way. Kid was on the fast track at Price Waterhouse. Partner at twenty-nine. National audit manager."

"Sounds like a real killer," said Glendenning. "Ought to have 'em quaking in their boots."

"Come on now, Glen. He's the new kind of soldier. You know, brains instead of brawn. Different war we're fighting this time."

"That's what they tell me. In the end, though, you still have to shoot the bad guys."

"Don't worry about Adam," said Halsey, his voice quieter, more confident, as if vouchsafing a secret. "He can hold his own."

We'd awakened something old and long dormant. It made me hesitate. Made me not want to finish the circle. Stubbornness, and fear. I didn't completely understand what I was feeling. It was someone else's magic, someone's spell. We'd triggered it, but I didn't know what it would do.

We could raise our dead but it would be like walking a tightrope between the other spell and . . . something.

PRAISE FOR THE NOVELS OF LAURELL K. HAMILTON, FEATURING ANITA BLAKE, VAMPIRE HUNTER:

"I was enthralled . . . a departure from the usual type of vampire tale which will have a wide appeal to any reader hunting for both chills and fun."

—Andre Norton

"Edge-of-the-seat excitement."

—*Locus*

"Anita Blake's world is a welcome addition to both the hard-boiled detective and the dark fantasy genres. Smart and scary, Anita's adventures will keep you reading—and have you looking over your shoulder when you're done!"

—Richard Knaak, author of *Frostwing*

"A fast-paced delight, with its strange characters, snappy dialogue, and brutal action."

—*VOYA*

"Anita Blake is . . . fast, feisty and far from frilly. A lot of fun to curl up with . . ."

—*Bakka Books*

Ace Books by Laurell K. Hamilton

BLOODY BONES

LAURELL K. HAMILTON

ACE BOOKS, NEW YORK

This book is an Ace original edition, and has never been previously published.

BLOODY BONES

An Ace Book / published by arrangement with the author

PRINTING HISTORY
Ace edition / October 1996

All rights reserved.
Copyright © 1996 by Laurell K. Hamilton.
Cover art by Craig White.
This book, or parts thereof, may not be reproduced in any form without permission.
For information address: The Berkley Publishing Group, a division of Penguin Putnam Inc., 375 Hudson Street, New York, New York 10014.

Visit our website at
www.penguinputnam.com

ISBN: 0-441-00374-5

ACE®
Ace Books are published by The Berkley Publishing Group, a division of Penguin Putnam Inc., 375 Hudson Street, New York, New York 10014. ACE and the "A" design are trademarks belonging to Penguin Putnam Inc.

PRINTED IN THE UNITED STATES OF AMERICA

20   19   18   17   16   15

IN LOVING MEMORY OF MY MOTHER,
SUSIE MAY GENTRY KLEIN.
WOULD THAT WE HAD HAD MORE TIME.

MISS YOU.

ACKNOWLEDGMENTS

As always to my husband, Gary, more precious to me now than ever. To my editor, Ginjer Buchanan, whose input changed Serephina for the better. Paty Cockrum, who you can blame for the bathtub scene. Marella Sands, who was right about our reaction to Stirling. Mark Sumner for emergency reading, and questions. Who else can I call at midnight and know I won't wake them? Deborah Millitello as always for emergency phone calls and hand-holding. Rett MacPherson, who heard parts of this book over the phone. To Tom Drennan and N. L. Drew, new talent in the group. Alternate Historians forever. Jean-Claude, truce at last. Sergeant St. Clair, Public Information and Education Officer for the Missouri State Highway Patrol, who answered my last-minute questions. Brynda Mitchell, thanks for the penguin. Thanks to everyone who has written to us.

BLOODY
BONES

1

IT WAS ST. Patrick's Day, and the only green I was wearing was a button that read, "Pinch me and you're dead
meat." I'd started work last night with a green blouse on, but
I'd gotten blood all over it from a beheaded chicken. Larry
Kirkland, zombie-raiser in training, had dropped the decapitated bird. It did the little headless chicken dance and
sprayed both of us with blood. I finally caught the damn
thing, but the blouse was ruined.

I had to run home and change. The only thing not ruined
was the charcoal grey suit jacket that had been in the car. I
put it back on over a black blouse, black skirt, dark hose,
and black pumps. Bert, my boss, didn't like us wearing
black to work, but if I had to be at the office at seven o'clock
without any sleep at all, he would just have to live with it.

I huddled over my coffee mug, drinking it as black as I
could swallow it. It wasn't helping much. I stared at a series
of 8-by-10 glossy blowups spread across my desktop. The
first picture was of a hill that had been scraped open, probably by a bulldozer. A skeletal hand reached out of the raw
earth. The next photo showed that someone had tried to
carefully scrape away the dirt, showing the splintered coffin
and bones to one side of the coffin. A new body. The bulldozer had been brought in again. It had plowed up the red
earth and found a boneyard. Bones studded the earth like
scattered flowers.

One skull spread its unhinged jaws in a silent scream. A
scraggle of pale hair still clung to the skull. The dark,
stained cloth wrapped around the corpse was the remnants
of a dress. I spotted at least three femurs next to the upper

half of a skull. Unless the corpse had had three legs, we were looking at a real mess.

The pictures were well done in a gruesome sort of way. The color made it easier to differentiate the corpses, but the high gloss was a little much. It looked like morgue photos done by a fashion photographer. There was probably an art gallery in New York that would hang the damn things and serve cheese and wine while people walked around saying, "Powerful, don't you think? Very powerful."

They were powerful, and sad.

There was nothing but the photos. No explanation. Bert had said to come to his office after I'd looked at them. He'd explain everything. Yeah, I believed that. The Easter Bunny is a friend of mine, too.

I gathered the pictures up, slipped them into the envelope, picked my coffee mug up in the other hand, and went for the door.

There was no one at the desk. Craig had gone home. Mary, our daytime secretary, didn't get in until eight. There was a two-hour space of time when the office was un-manned. That Bert had called me into the office when we were the only ones there bothered me a lot. Why the se-crecy?

Bert's office door was open. He sat behind his desk, drinking coffee, shuffling some papers around. He glanced up, smiled, and motioned me closer. The smile bothered me. Bert was never pleasant unless he wanted something.

His thousand-dollar suit framed a white-on-white shirt and tie. His grey eyes sparkled with good cheer. His eyes are the color of dirty window glass, so sparkling is a real effort. His snow-blond hair had been freshly buzzed. The crewcut was so short I could see scalp.

"Have a seat, Anita."

I tossed the envelope on his desk and sat down. "What are you up to, Bert?"

His smile widened. He usually didn't waste the smile on anybody but clients. He certainly didn't waste it on me. "You looked at the pictures?"

"Yeah, what of it?"

"Could you raise them from the dead?"

I frowned at him and sipped my coffee. "How old are they?"

"You couldn't tell from the pictures?"

"In person I could tell you, but not just from pictures. Answer the question."

"Around two hundred years."

I just stared at him. "Most animators couldn't raise a zombie that old without a human sacrifice."

"But you can," he said.

"Yeah. I didn't see any headstones in the pictures. Do we have any names?"

"Why?"

I shook my head. He'd been the boss for five years, started the company when it was just him and Manny, and he didn't know shit about raising the dead. "How can you hang around a bunch of zombie-raisers for this many years and know so little about what we do?"

The smile slipped a little, the glow beginning to fade from his eyes. "Why do you need names?"

"You use names to call the zombie from the grave."

"Without a name you can't raise them?"

"Theoretically, no," I said.

"But you can do it," he said. I didn't like how sure he was.

"Yeah, I can do it. John can probably do it, too."

He shook his head. "They don't want John."

I finished the last of my coffee. "Who's they?"

"Beadle, Beadle, Stirling, and Lowenstein."

"A law firm," I said.

He nodded.

"No more games, Bert. Just tell me what the hell's going on."

"Beadle, Beadle, Stirling, and Lowenstein have some clients building a very plush resort in the mountains near Branson. A very exclusive resort. A place where the wealthy country stars that don't own a house in the area can go to get away from the crowds. Millions of dollars are at stake."

"What's the old cemetery have to do with it?"

"The land they're building on was in dispute between two

families. The courts decided the Kellys owned the land, and they were paid a great deal of money. The Bouvier family claimed it was their land and there was a family plot on it to prove it. No one could find the cemetery."

Ah. "They found it," I said.

"They found an old cemetery, but not necessarily the Bouvier family plot."

"So they want to raise the dead and ask who they are?"

"Exactly."

I shrugged. "I can raise a couple of the corpses in the coffins. Ask who they are. What happens if their last name is Bouvier?"

"They have to buy the land a second time. They think some of the corpses are Bouviers. That's why they want all the bodies raised."

I raised my eyebrows. "You're joking."

He shook his head, looking pleased. "Can you do it?"

"I don't know. Give me the pictures again." I set my coffee mug on his desk and took the pictures back. "Bert, they've screwed this six ways to Sunday. It's a mass grave, thanks to the bulldozers. The bones are all mixed together. I've only read about one case of anyone raising a zombie from a mass grave. But they were calling a specific person. They had a name." I shook my head. "Without a name it may not be possible."

"Would you be willing to try?"

I spread the pictures over the desk, staring at them. The top half of a skull had turned upside down like a bowl. Two finger bones attached by something dry and desiccated that must once had been human tissue lay next to it. Bones, bones everywhere but not a name to speak.

Could I do it? I honestly didn't know. Did I want to try? Yeah. I did.

"I'd be willing to try."

"Wonderful."

"Raising them a few every night is going to take weeks, even if I can do it. With John's help it would be quicker."

"It will cost them millions to delay that long," Bert said.

"There's no other way to do it."

"You raised the Davidsons' entire family plot, including Great-Grandpa. You weren't even supposed to raise him. You can raise more than one at a time."

I shook my head. "That was an accident. I was showing off. They wanted to raise three family members. I thought I could save them money by doing it in one shot."

"You raised ten family members, Anita. They only asked for three."

"So?"

"So can you raise the entire cemetery in one night?"

"You're crazy," I said.

"Can you do it?"

I opened my mouth to say no, and closed it. I had raised an entire cemetery once. Not all of them had been two centuries old, but some of them had been older, nearly three hundred. And I raised them all. Of course, I had two human sacrifices to ride for power. It was a long story how I ended up with two people dying inside a circle of power. Self-defense, but the magic didn't care. Death is death.

Could I do it? "I really don't know, Bert."

"That's not a no," he said. He had an eager, anticipatory look on his face.

"They must have offered you a bundle of money," I said.

He smiled. "We're bidding on the project."

"We're what?"

"They sent this package to us, the Resurrection Company in California and the Essential Spark in New Orleans."

"They prefer Élan Vital to the English translation," I said. Frankly, it sounded more like a beauty salon than an animating firm, but nobody had asked me. "So what? The lowest bid gets it?"

"That was their plan," Bert said.

He looked entirely too satisfied with himself. "What?" I asked.

"Let me play it back to you," he said. "There are what, three animators in the entire country that could raise a zombie that old without a human sacrifice? You and John are two of them. I'm including Phillipa Freestone of Resurrection in this."

"Probably," I said.

He nodded. "Okay. Could Phillipa raise without a name?"

"I don't have any way of knowing that. John could. Maybe she could."

"Could either she or John raise from the mass bones, not the ones in the coffin?"

That stopped me. "I don't know."

"Would either of them stand a chance of raising the entire graveyard?" He was staring at me very steadily.

"You're enjoying this too much," I said.

"Just answer the question, Anita."

"I know John couldn't do it. I don't think Phillipa is as good as John, so no, they couldn't do it."

"I'm going to up the bid," Bert said.

I laughed. "Up the bid?"

"Nobody else can do it. Nobody but you. They tried treating this like any other construction problem. But there aren't going to be any other bids, now are there?"

"Probably not," I said.

"Then I'm going to take them to the cleaners," he said with a smile.

I shook my head. "You greedy son of a bitch."

"You get a share of the fee, you know."

"I know." We looked at each other. "What if I try and can't raise them all in one night?"

"You'll still be able to raise them all eventually, won't you?"

"Probably." I stood, picking up my coffee mug. "But I wouldn't spend the check until after I've done it. I'm going to go get some sleep."

"They want the bid this morning. If they accept our terms, they'll fly you up in a private helicopter."

"Helicopter—you know I hate to fly."

"For this much money you'll fly."

"Great."

"Be ready to go at a moment's notice."

"Don't push it, Bert." I hesitated at the door. "Let me take Larry with me."

"Why? If John can't do it, then Larry certainly can't."

I shrugged. "Maybe not, but there are ways to combine power during a raising. If I can't do it alone, maybe I can get a boost from our trainee."

He looked thoughtful. "Why not take John? Combined, you could do it."

"Only if he'd give his power willingly to me. You think he'd do that?"

Bert shook his head.

"You going to tell him that the client didn't want him? That you offered him to the client and they asked for me by name?"

"No," Bert said.

"That's why you're doing it like this; no witnesses."

"Time is of the essence, Anita."

"Sure, Bert, but you didn't want to face Mr. John Burke with yet another client that wants me over him."

Bert looked down at his blunt-fingered hands clasped on the desktop. He looked up, grey eyes serious. "John is almost as good as you are, Anita. I don't want to lose him."

"You think he'll walk if one more client asks for me?"

"His pride's hurt," Bert said.

"And there's so much of it to hurt," I said.

Bert smiled. "You needling him doesn't help."

I shrugged. It sounded petty to say he'd started it, but he had. We'd tried dating, and John couldn't handle me being a female version of him. No; he couldn't handle me being a better version of him.

"Try to behave yourself, Anita. Larry's not up to speed yet; we need John."

"I always behave myself, Bert."

He sighed. "If you didn't make me so much money, I wouldn't put up with your shit."

"Ditto," I said.

That about summed up our relationship. Commerce at its best. We didn't like each other, but we could do business together. Free enterprise at work.

2

AT NOON BERT called and said we had it. "Be at the office packed and ready to go at two o'clock. Mr. Lionel Bayard will fly up with you and Larry."

"Who's Lionel Bayard?"

"A junior partner in the firm of Beadle, Beadle, Stirling, and Lowenstein. He likes the sound of his own voice. Don't give him a rough time about it."

"Who, me?"

"Anita, don't tease the help. He may be wearing a three-thousand-dollar suit, but he's still the help."

"I'll save it up for one of the partners. Surely Beadle, Beadle, Stirling, or Lowenstein will appear in person sometime this weekend."

"Don't tease the bosses either," he said.

"Anything you say." My voice was utterly mild.

"You'll do whatever you want no matter what I say, won't you?"

"Gee, Bert, who says you can't teach an old dog new tricks?"

"Just be here at two o'clock. I called Larry. He'll be here."

"I'll be there, Bert. I've got one stop to make, so if I'm a few minutes late, don't worry."

"Don't be late."

"Be there as soon as I can." I hung up before he could argue with me.

I had to shower, change, and go to Seckman Junior High School. Richard Zeeman taught science there. We had a date set up for tomorrow. At one point Richard had asked me to marry him. That was sort of on hold, but I did owe him more than a message on his answering machine, saying sorry, honey, can't make the date. I'm going to be out of town. A message would have been easier for me, but cowardly.

I packed one suitcase. It was enough for four days and

then some. If you pack extra underwear and clothes that mix and match, you can live for a week out of a small suitcase.

I did add a few extras. The Firestar 9mm and its inner pants holster. Enough extra ammo to sink a battleship and two knives plus wrist sheaths. I'd had four knives. All hand-crafted for little ol' *moi*. Two of them had been lost beyond recovery. I was having them replaced, but hand forging takes time, especially when you insist on the highest silver content possible in the steel. Two knives, two guns should be enough for one weekend business trip. I'd wear the Browning Hi-Power.

Packing wasn't a problem. What to wear today was the problem. They'd want me to raise them tonight if I could. Hell, the helicopter might fly directly to the construction site. Which meant I'd be walking over raw dirt, bones, shattered coffins. It didn't sound like high-heel territory. Yet, if a junior partner was wearing a three-thousand-dollar suit, the people who'd just hired me would expect me to look the part. I could either dress professionally or in feathers and blood. I'd actually had one client who was disappointed that I didn't show up nude smeared with blood. There could have been more than one reason for his disappointment. I don't think I've ever had a client that would have objected to some kind of ceremonial getup, but jeans and jogging shoes didn't seem to inspire confidence. Don't ask me why.

I could pack my coverall and put it over whatever I wore. Yeah, I liked that. Veronica Sims—Ronnie, my very best friend—had talked me into buying a fashionably short navy skirt. It was short enough that I was a little embarrassed, but the skirt fit inside the coverall. The skirt didn't wrinkle or bunch up after I'd worn the outfit to vampire stakings or murder scenes. Take the coverall off, and I was set to go to the office or out for the evening. I was so pleased, I went out and bought two more in different colors.

One was crimson, the other purple. I hadn't been able to find one in black yet. At least not one that wasn't so short that I refused to wear it. Admittedly, the short skirts made me look taller. They even made me look leggy. When you're five-foot-three, that's saying something. But the purple didn't match much that I owned, so crimson it was.

I'd found a short-sleeved blouse that was the exact same shade of red. Red with violet undertones, a cold, hard color that looked great with my pale skin, black hair, and dark brown eyes. The shoulder holster and 9mm Browning Hi-Power looked very dramatic against it. A black belt cinched tight at the waist held down the loops on the holster. A black jacket with rolled-back sleeves went over everything to hide the gun. I twirled in front of the mirror in my bedroom. The skirt wasn't much longer than the jacket, but you couldn't see the gun. At least not easily. Unless you're willing to have things tailor-made, it's hard to hide a gun, especially in women's dress-up clothes.

I put on just enough makeup so the red didn't overwhelm me. I was also going to be saying good-bye to Richard for several days. A little makeup couldn't hurt. When I say makeup, I mean eye shadow, blush, lipstick, and that's it. Outside of a television interview that Bert talked me into, I don't wear base.

Except for the hose and black high heels, which I would've had to wear no matter what skirt I wore, the outfit was comfortable. As long as I remembered not to bend directly at the waist, I was safe.

The only jewelry I wore was the silver cross tucked into the blouse, and the watch on my wrist. My dress watch had broken and I just had never gotten around to getting it fixed. The present watch was a man's black diving watch that looked out of place on my small wrist. But hey, it glowed in the dark if you pressed a button. It showed me the date, what day it was, and could time a run. I hadn't found a woman's watch that could do all that.

I didn't have to cancel running with Ronnie tomorrow morning. She was out of town on a case. A private detective's work is never done.

I loaded the suitcase into my Jeep and was on the way to Richard's school by one o'clock. I was going to be late to the office. Oh, well. They'd wait for me or they wouldn't. It wouldn't break my heart to miss the helicopter ride. I hated planes, but a helicopter . . . scared the shit out of me.

I hadn't been afraid of flying until I was on a plane that plunged several thousand feet in seconds. The stewardess ended up plastered against the ceiling, covered in coffee. People screamed and prayed. The elderly woman beside me recited the Lord's Prayer in German. She'd been so scared, tears had come down her face. I offered her my hand, and she gripped it. I knew I was going to die and there was nothing I could do to prevent it. But we would die holding on to human hands. Die covered in human tears, and human prayers. Then the plane straightened out and suddenly we were safe. I haven't trusted air transportation since.

Normally in St. Louis there is no real spring. There's winter, two days of mild weather, and summer heat. This year spring had come early and stayed. The air was soft against your skin. The wind smelled of green growing things, and winter seemed to have been a bad dream. Redbuds bent from the trees on either side of the road. Tiny purple blossoms like a delicate lavender mist here and there through the naked trees. There were no leaves yet, but there was a hint of green. Like someone had taken a giant paintbrush and tinted everything. Look directly at them and the trees were bare and black, but look sideways, not at a particular tree but at all the trees, and there was a touch of green.

270 South is about as pleasant as a highway can be; it gets you where you're going fairly fast, and it's over quickly. I exited at Tesson Ferry Road. The road is thick with strip malls, a hospital, and fast-food restaurants, and when you leave the commerce behind you hit new housing developments so thick they nearly touch. There are still stands of woods and open spaces, but they won't last.

The turn to Old 21 is at the crest of a hill just past the Meramec River. It is mostly houses with a few gas stations, the area water district office, and a large gas field to the right. Where the hills march out and out.

At the first stoplight I turned left past a little shopping area. The road is a curving narrow thing that snakes between houses and woods. There were glimpses of daffodils in the yards. The road dips down into a valley, and at the bottom of a steep hill is a stop sign. The road climbs quickly to the crest of a hill, to a T, turn left and you're almost there.

The one-story school sits on the floor of a wide, flat valley surrounded by hills. Having been raised in Indiana farm country, I'd have called them mountains once. The elementary school sits separate, but close enough to share a playground. If you got recess in junior high. When I was too little to go to junior high, it seemed you did get recess. By the time I got there, you didn't. The way of the world.

I parked as close to the building as I could. This was my second visit to Richard's school, and my first during the actual school day. We'd come once to get some papers he'd forgotten. No students then. I entered the main entrance and ran into a crowd. It must have been between classes when they moved the warm bodies from one room to another.

I was instantly aware that I was about the same height as or shorter than everyone I saw. There was something claustrophobic about being jostled by the book-carrying, backpack-wearing crowd. There had to be a circle of Hell where you were eternally fourteen, eternally in junior high. One of the lower circles.

I flowed with the crowd towards Richard's room. I admit I took comfort in the fact that I was better dressed than most of the girls. Petty as hell, but I had been chunky in junior high. There isn't a lot of difference between chunky and fat when it comes to teasing. I'd had my growth spurt and never been fat again. That's right; I'd been even tinier once. Shortest kid in school for years and years.

I stood to one side of the doorway, letting the students come and go. Richard was showing something in a textbook to a young girl. She was blonde, wearing a flannel shirt over a black dress that was three sizes too big for her. She was wearing what looked like black combat boots with heavy white socks rolled over the tops of them. The outfit was very now. The look of adoration on her face was not. She was shiny and eager just because Mr. Zeeman was giving her some one-on-one help.

I had to admit that Richard was worth a crush or two. His

thick brown hair was tied back in a ponytail that gave the illusion that his hair was very short and close to his head. He has high, full cheekbones and a strong jaw, with a dimple that softens his face and makes him look almost too perfect. His eyes are a solid chocolate brown with those thick lashes that so many men have and women want. The bright yellow shirt made his permanently tanned skin seem even darker. His tie was a dark, rich green that matched the dress slacks he wore. His jacket was draped across the back of his desk chair. The muscles in his upper arms worked against the cloth of his shirt as he held the book.

The class was mostly seated, the hallway nearly silent. He closed the book and handed it to the girl. She smiled and scrambled for the door, late to her next class. Her eyes flicked over me as she passed, wondering what I was doing there.

She wasn't the only one. Several of the seated students were glancing my way. I stepped into the room.

Richard smiled. It warmed me down to my toes. The smile saved him from being too handsome. It wasn't that it wasn't a great smile. He could have done toothpaste commercials. But the smile was a little boy's smile, open and welcoming. There was no guile to Richard, no deep, dark plan. He was the world's biggest Boy Scout. The smile showed that.

I wanted to go to him, have him wrap his arms around me. I had a horrible urge to grab his tie and lead him out of the room. I wanted to touch his chest underneath the yellow shirt. The urge was so strong, I put my hands in the pockets of my jacket. Mustn't shock the students. Richard affects me like that sometimes. Okay, most of the time when he's not furry, or licking blood off his fingers. He's a werewolf. Did I mention that? No one at the school knows. If they did, he'd be out of a job. People don't like lycanthropes teaching their precious kiddies. It's illegal to discriminate against someone for a disease, but everyone does it. Why should the educational system be different?

He touched my cheek, just his fingertips. I turned my face into his hand, brushing lips against his fingers. So much for being cool in front of the kiddies. There were a few oohs and nervous laughs.

"I'll be right back, guys." More oohs, louder laughter, one "Way to go, Mr. Zeeman." Richard motioned me out the door and I went, hands still in my pockets. Normally, I'd have said I wasn't going to embarrass myself in front of a bunch of eighth-graders, but lately I wasn't entirely trustworthy.

Richard led me a little ways from his classroom into the deserted hallway. He leaned up against the wall of lockers and looked down at me. The little-boy smile was gone. The look in his dark eyes made me shiver. I ran my hand down his tie, smoothing it against his chest.

"Am I allowed to kiss you, or would that scandalize the kiddies?" I didn't look up at him as I asked. I didn't want him to see the raw need in my eyes. It was embarrassing enough that I knew he sensed it. You can't hide lust from a werewolf. They can smell it.

"I'll risk it." His voice was soft, low, with a warm edge that made my stomach clench.

I felt him bend over me. I raised my face to his. His lips were so soft. I leaned against his body, palms flat against his chest. I could feel his nipples harden under my skin. My hands slid to his waist, smoothing along the cloth of his shirt. I wanted to pull his shirt out of his pants and run my hands over bare skin. I stepped back from him feeling just a little breathless.

It was my idea that we wouldn't have sex before marriage. My idea. But damn, it was hard. The more we dated, the harder it got.

"Jesus, Richard." I shook my head. "It gets harder, doesn't it?"

Richard's smile didn't look innocent or Boy Scoutish in the least. "Yes, it does."

Heat rushed up my face. "I didn't mean that."

"I know what you meant." His voice was gentle, taking the sting out of the teasing.

My face was still hot with embarrassment, but my voice

was steady. Point for me. "I've got to go out of town on business."

"Zombie, vampire, or police?"

"Zombie."

"Good."

I looked up at him. "Why good?"

"I worry more when you go away on police business, or vampire stakings. You know that."

I nodded. "Yeah, I know that." We stood there in the hall-way, staring at each other. If things had been different, we'd be engaged, maybe planning a wedding. All this sexual tension would have been coming to some kind of conclusion. As it was . . .

"I'm going to be late as it is. I've got to go."

"Are you going to tell Jean-Claude bye in person?" His face was neutral when he asked, but his eyes weren't.

"It's daylight. He's in his coffin."

"Ah," Richard said.

"I didn't have a date planned with him this weekend, so I don't owe him an explanation. Is that what you wanted to hear?"

"Close enough," he said. He took a step away from the lockers, bringing our bodies very close together. He bent to kiss me good-bye. Giggles erupted down the hall.

We turned to see most of his class huddled in the doorway gazing at us. Great.

Richard smiled. He raised his voice enough so they'd hear him. "Back inside, you monsters."

There were catcalls, and one small brunette girl gave me a very dirty look. I think there must have been a lot of girls that had a crush on Mr. Zeeman.

"The natives are restless. I've got to get back."

I nodded. "I'm hoping to be back by Monday."

"We'll go hiking next weekend, then."

"I put Jean-Claude off this weekend. I can't not see him two weeks in a row."

Richard's face clouded up with the beginnings of anger. "Hike during the day, see the vampire at night. Only fair."

"I don't like this any better than you do," I said.

"I wish I believed that."

"Richard."

He gave a long sigh. The anger sort of leaked out of him. I never understood how he did that. He could be furious one minute and calm the next. Both emotions seemed genuine. Once I was angry, I was angry. Maybe it's a character flaw?

"I'm sorry, Anita. It's not like you're dating him behind my back."

"I would never do anything behind your back; you know that."

He nodded. "I know that." He glanced back at his classroom. "I've got to go before they set the room on fire." He walked down the hallway without looking back.

I almost called after him, but I let him go. The mood was sort of spoiled. Nothing like knowing your girlfriend is dating someone else to take the wind out of your sails. I wouldn't have put up with it if it was the other way around. A double standard that, but one we could all three live with. If living was the term for Jean-Claude.

Oh, hell, my personal life was too confusing for words. I walked off down the hall, having to pass by his open classroom door. My high heels made loud, rackety echoes. I didn't try to catch a last glimpse of him. It would make me feel worse about leaving.

It hadn't been my idea to date the Master of the City. Jean-Claude had given me two choices; either he could kill Richard, or I could date both of them. It had seemed a good idea at the time. Five weeks later I wasn't so sure.

It had been my morals that had kept Richard and me from consummating our relationship. Consummating, nice euphemism. But Jean-Claude had made it clear that if I did something with Richard, I had to do it with him too. Jean-Claude was trying to woo me. If Richard could touch me but he couldn't, it wasn't fair. He had a point, I guess. But the thought of having to have sex with the vampire was more likely to keep me chaste than any high ideals.

I couldn't date both of them indefinitely. The sexual tension alone was killing me. I could move. Richard might even let me do that. He wouldn't like it, but if I wanted free of him, he'd let me go. Jean-Claude, on the other hand . . . He'd never let me go. The question was, did I want him to let me go? Answer: hell, yes. The real trick was how to break free without anybody dying.

Yeah, that was the $64,000 question. Trouble was, I didn't have an answer. We were going to need one sooner or later. And later was getting closer all the time.

3

I HUDDLED AGAINST the side of the helicopter, one hand in a death grip on the strap that was bolted to the wall. I wanted to use both hands to hold on, as if by holding very tightly to the stupid strap it would save me when the helicopter plummeted to earth. I used one hand because two hands looked cowardly. I was wearing a headset, sort of like ear protection for the shooting range, but with a microphone so you could talk above the teeth-rattling noise. I hadn't realized that most of a helicopter was clear, like being suspended in a great buzzing, vibrating bubble. I kept my eyes closed as much as possible.

"Are you all right, Ms. Blake?" Lionel Bayard asked.

The voice startled me. "Yeah, I'm fine."

"You don't look well."

"I don't like to fly," I said.

He gave a weak smile. I don't think I was inspiring confidence in Lionel Bayard, lawyer and flunkie of Beadle, Beadle, Stirling, and Lowenstein. Lionel Bayard was a small, neat man with a tiny blond mustache that looked like it was as much facial hair as he would ever get. His triangular jaw was as smooth as my own. Maybe the mustache was glued on. His brown suit with a thin yellow tweed fit his body like a well-tailored glove. His thin tie was brown-and-yellow striped with a gold tie tack. The tie tack was monogrammed. His slender leather briefcase was monogrammed as well. Everything matched, down to his gold-tasseled loafers.

Larry twisted in his seat. He was sitting beside the pilot. "You're really afraid of flying?" I could see his lips move, but all the sound came out of my headset; without them we'd never have been able to talk over the noise. He sounded amused.

"Yes, Larry, I'm really afraid of flying." I hoped sarcasm traveled the headsets as clearly as amusement did.

Larry laughed. Evidently, sarcasm traveled. Larry looked freshly scrubbed. He was dressed in his other blue suit, his white shirt—which was one of three he owned—and his second-best tie. His best tie had blood all over it. He was still in college, working weekends for us until he graduated. His short hair was the color of a surprised carrot. He was freckled and about my height, short, with pale blue eyes. He looked like a grown-up Opie.

Bayard was working hard at not frowning at me. The effort showed enough that he shouldn't have bothered. "Are you sure you're up to this assignment?"

I met his brown eyes. "You better hope I am, Mr. Bayard, because I'm all you got."

"I am aware of your specialized skills, Ms. Blake. I spent the last twelve hours contacting every animating firm in the United States. Phillipa Freestone of the Resurrection Company told me she couldn't do what we wanted, that the only person in the country who might be able to do it was Anita Blake. Élan Vital in New Orleans told us the same thing. They mentioned John Burke but weren't confident that he could do all we wanted. We must have all the dead raised or it's useless to us."

"Did my boss explain to you that I am not a hundred percent sure that I can do it?"

Bayard blinked at me. "Mr. Vaughn seemed very confident that you could do what we asked."

"Bert can be as confident as he wants. He doesn't have to raise this mess."

"I realize the earthmoving equipment has complicated your task, Ms. Blake, but we did not do it deliberately."

I let that go. I'd seen the pictures. They'd tried to cover it up. If the construction crew hadn't been local with some Bouvier sympathizers, they'd have plowed up the boneyard, poured some concrete, and voilá, no evidence.

"Whatever. I'll do what I can with what you've left me."

"Would it have been that much easier if you had been brought in before the graves were disturbed?"

"Yeah."

He sighed. It vibrated through the headphones. "Then my apologies."

I shrugged. "Unless you did it personally, you're not the one who owes me an apology."

He shifted a little in his seat. "I did not order the digging. Mr. Stirling is on site."

"*The* Mr. Stirling?" I asked.

Bayard didn't seem to get the humor. "Yes, that Mr. Stirling." Or maybe he really expected me to know the name.

"You always have a senior partner looking over your shoulder?"

He used one finger to adjust his gold-framed glasses. It looked like an old gesture from a time before new glasses and designer suits. "With this much money at stake, Mr. Stirling thought he should be in the area in case there were more problems."

"More problems?" I asked.

He blinked at me rapidly, like a well-groomed rabbit. "The Bouvier matter."

He was lying. "What else is going wrong with your little project?"

"Whatever do you mean, Ms. Blake?" His manicured fingers smoothed down his tie.

"You've had more problems than just the Bouviers." I made it a statement.

"Any problems we may or may not be having, Ms. Blake, are not your concern. We hired you to raise the dead and establish the identity of said deceased persons. Beyond that, you have no duties here."

"Have you ever raised a zombie, Mr. Bayard?"

He blinked again. "Of course not." He sounded offended.

"Then how do you know the other problems won't affect my job?"

Small frown lines formed between his eyebrows. He was a lawyer and was earning a good living, but thinking seemed to be hard for him. Made you wonder where he'd graduated from.

"I don't see how our little difficulties could affect your job."

"You've just admitted you don't know anything about my job," I said. "How do you know what will affect it and what won't?" Alright, I was fishing. Bayard was probably right. The other problems probably wouldn't affect me, but you never know. I don't like being kept in the dark. And I don't like being lied to, not even by omission.

"I think Mr. Stirling would have to make the call about whether you are enlightened or not."

"Not senior enough to make the decision," I said.

"No," Bayard said, "I am not."

Geez, some people you can't even needle. I glanced at Larry. He shrugged. "Looks like we're going to land."

I glanced out at the rapidly growing land. We were in the middle of the Ozark Mountains, hovering over a blasted scar of reddish naked earth. The construction site, I presume.

The ground swelled up to meet us. I closed my eyes and swallowed hard. The ride was almost over. I would not throw up this close to the ground. The ride was almost over. Almost over. Almost over. There was a bump that made me gasp.

"We've landed," Larry said. "You can open your eyes now."

I did. "You are enjoying the hell out of this, aren't you?"

He grinned. "I don't get to see you out of your element often."

The helicopter was surrounded by a fog of reddish dirt. The blades began to slow with a thick *whump, whump* sound. As the blades stopped, the dirt settled down and we could see where we were.

We were in a small, flat area between a cluster of mountains. It looked like it had once been a narrow valley, but bulldozers had widened it, flattened it, made it a landing pad. The earth was so red it looked like a river of rust. The mountain in front of the helicopter was one red mound. Heavy equipment and cars were clustered to the far side of the valley. Men were clustered around the equipment, shielding their eyes from the dust.

When the blades came to a sliding stop, Bayard unbuckled his seat belt. I did, too. We lifted off the headsets and Bayard opened his door. I opened mine and found that the ground was farther away than you'd think. I had to expose a long line of thigh to touch the ground.

The construction workers were appreciative. Whistles, catcalls, and one offer to check under my skirt. No, those weren't the exact words used.

A tall man in a white hard hat strode towards us. He was wearing a pair of tan coveralls, but his dirt-covered shoes were Gucci and his tan was health-club perfect. A man and a woman followed at his back.

The man looked like the real foreman. He was dressed in jeans and a work shirt with the sleeves rolled over muscular forearms. Not from racquetball or a little tennis, but from plain hard work.

The woman wore the traditional skirt suit complete with little blousy tie at her throat. The suit was expensive, but was an unfortunate shade of puce that did nothing for the woman's auburn hair but did match the blush that she'd smeared on her cheeks. I checked her neckline, and yes, she did have a pale line just above her collar where the base had not been blended in. She looked like she'd been made up at clown school.

She didn't look that young. You'd think someone somewhere would have clued her in to how bad she looked. Of course, I wasn't going to tell her either. Who was I to criticize?

Stirling had the palest grey eyes I'd ever seen. The irises were only a few shades darker than the whites of his eyes. He stood there with his entourage behind him. He looked me up and down. He didn't seem to like what he saw. His strange eyes flicked to Larry in his cheap, wrinkled suit. Mr. Stirling frowned.

Bayard came around, smoothing his jacket into place. "Mr. Stirling, this is Anita Blake. Ms. Blake, this is Raymond Stirling."

He just stood there, looking at me like he was disappointed. The woman had a clipboard notebook, pen poised. Had to be his secretary. She looked worried, as if it was very important that Mr. Raymond Stirling like us.

I was beginning not to care if he liked us or not. What I wanted to say was, "You got a problem?" What I said was, "Is there a problem, Mr. Stirling?" Bert would have been pleased.

"You're not what I expected, Ms. Blake."

"How so?"

"Pretty, for one thing." It wasn't a compliment.

"And?"

He motioned at my outfit. "You're not dressed appropriately for the job."

"Your secretary's wearing heels."

"Ms. Harrison's attire is not your concern."

"And my attire is none of yours."

"Fair enough, but you're going to have a hell of time getting up that mountain in those shoes."

"I've got a coverall and Nikes in my suitcase."

"I don't think I like your attitude, Ms. Blake."

"I know I don't like yours," I said.

The foreman behind him was having trouble not smiling. His eyes were getting shiny with the effort. Ms. Harrison looked a little scared. Bayard had moved to one side, closer to Stirling. Making clear whose side he was on. Coward.

Larry moved closer to me.

"Do you want this job, Ms. Blake?"

"Not enough to take grief about it, no."

Ms. Harrison looked like she'd swallowed a bug. A big, nasty, squirming bug. I think I'd missed my cue to fall down and worship at her boss's feet.

The foreman coughed behind his hand. Stirling glanced at

him, then back to me. "Are you always this arrogant?" he asked.

I sighed. "I prefer the word 'confident' to 'arrogant,' but I'll tell you what. I'll tone it down if you will."

"I am so sorry, Mr. Stirling," Bayard said. "I apologize. I had no idea . . ."

"Shut up, Lionel," Stirling said.

Lionel shut up.

Stirling was looking at me with his strange pale eyes. He nodded. "Agreed, Ms. Blake." He smiled. "I'll tone it down."

"Great," I said.

"All right, Ms. Blake, let's go up to the top and see if you're really as good as you think you are."

"I can look at the graveyard, but until full dark I can't do anything else."

He frowned and glanced at Bayard. "Lionel." That one word had a lot of heat in it. Anger looking for a target. He'd stop picking on me, but Lionel was fair game.

"I did fax you a memo, sir, as soon as I realized that Ms. Blake would be unable to help us until after dark."

Good man. When in doubt, cover your ass with paper.

Stirling glared at him. Bayard looked apologetic but he stood his ground, safe behind his memo.

"I called Beau and had him bring everybody down here on the understanding we could get some work done today." His gaze was very steady on Bayard. Lionel wilted just a little; evidently one memo was not protection enough.

"Mr. Stirling, even if I can raise the graveyard in one night, and that's a big if, what if the dead are all Bouviers? What if it is their family plot? My understanding is that construction will stop until you rebuy the land."

"They don't want to sell," Beau said.

Stirling glared at him. The foreman just smiled softly.

"Are you saying that the entire project is off if this is the Bouvier family plot?" I asked Bayard. "Why, Lionel, you didn't tell me that."

"There was no need for you to know," Bayard said.

"Why wouldn't they want to sell the land for a million dollars?" Larry asked. It was a good question.

Stirling looked at him like he'd just appeared out of thin air. Evidently, the flunkies weren't supposed to talk. "Magnus and Dorcas Bouvier have only a restaurant, called Bloody Bones. It is nothing. I have no idea why they wouldn't want to be millionaires."

"Bloody Bones? What kind of name is that for a restaurant?" Larry asked.

I shrugged. "It doesn't exactly say bon appetit." I looked at Stirling. He looked angry but that was all. I would have bet a million dollars that he knew exactly why the Bouviers didn't want to sell. But it didn't show on his face. His cards were close to his chest and unreadable.

I turned to Bayard. There was an unhealthy flush to his cheeks, and he avoided my gaze. I'd play poker with Bayard any day. But not in front of his boss.

"Fine. I'll change into something more bulky and we'll go take a look." The pilot handed out my suitcase. The coverall and shoes were on top.

Larry came up to me. "Gee, I wished I'd thought of the coverall. This suit's not going to survive the trip."

I pulled out two pairs of coveralls. "Be prepared," I said. He grinned. "Thanks."

I shrugged. "One good thing about being nearly the same size." I slipped off the black jacket, which left the gun in plain sight.

"Ms. Blake," Stirling said. "Why are you armed?"

I sighed. I was tired of Raymond. I hadn't even gone up the hill and I didn't want to go. The last thing I wanted to do was stand here and debate whether I needed a gun. The red blouse was short-sleeved. Visual aids are always better than lectures.

I walked over to him with my arms bent outward, exposing the inside of both forearms. There's a rather neat knife scar on my right arm, nothing too dramatic. My left arm is a mess. It had only been a little over a month since a shapeshifting leopard had opened my arm. A nice doctor had stitched it back together, but there is only so much you can do with claw marks. The cross-shaped burn scar that some inventive vampire servants had put on me was now a little crooked because of the claws. The mound of scar tissue at the bend of my arm where a vampire had bitten through the flesh and gnawed the bone dribbled white scars like water.

"Jesus," Beau said.

Stirling looked a touch pale but he held up well, like he'd seen worse. Bayard looked green. Ms. Harrison paled so that the makeup floated on her suddenly pale skin like impressionist water lilies.

"I don't go anywhere unarmed, Mr. Stirling. Live with it, because I have to."

He nodded, eyes very serious. "Fine, Ms. Blake. Is your assistant armed as well?"

"No," I said.

He nodded again. "Fine. Change, and when you're ready we'll go up."

Larry was zipping up his coverall when I walked back. "I could have been armed, you know," he said.

"You brought your gun?" I asked.

He nodded.

"Unloaded in your suitcase?"

"Just like you told me."

"Good." I let it go. Larry wanted to be a vampire executioner as well as an animator, which meant he needed to know how to use a gun. A gun with silver-plated bullets that could slow a vampire down. We'd work up to shotguns, which could take out a head and heart from a relatively safe distance. Beat the hell out of staking.

I'd gotten him a carry permit on the condition he didn't carry it concealed until I thought he was a good enough shot not to blow a hole in himself or me. I'd gotten him the permit mainly so we could carry it around in the car and go to the range in any spare moments.

The coverall went over the skirt like magic. I took off the heels and put the Nikes on. I left the coverall unzipped enough that I could go for the gun if needed, and I was set to go.

"Are you going up with us, Mr. Stirling?"

"Yes," he said.

"Then lead the way," I said.

He walked past me, glancing at the coveralls. Or maybe visualizing the gun under it. Beau started to follow but Stirling said, "No, I'll take her up alone."

Silence among the three flunkies. I'd expected Ms. Harrison to stay behind in her high-heeled pumps, but I'd been sure the two men would come along. So, from the looks on their faces, had they.

"Wait a minute. You said 'her.' You want Larry to wait down here, too?"

"Yes."

I shook my head. "He's in training. You can't learn if you don't see it done."

"Will you be doing anything that he needs to see today?"

I thought about that for a minute. "I guess not."

"I do get to come up after dark?" Larry asked.

"You'll get to see the down and dirty, Larry. Don't worry."

"Of course," Stirling said. "I have no problem with your associate doing his job."

"Why can't he come along now?" I asked.

"At the price we're paying, humor me, Ms. Blake."

He was being strangely polite, so I nodded. "Okay."

"Mr. Stirling," Bayard said, "are you sure you should go up alone?"

"Why ever not, Lionel?"

Bayard opened his mouth, closed it, then said, "No reason, Mr. Stirling."

Beau shrugged. "I'll tell the men to go home for the day." He started to turn away, then stopped. "Do you want the crew back tomorrow?"

Stirling looked at me. "Ms. Blake?"

I shook my head. "I don't know yet."

"What's your best guess?" he asked.

I looked over at the waiting men. "Do they get paid whether they show up or not?"

"Only if they show up," Stirling said.

"Then no work tomorrow. I can't guarantee they'll have anything to do."

Stirling nodded. "You heard her, Beau."

Beau looked at me, then back to Stirling. He had a strange look on his face, half amused, half something I couldn't read. "Anything you say, Mr. Stirling, Ms. Blake." He turned and strode off over the raw ground, waving at the men as he moved. The men began to leave long before he got to them.

"What do you want us to do, Mr. Stirling?" Bayard asked.

"Wait for us."

"The helicopter, too? It has to leave before dark."

"Will we be down before dark, Ms. Blake?"

"Sure. I'm just going to take a quick look around. I'll need to get back in here after dark, though."

"I'll give you a car and driver for your stay."

"Thanks."

"Shall we, Ms. Blake?" He motioned me forward. Something had changed in the way he was treating me. I couldn't put my finger on it, but I didn't like it.

"After you, Mr. Stirling."

He nodded and took the lead, striding over the red earth in his thousand-dollar shoes.

Larry and I exchanged glances. "I won't be long, Larry."

"Us flunkies aren't going anywhere," he said.

I smiled. He smiled. I shrugged. Why did Stirling want it to be just the two of us? I watched the senior partner's broad back as he marched across the torn earth. I followed him. I'd find out what the secrecy was all about when we got to the top. I was betting I wouldn't like what I'd hear. Just me and the big cheese on top of the mountain with the dead. What could be better?

4

THE VIEW FROM the top of the mountain was worth the hike. Trees stretched out and out to the horizon. We stood in a circle of forest that showed no hand of man as far as the eye could see. That first blush of green was more pronounced here. But the thing you noticed most was the lavender color of redbuds through the dark trees. Redbuds are such delicate things that if they came out in the height of summer they'd get lost in all the leaves and flowers, but here with nothing but naked trees the redbuds were eye-catching. A few dogwoods had started to bloom, adding their white to the lavender. Spring in the Ozarks, ah.

"The view is magnificent," I said.

"Yes," Stirling said, "it is, isn't it?"

My black Nikes were covered in rust-colored dirt. The raw, wounded earth filled the mountaintop. This hilltop had probably been just as pretty as the rest once. There was an arm bone sticking out of the dirt next to my feet. The lower arm, judging from the length. The bones were slender and still connected by a dry remnant of tissue.

Once I'd seen one bone, my eyes found more to look at. It was like one of those magic-eye pictures where you stare and stare and suddenly see what's there. I saw them all, studding the ground like hands reaching up through a river of rust.

There were a few splintered coffins, their broken halves spilling out into the air, but mostly it was just bones. I knelt and put my hands palm down on the ruined earth. I tried to get some sense of the dead. There was something faint and far-off like a whiff of perfume, but it was no good. In the bright spring sunlight I couldn't work my . . . magic. Raising the dead isn't evil, but it does require darkness. I don't know why.

I stood up, brushing my hands against the coverall, trying to clean the red dust away. Stirling was standing at the edge of the naked dirt staring off into space. There was a distance to his gaze that said he wasn't admiring the trees.

He spoke without looking at me. "I can't bully you, can I, Ms. Blake?"

"Nope," I said.

He turned to me with a smile, but it left his eyes empty, haunted. "I invested everything I had into this project. Not just my money, but clients' money. Do you understand what I am saying, Ms. Blake?"

"If the bodies up here are Bouviers, you're screwed."

"How eloquently you put it."

"Why are we up here alone, Mr. Stirling? Why all the skullduggery?"

He took a deep breath of the gentle air and said, "I want you to say they aren't Bouvier ancestors even if they are." He looked at me when he said it. Watched my face.

I smiled and shook my head. "I won't lie for you."

"Can't you make the zombies lie?"

"The dead are very honest, Mr. Stirling. They don't lie."

He took a step towards me, face very sincere. "My entire future is riding on you, Ms. Blake."

"No, Mr. Stirling, your future rides on the dead at your feet. Whatever comes out of their mouths will decide it."

He nodded. "I suppose that is fair."

"Fair or not, it's the truth."

He nodded again. Some light had gone out of his face, like someone had turned down the power. The lines in his face were suddenly clearer. He aged ten years in a few seconds. When he met my gaze, his dramatic eyes were woeful.

"I'll give you a piece of the profits, Ms. Blake. You could be a billionaire in a few years."

"You know bribing won't work."

"I knew it wouldn't work just a few minutes after we met, but I had to try."

"You really do believe this is the Bouvier family plot, don't you?" I asked.

He took a deep breath and walked away from me to gaze off at the trees. He wasn't going to answer my question, but he didn't have to. He wouldn't be so desperate if he didn't believe he was screwed.

"Why won't the Bouviers sell?"

He glanced back at me. "I don't know."

"Look, Stirling, there are just the two of us up here, nobody to impress, no witnesses. You know why they won't sell. Just tell me."

"I don't know, Ms. Blake," he said.

"You're a control freak, Mr. Stirling. You've overseen every detail of this deal. You have personally seen that every 'i' was dotted, every 't' crossed. This is your baby. You know everything about the Bouviers and their problem. Just tell me."

He just looked at me. His pale eyes were opaque, empty as a window with no one home. He knew, but he wasn't going to tell me. Why?

"What *do* you know about the Bouviers?"

"The locals think they're witches. They do a little fortune-telling, a few harmless spells." There was something about the way he said it, too casual, too offhand. Made me want to meet the Bouviers in person.

"They any good at magic?" I asked.

"How am I supposed to know?"

I shrugged. "Just curious. Is there a reason why it had to be this mountain?"

"Look at it." He spread his arms wide. "It's perfect. It is perfect."

"It is a great view," I said. "But wouldn't the view be equally good over on that mountaintop? Why did you have to have this one? Why did you have to have the Bouviers' mountain?"

His shoulders slumped; then he straightened and glared at me. "I wanted this land, and I got it."

"You got it. Trick is, Raymond, can you keep it?"

"If you are not going to help me, then don't taunt me. And don't call me Raymond."

I opened my mouth to say something else and my beeper went off. I fished under the coverall for it, and checked the number. "Shit," I said.

"What's wrong?"

"I'm being paged by the police. I've got to get to a phone."

He frowned at me. "Why would the police be calling you?"

So much for being a household name. "I'm the legal vampire executioner for a three-state area. I'm attached to the Regional Preternatural Investigation Team."

He was looking very steadily at me. "You surprise me, Ms. Blake. Not many people do that."

"I need to find a phone."

"I have a portable with a battery pack at the bottom of this damned hill."

"Great. I'm ready to head down if you are."

He did one last turn, taking in that breath-stealing billion-dollar view. "Yes, I'm ready to go down."

It was an interesting choice of words, a Freudian slip you might say. Stirling had wanted this land for some perverse reason. Maybe because he was told he couldn't have it. Some people are like that. The more you say no, the more they want you. It reminded me of a certain master vampire I knew.

Tonight I'd walk the land, visit with the dead. It would probably be tomorrow night before I actually tried to raise them. If the police matter was pressing enough, it might be longer. I hoped it wasn't pressing. Pressing usually meant dead bodies. When the monsters are involved, it's never just one dead body. One way or another, the dead multiply.

5

WE GOT BACK to the valley. The construction crew was gone except for Beau the foreman. Ms. Harrison and Bayard stood next to the helicopter, as if huddling against the wilderness. Larry and the pilot stood to one side, smoking, sharing that comradery of all people who are determined to blacken their lungs.

Stirling walked towards them all, his stride firm and confident once more. He'd left his doubts on top of the mountain, or so it seemed. He was the impervious senior partner once more. Illusion is all.

"Bayard, get the phone. Ms. Blake needs to use it."

Bayard gave a startled little jump, like he'd been caught doing something he shouldn't have. Ms. Harrison looked a little flushed. Was there romance in the air? And was that not allowed? No fraternizing among the flunkies.

Bayard ran off across the dirt towards the last car. He fetched what looked like a small, black leather backpack with a handle. He pulled a phone out and handed it to me. It looked like an antennaed walkie-talkie.

Larry walked over smelling of smoke. "What's up?"

"I got beeped."

"Bert?"

I shook my head. "Police." I walked a little ways from our group. Larry was polite enough to stay with them, though he didn't have to. I dialed Dolph's number. Detective Sergeant Rudolf Storr was head of the Regional Preternatural Investigation Team.

He answered on the second ring. "Anita?"

"Yeah, Dolph, it's me. What's up?"

"Three dead bodies."

"Three? Shit," I said.

"Yeah," he said.

"I can't be there soon, Dolph."

"Yes, you can," he said.

There was something in his voice. "What's that supposed to mean?"

"The victims are right near you."

"Near Branson?"

"Twenty-five minutes east of Branson," he said.

"I'm already forty miles from Branson in the middle of freaking nowhere."

"The middle of nowhere is where this one is," Dolph said.

"Are you guys flying up?" I asked.

"No, we got a vampire victim in town."

"Jesus, are the other three vamp victims?"

"I don't think so," he said.

"What do you mean, you don't think so?" I asked.

"Missouri State Highway Patrol has this one. Sergeant Freemont is the investigator in charge. She doesn't think it was a vampire because the bodies are cut up. Pieces of the bodies are missing. I had to do a lot of tap dancing to get that much information out of her. Sergeant Freemont seems convinced that RPIT is going to come in and steal all the glory. She was particularly worried about our headline-stealing pet zombie queen."

"It's the pet part that I mind the most," I said. "But she sounds charming."

"I'll bet she's even more charming in person," Dolph said.

"And I get to meet her?"

"Given the choice between a large chunk of the squad coming down later and just you right now, she chose you. I think she sees you alone, without us to back you up, as the lesser evil."

"Nice to be the lesser evil for a change," I said.

"You might get upgraded," Dolph said. "She doesn't know you too well yet."

"Thanks for the vote of confidence. Let me test my understanding here. None of you are coming up to the scene?"

"Not right away. You know we're shorthanded until Zerbrowski gets back on duty."

"What does the Missouri State Highway Patrol think about a civilian helping them in a murder investigation?"

"I made it clear that you are a valuable member of my squad."

"Thanks for the compliment, but I still don't have a badge to flash."

"You may if that new federal law goes into effect," Dolph said.

"Don't remind me."

"Don't you want to be a federal marshal?" His voice was very mild. Nah, amused.

"I agreed they should license us, but giving us what amounts to federal marshal status is ridiculous."

"You could handle it."

"But who else? John Burke with the power of the law behind him? Give me a break."

"It won't get passed, Anita. The pro-vampire lobby is too strong."

"From your lips to God's ear. Unless they revoke the need for court orders of execution, it won't make killing them any easier, and they won't do that. I've already gone out of state to execute vamps. I don't need no stinking badge."

Dolph laughed. "If you run into trouble, give a yell."

"I really don't like this, Dolph. I'm out here investigating a murder without any official status."

"See, you do need a badge." I heard him sigh over the phone. "Look, Anita, I wouldn't leave you solo if we didn't have problems of our own. I've got a body on the ground here. When I can, I'll send somebody. Hell, I'd like you to come take a look at our corpse. You're our resident monster expert."

"Give me some details and I'll try to play Kreskin."

"Male, early twenties, rigor hasn't set in."

"Where's the body?"

"His apartment."

"How'd you get there so soon?"

"Neighbor heard a fight, called 911. They called us."

"Give me his name."

"Fredrick Michael Summers, Freddy Summers."

"He got any old vampire bites on his body? Healed bites?"

"Yeah, quite a few. Looks like a damn pincushion. How'd you know?"

"What's the first rule of a homicide?" I said. "You check the nearest and dearest. If he had a vamp lover, there'd be healed bite marks. The more of them, the longer the relationship has gone on. No vamp can bite a victim three times within a month without running the risk of killing them and raising them as a vamp. You can have different vamps bite somebody, but that would make Freddy a vampire junkie.

Ask the neighbors if there were a lot of different guys or girls going in and out at night."

"It never occurred to me that a vampire could be someone's nearest and dearest," Dolph said.

"Legally, they're people. Means they get to have sweethearts, too."

"I'll check the bite radiuses," Dolph said, "If they match one vamp, a lover; different ones, and our boy was doing groups."

"Hope for a lover," I said. "If it's all one vamp, he might even rise from the dead."

"Most vamps know enough to slit the throat or take the head," he said.

"Doesn't sound well planned. Crime of passion, maybe."

"Maybe. Freemont is holding the bodies for you. Eagerly awaiting your expertise."

"I bet."

"Don't bust Freemont's balls on this, Anita."

"I won't start anything, Dolph."

"Be polite," he said.

"Always," I said in my mildest voice.

He sighed. "Try to remember that the staties may never have seen bodies with pieces missing."

It was my turn to sigh. "I'll be good, scout's honor. Do you have directions?" I got a small notebook with a pen stuck in its spiral top out of a pocket of the coverall. I'd started carrying notebooks just for such occasions.

He gave me what Freemont had given him. "If you see anything fishy at the crime scene, keep the scene intact and I'll try to send some people down. Otherwise, look over the victim, give the staties your opinion, and let them do their job."

"You really think Freemont would let me close up her shop and force her to wait for RPIT?"

Silence for a second; then, "Do the best you can, Anita. Call if we can do anything from this end."

"Yeah, sure."

"I'd rather have you on a murder than a lot of the cops I know," Dolph said.

That was a very big compliment coming from Dolph. He is the world's ultimate policeman. "Thanks, Dolph."

I was talking to empty air. Dolph had hung up. He was always doing that. I hit the button, turning the phone off, and just stood there for a minute.

I didn't like being out here in unfamiliar territory with unfamiliar police, and partially eaten victims. Hanging around with the Spook Squad legitimized me. I'd even pulled that "I'm with the squad" at crime scenes. I had a little ID badge that clipped to my clothes. It wasn't a police badge, but it did look official. But pretending on home turf, where I knew I could run to Dolph if I got in trouble for it, was one thing; out here with no backup was another story.

The police have absolutely no sense of humor about civilians meddling in their homicide cases. Can't really blame them. I wasn't really a civilian, but I had no official status. No clout. Maybe the new law would be a good thing.

I shook my head. Theoretically, I'd be able to go into any police station in the country and demand help, or involve myself uninvited in any case. Theoretically. In the real world, the cops would hate it. I'd be as welcome as a wet dog on a cold night. Not federal, not local, and there weren't enough licensed vamp executioners in the country to fill a dozen slots. I could only name eight of us; two of those were retired.

Most of them specialized in vampires. I was one of the few who would look at other types of kills. There was talk of the new law being expanded to include all preternatural kills. Most of the vampire executioners would be out of their depth. It was an informal apprenticeship. I had a college degree in preternatural biology, but that wasn't common. Most of the rogue lycanthropes, occasional trolls run amok, and other more solid beasties were taken out by bounty hunters. But the new law wouldn't give special powers to bounty hunters. Vampire executioners, most of them, worked very strictly within the confines of the law. Or maybe we just had better press.

I'd been screaming about vamps being monsters for years. But until a senator's daughter got herself attacked just a few weeks ago, nobody did shit. Now suddenly it's a cause celebre. The legitimate vampire community delivered the supposed attacker in a sack to the senator's home. They left his head and torso intact, which meant even without arms and legs he wouldn't die. He confessed to the attack. He'd been the new dead and just got carried away on a date, like any other twenty-one-year-old red-blooded male. Yeah, right.

The local hitter, Gerald Mallory, had done the execution. He's based out of Washington, D.C. He has to be in his sixties now. He still uses a stake and hammer. Can you believe it?

There had been some talk that cutting off their arms and legs would allow us to keep vamps in jail. This was vetoed mainly on the grounds of cruel and unusual punishment. It also wouldn't have worked, not for the really old vampires. It isn't just their bodies that are dangerous.

Besides, I didn't believe in torture. If cutting someone's arms and legs off and putting them in a little box for all eternity isn't torture, I don't know what is.

I walked back to the group. I handed the phone to Bayard. "I hope it isn't bad news," he said.

"Not personally," I said.

He looked puzzled. Not an uncommon occurrence for Lionel.

I talked directly to Stirling. "I've got to go to a crime scene near here. Is there someplace to rent a car?"

He shook his head. "I said you'd have a car and driver while you were here. I meant it."

"Thanks. I'm not so sure about the driver, though. This is a crime scene they won't want civilians hanging around."

"A car, then; no driver. Lionel, see that Ms. Blake gets anything she wants."

"Yes, sir."

"I'll meet you back here at full dark, Ms. Blake."

"I'll be here at dusk if I can, Mr. Stirling, but the police matter takes precedence."

He frowned at me. "You are working for me, Ms. Blake."

"Yes, but I'm also a licensed vampire executioner. Cooperation with the local police takes precedence."

"So it's a vampire kill?"

"I am not free to share police information with anyone," I said. But I cursed myself. By bringing up the word "vampire," I'd started a rumor that would grow with the telling. Damn.

"I can't leave the investigation early just to come look at your mountain. I'll be here when I can. I'll definitely look the dead over before daylight, so you won't really lose any time."

He didn't like it, but he let it go. "Fine, Ms. Blake. I will wait here for you even if it takes all night. I'm curious about what you do. I've never seen a zombie raised before."

"I won't raise the dead tonight, Mr. Stirling. We've been over that."

"Of course." He just looked at me. For some reason it was hard to meet his pale eyes. I made myself meet his gaze and didn't look away, but it was an effort. It was like he was willing me to do something, trying to compel me with his eyes like a vampire. But a vampire, even a little one, he was not.

He blinked and walked away without saying another word. Ms. Harrison toddled after him in her high heels on the uneven ground. Beau nodded at me and followed. I guess they'd all come in the same car. Or maybe Beau was Stirling's driver. What a joyous job that must be.

"We'll fly you to the hotel where we booked your rooms. You can unpack, and I'll have a car brought around for you," Bayard said.

"No unpacking, just a car. Murder scenes age fast," I said.

He nodded. "As you like. If you'll get back into the helicopter, we'll be off."

It wasn't until I was taking off the coveralls and repacking both of them that I realized I could have gone with Mr. Stirling. I could have driven out of here, instead of flying. Shit.

6

BAYARD HAD GOTTEN us a black Jeep with black-tinted windows and more bells and whistles than I could even guess at. I'd been worried they'd saddle me with a Cadillac or something equally ridiculous. Bayard had given me the keys with the comment, "Some of these roads are not even paved. I thought you might need something more substantial than just a car."

I resisted the urge to pat him on the head and say "Good flunkie." Hell, he'd made a great choice. Maybe he'd make full partner someday after all.

The trees made long, thin shadows across the road. In the valleys between mountains, the sunlight had softened to a late-afternoon haze. We might make it back to the graveyard by full dark.

Yes, we. Larry sat beside me in his wrinkled blue suit. The cops wouldn't mind his cheap suit. My outfit, on the other hand, might raise a few eyebrows. There aren't many female cops out in the boonies. And fewer who wear short red skirts. I was beginning to really regret my choice of clothes. Insecure: who, me?

Larry's face was shiny with excitement. His eyes sparkled like a kid's on Christmas Day. He was drumming his fingers on the armrest. Nervous tension.

"How you doing?"

"I've never been to a murder scene before," he said.

"There's always a first time."

"Thanks for letting me come along."

"Just remember the rules."

He laughed. "Don't touch anything. Don't walk through the blood. Don't speak unless spoken to." He frowned. "Why the last? I understand all the others, but why can't I talk?"

"I'm a member of the Regional Preternatural Investigation Team. You're not. If you go around saying golly gee whiz a dead body, they may catch on."

"I won't embarrass you." He sounded insulted; then a thought occurred to him. "Are we impersonating police officers?"

"No. Keep repeating I'm a member of the Spook Squad, I'm a member of the Spook Squad, I'm a member of the Spook Squad."

"But I'm not," he said.

"That's why I don't want you talking."

"Oh," he said. He settled back into his seat, a little of the shine dimming around the edges. "I've never actually seen a freshly dead body before."

"You raise the dead for a living, Larry. You see corpses all the time."

"It's not the same thing, Anita." He sounded grumpy.

I glanced at him. He had slumped down as far into the seat as the seat belt would allow, arms crossed over his chest. We were at the crest of a hill. A band of sunlight fell like an explosion over his orange hair. His blue eyes looked translucent for a moment as we passed from light into shadow. He looked all scrunched and sulky.

"Have you ever seen a dead person outside of a funeral or a freshly raised zombie?"

He was quiet for a minute. I concentrated on driving, letting the silence fill the Jeep. It was a comfortable silence, at least for me.

"No," he said at last. He sounded like a little boy who had been told he couldn't go outside and play.

"I'm not always good around fresh bodies either," I said.

He looked at me sort of sideways. "What do you mean?"

It was my turn to scrunch into the seat. I fought the urge and sat up straighter. "I threw up on a murder victim once." Even saying it very fast, it was still embarrassing.

Larry scooted up in his seat, grinning. "You're just telling me that to make me feel better."

"Would I tell a story like that about myself if it wasn't true?" I asked.

"You really threw up on a body at a crime scene?"

"You don't have to sound so happy about it," I said.

He giggled. I swear he giggled. "I don't think I'll throw up on the body."

I shrugged. "Three bodies, with parts missing. Don't make promises you can't keep."

He swallowed loud enough for me to hear it. "What do they mean, parts missing?"

"We'll find out," I said. "This isn't part of your job description, Larry. I get paid for helping the cops; you don't."

"Will it be awful?" His voice was low, uncertain.

Chopped-up bodies. Was he kidding? "I don't know until we get there."

"But what do you think?" He was staring at me very earnestly.

I glanced back at the road, then at Larry. He looked very solemn, like a relative who'd asked the doctor for the truth. If he would be brave, I could be truthful. "Yeah, it'll be awful."

7

IT WAS AWFUL. Larry had managed to stagger from the crime scene before he threw up. The only comfort I could offer him was that he wasn't the only one. Some of the cops were looking a little green around the edges, too. I hadn't thrown up yet, but I was keeping it as an option for later.

The bodies lay in a small hollow near the base of a hill. The ground was nearly knee-deep with leaves. Nobody rakes in the woods. The drought had dried the leaves to a fine, biting crunch underfoot. The hollow was ringed by naked trees and bushes with branches like thin brown whips. When the leaves came out, the hollow would be hidden on all sides.

The body nearest to me was a blond man with hair cut so short it looked like an old-fashioned butch. Blood pooled around the eyeballs, flowing from them down the face.

There was something wrong with the face, besides the eyes, but I couldn't quite figure out what. I knelt in the dry leaves, glad that the leg of the coverall was protecting my hose from the leaves and the blood. Blood had pooled to either side of the boy's face, soaking into the leaves. The blood had dried to a tacky maroon substance. It looked like the teenager's eyes had been crying dark tears.

I touched the tip of my gloved fingers to the blond's chin. It moved in a boneless, wiggling movement that chins were not meant to do.

I swallowed hard and tried to take shallow breaths. I was glad it was still spring. If the bodies had been sitting this long in full summer heat, they'd have been ripe in more ways than one. Cool weather was a blessing.

I put my hands in the leaves and bent from the waist in an awkward sort of push-up motion. I was trying to see under his chin without moving the body again. There, nearly lost in the blood on the neck, was a puncture mark. A puncture mark wider than my outspread hand. I'd seen knife wounds and claw marks that could make a similar wound, but it was too big for a knife and too clean for a claw. Besides, what the hell had a claw that big? It looked like a massive blade had been shoved under the blond's chin, close enough to the front of his face to slice the eyes up from inside the head. That's why the eyes were bleeding, but still looked intact. The sword had nearly pulled the blond's face off his skull.

I ran my gloved fingers over the blond's short hair and found what I was looking for. The tip of the sword, if that's what it was, had come out the top of his head. Then the blade had been withdrawn and the blond had dropped to the leaves. Dead, I hoped, but dying I was sure of.

His legs were missing just below the hip joint. There was almost no blood where the legs had been bisected. They'd been cut off after he'd died. Small blessing, that. He'd died relatively quickly, and had not been tortured. There were worse ways to die.

I knelt by the stubs of his legs. The left bone had been cut clean with one blow. The right bone had splintered, as if the sword struck from the left side, cut the left cleanly, but only got a piece of the right leg. A second blow had been needed to sever the right leg.

Why take the legs? A trophy? Maybe. Serial killers took trophies, clothing, personal items, a body part. Maybe a trophy?

The other two boys were shorter, neither of them over five feet. Younger maybe, maybe not. They were both small and dark-haired, slender. Probably the kind of boys who looked pretty rather than handsome but, frankly, it was hard to tell.

One lay on his back almost opposite from the blond. One brown eye stared up at the sky, glassy and immobile, somehow unreal like the eyes of a taxidermy animal. The rest of his face was sliced in two huge gaping furrows, as if the tip of the sword had been used coming and going like a backhand slap. The third slice had taken out his neck. It was a very clean wound; they all were. The damn sword, or whatever it was, was incredibly sharp. But it was more than a good blade. No human could have been fast enough to take them all without a struggle. But most beasties that will kill a human being won't pick up a weapon to do it.

A lot of things will claw us apart, or eat us alive, but the list of preternatural beings that will cut us up with weapons is pretty small. A troll may tear up a tree and whap you to death, but it won't use a blade. Not only had this thing used a sword, not a common weapon, but it had some skill.

The blows to the face hadn't killed the boy. Why didn't the other two run? If the blond was killed first, why didn't this one run? Nothing was fast enough that it could take out three teenage boys with a sword before any of them could run. These were not quick blows. Whoever, or whatever, had done this had taken some time with each kill. But they all acted as if they'd been hit by surprise.

The boy had fallen onto his back in the leaves, hands clutching at his throat. The leaves had been scuffed away where his feet had kicked them. I took a shallow breath. I didn't want to probe the wounds, but I was beginning to have a nasty idea.

I knelt and traced the neck wound with my fingertips. The edges of the skin were so smooth. But it was still human flesh, human skin, blood dried to a thick stickiness. I swallowed hard and closed my eyes and let my fingers search for what I thought I'd find. The edge of the wound had two lips, starting about midway. I opened my eyes and traced the double wound with my fingers. My eyes still couldn't see it. There was too much blood. Once the wound was clean, you'd see it, but not here, not like this. The neck had been sliced twice, deeply. One cut was enough to kill. Why twice? Because they were hiding something on the neck.

Fang marks, maybe? Being killed by a vampire would explain why he hadn't tried to crawl away. He'd just lain in the leaves and kicked until he died.

I stared at the last teenager. He was crumpled on his right side. Blood had pooled under him. He was so cut up that at first my eyes didn't want to make sense of what I was seeing. I wanted to look away before my brain caught up to my eyes, but I didn't.

Where the face should have been was just a ripped, gapping hole. The creature had done the same thing to this one as to the blond, but it had been more thorough. The front of the skull had been ripped away. I glanced around, searching the leaves for the piece of bone and flesh, but didn't see it. I had to look back then, at the body. I knew what I was looking at now. I liked it better when I didn't.

The back of the skull was full of blood and gore, like a gruesome cup, but the brain was gone. The blade had sliced him open across the chest and stomach. His intestines spilled out in a thick, rubbery mass. What I thought was his stomach had spilled out from the wound like a balloon half-inflated. The left leg had been chopped off at the hip joint. The ragged cloth of his jeans clung to the hole like the petals of an unopened flower. The left arm had been ripped out just below the elbow. The bone of the humerus was dark with dried blood, sticking up at an odd angle as if the entire arm had been broken at the shoulder and no longer moved. More violent. Had this one struggled a little?

My eyes flicked back to his face. I didn't want to look again, but I hadn't really examined it. There was something horribly personal about disfiguring a person's face. If it had been humanly possible to do all this, I'd have said check their nearest and dearest. As a general rule, only people who love you will cut up your face. It implies passion that you can't get from strangers. One exception is serial killers. They're working through a pathology in which the victims can represent someone else. Someone that the killer has a personal passion for. When cutting up the faces of strangers they'd be symbolically cutting up, say, a hated father figure.

The fine bones of the boy's sinus cavities had been cracked open. The maxillary was gone, making the face look incomplete. Part of the mandible was still there, but it had been cracked apart back to the rear molars. Some trick of blood flow had left two teeth white and clean. One of the teeth had a filling in it. I stared at that ruined face. I'd been doing pretty good at thinking of it as so much meat, just dead meat. But dead meat didn't get cavities, didn't go to dentists. It was suddenly a teenager, or maybe even younger. I was only judging on height and the apparent age of the other two. Maybe this one with no face was a child, a tall child. A little boy.

The spring afternoon wavered around me. I took a deep breath to steady myself, and it was a mistake. I got a big whiff of bowels and stale death. I scrambled for the side of the hollow. Never throw up on the murder victims. Pisses off the cops.

I fell to my knees at the top of the small rise where all the cops were gathered. I hadn't exactly fallen so much as thrown myself down. I took deep, cleansing breaths of the cool air. It helped. A small breeze was blowing up here, thinning out the smell of death. It helped more.

Cops of all shapes and sizes were huddled at the top of the rise. Nobody was spending more time than they had to down among the dead. There were ambulances waiting on the distant road, but everybody else had had their piece of the bodies. They had been videotaped and trooped through with the crime scene technicians. Everybody had done their job, except me.

"Are you going to be sick, Ms. Blake?" The voice was that of Sergeant Freemont, Division of Drug and Crime

Control, DD/CC—affectionately known as D2C2. Her tone was gentle but disapproving. I understood the tone. We were the only two women at the crime scene, which meant we were playing with the big boys. You had to be tougher than the men, stronger, better, or they held it against you. Or they treated you like a girl. I was betting Sergeant Freemont hadn't gotten sick. She wouldn't have allowed it.

I took another cleansing breath and let it out. I looked up at her. From my knees she looked every inch of her five-foot-eight. Her hair was straight, dark, cut just below her chin. The ends were curled under to frame her face. Her pants were a bright sunny yellow, jacket black, blouse a softer yellow. I had a good view of her polished black loafers. There was a gold wedding band on her left hand, but no engagement ring. Deep smile lines put her on the far side of forty, but she wasn't smiling now.

I swallowed once more, trying not to taste that smell on the back of my tongue. I got to my feet. "No, Sergeant Freemont, I'm not going to be sick." I was glad that it was true. I just hoped she didn't make me go back down into the hollow. I'd toss my cookies if I had to look at the bodies again.

"What did that?" She asked. I didn't turn and look where she pointed. I knew what was down there.

I shrugged. "I don't know."

Her brown eyes were neutral and unreadable, good cop eyes. She frowned. "What do you mean, you don't know? You're supposed to be the monster expert."

I let the "supposed to be" go. She hadn't called me a zombie queen to my face; in fact she'd been very polite, correct, but there was no warmth to it. She wasn't impressed, and in her quiet way, with a look or the slightest inflection, she let me know. I was going to have to pull a very big corpse out of my hat to impress Sergeant Freemont, DD/CC. So far I wasn't even close.

Larry walked up to us. His face was the color of yellow-green tissue paper. It clashed with his red hair. His eyes were red-rimmed where his eyes had teared while he threw up. If it's violent enough, sometimes you cry while you vomit.

I didn't ask Larry if he was okay; the answer was too obvious. But he was on his feet, ambulatory. If he didn't faint, he'd be fine.

"What do you want from me, Sergeant?" I asked. I'd been more than patient. For me, I'd been downright conciliatory. Dolph would be proud. Bert would have been amazed.

She crossed her arms over her stomach. "I let Sergeant Storr talk me into letting you see the crime scene. He said you were the best. According to the newspapers, you just do a little magic and figure it all out. Or maybe you can just raise the dead and ask them who killed them."

I took a deep breath and let it out. I didn't use magic to solve crimes, as a general rule; I used knowledge, but saying so would be defending myself. I didn't need to prove anything to Freemont. "Don't believe everything you read in the papers, Sergeant Freemont. As for raising the dead, it won't work with these three."

"Are you telling me you can't raise zombies, either?" She shook her head. "If you can't help us then go home, Ms. Blake."

I glanced at Larry. He gave a small shrug. He still looked shaky. I don't think he had the energy yet to tell me to behave myself. Or maybe he was as tired of Freemont as I was.

"I could raise them as zombies, Sergeant, but you have to have a mouth and a working throat to talk with."

"They could write it down," Freemont said.

It was a good suggestion. It made me think better of her. If she was a good cop, I could put up with a little hostility. As long as I never had to see another set of bodies like the ones below, I could put up with a lot of hostility.

"Maybe, but the dead often lose higher brain function faster after a traumatic death. They might not be able to write, but even if they could, they might not know what killed them."

"But they saw it," Larry said. His voice sounded hoarse, and he coughed gently behind his hand to clear it.

"None of them tried to run away, Larry. Why?"

"Why are you asking him?" Freemont said.

"He's in training," I said.

"Training? You brought a trainee in on my murder case?"

I stared up at her. "I don't tell you how to do your job. Don't tell me how to do mine."

"You haven't done a damn thing yet. Except for your assistant throwing up in the bushes."

An unhealthy flush crept up Larry's neck. Embarrassed when he was almost too nauseated to stand.

"Larry wasn't the only one upchucking in the weeds, just the only one without a badge." I shook my head. "We don't need this shit." I brushed past Freemont. "Come on, Larry."

Larry followed, obedient to the last.

"I don't want any of this leaked to the press, Ms. Blake. If the media gets hold of it, I'll know where it came from." She wasn't yelling, but her voice carried.

I turned. I wasn't yelling either, but everyone could hear me. "You have an unknown preternatural creature that uses a sword, and is faster than a vampire."

Something flickered across her face, like maybe I'd finally done something interesting. "How do you know it's faster than a vampire?"

"None of the boys tried to get away. All of them died where they stood. Either it's faster, or it has some amazing mind control."

"It's not a lycanthrope, then?"

"Even a lycanthrope isn't that fast, and they don't have the ability to cloud men's minds. If a lycanthrope came in there with a sword, the boys would have screamed and run. There would have at least been signs of a struggle."

Freemont just stood there looking. It was a very serious look, like she was weighing and measuring me. She still wasn't happy with me, but she was listening.

"I can help you, Sergeant Freemont. I can help you figure out what did this, maybe, before it does it again."

Her quiet, confident mask crumbled around the edge for a second. If I hadn't been staring at her neutral brown eyes, I'd have missed it.

"Shit," I said, loud. I walked back over to her and lowered my voice. "That's it, isn't it? These aren't the first killings."

She glanced down at the ground, then met my eyes, jaw

sort of thrust forward. Her eyes weren't neutral now; they were just a little bit scared. Not for herself, but for what she'd done, or not done.

"The State Highway Patrol can handle a homicide." Her voice was the gentlest I'd heard it.

"How many?" I asked.

"Two before. A couple of teenagers, boy and a girl. Probably necking in the woods." Her voice was soft, almost tired.

"What's the M.E. say?"

"You're right," she said. "It was a blade, probably a sword. The monsters don't use weapons, Ms. Blake. I thought it was the girl's ex-boyfriend. He's got a collection of Civil War memorabilia, including swords. It seemed pretty cut-and-dried."

I nodded. "Sounds logical."

"None of his swords matched the blows, but I thought he'd ditched the murder weapon. I didn't think . . ." She looked away from me, hands shoved so hard into her pants pockets I thought they'd split the cloth. "The first scene wasn't like this. They were killed with the first blow; it pinned them through the chest into the ground. A human being could have done that." She looked back at me as if wanting me to agree with her. I did.

"Were their bodies cut up beyond the death wound?"

She nodded. "Disfigured faces, her left hand missing. The one that had worn the ex-boyfriend's ring."

"Were their throats cut?"

She frowned, thinking, then nodded. "Hers was. Not much blood either, like it'd been done after she died."

My turn to nod. "Great."

"Great?" Larry asked.

"I think you've got a vampire on your hands, Sergeant Freemont."

They both frowned at me. "Look at the body parts that are missing. The legs of the one boy were cut off after he died. The femoral artery is in the thigh near the groin. I've seen vamps take blood from that in preference to the neck. Cut off the legs, and no fang marks."

"What about the other two?" Freemont asked.

"Maybe the smallest boy was bitten. His neck was sliced twice for no reason. Maybe it was just a little extra violence like the disfigurement of the face. I don't know. But a vamp can take blood from the wrist, the bend of the arm. All parts that are missing."

"One of their brains is missing," Freemont said.

Larry swayed gently beside me. He wiped a hand over his suddenly sweating face.

"You going to be alright?" I asked.

He nodded, not trusting his voice. Brave Larry.

"What better way to throw us off the track than to take something a vamp wouldn't be interested in?" I said.

"Okay, say it makes some sense. Why this way? This is . . ." She spread her hands wide, staring down at the carnage. She was the only one of the three of us still looking at it. "This is nuts. If it was human, I'd say we had a serial killer on our hands."

"We may have," I said softly.

Freemont stared at me. "What the hell do you mean?"

"A vampire was a person once. Just being dead doesn't cure you of any problems you had as a live human being. If you have a violent pathology before death, that won't change just because you're dead."

Freemont looked at me like I was the one who was crazy. I think it was the word "dead" that was bothering her. Once her suspects were dead, they weren't suspects anymore. I tried again. "Say Johnny is a serial killer. He becomes a vampire. Why should being a vampire make him suddenly less violent? Why not more violent?"

"Oh, my God," Larry said.

Freemont took a deep breath in through her nose and let it out slow. "Okay, maybe you're right. I'm not saying you are. I've seen pictures of vampire victims and they don't look like this, but if you are, what do you need from me?"

"The pictures from the first crime scene. And a look at where it happened."

"I'll send the file to your hotel," she said.

"Where was the couple killed?"

"Just a few hundred yards from here."

"Let's go take a look."

"I'll have one of the troopers take you over," she said.

"This is a damn small geographic area. I assume you searched it."

"With a fine-tooth comb. But frankly, Ms. Blake, I wasn't sure what we were looking for. The leaves and the dry weather make it almost impossible to find tracks."

"Yeah," I said. "Tracks would help." I glanced back the way I'd come. The leaves were disturbed coming up the hill. "If it is a vampire . . ."

Freemont cut me off. "What do you mean, if?"

I met her suddenly accusing eyes. "Look, Sergeant, if it is a vampire it has more mind control than I've ever seen. I've never met a vampire, even a master vampire, that could hold three humans in thrall while he killed them. Until I saw this, I'd have said it couldn't be done."

"What else could it be?" Larry asked.

I shrugged. "I think it's a vamp, but if I said I was a hundred percent sure, I'd be lying. I try not to lie to the police. There may be no tracks up the hill even if the ground was soft, because the vampire could have flown in."

"Like a bat?" Freemont asked.

"No, they don't change shape into a bat, but they can . . ." I searched for a word and there wasn't one. "They can levitate, sort of fly. I've seen it. I can't explain it, but I've seen it."

"A serial killer vampire." She shook her head, the lines near her mouth deepening. "The Feds are going to be all over this."

"No joke," I said. "Did you find the missing body parts?"

"No, I thought maybe it had eaten them."

"If it ate that much, why not more? If it ate, why no teeth marks? If it ate, why not some scattered body parts, like crumbs?"

She clenched her hands into fists. "You've made your point. It was a vampire. Even a dumb cop knows they don't eat flesh." She turned her brown eyes to me, and there was a lot of anger in them. Not at me, exactly, but I might make a good target. I stared back at her, not flinching. She looked away first. Maybe I wouldn't make a good target.

"I don't like having a civilian contractor in on a homicide investigation, but you spotted things down there that I missed. You're either very good, or you know something that you aren't telling me."

I could have just said I'm good at my job, but I didn't. Didn't want the police thinking I was holding out information when I wasn't. "I've got one advantage over a normal homicide detective, I expect it to be a monster. No one ever calls me in if it's just a stabbing, or a hit-and-run. I don't spend a lot of time trying to come up with nice, normal explanations. It means I get to ignore a lot of theories."

She nodded. "Alright, if you help me catch this thing, I don't care what you do for a living."

"Glad to hear it," I said.

"But no reporters, no media. I am in charge here. This is my investigation. I decide when we go public. Is that clear?"

"Sure."

She stared at me like she didn't believe me. "I mean it about the media, Ms. Blake."

"I don't have a problem with no media, Sergeant Freemont. I prefer it that way."

"For a person who doesn't want the media around, you get a lot of attention."

I shrugged. "I'm involved in only sensational cases, detective. Cases that make good press, good sound bites. I slay vampires, for God's sake; it makes great headlines."

"As long as we understand each other, Ms. Blake."

"No media; it's not a hard concept," I said.

She nodded. "I'll have someone walk you over to the first crime scene. I'll see you get the file at your hotel." She started to turn away.

"Sergeant Freemont?"

She turned back, but it was not a friendly look. "What is it now, Ms. Blake? You've done your job."

"You can't treat this like a human serial killer."

"I'm in charge of this investigation, Ms. Blake. I can do what I damn well please."

I stared up at her, met her hostile eyes. I wasn't feeling too friendly myself. "I am not trying to steal your thunder here. But vampires aren't just people with fangs. If the vamp could catch their minds and hold them while he slaughtered each of them in turn, he could capture your mind, anyone's mind. A vampire that talented could make you think black was white. Do you understand me?"

"It's daylight, Ms. Blake; if it's a vampire then we find it and stake it."

"You'll need a court order of execution."

"We'll get one."

"When you get it, I'll come back and finish the job."

"I think we can handle it."

"You ever stake a vampire?" I asked.

She just looked at me. "No, but I've shot a man. It can't be that much harder."

"It's not harder in the way you mean," I said. "But it's a hell of a lot more dangerous."

She shook her head. "Until the Feds get here, I'm in charge, and not you or anyone else is taking over. Is that clear, Ms. Blake?"

I nodded. "Crystal, Sergeant Freemont." I stared at the cross-shaped pin in the lapel of her suit jacket. Most plain-clothesmen had a cross-shaped tie tack. Standard police issue across the country. "You do have silver ammo, right?"

"I'll take care of my men, Ms. Blake."

I raised my hands slightly. So much for girl talk. "Fine, we're leaving. You've got my beeper number. Use it if you need it, Detective Freemont."

"I won't need it."

I took a deep breath and swallowed a lot of words. Picking a fight with the cop in charge of a murder investigation was not the way to get invited back to play. I walked past her without saying good-bye. If I opened my mouth, I wasn't sure what would come out. Nothing pleasant, and nothing useful.

8

PEOPLE WHO DON'T camp much think darkness falls from the sky. It doesn't. Darkness slides from the trees and fills them first, then spreads outward to the open places. It was so dark under the trees that I wished for a flashlight. When we stumbled to the road, and our waiting Jeep, it was only dusk.

Larry looked up at the coming night, and said, "We can get back and walk the graveyard for Stirling."

"First let's eat," I said.

He looked at me. "You wanting to stop for food, that's a first. I usually have to beg for drive-up."

"I forgot to eat lunch," I said.

He grinned. "That I believe." The smile faded slowly from his face. "The first time you offer me food voluntarily, and I don't think I can eat." He stared at me. There was enough light left for me to see him search my face. "Could you really eat after what we just saw?"

I looked at him. I didn't know what to say. Not so long ago, the answer would have been no. "Well, I wouldn't want to face a plate of spaghetti, or steak tartare, but yeah, I could eat."

He shook his head. "What the heck is steak tartare?"

"Raw beef, pretty much," I said.

He swallowed hard, looking just a little paler than he had a second ago. "How can you even think of stuff like that so soon after . . ." He let the words trail off. We'd both seen it; no words were needed.

I shrugged. "I've been going to murder scenes for nearly three years, Larry. You learn to survive. Which means you learn to eat after seeing cut-up bodies." I didn't add that I'd seen worse. I'd seen human bodies reduced to a roomful of blood and gobbets of unrecognizable flesh. Not enough left to fill a gallon-size baggie. I hadn't gone out for Big Macs after that one.

"Are you up to at least trying to eat?"

He was looking at me sort of suspiciously. "Where did you have in mind?"

I untied the Nikes and stepped carefully on the gravel road. Didn't want to snag the hose. I unzipped the coverall and stepped out of it. Larry did the same, but he tried to keep his shoes on. He managed to work his feet through, but it required some hopping on one leg.

I folded my coverall carefully so the blood wouldn't touch the Jeep's immaculate interior. I tossed the Nikes into the back floorboard and got the high heels out.

Larry was trying to brush wrinkles from his suit pants, but some things only a dry cleaner could fix.

"How would you like to go to Bloody Bones?" I asked.

He looked up at me, hands still patting at the wrinkles. He frowned. "Where?"

"It's the restaurant that Magnus Bouvier owns. Stirling mentioned it."

"Did he tell us where it was?" Larry said.

"No, but I asked one of the local cops for restaurants, and Bloody Bones isn't that far from here."

Larry squinted suspiciously at me. "Why do you want to go there?"

"I want to talk to Magnus Bouvier."

"Why?" he asked.

It was a good question. I wasn't sure I had a good answer. I shrugged and climbed into the Jeep. Larry had no choice but to join me, unless he didn't want to continue the conversation. When we were all settled in the Jeep, I still didn't have a really good answer.

"I don't like Stirling. I don't trust him."

"I got the impression you didn't like him," Larry said, his voice very dry. "But why not trust him?"

"Do you trust him?" I asked.

Larry frowned and thought about it. He shook his head. "Not as far as I could throw him."

"See?" I said.

"I guess so, but you think talking to Bouvier will help?"

"I hope so. I don't like raising the dead for people I don't trust. Especially something this big."

"Okay, so we go eat dinner at Bouvier's restaurant and talk to him; then what?"

"If we don't learn anything new, we go see Stirling and walk the graveyard for him."

Larry was looking at me like he wasn't sure he trusted me. "What are you up to?"

"Don't you want to know why Stirling had to have that mountain? Why the Bouviers' mountain and not someone else's?"

Larry looked at me. "You've been hanging around the police too long. You don't trust anybody."

"The cops didn't teach me that, Larry; it's natural talent." I put the Jeep in gear and off we went.

The trees made long, thin shadows. In the valleys between mountains, the shadows formed pools of coming night. We should have driven straight to the graveyard. Just walking the cemetery wouldn't hurt anything. But if I couldn't go vampire hunting, I could question Magnus Bouvier. That part of my job nobody could chase me out of.

I didn't really want to go vampire hunting. It was almost dark. Hunting vamps after dark was a good way to get killed. Especially one that could control minds like this one could. A vampire can cloud your mind and even hurt you, if its control is good enough, and you won't mind. But once its concentration is off you, onto someone else, and that person starts screaming, you'll wake up. You'll run. But the boys hadn't run. They hadn't woken up. They'd just died.

If this thing wasn't stopped, other people would die. I could almost guarantee it. Freemont should have let me stay. They needed a vampire expert with them on this one. They needed me. Okay, they really needed police with expertise in monsters, but they didn't have that. It had only been three years since Addison v. Clark made vampires legally alive. Three years ago Washington had made the blood-suckers living citizens with rights. Nobody had thought what that meant for the police. Before the law changed, preternatural crime was handled by bounty hunters, vampire hunters. Those private citizens with enough experience to keep them alive. Most of us had some sort of preternatural power that helped give us an edge against the monsters. Most cops didn't.

Ordinarily human beings didn't fare well against the monsters. There have always been a few of us who had a talent for taking out the beasties. We've done a good job, but suddenly the cops are expected to take over. No extra training, no extra manpower, nothing. Hell, most police departments wouldn't even spring for the silver ammunition.

It had taken this long for Washington, D.C., to realize they might have been hasty. That maybe, just maybe, the monsters were really monsters and the police needed some extra training. It would take years to train the cops, so they were going to short-circuit the process, just make cops out of all the vampire hunters and monster slayers. For myself, personally, it might work. I would've loved to have a badge to shove in Freemont's face. She couldn't have chased me off then, not if it was federal. But for most vampire hunters, it was going to be a mess. You needed more than preternatural expertise to work a homicide case. You sure as hell needed more than vampire expertise to carry a badge.

There were no easy answers. But out there in the coming darkness were a bunch of police hunting a vampire that could do things I never thought they could do. If I had a badge, I could be with them. I wasn't an automatic safety zone, but I knew a damn sight more than a state cop who had "seen" pictures of vampire victims. Freemont had never seen the real thing. Here was hoping she survived her first encounter.

9

BLOODY BONES BAR and grill lay up a red gravel road. Someone had butchered the trees back to either side, so the Jeep climbed upward towards a black blanket of sky, sprinkled with a million stars. The shine of stars was the only light in sight.

"It is really dark out here," Larry said.

"No streetlights," I said.

"Shouldn't we see the lights from the restaurant by now?"

"I don't know." I was staring at the broken trees. The trunks gleamed white and ragged. It had been done recently, as if someone had gone mad with an axe, or maybe a sword, or something big had ripped off the trunks.

I slowed down, scanning the darkness. Was I wrong? Was it trolls? Was there a Greater Ozark Mountain Troll left in these mountains? One that would use a sword? I was a big believer in a first time for everything.

I brought the Jeep almost to a stop.

"What's wrong?" Larry asked.

I hit the emergency flashers. The road was narrow, barely two cars wide, but it was going uphill. Anybody coming down wouldn't see the Jeep right away. The lights helped, but if someone was speeding . . . Hell, I was going to do it; why quibble? I put the Jeep in park and got out.

"Where are you going?"

"I'm wondering if a troll ripped the trees apart."

Larry started to get out on his side. I stopped him. "Slide over on my side if you want to get out."

"Why?"

"You're not armed." I got the Browning out. It was a solid, comforting weight, but truthfully, against something the size of one of the great mountain trolls, it wasn't too useful. Maybe with exploding bullets, but short of that a 9mm wasn't the gun for hunting something the size of a small elephant.

Larry closed his door and slid across. "You really think there's a troll out here?"

I stared off into the darkness. Nothing moved. "I don't know." I moved to a dry gully that cut the edge of the road. I stepped very carefully into it. The heels sank in the dry, sandy soil. I grabbed a handful of weeds with my left hand and levered myself up the slope. I had to grab one of the butchered trunks to keep from sliding backwards in the loose leaves and pine needles.

My hand came up against thick sap. I fought the urge to jerk away, forcing myself to keep hold of the sticky bark.

Larry scrambled up the bank, slick-soled dress shoes sliding in the dry leaves. I didn't have a free hand to offer him. He caught himself in a sort of half push-up, and used the weeds to move up beside me. "Damn dress shoes."

"At least you're not in heels," I said.

"And don't think I'm not grateful," he said. "I'd break my neck."

Nothing moved in the dark, dark night except us. There was the sound of spring peepers close by, musical, but nothing bigger. I let out a breath I hadn't realized I was holding. I pulled myself up to more solid footing and looked at the trees.

"What are we looking for?" Larry asked.

"An axe makes a wide, smooth stroke. If a troll snapped the trunks, they'll be ragged and full of jagged points of wood."

"Looks smooth to me," he said. He ran his fingertips over the naked wood. "But it doesn't look like an axe."

The wood was too smooth. An axe will come in at an angle. This was almost flat, like each tree had been felled with a single stroke, two at most. Some of the trees had been nearly a foot in diameter. No human could do that, even with an axe.

"Who could have done this?"

I searched the darkness, fighting an urge to aim the gun into the dark, but I kept it skyward. Safety first. "A vampire with a sword, maybe."

He stared off into the darkness. "You mean the one that killed the guys? Why would the vampire chop down a bunch of trees after he killed them?"

It was a good question. A great question. But like with so many questions today, I didn't have a good answer. "I don't know. Let's get back to the car."

We scrambled back the way we'd come. Neither of us fell down this time. A record.

When we were at the car I put the gun away. I probably hadn't needed it at all, but then again . . . something cut down those trees.

I used the aloe and lanolin baby wipes that I kept in the car to wipe off blood, to wipe the sap from my hand. The wipes worked nearly as well on tree blood as it did on human.

We drove on, searching for lights. We had to be close to Bloody Bones, unless the directions were way off. Here's hoping they weren't.

"Is that a torch?" Larry asked.

I stared into the darkness. There was a flicker of fire, too high off the ground to be a campfire. Two torches on long poles illuminated a wide gravel turnaround to the left of the road. The trees had been pushed back here, too, but years ago. It was an old, established clearing. The trees formed a backdrop for a one-story building. A wooden sign hung from the eaves. It was hard to read by torchlight, but it might have read "Bloody Bones."

Dark wooden shingles covered the roof and climbed down the walls, so that the entire building looked like a natural growth that had sprung from the red clay soil. About twenty cars and trucks were parked haphazardly on the dark gravel.

The sign swung in the wind, the torchlight reflecting off the deeply carved words. "Bloody Bones" was carved in smooth, curving letters.

I walked carefully over the gravel in my high heels. Larry's dress shoes worked better on gravel than mine did. "Bloody Bones is a strange name for a bar and grill."

"Maybe they serve ribs," I said.

He made a face at me. "I could not face barbecue anything right now."

"It wouldn't be my first choice either."

The door swung inward directly into the bar. The door swung shut and we were plunged into a fire-shot twilight. Most bars are gloomy places to drink and hide. A place of refuge from the noisy shiny world outside. But as refuges went, this was a good one. There was a bar along one side of the room, and a dozen small tables scattered on the dark polished wood floor. There was a small stage to the left and a jukebox near the back wall where a small hallway probably led to bathrooms and the kitchen beyond.

Every surface was dark wood and polished 'til it shone. Candles with chimney glass over them shone from the walls. A chandelier with more chimney glass and candles hung from the low, dark wood ceiling. The wood was the darkest of mirrors, glowing in the light rather than reflecting it.

The beams that supported the ceiling were carved with fruiting vines and stray leaves that looked like oaks. Every face was turned towards us like a bad western. A lot of the faces were male; the eyes slid over me, saw Larry, and most went back to their drinks. A few stayed hopeful, but I ignored them. It was too early in the night for anybody to be drunk enough to give me grief. Besides, we were armed.

The women were grouped three deep at the bar. They were dressed for a Friday night, if you planned to spend Friday night on a street corner propositioning strangers. They stared at Larry like they wondered if he'd be good to eat. Me, they seemed to hate on sight. If I knew any of them, I'd have said they were jealous, but I'm not the kind of woman to elicit jealousy on sight. Not tall enough, not blonde enough, not Nordic enough, not exotic enough. I'm pretty, but I'm not beautiful. The women looked at me like they saw something I didn't. It made me glance behind me to see if someone had come in behind us, even though I knew no one had.

"What going on?" Larry whispered.

That was another thing. It was quiet. I'd never been in a bar on a Friday night that you could whisper in and be heard.

"I don't know," I said softly.

The women at the bar parted like someone had asked, giving us a clear view of the bar. There was a man behind the bar. I thought what beautiful hair *she* had when I first saw him. The hair fell to his waist like thick, chestnut-colored water. The candle flames gleamed in his hair the same way they shone in the polished wood of the bar.

He raised startling blue-green eyes, like deep sea water, to us. He was dark and lovely rather than handsome, androgynous as a cat. He was exotic as hell and I suddenly understood why the bar was three deep in women.

He sat an amber-filled glass down on a tiny napkin and said, "You're up, Earl." His voice was surprisingly low, like he'd sing deep bass.

A man got up from the tables, Earl probably. He was a large, lumbering man, formed of soft squares like a gentler version of Boris Karloff's monster. Not a cover boy. He reached for his drink, and his arm brushed the back of one of the women. The woman turned, angry. I expected her to tell him to go to hell, but the bartender touched her arm. She was suddenly very still, as if listening to voices I couldn't hear.

The air wavered. I was suddenly very aware that Earl smelled of soap and water. His hair was still damp from the shower. I could lick the water from his skin, feel those big hands on my body.

I shook my head and stepped back into Larry. He caught my arm. "What's wrong?"

I stared at him, clutching his arm, my fingers digging through the cloth of his suit, until I could feel his arm solid under my hand. I turned back to the bar.

Earl and the woman had gone to sit at a table. She was kissing the palm of his calloused hand.

"Jesus," I said.

"What's wrong, Anita?" Larry asked.

I took a deep breath and stood away from him. "I'm okay; it was just unexpected."

"What was?"

"Magic." I stepped up to the bar.

Those amazing eyes stared back at me, but there was no power to them. It wasn't like dealing with a vampire. I could gaze into those beautiful eyes forever, and they would still just be eyes. Sort of.

I placed my hands on the gleaming wood of the bar. More vines and leaves curved around the edge of the heavy wood. I ran my fingers over the deep set carvings. Hand-carved, all of it.

His fingertips caressed the wood like it was skin. It was a proprietal touch, the way some men touch their girlfriends when they're into ownership. I was betting that he'd carved every inch of it.

A brunette in a dress two sizes smaller than it should have been touched his arm. "Magnus, you don't need a stranger."

Magnus Bouvier turned to the brunette. He trailed those caressing fingertips down her arm. She shivered. He raised her hand gently from his arm, pressing his lips to the back of her hand. "Pick anyone you want, darlin'. You are too beautiful to be denied tonight."

She wasn't beautiful. Her eyes were small and muddy brown, her chin too sharp, nose too large for a thin face. I was staring right at her from not a foot away, and her face smoothed. Her eyes were suddenly large and sparkling, her thin lips full and moist. It was like seeing her through one of those soft filters they used during the sixties, except more.

I glanced at Larry. He looked like he'd been hit by a truck. A slim, lovely truck. I stared out over the bar, and every other male in the place except Earl was staring at the woman in exactly the same way, as if she'd just appeared before them like Cinderella transformed by her fairy godmother. Not a bad analogy.

I turned back to Magnus Bouvier. He was not staring at the woman. He was staring at me.

I leaned into the bar, meeting his gaze. He smiled slightly. I said, "Love charms are illegal."

The smile widened. "You're much too pretty to be the police." He reached out to touch my arm.

"Touch me and I'll have you arrested for using undue preternatural influence."

"It's a misdemeanor," he said.

"Not if you're not human, it isn't," I said.

He blinked at me. I didn't know him well enough to be sure, but I think I surprised him, like I should have believed he was human. Yeah, right.

"Let's talk at a table," he said.

"Fine with me."

"Dorrie, can you take over for a few minutes?"

A woman came behind the bar. She had the same thick chestnut hair, but it was tied back from her face in a severe ponytail, high and tight on her head. The long, shining tail of hair swung as she moved, like it was alive. Her face, free of hair and makeup, was triangular, exotic, catlike. Her eyes were the same startling seawater green as Magnus's.

The men nearest the bar watched her out of the corners of their eyes, as if afraid to look directly at her. Larry stared at her open-mouthed.

"I'll watch the bar, but that's all," she said. She turned those eyes to Larry and said, "What are you staring at?" Her voice was harsh, thick with scorn.

Larry blinked, closed his mouth, and stuttered. "N-nothing."

She glared at him like she knew he was lying. I got an inkling why the men weren't staring at her.

"Dorcas, be nice to the customers."

She glared at Magnus; he smiled, but he backed down. Magnus stepped out from behind the bar. He was wearing a soft blue dress shirt untucked over jeans so faded they were almost white. The shirt hit him at nearly mid-thigh; he'd had to roll the sleeves over his forearms. Black and silver cowboy boots completed the outfit. Everything but the boots looked borrowed. He should have looked sloppy, too casual among everyone else duded up for a Friday night, but he didn't. His utter confidence made the outfit seem perfect. A woman at one of the tables grabbed the hem of his shirt as he moved passed. He pulled it out of her hands with a playful smile.

Magnus led us to a table near the empty stage. He stood, letting me choose my seat; very gentlemanly of him. I sat with my back to the wall so I could see both doors and the room. It was sort of cowboyish, but magic rode the air. Illegal magic.

Larry sat to my right. He'd watched me and scooted his chair a little back from the table so he could see the room too. It was almost frightening how seriously Larry watched what I did. It would keep him alive, but it was like being followed around by a three-year-old with a carry permit. Kind of intimidating.

Magnus smiled at us both, indulgently, like we were doing something cute or amusing. I wasn't in the mood to be amusing.

"Love charms are illegal," I said.

"You said that already," Magnus said. He flashed me a smile that I think was meant to be charming and harmless. It wasn't. There wasn't anything he could do to make himself less than exotic. He sure as hell wasn't harmless.

I stared at him until the smile wilted around the edges, and he swallowed. He spread his long-fingered hands on the tabletop, staring at them. When he looked up, the smile was gone. He looked solemn, a little nervous even. Good.

"It's not a charm," he said.

"The hell it isn't," I said.

"It isn't. A spell, but nothing as mundane as a charm."

"You're splitting hairs," I said.

Larry was staring at us intently. "Was that stuff at the bar a love charm?"

"What stuff at the bar?" Magnus's face was incredibly mild, as if he thought Larry would believe him.

Larry looked at me. "Is he kidding? The woman went from a three to a twenty-three. It had to be magic."

Magnus turned his attention to Larry for the first time, excluding me—and I felt excluded. It was like a ray of sunshine had moved away from me, and I was just a little colder, a little more in the dark.

I shook my head. "Cut the glamor crap."

Magnus turned back to me, and for a minute I felt that warmth. "Stop it."

"What?"

I stood up. "Fine; let's see how funny you think you are in jail."

Magnus encircled my wrist with his hand. His skin should have been work-roughened, but it wasn't. His skin was unnaturally soft, like living velvet. Of course, that could have been illusionary, too.

I tried to pull my hand away, but his grip tightened. I kept pulling, and he kept tightening with that certainty of some-one who knew that I couldn't get away. He was wrong. It wasn't just a matter of strength, it was a matter of leverage.

I turned my wrist towards his fingers in a quick turning motion, jerking at the same time. His fingers slid over my skin trying to dig in, but it was over. My wrist felt rubbed raw where his finger had scraped along the skin. It wasn't bleeding, but it hurt anyway. It would have felt better if I rubbed it, but I wouldn't give him the satisfaction. I was, after all, a tough-as-nails vampire slayer. Besides, it would have ruined some of the effect, and I liked the surprise on Magnus's face.

"Most women don't pull away once I've touched them."

"You use magic on me one more time, and I'll feed you to the cops."

He stared up at me, a thoughtful look on his face. He nodded. "You win. No more magic on you or your friend."

"Or anyone else," I said. I sat back down carefully, putting a little more distance between me and him. I angled the chair just a little to one side so the grab for my gun would be smoother. I didn't think I'd have to shoot him, but my wrist was aching where he'd squeezed. I had arm wres-tled with vampires and shapeshifters. I knew preternatural strength when I felt it. He had it. He could have squeezed until my bones popped out of my skin, but he hadn't squeezed fast enough. He hadn't really wanted to hurt me. His mistake.

"Oh, my customers wouldn't like the magic going away," he said.

"You can't manipulate them like this. It is illegal, and I will turn you in for it."

"But everyone knows that Friday night is lovers' night at Bloody Bones," Magnus said.

"What's lovers' night?" Larry asked.

Magnus smiled, already regaining some of his easy charm, but that flicker of warmth was gone. He was being true to his word, as far as I could tell. Even vampires couldn't work mind control on me without my knowing it. That Magnus could made me nervous.

"I make everyone beautiful or handsome, or sexy, tonight. For a few hours you can be the lover of your own dreams, and someone else's. Though I wouldn't spend the night. The glamor doesn't last that long."

"What are you?" Larry asked.

"What looks like *Homo sapiens*, can breed with *Homo sapiens*, but isn't *Homo sapiens*?" I asked.

Larry's eyes widened. "*Homo arcanus*. He's a fairie?"

"Please keep your voice down," Magnus said. He glanced around at the near tables. No one was playing much attention to us. They were too busy gazing into each other's magically enhanced eyes.

"You can't be passing for human," I said.

"The Bouviers have told the future and made love charms for centuries around here."

"You said it wasn't a love charm," I said.

"They think it is, but you know what it is."

"Glamor," I said.

"What's glamor?" Larry asked.

"It's fairie magic. It's what allows them to cloud our minds, make things seem better or worse than they are."

Magnus nodded, smiling, as if pleased that I knew so much. "Exactly; it's really a minor magic compared to some."

I shook my head. "I've read about glamor, and it doesn't work this well unless you're high court, *Daoine Sidhe*. The seelie court of fairyland doesn't interbreed with mortals often. At least not commoners. The unseelie court, on the other hand, does."

He stared at me with his beautiful eyes, looking, even without glamor, so gorgeous you wanted to touch him. Wanted to see if his hair was as luxuriant as it looked. He was like a really fine sculpture; you wanted to run your hands over it and feel the lines.

Magnus smiled gently. "The unseelie court is evil, cruel. What I do here is not evil. For one night these people can come here and be their own fantasies. They think it's love charms, and I let them. We all keep the secret of this small illegal act. The local police know. They even come down once in a while and join in."

"But it's not love charms."

"No, it's natural talent on my part. Using my own home-grown magic isn't illegal if everyone knows I'm doing it."

"So you pretend it's love charms, and everyone looks the other way because they're having a good time, but it's really fairie glamor, which isn't illegal with permission of the participants."

"Exactly," he said.

"Which makes it all legal."

He nodded. "Now if I was descended from the dark side of fairie, would I do anything to bring pleasure to so many?"

"If it suited your needs, yeah."

"Isn't there a ban on unseelie court moving to this country?" Larry asked.

"Yeah," I said.

"Not if my family moved here before the ban went into effect. The Bouviers have been here for nearly three hundred years."

"Not possible," I said. "Nobody but the Indians have been here that long."

"Llyn Bouvier was a French fur trapper. He was the first European to set foot on this land. He married into the local tribe, Christianized them."

"Bully for him. So how come you didn't want to sell to Raymond Stirling?"

He blinked at me. "It would disappoint me greatly to find out you are working for him."

"Sorry to disappoint you," I said.

"What are you?"

He hadn't asked who, he'd asked what. It was a very different question. It sort of stopped me for a second.

"I'm Anita Blake; this is Larry Kirkland. We're animators."

"I take it you don't draw cartoons," he said.

It made me smile. "No. We raise the dead; 'animate' from the Latin, to give life."

"Is that all you do?" He was staring at me very intently,

like there was something written on the inside of my skull and he was trying to read it.

It was an uncomfortable level of scrutiny, but I've been stared at by the best. I met his eyes and answered. "I'm a licensed vampire executioner."

He shook his head gently. "I didn't ask what you did for a living. I asked what you were."

I frowned. "Maybe I don't understand the question."

"Perhaps you don't, but your friend asked what I was. You said I was a fairie. I ask you what you are, and you describe your job. It would be like me saying I'm a bartender."

"I don't know how to answer you, then," I said.

He was still staring at me. "Yes, you do. I can see a word in your eyes. One word."

When he said it, a word did come to mind. "Necromancer. I'm a necromancer."

Magnus nodded. "Does Mr. Stirling know what you are?"

"I doubt he'd understand even if I told him."

"Do you really have the ability to control all types of undead?" Magnus asked.

"Can you really make a hundred shoes in a single night?" I asked.

Magnus smiled. "Wrong kind of fairie."

"Yeah," I said.

"If you're working for Stirling, why are you here? I hope you didn't come here to try to persuade me to sell. I'd hate to have to say no to such a lovely woman."

"Can the compliments, Magnus. It won't get you anywhere."

"What would get me somewhere?"

I sighed. "I've got too many men on my plate now."

"That's the God's honest truth," Larry muttered.

I frowned at him.

"I'm not asking you out on a date. I'm asking you into my bed."

I frowned at Magnus. No, glared was a better word. "Not in this lifetime."

"Sex between supernatural beings is always amazing, Anita."

"I'm not a supernatural being."

"Now who's splitting hairs?"

I didn't know what to say to that, so I said nothing. I rarely get in trouble with silence.

Magnus smiled. "I've made you uncomfortable. I am sorry, but I'd never have forgiven myself if I hadn't asked. It's been a long time since I was with anyone who wasn't straight human. Let me buy you both drinks, to make up for my rudeness."

I shook my head. "Menus would be fine. We haven't eaten yet."

"The meals will be on the house."

"No," I said.

"Why not?"

"Because I don't particularly like you, and I don't take favors from people I don't like."

He sat back in his chair, a strange, almost startled expression on his face. "You are direct."

"You have no idea," Larry said.

I resisted the urge to kick Larry under the table and said, "Can we have some menus?"

He raised a hand and called, "Two menus, Dorrie."

Dorrie brought them over. "I'm part owner of this place, not your waitress, Magnus. Hurry it up."

"Don't forget that appointment I've got tonight, Dorrie." His voice was mild. She wasn't fooled.

"You aren't leaving me alone with these people. I will not . . ." She glanced at us. "I don't approve of lovers' night. You know that."

"I'll take care of everybody before I leave. You won't have to sully your morals."

She glared at all of us in turn. "You're leaving with them?"

"No," he said.

She turned on her heel and stalked back to the bar. The men who weren't paired off watched her swaying back, carefully, not staring until she couldn't see them.

"Your sister doesn't approve of abusing glamor?" I asked.

"Dorrie doesn't approve of a lot of things."

"She has morals."

"Implying I don't," he said.

I shrugged. "You said it, not me."

"She always this judgmental?" he asked Larry.

Larry nodded. "Usually."

"Let's just order our food," I said.

Larry smiled, but he looked down at the menu.

It was a laminated piece of paper printed on both sides. I ordered a cheeseburger, well done, house fries, and a large Coke. I hadn't had caffeine in several hours; I was running low.

Larry was frowning at the menu. "I don't think I could eat a hamburger right now."

"They've got salads," I said.

Magnus laid his fingertips against the back of Larry's hand. "Something swims up behind your eyes. Something . . . awful just behind your eyes."

Larry stared at him. "I don't know what you mean."

I grabbed Magnus's wrist and pulled him away from Larry. He turned his eyes to me, but there was more than just their color to make them hard to stare at. The pupil of his eyes had spiraled down like the eye of a bird. Human eyes just didn't do that.

I was suddenly very aware that I was still holding his wrist. I drew my hand away. "Stop reading us, Magnus."

"You wore gloves, or I'd be able to tell what you'd touched," he said.

"It's an ongoing police investigation. Anything you discern by psychic means must be held confidential, or you're liable just as if you stole information out of our files."

"Do you always do that?" he asked.

"What?"

"Quote the law when you're nervous."

"Sometimes," I said.

"I saw blood, that's all. My gifts are rather limited in the area of far-seeing. You should shake Dorrie's hand. Far-seeing is her strong suit."

"Thanks, but no thanks," Larry said.

He smiled. "You are not police, or you wouldn't have

threatened me with the police, but you were with them earlier. Why?"

"I thought all you saw was blood," I said.

He had the grace to look embarrassed; nice to know he could be embarrassed. "A little bit more, perhaps."

"Touch clairvoyance isn't a traditional fey power."

"Our many-times-great-grandmother was the daughter of a shaman, so the story goes."

"Getting magic from both sides of the family tree," I said. "Dirty pool."

"Clairvoyance isn't magic," Larry said.

"A really good clairvoyant will make you think it is," I said. I stared at Magnus. The last clairvoyant who had touched me and seen blood had been horrified. He hadn't wanted to touch me again. He hadn't wanted me anywhere near him. Magnus didn't look horrified, and he'd offered to have sex with me. Different strokes for different folks.

"I'll take your order through to the kitchen myself, if you'll just decide what you want," he said.

Larry stared at the menu. "A salad, I guess. No dressing." He thought about it some more. "No tomatoes."

Magnus started to stand.

"Why won't you sell to Stirling?" I asked.

Magnus cocked his head to one side, smiling. "The land has been in our family for centuries. It's our land."

I looked at him and couldn't read his face. It could have been the absolute truth, or a bold-faced lie.

"So the only reason you don't want to be a millionaire is because of what . . . family tradition?"

The smile deepened. He leaned closer, long hair spilling forward. He whispered, and it was quiet enough that he needed to whisper. "Money is not everything, Anita. Though Stirling seems to think it is."

His face was very close, just barely far enough away for me not to complain. I could smell his aftershave, faint as if you'd have to get very near his skin to smell it, but it would be worth the effort.

"What do you want, Magnus, if it's not money?" I stared at him from too close. His long hair trailed over my hand.

"I told you what I wanted."

Even without the glamor he was trying to sweet-talk me, distract me. "What happened to the trees out by your road?" I didn't distract that easily.

He blinked long lashes. Something slid behind his eyes. "I happened."

"You cut down those trees?" Larry asked.

Magnus turned to him, and I was glad not to be staring at him from inches away. "Sadly, yes."

"Why?" I asked.

He straightened up, suddenly businesslike. "I got drunk and went on a little rampage." He shrugged. "Embarrassing, isn't it?"

"That's one word for it," I said.

"I'll go get your food. One naked salad coming up."

"You remember what I'm getting?" I asked.

"Meat burned to death; I remember."

"You sound like a vegetarian."

"Oh, no," he said. "I eat all sorts of things."

He walked away through the crowd before I could decide if I'd been insulted or not. Just as well. For the life of me, I couldn't think of a good comeback line.

10

DORCAS BROUGHT OUR food without a word. She seemed angry—maybe not at us, but with us. Or with everything. I sympathized. Magnus went behind the bar, spreading his own special brand of magic to his customers once more. He glanced our way and smiled but didn't come back to finish our talk. Of course; we'd been finished. I was all out of questions.

I took a bite of my cheeseburger. It was almost crispy around the edges, not a smidgen of pink in the center. Perfect.

"What's wrong?" Larry asked. He was nibbling at a lettuce leaf.

I swallowed. "Why should something be wrong?"

"You're frowning," he said.

"Magnus didn't come back to the table."

"So? He answered all our questions."

"Maybe we just don't know the right questions to ask."

"You suspect him of something now?" Larry shook his head. "You have been hanging around with cops too long, Anita. You think everyone's up to something."

"They usually are." I took another bite of burger.

Larry squinched his eyes tight.

"What's wrong with you?" I asked.

"There's juice coming out of your burger. How can you eat that after what we just saw?"

"I guess this means you don't want me to put ketchup on my fries."

He looked at me with something near physical pain on his face. "How can you make jokes?"

My beeper went off. Had they found the vampire? I hit the button, and Dolph's number flashed at me. Now what?

"It's Dolph. Eat hearty. I'll phone from the Jeep and be back."

Larry stood up with me. He put a tip on the table and left his salad nearly untouched. "I'm done."

"Well, I'm not. Have Magnus pack my meal to go." I left him staring forlornly down at my half-eaten burger.

"You're not going to eat it in the car, are you?"

"Just have it packed up." I went for the Jeep and its fancy phone.

Dolph answered on the third ring. "Anita?"

"Yeah, Dolph, it's me. What's up?"

"Vampire victim out near you."

"Shit, another one."

"What do you mean another one?"

That stopped me. "Freemont didn't call you after I talked to her?"

"Yeah, she said good things about you."

"That surprises me; she wasn't too friendly."

"How not friendly?"

"She wouldn't let me hunt vampires with her."

"Tell me," Dolph said.

I told him.

Dolph was quiet for a very long time after I finished.

"You still there, Dolph?"

"I'm here. I wish I wasn't."

"What's going on, Dolph? Why would Freemont call and tell you what a good job I'm doing, but not ask for the squad's help on something this big?"

"I bet she hasn't called the Feds either," Dolph said.

"What's going on, Dolph?"

"I think Detective Freemont is pulling a Lone Ranger on us."

"The federal boys are going to want a piece of this. The first vampire serial killer in recorded history. Freemont can't keep it to herself."

"I know," Dolph said.

"What are we going to do?"

"The body on the ground this time sounds like a straight-forward vampire kill. It's classic, bite marks, no other damage to the body. Could it be a different vamp?"

"Could be," I said.

"You sound doubtful."

"Two rogue vamps in this small a geographical area, this far from a city, doesn't seem likely."

"The body wasn't cut up."

"There is that," I said.

"How sure are you that the first killer is a vamp? Is there anything else it could be?"

I opened my mouth to say no, and closed it. Anybody who could cut down all those trees in one drunken brawl could certainly cut up people. Magnus had his glamor. I wasn't sure it was capable of doing what I'd seen in the clearing, but . . .

"Anita?"

"I might have an alternative."

"What?"

"Who," I said. I hated giving Magnus up to the cops. He'd

kept his secret so long, but . . . what if the question I should ask was, had he killed five people? I'd felt the strength in his hands. I remembered the clean trunks of the trees, cut by just one blow, two at most. I flashed on the murder scene. The blood, the naked bone. I couldn't rule Magnus out, and I couldn't afford to be wrong.

I gave him up to Dolph. "Can you keep the part about him being fairie out of it for a while?"

"Why?"

"Because if he didn't do it, then his life is ruined."

"A lot of people have fey blood in them, Anita."

"Tell that to the college student last year whose fiance beat her to death when he found out he was about to marry a fairie. He protested in court that he hadn't meant to kill her. The fey were supposed to be hard to kill, weren't they?"

"Not everyone is like that, Anita."

"Not everyone, but enough."

"I'll try, Anita, but I can't promise."

"Fair enough," I said. "Where's the new victim?"

"Monkey's Eyebrow," he said.

"What?"

"That's the name of the town."

"Jesus. Monkey's Eyebrow, Missouri. Let me guess. It's a small town."

"Big enough to have a sheriff and a murder."

"Sorry. Do you have directions?" I fished my small, spiral-bound notebook out of the pocket of the black jacket.

He gave me directions. "Sheriff St. John is holding the body for you. He called us first. Since Freemont wants to go it alone, we'll let her."

"You're not going to tell her?"

"No."

"I don't suppose Monkey's Eyebrow has a crime scene unit, Dolph. If we don't have Freemont come in with her people, we're going to need somebody. Can you guys come down yet?"

"We're still working our own murder. But since Sheriff St. John called us in for his murder, we'll be in the area as soon as we can get there. Not tonight, but tomorrow."

"Freemont's supposed to send over crime-scene photos from the first couple that was killed. I bet if I asked she might send over photos from the second scene, too. Show-and-tell tomorrow when you get here."

"Freemont may be suspicious about you asking for more pictures," Dolph said.

"I'll tell her I want them for comparison. She may be trying to hog the case for herself, but she wants it solved. She just wants to solve it herself."

"She's a glory hound," Dolph said.

"Looks that way."

"I don't know if I'll be able to keep Freemont out of the second case or not, but I'll try to give you some lead time, so you can look around without her breathing down your neck."

"Much appreciated."

"She said you had your assistant with you at the crime scene. Had to be Larry Kirkland, right?"

"Right."

"What are you doing bringing him to crime scenes?"

"He'll have a degree in preternatural biology this spring. He's an animator and a vampire slayer. I can't be every-where, Dolph. If I think he can handle it, I thought it might be nice to have two monster experts."

"It might. Freemont said Larry lost his lunch all over the crime scene."

"He didn't throw up on the crime scene, just near it."

There was a moment of silence. "Better than throwing up on the body."

"I'm never going to live that down, am I?"

"No," Dolph said, "you aren't."

"Great. Larry and I will get out there as soon as we can. It's about a thirty-minute drive, maybe more."

"I'll tell Sheriff St. John you're on your way." He hung up.

I hung up. Dolph was training me never to say good-bye over the phone.

LARRY SLUMPED IN the seat as far as the seat belt would let him. His hands were clenched tight in his lap. He stared out into the dark like he was seeing something besides the passing scenery. Images of butchered teenagers dancing in his head, I bet. They weren't dancing in mine. Not. I might see them in my dreams, but not awake, not yet.

"How bad will this one be?" he asked. His voice sounded quiet, strained.

"I don't know. It's a vampire victim. Could be neat, just a couple of puncture wounds; could be carnage."

"Carnage like the three boys?"

"Dolph said no, said it's classic, just bite marks."

"So it won't be messy?" His voice was squeezed down to a near whisper.

"Won't know until we get there," I said.

"You couldn't just comfort me?" His voice sounded so small, so uncertain that I almost offered to turn the Jeep around. He didn't have to see another murder scene. It was my job, but it wasn't his job, not yet.

"You don't ever have to see another murder scene, Larry."

He turned his head and looked at me. "What do you mean?"

"You've had your quota of blood and guts for one day. I can turn around and drop you back at the hotel."

"If I don't come tonight, what happens next time?"

"If you aren't cut out for this kind of work, you aren't cut out for it. No shame in that."

"What about next time?" he asked.

"There won't be a next time."

"You aren't getting rid of me that easy," he said.

I hoped the darkness hid the smile on my face. I kept it small.

"Tell me about vampires, Anita. I thought a vampire couldn't drink enough blood in one night to kill somebody."

"Pretty to think so," I said.

"They told us in college that a vampire couldn't drain a human being with one bite. Are you saying that's not true?"

"They can't drink a human dry with one bite, in one night, but they can drain one with one bite."

He frowned at me. "What's that supposed to mean?"

"They can pierce the flesh and drain the blood without drinking it."

"How?" he asked.

"Just put the fangs in, start the blood flow, and let the blood fall down your body onto the ground."

"But that's not taking blood for food, that's just murder," Larry said.

"And your point is?" I said.

"Hey, isn't that our turnoff?"

I caught a glimpse of the road sign. "Damn." I slowed down, but couldn't see over the crest of the hill. I didn't dare U-turn until I was sure there were no cars coming the other way. It was another half mile before we came to a gravel road. There was a row of mailboxes beside the road.

Trees grew so close to the road that even winter-bare they covered the one-lane road in shadows. There was no place to turn around. Hell, if a second car had come, one of us would have had to back up.

The road rose up and up, as if it were going to go straight into the sky. At the crest of the hill I could see nothing in front of the car. I had to simply trust that there was more road in front of us, rather than some endless precipice.

"Jesus, this is steep," Larry said.

I eased the Jeep forward and the tires touched road. My shoulders loosened just a little. There was a house just up ahead. The porch light was on, like they were expecting company. The bare light bulb was not kind. The house was unpainted wood with a rusting tin roof. Its raised porch sagged under the weight of the front seat of a car that was sitting by the screen door. I turned around in the dirt in front of the house that passed for a front yard. It looked like we weren't the first car to do it. There were deep wheel ruts in the powder-dry dirt from years of cars turning in and out.

By the time we got down to the end of the road, the darkness was pure as velvet. I hit the Jeep's high beams, but it was like driving in a tunnel. The world existed only in the light; everything else was blackness.

"I'd give a lot for a few streetlights right now," Larry said.

"Me, too. Help me spot our road. I don't want to drive past it twice."

He leaned forward in his seat, straining against the shoulder belt. "There." He pointed as he spoke. I slowed and turned carefully onto the road. The headlights filled the tunnel of trees. This road was just bare red earth. The dirt rose in a mist around the Jeep. For once I was glad of the drought. Mud would have been a real bitch on a dirt road.

The road was wide enough that if you had nerves of steel, or were driving someone else's car, you could drive two cars abreast. A stream cut across the road, with a ditch at least fifteen feet deep. The bridge was nothing but planks laid across some beams. No rails, no nothing. As the Jeep crept over the bridge, the planks rattled and moved. They weren't nailed in. God.

Larry was staring at the drop, his face pressed against the tinted glass. "This bridge isn't much wider than the car."

"Thanks for telling me, Larry. I'd have never noticed on my own."

"Sorry."

Past the bridge, the road was still wide enough for two cars. I guess if two cars met at the bridge they took turns. There was probably some traffic law to cover it. First car on the left gets to go first, maybe.

At the crest of the hill, lights showed in the distance. Police lights strobed the darkness like muticolored lightning. They were farther away than they looked. We had two more hills to go up and down before the lights reflected off the bare trees, making them look black and unreal. The road spilled into a wide clearing. A lawn spread up from the road, surrounding a large white house. It was a real house with siding and shutters and a wraparound porch. It was two-storied and edged with neatly trimmed shrubs. The driveway was white gravel, which meant someone had shipped it in. Narcissus edged the driveway in two thick stripes.

A uniformed policeman stopped us in the foot of the sloping drive. He was tall, big through the shoulders, and had dark hair. He shined a flashlight into the car. "I'm sorry, miss, but you can't go up there right now."

I flashed my ID at him and said, "I'm Anita Blake. I'm with the Regional Preternatural Investigation Team. I was told Sheriff St. John is expecting me."

He leaned into the open window and flashed his light at Larry. "Who's this?"

"Larry Kirkland. He's with me."

He stared at Larry for a few seconds. Larry smiled, doing his best to look harmless. He's almost as good at it as I am.

I had a good view of the cop's gun as he leaned into the window. It was a Colt .45. Big gun, but he had the hands for it. I caught a whiff of his aftershave; Brut. He'd leaned too far into the window to look at Larry. If I'd had a gun hidden in my lap, I could have fed it to him. He was big, and I bet sheer size saw him through a lot, but it was careless. Guns don't care how big you are.

He nodded and pulled out the car. "Go on up to the house. Sheriff's expecting you." He didn't sound particularly happy about that.

"You got a problem?" I asked.

He gave a smile, but it was sour. He shook his head. "It's our case. I don't think we need any help; that includes you."

"You got a name?" I asked.

"Coltrain. Deputy Zack Coltrain."

"Well, Deputy Coltrain, we'll see you up at the house."

"I guess you will, Miss Blake."

He thought I was a cop and deliberately didn't call me "officer" or "detective." I let it go. If I really had a professional title I'd have demanded it, but getting into an argument because he wouldn't call me "detective" when I wasn't one seemed counterproductive.

I drove up and parked between the police cars. I clipped my ID to my lapel. We walked up the pale curve of sidewalk, and no one stopped us. We stood outside the door in a silence that was almost eerie. I'd been to a lot of murder scenes. One thing they weren't was silent. There was no sta-

tic crackle of police radios, no men milling around. Murder
scenes were always thick with people: plainclothes detectives, uniforms, crime scene techs, people taking photographs, video, the ambulance waiting to take the body
away. We stood on the freshly swept porch in the cool spring
night with the only sounds the calls of frogs. The high-
pitched, peeping sound played oddly with the swirling police lights.

"Are we waiting for something?" Larry asked.

"No," I said. I rang the glowing doorbell. The sound gave
a rich *bong* deep within the house. A small dog barked furiously, somewhere deep in the house. The door opened. A
woman stood framed in the light from the hall, placing most
of her in shadow. The police lights strobed across her face,
painting in neon Crayola flashes. She was about my height
with dark hair that was either naturally curly or had a really
good perm. But she'd done more with it than I did, and it
framed her face neatly. Mine always looked sort of unruly.
She was wearing a button-down shirt with long sleeves untucked over jeans. She looked about seventeen, but I wasn't
fooled. I looked young for my age, too. Heck, so did Larry.
It can't just be being short, can it?

"You aren't the state police," she said. She seemed very
sure of that.

"I'm with the Regional Preternatural Investigation Team,"
I said. "Anita Blake. This is my colleague Larry Kirkland."

Larry smiled and nodded.

The woman moved back out of the door, and the light
from the hallway fell full on her face. It added five years to
her age, but they were a good five years. It took me a minute
to realize she was wearing very understated makeup.
"Please come in, Miss Blake. My husband, David is waiting
with the body." She shook her head. "It's awful."

She peered out into the colored darkness before she
closed the door. "David told him to turn off those lights. We
don't want everyone for miles to know what's happened."

"What's your name?" I asked.

She blushed slightly. "I'm sorry; I'm not usually this scattered. I'm Beth St. John. My husband is the sheriff. I've

been sitting with the parents." She made a small motion towards a set of double doors to the left of the main entrance.

The dog was still barking behind those doors like a small furry machine gun. A man's voice said, "Quiet Raven." The barking stopped.

We were standing in an entryway that had a ceiling that soared up to the roof, as if the architect had cut a piece out of the room above us to create the sweeping space. A crystal chandelier sparkled light down on us. The light cut a rectangle out of the darkened room to our right. There was a glimpse of a cherrywood dining room set so polished it gleamed.

The hallway cut straight back to a distant door that probably led to the kitchen. Stairs ran along the wall with the double doors. The bannister and door edges were white, the carpet was pale blue, the wallpaper white with tiny blue flowers and tinier leaves. It was open and airy, bright and welcoming, and utterly quiet. If we could have found a piece of uncarpeted floor, we would have dropped a pin and listened to it bounce.

Beth St. John led us up the blue-and-white stairway. In the center of the hallway on the right-hand side was a series of family portraits. They began with a smiling couple; smiling couple and smiling baby; smiling couple and one smiling baby, one crying baby. I walked down the hallway, watching the years pass by. The babies became children, a girl and a boy. A miniature black poodle appeared in the pictures. The girl was the oldest, but only by about a year. The parents grew older, but didn't seem to mind. The parents and the girl smiled; sometimes the boy did, sometimes he didn't. The boy smiled more on the other wall, where the camera had caught him tanned with a fish, or with hair slicked back from just coming out of the pool. The girl smiled everywhere you looked. I wondered which of them was dead.

There was a window at the end of the hallway. The white drapes framed it; no one had bothered to draw them. The window looked like a black mirror. The darkness pressed against the glass like it had weight.

Beth St. John knocked on the last door to the right, next

to that pressing darkness. "David, the detectives are here." I let that slide. The sin of omission is a many-splendored thing.

I heard movement in the room, but she stepped back before the door could open. Beth St. John backed up into the middle of the hallway so there would be no chance of her seeing inside the room. Her eyes flicked from one picture to another, catching glimpses of smiling faces. She put a slender hand to her chest, as if she was having trouble breathing.

"I'm going to go make coffee. Do you want some?" Her voice was strained around the edges.

"Sure," I said.

"Sounds good," Larry said.

She gave a weak smile and marched down the hallway. She did not run, which got her a lot of brownie points in my book. I was betting it was Beth St. John's first murder scene.

The door opened. David St. John was wearing a pale blue uniform that matched the one his deputy wore, but there the resemblance ended. He was about five-foot-ten, thin without being skinny, like a marathon runner. His hair was a paler, browner version of Larry's red. You noticed his glasses before you noticed his eyes, but the eyes were worth noticing. A perfect pale green like a cat's. Except for the eyes it was a very ordinary face, but it was one of those faces you wouldn't grow tired of.

He offered me his hand. I took it. He barely touched my hand, as if afraid to squeeze. A lot of men did that, but at least he offered to shake hands; most don't bother.

"I'm Sheriff St. John. You must be Anita Blake. Sergeant Storr told me you'd be coming." He glanced at Larry. "Who's this?"

"Larry Kirkland."

St. John's eyes narrowed. He stepped fully into the hallway, closing the door behind him. "Sergeant Storr didn't mention anyone else. Can I see some ID?"

I unclipped my badge ID. He looked at it and shook his head. "You're not a detective."

"No, I'm not." I was mentally cursing Dolph. I'd known it wouldn't work.

"How about him?" He jerked his chin at Larry.

"All I have on me is a driver's license," Larry said.

"Who are you?" the sheriff asked.

"I am Anita Blake. I am part of the Spook Squad. I just don't happen to have a badge. Larry is a trainee." I fished my new vampire executioner's license out of my jacket pocket. It looked like a glorified driver's license, but it was the best I had.

He peered at the license. "You're a vampire hunter? It's a little early for you to be called in. I don't know who did it yet."

"I'm attached to Sergeant Storr's squad. I come in at the start of a case instead of the end. It tends to keep the body count down that way."

He handed back the license. "I didn't think Brewster's law had gone into effect."

Brewster was the senator whose daughter got eaten. "It hasn't. I've been working with the police for a long time."

"How long?"

"Nearly three years."

He smiled. "Longer than I've been sheriff." He nodded, almost as if he'd answered a question for himself. "Sergeant Storr said if anybody could help me solve this, it was you. If the head of RPIT has that much confidence in you, I'm not going to refuse the help. We've never had a vampire kill out here, ever."

"Vampires tend to stay near cities," I said. "They can hide their victims better that way."

"Well, no one tried to hide this one." He pushed the door open and made a little arm gesture, ushering us in.

The wallpaper was all pink roses, big old-fashioned cabbage roses. There was an honest-to-God vanity, with a raised mirror and everything, that looked like it might be an antique, but everything else was white wicker and pink lace. It looked like the room for a much younger girl.

The girl lay on the narrow bed. The bedspread matched the wallpaper. The sheets twisted up underneath her body were jellybean pink. Her head lay on the edge of the pillows, as if it had slipped to one side after she was laid on them.

The pink curtains fanned against the open window. A cool breeze crawled through the room, ruffling her thick black hair. It had been curled and styled with hair gel. There was a small red stain under her face and neck where the sheets had soaked up some blood. I was betting there was a bite mark on that side of the neck. She wore makeup not nearly as well applied as Beth St. John's, but the attempt had been made. The lipstick was badly smeared. One arm hung off into space, the hand half-cupped as if reaching for something. The nails were shiny with fresh red nail polish. Her long legs were spread-eagled on the bed. There were two fang marks high on her inner thigh—not fresh, though. Her toenails were painted to match her fingers.

She was still almost wearing the black teddy she'd started the night in. The straps had been pushed down her shoulders, exposing small, well-formed breasts. The crotch had been ripped out, or was one of the ones that snapped open, because the bottom was pushed up nearly to her waist until the teddy was little more than a belt. With her legs spread wide, she was completely exposed.

That, more than anything, pissed me off. He could have at least covered her up, not left her like some whore. It was arrogant and cruel.

Larry was standing across the room at the other window. It was open too, spilling cool air into the room.

"Have you touched anything?"

St. John shook his head.

"Have you taken any photos?"

"No."

I took a deep breath, reminding myself that I was a guest here and had no official status. I could not afford to piss him off. "What have you done?"

"Called you, and the state cops."

I nodded. "How long ago did you find the body?"

He checked his watch. "An hour ago. How did you get here so fast?"

"I wasn't ten miles away," I said.

"Lucky for me," he said.

I looked at the girl's body. "Yeah."

Larry was hugging the windowsill, gripping it with his hands. "Larry, why don't you run down to the Jeep and get some gloves out of my bag?"

"Gloves?"

"I've got a box of surgical gloves in with my animating stuff. Bring the box."

He swallowed hard and nodded. Every freckle stood out on his face like ink spots. He moved very quickly to the door and shut it behind him. I had two sets of gloves in my jacket pocket, but Larry needed air.

"This his first murder?"

"Second," I said. "How old is the girl?"

"Seventeen," he said.

"Then it's murder even if she consented."

"Consented? What are you talking about?" There was the very first hint of anger in his voice.

"What do you think happened here, Sheriff?"

"A vampire climbed in her window while she was getting ready for bed and killed her."

"Where's all the blood?"

"There's more blood under her neck. You can't see the mark, but that's where he drained her."

"That's not enough blood to kill her."

"He drank the rest." He sounded a little outraged.

I shook my head. "No single vampire can consume the entire blood supply of an adult human in one sitting."

"Then there was more than one," he said.

"You mean the bites on her thighs?"

"Yeah, yeah." He paced the pink shag carpet in quick, nervous strides.

"Those marks are at least a couple of days old," I said.

"So he hypnotized her twice before, but this time he killed her."

"It's awfully early for a teenager to be going to bed."

"Her mother said she wasn't feeling well."

That I believed. Even if you want it to happen, that much blood loss can take the sparkle out of your step.

"She fixed her hair and makeup before she went to bed," I said.

"So?"

"Did you know this girl?"

"Yes, hell yes. This is a small town, Miss Blake. We all know each other. She was a good kid, never in any trouble. You never found her parked with a boy, or out drinking. She was a good girl."

"I believe she was a good girl, Sheriff St. John. Being murdered doesn't make you a bad person."

He nodded, but his eyes were sort of wild, too much white showing. I wanted to ask how many murders he'd seen, but didn't. Whether this was his first or his twenty-first, he was sheriff.

"What do you think happened here, Sheriff?" I'd asked the question once, but I was willing to try it again.

"A vampire raped and killed Ellie Quinlan, that's what happened here." He said it almost defiantly, like he didn't believe it either."

"This wasn't rape, Sheriff. Ellie Quinlan invited her killer into this room."

He paced to the far window and stood like Larry had, staring out into the darkness. He wrapped his arms around himself like he was hugging himself. "How am I going to tell her parents, her kid brother, that she let some . . . thing make love to her? That she'd been letting it feed off her? How can I tell them that?"

"Well, in three nights, two counting tonight, Ellie can rise from the dead and tell them herself."

He turned back to me, his face pale with shock. He shook his head slowly. "They want her staked."

"What?"

"They want her staked. They don't want her to rise as a vampire."

I stared down at the still-warm body. I shook my head. "She'll rise in two more nights."

"The family doesn't want it."

"If she was a vampire, it would be murder to stake her just because her family doesn't want her to be one."

"But she's not a vampire yet," St. John said. "She's a corpse."

"The coroner will have to certify death before she can be staked. That can take a little time."

He shook his head. "I know Doc Campbell; he'll speed it along for us."

I stood there, staring down at the girl. "She didn't plan to die, Sheriff. This isn't a suicide. She's planning on coming back."

"You can't know that."

I stared at him. "I do know that, and so do you. If we stake her before she can rise from the dead, it's murder."

"Not according to the law."

"I am not going to take out the head and heart of a seventeen-year-old girl just because her parents don't like the lifestyle she's chosen."

"She's dead, Miss Blake."

"It's Ms. Blake, and I know she's dead. I know what she'll become. Probably better than you do."

"Then you understand why they want it done."

I looked at him. I did understand. There was a time when I could have done it and felt good about it. Felt like I was helping the family, freeing her soul. Now, I just wasn't sure anymore.

"Let her parents think about it for twenty-four hours. Trust me on this. They're horrified right now, and grief-stricken; are they really in a position to decide what happens to her?"

"They're her parents."

"Yeah, and two days from now would they rather have her on her feet, talking to them, or dead in a box?"

"She'll be a monster," he said.

"Maybe, probably, but I think we should hold off for just a little while until they've had some time. I think the immediate problem is the blood-sucker that did this."

"I agree, we find him and kill him."

"We can't kill him without a court order of execution," I said.

"I know the local judge. I can get you a court order."

"I bet you can."

"What's the matter with you? Don't you want to kill him?"

I looked at the girl. If he'd really wanted her to rise as a vampire, he'd have taken the body with him. He'd have hidden her until she rose to keep her safe from people like me. If he cared for her. "Yeah, I'll kill him for you."

"Alright, what can we do?"

"Well, first, the killing took place just after dark, so his daytime resting place had to be very near here. Are there any old houses, caves, some place where you could hide a coffin?"

"There's an old homestead about a mile from here, and I know there's a cave down along the stream. I used to go there when I was little. We all did."

"Here's the deal, Sheriff. If we go out into the dark after him now, he'll probably kill some of us. But if we don't try it tonight, he'll move his coffin. We might not find him again."

"We'll look for him tonight. Now."

"How long have you and your wife been married?" I asked.

"Five years; why?"

"You love her?"

"Yes, we were high school sweethearts. What kind of question is that?"

"If you go out after the vampire, you may never see her again. If you've never hunted one out there at night in its own territory, you don't know what we're up against, and nothing I can tell you will prepare you for it. But think about never seeing Beth again. Never holding her hand. Never hearing her voice. We can go out in the morning. The vampire may not move its coffin tonight, or it might move from the cave to the homestead, or vice versa. We might catch it tomorrow without risking anybody's life."

"Do you think it won't move tonight?"

I took a deep breath and wanted to lie. God knows I wanted to lie. "No, I think it'll leave the immediate area tonight. That's probably why he came just after full dark. It gives him all night to run."

"Then we go after him."

I nodded. "Okay, but we have to have some ground rules here. I'm in charge. I've done this before and I'm still alive; that makes me an expert. If you do everything I say, maybe, just maybe, we can all live until morning."

"Except for the vampire," St. John said.

"Yeah, sure." It had been a long time since I had gone up against a vampire at night in the open. My vampire kit was at home in my closet. It was illegal to carry it with me without a specific court order of execution. I had the cross I was wearing, the two handguns, the two knives, and that was it. No holy water, no extra crosses, no shotgun. Hell, no stake and mallet.

"Do you have silver bullets?"

"I can get some."

"Do it, and find me a shotgun and silver ammo for that too. Is there a Catholic or Episcopalian church around here?"

"Of course," he said.

"We need some holy water and holy wafer, the host."

"I know you can throw the holy water on the vampire, but I didn't know you could throw the host."

I had to smile. "They aren't like little holy grenades. I want the host to give to the Quinlans so they can put one at every windowsill, every doorsill."

"You think it'll come for them?"

"No, but the girl invited it in, only she can revoke the invitation, and she's dead. Until we get the bastard, better safe than sorry."

He hesitated, then nodded. "I'll go to the church. I'll see what I can do." He went for the door.

"And, Sheriff?"

He stopped and turned to me.

"I want that court order in my hands before we leave. I'm not going to be up on murder charges."

He nodded, sort of nervously, head bobbing like one of those dogs you see in the backs of cars. "You'll have it, Ms. Blake." He left, closing the door behind him.

I was left alone with the dead girl. She lay there pale and

unmoving, growing colder, deader. If her parents had their way, it would be permanent. And it would be my job to make it happen. There were schoolbooks scattered beside the bed, as if she had been studying in bed before he came. I pushed one of the book covers closed with my toe, careful not to rearrange it. Calculus. She'd been studying calculus before she put on her makeup and black teddy. Shit.

12

WHILE WE WAITED for the court order, I talked to the family. Not my favorite thing to do, but necessary. This hadn't been a random attack, which meant they probably knew the vampire, or had known him before he died.

The living room continued the pastel theme, blue predominating. Beth St. John had made coffee. She'd shanghaied Larry into carrying up a tray. I guess she didn't want to see the body again. Couldn't say I blamed her. I'd seen bloodier murder scenes, a lot bloodier, but each death has its own peculiar poignancy. There was something very piteous about Ellie Quinlan stretched across her pink candy sheets, and I hadn't known her. Beth St. John had. Made it hard.

The family sat huddled on the white sofa. The man was broad, not fat, but square like a linebacker. He had short black hair that was going nicely grey at the sideburns. Very distinguished. His complexion was ruddy, not tanned, but colorful just the same. He was dressed in a white dress shirt unbuttoned at the neck, but sleeves still sporting their cufflinks. His face was very tight, immobile like a mask, as if underneath something entirely different was going on. He looked calm, composed, but the effort thrummed along his skin. Anger glittered in his dark eyes.

His arm was around his wife's shoulders. She leaned into him crying softly, eyes closed as if that would make it better. Her eye makeup had smeared in long, multicolored streaks like an oil slick down her cheeks. She had thick black hair done in some short, complicated style that looked too stiff to touch. She wore a long-sleeved, button-down blouse with a delicate flower pattern on it, pink predominating. Her slacks were a matching pink. Her feet were bare except for dark hose. A delicate gold cross and wedding rings were her only jewelry.

The boy was only about my height and slender as a willow. He hadn't hit his growth spurt yet, and it made him look younger than he was. His face had that soft, perfect skin that said he'd never had a pimple and shaving was a distant dream. If the girl was seventeen, he had to be at least fifteen, maybe sixteen. He could have passed for twelve. A perfect victim, except for his eyes and the way he held himself. Even in the midst of grief with the lines of tears drying on his face, he looked sure of himself, self-possessed. His eyes held a quick intelligence and a rage that would hold the bullies at bay.

His hair was the perfect black of his father's, but it was baby fine, probably the natural texture of Mrs. Quinlan's before she styled it to death.

A little black poodle was in his lap. It had barked like a machine gun, rat-a-tat-tat, yip-yip-yip until he'd picked it up and held it. A soft growl tickled out of its curly jaws.

"Hush, Raven," the boy said. He petted the dog as he said it, thus rewarding the growling. The dog growled again; he petted it again. I decided to ignore it. If the poodle got loose, I figured I could take it. I was armed.

"Mr. and Mrs. Quinlan, my name's Anita Blake. I need to ask you a few questions."

"Have you staked the body yet?" the man asked.

"No, Mr. Quinlan, the sheriff and I agreed to wait twenty-four hours."

"Her immortal soul is in jeopardy. We want it done now."

"If you still want it done tomorrow night, I'll do it."

"We want it done now." He was holding his wife very tight, fingers digging into her shoulder.

She opened her eyes and blinked at him. "Jeffrey, please, you're hurting me."

He swallowed hard and loosened his grip. "I'm sorry, Sally. I'm sorry." The apology seemed to take some of the anger out of him. The lines in his face softened. He shook his head. "We must save her soul. Her life is gone, but her soul remains. We must save that at least."

There had been a time when I believed that, too. Down to my toes I thought all vampires were evil. Now, I wasn't so sure. I knew too many of them who didn't seem that bad. I knew evil when I felt it, and that wasn't what they were. I didn't know what they were, but were they damned? According to the Catholic Church, yes, they were, and so was the girl upstairs. But then, according to the Church, so was I. I'd become Episcopalian when the church declared all animators excommunicates.

"Are you Catholic, Mr. Quinlan?"

"Yes; what difference does that make?"

"I was raised Catholic. So I understand your beliefs."

"They are not beliefs, Miss . . . What is your name?"

"Blake, Anita Blake."

"They are not beliefs, Miss Blake. They are facts. Ellie's immortal soul is in danger of eternal damnation. We must help her."

"Do you understand what you're asking me to do?" I asked.

"To save her."

I shook my head. Mrs. Quinlan was looking at me. Her eyes were very intent. I was betting I could cause a little family disagreement.

"I will put a stake through her heart and chop off her head." I left the fact out that most of my executions were done with a shotgun now, at close range. It was messy and you needed a closed coffin, but it was a lot easier on me and a quicker death for the vampire.

Mrs. Quinlan started to cry again, huddling against her husband. She buried her face against him, smearing makeup on his clean white shirt.

"Are you trying to upset my wife?"

"No, sir, but I want you all to realize that two nights from now Ellie will rise as a vampire. She'll walk and talk. Eventually, she'll be able to be around you. If I stake her, all she'll be is dead."

"She is already dead. We want you to do your job," he said.

Mrs. Quinlan wouldn't look at me. Either she believed as strongly as her hubby, or she wouldn't fight him. Not even for her daughter's continued existence.

I let it go. I could stall for twenty-four hours. I doubted that Mr. Quinlan was going to change his mind. I had hopes for Mrs. Quinlan.

"Does the poodle always bark at strangers?"

They all three blinked at me like rabbits caught in headlights. The change of subject was too abrupt for their grief.

"What has that got to do with anything?" he asked.

"There is a murderous vampire out there somewhere. I'm going to catch him, but I need your help. So please just answer my questions as best you can."

"What does the dog have to do with it?"

I sighed and sipped my coffee. He had just found his daughter dead, murdered, raped, I'm sure he'd told himself. The horror of it cut him some slack, but he was beginning to use it up.

"The poodle barked its head off when I came to the door. Does it bark every time a stranger comes to the house?"

The boy saw what I was getting at. "Yeah, Raven always barks at strangers."

I ignored his parents and talked to the most reasonable person in the room. "What's your name?"

"Jeff," he said. God, Jeffrey Junior, of course.

"How many times would I have to come to the house before Raven stopped barking at me?"

He thought about that, rolling his lower lip under, really thinking about it.

Mrs. Quinlan sat up, a little apart from her husband. "Raven always barks when someone comes to the door. Even if she knows you."

"Did she bark tonight?"

The parents frowned at me. Jeff said, "Yeah. She barked like crazy until Ellie let her in her room just after dark. Ellie let her in, then a few minutes later Raven came back downstairs."

"How'd you find the body?"

"Raven started barking again and wouldn't stop. Ellie didn't let her in. Ellie always lets her in. I mean, I'm not allowed in her room, but Raven gets to go in even when Ellie wants her privacy." He made that last word sound like he usually said it with a lot of eye-rolling.

"I knocked at the door and she didn't answer. Raven was scratching at the door. It was locked. She locked her door a lot, but she wouldn't answer." A tear escaped from his wide eyes. "I went and got Dad."

"You unlocked the door, Mr. Quinlan?"

He nodded. "Yes, and she was just lying there. I couldn't bear to touch her. She's unclean now. I . . ." He was choking on tears, trying so hard not to cry that his face was turning purple.

Jeff came and put his arm around his dad, leaning against his mother, the poodle still gripped in his other arm. The dog whined softly, licked the makeup from Mrs. Quinlan's face. The woman looked up and gave a choked laugh, petting the curly fur.

I wanted to leave. I wanted to let them huddle together and grieve. Hell, the death was so fresh, they hadn't gotten to grieving yet. They were still in shock. But I couldn't leave. Sheriff St. John would be back with the warrant, and I needed as much information as I could get before we braved the darkness.

Larry was sitting in the corner in a pale blue chair. He was being so quiet you'd almost forget he was there. But his eyes were eager, noticing everything, filing it all away. When I first realized he damn near memorized everything I said and did, it was intimidating. Now I counted on it.

Beth St. John came into the room with a tray of sandwiches, coffee, and soft drinks. I didn't remember anybody asking for them, but I think Beth was needing something to do besides sit here and watch the Quinlans cry. Me, too.

She set the tray on the coffee table between the couch and the love seat. The Quinlans ignored it. I took a fresh mug of coffee. Grilling grieving families always goes down better with caffeine.

The group huddle broke up. The poodle was transferred to the wife's arms, and the two men sat on either side of her. Jeffrey and Jeff looked at me with identical eyes. It was almost eerie. Genetics at work.

"The vampire had to be in the room with Ellie when she let the dog in at full dark," I said.

"My daughter would not have let in her murderer."

"If she was eighteen, Mr. Quinlan, it wouldn't be murder."

"Being made a vampire against your will is still murder, Miss Blake."

I was getting tired of everyone calling me "Miss," but the grieving father could do it a few more times. "I believe your daughter knew the vampire. I believe she let him in willingly."

"You are crazy. Beth, go get the sheriff. I want this woman out of my house."

Beth stood up uncertainly. "David's gone to get some things, Jeffrey. I . . . Deputy Coltrain's upstairs with the body, but . . ."

"Then get him down here."

Beth looked at me, then back to him. She gripped her small hands together, almost wringing them. "Jeffrey, she's a licensed vampire hunter. She's done this a lot. Listen to her."

He stood up. "My daughter was raped and murdered by some soulless, blood-sucking animal, and I want this woman out of my house, now." If he hadn't been crying at the same time, I'd have been pissed.

Beth looked at me. She was willing to stand up to him if I needed her to. Mucho points for her. "Has anyone you know vanished or died recently?" I asked.

Quinlan squinted at me. He looked confused. The change of subject again was just too abrupt. I was hoping I could distract him from throwing me out long enough to learn something.

"What?"

"Has anyone you know gone missing or died recently?"
He shook his head. "No."

"Andy's missing," Jeff said.

Quinlan shook his head again. "That boy is no concern of ours."

"Who's Andy?" I asked.

"Ellie's boyfriend."

"He is not her boyfriend," Quinlan said.

I caught Jeff's gaze. The look said it all. Andy had been a boyfriend, and dear old dad hadn't liked him one little bit.

"Why didn't you like Andy, Mr. Quinlan?"

"He was a criminal."

I raised my eyebrows. "In what way?"

"He was arrested for drug abuse."

"He smoked some pot," Jeff said.

I was beginning to wish I could just go off and talk with Jeff. He seemed to know what was going on and wasn't trying to hide it. Trick was how to manage it.

"He was a corrupting influence on my daughter, and I put a stop to it."

"And he's missing?" I asked.

"Yes," Jeff said.

"I will answer Miss Blake's questions, Jeff. I am the man of the house."

Jesus, man of the house. Hadn't heard that in a while. "I'd like to see the rest of the house in case the vampire entered somewhere other than her room. If Jeff could show me the doors, I'd appreciate it."

"I can show you around, Miss Blake," Quinlan said.

"I'm sure your wife needs you right now, Mr. Quinlan. Jeff can show me around, but only you can comfort your wife."

Mrs. Quinlan looked up at him, then at me, as if she wasn't sure she wanted to be comforted, but I knew the image would appeal to him.

He nodded. "Perhaps you're right." He touched his wife's shoulder. "Sally needs me right now."

Sally cooperated with fresh crying, using the poodle as a sort of impromptu handkerchief. The poodle squirmed and whined. Quinlan sat down and took his wife in his arms. The dog squirmed free and trotted over to Jeff.

I stood. Larry stood. I moved toward the door and looked back at the boy. Jeff stood and the poodle trotted at his side. I opened the doors and ushered us all outside. Raven the poodle eyed me suspiciously, but she came along.

I caught a last glimpse of Beth St. John gazing at the door as if she wanted to go with us, but she sat down beside the unwanted sandwiches and the cooling coffee. She sat like a good soldier. She would not abandon her post.

I closed the door, feeling cowardly. I was glad it wasn't my job to hold the Quinlans' hands. Facing the vampire even in the dark didn't seem so bad by comparison. Of course, I was still safe inside the house. Out there in the dark with the vampire, I might feel different.

13

WE STOOD OUT in the entryway. The air felt cooler out here, easier to breathe. Had to be my imagination. The poodle was sniffing at my foot. She gave a low growl and Jeff picked her up, tucking her under one arm, in a familiar gesture like he'd done it a hundred times before.

"You don't really want to see the doors, do you?" He asked.

"No," I said.

"Dad's all right. He's just . . ." He shrugged. "He's just right, and everyone else is wrong. He doesn't mean anything by it."

"I know. He's scared right now, too. That makes everyone bitchy."

Jeff grinned. I wasn't sure if it was the "scared" comment or the word "bitchy." Probably didn't hear many people saying either about his dad.

"How serious were Andy and your sister?"

He glanced at the closed doors and lowered his voice just a little. "Dad'll say not very, but they were serious. Real serious." He glanced at the door again.

"We can go somewhere else to talk," I said. "Your choice of rooms."

He looked at me. "You're really a vampire hunter?" If the circumstances had been different, he would have been enjoying himself. It's hard not to think it's cool to put stakes through people's chests.

"Yeah, and we raise zombies, too."

"Both of you?" He sounded surprised.

"I'm a full-fledged animator," Larry said.

Jeff shook his head. "We can talk in my room." He led the way up the stairs. We followed.

If I'd been a cop, questioning a juvenile without a guardian or lawyer present would have been illegal, but I wasn't a cop. And he wasn't a suspect. Just gathering information, folks. Just grilling a sixteen-year-old boy about his sister's sex life. Murder investigations are never pleasant, and some of that unpleasantness has nothing to do with the corpse.

Jeff hesitated at the head of the stairs, peering down the hallway. Deputy Coltrain was standing outside Ellie's room, back stiff, hands behind his back, alert for intruders. The door was open. Too hard to stand in the room with the body, I guess. He saw Jeff and closed the door, still standing in front of it. Nice of Coltrain to make sure Jeff didn't see the body. But standing outside the closed door was not the best idea. A vampire, if it was old enough, could have come in the room behind him and opened the door before he could have drawn his gun. The undead make no noise.

I debated on whether to tell him that. I let it go. If the vamp had meant to take out more people, it could have. He could have taken out the entire family. Instead, when the dog barked he panicked and ran. This was not an ancient bloodsucker. This was someone who was new at the job. I was betting on the boyfriend, Andy, but I'd keep an open mind. Andy might have just driven to California to find fame and fortune, but I doubted it.

Jeff opened the door near the head of the stairs and went in. His room was smaller than his sister's. Being firstborn does have its advantages. The wallpaper was tan with cowboys and Indians on it. The bed had a matching spread. It was the room of a much younger person, just like his sister's. The walls were bare, no pinups, no sports figures. There was a desk stacked high with books. A small pile of clothes lay near the closet door. Raven the poodle sniffed the clothes. Jeff shooed her away and kicked the clothes into the closet and closed the door.

"Sit down anywhere you can." He pulled the desk chair out a little, then stood near the window, not sure what to do. I doubted he had many adults up to his room for a talk. Parents didn't count. Though frankly I couldn't imagine either of the Quinlans coming in for a quiet chat.

I took the chair. I figured Jeff would feel more comfortable lounging on his bed with Larry than with me. Besides, I wasn't used to wearing skirts this short yet, and every once in a while I forgot. The chair seemed safer.

Larry sat down on the bed with his back pressed against the wall. Jeff sat down next to him, propping some of the pillows into the corner for a back rest. Raven jumped up on the bed, circled his lap twice, and lay down. Cozy.

"How hot an item were Andy and your sister?" No prelims; off with the clothes.

He glanced at both of us. Larry gave him an encouraging smile. He shifted more securely against his mound of pillows and said, "Pretty hot. I mean, they hung all over each other at school."

"Embarrassing," I said.

"Yeah. I mean, she was my sister. She's only a year older than me, and there's this guy pawing her." He shook his head. He rubbed the poodle's ears, hands moving down her small curly body. He petted her like it was habit, a comfort measure.

"Did you like Andy?"

He shrugged. "He was older and sort of cool, but no, I thought Ellie could have done better."

"How so?"

"He did smoke pot and didn't have any plans for college. Andy wasn't going anywhere. It was like the fact that he loved my sister was everything. Like they'd live on love or something stupid like that."

I agreed that that was stupid. "When your dad put a stop to it, did it stop?"

He grinned at me. "No. They just started sneaking around. I think if anything, telling Ellie she couldn't see him made it worse."

"It usually does," I said. "When did Andy disappear?"

"About two weeks ago. His car went missing, too, so everybody thought he'd run off, but he wouldn't have left Ellie behind. He was sort of creepy, but he wouldn't have left her."

"Was Ellie upset at being left behind?"

He frowned, hugging the dog against his chest. Raven licked his chin with her small pink tongue. "That was the weird part. I mean, I know she had to pretend not to care in front of Mom and Dad, but even at school or out with our friends she didn't seem to care. I was kinda glad. I mean, Andy was a loser, but it was like she didn't believe he was gone or knew something the rest of us didn't. I thought he'd just gone off to find like an out-of-town job and was going to send for her."

"Maybe he did," I said.

The frown deepened between his smooth, unblemished brows. "What do you mean?"

"I think Andy may be the vampire that did your sister."

A look of disgust crumbled his face even further. "I don't believe that. Andy loved Ellie; he wouldn't kill her."

"If he's a vampire, Jeff, he wouldn't think turning her into the undead is killing her. He'd probably think of it as bringing her over."

Jeff shook his head. Raven wiggled out of his grasp as if he was squeezing too hard. She hopped off his lap and lay down on the covers. "Andy wouldn't hurt Ellie. Doesn't it hurt to die?"

"Probably," I said.

"The bushes underneath her end window are all crushed," Larry said.

I looked at him. "Say again."

He smiled, pleased with himself. "I took a look around outside. That's what took me so long when you sent me out for gloves that you didn't need. The bushes under the end window to the girl's room are all smashed like something heavy fell on them."

I had a moment to visualize Larry out in the dark all alone, unarmed except for his cross. The thought made my skin cold. I opened my mouth to yell at him and closed it. Never dress anyone down in public unless it's an object lesson. I said, "Any tracks?" I gave myself a dozen brownie points for not yelling.

"Do I look like Tonto? Besides, the ground is just grass and it's been so dry lately. I don't think there'd be any tracks." He frowned at me. "Can you track vampires?"

"Not normally, but if this one is as new as I think he is, then maybe." I nodded. "Yeah." I stood up. "I've got to go ask the deputy something. Thank you for your help, Jeff." I offered him my hand to shake. He took it. His handshake was a little uncertain, as if he wasn't used to it.

I went for the door and Larry followed.

"You will find him and kill him, even if it's Andy?" Jeff asked.

I turned back and looked at him. His dark eyes were still intelligent, still full of purpose, but there was also a little boy needing reassurance.

"Yeah, we'll find him."

"And kill him?"

"And kill him," I said.

"Good," he said. "Good."

I wasn't sure if "good" was the word I would have chosen, but it wasn't my sister lying dead in the other room.

"You got a cross?" I asked.

He frowned, but said, "Yeah."

"You wearing it?"

He shook his head.

"Get it and wear it until we catch him. Okay?"

"You think he'll come back?" Fear glittered at the edge of his eyes.

"No, but you never know, Jeff. Just humor me."

He got up and went to his bureau. There was a line of glittering chain on one corner of the mirror. When he picked it up, a tiny gold cross dangled from it. I watched him put it on. The dog watched it all with anxious eyes.

I smiled. "We'll see you later."

He nodded, fingering the cross, scared now underneath the shock. We left him in the tender care of Raven.

"You really think the vamp will come back to the house?" Larry asked.

"No," I said, "but just in case your little visit out into the dark gives him ideas, I want Jeff to at least have a cross on."

"Heh," he said. "I found a clue."

Deputy Coltrain was watching us, but we were running out of privacy. I kept my voice down and hoped that was enough. "Yeah, and you went out, alone, unarmed, in the dark with a vampire that had already killed once on the loose."

"You said it was a really new vampire."

"Not before you went out after the gloves."

"Maybe I figured out that it was a new one all on my own," he said. He was looking stubborn, like far from taking my warning to heart, he just might do it again."

"New vampires can still kill you, Larry."

"With a cross on?"

He had a point. Very few of the new dead could get past the pain of a cross, or play enough head games to get you to take it off voluntarily.

"Fine, Larry, but where's the vampire that made him? That one may be a couple of centuries old, and it's out in the dark, too."

He went a little pale around the edges. "I never thought of that."

"I did."

He gave a shrug and had the grace to look embarrassed. "That's why you're the boss."

"That's right," I said.

"All right, all right. I promise to be good."

"Great; now let's go ask Deputy Coltrain if he knows any-one who could track our vampire."

"Can you really track a vampire like that?"

"I don't know, but with one less than two weeks old, one that falls out a window and into some shrubs, you might be able to. They at least might be able to narrow down where we should look first."

He was grinning very broadly at me.

"Yeah, knowing it fell out the window is useful informa-tion. It might not have occurred to me to check for tracks outside the window."

If he grinned any wider, he was going to pull something.

"And if a vampire old enough to get past your cross had eaten your face, I'd have never known about the shrubs."

"Ah, Anita. I done good."

I shook my head. For all that Larry had seen of vampires, it wasn't enough. He still didn't fully appreciate what they were. He didn't have any scars yet. If he stayed in the busi-ness long enough to get his license, that would change.

God help him.

14

THE WIND WAS cool and smelled of rain. I turned my face to the soft touch of it. The air smelled of green growing things. It smelled clean and new. I stood on the grass look-ing upward. Ellie Quinlan's window shone like a soft yellow beacon. Ellie had opened the windows, but her father had turned on the lights. She had met her vampire lover in dark-ness. The better not to see him for the walking corpse he was.

I had the coverall back on, unzipped halfway so I could get to the Browning. I'd only brought an inner pants holster for the Firestar, so I shoved it into a pocket of the coveralls.

Not handy for a quick draw, but better than not having it. An inner pants holster just doesn't work well with a skirt on.

Larry had his very own gun in a shoulder rig. He stood beside me shrugging his shoulders, trying to get the straps more comfortable. It isn't really uncomfortable if it's a good fit, but it isn't really comfortable either. It's sort of like a bra. They fit and they are necessary, but they are never completely comfortable.

He was wearing the extra coverall unzipped and flapping nearly to his hips. A flashlight flicked over us, glinting on Larry's cross. The light swept over me, glaring in my eyes. "Now that you've ruined my night vision, get that damn thing out of my eyes."

Deep masculine laughter came from behind the brilliant beam of light. Two state cops had arrived just in time to join us on the hunt. Oh, joy.

"Wallace," a man's voice said, "do what the lady says." The voice was deep and vaguely threatening. A voice to say, "lean on the hood of the car and spread 'em." And you'd do it or else.

Officer Granger walked up to us, his flashlight pointed at the ground. He wasn't as tall as Wallace, and a gut was beginning to creep over his belt, but he moved through the dark like he knew what he was doing. Like maybe he'd hunted in the dark before. Maybe not vampires but something. Maybe men.

Wallace walked over to us, flashlight swimming around us like an oversized firefly. It wasn't in my eyes, but it was still not helping my night vision.

"Turn off the flashlight . . . please," I said.

Wallace took a step closer, looming over me. He was tall, built like a football player, with long legs. A running back, maybe. He and Deputy Coltrain could arm wrestle later. Right now I just wanted him to back the fuck off me.

"Turn it off, Wallace," Granger said. He'd already clicked off his own.

"I won't be able to see a damn thing," he protested.

"Afraid of the dark?" I asked, smiling up at him.

Larry laughed. It was the wrong thing to do.

Wallace turned on him. "You think that's funny?" He stepped up to Larry until they were almost touching, using his size to intimidate. But Larry's like me; he's been small all his life. He'd been bullied by the best. He stood his ground.

"Are you?" Larry asked.

"Am I what?" Wallace asked.

"Afraid of the dark?"

Animating wasn't the only thing Larry was learning from me. Unfortunately for Larry, he was a boy. I could get away with being a pain in the ass and most people wouldn't take a swing at me. Larry wasn't so lucky.

Wallace balled his hands into Larry's coverall and lifted him to tiptoes. His flashlight fell to the grass, rolling around spotlighting our ankles.

Officer Granger stepped up close to them but didn't touch Wallace. Even in the dark you could see the tension in his shoulders and arms. Not from lifting Larry, but from wanting to hit him and resisting the urge.

"Ease down, Wallace. He didn't mean anything."

Wallace didn't say anything, he just pulled Larry closer to him, leaning over to put his face next to Larry's. A square of yellow light fell across his face. The muscle along the edge of his jaw was jutting out, throbbing like it would pop out of his face. There was a scar under the bone of his jawline. A scar that disappeared into the collar of his jacket.

Wallace nearly put his face nose to nose with Larry. "I-am-not-afraid-of-anything." Each word was squeezed out.

I stepped up close to him. He was bent down to intimidate Larry, so I could whisper in his ear. "Nice scar, Wallace."

He jumped like I'd bit him. He released Larry so suddenly that Larry stumbled. He whirled, one big hand raised to smash my face. At least he'd let go of Larry.

He swung at me. I swept his arm to one side and past me. He stumbled. I brought my knee up into his stomach hard. It took a lot not to follow through and really hurt him. He was a cop. One of the good guys. You don't beat up on them. I stepped back, out of reach, and hoped that one near miss had cooled him down. I could have hurt him badly in the initial rush, but now he'd be ready. Harder to hurt.

He was nearly a foot taller than me and outweighed me by more than a hundred pounds. If the fight turned serious, I was in trouble. I hoped I wouldn't regret my gallant gesture.

Wallace ended on all fours near the shrubs by the house. He got to his feet quicker than I wanted him to, but he stayed half bent over, hands on his knees. He looked up at me. I wasn't sure what his expression meant, but it wasn't completely hostile. It was more a considering sort of look, as if I'd surprised him. I get that look a lot.

"You all right now, Wallace?" Granger asked.

Wallace nodded. Hard to talk after a good gut shot.

Granger glanced at me. "You all right, Ms. Blake?"

"I'm fine."

He nodded. "Yes, you are."

Larry moved up beside me. He was standing too close. If Wallace came back at me, I would need more room to maneuver. I knew that Larry meant it as a show of support. After we got Larry's shooting up to speed, we'd have to work on some basic hand-to-hand techniques.

Why was I training him to shoot before I taught him to fight? Because you don't arm wrestle vampires. You shoot them. He would live through a beating from Officer Wallace. He wouldn't live through a vampire attack. Not if he couldn't shoot.

"Were you with him when he got that scar?" I asked.

Granger shook his head. "His first partner didn't make it."

"Vampire got him?"

He nodded.

Wallace stood up sort of slow. He arched his back just a bit, as if working the kinks out. "Nice shot," he said.

I shrugged. "It was my knee, not my fist."

"Still a good shot. I don't have any excuses good enough for what I just did."

"No," I said, "you don't."

He just looked down at the ground, then up. "I don't know what made me do it."

"Let's take a little walk." I started off into the dark without looking back, as if I had no doubt he'd follow me. This technique works more often than you think it would.

He followed me. He had stopped to pick up his flashlight, but bravely turned it off.

I stopped just short of the woods and stared off into the trees, letting my eyes adjust to the dark. I didn't look at anything in particular. I let my eyes just sort of see everything. I was looking for movement. Any movement. The tree limbs moved fitfully in the spring wind, but it was a general movement like ocean waves. The trees weren't what worried me.

Wallace tapped the darkened flashlight against his thigh. A soft *whap, whap*. I wanted to tell him to stop but didn't. If it comforted him, I could live with it.

I let the silence stretch between us. The wind picked up, filling the night with a rushing, hurrying sound. You could smell the rain on the wind.

He gripped the flashlight in both hands. I could hear his intake of breath above the wind. "What was that?"

"The wind," I said.

"Are you sure?"

"Pretty much."

"What do you want?" he asked.

"Is this the first vamp you've gone after since your partner's death?"

He looked at me. "Granger told you?"

"Yeah, but I saw your neck. I was pretty sure what had done it."

I wanted to tell him it was okay to be scared. Hell, I was scared, but he was a cop and a man, and I didn't know him well enough to know how he'd take a pep talk from me. But I had to know if he'd follow me into those woods. I had to know if I could depend on him. If he stayed this scared, I couldn't.

"What happened?" I asked. Maybe talking about it right now was the wrong thing to do, but ignoring it wasn't working very well.

He shook his head. "Headquarters says you're in charge, Ms. Blake. Fine, I'll do what I'm told. But I don't have to answer personal questions."

It was too much trouble to shrug out of the overall, and I really didn't want my arms trapped. I undid one button on my blouse and spread the cloth.

"What are you doing?"

"How good's your night vision?"

"Why?"

"Can you see the scar?"

"What are you talking about?" He sounded suspicious. Suspicious that I was crazy, maybe.

My night vision would have picked it up, but most people don't have my eyes. "Give me your hand."

"Why?"

"I am about to give you a once-in-a-lifetime offer. Just give me your damn hand."

He did, sort of hesitatingly, glancing back at the waiting men.

His hand was cold to the touch. He was one scared puppy. I traced his large, blunt fingers along my collarbone. The moment he touched the scar tissue, his hand jerked like he'd had an electric shock. I pulled my hand away, and he traced the scar again on his own.

He took his hand back, slowly, rubbing his fingers together like he was remembering the feel of my skin. "What did that?"

"Same thing that did your neck. A vampire that wasn't neat with its food."

"Jesus," he said.

"Yeah," I said. I rebuttoned my blouse. "Tell me what happened, Wallace. Please."

He looked at me for a moment longer, then nodded. "Harry, my partner, and me, we got a call that someone had found a body with its throat torn out." He made the words very bland, ordinary, but I knew he was seeing it in his head. Watching it all happen again behind his eyeballs.

"It was a construction site. Just us in the middle of the place with our flashlights. There was a sound like wind whistling, and something hit Harry. He went down with a man on top of him. He screamed, and I had my gun out. I fired into the man's back. I hit him solid three, four times.

He turned on me and his face was bloody. I didn't have time to wonder why, 'cause he jumped me. I emptied my gun into him before I hit the ground."

He took a deep breath, big hands twisting back and forth on the flashlight. He was looking off into the trees, too, but not for vampires, or at least not for this one.

"He ripped my jacket and shirt like they were paper. I tried to fight him, but . . ." He shook his head. "He caught me with his eyes. He caught me with his eyes, and when he tore into my neck, I wanted him to do it, wanted it worse than I've ever wanted anything in my life."

He turned a little away from me, as if not meeting my eyes wasn't enough. "When I woke up, he was just gone. Harry was dead. The girl was dead. I was alive."

He turned to me finally, looked me straight in the eyes and said, "Why didn't he kill me, Ms. Blake?"

I looked into his earnest eyes and didn't have a good answer. "I don't know, Wallace. He wanted to make you one of them, maybe. I don't know why you and not Harry. You ever catch him?"

"The local master sent his head in a box to the station. The note apologized for his uncivilized behavior. That's what the note said, 'uncivilized behavior.'"

"It's hard to look at it as murder when you feed off humans yourself."

"Do they all do that? Feed off people?"

"I've never met one that didn't."

"Can't they eat animals?"

"Theoretically, yes. In practice it seems to lack certain nutrients." Truth was, feeding was too close to sex for most vamps. They weren't into bestiality, so they didn't feed off animals. I didn't think the sex analogy would go over well with Officer Wallace.

"Can you do this, Wallace?"

"What do you mean?"

"Can you go out into the dark and hunt vampires?"

"It's my job."

"I didn't ask if it was your job. I asked if you can go out into that darkness and hunt vampires."

"You think there's more than one?"

"Always best to assume so," I said.

He nodded. "Yeah, I guess so."

"Scared?" I asked.

"Are you?"

I looked off into the windswept night. The trees tossed and moaned in the wind. There was movement everywhere. Soon there would be rain, and what light the stars gave would be gone.

"Yeah, I'm scared."

"But you're a vampire hunter," he said. "How can you do this night after night if it scares you?"

"Doesn't it scare you to know that every time you pull over some yahoo for a traffic violation that he could be armed? You walk up on that car and never know."

"It's my job."

"And this is my job."

"But you're scared?"

"Down to my toes."

Larry called, "The sheriff's back. He's got the warrant."

Wallace and I looked at each other. "You got silver bullets?" I asked.

"Yes."

I smiled. "Then let's go. You'll be fine," I said. I believed it. Wallace would do his job. I would do my job. We would all do our jobs. And come morning, some of us would be alive and some of us wouldn't. Of course, maybe there was just the one newly dead vampire to deal with. If so, we might all see the sunrise. But I hadn't lived this long assuming the best. Assuming the worst was always safer. And usually truer.

15

I'D GOTTEN USED to the sawed-off shotgun that I had at home. Yeah, it is illegal, but it's easy to carry and makes mincemeat out of vampires. What more could a modern vampire hunter want? The Ithaca pump action 12 gauge was close.

"Why don't I get a shotgun?" Larry asked.

I just looked at him. He looked serious. I shook my head. "When you can handle the nine, we'll talk about shotguns."

"Great."

Oh, for the enthusiasm of youth. Larry was only four years younger than I was. Sometimes it seemed like a million.

"He's not going to shoot us in the back by accident, is he?" Deputy Coltrain asked.

I smiled, not sweetly. "He promised not to."

Coltrain looked at me like he wasn't sure I was kidding.

Sheriff St. John joined us at the edge of the woods. He had a shotgun, too. I had to trust that he knew how to use it. Wallace had the shotgun from their unit. His partner Granger had a wicked-looking rifle like something a sniper would carry. It looked like the wrong tool for tonight's job, and I had said so. Granger had just looked at me. I'd shrugged and let it go. It was his neck and his gun.

I looked around at them. They looked at me. Waiting for me to give the word.

"Everybody got their holy water?" I asked.

Larry patted his coverall pocket. Everyone else nodded, or mumbled yes.

"Remember the three rules of vampire hunting. One: Never, ever look them in the eyes. Two: Never, ever give up your cross. Three: Aim for the head and heart. Even with silver ammo, it won't be a killing blow anywhere else." I felt like a kindergarten teacher sending her kiddies off to a hostile playground. "Don't panic if you get bitten. The bite can be cleansed. As long as they don't mesmerize you with their eyes, you can still fight."

I looked at them, all silent, all taller than me, even Larry by an inch or two. They could all arm wrestle me and win. So why did I want to order them all into the house where'd they'd be safe? Heck, we could all go inside. Have a nice cup of hot cocoa. Tell the Quinlans their little girl would be fine. I mean, liquid diets are in with teens. Right?

I took a deep breath and let it out slow. "Let's do it, boys. We're wasting starlight." Either nobody got my John Wayne reference, or nobody thought it was funny. Hard to tell which.

I had to let St. John lead the way into the black trees. I didn't know the area. He did. But I didn't like him taking point. I didn't like it at all. I wanted to bring him back to his wife. His high school sweetheart. Five years married and still in love. Jesus, I didn't want to get him killed.

The trees closed around us. St. John threaded his way through them like he knew what he was doing. There was very little undergrowth this time of year. It made it easier, but there is still an art to going through thick woods, especially in the dark. You can't really see even with a flashlight. You have to sort of give yourself over to the trees the way you give yourself to water when you swim. You don't really concentrate on the water, or even on your own body. You concentrate on the rhythm of your body cutting, sliding through the cool liquid. For the forest you find a rhythm, too. You concentrate on sliding your body through the natural openings. Finding the place where the forest itself will let you through. If you fight it, it will fight you back. And, just like water, it can kill you. Anyone who doesn't believe that the forest is a deadly place has never been lost in one.

St. John knew how to move, and so did I. I was pretty pleased at that, actually. I'd been a city girl for a long time. Larry stumbled into me. I had to brace, or we'd have both gone down.

"Sorry," he said, pushing himself away from me.

"How ya doing up there, vampire hunter?" Coltrain called. He was bringing up the rear. I had to go second to back up St. John, and I wouldn't let Larry take rear. Coltrain had wanted it. Said he and the sheriff would guard our ass. Fine with me.

"Yell a little louder," Wallace said. "I don't think the vampire heard you."

"I don't need no statie telling me how to do my job."

"It knows we're here," I said.

That stopped them. They both looked at me. Granger, who was just ahead of Wallace, looked at me, too. I had everyone's attention.

"Even if the vampire is only a few weeks old, its hearing is incredibly acute. It knows we're here. It knows we're coming. It doesn't matter if we're quiet or have a brass band. It's all the same. We won't surprise it in the dark." It would probably surprise us, but I didn't add that part aloud. We were all thinking it anyway.

"We are wasting time here, Deputy," St. John said.

Coltrain didn't apologize or even look sorry. Wallace did. "I'm sorry, Sheriff. It won't happen again."

St. John nodded and turned without another word and led us farther into the woods.

Coltrain made a small humphing sound but let it go. Whatever he said, I didn't think Wallace would rise to bait again. At least I hoped not. I didn't care if he was scared; we had enough problems without fighting among ourselves.

The trees rustled and swayed around us. Last year's dead leaves crunched underfoot. Someone cursed softly behind me. The wind blew in a wild gust, streaming my hair back from my face. Up ahead the quality of darkness was different. We were approaching the clearing.

St. John stopped just short of the tree line. He glanced back at me. "How do you want to do this?"

I could taste the rain on the wind coming closer. If possible, I wanted us out of here before it came. Visibility sucked as it was.

"We kill it, and we get the hell back to the house. It's not a hard plan."

He nodded, as if I'd said something profound.

Wish I had.

A figure stepped in front of us. One minute nothing, the next there he was. Darkness and shadows, magic. He grabbed St. John as he went for his gun and threw him out into the clearing in a high looping arch.

I shot the vampire in the chest at almost point-blank

range. He collapsed to his knees. I caught a glimpse of the whites of his eyes, like he couldn't believe it. I had to pump the shotgun to jack another shell in place.

Granger's rifle exploded behind me like a cannon. Someone screamed. I shot the vampire between the eyes. His head splattered into the leaves. I turned with the shotgun to my shoulder before the body hit the ground.

Larry was on the ground with a vamp on top of him. I had a glimpse of long brown hair before his cross flared to life in a brilliant flash of blue-white fire. She flung herself backwards with a scream, scrambling into the dark. Gone.

A vamp with long blonde hair held Granger in her slender arms, head pressed to his neck. I couldn't use the shotgun. They were pressed too close together. At this range I'd kill them both.

I dropped the shotgun into Larry's surprised lap. He was still lying on the ground, blinking. I drew the Browning and fired into the vampire's broad chest. She jerked but didn't let go of Granger. The vampire looked at me, the man still clasped to her chest. She hissed at me. I fired a round into her gaping mouth. It blew the back of her head out.

The vamp shuddered. I fired a second round into her head. She let go of Granger and fell to the leaves in convulsions. Granger just lay there. In the dark I couldn't see his face or neck. Dead or alive, I'd done all I could.

Larry was on his feet, shotgun awkward in his hands.

There was a scream, low and pain-filled. Wallace was on the ground with a slender-bodied vamp on top of him. Fangs sunk in his arm. The bone broke with a loud, brittle snap. He screamed again.

I had a glimpse of Coltrain standing, frozen, just beyond. There was movement behind him. I stared straight at it, waiting for the vampire to take shape from the shadows, but something gleamed. A dull silver blade flashed into sight. I stared straight at it, but I lost a second somehow. The next thing I knew the blade tip exploded from Coltrain's throat. I lost another second, blinking at shadows, and the vampire tore the blade from his throat and was gone. It scuttled through the trees like nothing human, unbelievably fast, like a nightmare seen from the corner of your eye.

Larry raised the shotgun to his shoulder, aimed in Wallace's direction. I grabbed it from him, and something smashed into my back and rode me into the leaves. A hand pressed my face into the dry, crackling leaves. A second hand ripped the back of my coverall so violently it wrenched one shoulder. There was an explosion just behind my head, and the vampire was gone. I rolled over, ears ringing.

Larry was standing over me with his arm extended, gun out. Whatever he'd shot was gone out in the dark.

My left shoulder was hurt, but not as badly as it might be if I didn't get up. I struggled to my feet. The vampires were gone.

Wallace was sitting up, cradling his arm. Coltrain lay on the ground without moving. A sound behind us. I turned, Browning pointed. Larry was turning too, but too slow. I sighted down the barrel, and it was St. John.

"Don't shoot. It's me."

Larry held his gun two-handed pointed at the ground. "Sweet Jesus," he said.

Amen. "What happened to you?"

"The fall knocked me out. I followed the sound of shots," St. John said.

A gust of wind slapped against us. It smelled so strongly of rain I almost felt it on my skin.

"Check Granger's pulse, Larry," I said.

"What?" Larry looked shell-shocked.

"See if he's alive." It was a messy job, and I'd have done it myself, but I trusted me more than Larry to keep the vampires away. He'd saved me once tonight, but I still trusted me more.

St. John walked past us. He touched Wallace, who nodded. "My arm's broke, but I'll live." St. John went to Coltrain's still form.

Larry knelt by Granger. He switched his gun to his left hand, not the best thing to do, but I understood. Hard to check for a pulse in the dark on a throat warm with blood; better to use your dominant hand.

"I've got a pulse." He looked up, his broad smile a dim whiteness in the dark.

"Coltrain's dead," St. John said. "God help me, he's dead." He raised a hand and the skin glistened with blood, black in the dim light. "He's nearly decapitated. What did this?"

"Sword," I said. I'd seen it. Watched it happen. But all I could remember was a black shape larger than a human being. Or larger than most. A shadow with a sword was all I'd seen, and I'd been looking right at it.

Something flowed across my skin, and it wasn't the wind. Power filled the spring night like water. "There's something old out here," I said.

"What are you talking about?" St. John said.

"An ancient vampire. It's here. I can feel it." I searched the darkness, but nothing moved but the trees, the wind. There was nothing to see. Nothing to fight. But it was here and it was close. Sword in hand, maybe.

Granger sat up so suddenly that Larry fell back into the leaves with a squeak. The big man's eyes turned to me. I saw his hand go for his gun, and I knew what the vampire was doing.

I pointed the Browning at his head and waited. I had to be sure.

Granger didn't hunt for his dropped rifle. He drew his sidearm and pointed it very slowly, as if he didn't want to do it. He pointed it at Larry from less than a foot away.

Wallace yelled, "Granger, what the fuck are you doing?" I fired.

Granger jerked; the gun wavered, then his hand came back up. I fired again, and again. His hand fell slowly to the ground, gun still in it. He fell straight back into the leaves.

"Granger!" Wallace was screaming, crawling toward his partner. Shit.

I got there first and kicked the gun out of his hand. If he'd twitched, I'd have shot him again. He didn't twitch. He just lay there, dead.

Wallace tried to cradle him one-handed. "Why'd you shoot him? Why?"

"He was going to kill Larry. You saw it."

"Why?"

"The vamp that bit him. His master is out here. And he's a powerful son of a bitch. He used him."

Wallace had Granger's bloody head in his lap, his own ravaged arm pressed to Granger's chest. He was crying.

Shit.

A sound rode the rising wind. A sharp, furious barking. A woman's scream, high and clear, cut across the sound.

"Oh, God," I whispered.

"Beth." St. John was on his feet running before I could say anything.

I grabbed Wallace's shoulder, pulling on his jacket. He looked up.

"What's happening?"

"They're in the house," I said. "Can you walk?"

He nodded. I helped him to his feet.

Another scream came. It wasn't the same scream. A man this time, or a boy.

"Stay with him, Larry. Get to the house as soon as you can."

"What if they're trying to split us up?" Larry asked.

"Then it's going to work," I said. "Shoot anything that moves." I touched his arm, as if that would make him more real, keep him safe. It wouldn't, but it was all I had. I had to go for the house. Larry had signed up to be a monster slayer. The Quinlans and Beth St. John hadn't.

I holstered the Browning, kept a two-handed grip on the shotgun, and threw myself into the trees. I ran, not trying to see where I was going. Rushing through openings in the trees that I wasn't sure were there, but they were. I jumped over a log and nearly fell but caught myself and kept running. A branch slashed my face, bringing tears to my eye. The forest that had seemed passable before was now a maze of roots and branches that grabbed and tripped. I was running blind. It was not a good way to stay alive with vampires in the dark. I spilled out onto the Quinlans' lawn on my knees, shotgun tightly gripped.

The front door was open. Light spilled in a warm rectangle. Shots sounded from inside the house. I got to my feet and ran for the light.

The poodle lay broken by the door, crumpled like someone had tried to force it into a ball.

The doors to the living room were open. A second shot sounded. I went in to the left of the door, wall at my back, shotgun ready.

Mr. and Mrs. Quinlan were huddled in the far corner with their crosses held out before them. The metal glowed with a white-hot light like burning magnesium.

The thing in front of them didn't look much like a vampire. It looked like a skeleton with muscle and flesh stretched over a bone frame. It was stretched impossibly thin and tall. A sword rode its back, gleaming and wide as a scimitar. Coltrain's killer?

St. John was firing into the brown-haired vamp from the woods. She had long brown hair parted in the middle, straight and lovely, framing a face that was blood-smeared and stretched wide over fangs.

I had a glimpse of Beth St. John on the floor behind her. She wasn't moving.

St. John kept firing into the vampire's body. She just kept coming. Blood blossomed on the front of her jean jacket. His gun clicked, empty. The vampire staggered, then fell to her knees. She fell forward on all fours, and you could see that her back was so much raw meat. She lay gasping on the floor while St. John reloaded.

I got to my feet, trying to keep an eye on the door just in case this wasn't all. I walked towards the Quinlans and the thing that stood in front of them. I needed a better angle before I used the shotgun. Didn't want to catch them in the shot pattern.

The thing turned on me. I had a glimpse of a face that was neither human nor animal, but stretched thin and alien with fangs and blind, glowing eyes. It shrank, and skin flowed over the bare flesh, covered the nearly naked bone. I'd never seen anything like it. When I aimed the shotgun, I was looking into what could have passed for a human face. Long white hair framed a fine-boned face, and it ran—if running was the word for that blur of motion. It ran like some of them flew, almost like it was doing something else altogether, but I had no better word for it. Some of them flew; this one ran. It was gone before I could pull the trigger.

I was left staring at the open door where the barrel had followed its movement. Could I have fired? Had I hesitated? I didn't think so, but I wasn't sure. It was like in the woods when Coltrain died, like I'd missed a few seconds. The vampire had to be our killer, but the only thing I'd seen clearly in the woods had been the sword.

St. John shot into the fallen vampire. He fired until his gun clicked empty again. The gun went click, click, click.

I walked over to him. The vampire's head was bloody meat and heavier, wetter things. There was no face left. "It's dead, St. John. You killed it."

He just stared at it, down the barrel of his empty gun. He was shaking. He collapsed to his knees suddenly, as if he just couldn't stand any longer. He crawled over to his wife, gun left behind him on the carpet. He cradled her in his arms, half-lifting, rocking her. She was soaked with blood. Her throat was so much raw meat on one side.

St. John was making a high, keening sound deep in his throat.

The Quinlans's crosses had stopped glowing. They stood still clinging to each other, blinking as if blinded by the light.

"Jeff—he took Jeff," Mrs. Quinlan said.

I looked at her. Her eyes were too wide. "He took Jeff."

"Who took Jeff?" I asked.

"The big one," Mr. Quinlan said. "That thing, that thing told Jeff to take his cross off, and Jeff did it." He looked at me with startled eyes. "Why did he do that? Why did he take it off?"

"The vampire caught him with his eyes," I said. "He couldn't help himself."

"If his faith had been stronger, he wouldn't have given in," Quinlan said.

"It wasn't your son's fault."

Quinlan shook his head. "He wasn't strong enough."

I turned away from him. Which put me staring at St. John. He had folded as much of his wife's body into his lap and arms as he could. He rocked her, eyes distant. He wasn't seeing this room. He'd gone somewhere deep inside. Someplace better. I hoped.

I went for the door. I didn't have to see this. Watching St. John rock his wife's body was not part of my job description. Honest.

I sat down on the stairs where I could see the door, the hallway, and the stairs as far as the landing. St. John started singing in a strange, broken voice. It took me a few minutes to figure out what he was singing. It was "You Are So Beautiful." I got up and went for the outer door. Larry and Wallace were just limping up onto the porch.

I just shook my head and kept walking. I was almost to the driveway before I couldn't hear the singing. I stood there taking deep breaths, letting them out slowly. I concentrated on my breathing, concentrated on the sound of frogs and wind. I concentrated on anything but the sound that was building in my throat. I stood there in the dark, in the open, knowing it was dangerous, and not sure I cared. I stood there until I was sure I wasn't going to start screaming. Then I turned and went back to the house.

It was the bravest thing I'd done all night.

16

DETECTIVE FREEMONT SAT on one end of the Quinlans' couch and I perched on the other. We were as far away from each other as we could get and share it. Only pride kept me from taking a chair. I wouldn't flinch under her cool cop eyes. So I stayed nailed to my end of the couch, but it was an effort.

Her voice was low and careful, every word enunciated, as

if she thought she might yell if she rushed the words. "Why didn't you call and tell me you had a second vampire kill?"

"Sheriff St. John called the state cops. I assumed you'd be told."

"Well, I wasn't."

I stared up into her cool eyes. "You're twenty minutes away with a crime scene unit looking into a possible vampire kill. Why wouldn't they send you over to a second vampire scene?"

Freemont's eyes shifted to one side, then back to me. Her cool cop eyes had melted just a little. It was hard to read for sure, but she looked uneasy. Maybe even scared.

"You haven't told them it was a vampire kill, have you?"

Her eyes flinched.

"Shit, Freemont. I know you don't want the Feds to steal your case, but withholding information from your own people . . . Bet your superiors aren't happy with you."

"That's my business."

"Fine. Whatever plan you've got, more power to you, but why are you pissed at me?"

She took a deep, shaking breath and blew it out like a runner trying to get that extra kick. "How sure are you the vampire used a sword?"

"You saw the body," I said.

She nodded. "A vampire could have ripped the neck apart."

"I saw a blade, Freemont."

"The ME will either back you up, or not."

"Why don't you want this to be vampires?"

She smiled. "I thought I had this case all solved. Thought I'd make an arrest this morning. I didn't think it was vampires."

I stared at her. I wasn't smiling. "If it wasn't vamps, then what was it?"

"Fairies."

I stared at her for a heartbeat. "What do you mean?"

"Your boss, Sergeant Storr, called me. Told me what you'd found out about Magnus Bouvier. He's got no alibi for the time of the killings, and even you think he could have done it."

"Because he could have done it, doesn't mean he did," I said.

Freemont shrugged. "He ran when we tried to question him. Innocent people don't run."

"What do you mean, he ran? If you were there questioning him, how could he run?"

Freemont settled back into the couch, hands clasped together so tightly her fingers were mottled. "He used magic to cloud our minds, and made his escape."

"What sort of magic?"

Freemont shook her head. "What do you want me to say, Ms. Preternatural Expert? Four of us sat there in his restaurant like idiots while he just walked out. We didn't even see him get up from the table."

She looked at me, no smiles. Her eyes were back to that neutral coolness. You could stare all day at someone with eyes like that and keep all your secrets safe.

"He looked human to me, Blake. He looked like a nice, normal guy. I wouldn't have picked him out of a crowd. How did you know what he was?"

I opened my mouth, and closed it. I wasn't exactly sure how to answer the question. "He tried to use glamor on me, but I knew what was happening."

"What's glamor, and how did you know he was using a spell on you?"

"Glamor isn't exactly a spell," I said. I always hated explaining preternatural things to people who had no skill in the area. It was like having quantum physics explained to me. I could follow the concepts, but I had to take their word for it on the math. The math was beyond me, hated to admit it, but it was. But not understanding quantum physics wouldn't get me killed. Not understanding preternatural creatures might get Freemont killed.

"I'm not stupid, Blake. Explain it to me."

"I don't think you're stupid, Detective Freemont. It's just hard to explain. I was riding with two uniforms in St. Louis. They were transporting me from a crime scene, playing taxi.

The driver spotted this guy just walking along. He pulled over, put him up against a car. The guy was carrying a weapon, and was wanted in another state for armed robbery. If I'd been in a room with him, I'd have noticed the gun, but just passing by in a car, no way. I wouldn't have seen it. Even his partner asked him how he spotted him. He couldn't explain so that we could do it, but he knew how to do it."

"So it's practice?" Freemont said.

I sighed. "In part, but hell, Detective, I raise the dead for a living. I have some preternatural abilities. It gives me a leg up."

"How the hell are we supposed to police creatures, Ms. Blake? If Bouvier had pulled a gun, we'd have sat there and let him shoot us. We just sort of woke up and he wasn't there anymore. I've never seen anything like it."

"There are things you can do to protect yourself from fairie glamor," I said.

"What?"

"A four-leaf clover will break glamor, but it won't keep the fey from killing you by hand. There are other plants you can wear, or carry that break glamor: Saint-John's-wort, red verbena, daisies, rowan, and ash. My choice would be an ointment made of either four-leaf clovers or Saint-John's-wort. Spread it on your eyelids, mouth, ears, and hands. It'll make you proof against glamor."

"Where do I get this stuff?"

I thought about that for a second. "Well, in St. Louis I'd know where to go. Here, try health-food stores and occult shops. Any fairie ointment will be hard to find because we don't have any fairies native to this country. Ointment from four-leaf clovers is very expensive, and rare. Try for the Saint-John's-wort."

She sighed. "Will this ointment work on any mind control, like for vamps?"

"Nope," I said. "You could drop a vamp in a whole tub of Saint-John's-wort and it wouldn't give a damn."

"What do you do against vampires, then?"

"Keep your cross, avoid eye contact, pray. They can do things that'll make Magnus look like an amateur."

She rubbed her eyes, smearing eye shadow on the ball of her thumb. She suddenly looked tired. "How do we protect the public against something like that?"

"You don't," I said.

"Yes, we do," she said. "We have to; it's our job."

I didn't know what to say to that, so I didn't try. "So you thought it was Magnus because he ran, and he doesn't have an alibi?"

"Why else would he run?"

"I don't know," I said. "But he didn't do it. I saw the thing in the woods. It wasn't Magnus. Hell, I've only heard about vampires forming from shadows. I'd never seen it before."

She looked at me. "You've never seen it before. That's not comforting."

"It wasn't meant to be. But since it wasn't Magnus, you can call off the warrant."

She shook her head. "He used magic on police officers while committing a crime. That's a class C felony."

"What was his crime?"

"Escaping."

"But he wasn't under arrest."

"I had a warrant for his arrest," she said.

"You didn't have enough for a warrant," I said.

"Helps to know the right judge."

"He didn't kill those kids, or Coltrain."

"You pointed the finger at him," she said.

"Just an alternate possibility. With five people dead, I couldn't afford to be wrong."

She stood. "Well, you got your wish. It was vampires, and I don't know why the hell Magnus Bouvier ran from us. But just using magic on a police officer is a felony."

"Even if he was innocent of the original crime you were trying to bring him in on?" I asked.

"Felonious use of magic is a serious crime, Ms. Blake. There's a warrant for his arrest. You see him, you remember that."

"I know Magnus isn't nice people, Detective Freemont. I don't know why he ran, but if you put out the word that he used magic on cops, someone'll shoot him."

"He's dangerous, Ms. Blake."

"Yeah, but so are a lot of people, Detective. You don't hunt them down and arrest them for it."

She nodded. "We've all got prejudices, Ms. Blake; makes us all wrong once in a while. At least here we know what did it."

"Yeah," I said. "We know what did it."

"Do you know when the girl's body was taken?" she asked. She got a notebook out of her coat pocket. Down to business.

I shook my head. "No. It was just gone when I went up."

"What made you think to check on the body?"

I looked at her. Her eyes were pleasant and unreadable. "They'd gone to a lot of trouble to make her one of them. I thought they might try to get her. They did."

"The father's making noises that he asked you to stake her body before you went out after the vampires. Is that true?" Her voice was soft, matter-of-fact. But she was paying attention to the answers. She didn't take as many notes as Dolph did. The notebook seemed to be more something to do with her hands than anything else. I was finally seeing Freemont doing her job. She seemed good at it. That was reassuring.

"Yeah, that's true."

"Why didn't you stake the girl when the parents requested it?"

"I had a father. A widower. His daughter and only child got bit. He wanted her staked. I did it that night, right away. Next morning he's in my office crying, wanting me to undo it. Wanting me to bring her back as a vampire." I leaned back into the couch, hugging myself. "You put a stake through a new vamp's heart, and it's dead for good."

"I thought you had to take a vampire's head to be sure."

"You do," I said. "If I had staked the Quinlan girl, I would have taken out her heart, cut off her head." I shook my head. "There isn't much left."

She drew something on her note pad. I couldn't see what. I was betting it was a doodle and not a word. "I see why you wanted to wait, but Mr. Quinlan is talking about suing you."

"Yeah, I know."

Freemont raised her eyebrows. "Just thought you'd want to know."

"Thanks."

"We haven't found the boy's body yet."

"I don't think you will," I said.

Her eyes didn't look pleasant anymore. They looked narrow and suspicious. "Why?"

"If they wanted to kill him, they could have done it here, tonight. I think they want to make him one of them."

"Why?"

I shrugged. "I don't know. But usually when a vampire takes this personal an interest in a family, there's a reason for it."

"You mean a motive?"

I nodded. "You've seen the Quinlans. They're devout Catholics. The church sees vampirism as suicide. Their children will be damned for all eternity if they become vampires."

"Worse than just killing them," she said.

"To the Quinlans, I think so."

"You think the vampires will be back to get the parents?"

I thought about that for a minute. "Hell, I don't know. I mean, before vampires were legal you had some cases where a master vamp would take out entire families. Sometimes befriend them first. Sometimes just for revenge for some slight. But since they've been legal, I don't know why the vamp would do it. I mean, the vampire can take them to court. What could the Quinlans have done that was bad enough for this?"

The doors opened. Freemont turned, a frown already in place. Two men appeared in the doorway. They were both dressed in dark suits, dark ties, white shirts. Standard federal issue. One was short and white, the other tall and black. That alone should have made them look different, but there was a sameness to them, like the same cookie cutter had been used no matter how well cooked the outside was.

The shorter of the two flipped his badge at us. "I'm Special Agent Bradford, this is Agent Elwood. Which one of you is Detective Freemont?"

Freemont walked towards them with her hand out. Showing she was unarmed and friendly. Yeah, right. "I'm Detective Freemont. This is Anita Blake."

I appreciated being included in the introductions. I stood up and joined the foursome.

Agent Bradford looked at me for a long time. Long enough that it got on my nerves. "Is there something wrong, Agent Bradford?"

He shook his head. "I attended Sergeant Storr's lectures at Quantico. The way he talked about you, I thought you'd be bigger." He smiled when he said it, halfway between friendly and condescending.

A lot of scathing comebacks came to mind, but never get in a pissing contest with the Feds. You'll lose. "Sorry to disappoint you."

"We've already talked with Officer Wallace. He makes you sound taller, too."

I shrugged. "Hard to make me sound shorter."

He smiled. "We'd like to speak with Detective Freemont in private, Ms. Blake. But don't go far; we'll want a statement from you and your associate, Mr. Kirkland."

"Sure."

"I took Ms. Blake's statement personally," Freemont said. "I don't think we need her any more tonight."

Bradford looked at her. "I think we'll be the judge of that."

"If Ms. Blake had called me in when there was only one body on the ground, there wouldn't be two dead policemen, and a dead civilian," Freemont said.

I just looked at her. Somebody's ass was going to be in a sling, and Freemont didn't want it to be hers. Fine.

"Don't forget the missing boy," I said. Everyone looked at me. "You want to start pointing fingers, fine; there's enough blame to go around. If you hadn't chased me off earlier, I might have called you in, but I did call the state police. If you'd told your superiors everything I told you, they'd have connected the two cases, and you'd have been here anyway."

"I had enough men with me to cover the house and the civilians," Freemont said. "Not including me cost lives."

I nodded. "Probably. But you'd have come down here and kicked me out again. You'd have taken St. John and his people out in the dark with five vampires, one of them ancient, when all you've seen is pictures of vampire kills. They'd have slaughtered you, but maybe, just maybe, Beth St. John would be alive. Maybe Jeff Quinlan would still be here."

I stared up at her, and watched the anger drain from her eyes. We looked at each other. "It took both of us to fuck this one up, Sergeant." I turned back to the two agents. "I'll wait outside."

"Wait," Bradford said. "Storr said that sometimes the legal vampire community will help on a case like this. Who do I talk to down here?"

"Why would they hunt down one of their own?" Agent Elwood asked.

"This kind of shit is bad for business. Especially right now with Senator Brewster's daughter getting killed. Vampires don't need any more bad publicity. Most of them like being legal. They like the fact that killing them is murder."

"So who do I talk to?" Bradford asked.

I sighed. "In this area, I don't know. I'm not a hometown girl."

"How do I go about finding out who to talk to?"

"I might be able to help you there."

"How?"

I shook my head. "I know someone who might know a name. I'm not trying to give you a hard time here, but a lot of the monsters don't like dealing with cops. It just hasn't been that long ago that the police shot them on sight."

"So you're saying the vampires will talk to you and not to us?" Elwood said.

"Something like that."

"That makes no sense. You're a vampire executioner. Your job is to kill them. Why would they believe you and not us?" he asked.

I didn't know how to explain it, and wasn't sure I wanted to. "I also raise zombies, Agent Elwood. I think they sort of consider me one of the monsters."

"Even though you're their version of an electric chair."

"Even though."

"That's not logical."

I laughed then; I couldn't help it. "God, has anything that happened here tonight been logical?"

Elwood gave a very small smile. I pegged him as the newer of the two. I don't think he'd gotten over the thought that FBI agents don't smile.

"You wouldn't be withholding information from the FBI, would you, Ms. Blake?" Bradford asked.

"If I come up with a vampire in this area that will talk to you, I'll give you the name."

Bradford stared at me. "How about if you come up with any vampires in this area, you give us the names. Let us worry about whether they'll talk to us or not."

I looked at him for a heartbeat and lied. "Sure." If I expected the monsters to help me, I couldn't give them all over to the cops. Only a select few.

He looked like he didn't believe me, but couldn't quite call me a liar to my face. "When we find the vampires responsible, we'll be sure to call you in for the kill."

That was more than Freemont had been willing to do. The night was looking up. "Beep me any time."

"We'll talk to Sergeant Freemont now, Ms. Blake." I was dismissed. Fine with me. He offered his hand. I took it. We shook. Agent Elwood and I shook. Everyone smiled. I left.

Larry was waiting out in the entryway. He got up off the stairs where he'd been sitting. "What now?"

"I need to make a phone call."

"Who to?"

Two more men with "Federal Agent" tattooed on their foreheads walked up the hallway from the direction of the kitchen. I shook my head and went out the door into the cool windy night. The place was swarming with cops. I'd never seen so many federal agents in my life. But hey, the very first vampire serial killer was news. Everyone would want a piece. Watching everyone mill around on the carefully tended lawn, I suddenly wanted to go home. To just pack up and go home. It was still early. Hours and hours left of darkness. It only seemed like it had been an eternity since we left the graveyard. Hell, there'd be time to go back and look at Stirling's boneyard before dawn.

I got in the jeep that Bayard had loaned us. I'd use the nifty portable phone it came with.

Larry got in the passenger side.

"Private call."

"Come on, Anita."

"Out, Larry."

"Out in the dark with the vampires." He blinked his big blue eyes at me.

"The place is lousy with cops. I think you'll be safe. Out."

He got out, grumbling under his breath. He could grumble all he wanted to. Larry wanted to be a vampire hunter, fine; but he didn't have to be as intimately involved with the monsters as I was. I was trying to keep him as out of it as I could. Not easy, but worth the effort.

I'd lied to the nice agents. It wasn't the fact that I raised zombies that got me in good with the vampires. It was the fact that the Master of the City, of St. Louis, had the hots for me. Was maybe in love with me, or at least thought he was.

I knew the number by heart, which was a bad sign all on its own. "Guilty Pleasures, where your darkest fantasies come true. This is Robert. How may I help you?"

Great; Robert, one of my least favorite vampires. "Hi, Robert, this is Anita. I need to speak to Jean-Claude."

He hesitated, then said, "I'll transfer you to his office phone. It's a new system, so if I disconnect you, call back."

The phone clicked before I could answer. A moment of silence, and the voice came on the line. You can criticize a lot about Jean-Claude, but he gives good phone.

"Good evening, *ma petite*." That was it, all he said, but even over the buzzing phone his voice was like fur inside my skull.

"I'm near Branson. I need to contact the Master of the City down here."

"No 'Good evening, Jean-Claude, how are you doing?'? Just down to business. How terribly rude, *ma petite*."

"Look, I don't have time for games right now. Some vampires down here are on the rampage. They've kidnapped a young boy. I want to find him before they can make him one of them."

"How young is the boy?"

"Sixteen."

"In centuries past, *ma petite*, that was not considered a child."

"It isn't legal age right this minute."

"Did he go willingly?"

"No."

"You know that for a fact, or were you merely told he was kidnapped?"

"I talked to him before. He didn't go willingly."

Jean-Claude sighed. The sound slithered down my skin like cool fingers. "What do you want of me, *ma petite*?"

"I want to talk to the Master of the City down here. I need the name. I'm assuming you do know who the Master is down here?"

"Of course, but it is not that simple."

"We only have three nights to save him, and a hell of a lot less if they just want a snack."

"The Master will not talk to you without a guide to take you in."

"Send someone, then."

"Who? Robert? Willie? Neither of them is powerful enough to be your escort."

"If you mean they can't protect me, I can protect myself."

"I know you can take care of yourself, *ma petite*. You have made that abundantly clear. But you do not look as dangerous as you are. You might have to shoot one or two to teach them their place. If you got out alive, they would not help you."

"I want to get this boy back intact, Jean-Claude. Work with me here."

"*Ma petite* . . ."

I had an image of Jeff Quinlan's brown eyes. His room with its cowboy wallpaper. "Help me, Jean-Claude."

He was silent for a moment. "I am the only one powerful enough to be your escort. Do you wish me to drop everything and rush down to you?"

It was my turn to be quiet. Put like that, it didn't sound right. It sounded like a big favor. I didn't want to be indebted to him. But I'd probably live through owing him a favor. Jeff Quinlan might not.

"Fine," I said.

"You want me to come help you?"

I gritted my teeth and said, "Yes."

"I will fly down tomorrow night."

"Tonight."

"*Ma petite, ma petite*, what am I to do with you?"

"You said you'd help me."

"And I will, but these things take time."

"What things?"

"It might be helpful if you thought of Branson as a foreign country. A potentially hostile foreign country where I am working to get us safe passage. There are customs to be observed. If I barge in, it will be seen as a declaration of war."

"Isn't there any way to start tonight?" I asked. "Short of starting a war?"

"Perhaps, but if you wait one more night, *ma petite*, we can enter much more safely."

"We can take care of ourselves. Jeff Quinlan can't."

"That is his name?"

"Yeah."

He took a deep breath and let it out in a sigh that made me shiver. I would have told him to stop that, but it would have amused him, so I didn't.

"I will fly down tonight. How do I contact you?"

I gave him the name of my hotel and then, with a sigh, my beeper number.

"I will call you when I arrive."

"How long will it take you to fly this far?"

"Anita, do you think I am going to fly myself down, as a bird would?"

I didn't like the faint amusement in his voice, but I answered truthfully. "It was a thought."

He laughed, and it raised goose-bumps on my arms. "Oh, *ma petite, ma petite*, you are precious."

Just what I wanted to hear. "So how are you getting here?"

"My private jet."

Of course, he had a private jet. "When can you be here?"

"I will be there as soon as I can, my impatient flower."

"I prefer *ma petite* to flower."

"As you like, *ma petite*."

"I want to see the Master of Branson tonight before dawn."

"You have made that abundantly clear, and I will try."

"Do more than try."

"You are feeling guilty about this boy; why?"

"I'm not feeling guilty."

"Responsible, then," he said.

I sat there, not sure what to say. He was right. "I don't suppose you read my mind just then?"

"No, *ma petite*, just your voice and your impatience."

I hated that he knew me that well. Hated it. "Yeah, I feel responsible."

"Why?"

"I was in charge."

"Did you do all you could to keep him safe?"

"I had hosts put at every entrance."

"Someone let them in, then?"

"They had a doggie door that exited through the garage, into the house wall. They didn't want to cut a hole through any of the outer doors."

"Was there a child vampire among them?"

"No."

"Then how?"

I described the thin, skeletal vampire. "It was almost a form change. He changed back in seconds. Once he changed back, he could have passed for human in dim light. I've never seen anything like it."

"I've only seen the ability once," he said.

"You know who it is, don't you?"

"I will be with you as soon as I am able, *ma petite*."

"You sound serious all of a sudden; why?"

He gave a small laugh, but this one was bitter, like swallowing broken glass. It hurt just to hear it. "You know me too well, *ma petite*."

"Just answer the question."

"Did the boy who was taken look younger than his years?"

"Yeah; why?"

Silence thick enough to slice was the only answer.

"Talk to me, Jean-Claude."

"Have there been any other young boys gone missing?"

"Not to my knowledge, but I haven't asked."

"Ask," he said.

"How young?"

"Twelve, fourteen, older if they look young enough."

"Like Jeff Quinlan," I said.

"I fear so."

"Is this vampire into more than just kidnapping?"

"What do you mean, *ma petite*?"

"Murder, not just biting them, but murder."

"What sort of murder?"

I hesitated. I didn't discuss ongoing police investigations with the monsters.

"I know you do not trust me, *ma petite*, but it is important. Tell me of these deaths, please."

He didn't say please very often. I told him. Not in great detail, but enough.

"Were they violated?"

"What do you mean, violated?" I asked.

"Violated, *ma petite*, violated. There are other words for it, but none better for children."

"Oh," I said. "I don't know if they were sexually assaulted. They were still clothed."

"There are things that can be done without removing clothing, *ma petite*. But the abuse would have happened before the killings. Systematic abuse over a period of weeks or months."

"I'll find out if they were assaulted." An idea occurred to me. "Would this vamp ever do a girl?"

"By 'do,' you mean sex?"

"Yeah."

"If pressed for company, he would take a young girl, prepubescent, but only if he could find nothing else."

I swallowed hard. We were talking about children like they were things, objects. "No, this girl looked like a woman. She didn't look young."

"Then, no, he would not willingly touch her."

"What do you mean, willingly? What other choice would there be?"

"His master could order him to do it, and he might, if he feared the master enough. Though I cannot think of many people that he would fear enough to do something he found repugnant."

"You know this vampire. Who is he? Give me a name."

"When I arrive, *ma petite*."

"Just give me the name."

"So you can give it to the police?"

"That is their job."

"No, *ma petite*. If it is who I think it is, it will not be a matter for the police."

"Why not?"

"Put simply, he is too dangerous and too exotic to be revealed to the general public. If mortals found out we could have among us such things, they might turn on us all together. You must be aware of that nasty law floating around the Senate."

"I'm aware."

"Then you must understand my caution."

"Maybe, but if more people die because of your caution, it's going to help Brewster's law get passed. You think about that."

"Oh, I am, *ma petite*. Trust that I am. Now farewell. I have much to do." He hung up.

I sat there staring at the phone. Damn him. What did he mean by exotic? What could this new vampire do that others couldn't? He could slim himself down enough to fit through a doggie door. Maybe it made Houdini jealous, but it was hardly a crime. But I remembered its face. Not human. Not even just a corpse's face. It had been something else altogether. Something different. And I remembered those few seconds I lost, twice. Me, the great vampire hunter, helpless as any civilian for just a heartbeat. With vampires, a heartbeat was enough.

Visions of such things would get you talking of demons, which Quinlan had done briefly. The police ignored him, and I didn't back up his story. Quinlan had never met a real demon, or he wouldn't have made the mistake. Once you've been in the presence of demons, you never forget it. I'd rather fight a dozen vampires than one demonic presence. They don't give a shit about silver bullets.

17

IT WAS AFTER 2:00 A.M. before we got back to the grave-yard. The Feds had kept us forever, like they didn't believe we were telling them the whole truth. Fancy that. I hated being accused of concealing evidence when I wasn't. Made me want to lie to them just so they wouldn't be disappointed. I think Freemont had painted a less than charitable picture of me. That'll teach me to be generous. But it seemed petty to point fingers at each other, and say she did it, when Beth St. John's blood was still wet on the carpet.

The wind that had all but promised rain had drifted away. The thick clouds that had obscured the woods while we were playing tag with vampires were suddenly gone. The moon rode high and two days past full. Since dating Richard, I'd paid more attention to the lunar cycles. Fancy that.

The moon sailed the shining night sky, gleaming like it had been polished. The moonlight was so strong it cast faint shadows. You didn't need a flashlight, but Raymond Stirling had one. A big freaking halogen torch that filled his hand like a captive sun.

I watched him start to point it at Larry and me. I raised an arm and said, "Don't point it at us. You'll ruin our night vision." It wasn't very diplomatic, but I was tired, and it had been a long night.

He hesitated in mid-motion. I didn't have to see his face to know he didn't like it. Men like Raymond give orders better than they take them.

He clicked off the light. Good for him. He waited with Ms. Harrison, Bayard, and Beau gathered around him. He was the only one with a flashlight. I bet that his entourage wasn't worried about night vision, and would have liked to have had a light.

Larry and I were still wearing the coveralls. I was getting tired of mine. What I really wanted to do was go back to the hotel and sleep. But once Jean-Claude arrived I wouldn't be sleeping anyway; might as well work. Besides, Stirling was my only paying client. Well, yeah I do get money for killing vampires if it's a legal kill, but it's not a lot of money. Stirling was financing this trip. He deserved his money's worth, I guess.

"We've been waiting for a very long time, Ms. Blake."

"I'm sorry that the death of a young girl inconvenienced you, Mr. Stirling. Shall we go up?"

"I am not unsympathetic to another's loss, Ms. Blake, and I resent the implication that I am." He stood there in the moonlit dark, very straight, very commanding. Ms. Harrison and Bayard moved a little closer, showing support. Beau just stood there, looking sort of amused behind Stirling's back. He was wearing a black slicker with a hood. He looked like a phantom.

I looked up at the clear, sparkling sky. Looked at Beau. He grinned broadly enough for his teeth to flash in the moonlight. I just shook my head and let it go. Maybe he'd been a Boy Scout, always prepared and all that.

"Fine, whatever you say. Let's get this over with." I didn't wait for them. I just walked past them and started up.

Larry, at my side, said, "You're being rude."

I glanced at him.

"Yeah, I am."

"He is a paying client, Anita."

"Look, I don't need you to chastise me, okay?"

"What's wrong with you?"

I stopped. "What we just left is what's wrong with me. I'd think it'd bother you a little more, too."

"It bothers me, but I don't have to take it out on everyone else."

I took a deep breath and let it out slow. He was right. Damn. "Alright, you've made your point. I'll try to be nicer."

Stirling marched up to us, entourage in tow. "Are you coming, Ms. Blake?" He walked past us, his back ramrod-straight.

Ms. Harrison stumbled, and only Bayard's grab on her elbow kept her from falling flat on her butt. She was still wearing her high heels. Maybe it was against the executive secretary code to wear tennis shoes.

Beau followed with his black slicker flapping around his long legs. It made a distinctive *slap-slap* sound that was most irritating.

Okay, maybe everything was irritating right now. I was feeling decidedly grumpy. Jeff Quinlan was out there somewhere. He was either already dead or had one bite by now. It wasn't my fault. I'd told his father to put a piece of the host in front of every entrance. I would have thought of the doggie door if I'd seen it, but I'd never gone that far into the house. Even I would have thought it was paranoid to guard the doggie entrance. But I would have done it, and Beth St. John would be alive.

I'd dropped the ball. I couldn't bring Beth St. John back, but I could save Jeff. And I would. I would. I didn't want to avenge him by killing the vampire that killed him. For once I wanted to be in time. For once I wanted to save someone and leave revenge for someone else.

Was Jeff being violated, right this minute? Was that thing I'd seen in the Quinlans' living room doing more than just biting his neck? God, I hoped not. I was pretty sure I could bring Jeff back from a vampire bite, but combine that with rape by a monster, and I wasn't so sure. What if I found him and there wasn't much left to save? The mind is a surprisingly fragile thing sometimes.

I prayed as we walked up the hill. I prayed and felt a measure of calm return. No visions. No angels singing. But a feeling of peace flowed over me. I took a deep breath, and something hard and tight and ugly in my heart let go. I took it as a good sign that I'd get to Jeff in time. But part of me was skeptical. God doesn't always save someone. Often He just helps you live through the loss. I guess I don't entirely trust God. I never doubt Him, but His motives are too beyond me. Through a glass darkly and all that. Just once I'd like to see through the damn glass clearly.

The moon shone down on the top of the hill like silver fire. The air was almost luminescent. The rain was gone, giving its blessing somewhere else. Heaven knows we could have used the rain, but personally I was just as glad I didn't have to walk the raw dirt in a downpour. Mud would have been just too perfect.

"Well, Ms. Blake, shall we begin?" Stirling asked.

I glanced at him. "Yeah." I took a breath and swallowed the blunt things I wanted to say. Larry was right. Stirling was a pain in the ass, but he wasn't who I was mad at. He was just a convenient target.

"Mr. Kirkland and I will walk the graveyard. But you need to stay here. Other people moving around are very distracting." There; that was diplomatic.

"If you were going to make us stand here like an audience, you could have said so at the bottom of this mountain. And saved us the walk."

So much for diplomacy. "Would you have liked me telling you to stay at the bottom of the hill where you couldn't see what we were doing?"

He thought about that for a minute. "No, I suppose I wouldn't have liked it."

"Then what are you complaining about?"

"Anita," Larry said very softly under his breath.

I ignored him. "Look, Mr. Stirling, it has been a really

rough night. I am just out of niceness right now. Please, just let me do my job. The faster I get this done, the sooner we go home. Okay?"

Honesty. I was hoping profound honesty would work. It was about all I had left.

He hesitated a minute, then nodded. "All right, Ms. Blake. Do your job, but know this. You have been decidedly unpleasant. It better be pretty spectacular."

I opened my mouth, and Larry touched my arm. He gripped my arm not too hard, but hard enough. I swallowed what I was going to say and walked away from all of them. Larry trailed after me. Brave Larry.

"What's the matter with you tonight?" he asked when we were out of earshot of Stirling and Co.

"I told you."

"No," he said, "it isn't just the murder tonight. Hell, I've seen you kill people and be less upset afterwards. What's wrong?"

I stopped walking and just stood there for a minute. He'd seen me kill people and be less upset. Was that true? I thought about it for a heartbeat. It was true. That was pretty damn sad.

I knew what was wrong. I'd seen too many slaughtered people in the last few months. Too much blood. Too much killing. I'd done some of the killing. Not all of it had been sanctioned by the state. I also wanted to be looking for Jeff Quinlan. I couldn't do anything until Jean-Claude arrived. I really couldn't. But I felt like my job was interfering with my police work. Was that a bad sign? Or a good one?

I took a deep breath of the cool mountain air. I let it out very slowly, concentrating on just breathing, in and out, in and out. When I felt calm again, I looked at Larry.

"I'm just a little on edge tonight, Larry. I'll be alright."

"If I said a little on edge with a surprised lilt in my voice, would you get mad?"

I smiled. "Yeah, I would."

"You've been in a blacker mood than usual since you talked to Jean-Claude. What's up?"

I stared into his smiling face and didn't want to tell him.

He wasn't that much older than Jeff Quinlan, four years. He could still have passed for a high-schooler. "Fine," I said, and told him.

"A vampire pedophile; isn't that against the rules?"

"What rules?"

"That you can only be one kind of monster at a time."

"It kind of caught me off guard, too."

A strange look flashed across his face. "Sweet Jesus, Jeff Quinlan is with that thing." He looked at me, all the horror, all the pain, or as much as he could imagine, flowing across his face. "We have to do something, Anita. We have to save him." He turned as if to go back down the mountain.

I grabbed his arm. "We can't do anything until Jean-Claude arrives."

"But we can't just do nothing."

"We aren't doing nothing. We're doing our job."

"But how can we . . ."

"Because we can't do anything else right now."

Larry looked at me for a second, then nodded. "Okay; if you can be calm, so can I."

"Good man."

"Thanks. Now show me this nifty trick you've been talking about. I've never heard of anyone who could read the dead without raising them first."

Truthfully, I didn't know if Larry could do it. But telling him he might not be able to was not going to help his confidence. Magic, if that was the right word, often rises and falls on your own belief in your abilities. I've seen very powerful people completely crippled by self-doubt.

"I'm going to walk the cemetery." I tried to think of how to put it into words. How do you explain something that you don't fully understand yourself?

I have always had an affinity with the dead. Even as a small child, I always knew if the soul had fled the body. I remember my great-aunt Katerine's funeral. I'm named after her, my middle name. She was my father's favorite aunt. We went early to view the body and make sure everything was ready. I felt her soul hovering above the coffin. I looked up expecting to see it, but there was nothing for my eyes to hold onto. I've never seen a soul. I've felt them, but I've never seen one.

I know now that Aunt Katerine's soul hung around a long time. Most souls leave within three days, some leave instantly, some don't. My mother's soul was gone by the time the funeral arrived. I didn't feel her there. There was nothing but a closed coffin and a blanket of pink roses over the coffin, as if the coffin would get cold.

It was at home where I felt my mother hovering close. Not her soul, not really, but some piece of her that couldn't let go immediately. I would hear her footsteps in the hall outside my bedroom as if she was coming to kiss me good night. She moved through the house for months, and I found it comforting. When she finally left, I was ready to let her go. I never told my father. I was only eight, but even then I knew that he couldn't hear her. Maybe he heard other things. I don't know. My father and I never talked much about my mother's death. It made him cry.

I'd been able to sense ghosts long before I could raise the dead. What I was about to do was just an extension of that, or maybe a combination of both skills. I don't know. But it was like trying to explain that there was a soul hovering over Aunt Katerine's coffin. Either you knew the soul was there or you didn't. Words didn't quite cover it.

"Can you see ghosts?"

"You mean right now?"

I smiled and shook my head. "No, just in general."

"Well, I knew the Calvin house wasn't haunted, no matter how many stories people made up. But there was a little cave near town that had something in it. Something not nice."

"Was it a ghost?"

He shrugged. "I never tried to find out, but nobody else seemed able to feel it."

"Do you know when the soul leaves the body? I mean, can you tell it?"

"Sure." He said it like, Couldn't everybody do that?

I had to smile. "Good enough. I'm just going to do it. I don't know what you'll see, if anything. I know that Raymond is going to be disappointed because he won't see anything, unless he's a lot more talented than he looks."

"What are you going to do, Anita? They never talked about 'walking a cemetery' in college."

"It's not like a magic spell, a few words or gestures and it works. It isn't anything like that." I struggled to put into words something that we had no vocabulary for. "It's closer to psychic ability than magic. It's not physical. It's not a muscle to move, or even a thought. It's . . . I just do it. Let me get started; then if I can, I'll bring you in or try and talk to you while I do it. Okay?"

He shrugged. "I guess so. I still don't understand what the heck you're doing, but that's okay. I usually don't know what's going on."

"But you always figure it out," I said.

He grinned. "I do, don't I?"

"You bet."

I stood in nearly the dead center of the raw earth. Not so long ago I was afraid of what I was about to do. It wasn't really frightening in and of itself. I was scared of the fact that I could do it at all. It wasn't a very human thing to be able to do. But then, lately I'd been rethinking exactly what made you human, and what made you one of the monsters. Once I'd been very sure of myself, and everyone else. I wasn't so sure anymore. Besides, I'd been practicing.

Of course, I'd been practicing in empty graveyards where there was nothing but me and the dead. Okay, night insects, but arthropods never bothered my concentration. People did.

Even with my back turned, I could feel Larry like a warm presence behind me. It bugged me. "Can you move back farther?"

"Sure; how far?"

I shook my head. "As far as you can get and still be in sight."

He raised his eyebrows. "Do you want me to go over and wait with Mr. Stirling?"

"If you can stand it."

"I can stand it. I schmooze clients better than you do."

That was the God's honest truth. "Great. When I call you over, come slowly. I've never tried to talk to someone while I do this."

"Whatever you say." He gave a laugh that was almost nervous. "I can't wait to see this."

I let that go, and turned away. I walked away from him. When I glanced back, he was walking to the others. I hoped Larry wouldn't be disappointed. I still wasn't sure if he'd be able to even sense anything. I turned my back on all of them. Seeing them huddled there would distract me, that much I was sure of.

The top of the mountain had been stripped. It was like standing on the edge of the world looking down. The moonlight bathed everything in a soft glow. It was so bright up here near the sky without any trees to hide it that the air itself glowed with diffused light. A gentle wind traced just about head-high. It smelled green and fresh, almost as if the rain had actually fallen. I closed my eyes and let the wind touch my skin, ruffle my hair. There was almost no sound but the singing of insects from below. Nothing but the wind, me, and the dead.

I couldn't tell Larry exactly how to do it, because I wasn't completely sure myself. If it was a muscle, I would move it. If it was a thought, I would think it. If it was a magic word, I would say it. It is none of those things. It is like my skin opens up. All my nerve endings naked to the wind. My skin grew cool. It's like a cool wind eminates from my body. It isn't really wind. You can't see it. You can't feel it, or no one else can. But it's there. It's real.

The cool fingers of "wind" stretched outward from me. Within a ten- to fifteen-foot radius I would be able to search the graves. As I moved, the circle would move with me, searching.

I raised my arm and waved. I didn't turn around to see if Larry saw me. I stayed tight inside my private circle. I was holding it in, trying not to start searching the dead until Larry got over here. I was hoping he'd be able to sense what was going on. Seemed logical that it would be easier to figure out if he saw it from the beginning.

I heard his footsteps on the dry earth. They seemed thunderously loud, as if I could hear every grain of dirt under his shoes.

He stopped behind me. "Jesus, what is that?"

"What?" My voice sounded distant and loud at the same time.

"Wind, a cold wind." He sounded a little scared. Good. You should always be a little afraid when you do magic. It's when you start taking it for granted that you get in trouble.

"Come closer, but don't touch me." I wasn't sure on that last, but it sounded like a good idea. Better cautious than not.

He came slowly, one hand held out like he was feeling the wind against his skin. "Jesus, Mary, and Joseph. Anita, it's coming from you. The wind is coming from you."

"Yes," I said.

His eyes were wide. He looked like his voice sounded, a little scared.

"If I stood right next to Stirling, he wouldn't feel a thing. None of them would."

Larry shook his head. "How could they miss it?" His hand hovered just off my body, almost touching but not quite. "It's colder, or stronger, or something the closer I get to your body."

"Interesting," I said.

"What now?" he asked.

"Now, I touch the dead." I let go of it, like unclenching a hand. The fingers of "wind" stretched downward. How does it feel to go through solid earth and touch the dead beneath? Like nothing human. It was as if the invisible fingers could melt through the dirt searching for the dead. This time we didn't have to search far. The earth was disturbed, and the dead lay on top of the raw land.

I'd never tried this in anything but a well-organized cemetery. Where each grave, each body, was distinct. The wind touched Larry like a stone in a stream. The power rippled around him. He was alive, and it disturbed us. But we'd been practicing, and we could work around him.

I was standing on top of bones. Under the earth where

eyes could not see. I tried to step off them, and only stepped on more. The earth was thick with bodies, like raisins in a pudding. No eating around them.

I stood on top on a raft of bones in a sea of dry, red earth. Everywhere I touched was a body—a piece of bone. There was no clear space. No breathing space. I stood there, huddled in on myself, trying to sort through what I was sensing.

The rib cage just to the left belonged with the thighbone yards away. The wind leaked out and touched piece after piece. I could have put the skeleton back together like a giant jigsaw puzzle. That was what my power would do if I tried to raise it.

I moved, stepping on the dead, and everywhere I walked I put bodies together. The pieces stayed separate, but I remembered.

Larry moved with me. He moved surprisingly smoothly through the power, like a swimmer leaving the smallest possible ripples behind.

A ghost flared to life like a pale, dancing flame. I walked towards it. It rose like a swaying snake, watching me without eyes. There was that thread of hostility that some ghosts seem to feel towards the living. A jealousy. But if I'd been tied to some forsaken piece of earth for a hundred years or more, I might be hostile, too.

"What is that?" Larry whispered.

"What do you see?" I asked.

"I think it's a ghost. I've just never seen one materialize before." He reached out as if to touch it.

I grabbed his wrist before he could ever have reached. I felt his power flare to life in a rush of wind that should have poured my hair back from my face.

The circle suddenly widened, like a camera lens spreading wide. The dead awoke under our combined power like twigs touched by fire. Our power spread over them, and they gave up their secrets. Bits of muscle withered to bone, gaping skulls, all the pieces were there. All we had to do was call them forth. Two more ghosts rose from the ground like smoke. It was a lot of active ghosts for this small and this old a cemetery. And they were all angry at being disturbed. The level of hostility was unusual.

Combining our powers hadn't doubled the circle—it had quadrupled it.

The nearest ghost stood like a white pillar of flame. It was strong, powerful. A full-blown ghost in a graveyard that hadn't seen a burial in over two hundred years.

I stared at it. Larry stared at it. As long as we didn't touch it, we were safe. Heck, we were safe even if we did touch it. Ghosts can't cause physical harm, not really. They can grab you, but if you ignore them they fall away. If you pay attention, they can be bothersome. Frightening, but if a spirit causes real harm it isn't just a ghost. Demon, evil sorcerous dead, but not a normal ghost.

Staring at the wavering shape, I wasn't at all sure this was a normal ghost. Ghosts wear out. They fade to haunts, which don't usually materialize, hot spots that can give you a jolt, then just shivery places. Ghosts do not last forever. These looked pretty damn solid. For ghosts.

"Stop!" a man's voice yelled.

Larry and I turned towards the voice. Magnus Bouvier scrambled up the side of the mountain opposite from where we had walked up. His hair fell across his face, hiding everything but his eyes from the moonlight. His eyes glowed in the dark, reflecting lights I could not see.

"Stop!" He was waving his hands. His long-sleeved shirt was untucked over jeans. He hit the circle of wind and froze. He put his hands up as if he was trying to touch it.

Two people in one night who could sense the power. Unusual, but sort of cool. If Magnus hadn't been on the run from the police, we could have sat down and had a nice talk about it.

"We told you to stay off this land, Mr. Bouvier," Stirling said.

Bouvier looked at him, turning his head slowly as if concentrating on anything besides the feel of power was hard.

"We've tried being nice about this," Stirling said. "We are not going to be nice any longer. Beau."

The pump action on a shotgun is a very distinctive sound.

I turned towards the sound, gun in hand. I don't remember thinking about it. I was just looking down the barrel of a gun at Beau. He was cradling a shotgun in his arms, not aimed at anything. That saved him. I know if it had been pointed near us, I'd have shot him.

I was still seeing double. I could see the graveyard behind my eyes where there is no optic nerve. The cemetery was mine. I knew the bodies. I knew the ghosts. I knew where all the pieces lay. I stared down the gun, seeing Beau and the shotgun, but inside my head the dead still reached out for their scattered parts.

The ghosts were still real. The power had agitated them. They'd dance and sway on their own for a while. But they'd fade back into the ground. There was more than one way to raise the dead, but not permanently.

I couldn't look away from the shotgun to see what Bouvier was doing. "Anita, please don't raise the dead." His surprisingly deep voice held a note of pleading.

I fought an urge to glance at him. "Why not, Magnus?"

"Get off my land," Stirling said.

"This is not your land."

"Get off my land or you will be shot for trespassing."

Beau glanced my way. "Mr. Stirling?" He was being very careful that the shotgun stayed loose, and harmless, in his hands.

"Beau, show him we mean business."

"Mr. Stirling," he said again, with a little more urgency in his voice.

"Do what I pay you for," Stirling said.

He started to raise the shotgun to his shoulder, but slowly, watching me.

"Don't do it," I said. I let my breath out all the way until my body was still and quiet. There was nothing but the gun and what I was aiming at.

Beau lowered the shotgun.

I took a breath and said, "Put it on the ground, now."

"Ms. Blake, this is none of your business," Stirling said.

"You are not going to shoot someone for trespassing on a piece of land while I watch."

Larry had his gun out too, now. It wasn't pointed at anybody in particular, which I was grateful for. Pointed guns have a tendency to go off if you don't know what you're doing.

"On the ground, Beau, now. I won't ask a third time."

He laid the shotgun on the ground.

"I pay your salary."

"You don't pay me enough to get killed."

Stirling made an exasperated sound and moved forward as if he would pick up the gun himself.

"Don't touch it, Raymond. You'll bleed just as easy as anybody else."

He turned to me. "I cannot believe that you would hold me at gunpoint on my own property."

I lowered my gun arm just a touch; it gets shaky if you hold a shooting pose too long. "I cannot believe that you had Beau come up here armed. You knew my little show would attract Bouvier. You knew it and planned for it. You cold-blooded son of a bitch."

"Mr. Kirkland, are you going to let her talk to me like that? I am a client."

Larry shook his head. "I'm with her on this one, Mr. Stirling. You were going to ambush that man. Murder him. Why?"

"Good question," I said. "Why are you so afraid of the Bouvier family? Or is it just him that you're afraid of?"

"I am afraid of no one. Come along; we will leave you to your new friend." He marched away, and the others followed. Beau sort of hesitated.

"I'll bring the shotgun down for you," I said.

He nodded. "Figured that."

"And you better not be waiting down there with another gun."

He looked at me for a long minute. At both of us. He shook his head. "I'm going home to my wife."

"You do that, Beau," I said.

He walked away, black slicker flapping against his legs. He hesitated, then said, "I'm out of it from now on. Money doesn't spend if you're dead."

I knew a few vampires that would argue with him, but I said, "Glad to hear it."

"I just don't want to get shot," he said. He walked away down the slope, out of sight.

I stood there with the Browning pointed skyward. I turned in a slow circle, surveying the mountaintop. We were alone, the three of us. So why didn't I want to put my gun up?

Magnus took a step up the slope and stopped. He raised slender hands towards the power-charged air. He trailed fingertips down it, like it was water. I felt the ripples of his touch shiver down my skin, tremble through my magic.

No, I wasn't putting my gun up yet.

"What was that?" Larry asked. His gun was still out, pointed at the ground.

Bouvier moved his gleaming eyes to Larry. "He is not a necromancer, Anita, but he is more than he seems."

"Aren't we all," I said. "Why didn't you want me to raise the dead, Magnus?"

He stared up at me. His eyes were full of glinting lights like reflections in a pool, but the reflections were of things that were not there.

"Answer me, Magnus."

"Or what?" he asked. "You'll shoot me?"

"Maybe," I said.

The slope made him shorter than I was, so I was looking down on him. "I didn't believe anyone could raise dead this old without a human sacrifice. I thought you'd take Stirling's money, try, fail, and go home." He took a step forward, trailing his hands through the power again, as if he were testing it. As if he weren't sure he could cross into it. The touch made Larry gasp.

"With this power you can raise some of them, maybe enough of them," Magnus said.

"Enough for what?" I asked.

He stared up at me, as if he hadn't meant to speak aloud. "You mustn't raise the dead on this mountain, Anita, Larry. You must not."

"Give us a reason not to," I said.

He smiled up at me. "I don't suppose just because I asked."

I shook my head. "Not hardly."

"This would be so much easier if glamor worked on you." He took another step up the slope. "Of course, if glamor worked on you, we wouldn't be here, would we?"

If he wouldn't answer one question, I'd try another one. "Why'd you run from the police?"

He took another step closer, and I backed up. He'd done nothing overtly threatening, but there was something about him as he stood there, something alien.

There were images in his eyes that made me want to glance behind to see what was reflecting in his eyes. I could almost see trees, water . . . It was like the things you see out of the corner of your eye, except in color.

"You told the police my secret; why?"

"I had to."

"You really think I did those awful things to those boys?" He took another step, moving into the flow of power, but he didn't slip easily as Larry had. Magnus was like a mountain, huge, forcing the power to go wide around him, as if he filled more space magically than could be seen with the naked eye.

I pointed the Browning two-handed at his chest. "No, I don't."

"Then why point a gun at me?"

"Why all this fey magic shit?"

He smiled. "I performed a lot of glamor tonight. It's like a high."

"You feed off your customers," I said. "You don't just do it for business. You siphon them; that's fucking unseelie court."

He gave a graceful shrug. "I am what I am."

"How'd you know the victims were boys?" I asked.

Larry moved to my left, gun pointed carefully at the ground. I'd yelled at him for pointing guns at people too soon.

"The police said so."

"Liar."

He smiled gently. "One of them touched me. I saw it all."

"Convenient," I said.

He reached out towards me. "Don't even think it."

Larry pointed his gun at Magnus. "What's going on, Anita?"

"I'm not sure."

"I can't allow you to raise the dead here. I am sorry."

"How are you going to stop us?" I asked.

He stared at me, and I felt something push against my magic, like something large swimming just out of sight in the dark. It made me gasp.

"Freeze, right there, or I will pull this trigger."

"I haven't moved a muscle," he said softly.

"No games, Magnus; you're too damn close to being dead."

"What did he just do?" Larry asked. There was a fine tremor in his two-handed grip.

"Later," I said. "Clasp your hands on top of your head, Magnus, slowly, very slowly."

"Are you going to take me in, as they say on television?"

"Yeah," I said. "You've got a better chance of getting to the jail alive with me than with most of the cops."

"I don't think I'll go with you." Staring down two guns, and he still sounded sure of himself. He was either stupid or knew something I didn't. I didn't think he was stupid.

"Tell me when to shoot him," Larry said.

"When I shoot him, you can shoot him, too."

"Okay," Larry said.

Magnus looked from one to the other of us. "You would take my life for such a small thing?"

"In a heartbeat," I said. "Now clasp your hands slowly on top of your head."

"If I don't?"

"I don't bluff, Magnus."

"Do you have silver bullets in those guns?"

I just stared at him. I could feel Larry shift slightly beside me. You can only point a gun so long without getting tired, or antsy.

"I'll bet they're silver. Silver isn't very effective against fairies."

"Cold iron works best," I said. "I remember."

"Even normal lead bullets would be better than silver. The metal of the moon is a friend to the fey."

"Hands, now, or we find out how fairie flesh holds up to silver bullets."

He raised his hands slowly, gracefully upward. His hands were above shoulder level when he threw himself backwards, falling down the slope. I fired, but he kept on rolling down the earth, and somehow I couldn't quite see him. It was like the air blurred around him.

Larry and I stood at the top of the slope and fired down on him, and I don't think either of us hit him.

He scrambled down the raw earth faster than he looked because he got harder to see even in the moonlight until he vanished into the underbrush left near the midpoint on that side.

"Please tell me he didn't just go poof," Larry said.

"He didn't just go poof," I said.

"What did he do, then?"

"How the hell do I know. This wasn't covered in Fairies 301." I shook my head. "Let's get out of here. I don't know what's going on, but whatever it is, I think we lost our client."

"You think we lost our hotel rooms?"

"I don't know, Larry. Let's go find out." I clicked the safety on the Browning but left it out in my hand. I'd have left the safety off, but that didn't seem wise while stumbling down a rocky mountainside even in the moonlight.

"I think you can put the gun up now, Larry." He hadn't put his safety on.

"You aren't."

"But I've got the safety on."

"Oh." He looked a little sheepish, but he clicked the safety on and holstered it. "You think they would have really killed him?"

"I don't know. Maybe. Beau would have shot at him, but see how much good it did us."

"Why does Stirling want Magnus dead?"

"I don't know."

"Why did Magnus run from the police?"

"I don't know."

"It makes me nervous when you keep answering all my questions with 'I don't know.'"

"Me, too," I said.

I glanced back once just before we lost sight of the mountaintop. The ghosts twisted and flared like candle flames, cool white flames. I knew something else I hadn't known before tonight. Some of the bodies were nearly three hundred years old. A hundred years older than Stirling had told us they were. A hundred years makes a lot of difference in a zombie raising. Why had he lied? Afraid I'd refuse, maybe. Maybe. Some of the bodies were Indian remains. Bits and pieces of jewelry, animal bone, stuff that wasn't European. The Indians in this area didn't bury their dead, at least not in simple graves. And this wasn't a mound.

Something was going on, and I didn't have the faintest idea what it was. But I'd find out. Maybe tomorrow after we got new hotel rooms, gave back the nifty jeep, rented a new car, and told Bert we no longer had a client. Maybe I'd let Larry break the news to him. What are apprentices for if they can't do some of the grunt work?

Okay, okay, I'd tell Bert myself, but I wasn't looking forward to it.

18

STIRLING AND CO. were gone when we trudged down off the mountain. We drove the Jeep back to the hotel. I was frankly surprised they hadn't taken the Jeep with them and left us to walk. Stirling didn't strike me as a man who liked having guns pointed at him. But then, who does?

Larry's room was first down the hall. He hesitated with

his room card in the lock. "You think the rooms are paid for tonight, or do we pack?"

"We pack," I said.

He nodded, and shoved the card in its little slot. The door handle turned, and in he went. I went to the next door and put in my own card. There was a connecting door between the rooms. We hadn't unlocked it, but it was there. Personally I liked my privacy, even from my friends. And especially from my coworkers.

The room's silence flowed around me. It was wonderful. A few minutes of quiet before I faced Bert and told him all that money had just flown the coop.

The room was a suite with an outer room and a separate bedroom. My apartment wasn't much bigger. There was a bar set into the left-hand wall. Being a teetotaler, that was a real plus for me. The walls were a soft pink with a delicate pattern of gilt-edged leaves, the carpet a deep burgundy. The full-sized couch was a purple so dark it looked nearly black. A love seat matched it. Two armchairs were done in a purple, burgundy, and white floral pattern. All exposed wood was very dark and highly polished. I had suspected I had some kind of honeymoon suite until I saw Larry's room. It was nearly a mirror of mine, but done in shades of green.

A cherrywood desk that looked like a genuine antique sat against the far wall. The connecting door was beside it but opened opposite so you wouldn't accidentally bump the desk. Monogrammed stationery graced the desk, along with a second telephone line for your modem I guess.

I don't know if I'd ever stayed in a room this expensive. I doubted seriously if Beadle, Beadle, Stirling, and Lowenstein would want to pick up the tab now.

A sound jerked me around. The Browning sort of materialized in my hand. I was staring down the barrel at Jean-Claude. He stood in the doorway leading to the bedroom. The shirt had long, full sleeves that had been gathered in three puffs down the length of the arm to end in a spill of cloth that framed his long, pale fingers. The collar was high and tied with a white cravat that spilled lace down the front of him tucked into a vest. It was black and velvety with pinpricks of silver on it. Thigh-high black boots fit his legs like a second skin.

His hair was nearly as black as the vest, making it hard to tell where the curls ended and the velvety cloth began. A silver and onyx stickpin that I'd seen before pierced the white lace at his chest.

"Well, *ma petite*, are you going to shoot me?"

I was still standing there with the gun pointed at him. He had not moved. He had been very careful to do nothing that could be taken as threatening. His blue, blue eyes stared at me. Serious, waiting.

I pointed the gun at the ceiling and let out a breath I hadn't realized I was holding. "How the hell did you get in here?"

He smiled then, and pushed away from the doorjamb. He walked into the room with that wonderful gliding motion of his. Part cat, part dancer, part something else. Whatever the "else" was, it wasn't human.

I put the gun away, though I wasn't sure I wanted to. It made me feel better having it in my hand. Trouble was, a gun wouldn't help me against Jean-Claude. Oh, if I was going to kill him it would, but that's not what we were doing lately. Lately we were—dating. Can you stand it? I wasn't sure I could.

"The desk clerk let me in." His voice was very mild, amused, whether with himself or with me it was hard to tell.

"Why would he do that?"

"Because I asked him to." He walked around me like a shark circling its prey.

I didn't turn with him. I stared straight ahead and let him circle me. It would only amuse him if I kept him in sight. The hairs at the back of my neck stood up. I took a step forward and felt his hand fall back. He'd been about to touch my shoulder. I didn't want him to touch me.

"You used mind tricks on the desk clerk?"

"Yes," he said. That one word was full of so much more. I turned towards him so I could see his face.

He was staring at my legs. He raised his face to mine, and somehow that onc quick gaze took in my entire body. His midnight blue eyes looked even darker than usual. We weren't sure how I was able to meet his gaze. I was beginning to suspect that being a necromancer had more fringe benefits than just being good with zombies.

"Red becomes you, *ma petite*." His voice had grown softer, deeper. He moved closer to me, not touching. He knew better than that, but somehow his eyes showed where his hands wanted to be. "I like this very much."

His voice was soft and warm, and far more intimate than his words. "Your legs are wonderful." His words were growing softer. A whisper in the dark that hovered around my body like a line of warmth. His voice was always like that, touchable. He still had the best voice I'd ever heard.

"Stop it, Jean-Claude. I'm too short to have wonderful legs."

"I do not understand this modern obsession with height." He ran his hands just above my hose, so close I could almost feel it like a breath of warmth against my skin.

"Stop it," I said.

"Stop what?" His voice was utterly mild, harmless. Ri—ight.

I shook my head. Asking Jean-Claude not to be a pain in the ass was like asking rain not to be wet. Why try?

"Fine, flirt all you want, but keep in mind that you're here to save the life of a young boy. A young boy who may be being raped while we sit here and waste time."

He sighed deeply and walked towards me. Something must have shown on my face because he sat down in the other chair, not trying to come closer. "You have a habit, *ma petite*, of taking all the fun out of seducing you."

"Yippee," I said. "Now, can we get down to business?"

He smiled his lovely, perfect smile. "I had arranged to meet with the Master of Branson tonight."

"Just like that," I said.

"Isn't that what you wanted me to do?" he asked. His voice held that amused edge again.

"Yeah. I'm just not used to you giving me exactly what I ask for."

"I would give you anything you wanted, *ma petite*, if you would only let me."

"I wanted you out of my life. You don't seem to want to do that."

He sighed. "No, *ma petite*, I do not want to do that." He let it go at that. No accusations about me wanting to be with Richard instead of him. No vague threats on Richard's life. It was sort of odd.

"You're up to something," I said.

He turned, eyes wide, long fingers pressed to his heart. "*Moi?*"

"Yeah, you," I said. I shook my head and let it go. He was up to something. I knew him well enough to know the signs, but I also knew him well enough to know that he wouldn't tell me until he was good and ready. Nobody kept a secret like Jean-Claude, and nobody else had as many of them. There was no deceit in Richard. Jean-Claude lived and breathed it.

"I've got to change and pack before we can leave."

"Change your lovely red skirt, why? Because I like it?"

"Not just that," I said, "though admittedly it's a plus. I can't wear my inner pants holster with the skirt."

"I will not argue that having a second gun will help our show of force tomorrow night."

I stopped and turned. "What do you mean, tomorrow night?"

He spread his hands wide. "It is too close to dawn, *ma petite*. We cannot even drive to the master's lair before the sun rises."

"Dammit," I said softly and with feeling.

"I did my part, *ma petite*. But even I cannot stop the sun from rising."

I leaned against the back of the love seat, hands gripping the edge hard enough to hurt. I shook my head. "We're going to be too late to save him."

"*Ma petite, ma petite*." He knelt in front of me, staring up at me. "Why does this boy bother you so very much? Why is his life so precious to you?"

I stared down into Jean-Claude's perfect face, and had no answer. "I don't know."

He laid his hands on top of my hands. "You're hurting yourself, *ma petite*."

I moved my hands out from under his, crossing my arms over my stomach. Jean-Claude remained kneeling, a hand on either side of me. He was entirely too close to me, and I was suddenly very aware of how short the skirt was.

"I have to go pack," I said.

"Why? Don't you like your room?" Without moving, he seemed closer somehow. I could feel the line of his body against my legs like heat.

"Move," I said.

He leaned backwards, sitting on his heels, forcing me to move past him. The hem of my skirt brushed his cheek as I walked past. "You are such a pain in the ass."

"So nice of you to notice, *ma petite*. Now, why are you leaving this lovely room?"

"A client's paying for the room, and he's not a client anymore."

"Why ever not, *ma petite*?"

"I pulled a gun on him."

His eyes widened, his face a perfect mask of surprise. The mask slipped and he stared at me with ancient eyes. Eyes that had seen much but still didn't know what to make of me. "Why would you do that?"

"They were going to shoot a man for trespassing."

"Was he trespassing?"

"Technically, yeah."

Jean-Claude just looked at me. "Does he not have the right to protect his own land?"

"No, not if it means killing people. A piece of land isn't worth killing over."

"Protecting our lands has been a valid excuse for slaughter since the beginning of time, *ma petite*. Did you suddenly change the rules?"

"I wasn't going to stand there and watch them kill a man for walking on a piece of ground. Besides, I think it was a setup."

"A setup? You mean a plot to kill the man."

"Yeah."

"Were you part of this plot?"

"I may have been bait. He could feel my power over the dead. It called to him."

"Now that is interesting. What is this man's name?"

"You give me the name of the mystery vampire first."

"Xavier," he said.

"Just like that. Why wouldn't you give me the name earlier?"

"I do not want the police to have it."

"Why not?"

"I explained all that. Now, the name of the man you saved tonight."

I stared at him, and didn't want to give it to him. I didn't like how interested he was in the name. But a deal was a deal. "Bouvier, Magnus Bouvier."

"I do not know the name."

"Should you?"

He just smiled at me. It meant nothing and everything.

"You are an irritating son of a bitch."

"Ah, *ma petite*, how can I resist you when you whisper such sweet endearments to me?"

I glared at him, which made him smile wider. There was just the faintest hint of fang peeking into view.

Someone knocked on the door. Probably the manager telling me to get out. I walked to the door. I didn't bother looking through the peephole, so I was caught off guard by who was outside. It was Lionel Bayard.

Had he come to throw us out in person?

I stood there for a second, looking at him. He spoke first, clearing his throat nervously. "Ms. Blake, may I speak with you for a moment?"

He was being awfully polite for someone who had come to kick us out. "I'm listening, Mr. Bayard."

"I really don't think the hallway is the place to discuss this."

I stepped to one side, ushering him into the room. He stepped past me, hands smoothing his tie. His gaze flicked to Jean-Claude, who was standing now. Jean-Claude smiled at Bayard. Pleasant, charming.

"I didn't realize you had company, Ms. Blake. I can come back."

I closed the door. "No, Mr. Bayard, it's all right. I told Jean-Claude about our misunderstanding this evening."

"Ah, yes, uh . . . " Bayard looked from one to the other of us, as if not sure what to say.

Jean-Claude didn't so much sit in the chair as fold his body around it. The movement was almost catlike. "Anita and I have no secrets from one another, Mr. . . . "

"Bayard, Lionel Bayard." He walked over and offered his hand to Jean-Claude. Jean-Claude raised an eyebrow but took the offered hand.

The handshake seemed to make Bayard feel better. A normal gesture. He didn't know what Jean-Claude was. How he could look at him and think him human was beyond me. I'd only seen one vampire that could have passed for human, and he hadn't been human at all. Bayard turned back to me, adjusting his glasses, which didn't need adjusting. That nervous little gesture again. Something was up.

"What's up, Bayard?" I asked. I'd closed the door and was leaning to one side of it, arms crossed over my stomach.

"I'm here to offer our most sincere apologies for earlier tonight."

I just stared at him. "You're apologizing to me?"

"Yes. Mr. Stirling was overzealous. Why, if you had not been there to bring us all to our senses, a great tragedy might have occurred."

I tried to keep my face blank. I wanted to frown at him, or look confused. "Stirling's not mad at me?"

"On the contrary, Ms. Blake. He's grateful to you."

I didn't believe that. "Really," I said.

"Oh, yes. In fact, I've been authorized to offer you a bonus."

"Why?"

"To make up for our behavior tonight."

"Your behavior was fine," I said.

He smiled modestly. His act was about as sincere as faux pearls, but not half so realistic.

"How much is the bonus?"

"Twenty thousand," he said.

I stayed leaning against the wall, staring at him. "No."

He blinked at me. "Excuse me?"

"I don't want the bonus."

"I'm not authorized to go higher than twenty thousand, but I could speak with Mr. Stirling. Perhaps he would go higher."

I shook my head and pushed away from the wall. "I don't want more money. I don't want the bonus at all."

"You aren't quitting on us, are you, Ms. Blake?" He was blinking so fast I thought he'd pass out. Me quitting bothered him. A lot.

"No, I'm not quitting. But you're already paying an enormous fee. You don't need to pay more."

"Mr. Stirling is just very anxious that he has not offended you."

I let that one go. Too easy. "Tell Mr. Stirling I'd have thought better of his apology if it had been delivered in person."

"Mr. Stirling is a very busy man. He would have come himself, but he had pressing business."

I wondered how often Bayard had to apologize for the big man. I wondered how often the apology was for telling a fellow flunkie to shoot someone. "Fine, you've delivered the message. Tell Mr. Stirling that it isn't the gunfight that's going to make me bail. I read the cemetery tonight. Some of the corpses are closer to three hundred than two hundred. Three hundred years, Lionel; that's an old zombie."

"Can you raise them?" He had stepped closer, hands fidgeting with his lapels. He was close to invading my space. I'd have rather had Jean-Claude next to me.

"Maybe. The question isn't can I, but will I, Lionel."

"What do you mean?"

"You lied to me, Lionel. You underestimated the age of the dead by nearly a century."

"Not deliberately, Ms. Blake, I assure you. I merely repeated what our research department told me. I did not deliberately mislead you."

"Sure."

He reached out almost like he wanted to touch me. I moved back, just enough. He seemed terribly intense. He let his hand drop. "Please, Ms. Blake, I did not lie on purpose."

"The problem, Lionel, is that I'm not sure I can raise zombies this old without a human sacrifice. Even I have my limits."

"So nice to know," Jean-Claude said softly.

I frowned at him. He smiled.

"You will try, won't you, Ms. Blake?"

"Maybe. I haven't decided yet."

He shook his head. "We will do anything to make this oversight up to you, Ms. Blake. It is entirely my fault that I did not double-check the research department's findings. Is there anything that I can do personally to make it up to you?"

"Just leave. I'll call your office tomorrow to discuss details. I may need some extra . . . paraphernalia to attempt the raising."

"Anything, anything at all, Ms. Blake."

"Fine; I'll call." I opened the door and stood by it. I thought it was enough of a hint. It was. Bayard went to the door and almost backed out, apologizing as he went.

I closed the door and stood there for a minute.

"That little man is up to something," Jean-Claude said.

I turned and looked at him. He was still curled in the chair, looking scrumptious.

"I didn't need vampiric powers to tell me that."

"Neither," he said, "did I." He rose from the chair easily. If I'd curled up in a chair like that, I'd have been stiff.

"I've got to tell Larry that he can stop packing. I don't understand why we're still hired, but we are."

"Can anyone else raise the graveyard?"

"Not without a human sacrifice, maybe not even then," I said.

"They need you, *ma petite*. From the little man's anxiety, they must need the dead raised very badly."

"Millions of dollars are at stake."

"I do not think money is all that is at stake," he said.

I shook my head. "Me either."

He came to join me by the door. "What extra paraphernalia will you need to raise a three-hundred-year-old corpse, *ma petite*?"

I shrugged. "A bigger death. I'd originally thought to use a couple of goats." I opened the door.

"What are you thinking about using now?"

"An elephant, maybe," I said.

We were out in the hall and he was staring at me.

"I'm kidding. Honest. Besides, elephants are an endangered species. I was thinking maybe a cow."

Jean-Claude stared down at me for a long space of moments, his face very serious. "Remember, *ma petite*, I can tell if you are lying."

"What's that supposed to mean?"

"You meant the elephant comment."

I frowned up at him. What could I say? "Okay, but just for a minute. I wouldn't really do in an elephant. I'm telling the truth."

"Yes, *ma petite*, I know."

I hadn't really meant the crack about the elephant. Not really. It was just the biggest animal I could think of on short notice. And if I was going to attempt to raise several three-hundred-year-old corpses, I was going to need something big. I didn't think a cow would do. Hell, I didn't think a herd of cows would do it. I just hadn't thought of a good alternative yet.

But no elephants, I promise. Besides, can you imagine trying to slit the throat of an elephant? The logistics of just getting one to hold still while you killed it were mind-boggling. There's a reason why most sacrifices are our size or smaller. Makes it easier to hold them down.

"We can't just leave Jeff with that monster," Larry said. He was standing in the middle of his forest green carpet. Jean-Claude was sitting in the corner of the green patterned couch. He was looking amused, like a cat that had found a very interesting mouse.

"We aren't leaving him," I said. "We just can't go looking for him tonight."

He whirled and pointed a finger at Jean-Claude. "Why, because he says so?"

Jean-Claude's smile widened. Definitely amused.

"Check the time, Larry. It'll be dawn soon. All the vampires will be asnooze in their coffins."

Larry shook his head. The look on his face reminded me of me. Stubborn, not wanting to accept it. "We have to do something, Anita."

"We can't talk to vampires during daylight hours, Larry. That's just the way it is."

"And what happens to Jeff today, while we wait for the sun to go down?" His pale skin had gone almost white. His freckles looked like brown ink spots. His pale blue eyes glittered like angry glass. I'd never seen Larry so mad. Hell, I'd never seen him angry.

I glanced at Jean-Claude; he just looked at me. I was on my own. Wasn't I always. "Xavier will have to sleep. He won't be able to harm Jeff once the sun rises."

Larry shook his head. "Will we get him back in time?"

I wanted to say "Sure," but I wouldn't lie. "I don't know. I hope so."

His soft, Howdy-Doody face was set in very stubborn lines. I looked at him and understood why so many people underestimate me. He looked so harmless. Hell, he was sort of harmless, but he was armed now, and learning how to be dangerous. And in his face for the first time I saw a grim purpose building. I'd planned on leaving him behind when I went to talk to the Master of Branson. Looking at him now, I wasn't sure he was going to let me do that. He'd had his first vampire hunt tonight. I'd managed to keep him out of the rough stuff until now. But it wasn't going to last. I'd been hoping he'd give up the idea of hunting vampires. Staring into his glittering eyes, I realized I was the one who was fooling myself. In his own way Larry was as stubborn as I was. Frightening thought, that. But for tonight he was safe.

"You couldn't just comfort me? Tell me we'll find him?" Larry asked.

I smiled. "I try not to lie to you, if I can avoid it."

"For once," Larry said, "I'd have liked to have heard the lie."

"Sorry," I said.

He took in a deep breath and let it out slow. His anger was gone just like that. Larry didn't know what it was to hold onto his rage. He didn't brood over things. One of the main differences between us. I never forgave anyone for anything. A character flaw to be sure, but hell, everyone's got to have at least one.

There was a knock on the door. Larry went for the door.

Jean-Claude was suddenly standing by me. I hadn't seen him move. Hadn't heard his leather boots slither over the carpet. Nothing. Magic. My heart was suddenly thudding in my throat.

"Stomp your feet or something when you do that."

"Do what, *ma petite*?"

I glared up at him. "That wasn't a mind trick, was it?"

"No," he said. That one word slithered across my skin like a low creeping breeze.

"Damn you," I said softly and with feeling.

He smiled. "We've been over that, *ma petite*; you are too late."

Larry had closed the door. "There's a guy out in the hall says he's with Jean-Claude."

"A guy or a vampire?" I asked.

Larry frowned. "Not a vampire, but if you mean human I wouldn't go that far."

"You expecting company?" I asked.

"Yes, I am."

"Who?"

He stalked to the door and put a hand on the doorknob. "Someone I believe you've already met." He opened the door with a flourish, stepping to one side to let me have a clear view.

Jason stood in the open door, smiling, relaxed. He was my height exactly, not something you find in a man often. Straight blond hair barely touched the top of his collar; his eyes were the innocent blue of spring skies. The last time I'd seen him he'd been trying to eat me. Werewolves will do that sometimes.

He was dressed in an oversized black sweater that hit him almost at mid-thigh. He'd had to roll the sleeves over his wrists. His pants were leather, laced up the side from waist to mid-calf, where the laces vanished into boots. The lacings were loose enough that there was a pale line of flesh all the way down.

"Hello, Anita."

"Hi, Jason. What are you doing here?"

He had the grace to look embarrassed. "I'm Jean-Claude's new pet."

He said the last word like it was alright. Richard wouldn't have said it that way.

"You didn't tell me you brought company," I said.

"We are going to be calling on the Master of the City. We must make a good show of it."

"So a werewolf, and what . . . me?"

He sighed. "Yes, *ma petite*, whether you bear my marks or not, most consider you my human servant." He raised a hand. "Please, Anita, I know you are not my human servant in the technical sense. But you have helped me defend my territory. You have killed to protect me. That is the best definition of what a human servant does."

"So, what? I have to pretend to be your human servant on this visit?"

"Something like that," he said.

"Forget it."

"Anita, I need a show of strength here. Branson was part of Nikolaos's territory. I gave it up because the population density could support another group. But it was still my land, and now it's not. Some view that as weakness rather than practicality."

"So without any marks at all you've finally got me to play servant for you. You manipulative son of a bitch."

"You asked me down here, *ma petite*." A thread of warmth cut through his words. He stalked towards me. "I am doing you a favor, do not forget that."

"I don't think you'll let me forget," I said.

He made a harsh sound, as if he had no words for his anger. "Why do I put up with you? You insult me at every turn. There are many who would give their souls for what I offer you."

He stood in front of me, eyes like dark sapphires, skin white as marble. His skin glowed like there was a light inside him. He looked like some kind of live sculpture made of light, jewels, and stone.

He was impressive and scary, but I'd seen it before. "Cut the vampire powers shit, Jean-Claude. It's almost dawn; don't you have a coffin to crawl into somewhere?"

He laughed, but it wasn't pleasant, it was bitter like the touch of steel wool. Something to irritate rather than entice. "Our luggage has not arrived, has it, my wolf?"

"No, master," Jason said.

"Your coffin hasn't arrived?" I asked.

"Either I have chosen a very lax skycab, or . . ." He let the words trail off, face bland and pleasant.

"Or what?" Larry asked.

"*Ma petite.*"

"You think the local master took your coffin," I said.

"A punishment for entering her territory without observing all the social niceties." He looked at me when he said it.

"I suppose that's my fault," I said.

He gave that infuriating shrug. "I could have said no, *ma petite.*"

"Stop being so civilized about it."

"Would you be happier if I was angry?" His voice was very mild when he said it.

"Maybe," I said. It would have made me feel less guilty, but I didn't say that out loud.

"Go to the airport and find our luggage if you can, Jason. Bring it back to Anita's room."

"Wait a minute. You are not moving into my room."

"It is nearly dawn, *ma petite.* I have no choice. Tomorrow we will find other accommodations."

"You planned this."

He gave a short, bitter laugh. "Even my deviousness knows some bounds, *ma petite.* I would not willingly be without my coffin this close to dawn."

"What are you going to do without your coffin?" Larry asked. He looked anxious.

Jean-Claude smiled. "Do not fear, Lawrence, all I need is darkness, or rather lack of sunlight. The coffin itself is not absolutely necessary, simply more secure."

"I've never known a vampire that didn't sleep in a coffin," I said.

"If I am underground in a secure place, I forego my coffin. Though truthfully, once daylight finds me I am insensible and could sleep on a bed of nails and not know it."

I wasn't sure I believed him. He worked harder than most at passing for human.

"You will see the truth of my words soon enough, *ma petite*."

"That's what I'm afraid of," I said.

"You can sleep on the couch if you prefer, but I am telling you truly that once full daylight arrives I will be harmless, helpless if you like. I would be unable to molest you even if I wanted to."

"And what other fairy tales am I supposed to believe? I've seen you move around after dawn, hidden from light, but you worked just fine."

"After eight hours or so of sleep, if it is still daylight I can move around, true, but I doubt you will stay abed for eight hours. You have clients or something, a murder investigation, some business that will take you out and about."

"If I leave you alone, who'll see that some maid doesn't come in, pull the curtains back and French fry you?"

The smile widened. "Concern over my well-being. I am touched."

I looked at him. He looked pleasant, amused, but it was a mask. His expression when he didn't want you to know what he was thinking, but didn't want you to know that he didn't want you to know. "What are you up to?"

"For once, *ma petite*, nothing."

"Yeah, right."

"If I find the coffin, I'll need to rent a truck," Jason said.

"You can use our Jeep," Larry said.

I glared at him. "No, he can't."

"Think of it as expediency, *ma petite*. If Jason must rent a truck, then I may have to spend another day in your bed. I know you do not want that." There was amusement in his voice, and an undercurrent of something else. It might have been bitterness.

"I'll drive," Larry said.

"No, you won't," I said.

"It's almost dawn, Anita. I'll be alright."

I shook my head. "No."

"You can't treat me like a kid brother forever. I can drive the Jeep."

"I promise not to eat him," Jason said.

Larry held out his hand for the keys. "You have to trust me sometime."

I just looked at him.

"I promise to shoot anything, human or monster, that threatens me while I'm gone." He made the Boy Scout sign, three fingers to heaven. "You can bail me out of jail and explain that I was just following orders."

I sighed. "Alright, dammit." I gave him the keys.

He grinned at me. "Thanks."

I shook my head. "Just hurry back, okay?"

"Anything you say."

"Just get out of here, and be careful."

Larry left with Jason trailing behind. I stared at the door after it closed, wondering if I should have gone with them. Knowing that Larry would have gotten mad, but mad was better than dead. Hell, it was a simple errand; go to the airport and pick up a coffin. What could go wrong with less than an hour of darkness left? Shit.

"You cannot protect him, Anita."

"I can try."

Jean-Claude gave that infuriating shrug that meant anything you wanted it to mean, and nothing at all. "Shall we retire to your room, *ma petite*?"

I opened my mouth to tell him he could bunk with Larry, but didn't say it. I didn't really believe he'd munch on Larry, but I was sure he wouldn't munch on me. "Sure," I said.

He looked a little surprised, as if he'd expected an argument. But I was all out of argument tonight. He could have the bed. I'd take the couch. What could be more innocent? Biker Nuns from Hell, but besides that.

19

I COULD FEEL dawn pressing against the windows like a cool hand when we got back to my room. It was very near. Jean-Claude smiled at me. "The first time I manage to share a hotel room with you, and there is no time." He gave an elaborate sigh. "Things never work as I plan with you, *ma petite*."

"Maybe that's a hint," I said.

"Perhaps." He glanced at the closed drapes. "I must go, *ma petite*. Until darkness." He shut the bedroom door a little hurriedly. I could feel the coming light pressing around the building. I'd noticed over the years of hunting vamps that I'd become aware of dawn, and sunset. There had been times when I'd struggled from disaster to disaster just to stay alive until that soft growing pressure of light could sweep the sky and save my cookies. For the first time I wondered what it would be like to see it as a danger instead of a blessing.

After he'd closed the door I realized my suitcase was in the bedroom. Damn. I hesitated, and finally knocked. No answer. I opened the door just a crack, then farther. He wasn't in there. Water ran in the bathroom. A line of light showed under the door. What did vampires do in bathrooms? Better not to know.

I grabbed my suitcase from the floor and carried it out before the bathroom door could open. I did not want to see him again. I did not want to see what happened to him when the sun rose.

When the sun had risen enough to pulse against the closed drapes like pale lemon liquid, I changed into a t-shirt and

jeans. I had a robe with me, but if I was going to greet both
Larry and Jason I wanted to be wearing some pants.

I called down for extra blankets and a pillow. No one
bitched that it was a quarter past dawn, and a strange time to
need bedclothes. They just brought the stuff. True class. The
maid didn't even glance at the closed bedroom door.

I spread the blanket on the couch and stared at it. It was a
pretty couch but didn't look terribly comfortable. Oh, well,
virtue had its punishments. Of course, maybe it wasn't
virtue that kept me out of the bedroom. If it had been
Richard curled up in the next room, then only moral forti-
tude would have kept me out. With Jean-Claude . . . I had
never seen him after dawn when he was dead to the world. I
wasn't sure I wanted to see. I knew I didn't want to cuddle
up next to him while the warmth left his body.

There was a knock on the door. I hesitated. It was probably
Larry, but then again . . . I went to the door with the Brown-
ing naked in my hand. Beau had had a shotgun last night.
Paranoia, or caution; hard to tell the difference sometimes.

I stood to one side of the door and said, "Yes."

"Anita, it's us."

I hit the safety and put the barrel of the Browning down
the front of my jeans. It was too big a gun to wear in an inner
pants holster, but for temporary holding, that worked.

I opened the door.

Larry leaned against the doorjamb, looking rumpled and
tired. He had a McDonald's sack in one hand, and four cups
shoved into one of those Styrofoam holders. Two of the cups
held coffee, the other two sodas.

Jason had a large leather suitcase under each arm, a battered, much smaller suitcase in his right hand, and a second
McDonald's bag in his left. He didn't look the least bit tired.
A morning person, even after no sleep at all. It was disgust-
ing. His eyes flicked to the gun shoved in my waistband. He
noticed, but he didn't comment. Point for him.

Larry never even blinked at the gun.

"Food?" I asked.

"I didn't eat much last night. Besides, Jason was hungry,
too," Larry said. He came inside, putting the drinks and food

on the wet bar. None of us drank; good to use the bar for something.

Jason walked through the door sideways with the suitcases and food, but there was no effort to it. He wasn't straining one little bit to carry it all.

"Showoff," I said.

He sat the luggage on the floor. "This isn't even close to showing off," he said.

I locked the door behind them. "I suppose you can bring the coffin up single-handedly."

"No, but not because it's heavy. It's just too long. The balance isn't right."

Great. Super werewolf. Though for all I knew, all lycanthropes could lift that much weight. Maybe Richard could lift coffins with one arm. It was not a comforting thought.

Jason started laying food out on the bar. Larry had already climbed onto one of the bar stools. He was pouring sugar into one of the coffees.

"Did you just leave the coffin in the lobby?" I asked. I had to lay the Browning on the bar to sit down. I was just too short-waisted to have it down my pants.

Larry sat the unopened coffee in front of me. "It's missing."

I stared at him. "You found the suitcases but not the coffin?"

"Yep," Jason said, as he finished dividing the food into three piles. He'd pushed some of it in front of both of us, but the lion's share was in front of him.

"How can you eat this early in the morning?"

"I'm always hungry," he said. He looked at me sort of expectantly.

I let it slide. It was too easy.

"Come on, I fed you that one," he said.

"You don't seem particularly worried," I said.

He shrugged, and slid onto a bar stool. "What do you want me to say? I've seen some weird shit since I became a werewolf. If I got hysterical every time something went wrong, every time someone I knew died, I'd be in the loony bin by now."

"I thought fights for dominance in the pack, except for pack leader, weren't to the death," I said.

"People forget," he said.

"I'll have to talk to Richard when I get back in town. He hasn't been mentioning any of this."

"Nothing to mention," Jason said. "Just business as usual."

Great. "Did anybody see who took the coffin?"

Larry answered, his voice sluggish even with the caffeine and sugar. There's only so much you can do on no sleep at all. "No one saw anybody take it. In fact, the only guy left from the night shift said, 'I just turned away for a second, and it wasn't there. Just the luggage standing there by itself.'"

"Shit," I said.

"Why take the coffin?" he asked. He drank most of his coffee. His Egg McMuffin sat untouched in front of him. They'd put hotcakes in front of me with a little tub of syrup beside it.

"Your breakfast is getting cold," Jason said.

He was enjoying himself too much. I frowned at him, but I opened my coffee. I didn't want the food. "I think the master is flexing a little muscle. What do you think, Jason?" I kept my voice casual.

He smiled at me around a mouthful of food, swallowed, and said, "I think whatever Jean-Claude wants me to think."

Maybe my voice had been too casual. I should really give up on subtlety; I just wasn't good enough at it. "Did he tell you not to talk to me?"

"No, just to be careful what I said."

"He says jump, and you say how high; is that it?"

"That's it." He ate a bite of scrambled egg, his face peaceful.

"Doesn't that bother you?"

"I don't make the rules, Anita. I'm not an alpha anything."

"And it doesn't bother you?" I asked.

He shrugged. "Sometimes, but there's nothing I can do about it. Why fight it?"

"I don't understand that at all," Larry said.

"Me either."

"You don't have to understand it," he said. He couldn't have been more than twenty, but the look in his eyes wasn't young.

It was the look of someone who'd seen a lot, done a lot, and not all of it nice. It was the look I was dreading to see on Larry's face someday. They were nearly the same age; what had people been doing to Jason to give him such jaded eyes?

"What do we do now?" Larry asked.

"You're the vampire experts. I'm just Jean-Claude's pet."

He said it like it didn't bother him. It would have bothered me. I shook my head. "I'm going to call the cops, then get some sleep."

"What are you going to tell them?" Jason asked.

"I'm going to tell them about Xavier."

"Did Jean-Claude say you could tell the cops?"

I looked at him. "I didn't ask for permission."

"Jean-Claude wouldn't like you bringing in the police."

I just stared at him.

He blinked at me. "Don't do it just because I said that, please."

"He knows you pretty well for someone who's only met you twice," Larry said.

"Three times," I said. "Two out of three times, he's tried to eat me."

Larry's eyes widened a little. "You're kidding."

"She just looks so tasty," Jason said.

"I've had about enough of you," I said.

"What's wrong? Jean-Claude and Richard both tease you."

"I'm dating both of them," I said. "I'm not dating you."

"Maybe you've got a thing for monsters. I can be just as scary as the next guy."

I stared at him. "No," I said, "you can't. That's why you're not alpha. That's why you're Jean-Claude's pet, because you aren't scary enough."

Something flowed through his pale blue eyes. Something angry and dangerous. Sitting there with his forkful of scrambled eggs, and a Coke in one hand, he was suddenly different. It was hard to put into words, but it raised the hair on the back of my neck.

"Ease down, wolf-boy," I said. My voice was soft, careful. I was sitting less than a foot away from him. At this distance he could jump me easy. The Browning was an inch away from my right hand, but I knew better. I might grab the gun, but I'd never get it pointed in time. I'd seen him move before, and I wasn't quick enough. Lack of sleep was making me trusting, or stupid. Same thing.

A low, trickling growl rumbled out of him. My pulse beat a little faster.

Larry's gun was suddenly pointing past my nose at the werewolf's face. "Don't," Larry said. His voice was low and even, and very damn serious.

I eased back off the bar stool, bringing the Browning with me. Didn't really want Larry's gun to go off right next to my face.

I pointed my gun at Jason's chest, one-handed, almost casual. "Don't ever threaten me again."

Jason stared at me. His beast lurked just behind his eyes like a wave rushing towards the shore.

"You start going furry, and I won't wait to find out if you're bluffing," I said.

Larry had one knee on the bar stool, gun still pointed nice and steady. I hoped he didn't fall off the bar stool and accidentally shoot Jason. If he shot him, I wanted it to be on purpose.

Jason's shoulders relaxed. His hands unclenched, leaving the fork and the drink on the bar. He closed his eyes and sat very still for nearly a full minute. Larry and I waited, guns still pointed. Larry's eyes flicked to me. I shook my head.

Jason opened his eyes and let out a deep, sighing breath. He looked normal again, that tension drained away. He grinned. "I had to try."

I took another step back, putting my back to the wall. Out of reach, I lowered the gun. Larry hesitated, but followed my lead.

"So you tried; now what?"

He shrugged. "You're dominant to me."

"Just like that," I said.

"Would you be happier if I made you fight me?"

I shook my head.

"But I backed her up," Larry said. "She didn't do it alone."

"Doesn't matter. You're loyal to her, would risk your life for her. There's more to being dominant than just muscle, or guns."

Larry looked puzzled. "What do you mean, dominant? I feel like I'm missing part of the conversation."

"Why are you working so damn hard at not being human, Jason?" I asked.

He smiled and went back to his breakfast.

"Answer me, Jason."

He finished off his eggs and said, "No."

"What's going on?" Larry said.

"Mind games," I said.

Larry made an exasperated noise. "Someone explain to me why we had to pull a gun on someone who's supposed to be on our side."

"Jean-Claude keeps telling me Richard isn't any more human than he is. Jason's little display helps emphasize that. Doesn't it, wolf-boy?"

Jason ate the rest of his food like we weren't there.

"Answer me," I said.

He turned on the bar stool, putting his elbows behind him. "I have too many masters now, Anita. I don't need another one."

"And I've got too many monsters messing with me right now. Don't add yourself to the list, Jason."

"Is it a short list?" he asked.

"Gets shorter all the time," I said.

He smiled and slid off the bar stool. "Is anybody tired but me?"

Larry and I stared at him. The werewolf didn't look tired—more than I could say for us mere humans.

Jason wasn't going to answer my questions, and they weren't important enough to shoot him over. Stalemate.

"Fine; where are you sleeping?" I asked.

"If you trust me not to eat him, in Larry's room."

"No way," I said.

"You want me here, with you?"

"I told him he could stay in my room on the ride over," Larry said.

"That was before he pulled the werewolf crap," I said.

Larry shrugged. "You've got the Master of the City tucked into your bed. I think I can handle one werewolf."

I didn't think so. But I didn't want to discuss it in front of the werewolf. "No, Larry."

He was instantly angry. "What do I have to do to prove myself to you?"

"Stay alive," I said.

"What's that supposed to mean?"

"You're not a shooter, Larry."

"I was willing to shoot him." Larry pointed to the smiling werewolf.

"I know."

"Because I'm not trigger-happy, you don't trust me to handle myself?"

I sighed. "Larry, please. If Jason turned furry in the middle of the day and killed you, I couldn't live with myself."

"And if he kills you?" Larry said.

"He won't."

"Why not?" Larry asked.

"Because Jean-Claude would kill him. If he hurt you, I'd kill him, but I don't know if Jean-Claude would avenge you. Jason's more frightened of Jean-Claude than he is of me. Aren't you, Jason?"

Jason had sat down on the end of the couch on my blanket. "Oh, yes."

"I don't know why," Larry said. "You're the one who kills for Jean-Claude. He never seems to kill anyone on his own."

"Larry, who would you be more afraid of, Jean-Claude or me?"

"You wouldn't hurt me," he said.

"If you had to face one of us, which would you prefer?"

Larry looked at me for a long time. The anger drained away, replaced by something tired and old in his eyes. "Him."

"For God's sake, why?" I asked.

"I've seen you kill a lot of people, Anita. A lot more than

Jean-Claude. He might try to frighten me to death, but you'd just kill me."

My mouth was open, just a little. "If you really believe that I'm more dangerous than Jean-Claude, then you haven't been paying attention."

"I didn't say you were more dangerous. I said you'd kill me quicker."

"That's why I'm not as afraid of Anita as I am of Jean-Claude," Jason said.

Larry looked at him. "What do you mean?"

"All she'll do is kill me, quick, neat. Jean-Claude wouldn't kill me quick, or easy. He'd make sure it hurt."

The two men stared at each other. Each one's logic was sound as far as it went. I was with Jason. "If you really believe what you're saying, Larry, then you haven't seen enough vampires."

"How am I ever going to see enough vampires if you keep me at arm's length, Anita?"

Had I really kept him out of it that much? Had I overprotected him? Let him see my ruthlessness but not Jean-Claude's?

"And I'm going to the master's tomorrow night. You are not leaving me behind anymore."

"You're right," I said. The answer seemed to surprise both of them.

"If you really believe that I'd kill someone quicker than Jean-Claude would, I have overprotected you. You have to understand how dangerous they are, Larry. How deadly, or someday I won't be around and you'll get killed."

I took a deep breath and let it out slowly. My stomach was tight with fear. Fear that Larry would get killed because I'd kept him out of it. It was something I hadn't anticipated.

"Come on, Jason," Larry said.

Jason stood up.

"No. Tomorrow you can be ass-deep in vampires with me watching. Until you understand how dangerous the monsters are, I don't want you alone with them."

His eyes were angry and hurt. I'd undercut his confidence, his self-esteem. But . . . what else could I do?

Larry turned abruptly on his heel and left. He didn't argue. He didn't say good-bye. He slammed the door behind him, and I fought an urge to follow him. What could I say? I leaned my forehead against the door, and whispered, "Damn."

"Do I get the couch?" Jason asked.

I turned and leaned against the door. I still had the Browning in my hand, though I wasn't sure why anymore. I was getting tired, sloppy. "No, I get the couch."

"Where do you want me, then?"

"I don't care; just not near me."

He ran his hands down the edge of the blanket, running the cloth between his fingers. "If you're really sleeping out here, I'd just as soon have the bed."

"It's taken," I said.

"How big is the bed?"

"King-size, but what difference does it make?"

"Jean-Claude won't mind if I share with him. He'd prefer it was you, but . . . " He shrugged.

I looked at him, at his tranquil, pleasant face. "Is this the first time you've shared a bed with Jean-Claude?"

"No," he said.

It must have shown on my face, because he lowered the high neck of the sweater enough for me to see two fang marks. I pushed away from the wall and walked closer. Close enough to see that the bite was almost healed.

"Sometimes he likes a snack when he first wakes up," Jason said.

"Jesus," I said.

Jason let go of the collar, and it slid over the bite like it wasn't there. The same way you'd hide a hickey. Jason sat there looking harmless. He was exactly my height, and had the face of a knowledgeable angel.

"Richard didn't let Jean-Claude snack on him," I said.

"No," he said.

"No. That's all you have to say."

"What do you want me to say, Anita?"

I thought about that for a second. "I want you to be out-raged. Angry."

"Why?"

I shook my head. "Go to bed, Jason. You're making me tired."

He went into the bedroom without another word. I didn't peek to see if he changed into a wolf and curled up on the carpet, or if he crawled into bed beside the corpse. None of my business, or at least nothing I wanted to see.

20

I PUT THE Browning under the pillow with the safety on. At home with the gun in the special holster I'd added to the headboard of the bed, the safety would have been off. But I'd look pretty silly if I accidentally shot myself during the night—day—trying to protect myself from werewolves.

The Firestar I put under the couch cushion, safety on. Normally it would have been in my luggage, but I was feeling just a little insecure.

The knives were in the luggage. Things weren't quite dangerous enough to wear the wrist sheaths to bed. Besides, they weren't very comfortable, not to sleep in, anyway.

I had just settled down for a long day's sleep when I realized I hadn't called Special Agent Bradford. Damn. I threw the blanket back and padded to the telephone in nothing but a t-shirt and undies. Yes, the Browning came with me. Doesn't do you a damn bit of good to have a weapon if it isn't with you.

I dialed the number and got no answer. Fancy that. Didn't everyone work twenty-four hours a day? I had his beeper number. Could the news about Xavier wait? Would even having the name help them? Agent Bradford had made it very clear that I was persona non grata. First, Freemont had blackballed me; second, the Quinlans were threatening to sue everybody unless I was kept away from the case. I'd done such a bang-up job protecting their family, they didn't want a repeat. They seemed to think I'd get their son killed. Fancy that.

I had Bradford's beeper number. He'd given strict orders that if I found out anything I was to tell him, and only him. Made me not want to tell him a bloody thing. But who was I to say the FBI didn't have a vampire file somewhere? Maybe the name would mean something to them. Maybe it would help them find Jeff. Besides, Jean-Claude hadn't told me not to give Xavier's name to the cops. I used the beeper number. I left my phone number. Now I could either go back to bed, and let his return call wake me, or I could sit in the chair for a few minutes and wait. I waited.

The phone rang in under five minutes. I like a man who returns his pages promptly. I said "Hello," in case it wasn't him. It was.

"Special Agent Bradford. This number was on my beeper." His voice was rough with sleep.

"This is Anita Blake."

A moment of silence, then, "Do you know what time it is?"

"I haven't been to bed yet, so yeah, I know what time it is."

Another silence. "What do you want, Ms. Blake?"

I took a deep breath and let it out slow. Getting mad would not be helpful. "I have a possible name for the vampire that's been slaughtering kids."

"What's the name?"

"Xavier."

"Last name?"

"Vampires don't have last names, as a general rule."

"Thank you for the name, Ms. Blake. How did you get it?"

I thought about that for a few seconds. I couldn't think of a really good answer. "It sort of fell into my lap."

"Why don't I believe that, Ms. Blake? I thought I'd made myself clear this evening. You are not to involve yourself in this case, in any way."

"Look, I didn't have to call, but I want Jeff Quinlan back

alive. I thought the FBI might be able to use the name of the vampire who took him."

"I want to know how you got the name," he said.

"An informant."

"I'd like to talk to this informant," he said.

"No," I said.

"Are you withholding information from a federal investigation, Ms. Blake?"

"No, Agent Bradford, I am going out of my way to share information."

He was quiet again. "Alright, Ms. Blake, you're right. Thank you for the name. We'll run it in the computers."

"This vampire has a history of harming preadolescent boys. He's a pedophile."

"Good lord, a vampire pedophile." He finally sounded genuinely interested in what I was saying. "And he has the Quinlan boy."

"Yeah," I said.

"I would really like to talk to this source of yours," he said.

"He's a little shy around the police."

"I could insist, Ms. Blake. We've got reports that a private jet flew in last night, and a coffin got unloaded. It's registered to a J. C. Corporation. They seem to own a lot of vampire-related, St. Louis-based businesses. Do you know anything about that, Ms. Blake?"

Lying to the FBI seemed like a bad idea, but I wasn't sure what they'd do with the truth. The Feds were investigating vampire crime, and suddenly a new vamp shows up in town. The least they would do was question him. The worst . . . well, there was the vampire in Mississippi that had been accidentally transferred to a cell with a window. The sun rose, and . . . French fried vampire. An ACLU lawyer had sued the cops' asses, and won, but that didn't bring the vamp back. Admittedly the dead vamp was one of the newly dead. Jean-Claude would have escaped fairly easily, but just escaping from the law by using vampire powers would get a warrant for his arrest. Sort of like what was happening to Magnus.

Besides, a vampire had killed a cop last night. The police might not be terribly careful with any vampire right now. The police are only human, after all.

"You still there, Blake?"

"I'm here."

"You didn't answer my question."

"Where was the coffin delivered?" I asked.

"It wasn't. It just disappeared."

"So what do you want from me?"

"There was some luggage that went with it. The luggage was picked up a little while ago by two young men. The description of one of them sounds a lot like Larry Kirkland."

"Is that so?"

"That's so."

We both sat on our ends of the phone waiting for someone to say something. "I could send some agents down to your hotel room."

"There are no coffins in my hotel room, Agent Bradford."

"You sure of that, Blake?"

"My hand to God."

"Do you know who runs this J. C. Corporation?"

"No." It was the truth. Until Bradford told me about it, I'd never heard of the J. C. Corporation. It would only have been an educated guess if I'd said Jean-Claude owned it. Okay, I was fooling myself, but so what?

"Do you know where the coffin was delivered?" he asked.

"Nope."

"Would you tell me if you knew?"

"If it would help find Jeff Quinlan, you bet."

"Alright, Blake, but no more helping. Stay the fuck out of this case. When we find the vampires we'll call you in, and you can do your job. You're a vampire hunter, not a cop. Try to remember that."

"Fine," I said.

"Good. Now I'm going back to sleep. I suggest you do the same. We'll find the vampires today, Blake. And let's just say I don't believe everything Freemont said. We'll call you in for the kill."

"Thanks."

"Good night, Blake."

"Good night, Bradford."

We hung up. I sat there for a minute, just letting it all sink in. If they found Jean-Claude in my room, what would they do? I'd seen the cops pop a comatose vampire in a body bag, transport it to the station house, and wait for nightfall to question it. I'd thought it was a bad idea because the vamp would wake up pissed. It did. I ended up killing it. I've always felt bad about that particular kill. It was an out-of-state job. The local cops invited me in to advise them. Once we found the vamp, they stopped listening to my advice. Reminded me of now. That vampire had also just been brought in for questioning.

I was suddenly tired. It was like the entire night just hit me in one grinding wave. Sleep dragged at me. I had to go to sleep. I couldn't help Jeff Quinlan, or anybody else, until I'd had a few hours of sleep. Besides, maybe the Feds would find him. Stranger things had happened.

I left a wake-up call with the desk for noon, and cuddled under the blanket. The Browning was lumpy under the pillow. At least I couldn't feel the Firestar under the couch cushion. I half wished I'd packed Sigmund, my stuffed toy penguin, but somehow having Jean-Claude or Jason find me sleeping with a stuffed toy bothered me almost as much as them trying to eat me. What price machismo?

21

SOMEONE WAS BANGING on the door. I opened my eyes to a room filled with soft, indirect sunlight. The curtains in here weren't nearly as thick as the ones in the bedroom. Which was why I was out here and Jean-Claude was in there.

I struggled into the jeans I'd left on the floor and yelled, "I'm coming."

The banging stopped, then it sounded like they kicked the door. Was this a federal wake-up call? I went to the door with the Browning in my hand. Somehow I didn't think the FBI would be so rude. I stood to the side of the door and asked, "Who is it?"

"It's Dorcas Bouvier." She kicked the door again. "Open this damn door."

I peeked through the little peephole. It was Dorcas Bouvier, or her evil twin. She didn't have a weapon in sight. I was probably safe. I put the Browning under the t-shirt in the waistband of my pants. The t-shirt was a large and fell to mid-thigh. It hid the gun and then some.

I unlocked the door and stood to one side. Dorcas shoved the door open, leaving it swinging open behind her. I closed and locked the door, leaning against it watching her.

Dorcas stalked through the room like some sort of exotic cat. Her waist-length, chestnut hair swung like a curtain as she moved. She finally turned and glared at me with those sea-green eyes that were a mirror of her brother's. The pupil had spiraled downward to a pinpoint, leaving the irises floating and making her look almost blind.

"Where is he?"

"Where's who?" I asked.

She glared at me and went for the bedroom door. I couldn't get there in time to stop her, and I wasn't willing to shoot her yet.

When I came up behind her she was two steps into the bedroom, back rigid, staring at the bed. It was worth staring at.

Jean-Claude lay on his back with the wine-dark sheets pulled up to mid-chest. One shoulder and a pale, pale arm were stretched across the dark sheets. In the semidarkness his hair blended with the pillow to leave his face white and nearly ethereal.

Jason lay on his stomach. The only things under the sheet were one leg and, barely, his buttocks. If he was wearing clothes, I couldn't tell. He raised up on his elbows and turned to us. His yellow hair had fallen into his face, and he blinked like he'd been deeply asleep. He smiled when he saw Dorcas Bouvier.

"It isn't Magnus," she said.

"No," I said, "it isn't. You want to talk outside?"

"Don't go on my account," Jason said. He rolled onto one elbow. The silken sheet slid across his hips as he moved.

Dorcas Bouvier turned on her heel and marched out of the room. I closed the door to the sound of Jason's laughter.

Dorcas looked shaken, embarrassed even. Good to see. I was embarrassed, too, but didn't know what to do about it. Trying to explain your way out of situations like this never works. People are always willing to believe the worst of you. So I didn't try. I just stood there looking at her. She wouldn't meet my eyes.

After a nice uncomfortable silence that caused heat to wash up her face, she said, "I don't know what to say. I thought my brother was in there. I . . . " She met my eyes finally. She was already regaining her composure, her surety of purpose. You could watch it solidify in her eyes. She was here for more than rousting her brother out of my bed.

"Why in the world would you think Magnus was here?"

"May I sit down?"

I motioned her to a seat. She sat in one of the chairs, spine very straight, perfect posture. My stepmother, Judith, would have been proud. I leaned on the arm of the couch because I couldn't sit down with the Browning down my pants. I wasn't sure how she'd take me being armed, so I didn't want to show the gun. Some people freeze up around firearms. Go figure.

"I know Magnus was with you last night."

"With me?" I said.

"I don't mean . . . " Heat crept up her face again. "I don't mean *with* you. I mean I know you saw him last night."

"He tell you that?"

She shook her head, making her hair slide like fur over her shoulders. It was eerily reminiscent of Magnus. "I saw you together."

I studied her face, trying to read past the embarrassment. "You weren't there last night."

"Where?" she asked.

I frowned at her. "How did you see us?"

"You admit you saw him last night, then," she said. Her eagerness came back in a rush.

"What I want to know is how you saw us together."

She took a deep breath. "That's my business."

"Magnus said his sister was better at visions than he was. Is that true?"

"What didn't he tell you?" she asked. She was angry again. Her emotions seemed to collide, spinning too fast over her face and voice.

"He didn't tell me why he ran from the police."

She looked down at her hands, folded in her lap. "I don't know why he ran. It doesn't make any sense." She looked back up at me. "I know he didn't kill those children."

"I agree," I said.

Surprise showed on her face. "I thought you told the police he did it."

I shook my head. "No, I told them he could have done it. I never said he did it."

"But . . . The detective was so sure. She said you'd told her."

I cursed softly under my breath. "Detective Freemont?"

"Yes."

"Don't believe everything she tells you, especially about me. She doesn't seem to like me very much."

"If you didn't tell them, then why are they so sure Magnus did these horrible things? He would have no reason to kill these people."

I shrugged. "Magnus isn't wanted for the killings anymore. Didn't anybody tell you that?"

She shook her head. "No. You mean he can come back home?"

I sighed. "It's not that simple. Magnus used glamor on the police to escape. That's a felony all on its own. The cops will kill him on sight, Ms. Bouvier. They don't mess around where magic is concerned. Can't say I blame them."

"I saw the two of you talking outside under the sky."

"I did see him last night."

"Did you tell the police?"

"No."

She stared at me. "Why not?"

"Magnus is probably guilty of something, or he wouldn't have run, but he deserves better treatment than he's getting."

"Yes," she said, "he does."

"What made you think he'd be in my bed?"

She looked down at her lap again. "Magnus can be very persuasive. I can't remember the last time a woman told him no. I apologize for assuming that about you." She stopped, glanced towards the bedroom, then back to me. She blushed again.

I was not going to explain how I ended up with two males in my bed. Surely it was obvious from the blanket and pillow that I'd slept out here. Surely.

"What do you want from me, Ms. Bouvier?"

"I want to find Magnus before he gets himself killed. I thought you could help me. How could you have betrayed Magnus to the police? Surely you know what it's like to be different."

I wanted to ask if it showed, if she could see "Necromancer" written across my forehead, but I didn't. If the answer was yes, I wasn't sure I wanted to know.

"If he hadn't run away, they would have simply questioned him. They didn't have enough to arrest him. Do you have any idea why he ran?"

She shook her head. "I've tried to think of something, anything, but it doesn't make any sense to me, Ms. Blake. My brother is a little amoral, but he's not a bad man."

I wasn't sure you could be a little amoral, but I let it slide. "If he turns himself in to me, I'll walk him into the police station. But short of that, I don't know what I can do."

"I've been everywhere I can think of, but he's just not there. I even checked the mound."

"The mound?" I asked.

She stared up at me. "He didn't tell you about the creature?"

I thought about lying to see if I could get information, but the look in her eyes told me I'd blown it. "He didn't mention any creature."

"Of course; if he had told you, the police would be down there with dynamite. Dynamite won't kill it, but it would screw our magical wards six ways to Sunday."

"What creature?" I asked.

"Is there anything Magnus told you that you didn't tell the police?" Dorcas asked.

I thought about that for a second. "No."

"He was right not to tell you."

"Maybe, but I'm trying to help him now."

"Do you have a guilty conscience?" she asked.

"Maybe," I said.

She looked at me. Her pupils had resurfaced, and she looked almost normal. Almost. "How can I trust you?"

"You probably can't. But I do want to help Magnus. Please talk to me, Ms. Bouvier."

"I have to have your word that you won't tell the police. I am serious, Ms. Blake. If the police interfere, they could loose the thing and people would die."

I debated but couldn't see any reason the police would need to know. "Okay, I give you my word."

"I may not have Magnus's way with glamor, but an oath to one of the fey is a serious matter, Ms. Blake. Lying to us tends to go badly."

"Is that a threat?"

"Think of it as a warning." The air moved between us like heat rising off a road. Her eyes swirled like miniature whirlpools.

Maybe I should have shown her my gun. "Don't threaten me, Dorcas. I'm not in the mood."

The magic seemed to seep away like water running into a crack in the rocks. You knew it was still there, below the surface. But for someone who had been threatened by werewolves and vampires, she paled in comparison. Magnus seemed to have most of the talent in the family. On the scale of scariness, Magnus was up there.

"Just so we understand each other, Ms. Blake. If you tell

the police and they let loose the creature, the deaths will be on your head."

"Alright, I'm impressed; now tell me about it."

"Did Magnus tell you about our ancestor, Llyn Bouvier?"

"Yeah, he was the first European in this area. He married into the local tribe. Converted them to Christianity. He was also fey."

She nodded. "He brought another fey with him."

"A wife?" I asked.

"No, he had captured one of the less intelligent fairies. He imprisoned it in a magically constructed box. It escaped and slaughtered nearly the entire tribe we're descended from. He finally managed to contain it with the help of an Indian shaman, or priest, but he never regained control over it. The best he could do was to imprison it."

"What kind of fairie did he bring over?"

"Bloody Bones isn't just the name of our bar," she said. "It's short for Rawhead and Bloody Bones."

My eyes widened. "But that's a nursery boggle; why would your ancestor want to capture one? They don't have any treasure, or wishes, to give out. Or am I wrong on that?"

"No, you're quite correct. Bloody Bones has no riches or gentle magic to grant wishes."

"Then why capture it?"

"Most children born of human and fairie blood don't have a lot of magic."

"That's what the legends say," I said, "but Magnus proves that wrong."

"Llyn Bouvier made a sort of pact for himself and his descendants. We would all have fey power, at a price."

She was dragging this out, and I was tired. "Just tell me, Ms. Bouvier. The suspense is getting irritating."

"Has it ever occurred to you that this might be embarrassing for me to admit?" she asked.

"No; if that's the case, I apologize."

"My ancestor imprisoned Bloody Bones so he could make a potion of its blood. But the potion had to be remade periodically, retaken, or his magic deserted him."

I stared at her. "How did the other fey take this little idea?"

"He was forced to flee Europe, or they would have killed him. It is forbidden among us to use each other like that."

"I can see why."

"His barbaric act gave us glamor. Power. But it was still purchased by blood, Ms. Blake. After Rawhead and Bloody Bones was imprisoned, my ancestor gave up his potion. He finally saw it as evil. Though his power faded, his children had the power of fairie in their blood. So here we are," she said.

"So you've got Rawhead and Bloody Bones hidden in some magic box somewhere?" I asked.

She smiled, and it made her face seem suddenly young and lovely. I had no way of judging her age. I couldn't see a line on her face. "When the magic failed the first time, Rawhead and Bloody Bones grew to its full size. It is bigger than a person, almost as big as a giant. It is imprisoned in a mound of earth and magic."

"You say it nearly wiped out an entire tribe way back when?"

She nodded.

I sighed. "I have to see where it's imprisoned."

"You promised . . ."

"I promised not to tell the police, but you've just told me there's a giant-sized creature capable of mass destruction imprisoned near here. I have to see that it's secure, that it's not going to break out and start slaughtering people."

"I assure you, Ms. Blake, our family has managed for centuries. We know what we're doing."

"If I can't tell the cops, I have to see for myself."

She stood up, trying to use her height to intimidate me. She wasn't even close. "And you'll bring the police, right? Do you think I'm that stupid?"

"I won't bring the cops, Ms. Bouvier, but I have to see it. If it does break out and I didn't warn the cops, then it would be my fault that no one was prepared."

"You can't prepare for Bloody Bones," she said. "It is immortal, Ms. Blake, truly immortal. It cannot die. You could cut off its head and it would not die. The police can do nothing but make things worse."

She had a point. "I still need to see for myself."

"You are a stubborn woman."

"Yeah, I can be a real pain in the ass, Ms. Bouvier. Let's not dance, just take me to see the prison, and if it's secure I'll leave you to it."

"If it's not secure enough for you?" she asked.

"We contact a witch and see what she recommends."

She frowned. "You wouldn't just go to the police?"

"If my home was robbed, I'd call the cops. If I need help with magic, I call somebody who can do magic."

"You are a strange woman, Ms. Blake. I don't understand you."

"There's a lot of that going around," I said. "Do I get to see where Rawhead and Bloody Bones is buried, or not?"

"Alright, I'll show you."

"When?"

"Without Magnus we're shorthanded at the bar, so not today. Come to the bar around three tomorrow. I'll take you from there."

"I have a coworker that I'd like to bring along," I said.

"One of those in the bedroom?"

"No."

"Why do you want to bring him?"

"Because I'm training him, and when will he ever get to see fey magic again?"

She seemed to think about it for a minute, then nodded. "Alright, you may bring one other person with you, but no more."

"Trust me, Ms. Bouvier, one is plenty."

"My friends call me Dorrie," she said. She held out her hand.

"I'm Anita." I shook her hand. She had a nice, firm grip for a woman. Sexist but true. Most women don't seem to know how to give a good handshake.

She held my hand longer than she had to. When she took her hand back, I remembered Magnus's clairvoyance. Dorrie turned those wide, eerie eyes to me. She held her hand to her chest like it hurt. "I see blood, and pain, and death. It follows you like a cloud, Anita Blake."

I watched horror seep into her eyes. Horror at the brief glimpse she'd had of me, my life, my past. I didn't look away. If you're not ashamed, you don't need to look away. Sometimes I would prefer a different line of work, but it's what I do, who I am.

The look faded from her eyes, and she blinked. "I won't underestimate you, Anita."

Dorrie looked normal again, or as normal as she had when she first came in, which wasn't very. Now for the first time I looked at her and wondered if I was seeing what was really there. Was she using glamor on me now, to appear normal? To appear less powerful than she was?

"I'll return the favor, Dorrie."

She flashed me that lovely smile again that made her seem young and vulnerable. Illusion, maybe? "Until tomorrow, then."

"Until tomorrow," I said.

She left, and I locked the door behind her. So Magnus's family were the guardians of a monster. Had that had something to do with why he ran? Dorrie didn't think it was a reason. She should know. But there was a feeling in the room of power gently moving on the air currents. A faint whiff of magic traced the air like perfume, and I hadn't known it until just before she left. Maybe Dorrie was just as good with glamor as Magnus, just more subtle. Could I really trust Dorrie Bouvier? Hmmm.

Why had I asked if Larry could go along? Because I knew it would please him. It might even make up for treating him so badly in front of Jason. But standing there, sensing Dorrie Bouvier's power hanging like a ghost in the air, I wasn't sure it was a good idea. Oh, hell, I knew it wasn't, but I was going, and Larry would go, too. He had a right to go. He even had a right to endanger himself. I couldn't keep him safe forever. He was going to have to learn to take care of himself. I hated it, but I knew it was true.

I wasn't ready to cut the apron strings, but I was going to have to lengthen them a bit. I was going to give Larry the proverbial rope. Here was hoping he didn't hang himself.

22

I SLEPT MOST of the day, and when I woke up, I discovered that nobody would let me come play. Everybody was running scared of the Quinlan lawsuit, and I was persona non grata everywhere I tried to go. Agent Bradford sent me packing, and threatened to have me jailed for obstruction of justice and hampering a police investigation. That's gratitude for you. The day was a bust. The only person who would talk to me was Dolph. All he could tell me was that they hadn't found any sign of Jeff Quinlan, or his sister's body. No one had seen Magnus either. The cops were questioning people, searching for clues, while I twiddled my thumbs, but neither of us came up with anything useful.

I watched darkness fall with a sense of relief; at least now we could get on with it. Larry had gone back to his room. I hadn't asked. Maybe he wanted to give me some privacy with Jean-Claude. Scary thought, that. At least Larry was talking to me. Nice that someone was.

I opened the drapes and watched the glass turn black. I'd brushed my teeth in Larry's room today. My own bathroom was suddenly off limits. I just didn't want to see Jason naked, and I certainly didn't want to see Jean-Claude. So, I borrowed part of Larry's room for the day.

I heard the bedroom door open but didn't turn. Somehow I knew who it was. "Hello, Jean-Claude."

"Good evening, *ma petite.*"

I turned. The room was almost in darkness. The only light was from the streetlights outside, and the glowing sign of the hotel. Jean-Claude stepped into that faint glow. His shirt had a collar so high it covered his neck completely. Mother-of-pearl buttons fastened the high collar so that his face was framed by the white, white fabric. There must have been a dozen buttons gleaming down the pleated front of his shirt. A black waist-high jacket that was almost too black to be seen hid the sleeves. Only the shirt's cuffs showed; wide and stiff, covering half his hand. He raised a hand to the light and the cuffs bent back underneath to give his hand a full range of motion. His tight black pants were stuffed into another pair of black boots. They came all the way up his legs, so that he was encased in leather; black on black buckled straps held the soft leather in place.

"Do you like it?" he asked.

"Yeah, it's spiffy."

"Spiffy?" There was an edge of humor to that one word.

"You just can't take a compliment," I said.

"My apologies, *ma petite*. It was a compliment. Thank you."

"Don't mention it. Can we go get your coffin now?"

He stepped out of the light, so I couldn't see his face. "You make it sound so simple, *ma petite.*"

"Isn't it?"

Silence then, so thick the room felt empty. I almost called out to him; instead I walked to the bar and turned on the track lighting above it. The soft white light glowed in the dark like a lighted cave. I felt better with the light. But with my back to where I thought he should be, I couldn't sense Jean-Claude. The room felt empty. I turned and there he was, sitting in one of the chairs. Even when I looked at him, there was no sense of movement. It was like a stop-action picture waiting for the switch to go on.

"I wish you wouldn't do that," I said.

He turned his head and looked at me. His eyes were solid darkness. The faint light picked up blue sparks from them. "Do what, *ma petite?*"

I shook my head. "Nothing. What's so complicated about tonight? I feel like you're not telling me everything."

He stood in one smooth motion almost like he skipped part of the process, and was just suddenly on his feet. "It is within our rules for Serephina to challenge me tonight."

"Is that the master's name, Serephina?"

He nodded.

"You don't think I'll tell the cops?"

"I will take you to her, *ma petite*. There will be no time for your impatience to make you foolish."

If I'd been stuck here all day with nothing much to do, but

had had the name, would I have tried to find her on my own? Yeah, I would have.

"Fine, let's go."

He paced the room, smiling and shaking his head. *"Ma petite,* do you understand what it will mean if she challenges me tonight?"

"It means we fight them, right?"

He stopped pacing and came into the light. He slid onto one of the bar stools. "There is no fear in you, none."

I shrugged. "Being afraid doesn't help. Being prepared does. Are you afraid of her?" I looked at him, trying to read that lovely mask.

"I do not fear her power. I believe us to be near equals in that, but let us say I am wary. All things being equal, I am still in her territory with only one of my wolves, my human servant, and Monsieur Lawrence. It is not the show of force I would have chosen to confront her after two centuries."

"Why didn't you bring more people? More werewolves, anyway."

"If I had had time to negotiate more of an entourage I would have, but with the rush . . ." He looked at me. "There was no time to bargain."

"Are you in danger?"

He laughed, and it wasn't entirely pleasant. "Am I in danger, she asks. When the council asked me to divide my lands, they promised to set in place someone of power equal to or less than mine. But they did not expect me to enter her territory so unprepared."

"Who are they? What council?"

He cocked his head to one side. "Have you really come among us so long and not heard of our council?"

"Just tell me," I said.

"We have a council, *ma petite.* It has existed for a very long time. It is not so much a governing body as a court, or police, perhaps. Before your courts made us citizens with rights, we had very few rules, and only one law. Thou shalt not draw attention to yourself. That's the law that Tepes forgot."

"Tepes," I said, "Vlad Tepes? You mean Dracula?"

Jean-Claude just looked at me. His face was perfectly blank, no expression. He looked like a particularly lovely statue, if a statue's eyes could glitter like sapphires. I could not read that expressionless face, nor was I meant to.

"I don't believe you."

"About the council, our law, or Tepes?"

"The last part."

"Oh, I assure you we did kill him."

"You make it sound like you were around when it happened. He died in, what, the 1300s?"

"Was it 1476, or was it 1477?" He made a great show of trying to remember.

"You are not that old," I said.

"Are you sure, *ma petite?*" He turned that unnervingly blank face to me; even his eyes went dead and empty. It was like looking at a well-constructed doll.

"Yeah, I'm sure."

He smiled, and sighed. Life, for lack of a better word, rushed back into his face, his body. It was like watching Pinocchio spring to life.

"Shit."

"So nice to know that I can still unnerve you from time to time, *ma petite.*"

I let that go. He knew exactly the effect he had on me. "If Serephina is your equal, then you take care of her, and I'll shoot everybody else."

"You know it will not be that simple."

"It never is."

He stared at me, smiling.

"Do you really think she'll challenge you?"

"No, but I wanted you to know that she could."

"Is there anything else I need to know?"

He smiled wide enough to flash a little bit of fang. He looked wonderful in the light. His skin was pale but not too pale. I touched his hand. "You're warm."

He glanced up at me. "Yes, *ma petite;* what of it?"

"You've slept an entire day. You should be cold to the touch until after you've fed."

He just looked at me with his drowning eyes.

"Shit," I said. I went for the bedroom. He didn't try to stop me. He didn't even try. It made me nervous. I was half-running by the time I hit the door.

All I could see was a pale outline on the bed. I turned on the switch by the door. The overhead light was glaring, and merciless.

Jason lay on his stomach, blond hair bright against the dark pillows. He was naked except for a pair of vibrant blue bikini briefs. I walked towards the bed, staring at his back, willing him to breathe. When I was almost at the bed I could see him breathe. Something tight in my chest loosened.

I had to kneel on the edge of the bed to reach him. I touched his shoulder. He moved under my hand. I rolled him onto his side, and he didn't try to help. He was totally passive. He stared up at me with heavy-lidded eyes. Two thin crimson lines flowed down his neck. Not a lot of blood, at least not spilled onto the sheets. I had no way of knowing how much he'd lost. How much Jean-Claude had taken.

Jason smiled at me. It was a slow, lazy smile.

"Are you alright?"

His hand slid around my waist as he rolled onto his back.

"I'll take that as a yes." I tried to back off the bed, but his arm was firm around me, holding me. He pulled me down to his chest. I pulled the Browning on the way down. He could have stopped me, but he didn't try.

I shoved the gun against his ribs. My other hand was pressed to his bare chest, trying to hold my face a little above his. He raised his face towards mine.

"I will pull this trigger."

He stopped with his face inches from mine. "I'll heal."

"Is one kiss worth getting a hole punched in your side?"

"I don't know," he said. "Everyone else seems to think so." His face moved towards me slowly, giving me plenty of time to decide.

"Jason, release her, now." Jean-Claude's voice filled the room with whispers like tiny echoes.

Jason let me go. I slid off the bed, the gun still naked in my hand.

"I need my wolf tonight, Anita. Try not to shoot him until after we've seen Serephina."

"Tell him to stop hitting on me," I said.

"Oh, I shall, *ma petite,* I shall."

Jason lay back against the pillows. He raised one knee, his hands lying across his stomach. He looked relaxed, lascivious, but his eyes stayed on Jean-Claude.

"You are almost the perfect pet, Jason, but do not provoke me."

"You never said she was off limits."

"I am saying it now," Jean-Claude said.

Jason sat up on the bed. "I'll be a perfect gentleman from now on."

"Yes," Jean-Claude said, "you will." He stood there in the doorway, still lovely to look at, but dangerous. You could feel it building in the room, whispering through his voice. "Leave us for a moment, *ma petite.*"

"We don't have time for this," I said.

Jean-Claude looked at me. His eyes were still a solid midnight blue; the whites had drowned. "Are you protecting him?"

"I don't want him hurt because he got out of hand with me."

"Yet you would have shot him."

I shrugged. "I never said I was consistent, just serious."

Jean-Claude laughed. The abrupt change in mood made both Jason and me jump. His laughter was rich and thick as chocolate, as if you could pull it from the air and eat it.

I glanced at Jason. He was watching Jean-Claude the way a well-trained dog will watch its master, looking for clues to what its master wanted next.

"Get dressed, my wolf, and you, *ma petite,* you must change as well."

I was wearing black jeans and a royal blue polo shirt. "What's wrong with what I'm wearing?"

"We must make a show of it tonight, *ma petite.* I would not ask if it were not important."

"I am not wearing a dress tonight."

He smiled. "Of course not. Just something a little more

stylish. If your young friend does not have anything suitable, I believe he and Jason are about the same size. I'm sure
we could find something."

"You'll have to talk to Larry about that."

Jean-Claude looked at me for a heartbeat. "As you like,
ma petite. Now, if you would leave Jason to dress? I will
stay in here until you have chosen more appropriate attire."

I wanted to argue. I didn't like being told what to wear, or
what not to wear. But I let it go. I'd been around vampires
enough to know they admired the spectacular, or the dangerous. If Jean-Claude said we needed to make a show of it,
maybe he was right. It wouldn't kill me to dress up a little.
It might get us all killed to refuse. I just didn't know the
rules in this situation. I suspected that there weren't any.

I hadn't packed with meeting a master vampire in mind,
so my choices were sort of limited. I settled for a crimson
blouse with a high collar and a spill of lace down the front.
There was even a little frilly cuff at each sleeve. It looked
like a cross between a Victorian blouse and a business shirt.
It would have looked very conservative if it hadn't been
screaming vermillion red. I hated the idea of wearing it, because I knew Jean-Claude would like it. Except for the
color, it looked like something he might wear.

I put the all-purpose black jacket over the blouse. With
both guns, both knives, and a cross around my neck inside
the blouse, I was ready to go.

"*Ma petite,* may we come out?"

"Sure."

He opened the door and took it all in with a glance. "You
look splendid, *ma petite*. I appreciate the makeup."

"I look pale in crimson without it."

"Of course; do you have other shoes?"

"I only have the Nikes and high heels. I move better in the
Nikes."

"The blouse was more than I hoped for; keep your jogging shoes. They are black, at least."

Jason walked out of the bedroom. He was wearing black
leather pants tight enough that I knew he wasn't wearing the
underwear anymore. The top was vaguely oriental with one

of those upright collars and one black button, the kind where a loop of thread comes over the button. The sleeves were full, and the collar was a soft shining blue that matched his eyes to perfection. It was embroidered in yellow so dark it looked gold, and darker blue thread. The sleeves, collar, and edge of the fabric were embroidered black on black. When Jason moved, the shirt gaped just a little, enough to show glimpses of his bare stomach. Soft black boots rode up over his knees.

"Well, I know who your tailor is," I said. I was going to be woefully underdressed.

"If you would fetch Monsieur Kirkland. When he is dressed, we can go."

"Larry may not want to change."

"Then he won't. I will not force him."

I looked at him, not quite sure I believed him, but I got Larry. He agreed to go into the bedroom and see what other goodies were in the luggage, but he didn't promise to change.

He came out still wearing dark blue jeans and Nikes. He had changed his t-shirt for a silk dress shirt that was a rich, vibrant blue. It made his eyes look even bluer than usual. A black leather jacket that was just a touch big in the shoulders hid his shoulder holster. I guess it was an improvement over the oversized flannel he'd been wearing. The collar of the shirt was spread over the jacket so that it framed his face.

"You should see some of the stuff in there," Larry said. He shook his head as if he still couldn't believe it. "I wouldn't even know how to get into some of it."

"You look nice," I said.

"Thanks."

"Can we go now?" I asked.

"Yes, *ma petite,* we can go. It will be interesting to meet Serephina after two centuries."

"I know this is old home week for you, but let's remember why we're here," I said. "Xavier has Jeff Quinlan. Who knows what he's doing to him? I want him home safe. It's the second night. We have to get to him tonight, or find someone else who can."

Jean-Claude nodded. "Then let us be off, *ma petite.* Serephina awaits us." He sounded almost eager, like he was looking forward to seeing her. For the first time I wondered if he and Serephina had been lovers. I knew Jean-Claude wasn't a virgin. I mean, get real. But knowing he had lovers and meeting one were two different things. I realized with a start that it would bother me.

He smiled at me, almost as if he knew what I was thinking. The whites of his eyes had reappeared. It made him look almost human. Almost.

23

JEAN-CLAUDE WALKED across the parking lot in his boots and jacket, looking like someone should be snapping his picture, or asking for an autograph. The rest of us followed like his entourage. Which was what we were, whether I liked it or not. But to save Jeff Quinlan I could do a little bootlicking. Even I will toady a little if it's in a good enough cause.

"You driving, or do I get directions to Serephina's house now?" I asked.

"I will tell you where to turn when it is time."

"You think I'm going to run to the cops with directions to her house?"

"No," he said. That was all he said.

I frowned at him, but we all got in the Jeep. Guess who got the front seat.

We drove out onto the main road, the Strip. The traffic was bumper-to-bumper. If traffic is bad, it can take a couple of hours to drive the four miles that make up the Strip. Jean-Claude had me turn on a small road. It looked like a driveway leading to yet another theater, but it turned out to be an access road. If you knew your way around the smaller roads, you could avoid most of the congestion.

You would never know from the main drag of Branson but just out of sight, over the next hill, is the real Ozarks. Mountains, forests, houses where people who don't make their living off tourists live. On the Strip it was all neon and artifice; within fifteen minutes we were surrounded by trees, on a road that wound through the Ozark Mountains.

Darkness closed around the Jeep. The only light was a spill of stars pressed against the blackness, and the tunnel of my own headlights.

"You seem to be looking forward to seeing Serephina, even with the coffin missing," I said.

Jean-Claude turned in his seat as far as the seat belt would allow. I'd insisted everybody wear seat belts, which amused the vampire. I guess it was silly to have a dead man buckle up, but hey, I was driving.

"I believe Serephina still thinks of me as the very young vampire she knew centuries ago. If she thought me a worthy opponent, she would have confronted me or my minions directly. She would not have simply stolen the coffin. She is overconfident."

"Speaking as one of your minions," Larry called from the back seat, "are you sure you're not the one who's overconfident?"

Jean-Claude glanced back at him. "Serephina was centuries old when I met her. The limit of a vampire's powers is well established after two or three centuries. I know her limits, Lawrence."

"Stop calling me Lawrence. The name's Larry."

Jean-Claude sighed. "You have trained him well."

"He came that way," I said.

"Pity."

Jean-Claude made this sound like a hostile family reunion, or is that an oxymoron? I hoped he was right, but one thing I've learned about vampires—they keep pulling new rabbits out of their cloaks. Big, fanged, carnivorous bunnies that'll eat your eyeballs if you're not paying attention.

"What's wolf-boy in the back going to do?"

"I do what I'm told," Jason said.

"Great," I said.

We drove in silence. Jean-Claude rarely sweats small talk, and I wasn't in the mood. We could all have a nice little visit, but out there somewhere Jeff Quinlan had woken to a second night in Xavier's tender care. Sort of ruined the mood for me.

"The turn is just ahead to your right, *ma petite.*" Jean-Claude's voice made me jump. I had sunk into the silence and the dark hush of the highway.

I slowed the Jeep. Didn't want to miss the turnoff. A gravel road, like a hundred other gravel roads, spilled off the main road. There was nothing to make it stand out. Nothing special.

The road was narrow with trees growing so close on either side it was like driving through a tunnel. The naked branches of trees curved around us like interlocking pieces of a wall. The headlights slid over the nearly naked trees, bouncing when the Jeep eased over a pothole. Naked wooden fingers tapped the roof of the Jeep. It was damn near claustrophobic.

"Geez," Larry said. He had pressed his face to the dark glass as far as the seat belt would allow. "If I didn't know there was a house down this road, I'd turn back."

"That is the idea," Jean-Claude said. "Many of the older ones value their privacy above almost all else."

The headlights picked up a hole that stretched across the entire road. It looked like a gully wash where rainwater had eaten the road away over decades.

Larry leaned over the back of the seat, straining against his seatbelt. "Where'd the road go?"

"The Jeep can make it," I said.

"Are you sure?" he asked.

"Pretty sure," I said.

Jean-Claude had settled back into the seat. He seemed totally relaxed, almost detached, like he was listening to music I couldn't hear, thinking thoughts that I never would understand.

Jason leaned forward, putting a hand on the back of my seat. "Why wouldn't she pave the road? She's been here almost a year."

I glanced back at Jason. It was interesting to find out that he knew more about Jean-Claude's business than I did.

"This is her moat," Jean-Claude said. "Her barrier against the curious. Many find our new status hard to accept and still closet themselves away."

The wheels slid over the edge. It was like driving into a crater. Miraculously, the Jeep crawled out the other side. If we'd been in a car, we'd have had to walk.

The road climbed upward for about a hundred yards, and suddenly on the right-hand side of the road was an opening. It didn't look big enough to drive the Jeep through, not without scratching the paint job to hell. The only thing that really told you it was a clearing was the moonlight pulsing against the darkness of the trees. That much moonlight meant something was there. Grass had grown over a scattering of gravel that might once have been a driveway.

"Is this it?" I asked, just to make sure.

"I believe so," Jean-Claude said.

I eased the Jeep into the trees and listened to branches slap the sides. I hoped Stirling's company owned the Jeep, and wasn't just renting. We crawled free of the trees with a last metallic *scritch.* An acre of open land spread out before us, silver-edged with moonlight. The grass was butchered short like someone had bush-hogged it last fall, and left it naked and unfinished through the winter. There was a neglected orchard behind the house. The land rose in a gentle slope up towards the foot of a mountain. Just beyond the bush-hogged grass was forest, thick and untouched.

A house sat in the middle of the gentle rise. The house was silver-grey in the moonlight. Curling flecks of paint clung here and there, like the last sad remnants of an accident victim's clothes. A large stone porch graced the front of the house, hid the door and windows in a well of shadow.

"Turn off the lights, *ma petite.*"

I looked at that dark porch and didn't want to hit the lights. The moonlight should have penetrated those shadows.

"*Ma petite,* the lights."

I hit the lights. The moonlight bathed us like a wash of

visible air. The porch stayed dark and still like a cup of ink. Jean-Claude undid his seat belt and slid out. The boys followed suit. I got out last.

Large, flat stones were set in the grass, forming a curving sidewalk to the foot of the steps that led up to the porch. There was a large picture window to one side of the peeling door. The glass was jagged. Someone had nailed plywood behind the broken window to keep out the night air.

The smaller window on the other side of the door was intact, but so covered in grime it was blind. The shadows were viscous, and seemed thick enough to touch. It reminded me of the darkness that the sword had come swinging out of. But it wasn't as thick. I could see through this darkness. There was nothing there but shadows.

"What's with the shadows?" I asked.

"A parlor trick," Jean-Claude said. "Nothing more." He glided up the steps without a backward glance. If he was worried, it didn't show. Jason glided up the steps behind him. Larry and I just walked up. It was the best we could do. The shadows were colder than they should have been, and Larry shivered beside me. But there was no sense of power to it. As Jean-Claude had said, a parlor trick.

The screen door had been ripped off its hinges. It lay on the porch, torn and forgotten. Even with the protection the porch offered, the inner door was warped and peeling, exposed to too much weather. Leaves lay in piles at the edges of the porch railings where the wind had blown them.

"Are you sure this is it?" Larry asked.

"I am sure," Jean-Claude said.

I understood the question. If it hadn't been for the shadows, I'd have said the house was deserted. "The shadows would discourage any casual passersby," I said.

"Well, I wouldn't come trick-or-treating," Larry said.

Jean-Claude glanced back at us. "Our hostess comes."

The pitted, broken door opened. I had expected a haunted-house *screech* of rusty hinges but the door opened smoothly. A woman stood in the doorway. The room behind her was dark, her body silhouetted against the room and the night. But even in the dark I knew two things: she was a vampire, and she wasn't old enough to be Serephina.

The vampire was only a few inches taller than I was. She raised an unlit candle in one hand. The hairs on the back of my neck stood at attention, as a trickle of power slid through the room. The candle flared to life, leaving stars dancing across my night vision.

The vampire had brown hair, cut so short the hair on either side of her head had been shaved. Silver stud earrings glittered up the curve of her ears. One long earring dangled from her left ear. It was a green enamel leaf on a silver chain. She wore a red leather dress that was so tight on top, it was how I'd known in the dark she was a girl. The skirt of the dress fell to her ankles, loose once you got past the hips. A leather formal; wow.

She grinned at us, flashing fangs. "I'm Ivy." Her voice had an edge of laughter to it, but unlike Jean-Claude's laugh that always felt vaguely sexual, or fattening, hers felt sharp as broken glass, meant to hurt, terrify, not titillate.

"Enter our dwelling, and be welcome." The words sounded too formal, like a rehearsed speech, or an incantation that you don't understand.

"Thank you, Ivy, for your most generous invitation," Jean-Claude said. He was suddenly holding her hand. I hadn't seen him reach for it. I hadn't seen him move. It was like I'd missed a frame of the film. From the look on Ivy's face, so had she. She looked pissed.

Jean-Claude raised her hand, very slowly, towards his lips. He never took his eyes off her. The way you bow to someone on the dojo mat, because if you look away they may spill you on your ass.

A line of wax trickled down the side of the white candle. She was holding it in her bare fist, no candle holder. Jean-Claude slowly raised her hand and laid his lips on the back of it. The wax dripped faster than it should have.

He released her hand in time for her to save herself, but she stood there and let the line of hot wax drip down her skin. Only the faintest flicker in her eyes showed that it hurt.

She left the wax to harden on her hand. A faint redness spread from the line of wax. She ignored it.

No more wax dripped from the candle. Usually when a candle runs that soon, it keeps running. The wax made a little golden pool at the top of the candle, like a drop of water under tension.

I glanced from one vampire to the other and shook my head. Does the term "childish" mean anything to you? I didn't say it out loud, though. For all I knew, this was some kind of ancient vampire ritual. Though I doubted it pretty damn sincerely.

"Aren't your companions going to come inside?" Ivy stepped aside with a swish of leather skirts, holding the candle high, lighting our way.

Jean-Claude stepped to the other side of the door so we would have to walk between the two vampires to get into the house. I trusted Jean-Claude not to munch on me. I even trusted him to keep Ivy from munching on me. But I didn't like how much fun Jean-Claude was having. Made me nervous. I've never been around vampires that were having a good time when it didn't get ugly.

Jason walked between them, into the house. Larry glanced at me. I shrugged and walked inside. He followed at my heels, trusting that if I went inside it would be okay. It probably would be. Probably.

24

THE DOOR CLOSED behind us, and I don't think anybody closed it, not with hands anyway. Safe or not, these little displays of power were getting on my nerves.

The air in the room was utterly still, stale. It smelled musty, dry, with an undertaste of mildew. You knew even with your eyes closed that these rooms had been empty for a very long time. There was an open archway to the left that led into a smaller room. I could see a bed, complete with bedspread and pillows, so covered in dust it looked grey. A vanity sat in one corner with its mirror reflecting the empty room.

There was no furniture left in the living room. The wooden floor was dust-coated. The hem of Ivy's dress trailed in the thick dust as she moved towards a door in the far wall. A thin line of light showed under that door. Golden and thicker than electricity. I was betting on more candles.

The door opened before Ivy reached it. A rich wave of light spilled out, brighter than it should have been because we'd been in the dark so long. A male vamp stood framed in the light. He was short, slender, with a face too young to be handsome, more pretty. He was so newly dead that his skin still held the tan he'd picked up at the beach, or lake, or some other sun-soaked place. He looked frightfully young to be dead. He had to be eighteen, anything younger and it was illegal, but he still looked delicate and half-finished. Jailbait forever.

"I'm Bruce." He seemed vaguely embarrassed. Maybe it was the clothes. He was dressed in a pale grey tux complete with tails, and a charcoal grey strip down the outside leg of the pants. His gloves were white and matched what could be seen of his shirt. His vest was a silky grey. His bow tie and cummerbund were a red that matched Ivy's dress. They looked like they were going to the prom.

Two man-sized candelabra stood on either side of the door, filling the room with moving, golden light. The room beyond was twice the size of the living room, and had probably been the kitchen once upon a time. But unlike the front rooms, there'd been some redecorating.

A Persian carpet was spread across the floor. The colors were so bright it looked like stained glass. Wall hangings covered the two longest walls. On one wall a unicorn fled from a pack of hounds. The other hanging was a battle scene so dimmed with age that parts of the figures had vanished into the cloth. Bright silken drapes covered the far end of the room, hung from the ceiling with heavy cords. A door opened to the left of the drapes.

Ivy sat the candle she'd been holding in an empty sconce on the candelabra. She moved in front of Jean-Claude. She had to tilt her head up to look him in the eyes. "You are beautiful." She ran her fingers along the edge of his jacket. "I thought they'd lied. That nobody could be that beautiful." She fingered the mother-of-pearl buttons, starting at his neck and working down. Jean-Claude moved her hand when she reached the last button before the shirt disappeared into his pants.

Ivy seemed to find that amusing. She stood on tiptoe, leaning her hands and forearms on his chest. Her mouth was tilted towards him, kissable. "Do you fuck as good as you look? They said you did. But you're sooo pretty. Nobody could be that good a lay."

Jean-Claude laid his fingers on either side of her face, cradling her jawline. He smiled at her.

Her red lips curved into a smile. She pressed against him, letting her full weight rest against his body.

Jean-Claude kept his light touch on her face as if she wasn't leaning full out against him.

Her smile began to fade, slipping from her face like the sun sinking below the earth. She slid slowly down to stand flat-footed in front of him. Her face was blank and empty in the cradle of his hands.

Bruce the vampire jerked her back by one arm. Ivy stumbled and would have fallen if he hadn't caught her. She looked around bewildered, as if she expected to be elsewhere.

Jean-Claude wasn't smiling now. "It has been a long time since I was anyone's meat that wanted me. A very long time."

Ivy stood half-collapsed in Bruce's arms. Her face was harsh with fear. She pushed away from Bruce to stand straight and alone. She tugged at the red dress as if to settle it into place. The fear was mostly gone from her face; just a certain tightness remained around the eyes.

"How did you do that?"

"Centuries of practice, little one."

Anger made her eyes dark. "You aren't supposed to be able to capture another vampire with your gaze."

"You aren't?" he asked, his voice lilting with amazement. "Don't you laugh at me."

I had some sympathy for her frustration. Jean-Claude can be such a pain in the ass when he wants to be.

"You were told to lead us somewhere, children; do so."

Ivy stood in front of him, hands balled into fists. Her anger spilled into her eyes, and the brown irises bled onto the whites of her eyes until she looked blind. Her power breathed through the room, creeping along the skin, raising the tiny hairs on my body as if a finger had been run just above them.

My hand started for the Browning. Old habits.

"No, Anita, that is not necessary," Jean-Claude said. "This little one cannot hurt me. She shows her fangs, but unless she wishes to die on this lovely carpet she had best remember who and what I am."

"I am the Master of the City!" His voice thundered through the house, echoing in the room until the air was so thick with echoes that it was like breathing his words.

When the sound died, I was shaking. Ivy had pulled herself together. She still looked angry, but her eyes had bled back to normal.

Bruce had laid a hand on her shoulder, as if he wasn't sure she would listen to reason. She shook off his hand and motioned gracefully towards the open door.

"We are to take you downstairs. Others await you there."

Jean-Claude gave a low theatrical bow, never taking his eyes from her. "After you, my sweet. A lady should always walk before a gentleman, never behind."

She smiled, suddenly pleased with herself again. "Then your human lady can walk beside me."

"I don't think so," I said.

She turned innocent brown eyes to me. "Are you not a lady, then?" She stalked towards me with an exaggerated sway of her hips. "Did you bring us someone who is not a lady, Jean-Claude?"

I heard him sigh. "Anita is a lady. Walk beside her, *ma petite,* but carefully."

"What does it matter what these assholes think of me?"

"If you are not a lady, then you are a whore. You do not want to know what would happen to a human whore within these walls." He seemed tired as he said it, as if he'd been there, done that, and hadn't had a good time.

Ivy smiled at me, giving me a big dose of brown eyes. I met her gaze and smiled.

She frowned. "You are human. You can't meet my gaze, not like that."

"Surprise, surprise," I said.

"Shall we go?" Jean-Claude said.

Ivy frowned again, but she stepped into that open door, and down a step or two, one hand on her dress to keep the hem from tripping her feet. She turned and looked back at me. "Are you coming?"

I asked Jean-Claude, "How careful do I need to be?"

Larry and Jason came to stand beside me.

"Defend yourself if they offer violence first. But do not shed the first blood, or strike the first blow. Defend, but do not attack, *ma petite.* We are playing games tonight, unless you make it more; the stakes are not that high."

I scowled at him. "I don't like this."

He smiled. "I know, but bear with us, *ma petite.* Remember the human you wish to save, and control that wonderful temper of yours."

"Well, human?" Ivy said. She was waiting for me on the steps. She looked like an impatient child, petulant.

"I'm coming," I said. I did not run to catch up with the waiting vampire. I walked at a normal pace, though the weight of her gaze made my skin itch. I stopped at the head of the stairs and peered downward. Cool, damp air pushed against my face. The smell was thick, enclosed, and mildewed. You knew there would be no windows, and somewhere water was eating the walls. A basement. I hated basements.

I took a deep breath of the fetid air and walked down the steps. They were the widest stairs I'd ever seen in a basement. The wood felt new and raw, like they hadn't taken time to stain or sand it. There was enough room for the two of us to share a step. I didn't want to share a step. Maybe she wasn't a threat to Jean-Claude, but I had no illusions about what she could do to me. She was a baby master, not full grown yet, but the power was there bubbling under the surface, crawling along my skin. I stopped a step above her, waiting for her to go down.

Ivy smiled. She could smell my fear. "If we are both ladies, then we should walk together. Come, Anita." She held out a hand to me. "Let us go down together."

I didn't want to be that close to her. If she tried to jump me, there wouldn't be time to do much. I might get a weapon out in time, I might not. It irritated me that I wasn't supposed to show a weapon first. And scared me. One of the things that's kept me alive is shooting first and asking questions later. Doing it the other way around was no way to stay alive.

"Is Jean-Claude's human servant afraid of me?" She stood there framed against the darkness beyond, smiling. The basement was like a great black pit behind her.

But she couldn't sense vampire marks, or she'd have known I wasn't his servant. She wasn't as hot as she thought she was. I hoped.

I ignored the outstretched hand, but walked down those two steps. My shoulder brushed her bare skin, and it felt like worms were crawling down my arm. I kept walking down the steps into the dark beyond, left hand in a death grip on the railing. I heard her high heels clattering down the steps to catch up with me. I could feel her irritation like heat rising from her skin. I heard the menfolk following us, but didn't look behind to check. We were playing chicken tonight. It was one of my best games.

We went down the steps together like horses pulling a carriage, my left hand on the railing, her hands lifting her dress. I kept up a pace that made gliding effortlessly impossible, unless she could levitate. She couldn't.

She grabbed my right arm and whirled me around to face her. I couldn't go for a gun. Because I was wearing wrist sheaths, I couldn't even go for a knife. I stood there nearly face to face with an angry vampire and couldn't reach a weapon. All that could save me was her not killing me. Trusting my life to Ivy's beneficence seemed like a bad bet.

Her anger spilled along my skin. Heat flowed down her body. I could feel her hand, hot, even through the leather jacket. I didn't try to pull away; things that can bench-press Toyotas don't let go. Her touch didn't burn, because it wasn't that kind of heat, but it was hard to convince my body that it wouldn't hurt eventually. Years of warnings, don't touch, it's hot. Heat flared along my body like I was standing next to a fire. If she hadn't been doing it unintentionally, it would have been impressive. Hell, it was still impressive. Give her a few centuries and she'd be scary as hell, as if she wasn't already.

I could still meet her eyes, drowning deep and glowing with their own light. That was going to do me a hell of a lot of good when she ripped my throat out.

"If you hurt her, Ivy, our truce is over." Jean-Claude glided down the steps to stand just above us. "You do not want the truce to be over, Ivy." He ran his fingertip along the edge of her jaw.

I felt the jolt of power jump from him, to her, to me. I gasped, but she let me go. My arm was numb at my side like it'd gone to sleep. I couldn't have held a gun. I wanted to ask what the hell he'd done, but didn't. As long as I got the use of my arm back, we could argue about it later.

Bruce pushed between us, hovering over Ivy like a worried boyfriend. Watching his face, I realized that was accurate. I was betting she'd brought him over.

Ivy pushed him away so hard that he went tumbling backwards down the stairs, lost in the thicker darkness. Everything seemed to be working on her just fine. I could barely feel my fingertips.

Heat rushed over me like a scalding wind, and swept outward into the dark. Torches flared to life in sconces along the walls with a *whoosh* and a shower of sparks. A large kerosene lamp suspended from the ceiling filled with fire.

Its glass chimney exploded in a shower of glass, its flame burning naked on the wick.

"Serephina will make you clean up your mess," Jean-Claude said. He made it sound like she'd spilled her milk.

Ivy walked down the rest of the steps in a hip-swinging glide. "Serephina will not care. Broken glass and flame have so many uses." I didn't like the way she phrased that.

The basement was black. Black walls, black floors, black ceiling. It was like being in a great dark box. Chains hung from the walls, some with what looked like fur on the cuffs. Straps dangled from the ceiling like obscene decorations. There were . . . devices placed throughout the room. I recognized some of them. A rack, an iron maiden, but most of it was like looking at bondage paraphernalia. You were pretty sure what the point was, but not how it worked. There were always more holes than I could figure out what to do with, and nothing ever seemed to come with instructions.

There was a drain in the floor, and a thin trickle of water ran down it. But I was betting that the drain wasn't there just for water.

Larry moved down the steps to stand beside me. "Are those what I think they are?"

"Yeah, they're torture devices." I forced my hand to make a fist, and another one. The feeling was coming back.

"I thought they weren't going to harm us," he said.

"I think it's supposed to scare us."

"It's working," he said.

I didn't like the decor much either, but I could feel my hand. I could have held a gun if I had to.

A door that I hadn't even seen opened to the left. A secret panel. A vampire came through the door. He had to bend nearly double to make it through the door frame. He unfolded, impossibly tall and thin, cadaverous. He had not fed tonight, and was wasting no power on looking pretty. His skin was the color of old parchment and clung to the bones of his face like a thin film barely covering his skull. His eyes were sunken and dull in his head, the dead blue of fish eyes. His sickly hands were long and bony with impossibly long fingers, like white spiders sticking from the sleeves of his black coat.

He stalked into the room with the edges of his black coat sweeping behind him like a cloak. He was dressed entirely in black; only his skin and the short cut white hair on his head betrayed him. As he moved through the black room, it looked like his head and hands were floating on their own.

I shook my head to clear the image. When I looked back, he seemed a touch more normal. "He's using his powers to make himself look frightening," I said.

"Yes, *ma petite,* he is." There was something in his voice that made me turn and look at him. His face was its usual lovely mask—but in his eyes, for just a second, I saw fear.

"What's going on, Jean-Claude?"

"The rules have not changed. Do not draw a weapon. Do not strike the first blow. They cannot harm us unless we break these rules."

"Why are you suddenly scared?"

"That is not Serephina," he said. His voice was very bland when he said it.

"What's that supposed to mean?"

He threw back his head and laughed. The sound reverberated through the room, echoing and outwardly joyous. But I could taste it on the back of my tongue, and it was bitter. "It means, *ma petite,* that I am a fool."

25

JEAN-CLAUDE'S LAUGHTER faded away in bits and pieces, like the sound was clinging to the walls. "Where is Serephina?" he asked.

Ivy and Bruce walked out of the room. I didn't know where they were going, but it had to be better than this. How many torture rooms could a house this size have? Don't answer that.

The tall vampire looked at us with his dead-fish eyes. There was no pull, nothing; it was like looking into the eyes of a corpse.

His voice, when it came, was almost shocking. It was rich and deep, resonant, but not with vampiric powers. It was the voice of an actor, or an opera singer. I watched it come out of the thin, lipless mouth and it still looked like a parlor trick, like the mouth should move out of sync with the words, but they didn't.

"You must pass through me before she will see you."

"You surprise me, Janos." Jean-Claude glided down the steps. I guess we were going down. Pity. "You are more powerful than Serephina. How is it you do her bidding?"

"When you have seen her, you will understand. Now come, all of you, join us. The night is young, and I want to see you all naked and bleeding before dawn."

"Who is this guy?" I asked. I could use my hand again; might as well smart off.

Jean-Claude stopped on the last step. Jason moved up, one step behind him. Larry and I stayed a little behind that. I don't think either of us was too eager to go down.

The vampire turned his dead eyes on me. "I am Janos."

"Dandy, but the rules say you can't bleed us, or anything else. Or did I miss something?"

"You miss very little, *ma petite,*" Jean-Claude said.

"You will not be harmed against your will," Janos said. "You must all consent for any harm to befall you."

"Then we're safe," I said.

He smiled, the skin of his face stretching like paper. I half-expected bone to break through, but it didn't. The smile was nicely hideous.

"We shall see."

Jean-Claude took that last step, and moved farther into the room. Jason followed, and after a moment's hesitation so did I. Larry followed me like a trooper.

"This room is your idea, Janos," Jean-Claude said.

"I do nothing without my master's consent."

"She cannot be your master, Janos. She is not powerful enough."

"Yet, here I am, Jean-Claude. Here I am."

Jean-Claude walked around the dark wood of the rack, trailing a pale hand over it. "Serephina was never much for torture. She was many things, but not sadistic." Jean-Claude came to stand in front of Janos. "I think you are master here and she is your stalking horse. She is known as master so all the challenges come her way. When she dies, you will find another puppet."

"I promise you, Jean-Claude, she is my master. Think of this room as my reward for being a faithful servant." He looked around the room with a proprietary smile, like a storekeeper admiring well-stocked shelves.

"What do you plan for us in this room of yours?"

"But wait a few moments, my impatient boy, and all will be revealed."

It was odd to have someone call Jean-Claude "boy," as if he were a much younger cousin that Janos had watched grow up. Had Janos known him when he was a little vampire? Freshly dead?

A woman's voice: "Where are you taking me? You're hurting me." Ivy and Bruce dragged a young woman through the side door. Literally dragged her. She had let her legs collapse, trying to use them like a dog does when you try to take it to the vet. But she only had two legs and a vampire on each arm. She wasn't having much luck slowing them down.

She had straight blonde hair that barely touched the tops of her shoulders. Her eyes were large and blue, and the makeup she'd started the night with was smeared from crying.

Ivy seemed to be having a good time. Bruce had very wide eyes. He was afraid of Janos. Hard not to be, I guess.

The girl stared wordlessly at Janos for a second, then screamed. Ivy cuffed her absently like you'd swat a barking dog. The girl whimpered and fell silent, staring at the floor, fresh tears trailing down her cheeks.

There was only Janos and the two youngsters in the room with us. I was betting we could take them. Two more vampires came in, but they didn't drag in the next girl. She walked in, eyes glittering with anger, back very straight, hands in fists at her sides. She was short, a little heavy, but not quite fat, as if a good burst of growth would take care of the weight. Her hair was a nondescript brown, glasses framed small brown eyes, freckles dusted her face. The personality that radiated from that face was not nondescript. I liked her instantly.

"Oh, Lisa," she said, "get up." She sounded embarrassed as well as angry.

The blonde girl, Lisa, just cried harder.

The two vamps that were guarding the second girl were not young. They were both tall, around six feet, dressed in black leather, one with her long yellow hair in a braid down her back, the other with black hair falling free around her face. Their bare arms were muscled and firm. They looked like female bodyguards from some bad spy movie.

The power that radiated from the two of them was not a B movie effect. It crept through the room like a current of water, thick and cool. When the line of power poured over my body it took my breath away. The power crawled into my bones and made them ache. Larry gasped behind me.

I glanced at him just to make sure he was gasping for the same reason I was. No new monsters behind us, just the power of the two new vamps.

"What are you guys doing, running a halfway house for all vampires over five hundred years?" I asked.

Everyone turned towards me. The two female vamps smiled, most unpleasantly. They looked at me like I was a piece of candy and they wondered what sort of center I had. Soft and gooey, or hard with a nut in the middle? I'd had men undress me with their eyes, but I'd never had anything trying to picture what I'd look like with my skin off. Yikes.

"Do you have something to add?" Janos asked.

"You can't just drag a couple of underage girls in here and expect us to do nothing."

"On the contrary, Anita, we expect you to do many things."

I didn't like the phrasing of that. "What's that supposed to mean?"

"First, the young women aren't underage, are you, girls?"

The second girl just glared at him. Lisa shook her head, still staring at the floor.

"Tell her your ages," Janos said.

Neither of them answered. Ivy yanked hard enough to make the blonde girl cry out.

"Eighteen. I'm eighteen." She collapsed on the floor in a sobbing heap, and the vampires let go of her so she could do it.

One of the female vamps said, "Your age, now." Her voice was like quiet thunder, a warning of the coming storm.

The second girl's eyes widened behind her glasses. "I'm nineteen." There was fear now peeking out from behind her anger.

"Fine; they're over eighteen, but an unwilling human is still an unwilling human, regardless of age," I said.

"Would you play policeman here, Anita?" Janos asked. He sounded amused.

"I won't just stand here and watch you hurt them."

"You have a high opinion of yourself, Anita. Confident. I like that. Always so much more entertaining to break someone strong. The weaklings fold and cry and snivel, but the brave ones, they almost demand that you hurt them." He stalked towards me, reaching out one white spider-hand. "Do you want me to hurt you?"

I remembered Jean-Claude's warning not to use weapons, but fuck it, I was going for the Browning.

Jean-Claude was just suddenly there, holding Janos's wrist. Janos seemed impressed. Truthfully, so was I. I hadn't seen him move, and apparently neither had Janos. A nifty trick, that.

I let my hand relax away from the gun, though I was pretty sure that drawing it would make me feel better. But the purpose of tonight's exercise was not to make me feel better, it was to stay alive.

"No harm to any of us; that was the promise," Jean-Claude said.

Janos drew his wrist from Jean-Claude's grasp slowly, almost lingeringly, as if he enjoyed it. "Once Serephina's promise is given, she keeps it."

"Then why are the young women here?"

"Those two"—he motioned to Larry and me—"would truly not stand by and watch harm come to strangers?" He sounded surprised, but not unhappy about it.

"Sadly, yes," Jean-Claude said.

"And if they join the fray, you will come in to protect her?" Janos asked.

"If I must."

Janos smiled, and I could hear his skin creak with the strain of holding in his bones. "Splendid."

I saw a tremor run through Jean-Claude's back, as if he had been caught off guard. I was just plain confused.

"The two young women came willingly into our house. They knew what we were, and agreed to help us entertain guests."

I glanced at the second girl. "Is that true?"

One of her vampire guards touched her shoulder, lightly, but it was enough. "We came willingly, but we didn't know . . ." The vampire's hand squeezed. The girl's face crumbled in pain but she made no sound.

"They came of their own free will, and they are of the age of consent," Janos said.

"So what happens now?" I asked.

"Ivy, chain that one over there." He pointed as he said it to some fur-lined manacles to the left of the door. Ivy and Bruce picked up the girl, pulled her to her feet, and led her stumbling to the wall.

"Her back facing the room, please."

I stepped next to Jean-Claude and whispered, though I knew within reason they'd hear, "I don't like this."

"Nor I, *ma petite.*"

"Can we stop it without breaking the truce?"

"Not unless they offer harm to us directly, no."

"What happens if I break the truce?"

"They will try to kill us, most likely."

There were five vampires in the room, three of them older than Jean-Claude. We would die. Dammit.

The blonde girl sobbed and struggled, pulling at her arms as the vampires chained her to the wall. She screamed and pulled so violently that without the fur lining she'd have bloodied her wrists.

A woman stepped into the room from the side door. She was tall, taller than Jean-Claude. Her skin was the color of coffee with two creams. Her dark hair fell in long cornrows to her waist. She was dressed in a black, patent leather body suit. It left very little to the imagination. She strode hard on her heels, a very human walk. But she wasn't human.

"Kissa," Jean-Claude said. "You are still with Serephina." He sounded surprised.

"Not all of us have your luck." Her voice was thick like honey. There was a smell like spices in the air, and I wasn't sure if it was her perfume or illusion.

Her high-boned face was empty of makeup and still she was beautiful—though I wondered what she'd look like if she weren't clouding my mind. Because surely no human could have radiated the raw sexuality that clung to Kissa like a touchable cloud.

"I am sorry you are here, Kissa."

She smiled. "Don't pity me, Jean-Claude. Serephina has promised you to me, before Janos breaks that beautiful body of yours."

Six vampires, four of them older than Jean-Claude. The odds were not going in our favor.

"Chain the other girl there." Janos motioned to a matching set of manacles to the right of the door.

The girl shook her head. "No way." She just refused to go, and she struggled better than the blonde. She threw her body on the ground and used every inch of it, not to fight, just not to go.

Two vampires several centuries old, powerful enough to make my teeth hurt, and they had to pick her up from both ends and carry her to the wall. She'd finally started to scream, one loud, ragged, rage-filled sound after another. The dark-haired vamp pinned her to the wall, and the other one chained her.

"I can't just watch this," Larry said. He was standing very

close to me; maybe he didn't know the vampires would hear his whispers.

It didn't really matter. "Neither can I."

We were going to get ourselves killed; might as well take as many of them with us as we could.

Jean-Claude turned around, as if he could smell us going for our guns. "*Ma petite,* Monsieur Kirkland, do not go for your weapons. They are treading legalities. The women have come to help entertain. They will not kill them."

"You're sure of that?" I asked.

He frowned. "I am sure of nothing anymore, but I believe that they will keep their word. The women are frightened and a little bruised, but they are not harmed."

"This isn't harm?" Larry asked. He looked outraged, and I couldn't blame him.

I answered him. "Vampires have a very unique sense of what's harmful, don't they, Jean-Claude?"

He met my gaze. "I see accusation in your eyes, but remember this, *ma petite,* you asked me to bring you here. So do not blame this particular problem on me."

"Is our entertainment so boring?" Janos asked.

"We were discussing whether to kill you all now, or later," I said, my voice very matter-of-fact.

Janos gave a low chuckle. "Please do break the truce, Anita. I would love to have an excuse to get you on one of my novelties. I think you would take a long time to break. Then again, it is sometimes the braggarts who break first."

"I don't brag, Janos. I tell the truth."

"She believes what she says," Kissa said.

"Yes, she has a disturbing hint of truth to her," Janos said. "Most tasty."

The blonde, Lisa, had stopped struggling against the chains. She sagged in them, nearly incoherent with crying. The other girl, now that she was chained, stood very still, but a fine trembling had started in her arms and hands. She balled her hands into fists, but could not stop the trembling.

"The women came for a little adventure. They are certainly getting their money's worth," Janos said.

The two female vamps opened panels in the black walls.

They each took out a long coil of whip. Neither of the girls could see. I was glad.

I couldn't stand and watch, I couldn't. It would kill something inside me to just stand and watch, even if it meant I died. I'd at least go down fighting, and I'd take some of them with me. Better than nothing. But before we all committed suicide, I'd try to talk. "If you're not trying to goad us into breaking the truce, then what the hell do you want?"

"Want?" Janos said. "Want? Why, many things, Anita."

I was beginning to hate the way he said my name, sort of half-amused, and intimate, like we were friends, or close enemies.

"What do you want, Janos?"

"Shouldn't you be negotiating for your people?" he asked Jean-Claude.

"Anita does well enough on her own," Jean-Claude said.

Janos gave another rictus smile. "Very well. What do we want?"

The vampires went to the girls. They held up the whips so the two girls could see them.

"What is that?" the blonde asked. "What is that?" Her voice was high and bubbly with fear.

"It's a whip," the second girl said. Firm and clipped, her voice did not betray her the way her trembling body did.

The two vampires backed away, just enough for good whipping distance, I guess.

"What the bloody hell do you want?" I asked.

"Are you familiar with the term 'whipping boy'?" Janos asked.

"It was a person used by royalty to be beaten in the place of the royal heir."

"Very good; so few young people have a sense of history."

"What does the history lesson have to do with anything?"

"The girls are whipping boys for your two young men," Janos said.

The two vampires snaked the whips along the floor, and cracked them nearly in unison, but neither whip touched the girls. The second girl screamed, a short, clipped sound, when the whip whistled into the wall next to her. The blonde just sank against the wall, sobbing, "Please, please, please," over and over in a ragged voice.

"Don't hurt them," Larry said. "Please."

"Would you take her place?" Janos asked.

I finally understood where we were heading. "You can't hurt us without our cooperation. You treacherous son of a bitch."

He smiled. "Answer me, lad. Would you take her place?"

Larry nodded.

I grabbed his arm. "No."

"Surely it is his choice," Janos said.

"Let go of my arm, Anita."

I stared at his eyes, searching to see if he understood what he was doing. "You don't know what a whip will do to human flesh. You don't know what you're offering."

"We can remedy that," Janos said.

The vampires ripped the backs of the girls' blouses with a harsh, quick tearing.

The blonde screamed.

"We can't just watch," Larry said.

He was right; whether I liked it or not, he was right.

"I've seen what a whip can do," Jason said suddenly. "Don't hurt them."

I stared at him. "You don't strike me as the self-sacrificing kind."

He shrugged. "We all have our moments."

"Would it make this an easier choice if I swore that if your young man takes the girl's place we will not cripple him?"

"How about kill him?" I said. "You can die of shock from a whipping."

"No killing, no crippling. We simply want our pound of flesh, and a quart of blood."

Something must have shown on our faces, because he laughed. "Figuratively speaking, of course. You will wear scars until you die, but no greater harm."

"This is ridiculous," I said. "We aren't going to do this."

"If we pull our guns, can we take them?" Larry asked.

I looked away from his earnest eyes. He touched my arm. "Anita?"

"We can take some of them with us," I said.

"But we'll still be dead, and once we're dead who'll help the girls?"

I shook my head. "There's got to be a better way."

Larry looked at Jean-Claude. "Will he keep his word? Will they not kill me?"

"Janos's word has always been reliable, or at least it was a couple of centuries ago."

"Can we trust them?" Jason asked.

"No," I said.

"Yes," Jean-Claude said.

I glared at him.

"I know you would rather shoot it out, but you would only succeed in getting us all killed. Or perhaps some of us made into vampires."

Larry touched my shoulders. He made me look at him. "It's alright."

"It's not alright," I said.

"Fine, but it's the best we can do right now."

"Don't do this."

"I don't have a choice," he said. "Besides, I'm a big boy, remember? I can take care of myself."

I hugged him. I didn't know what else to do.

"I'll be alright," he whispered.

I just nodded. I didn't trust my voice, and I try never to lie to my friends. He would not be alright. I knew it. He knew it. We all knew it.

Jason walked away from us towards the vampires. "Oh, no, my good shapeshifter, we don't want you chained to a wall."

"But you said . . ."

"I said you could save the girls, but not like that. Let the human take his lashes. All you must agree to is satisfying the desires of my two helpers, Bettina and Pallas."

Jason stared at the two vampires. They'd turned to face us. I suddenly tried to see them from the viewpoint of a twenty-year-old male. They were chesty, slim waisted; if

Pallas's face was a little too witchy-looking for my taste, and Bettina's eyes too small, that was just me. Neither of them was pretty, or even beautiful; they were handsome in the way that some tall, leggy women are. Handsome in a good way, if they had been human.

Jason frowned. "It seems I'm getting the better deal here."

"Would it make any difference if I said you had to do it here in this room, on the floor, in front of everyone?" Janos asked.

Jason thought about that for a minute. "If I say no, does the girl get whipped?"

Janos nodded.

"Then I agree," he said, but his voice was soft and uncertain. Being lascivious in private was one thing; doing it in public was different.

"Come then, shapeshifter, let the show begin." Janos made a sweeping motion with his white hands.

Jason glanced back at Jean-Claude like a kid on the first day of school wondering if the bullies were really going to hurt him. Jean-Claude gave no comfort. His face was as still and unreadable as a painting. He gave a small nod that could have meant anything from "It will be alright" to "Just do it."

I watched Jason's shoulders rise with a deep breath, and heard him blow it out like a runner before a race. Why is it that most things you might willingly do under other circumstances become distasteful when you have no choice?

"Have you ever been with one of us?" Janos asked.

Jason shook his head.

Janos put a long-fingered hand on Jason's shoulder. Jason didn't seem to enjoy that. Couldn't blame him. "There are many pleasures that await you, my young shapeshifter. Things that no human or wereanimal can give to you. Sensations that only the dead can offer."

The two female vampires had stepped to the far end of the room in a clear space on the black floor. The whips lay coiled at the feet of the two girls, as if they were a reminder of what would happen if anyone chickened out.

If Jason wanted to fuck a few vampires, that was fine with

me. Besides, he wasn't mine to protect. But the sex wasn't going to last forever. I couldn't let them have Larry. I couldn't stand by and watch him be tortured. I just couldn't. But if I pulled down the room, then even if we got out of the basement—highly doubtful all on its own—we'd have every vamp in the place after our ass. There would be more; there were always more. But what had Jean-Claude said? If they broke the truce first, we could draw weapons. It had possibilities.

The one with long blonde hair had undone her braid. She shook out her hair like it was a thick curtain of yellow waves. It hid her face for a moment, and she seemed softer, more human. Maybe it was illusion. Whatever, Jason touched that thick hair, wadded his hands into it, then slid his hands around her waist. If he was going to have to do it, it looked like he was going to have fun while he did. Nice to see someone who enjoys his work.

The dark-haired vamp came in from behind, pressing her leather-clad body against him. Jason was short enough that his face was about breast level for both of them. He buried his face in the blonde's chest. She unlaced the front of her leather vest, peeling it back so he could suck her breasts.

I turned away. I was never much for voyeurism. Had an embarrassing tendency to blush. Ivy and Bruce moved along the wall to stand near the corner next to the threesome. Bruce was fascinated and embarrassed, but he kept looking. There was no embarrassment on Ivy's face. She moved along the wall, her back pressed to it, hands feeling their way along. Her red lipsticked mouth was partially open. She slid down the wall, the red dress bunching around her thighs as she went to all fours. Watching them move along the wall brought my gaze back to the entertainment.

Jason's shirt was gone. Wearing nothing but his leather pants and his black boots, he matched the two vampires. He was on his knees, his back arched so he was cradled against the brunette behind him. She smoothed her hands down his naked chest. He turned, giving her his lips. The kiss was long and deep, and full of more probing than anybody but your doctor should be doing.

The blonde was sitting with her legs wide open in front of them, undoing Jason's pants. She'd already done something to her leather pants so that the crotch was open. She was a natural blonde. Why was I surprised?

Ivy stretched out a hand to pull at the other vampire's long yellow hair.

"Ivy," Janos said, "you were not invited."

She pulled her hand back but didn't back away. She was as close to the action as she could get and not be part of it. Bruce was still pinned to the wall, open-mouthed and a little sweaty, but he didn't seem to want to come closer.

Janos stood very calmly watching. He had a tight grin on his face, and for the first time there was some light in those dead-fish eyes. He was enjoying himself.

Jean-Claude was half-leaning, half-sitting against a metal frame that held the rough outline of a body. He was watching the show, but his face was still unreadable, a beautiful mask.

He saw me looking at him, but there was no change in his eyes. He was as closed and solitary as if he were standing in an empty room. He wasn't breathing that I could see. Did he have a heartbeat when he held himself so still? Or did everything stop?

Kissa stood by the door that we hadn't been through. She had her arms crossed over her stomach. For someone that had wanted to jump Jean-Claude's bones so badly, she didn't seem to like the show much. Or maybe she was the guard to keep Larry and me from running screaming from the room.

Larry had backed as far away from the action as he could get. He was pressed up against the wall, trying to find something to look at, but his eyes kept being drawn back to the other end of the room. It was like trying not to watch a train wreck. You didn't want to see it happen, but if it was going to happen you didn't quite want to look away either. When would you ever get the chance to see it again? A ménage à trois made up of two vampires and a werewolf couldn't be that common a sight for Larry. It wasn't even a common sight for me.

The two girls still chained to the wall couldn't see what was going on. Probably just as well.

A low moan broke from the other side of the room. It made me glance back. Jason's pants had been pulled partially down to reveal most of the smooth expanse of his buttocks. His arms were braced, leaving only his lower body touching the woman. His body rose and fell rhythmically. The blonde vampire writhed under him, another low moan escaping her throat. Her breasts spilled out of her black leather vest like an offering as she did a sort of sit-up to meet Jason's mouth.

The brunette licked a slow, pink tongue along his spine. His back convulsed with the sensation, or maybe it was another sensation. The effect looked the same.

I turned away, but the image was burned on my mind. I felt heat crawl up my neck. Damn. Larry's eyes widened and I watched the color drain from his face, until his skin was the surprised white of paper and his eyes too big for his face.

I fought it for a minute, but I turned back to see, like Lot's wife risking it all for one last forbidden glimpse. Jason had collapsed, his face lost in the blonde's hair. Her face was turned to the room. Her skin had thinned until you could see every bone in her face. Her full lips had thinned back, making her teeth look longer. She no longer had enough lips to hide her fangs.

The brunette knelt just behind them, her knees between both their legs. She lowered her hands from her face, and one half of that handsome face rotted away. She ran her hand through her long dark hair and it came away in clumps.

She turned her face towards the rest of us. The skin sloughed off the bones on the left side of her face and fell to the floor with a thick wet plop.

I swallowed hard enough that it hurt going down and backed up to stand by Larry. He wasn't white anymore; he was green.

"My turn now," one of the vampires said. My face turned back to the scene at the end of the room, almost against my will. I couldn't stand to watch, and couldn't stand to look away.

Jason rose in a sort of push-up motion. He caught a glimpse of the blonde's face and his shoulders tensed, the line of his spine tightening. He pulled away from her slowly, coming to his knees.

The brunette ran her fingers down his naked back. Her flesh sloughed away, leaving a trail of greenish slime behind. A tremor ran through his body that had nothing to do with sex.

From across the room I could see Jason's chest rise and fall faster and faster, as if he was hyperventilating. He stayed staring straight ahead, making no move to turn and look behind him, as if it would go away if he didn't look.

The brunette wrapped her decaying arms around his shoulders, leaned her rotted face next to his, and whispered something.

Jason struggled away from them, crawling against the wall. His bare chest was covered in bits of her flesh. His eyes were impossibly wide, showing too much white. He couldn't seem to get enough air. A strand of something thick and heavy slid slowly down his neck onto his chest. He batted at it like you would swat at a spider that you found crawling along your skin. He was pressed into the black wall with his pants nearly to his thighs.

The blonde rolled off her back and crawled towards him, reaching a hand out that was nothing but bones with bits of dried flesh. She seemed to be decaying in dry ground. The brunette was wet. She lay back on the floor, and some dark fluid rushed out from her to pool beneath her body. She'd undone her own leather shirt, and her breasts were like heavy bags of fluid.

"I'm ready for you," the brunette said. Her voice was still clear and solid. No human voice should have come out of those rotting lips.

The blonde grabbed Jason's arm, and he screamed.

Jean-Claude sat there watching, motionless, unmoved.

I found myself walking towards them. It surprised even me. I kept waiting for the smell that should have accompanied the rotting flesh, but with every step the air was clean.

I stood beside Jean-Claude and said, "Is this illusion?"

He wouldn't look at me. "No, *ma petite,* it is not an illusion."

I poked him in the arm, and it was hard and firm as wood. It didn't feel like flesh at all. "Is this illusion?"

"No, *ma petite.*" He looked at me at last, and his eyes were solid drowning blue. "Both forms were real." He stood, and even standing next to him I could not see him breathe.

The brunette was on all fours reaching for Jason with a hand that fell into wet pieces as it moved. Jason screamed and pressed himself into the wall as if he wanted to crawl through it. He hid his face like a child ignoring the monster under his bed, but this was no child, and he knew the monsters were real.

"Help him," I whispered, and I wasn't sure which of us I was talking to.

"I shall do what I can," Jean-Claude said. I was staring at him when I heard the next words in my head. His lips never moved. "If they break the truce first, *ma petite,* then you are free to slaughter everyone in this room."

I stared at him, but his face betrayed nothing. Only the echo of him inside my head told me I hadn't hallucinated it. There was no time to bitch about the fact that he'd invaded my head. Later; we could argue later.

"Janos." That one word reverberated through the room until it echoed up the soles of my feet like a deep bass drum.

Janos turned to look at Jean-Claude, his skeletal face set in a pleased expression. "You rang?"

"I challenge you." The three words were bland; they fell like off-key notes jangling along my nerves. If the tone bothered Janos, you couldn't tell it.

"You cannot prevail against me," Janos said.

"That remains to be seen, does it not?" Jean-Claude asked.

Janos smiled until the skin nearly snapped. "If by some miracle you best me, what do you want?"

"Safe passage for all my people." I cleared my throat. "And the two girls."

"And if I win," Janos said, "what do I get?"

"What do you want?"

"You know what we want."

"Say it," Jean-Claude said.

"You give up your safe passage. We get you, to do with as we like."

Jean-Claude gave a small nod. "So be it." He pointed at the rotting vampires. "Get them away from my wolf."

Janos smiled. "They will not hurt him, but if you fail . . . I'll make a gift of him to my two beauties."

A low sound like a swallowed scream crawled from Jason's throat. The brunette's hand started the crawl down his stomach to his privates. He screamed and pushed her away, but unless he resorted to violence he was trapped. And if we broke the truce first we were dead, but if they broke the truce . . .

Jean-Claude and Janos had moved back to the center of the room. They stood a few yards apart. Jean-Claude stood with his feet spaced as if he was bracing for a fight. Janos stood with his feet together, easy, unconcerned.

"You will lose everything, Jean-Claude; what are you up to?"

Jean-Claude just shook his head. "Challenge has been offered and accepted; what are you waiting on, Janos? Are you afraid of me at long last?"

"Afraid of you? Never, Jean-Claude. Not a hundred years ago, not a moment ago."

"Enough talk, Janos." His voice had gone low and soft, yet it carried through the entire room, and crawled up the black walls to rain down in drops of sound that were dark and anger-filled.

Janos laughed, but the sound had none of the touchable qualities of Jean-Claude's voice. "Let us dance." Silence fell so abruptly on the room I thought I'd gone deaf. Then I realized I could still hear my own heartbeat, the blood rushing in my own head. Waves of something rose between the two master vampires like heat rising off summer pavement. What poured along my skin wasn't heat, it was . . . power.

A whirling, rushing storm of power. I'd felt Jean-Claude go up against other vampires, and I'd never felt anything like this. My hair streamed in a wind that was coming from the two.

Jean-Claude's face was thinning down, his white skin glowing like polished alabaster. His eyes were blue flames that bled sapphire fire down every vein under his skin. His bones glowed gold. His humanity was folding away, and it wouldn't be enough. He would lose.

Unless they broke the truce first.

Kissa stood by the door, still guarding it. Her dark face was impassive. She was no help to me. The two rotted things still crawled over Jason. Only Ivy and Bruce were still standing. Bruce looked scared, Ivy looked excited. She watched the two master vamps with half-parted lips, her lower lip drawn under with concentration or excitement.

I'd been able to meet her eyes, and that had bothered her—a lot.

I crossed the room behind Jean-Claude. When I passed him, the current of power lashed out and curled around me like an arm. I kept walking and it slipped away, but my skin shivered where it had touched me. The shit was going to hit the fan unless I could stop it.

Kissa watched me move past her with narrowed eyes. I ignored her. One master vampire at a time. I walked past Bruce and stopped in front of Ivy. She stared past me at the two masters, ignoring me.

I opened my mouth. As I spoke, the silence split apart and sound came back to me ears with a nearly painful clap like a tiny sonic boom.

"I challenge you."

Ivy blinked at me as if I'd just appeared. "What did you say?"

"I challenge you," I said. I kept my face blank and tried very hard not to think about what I was doing.

Ivy laughed. "You are mad. I am a master vampire. You cannot challenge me."

"But I can meet your eyes," I said. I let a small smile play along my lips. I tried to keep my mind blank, no thought to betray me, no fear to leak out, but of course once I thought of fear it was there curling in my stomach.

She laughed, high and tinkling like broken glass. It nearly cut skin just to hear it. What the hell was I doing?

The wind rushed against my back, nearly flinging me into her. I glanced back in time to see Jean-Claude stagger and a splash of blood spill from his hand. Janos hadn't broken a sweat yet.

Whatever I was doing, I'd better do it fast.

"After Jean-Claude loses, I'm going to ask Janos to make him fuck me. Your master is going to be everybody's meat, and so will you."

My eyes flicked to the rotted things clawing at Jason. Incentive enough. I turned back to Ivy and met her brown eyes. "You won't do shit. You can't even outstare one puny human being."

She glared at me. Her anger was instantaneous, like fire springing out of a match. I watched the brown of her irises spread across her eyes from a space of less than ten inches. Her eyes were shining pools of dark light. My pulse threatened to choke me, and a little voice in my head was screaming, "Run away, run away." I stood there and stared her down.

She was a master vampire but a young one. A hundred years from now she'd have eaten me for breakfast, but right now, tonight, maybe, just maybe, she wouldn't.

She hissed at me, flashing her fangs.

"Oh, that's impressive," I said. "Like a dog showing its teeth."

"This dog could tear your throat out." Her voice had gone low and evil crawling along my spine, until I spent most of my effort not to shiver.

I didn't trust my voice not to shake, so I spoke low, and soft, and very clear. "Try it; see how far you get."

She darted forward, but I saw her move, felt her come for me. I threw myself backwards away from her, but she grabbed my arm and lifted me off my feet with her elbow braced so that she could hold me aloft. Her strength was incredible. She could have crushed my arm and I couldn't have done a damn thing about it.

Kissa was suddenly there. "Put her down, now!"

Ivy put me down. She threw me across the room. Air rushed past me, the world blurring so quickly it was like being blind. The air stopped rushing, and down I came.

26

FALLING DOES NOT cover the speed and abruptness of being thrown from less than ten feet high. I smacked into the wall and tried to slam my arms and hands against it to take some of the momentum before my head smacked into it. I slid down the wall, though slid implies something slow, and there was nothing slow about it. I collapsed at the base of the wall in a crumbled, breathless heap, blinking at bright jarring images that didn't quite make pictures yet.

The first image that came clear was a rotted face with a patch of long, dark hair dangling from its scalp. The vamp's tongue rolled behind broken teeth; something black and thicker than blood spilled with a plop out of her mouth.

I pushed to my knees and found skeletal arms wrapped around my shoulders. The blonde's dried, fang-filled mouth whispered in my ear. "Come to play." Something hard and stiff poked my ear. It was her tongue. I scrambled away, but claws caught in my jacket. Hands that should have been weak as dried sticks were like steel bands.

"They broke the truce, *ma petite*. I cannot hold him long."

I had a moment to glance up and find Jean-Claude on his knees with both hands extended towards Janos. Janos still stood, but he did nothing else. I had a few moments, nothing more.

I stopped trying to get free of the two vampires. They swarmed over me, and in the mess of arms and legs and body fluids, I drew the Browning. I fired it point-blank into the rotted one's chest. She staggered, but didn't go down. Fangs sank into my back, and I screamed.

A gun exploded from across the room, but there was no

time to look. Jason was suddenly there, pulling the blonde off me. I fired into the rotting skull of the brunette. She finally collapsed onto the floor in a puddle of liquid and jerking limbs.

I turned back to Jean-Claude and found him nearly prone on the floor, a pool of blood in front of him. He had one arm still held outward towards Janos.

Janos made a small, flicking motion, and blood flew in an arc from Jean-Claude's body. He collapsed to the floor, and power rushed outward, blowing back my hair. The world suddenly stank of rotting corpses.

I gagged and pulled the trigger on that long black body.

Janos turned. It seemed like slow motion, as if I had all the time in the world to aim and fire again, but somehow he was facing me when I pulled the trigger the second time. The bullet took him squarely in the chest. He staggered, but didn't go down.

I sighted on that round, skeletal head. His white hand came up and slashed the air. And impossibly, I felt like some invisible claw had slashed my arm. I fired, but my aim was a little off. The bullet grazed the side of his face.

He slashed at me again, and I saw blood start to drip down my hands. Scare tactics. It didn't hurt that much, not nearly as much as it would hurt if he got his hands on me for real.

A second gun sounded, and Janos staggered as a bullet took him in the shoulder. Larry was behind him, gun out.

My vision faded, as if fog was rolling in behind my eyes. I lowered my aim to the larger target of his upper body and pulled the trigger again. I heard Larry's bullet go high and wide into the wall behind me.

A startled, "Hey!" let me know Jason was still back there.

I saw Janos go for the door, like watching slow motion through a fog so thick I could barely see. I fired twice more and knew I hit him at least once. When he was out of the room I fell forward onto all fours, and waited for my vision to clear. Hoped it would clear.

Through my ruined vision I saw Jean-Claude still lying motionless in a pool of his own blood. The question that came into my head was, Is he dead? A stupid question about a vampire, but it was still the first thing I thought of.

I glanced behind me and found Jason scattering bits of the two female vampires around the floor. He was tearing at them with his bare hands, cracking their bones and throwing them far away from each other, as if by sheer destruction he could wash away what they'd done to him.

Bruce lay on his back by the wall. Blood had soaked into his tuxedo. I couldn't tell for sure, but he looked dead. Ivy and Kissa were nowhere to be seen.

Larry was still standing across the room, gun extended, as if he didn't realize that Janos was gone. He was frowning. Everybody was up, everybody was moving except Jean-Claude. Shit.

I crawled towards him, not trusting myself to stand with my vision so spotty. It seemed to take a long time to reach him, as if more than my eyesight wasn't working quite right.

My vision was mostly clear by the time I got to him. I knelt in a thick pool of his blood and stared down at him. How do you tell if a vampire is dead? Sometimes he didn't have a pulse, or a heartbeat, or didn't breathe. Shit, again.

I holstered the Browning. There was nothing here right now to shoot, and I needed my hands. I bled on my shirt and looked at my hands for the first time. It looked like fingernails had scraped down both of them, a little deeper than normal, but they'd heal. Probably wouldn't even be a scar.

I touched Jean-Claude's shoulder and the flesh was soft, very human. I rolled him over onto his back. His hand flopped against the floor with a bonelessness that only the dead have. Some trick of the night had made his face beautiful again. The most human I'd ever seen it, except for the fact that no one was that pretty.

I checked for the big pulse in his neck. I held my fingers against his cooling skin, and felt nothing. Something like tears welled against my eyes, and my throat was tight. But I wouldn't cry, not yet. I wasn't even sure I wanted to.

When is dead, dead for a vampire? Is there such a thing as CPR for the undead? Hell, he breathed some of the time.

He had a heart, and it beat most of the time. Not beating couldn't be a good thing.

I positioned his head, pinched his nose closed, and blew a breath into his mouth. His chest rose with it. I tried two more breaths, but he didn't breathe on his own. I unbuttoned his shirt and found the spot above his breastbone, and pressed, one, two, three, four, all the way to fifteen compressions. Two breaths.

Jason staggered over to me, then collapsed to his knees. "Is he gone?"

"I don't know." I pumped with everything I had in me, hard enough to break ribs on a human being, but he wasn't human. He lay there, his body moving only when I moved it, as loose and boneless as only the dead can be. His lips were half-parted, his closed eyes edged with the black lace of his thick eyelashes. His curling black hair still framed his pale face.

I'd pictured Jean-Claude dead. I'd even thought about killing him myself once or twice, but now that his death was a fact I didn't know how to feel. It didn't seem fair somehow. I'd brought him here. I'd asked him to come, and he came. And now he was dead, well and truly dead. And it was partially my fault, partially my doing. If I killed Jean-Claude, I wanted to actually pull the trigger and watch his eyes as he died. Not like this.

I stared down at him. I thought about no more Jean-Claude. This beautiful body rotting at last in the grave it so richly deserved. I shook my head. I couldn't let that happen, not if I could save him. I only knew one thing that all dead respected, craved. Blood. I tried to breathe life into him one more time, with one difference. I smeared my blood on his mouth first. My lips touched his, and I tasted the sweet, metallic taste of my own blood.

Nothing.

Larry knelt beside us. "Where did Janos go?"

He hadn't been able to see through the fog, but I didn't have time to explain. "Watch the door; shoot anything that comes through."

"Can I let the girls go?"

"Sure." I'd forgotten about the girls. I'd forgotten about Jeff Quinlan. I'd have traded them all for Jean-Claude to blink his eyes at me. Not if the choice had been offered to me as an either-or, but just now they were strangers. He wasn't.

"More blood, maybe," Jason said softly.

I looked at him. "You offering?"

"Neither of us can feed him back to full strength without dying, but I'll help," he said.

"You fed him once tonight already. Can you donate twice?"

"I'm a werewolf. I heal quick. Besides, my blood has more kick to it than a human's, more power."

I really looked at him then. He was covered in slime. A big black smear covered most of one cheek. His blue eyes didn't look wolfish; they looked haunted, hurt. There are things that harm a lot more than physically.

I took a deep breath and slid one of my knives out of its sheath. I sliced my left wrist. The pain was sharp and immediate. I placed the wound against Jean-Claude's lips. Blood welled into his mouth. Blood filled his mouth like wine pouring into a cup. It seeped out the corner of his mouth and slid down his cheek. I stroked his throat to make him swallow the blood.

How he'd laugh to know I'd finally opened a vein for him. More blood spilled from his unresponsive lips. Dammit.

I breathed into his mouth and got a taste of my own blood. I made his chest rise, breathing in my own blood. I thought one word at him: Live, live, live.

A shudder ran through the body. The throat convulsed, swallowed. I pulled back from him. He caught my wrist as I moved it back from his chin. His grip hurt. I could feel that unnatural strength that could break bone. His eyes were still closed; only the grip on my wrist let me know we were making progress.

I put a hand on his chest. He wasn't breathing on his own yet. No heartbeat. Was that bad? Good? Indifferent? Hell, I didn't know.

"Jean-Claude, can you hear me? It's Anita."

He raised up in a small motion and pressed my bleeding wrist to his mouth. He bit me, and I gasped. He used both hands to press my wrist to his mouth and sucked me. In the middle of sex it might have felt good; now it just hurt.

"Damn," I said.

"What's wrong?" Larry asked.

"It hurts," I said.

"I thought it was supposed to feel good," the blonde girl said.

I shook my head. "Not unless you're under hypnotic control."

"How long will this take?" Larry asked.

"As long as it takes," I said. "Watch the door."

"Which one?"

"Oh, hell, just shoot anything that comes through it." I was feeling light-headed. How much had he drunk?

"Jason, I'm getting a little woozy here." I tried to pull my wrist free, but his hands were like iron forged to my skin. "I can't get him off."

Jason pulled at the pale hands, but couldn't budge them. "I could tear the fingers off one at a time and get you loose, but . . ."

"Yeah, Jean-Claude would be pissed." Dizziness was coming in waves, nausea starting to build in the pit of my stomach. I had to get him off me.

"Let go of me, Jean-Claude. Let go of me, dammit!"

His eyes were still closed, his face blank. He fed like a baby with single-minded determination, but this baby was draining my life away. I could feel it going down my arm. My heart was beginning to pound in my ears as if I'd been running, pumping the blood faster. Feeding him faster. Killing me faster.

Spots were dancing in front of my eyes. The darkness beginning to eat the light. I drew the Browning.

"What are you doing?" Jason asked.

"He's going to kill me."

"He doesn't know what he's doing."

"I'll still be dead."

"Something's moving around at the head of the stairs," Larry called.

Great. "Jean-Claude, let go of me, now!"

I pressed the barrel of the gun to the flawless skin of his forehead. Darkness was eating my vision in great moving bites. Nausea burned up my throat.

I leaned over him and whispered, "Please, Jean-Claude, let me go. It's your *ma petite,* let me go." I sat back up.

"Vampires coming," Larry said. "Hurry up."

I stared down at that beautiful face locked on my arm, eating me alive, and squeezed. His eyes flew open. I moved my whole finger to keep from squeezing down.

He lay his head back onto the floor, still holding my wrist but no longer feeding. His mouth was crimson with my blood. The gun was still pointed at him.

"Ah, *ma petite,* haven't we done this before?"

"The gun," I said, "but not this." I drew my wrist from his reluctant hands and sat back with the Browning cradled in my lap. Nausea and darkness flew inside my head like clouds driven by the wind.

I saw Larry crouched by the foot of the stairs, gun out. But it was like looking down a tunnel, distant and not as important as it should have been.

Jason lay down on the bloody floor. I blinked at him. "The neck hurts less," he said, just as if I'd asked. Jean-Claude crawled on top of him. Jason turned his head to one side without being asked. Jean-Claude pressed his bloodstained mouth over the big pulse in Jason's neck. I saw the muscles in his mouth and jaw as he sank fangs into the tender skin.

Even if I'd known the neck hurt less, I wouldn't have offered it. It looked too much like sex. The wrist at least let me pretend we weren't doing something intimate.

"Anita!"

I turned back to the stairs. Larry was crouched there, alone, with his gun. The two girls had moved back away from the door. The blonde was having hysterics again. Couldn't really blame her.

I shook my head, lifted the Browning in a teacup grip, and pointed it at the door. I needed the extra arm to steady me.

There was a faint tremor to my arms that wasn't going to help my aim much.

Power breathed through the room, prickling along my skin. You could almost smell it like perfumed sheets in the dark. I wondered if Jean-Claude and I had given off that kind of power when he'd fed off me. I hadn't noticed it.

Something white appeared in the doorway. It took me a second to figure out what it was. A white handkerchief tied to a stick.

"What the fuck is that?" I asked.

"A flag of truce, *ma petite.*"

I didn't look away from the stairs to that thick, honey-dipped voice. Jean-Claude sounded better, or worse, than ever, each word like fur rubbing along my tired body. His voice was thick enough to wrap around all the aches and pains. He could make them go away. I just knew it.

I swallowed and lowered the gun towards the floor. "Stay the fuck out of my head."

"My apologies, *ma petite.* I can taste you in my mouth, feel your frantic heartbeat like a treasured memory. I will curb my enthusiasm, but with effort, Anita, with great effort." He sounded like I had let him have just a little sex, and he wanted more.

I glanced at him. He was sitting beside Jason's half-naked body. Jason was staring at the ceiling, eyes heavy-lidded like he was half-asleep. Blood trickled from two new puncture wounds in his neck. He didn't look like he'd felt much pain. In fact, it looked like it had felt good. I'd taken the edge off Jean-Claude's need, and Jason had gotten a smoother ride. Bully for him.

"May we talk?" A voice from the hallway, a man's. I couldn't place it. Hell, I was having trouble focusing on anything, let alone who the disembodied voices belonged to.

"Anita, what do you want me to do?" Larry asked.

"It's a flag of truce," I said. My words felt slurred, though they sounded clear enough. I felt almost drunk, or drugged. It was a bad drunk, a dangerous downer.

Magnus stepped into the doorway. For a second I thought I was seeing things. It was so damned unexpected. He was dressed all in white from his tux to his shoes. The cloth seemed to shine against his dark skin. His long hair was tied back with a loose white ribbon. He had the handkerchief-coated stick gripped in one hand. He walked down the steps in a graceful, almost dancelike movement. It wasn't a vampire's glide, but it was close.

Larry kept his gun trained on him. "Stay where you are," Larry said. He sounded a little scared, but like he meant it. The gun was pointed nice and steady.

"We've discussed the fact that silver bullets don't work on the fey."

"Who says this gun has silver bullets?" Larry said.

It was a good lie. I was proud of him. I was certainly too gone to have thought of it.

"Anita?" Magnus looked past Larry like he wasn't there, but he didn't come down those last few steps.

"I'd do what he says, Magnus. Now what do you want?"

Magnus smiled and spread his arms away from his body. To show he was unarmed, I guess. But I knew, and Larry knew, that weapons weren't what made him dangerous. "I mean you no harm. We know that Ivy broke the truce first. Serephina offers her most sincere apologies. She asks that you come directly to her audience chamber. No more tests. We have all been unforgivably rude to a visiting master."

"Do we believe him?" I asked of no one in particular.

"He speaks the truth," Jean-Claude said.

Great. "Let him pass, Larry."

"You sure that's a good idea?"

"No, but do it anyway."

Larry pointed his gun at the floor, but he didn't look happy. Magnus walked down the stairs, smiling, mostly at Larry. He walked past him and made a show of giving him his back. It was almost enough to make me wish Larry would shoot him.

He stopped a few feet in front of the rest of us. We were all still on the floor, sitting, or in Jason's case, lying. Magnus looked down at us, amused, or bemused.

"What the hell are you doing here?" I asked.

Jean-Claude glanced at me. "You seem to know each other."

"This is Magnus Bouvier," I said. "What are you doing here, with them?"

He loosened the tie at his collar and spread the stiff cloth. I was pretty sure what he was trying to show me, but I couldn't see from the floor. I wasn't at all sure I could stand without falling over. "If you want me to take a peek, you're going to have to come down here."

"With pleasure." He knelt in front of me less than two feet away. He had two healing bite marks on his neck.

"Shit, Magnus. Why?"

He looked at me, eyes flicking to my bloody wrist. "I might ask you the same thing."

"I donated blood to save his life. What's your excuse?"

He smiled. "Nothing half as nice as that." Magnus undid the ribbon and let his hair fall like a curtain around his shoulders. He looked at me with his turquoise blue eyes, and crawled on all fours towards Jean-Claude. He moved like he had muscles in places that people didn't. It was like watching a great cat move. People just didn't move like that.

He knelt in front of Jean-Claude, so close they were almost touching. He swept his hair to one side and offered his neck.

"No," Jean-Claude said.

"What's going on?" Larry asked.

It was a good question. I didn't have a good answer. I didn't even have a bad one.

Magnus slipped off his white jacket and let it slide to the floor. He undid the cuff to his right wrist and pushed the cloth back. He offered his bare wrist to Jean-Claude. The skin was smooth and unbroken. Jean-Claude took his hand and raised the skin to his lips.

I almost looked away, but in the end I didn't. Looking away is like lying to yourself. You pretend it isn't happening, but it is.

Jean-Claude brushed his lips across the skin, then released Magnus's hand. "The offer is generous, but I would be drunk indeed if I added your blood to theirs."

"Drunk?" I asked. "What the fuck are you talking about?"

"Ah, *ma petite,* you do have a way with words."

"Shut up."

"Losing a quantity of blood makes you grumpy," he said.

"Fuck off."

He laughed, and the sound was sweet. It had a taste just outside description, like some forbidden candy that was not just fattening but poisonous. But what a way to go.

Magnus stayed kneeling, staring at the laughing vampire. "You won't taste me?"

Jean-Claude shook his head, as if he didn't trust himself to speak. His eyes glittered with suppressed laughter.

"The blood has been offered." Magnus crawled back towards me. His hair had spilled forward on one side so one eye was lost, glittering like a jewel through his hair. Eyes just weren't supposed to be that color. He crawled up to me until our faces were inches apart. "A pint of blood, a pound of flesh." He whispered it, leaning in towards me as if for a kiss.

I leaned back, away from him, and overbalanced. I ended up on my back on the floor. It was not an improvement. Magnus crawled over me, still on all fours, hovering. I pressed the Browning into his chest.

"Back off, or bite it."

Magnus crawled backwards, but not very far. I sat up, keeping the gun on him one-handed. The barrel wavered a lot more than normal. "What was that all about?"

Jean-Claude said, "Janos spoke of taking blood and flesh from us this night. As an apology, Serephina offers us blood, and flesh."

I stared at Magnus, still on all fours, still looking feral and dangerous. I lowered the gun. "No, thanks."

Magnus sat back on the floor, smoothing his hands through his hair, brushing it back from his face. "You have refused Serephina's peace offerings. Do you refuse her apology as well?"

"Take us to Serephina, and you will have done what was asked of you," Jean-Claude said.

Magnus looked at me. "What of you, Anita? Are you content that I take you to Serephina? Do you accept her apology?"

I shook my head. "Why should I?"

"Anita is not a master," Jean-Claude said. "It is my vengeance, my pardon, you should be asking."

"I am doing what I was told," he said. "She challenged Ivy to a test of wills. Ivy lost."

"I didn't throw her across the room," I said.

Jean-Claude frowned. "She resorted to brute force, *ma petite*. She could not win by force of will or vampire wiles against a human being." He looked suddenly very serious. "She lost . . . to you."

"So?"

"So, *ma petite,* you declared yourself a master, and proved that claim."

I shook my head. "That's ridiculous; I'm not a vampire."

"I did not declare you a master vampire, *ma petite*. I said you were a master."

"A master what? Human being?"

It was his turn to shake his head. "I do not know, *ma petite.*" He turned to Magnus. "What does Serephina say?"

"Serephina says to bring her."

Jean-Claude nodded and stood like he was pulled by strings. He looked fresh and new, if a little bloodstained. How dare he look so good when I felt like shit?

He looked down at Jason and me. His strange good humor had returned. He smiled down at me, and even with blood staining his mouth he was beautiful. His eyes glittered with some amusing secret. He was full of himself in a way I'd never seen before.

"I do not know if my companions are able to walk. They're feeling a little drained." He chuckled at his own joke, putting a hand in front of his eyes, as if it was too funny even for him.

"You are drunk," I said.

He nodded. "I believe I am."

"You can't be drunk on blood."

"I've drunk deep of two mortals, but neither of you are human."

I didn't want to hear this. "What the hell are you talking about?"

"Necromancer with a chaser of werewolf; a drink to make any vampire giddy." He giggled. Jean-Claude never giggled.

I ignored him, if you can ignore an intoxicated vampire. "Jason, can you stand?"

"I think so." His voice was thick, heavy but not sleepy, more the languor after sex. Maybe I was glad my bite had hurt.

"Larry?"

Larry walked over to us, glancing at Magnus, gun naked in his hand. He didn't look happy. "Can we trust him?"

"We're going to," I said. "Help me stand up, and let's get out of here before fangface busts a gut."

Jean-Claude was doubled over with laughter. He seemed to think "fangface" was outrageously funny. Ye gods.

Larry helped me stand, and after a second of dizziness I was okay. He offered a hand to Jason without being asked. Jason swayed on his feet, but stayed standing.

"Can you walk?"

"If you can, I can," he said.

A man after my own heart. I took a step, another, and was on my way across the room. Jason and Larry followed. Jean-Claude staggered to his feet, still laughing softly.

Magnus was standing at the foot of the stairs, waiting for us. He had the jacket slung over one arm. He'd even found the ribbon to tie back his hair.

Jason walked wide around the torn bodies of his two would-be lovers and picked his shirt off the floor. The shirt covered the mess on his chest, but the goo was still on his face, and his hair was stiff and nearly as dark as his pants.

Even the back of Jean-Claude's clothes and hair were thick with congealing blood. I had my own share of blood and goop. Good thing I wore mostly black tonight; didn't show dirt as badly. The crimson blouse was looking a little worse for wear.

Larry was the only one without any blood or gore on him. Here was hoping he could keep up the good work.

The two girls had hidden under the stairs while we discussed things. I was betting it was the brown-haired girl's idea to hide. Lisa seemed too scared to think, let alone do anything smart. Not that I could blame her, but hysteria gets you nowhere but dead.

The brown-haired girl walked over to Larry. The blonde came along for the ride, her hands dug so tightly into the other one's torn blouse it would have taken surgery to remove them.

"We just want to go home now. Can we do that?" Her voice was a little breathy, but for the most part solid. I stared into her brown eyes and nodded.

Larry looked at me.

"Magnus," I said.

He raised his eyebrows, still waiting by the stairs like a tour guide, or a butler ready to escort us up. "You called?"

"I want the girls to leave now, safe."

He glanced at them. "I don't see why not. Serephina had us collect them mostly for your benefit, Anita. They've served their purpose."

I didn't like the way he said that last. "Safe, Magnus, no more harm. Are we clear on what that means?"

He smiled. "They walk out the door, and go home. Is that clear enough for you?"

"Why so cooperative all of a sudden?"

"Would letting them go be apology enough?" Magnus asked.

"Yeah, if they go free, unharmed. I'll accept her apology."

He nodded. "Then consider it done."

"Don't you have to check with your master first?"

"My master whispers sweetly to me, Anita, and I obey." He smiled while he said it, but there was a tightness around his eyes, an involuntary flexing of his hands.

"You don't like being her lap dog."

"Perhaps, but there's not much I can do about it." He started up the stairs. "Shall we go up?"

Jean-Claude paused at the bottom of the stairs. "Do you need some help, *ma petite?* I have taken quite a bit of your blood. You do not recover as quickly as my wolf."

Truthfully, the stairs looked longer going up than they had coming down. But I shook my head. "I can make it."

"Of that, *ma petite,* I have no doubt." He stepped close to me, but did not whisper; instead I felt him in my mind. "You are weak, *ma petite*. Let me help you."

"Stop doing that, dammit."

He smiled and sighed. "As you like, *ma petite."* He walked up the steps like he could have flown, barely touching them. Larry and the girls went up next; none of them seemed tired. I slogged up after them. Jason brought up the rear. He looked hollow-eyed. It may have felt good, but donating that much blood is still rough, even on the temporarily furry. If Jean-Claude had offered to carry him up the stairs, would he have agreed?

Jason caught me looking, but he didn't smile; he just stared back. Maybe he'd have said no, too. Weren't we all just being uncooperative tonight?

27

THE SILKEN DRAPES had been drawn aside. A throne sat in the far right-hand corner. There was no other word for it; "chair" just didn't cover that golden, bejeweled thing. Cushions were scattered on the floor around it, heaped like they should be covered with harem girls, or at least small pampered dogs. Nothing sat on them. It was like an empty stage waiting for the actors to appear.

A small wall-hanging on the back wall had been pushed aside to reveal a door. The door had been wedged open with a triangular piece of wood. The spring air poured through the open door, chasing back the smell of decay. I started to say "Come on, girls," but the wind changed. It blew harder, colder, and I knew it wasn't wind at all. My skin prickled, the fine muscles along my arms and shoulders twitching with it.

"What is that?" Larry asked.

"Ghosts," I said.

"Ghosts? What the hell are ghosts doing here?"

"Serephina can call ghosts," Jean-Claude said. "It is a unique ability among us."

Kissa appeared in the doorway. Her right arm hung loose at her side. Blood dripped down her arm in a slow, heavy line.

"Your handiwork?" I asked.

Larry nodded. "I shot her, but it didn't seem to slow her down much."

"You hurt her."

Larry widened his eyes. "Great." He didn't sound great when he said it. Wounded master vampires get cranky as hell.

"Serephina bids you come outside," Kissa said.

Magnus dropped to the cushions, boneless as a cat. He looked like he'd curled up there before.

"You aren't coming?" I asked.

"I've seen the show," he said.

Jean-Claude walked towards the door. Jason had moved up beside him, but back a couple of steps like a good dog.

The two girls were holding onto Larry's jacket. He had been the one who unchained them. They'd seen him shoot the bad guys. He was a hero. And like all good heroes, he'd get himself killed protecting them.

Jean-Claude was suddenly at my side. "What is wrong, *ma petite?*"

"Can the girls go out the front?"

"Why?"

"Because whatever's out there is big and bad, and I want them out of it."

"What's wrong?" Jason asked. He stood a little to one side. He was flexing his hands, closed, open, closed, open. He'd seemed a lot more relaxed thirty minutes ago, but then, weren't we all?

Jean-Claude turned to Kissa. "Was this one right?" He motioned to Magnus. "Are the girls free to go?"

"They may go; so says our master."

He turned to the girls. "Go," he said.

They looked at each other, then at Larry. "Alone?" the blonde said.

The brown-haired one shook her head. "Come on, Lisa, they're letting us go. Come on." She looked at Larry. "Thank you."

"Just go home," he said. "Be safe."

She nodded and started for the far door with Lisa clinging to her. They left the door to the room open, and we watched them walk out the front. Nothing swooped down upon them. No screams cut the night. What do you know?

"Are you ready now, *ma petite?* We must pay our respects." He took a step forward, looking at me. Jason already stood at his side, nervous hands and all.

I nodded and fell into step behind Jean-Claude. Larry stayed at my side like a second shadow. I could feel his fear like a trembling against my skin.

I understood why he was scared. Janos had beaten Jean-Claude. Janos was afraid of Serephina, which meant she could take Jean-Claude without raising a sweat. If she could take the vampire that was on our side, she wouldn't find us much of a challenge. If I was smart, I'd shoot her as soon as I saw her. Of course, we were here to ask for her help. It sort of cut my options.

The cool wind played in our hair like it had little hands. It was almost alive. I'd never felt any wind that could make me want to brush it off, like an overly amorous date. But I wasn't afraid. I should have been. Not of the ghosts, but of whatever had called them up. But I felt distant and faintly unreal. Blood loss will do that to you.

We walked out the door and down two small stone steps. Rows of small, gnarled fruit trees decorated the back of the house. There was a wall of darkness just beyond the orchard. It was a thick wall of shadows, so black that I couldn't see through it. The naked tree branches were framed against the blackness.

"What is that?" I asked.

"Some of us can weave shadows and darkness around us," Jean-Claude said.

"I know. I saw it when Coltrain was killed, but this is a freaking wall."

"It is impressive," he said. His voice was very bland, matter-of-fact. I glanced at him, but even in the bright moonlight I couldn't read his face.

A sparkle of white light showed behind the blackness. Beams of cold, pale light pierced the darkness. The light ate away at the dark like paper burns, the blackness crumbling, vanishing as the light consumed it. When the last of the darkness had shredded away, a pale figure stood among the trees.

Even from this distance you wouldn't have mistaken her for human, but then she wasn't trying to pass. A pale, white luminescence swirled above her head, a glowing cloud, yards across like colorless neon. Vague figures darted out from it, then swirled back.

"Is that what I think it is?" Larry asked.

"Ghosts," I said.

"Shit," he said.

"My thoughts exactly."

The ghosts flowed out into the trees. They hung on the dead branches like a froth of early blossoms, if blossoms could move and writhe and glow.

The strange wind blew against my face, sending my hair streaming backwards. A long, thin line of phosphorescent figures whirled out. The ghosts came sweeping towards us, low to the ground.

"Anita!"

"Just ignore them, Larry. They can't actually hurt you as long as you keep moving and ignore them."

The first ghost was long and thin with a wide, screaming mouth that looked like a smoke ring. It hit me at mid-chest; the shock ran through me like electricity. The small muscles in my arms jerked with it. Larry gasped.

"What the hell was that?" Jason asked.

I took a step forward. "Keep walking and ignore them."

I didn't mean to, but my pace took me ahead of Jean-Claude. The next ghost swept over my face. There was a moment of smothering but I kept walking and it passed.

Jean-Claude touched my arm. I stared into his face and wasn't sure what I saw. He was definitely trying to tell me something. He stepped out in front of me, still staring at me.

I nodded, and let him lead. It didn't cost me anything.

"I don't like this," Larry said in a singsong voice.

"Me either," Jason said. He was batting at a tiny swirl of whiteness like a tame mist. The more he swatted at it, the more solid it became. A face was forming out of the mist.

I walked back to Jason and grabbed his arms. "Ignore it."

The small ghost perched on his shoulder. It had a large, bulbous nose and two half-formed eyes.

Jason's arms tensed under my hands. "Every time you notice them, you give them power to manifest themselves," I said. A ghost hit me in the back. It was like a lump of moving ice in the center of my body. It crawled out the front of my body like a cold rope being pulled through me. The sensation was unnerving as hell, but it wasn't permanent. It didn't even really hurt.

The ghost dived into Jason's chest, and he cried out. Only my grip on his arms kept him from clawing at the thing. Every muscle in Jason's body twitched like a horse being eaten alive by flies. He sagged when the ghost was through him, looking at me with horror-filled eyes. It was nice to know he could be scared. The vampires seemed to have taken some of his courage with their rotting arms. Couldn't blame him. I'd have had screaming fits, too.

Larry jumped when a ghost popped through him, but that was all. His eyes were a little wide, but he knew where the danger lay, and it wasn't the ghosts.

Jean-Claude came to stand near us. "What is wrong, my wolf?" There was an undercurrent of warning, anger. His pet was not living up to his reputation.

"We're fine," I said. I squeezed Jason's hand; his eyes were still wide, but he nodded. "We'll be fine."

Jean-Claude walked towards the distant white figure once more, his movement graceful, unhurried, as if he wasn't as scared as the rest of us. Maybe he wasn't. I pulled Jason with me. Larry had moved to my back. The three of us walked like normal human beings behind Jean-Claude. We looked like good little soldiers except for the fact that I was holding the werewolf's hand. His hand was sweating against my skin. Couldn't afford to have a hysterical werewolf. My right hand was still free to go for a gun, or a knife. We'd hurt them once; if they didn't behave themselves, we could finish the job. Or at least go down trying.

Jean-Claude led us among the naked trees with the ghosts crawling over the bare branches like phantom snakes. He stopped a few feet away from the vampire. I almost expected him to bow, but he didn't. "Greetings, Serephina."

"Greetings, Jean-Claude." She was dressed in a simple white dress that fell in folds of shining cloth over her feet. White gloves covered her arms almost completely. Her hair was grey with streaks of white, left unadorned save for a headband of silver and pearls. It wasn't a headband, probably called a coronet or something. Her face was lined with age. Delicate makeup had been added, but not enough to hide the fact that she was old. Vampires didn't age. That was the whole point, wasn't it?

"Shall we go inside?" she asked.

"If you like," he said.

She gave a faint smile. "You may escort me inside, as you did of old."

"But it is not olden days, Serephina. We are both masters now."

"I have many masters serving me, Jean-Claude."

"I serve only myself," he said.

She stared at him for a space of heartbeats, then nodded. "You have made your point. Now be a gentleman."

Jean-Claude took a deep enough breath that I heard it sigh from his lips. He offered her his arm, and she slid one gloved hand through it, her hand resting on his wrist.

The ghosts floated downward behind her like a great flowing train. They brushed past the rest of us with a skin-prickling rush, then floated upward, hovering about ten feet off the ground.

"You may walk with us," Serephina said. "They will not molest you."

"Comforting," I said.

She smiled again. It was hard to tell in the moonlight and ghostly glow, but her eyes were pale, maybe grey, maybe blue. You didn't need to see the color to not like the look in them.

"I have looked forward to meeting you, necromancer."

"Wish I could say the same."

The smile didn't widen, and didn't fade; it didn't move at all. It was like her face was a well-constructed mask. I raised my glance to her eyes, for just a moment. They didn't try to suck me under, but there was an energy in them, a deep burning that pushed at the surface of her being like a banked fire; move a log just wrong, and the flames would come licking out and burn us all up. I couldn't judge her age; she was stopping me. I'd never met anyone that could actually stop me—trick me into believing them younger, yes, but not just glare at me and keep me from doing it.

She turned and walked through the door. Jean-Claude helped her up the steps, as if she needed it. The easy distance of the blood loss was receding, leaving me real, and alive, and wanting to stay that way. Maybe it was Jason's hand warm in my own. The sweat on his palm. The reality of him. I was suddenly scared, and she hadn't done a damn thing to me.

The ghosts flowed into the house, some pouring through the door, some sliding through the walls. Watching them pull free of the wood, you almost expected a sound, like a plop, but it was utterly quiet. The undead make no noise.

The ghosts bounced along the ceiling like helium-filled balloons, poured down the walls in back of the throne like milky water. They were translucent near the candle flames, like bubbles.

Serephina sat down in the corner on her throne. Magnus curled in the cushions at her feet. There was a flash of anger in his eyes, there, and gone. He wasn't enjoying being Serephina's boy toy. That got him an extra point in my book.

"Come sit by me, Jean-Claude," Serephina said. She motioned to the cushions on the opposite side from Magnus. They'd have made an interesting pair.

"No," Jean-Claude said. That one word was warning

enough. I drew my hand slowly from Jason's. If we really were going to fight, I'd need both hands.

Serephina laughed, and with that sound her power broke open and crashed on us poor humans.

The power rode down on me like pounding horses. My whole body vibrated with it. My mouth was too dry to swallow, and I couldn't quite get a full breath of air. She didn't have to touch me to hurt me. She could just sit on her throne and throw power at me. She could grind my bones into dust from a nice safe distance.

Something touched my arm. I jerked and turned, and it felt like slow motion. It has hard to focus on Jean-Claude's face, but once I did, the grinding power receded like the ocean pulling back from the shore.

I took a deep, shuddering breath, then another; every breath was firmer. "Illusion," I whispered. "Fucking illusion."

"Yes, *ma petite.*" He turned from me and went to Larry and Jason, who were still standing spellbound.

I looked back at the throne. The ghosts had formed a glowing nimbus around her; most impressive. But not nearly as impressive as her eyes. I had one wild glimpse of eyes that seemed to go on forever, then I stared at the hem of her white dress as hard as I could.

"Can you not meet my gaze?"

I shook my head. "No."

"Can you really be that powerful a necromancer when you cannot even meet my eyes?"

I wasn't just not meeting her eyes. I was hunched over. I straightened but didn't move my eyes. "You're only about six hundred years old." I raised my eyes slowly, inch by inch up the white dress until I could see her chin. "How the hell did you get to be this powerful in that amount of time?"

"Such bravado. Meet my eyes and I will answer you."

I shook my head. "I don't want to know that badly."

She chuckled, and the sound was low and dark. It slid down my spine like something loathsome and half-alive. "Ah, Janos, Ivy, so good of you to join us."

Janos glided through the door with Ivy at his side. Janos

looked more human than he had since I'd first met him. His skin was pale but fleshy. His face was still thin, and he couldn't have passed for completely human, but he looked less monstrous. He also looked healed.

"Shit."

"Is something wrong, necromancer?" Serephina asked.

"I hate to waste that many bullets."

She gave that low chuckle again. It made my skin feel tight. "Janos is very talented."

He walked past us. I could see bullet holes in his shirt. At least I'd ruined his wardrobe.

Ivy looked dandy. Had she run when the shooting started? Had she left Bruce to die?

Janos went down on one knee among the cushions. Ivy knelt with him. They stayed there, head bent, waiting for her to notice them.

Kissa moved to stand beside Magnus, bleeding, her arm held close to her side. But she glanced from the two kneeling vampires to Serephina, and back again. She looked . . . worried.

Something was up. Something unpleasant.

She left them kneeling, and said, "What business brings you to me, Jean-Claude?"

"I believe you have something that belongs to me," he said.

"Janos," she said.

Janos rose to his feet and went back out the door. He was out of sight only a moment, then came back carrying a large cloth sack like something Santa Claus would have carried. He untied the cord that held it shut and emptied the contents on the floor at Jean-Claude's feet. Splinters of wood, none of them big enough to make a decent stake, fell into a medium-sized pile. The wood was dark and polished where it wasn't white with new cuts.

"With my compliments," Janos said. He shook the last bits of wood out of the sack and knelt back on the steps.

Jean-Claude stared down at the splintered wood. "This is childish, Serephina. Something I would have expected from you centuries ago. Now . . ." He motioned at the ghosts, at everything. "How have you managed to subdue Janos? You feared him once."

"State your business, Jean-Claude, before I grow impatient and challenge you myself."

He smiled and gave a graceful bow, arms out to his sides like an actor. When he raised up, the smile was gone. His face was like a beautiful mask. "Xavier is in your territory," he said.

"Did you truly think I would feel the presence of your pet necromancer, and not sense Xavier? I know he is here. If he challenges me, I will deal with him. Speak the rest of your business, or was that it? Did you come all this way to warn me? How touching."

"I realize you are more powerful than Xavier now," Jean-Claude said, "but he is slaughtering humans. Not just the attack on the missing boy's home, but many deaths. He has gone back to cutting up his pets. He draws attention to us all."

"Then let the council kill him."

"You are master in this territory, Serephina; it is your task to police it."

"Do not presume to tell me my duties. I was centuries old when you died. You were nothing but a catamite for any vampire that wanted you. Our beautiful Jean-Claude." She made beautiful sound like a bad thing.

"I know what I was, Serephina. Now I am Master of the City and follow the council's laws. We are not to allow humans to be slaughtered in our territories. It is bad for business."

"Let Xavier kill hundreds. There are always more," she said.

"Nice attitude," I said.

She turned her attention to me, and I wished I hadn't said anything. Her power pulsed against me, like a great beating heart.

"How dare you disapprove of me," Serephina said. I heard the rustle of her silk dress as she stood. No one else moved, and I heard her dress slither across the cushions, sliding along the floor, as she came closer. I did not want her to touch me.

I stared up the line of her body, and saw her gloved hand strike outward. I gasped. Blood dripped down my hand.

"Shit!" It was a deeper cut than Janos had managed, and it hurt more. I met her eyes, anger making me brave, or stupid. Her eyes were pure white, like captive moons shining from her face. Those eyes called to me. I wanted to fling myself into her pale arms, to feel the touch of those soft lips, the sharp sweet caress of her teeth. I wanted to feel her body cradling mine. I wanted her to hold me like my mother once had. She would take care of me forever, and never leave, never die, never desert me.

That stopped me. I stood very still. I was standing at the edge of the pillows. The hem of her dress spilled at my feet. I could have reached out a hand and touched her.

Fear pounded my heart in my head. I could taste my pulse on my tongue.

She spread her arms wide. "Come to me, child, and I will always be with you. I will hold you forever."

Her voice was everything good; warmth, food, shelter from all the things that hurt, all the disappointment. I knew in that moment that all I had to do was step into her arms and all the bad things would go away.

I stood there with my hands balled into fists. My skin ached to have her touch me, hold me. Blood still dripped down my hand from where she'd cut me. I rubbed my fingers into the cut, making the pain sharp.

I shook my head.

"Come to me, child. I will be your mother forever."

I found my voice. It sounded rusty, choked, but it came. "Everything dies, bitch. You aren't immortal, none of you are."

I felt her power waver like a pebble thrown in a pool, and I moved back a step, then another. It took everything I had left not to run from that room, and to keep running. To run and run and run. Away from her.

I didn't run. In fact, I stayed about two steps back, looking around. People had been busy. Janos stood next to Jean-

Claude. They weren't trying their vampire wiles on each other, but the threat was open, and there. Kissa stood to one side, blood pooling on the pillows at her feet. There was a look on her face that I couldn't read. It was almost amazement. Ivy was standing now, staring at me, smiling, pleased that I'd nearly fallen into Serephina's arms.

I wasn't pleased. No one had ever come closer, not even Jean-Claude. I was beyond scared. My skin was cold. I had broken her hold over me, but it was temporary. She might not be able to trick me with her mind, but I'd felt her mind brush mine. If she wanted me, she could have me. It wouldn't be pretty. No illusions, no tricks, just brute fucking force and she could have me. I would never run into her arms, but she could crush my mind. That she could do.

The knowledge was almost calming. If there was nothing I could do to prevent it, might as well not worry about it. Worry about the things you can control; the rest will either work themselves out, or they'll kill you. Either way, no more worries.

"You are quite right, necromancer," Serephina said. "We are all mortal in this room. Vampires can live a long, long time. It makes us forget that we are mortal. But immortality eludes even us."

It wasn't a question, and I agreed with everything she said, so I just looked at her.

"Janos told me you had an aura of power, necromancer. He said he used it against you as he would another vampire. I did it just now when I slashed your hand. I have never known a human that could be harmed so."

"I don't know what you mean about an aura of power."

"It is what allowed you to slip my magic. No human could have withstood me, and few vampires."

"Glad I could do something to impress you."

"I never said I was impressed, necromancer."

I shrugged. "Fine, maybe you don't give a damn about humans, or keeping a low profile. I don't know about your council, or what they'll do to you for not helping us. But I do know what I'll do."

"What are you babbling about, human?"

"I am the vampire executioner for this state. Xavier and his crew took a young boy. I want him back, alive. You help me get him back alive, or I go to the courts and get a death warrant on you."

"Jean-Claude, talk to her, or I will kill her."

"She has the weight of human law behind her, Serephina."

"What is human law to us?"

"The council says that it rules us as it rules the humans. Refusing the human laws is the same as breaking with the council."

"I don't believe you."

"You can taste the truth of my words. I could never lie to you, not two hundred years ago, not now." His voice was very calm, very sure.

"When did this new law go into effect?"

"When the council saw the benefit of being mainstream. They want the money, the power, the freedom to walk the streets in safety. They don't want to hide anymore, Serephina."

"You believe what you say; that much is true," she said. She looked down at me, and the weight of that gaze even with me looking away was like a giant hand mashing me down. I stayed on my feet, but it was an effort. You should bow down to such power. Grovel before it. Worship it.

"Stop it, Serephina," I said. "Cheap mind tricks won't work, and you know it." The cold lump in my stomach wasn't so sure.

"You fear me, human. I can taste it on the back of my tongue."

Oh, goody. "Yeah, you scare me. You probably scare everybody in this room. So what?"

She drew herself up to every inch of her tall, thin frame. Her voice was suddenly soft, breathing down my skin like fur. "I will show you."

She gestured outward with one gloved hand. I tensed, waiting for another cut, but it never came. A scream cut the air and whirled me around.

Blood ran down Ivy's face. Another cut appeared on her

bare arm. Two more on her face. Long, slicing wounds with every gesture that Serephina made.

Ivy shrieked. "Serephina, please!" She fell to her knees among the bright cushions, one hand outstretched towards the master vampire. "Serephina, master, please."

Serephina walked around her, one gliding movement at a time. "If you had held your temper, they would all be ours now. I knew their hearts, their minds, their deepest fears. We would have broken them all. They would have broken the truce and we could have feasted on them to our blood's content."

She was almost even with me. I wanted to move back away from her, but she might see it as a sign of weakness. Her dress brushed my leg, and I didn't care. I did not want her to touch me. I moved back, and she caught my wrist. I hadn't even seen her move.

I stared at that silk-gloved hand as if a snake had just coiled around my wrist. Hell, I'd have rather had the snake.

"Come, necromancer; help me punish this bad vampire."

"No, thanks," I said. My voice sounded shaky. It matched the fluttering in my gut. She hadn't done anything to me yet except touch me, but touch makes all powers stronger. If she tried a mind trick now, I was finished.

"Ivy would have taken great delight in your pain, necromancer."

"That's her problem, not mine." I was staring very hard at the silky cloth of Serephina's dress. I had a terrible urge to look upward, to meet her eyes. I didn't think it was her power, just my own morbid compulsion. It's hard to be tough when you're staring at someone's body and being led around by the hand like a child.

Ivy lay on the floor, half-propped on her arms. Her lovely face was a mass of deep cuts. Bone gleamed in the candlelight from one cheek. Her right arm had a cut that showed muscle twitching and bloody.

Ivy stared up at me, and behind the pain was a hatred strong enough to light a match. The anger rose from her in slapping waves.

Serephina knelt beside her, drawing me down with her. I

glanced back at Jean-Claude. Janos had a white spider-hand on his chest. Larry mouthed the word "gun." I shook my head. She hadn't hurt me yet. Not yet.

The hand jerked my arm hard enough to wrench my head around to face her. We were eye to eye, suddenly, horribly. What I saw in her eyes wasn't horrible. Her eyes, which I would have sworn were some pale shade, looked solid wood brown. My mother's eyes.

I think she meant for it to be comforting, or seductive. It wasn't. My skin went cool with fear. "Stop it."

"You don't want me to stop," she said.

I tried to pull my arm out of her grasp. I might as well have tried to move the sun to a different part of the sky. "All you can offer me is death. My dead mother in your dead eyes." I stared into those brown eyes that I never thought to see this side of heaven. I yelled at my mother's eyes, because I couldn't look away. Serephina wouldn't let me, and I couldn't fight her on that, not while she touched me.

"You're a walking corpse, and everything else is just lies."

"I am not dead, Anita." There was an echo of my mother's voice in her words. She raised her other hand as if to caress my cheek.

I tried to close my eyes. Tried to look away. I couldn't. A strange paralysis was sliding over my body, like the feeling you get just on the edge of sleep when your body weighs a thousand pounds and every movement is nearly impossible.

That hand came for me in slow motion, and I knew if she touched me I would fall into her arms. I would cling to her and cry.

I remembered my mother's face the last time I'd seen her. The coffin had been dark wood covered in a blanket of pink roses. I knew Mommy was in there, but they wouldn't let me see. No one could see. Closed coffin, they said, closed coffin. Every adult in my life was having hysterics. The room was full of screams, sobbing. My father collapsed to the floor. He was useless to me. I wanted my mother. The latches on the coffin were silver. I opened them, and I heard a cry behind me. I didn't have much time. The lid was heavy, but I shoved it upward and it moved. I got a glimpse of white satin, and shadows. I raised my arms over my head with every ounce of strength and got a glimpse of something.

My Aunt Mattie grabbed me back. The lid clanged shut, and she snapped the lock back in place, dragging me away. I didn't struggle; I'd seen enough. It was like looking at one of those pictures that you know must look like something, but your eyes can't make sense of it. It took me years to make sense of it. But what I saw wasn't my mother. Couldn't be my beautiful mother. It had been a husk, something left behind. Something to hide in a dark box and let rot.

I opened my eyes, and Serephina had pale grey eyes. I pulled my wrist from her suddenly loose grasp and said, "Pain helps."

I stood and stepped away from her, and she didn't stop me. Which was good, because I was shaking all over, and it wasn't from the vampire. Memories have teeth, too.

She stayed kneeling by Ivy, and said, "Most impressive, necromancer. I will help you find this boy you seek."

Her sudden cooperation was unnerving. "Why?"

"Because since I attained my full powers, no one has ever slipped my illusions twice in one night. No one living or dead."

She grabbed Ivy by one bloody arm and pulled her into her lap to bleed on the white dress. Ivy gasped. "Remember this, young master vampire: This mortal did what you could not. She stood against me and won." She tossed her suddenly away, sending her sprawling across the floor. "You are not worthy of my sight. Get out."

Serephina stood. The fresh blood stood out in scarlet relief against her white dress and gloves. "You have impressed us. Now go, all of you." She turned and walked back to her throne. She didn't sit down. She stood with her back to us, one hand on the chair arm. Perhaps it was my imagination, but she seemed tired. Her ghosts flowed down to meet her in a swirling white mist. There weren't as many individual shapes as before, as if the phantoms had lost some of their solidity.

"Go," she said without turning around.

The back door was open, but Jean-Claude walked to the doorway that led out the front. I wasn't going to argue. I just wanted out. I didn't give a damn which door we took.

We walked coolly, calmly towards the door. I wanted to run. Larry stood next to me, and I could see the pulse in his throat jumping with the effort not to bolt. Jason reached the door a little ahead of us, but he waited and turned and motioned us through like a doorman, or a butler.

I caught a glimpse of his eyes, too wide, scared, and knew what the gesture had cost him. We went through; he followed. Jean-Claude brought up the rear. The doors slammed behind us, and we walked out. Just like that.

But for the first time I knew that I'd been let go. I hadn't fought my way out, or bluffed my way out. She could be impressed all she wanted, but she had allowed us to go. Being allowed to leave was not the same thing as winning.

I would never go back into that house voluntarily. I would never be near her willingly. Because I'd been impressive tonight, but I couldn't keep it up. Even now I knew that she could have me. This vampire had my ticket. Had a lie almost worth my immortal soul.

Damn.

28

JASON WALKED PAST me into the hotel room. He headed straight for the bathroom. "I'm taking a shower." It was pushy, but he did smell like a decayed corpse. We'd driven back with all the windows rolled down. Most of the time if you stink, you can't smell someone else. I had some of the rotted stuff on me, but I could still smell Jason. Some smells are too unique to ever really go away.

"Wait," Larry said.

Jason turned, but not like he was happy.

"Use my shower." He held up a hand before I could say anything. "It's an hour until dawn. If we want everybody tucked in before that, it makes sense to use both bathrooms."

"I thought we'd all sleep in this room tonight," I said.

"Why?" he asked.

Jean-Claude stood by the love seat looking lovely and unhelpful. Jason just looked impatient.

"Safety in numbers," I said.

Larry shook his head. "Alright, but I can take the werewolf next door and let him shower. Or don't you trust me to even do that?" He was getting angry again.

"I trust you, Larry. You did good tonight."

I expected a smile. I didn't get it. He looked very serious. "I killed that vampire Bruce."

I nodded. "I thought we were going to have to kill everything in the room."

"So did I." He sank into one of the chairs. "I've never killed anyone before."

"It was a vampire. It's not the same thing as killing a person."

"Yeah, right. And how many corpses have you given CPR to lately?"

I glanced at Jean-Claude smiling at me. I shrugged. "Just one. Can you give us some privacy here?" I asked.

"I will hear what you are saying no matter where I stand in this room," Jean-Claude said.

"Illusion is all; just back off," I said.

Jean-Claude bowed his head slightly and took Jason to one side of the room, near the windows. I knew he'd hear everything, but at least he wouldn't be standing over us.

"You don't really believe he's dead, do you?" Larry asked.

"You saw what happened to those two vampires," I said. "They are just rotting corpses; everything else is illusion."

"You think he ever looks like that?"

I looked at Jean-Claude's back for a minute. "I'm afraid I do."

"How can you date him after seeing that?"

I shook my head. "I don't know."

"Corpse or not, you tried to keep him alive." He reacted to the look on my face. "Alive, undead, whatever you want to call it, you tried to preserve it. You were scared he was really dead."

I just looked at him. "So?"

"So, I killed another living being, or undead being. Hell, Anita, Bruce was so newly dead he seemed human."

"Probably why one bullet to the chest finished him."

"How am I supposed to feel about that?"

"Killing him, you mean?"

"Yeah."

"They are monsters, Larry. Some of them are prettier than others, but they are monsters. Never doubt that."

"You can honestly tell me that you think Jean-Claude is a monster." It was more statement than question.

I almost looked at the monster in question, but I didn't. I'd looked at him enough for one night. "Yeah, I do."

"Now, ask her if she thinks she's a monster." Jean-Claude leaned on the back of the love seat, his arms crossed over his chest.

Larry looked a little startled, but he said, "Anita?"

I shrugged. "Sometimes."

Jean-Claude smiled. "See, Lawrence? Anita thinks we're all monsters."

"Larry's not," I said.

"Give him time."

That was a little too close to the truth. "I asked for privacy, or did you forget?"

"I forget nothing, *ma petite,* but time grows short. My wolf is not the only one that needs a bath. Only our young friend is still fresh."

I looked at Larry. There wasn't a drop of blood on him. He was the only one who hadn't wrestled with vampires tonight. He shrugged. "Sorry; I just couldn't get anybody to bleed on me tonight."

"Don't joke, Larry," I said. "With Serephina I think you'll get another chance."

"Sadly, true, *ma petite.*"

"How long can you go without a coffin?" I asked.

He smiled. "Concern over my well-being. I am touched."

"Don't give me crap. I opened a freaking vein for you tonight."

"If I have not thanked you for saving my life tonight, *ma petite,* my apologies."

I looked at him. He looked pleasant, amused, but it was a mask. His expression when he didn't want you to know what he was thinking, but didn't want you to know that he didn't want you to know. "Don't mention it."

"I will remember that you saved me, *ma petite.* You could have been free of me. Thank you."

It sounded sincere enough. "You're welcome."

"I need to get this crud off me," Jason said. He sounded just a touch frantic. I was betting he'd be trying to scrub off more than just dirt. But memories don't wash that easily. More's the pity.

"Go on, both of you. Jason can scrub up in Larry's room. It's only practical."

Larry grinned at me. "Thanks."

"I meant it when I said you did good tonight."

I finally got the smile I'd expected. "Come on, Jason, hot water and fresh towels await." Larry held the door for Jason and gave me a little salute. Geez.

Alone again with Jean-Claude. Would this night never end? "You never answered my question about the coffin," I said.

"I will be alright for another night or two."

"How did Serephina go from being your equal in power to being what we saw tonight?"

He shook his head. "I truly do not know, *ma petite.* She surprised me badly. She did not have to let us go tonight. As long as she did not harm us, we could have been her guests for the day."

"Are you surprised she let us go?" I asked.

"Yes," he said.

Jean-Claude pushed away from the love seat. "Take your shower, *ma petite.* I will await the young men's return."

"I thought you could go next, wash the blood out of your hair."

He put a hand up to the back of his hair. He grimaced at the feel of it. "Distasteful, but I want a bath, *ma petite*. It takes longer than a shower, so you go first."

I looked at him for a long moment.

"If you do not hurry, I will not have time for a bath before dawn. I would hate to sleep on your clean sheets covered in blood."

I took a deep breath and let it out slowly. "Fine; just be sure you stay out of the bathroom."

"My word of honor that I will not barge in on you."

"Yeah, right." Though, strangely enough, I believed him. Jean-Claude had been trying to seduce me for a long time. A frontal assault just wasn't his style. I went to take my shower.

29

RONNIE HAD DRAGGED me into Victoria's Secret. I had pointed out that no one would see my underwear or my nightclothes except other women in the gym locker room. Ronnie had replied, "You'll see them." The logic escaped me but she had talked me into a robe.

It was burgundy, the color of wine-dark peonies. It glowed against my pale skin and matched some of the bruises blossoming on my back. Nothing like getting thrown into a wall to give you a little color. The bite mark on my back wasn't very deep. Hard for humanoid fangs to sink in from that angle. The fang marks on my wrist were deeper. They were two neat little holes, almost dainty. It didn't hurt as much as it should have. Maybe vampires did have painkillers in their saliva, or maybe it was the fangs.

I still couldn't believe that I'd let him sink fangs into me. Shit.

I pulled the robe closer around me. The material was heavy enough to be cozy on a winter evening, and had wide silky cuffs, and more silk lining the edges. It looked vaguely Victorian, a little masculine. I looked delicate in it, like a Victorian doll that hadn't gotten completely dressed yet. I put on an oversized black t-shirt under the robe. It ruined some of the effect, but it beat the heck out of wearing nothing but a robe and underwear out to greet the boys.

I retrieved the Browning from the back of the stool where it had sat during my shower. I carried it with me to the bedroom, and hesitated. I always went armed. Hell, I slept with a gun, but I didn't feel like slipping on a holster. I put the Browning away and settled for slipping the Firestar into the robe pocket. Made the cloth hang funny, but if something nasty came through the door I was ready for it.

Jean-Claude was standing at the window when I opened the bedroom door. He had opened the drapes, and was leaning against the window's edge staring out into the darkness. He turned when the door opened, though I knew he'd heard me before that.

"Ma petite, you look lovely."

"It's the only robe I own," I said.

"Of course," he said. His face had that amused mask on it again; this time I would have liked to know what he was thinking. His midnight blue eyes were very intense; they didn't match the nonchalant expression. Maybe I didn't want to know what he was thinking.

"Where are Larry and Jason?"

"They have come and gone," he said.

"Gone?"

"Jason had a sudden craving, and Larry drove him in the Jeep."

I just looked at him. "There is such a thing as room service."

"It is the wee hours of the morning, *ma petite.* The room service menu is somewhat limited. Jason has donated blood twice to me tonight; he needed protein." Jean-Claude smiled. "It was either take-out, or he could eat Larry. I thought you'd prefer take-out."

"Very funny. You shouldn't have sent them alone."

"We are safe from Serephina tonight, *ma petite*, and as long as they stay in town, safe from Xavier."

"How can you be so sure?" I crossed my arms over my stomach.

He leaned his back against the window and looked at me. "Your Monsieur Kirkland handled himself well tonight. I think you worry unnecessarily about him."

"One night of heroics doesn't keep you safe," I said.

"It will be dawn soon, *ma petite;* even Xavier cannot bear the light of day. All the vampires will be seeking shelter. They will have no time to chase our young men."

I stared at him, trying to read past his pleasant face. "I wish I was as sure as you seem to be."

He smiled then, and pushed away from the wall. He slid out of his jacket and let it fall to the rose-colored carpet.

"What are you doing?"

"Undressing."

I jerked a thumb at the bedroom, "Undress in there."

He began unbuttoning his shirt.

"In the other room, right now," I said.

He pulled the white shirt out of his pants, working the last few buttons as he walked towards me. The flesh of his chest and stomach had more color than the shirt. He was pumped up and human-looking on blood, part of it mine. The dried bloodstains that had soaked through the shirt marred the pale perfection of his body.

I expected him to try to kiss me, or something, but he walked past me. The back of the shirt was brownish with dried blood. He peeled it off his skin with a sound like tearing. He dropped the shirt on the carpet and walked into the bedroom.

I stood there staring after him. There had been white scars on his back. At least I thought that's what they were. Hard to tell through all the blood. He left the bedroom door open, and in a few minutes I heard water running in the bathtub.

I sat down in one of the straight-back chairs. I wasn't sure what else I was supposed to do. Water ran for a long time, then silence, then sloshing water. He was in the tub. He hadn't closed the bathroom door first. Great.

"Ma petite," he called.

I sat there for a minute, unwilling to move.

"Ma petite, I know you are there. I can hear you breathing."

I walked to the edge of the bedroom door, very careful not to look inside. I leaned my back against the wall and crossed my arms. "What do you want?"

"There seem to be no clean towels."

"What am I supposed to do about it?"

"Could you call down to housekeeping and have some sent up?"

"I guess so."

"Thank you, *ma petite.*"

I stomped over to the phone, pissed. He'd known there were no clean towels before he got into the tub. Hell, I'd known there were no clean towels, but I'd been so busy listening to him splash around in the water I hadn't thought of it.

I was as mad at me as I was at him. He was always a tormenting son of a bitch. I was supposed to watch myself around him better than this. I was in a hotel room that looked like a freaking bridal suite with Jean-Claude all naked and soapy in the next room. After what I'd seen with Jason, there shouldn't have been this much sexual tension in the air, but there was. Maybe it was habit, or maybe Larry was right. I just didn't believe that Jean-Claude was a rotting corpse.

I called for more towels.

They would be happy to bring some up. No one bitched about the time. No one questioned. You can always tell how much you're paying for a room by how little they complain.

A maid brought me four big, soft towels. I looked at her for a full minute, hesitating. I could have her take the towels into Jean-Claude.

She said, "Ma'am?"

I took the towels, said thanks, and closed the door. I just couldn't let a strange woman see that I had a naked vampire in my tub. I wasn't even sure the vampire part was what made it embarrassing. Good girls do not end up with naked male anything in their bathtubs at four something in the morning. Maybe I wasn't a good girl. Maybe I never had been.

I hesitated at the bedroom door. The room was dark. The only light came from the bathroom, spilling in an oblong across the carpet.

I crushed the towels to my chest, took a deep breath, and stepped into the room. I could see the bathtub from here, but mercifully not all of it. I had a glimpse of white porcelain and a mound of white bubbles. Just seeing the bubble bath made the muscles in my shoulders relax a little. Bubbles can hide a multitude of sins.

I stopped at the bathroom door.

Jean-Claude lay back against the edge of the tub. His black hair was wet and had obviously been cleaned. Strands of it clung to his bare shoulders. His arms lay propped on the edge of the bathtub, his head resting against the dark tile of the wall. One pale hand was suspended in midair as if reaching for something, but the hand was utterly limp. His eyes were closed, making black half-moons against his pale cheeks. Beads of water clung to his face and what I could see of his body. He looked almost asleep.

His knee came up through the mound of bubbles, a surprising glimpse of bare wet skin. He turned his head and opened his eyes. The midnight blue of his eyes seemed darker. Maybe it was the way the water made his hair seem heavier, blacker.

I took a shallow breath and said, "Here are the towels."

"Could you place them here, please?" He gestured with that one half-suspended hand.

"Here" was the closed top of the toilet, which was close enough to the tub for grabbing. "I'll put them on the edge of the sink."

"I'll drip water all over the floor getting them from there," he said. His voice was neutral, no vampiric tricks, almost no tone at all.

He was right, and I was being silly. He wouldn't grab me and ravish me. If that'd been the plan, he could have done that years ago.

I placed the towels on the stool, eyes studiously anywhere but the tub.

"You must have questions about tonight," he said.

I glanced at him. The water on his naked torso caught the light like quicksilver. Suds clung to his chest, just under one nipple. I had a horrible urge to brush off the bubbles. I stepped back until I was standing by the far wall.

"It's not like you to offer answers," I said.

"I am feeling generous tonight." His voice had that quality that voices get when they are edging towards sleep.

"If you weren't naked in a tub of bubble bath, would you be offering to answer questions?"

He smiled then, a quick, familiar expression. "Perhaps not, but if I must answer your ravenous curiosity, isn't it more fun this way?"

"Fun for whom?"

"Both of us, if you would only admit it."

That got a smile from me, and I didn't want to smile. I didn't want to be enjoying watching him all soapy and wet. I wanted to be afraid of him, and I was, but I also wanted him. Wanted to run my hands down his wet flesh, wanted to touch what lay under those bubbles. I didn't want intercourse. I couldn't imagine that with him, but I wanted to do a little exploring. I hated that. He was a corpse; surely what I'd seen tonight convinced me of that.

"You're frowning, *ma petite;* why?"

"I asked you if the two rotting vampires were illusion, you said no. I asked if your form was real, you said yes. Both forms are real, you said."

"That is true," he said.

"Are you a rotting corpse?"

He settled lower in the warm, soapy water, drawing his arms into it, until only his head showed above the surface of the water. "That is not one of my forms."

"That isn't an answer."

He raised a pale hand from the water, a handful of bubbles cupped like a snowball. "There are different vampiric abilities, *ma petite;* you know that."

"What's that have to do with it?"

He raised his other hand and began to play with the bubbles, trailing them from hand to hand. "Janos and his two female companions are a different type of vampire than I am. Than most of us are. They are much rarer. If you ever see me as a rotted corpse, I will be well and truly dead. They can rot and reform, and it makes them much harder to kill. The only true surety is fire."

"Volunteering an awful lot of information, aren't you?"

He lowered his hands in the water, washing the soap away. He sat up a little straighter; suds clung to his body. "Perhaps I am afraid you will think that what happened with Jason would happen with us."

"We will never test that theory," I said.

"You sound so sure of that," he said. "Your lust perfumes the air, and yet you truly believe that we will never make love. How can you want me almost as much as I want you, yet be sure we will never know each other's bodies?"

I wasn't sure I had an answer for that one. I slid down the wall and sat with my knees drawn up to my chest. The pocket with the gun in it clunked against the wall. I moved the gun to a better position and said, "We just won't, Jean-Claude, not ever. I just can't." A part of me regretted that, but only part.

"Why, *ma petite?*"

"Sex is about trust. I'd have to trust someone implicitly to have sex with them. I don't trust you."

He stared at me with his blue, blue eyes, looking all scrumptious and wet. "You mean that, don't you?"

I nodded. "Yeah, I do."

"I do not understand you, *ma petite.* I try, but still I do not."

"You're pretty much a riddle to me, too. If that's any comfort."

"It isn't. If you were a woman who had casual lusts, we would have been in bed long ago." He sighed and sat up even straighter in the water so it hit him just above the waist. "Of course, if you were a woman of casual appetites, I don't think I would love you."

"You enjoy the chase, the challenge," I said.

"True, but it is more than that with you, if only you would believe me." He leaned forward, drawing his knees to his naked chest, rounding his shoulders to hug himself. White scars dribbled down his back from his shoulders to vanish into the water, not a lot of them, but enough.

"What made the scars on your back? Unless it was a holy item, you should have been able to heal them."

He laid his cheek on his knees so he could look at me. He looked younger, more human, vulnerable suddenly. "Not if the injury occurred before I died."

"Who whipped you?"

"I was the whipping boy for an aristocrat's son."

I stared at him. "You're telling me the truth, aren't you?"

"Yes."

"Is that why Janos chose whips tonight, to remind you where you came from?"

"Yes."

"You weren't born into the aristocracy?"

"I was born in a house with a dirt floor, *ma petite.*"

I looked at him. "Yeah, right."

He raised his head. "If I was going to make something up, *ma petite,* it would be more romantic, more entertaining than being a French peasant."

"So you were a servant in the castle?"

"I was their only son's constant companion. When he had clothes made, so did I. His tutor was my tutor. His riding instructor, mine. I learned swordplay and dancing and the proper way to eat at table. And when he was bad I was punished, because he was their only child, their only heir to an old family name. People speak of child abuse now." He leaned back in the tub, cuddling down into the warm water. "They complain of spanking. They have no idea what true abuse is. When I was a boy, parents thought nothing of taking a horse whip to a misbehaving child, or beating them bloody. Even the aristocrats beat their children. It was normal.

"But he was the only heir, the only child. So they paid money to my parents and took me. The lady of the manor chose me because I was fair of face. When the vampire who made me sought me out, she said my beauty called to her."

"Wait a minute."

He turned his head to give me the full weight of those dark blue eyes. I worked hard at not looking away.

"This gorgeous body and face is all vampire illusion, right? I mean, no one's this beautiful."

"I told you once that it was not my power that made you see me as you do, not most of the time at any rate."

"Serephina said you were a catamite for any vampire who would have you. What did she mean?"

"Vampires kill for food, but they bring others over for many reasons. Some for money, wealth, even title, love, but I was brought over for lust. When I was young and weak, they passed me around among them. One would grow tired of me, but there was always another."

I stared at him, horrified. "You're right. If you were going to make up a story, this wouldn't be it."

"The truth is so often disappointing, or ugly; don't you find that, *ma petite?*"

I nodded. "Yeah. Serephina was old. I thought vampires weren't supposed to age."

"Whatever age we die at is the age we remain."

"Did you know Serephina when you were young?"

"Yes."

"Did you sleep with her?"

"Yes."

"How could you let her touch you?"

"I was given to her as a gift by a master that makes even her new and improved powers seem weak. I had very little choice." He stared at me. "She knows what you want. Your greatest need, your most treasured wish, and she'll make it come true, or seem to. What did she offer you, *ma petite?* What could she offer you that nearly won you tonight?"

I looked away then; I didn't want to meet his eyes. "What did she offer you all those years ago?"

"Power."

I looked up at that. "Power?"

He nodded. "Power to escape them all."

"But you had to have the ability to be a master vampire inside you from the beginning. No one can give that to you," I said.

He smiled, but it wasn't a happy smile. "I know that now, but then I thought only she could save me from an eternity of . . ." His words trailed off and he submerged, leaving only a few black locks floating on the top of the water. He sat up with a loud breath of air, blinking the water from his eyes. The water had clumped his thick, dark eyelashes. He ran his hands through his wet hair, and it trailed over his shoulders.

"Your hair wasn't this long when we first met."

"You seem to prefer longer hair on your men."

"If you're dead, how can your hair grow?"

"That is a question for you to answer," he said. He ran his hands through his hair again, squeezing the ends out. He reached out a hand for a towel.

I scrambled to my feet. "I'll leave you to get dressed."

"Have Jason and Larry returned?" he asked.

"No."

"Then I won't be getting dressed." He stood, drawing the towel towards him. I had a glimpse of one side of his pale naked body, water streaming from it. The towel moved into view just in time. I fled.

30

I HUDDLED IN the straight-back chair farthest from the bedroom. But I was staring at the doorway. Shit. I wanted to run from the room, but why? It wasn't Jean-Claude I didn't trust. It was me. Fuck.

I touched the gun in my robe pocket. It was smooth and hard and reassuring, but it wouldn't help me now. Violence I understood; sex gave me more problems.

I honestly didn't want to sleep with him, but part of me was hoping for another glimpse of naked flesh. A long line of naked thigh, perhaps. Or maybe . . . I put the palms of my hands over my eyes, as if I could get the image out of my head by just pressing.

"Ma petite?" His voice sounded closer than the bathroom.

I didn't want to look, as if, just as Grandma Blake had said, I'd be struck blind. I felt him standing in front of me. Felt the movement of air. I lowered my hands a millimeter at a time. He was kneeling in front of me, one of the thick white towels wrapped around his waist.

I lowered my hands to my lap. Beads of water still clung to his skin. He'd combed his hair, but it was wet, slicked back, leaving his face plainer, more unadorned than normal. His eyes seemed bluer without his hair to frame them.

He put a hand on each chair arm and raised himself up. His lips brushed mine in a soft, nearly chaste kiss. He moved back from me, letting go of the chair.

I could taste my heart in my throat, and it wasn't fear.

Jean-Claude touched my hands, lifted them up. He placed my hands on his bare shoulders. The skin was warm, smooth, wet. He held my wrists in his hands, lightly, very lightly. I could have pulled away at any time. He ran my hands down his slick body.

I pulled my hands free. He said nothing, did nothing. He stayed kneeling, looking at me. Waiting. I could see the pulse in his neck jumping against the skin, and I wanted to touch it.

I slid my hands across his shoulders and lowered my face to his. He started to move into me for a kiss, but I slid my hand along his jaw and turned his head away. I touched lips to his neck and slid my mouth down his skin, until I could taste his pulse beating against my tongue. He tasted of perfumed soap, water, and clean skin.

I slid from the chair to the floor, kneeling in front of him. He was taller now, but not too tall. I licked water off his chest, and let myself do something I'd wanted to do for months. I ran my tongue over his nipple, and he shuddered against me.

I licked water off the center of his chest and ran my hands along his waist up the damp curve of his back.

He pulled the sash of my robe, and I didn't protest. I let his hands slide under the robe, around my waist, with nothing but the t-shirt between his flesh and mine. He ran his hands up my sides, his thumbs playing over my rib cage. The gun swung heavily in the loose cloth. It was annoying.

I raised my face to his. His arms slid behind my back, pressing me against the long wet line of his body. The towel was perilously loose.

His lips brushed mine; then the kiss became something more. Harder, nearly bruising, with his arms locked behind my shoulders. My hands slid down his waist, rubbed the sliding top of the towel, and found it had already slipped. My hand touched the smooth top of his buttocks. Only the pressure of our bodies kept the towel in place.

He ate at my mouth and I felt something sharp, painful. I jerked back and tasted blood.

Jean-Claude let me go. He sat back on his heels, the towel gathered in his lap. "I am sorry, *ma petite*. I got carried away."

I touched my mouth and came away with a spot of blood. "You nicked me."

He nodded. "I am truly sorry."

"I'll just bet you are," I said.

"Do not go all self-righteous on me, *ma petite*. You have finally admitted to yourself, to me, that you feel the pull of my body."

I sat on the floor by the chair with my robe in disarray. The t-shirt had ridden up to my waist. I guess it was a little too late to protest my innocence.

"Fine, lust; you happy?"

"Almost," he said, and now there was something in his eyes. Something dark and drowning, and older than it should have been.

"I can offer you my mortal body, and more, *ma petite*. It can be between us much more than any human lover could offer."

"Would I lose a little blood each time?"

"That was an accident," he said.

I stared at him, all pale and damp, kneeling on the floor with the white towel bundled into his lap, leaving nearly every inch of him bare.

"This is the first time I've cheated on Richard," I said.

"You have been dating me for weeks," he said.

I shook my head. "But I haven't been cheating. *This* is cheating."

"Then have you been cheating on me, with Richard?"

I didn't know what to say to that. "Go get dressed."

"Do you really want me to dress?" he asked.

I looked away. I was embarrassed now and uncomfortable. "Yes, please."

He stood up, the towel gripped in his hands. I looked down at the floor and didn't have to see his face to picture the smile on it.

He walked away from me, and didn't bother moving the towel around behind him. Muscles moved under his skin from calf to waist. He walked naked into the bedroom, and I enjoyed the view.

I touched my finger to my tongue. It was still bleeding. That's what I got for French kissing a vampire. Even thinking about it made me nervous.

"Ma petite?" he called from the other room.

"Yeah."

"Do you have a blow dryer?"

"In my suitcase. Help yourself."

Thankfully, I'd dragged my suitcase into the bedroom beside the bathroom door. One point for laziness. I was spared another glimpse of his naked body. Now that hormones were receding, I was embarrassed.

I heard the dryer and wondered if he was standing naked in front of the bathroom mirror while he dried his hair. I was very aware that all I had to do was go to the doorway and I could see for myself.

I stood up, pulled my t-shirt down, tied my robe securely in place, and sat down on the couch. My back was to the bedroom. I wouldn't be seeing anything else. I took the Firestar out of my pocket and laid it on the coffee table in front of me. The gun sat there looking very solid, very black, and somehow accusatory.

The dryer stopped, and he called to me again. *"Ma petite?"*

"What?"

"Come talk to me as the sun rises."

I glanced up at the window he had opened. The sky outside was less black, not light yet, but not pure darkness anymore. I closed the drapes and went to the bedroom. I left the gun on the table. The Browning was in the bedroom anyway.

Jean-Claude had neatly folded the bedspread and blanket at the foot of the bed. Only the wine-dark sheet covered him. He lay with his black hair soft and curling over the dark pillows. The sheet was bunched at his waist. "You can join me if you like."

I leaned against the wall and shook my head.

"I'm not offering sex, *ma petite;* dawn is too close for that. I offer you your half of the bed."

"I'll take the couch; thanks anyway."

He smiled, a slow knowing curve of lips—his old arrogance peeking back out. It was almost comforting to know nothing had really changed. "It is not me that you do not trust. It is you."

I shrugged.

He raised the sheet in front of his chest, an almost protective gesture. "It comes." Fear in his voice.

"What comes?"

"The sun."

I glanced at the closed drapes against the far wall. They were double thick, but a line of greyish light edged them. "You'll be alright like this without your coffin?"

"As long as no one opens the drapes." He looked at me for a long moment. "I love you, *ma petite,* as much as I'm able."

I didn't know what to say. Saying I lusted after him didn't seem appropriate. Saying I loved him would be a lie.

The light grew stronger, a white edge around the curtains. His body slumped back against the bed. He rolled onto his side, one hand outstretched, the other curling the sheets against his chest. He stared at the growing light, and I could taste his fear.

I knelt beside the bed. I almost took his hand but didn't. "What happens now?"

"You want the truth, then watch." I expected his eyes to flutter, his voice to grow sluggish as if he were falling asleep. It didn't happen that way. He closed his eyes all at once. Pain flashed across his face. He whispered, "It hurts." His face went slack. I'd seen people die, watched the light fade from their bodies. Felt their souls slip away. That was what I saw. He died. The light grew against the drapes, and when it was a solid white line, he died. His breath went out of him in a long rattle.

I knelt beside the bed and stared. I knew dead when I saw it, and this was it. Shit.

I put my arms on the bed and propped my chin on them. I watched him, waiting for him to breathe, to twitch, something. But there was nothing. I reached out to his one outstretched arm. My fingers hovered above his skin, then I touched him. The skin was still warm, still human, but he did not move. I checked his wrist, and there was no pulse. No blood moved in this body.

Did he know I was here? Did he feel me touching him? I stared at him for what seemed like a long time. So this answered the question. Vampires were dead. Whatever animated them was like my own power, some sort of necromancy. But I knew death when I saw it. It gave necrophilia a whole new slant.

Had I only imagined that I felt the brush of his soul leave his body? Surely vampires had no souls—that was part of the point—but I'd felt something leave. If not a soul, what? If a soul, where did it go for the daylight hours? Who watched all the vampires' souls while they lay dead?

There was a knock at the door, probably the other boys. I stood up, pulling my robe in tight. I was cold, and wasn't sure why. I went to answer the door. The cut on my tongue had almost stopped bleeding.

31

I DREAMED. IN the dream, someone held me in their lap. Smooth dark arms wrapped around me. I looked up into my mother's laughing face. She was the most beautiful woman in the world. I snuggled against her body, and the clean smell of her skin was there. She'd always smelled of Hypnotique bath powder. She bent and kissed me on the lips. I had forgotten the taste of her lipstick, the way she brushed my mouth with her thumb, and laughed because she'd gotten bright red lipstick on my small mouth.

Her thumb came away with something brighter than lipstick. Blood dripped down her thumb. She'd pricked her skin with a safety pin. It was bleeding. She held her thumb out to me and said, "Kiss it, Anita, make it all better."

But there was too much blood. It ran down her hand. I stared up at her laughing face, and blood ran down it like rain. I woke sitting bolt upright on the velvet couch, gasping for breath. I could still taste her lipstick on my mouth, and the smell of Hypnotique bath powder clung to me.

Larry sat up on the love seat, rubbing at his eyes. "What's wrong? Did we get our wake-up call?"

"No, I had a bad dream."

He nodded, stretching, then frowned. "Do you smell perfume?"

I stared at him. "What do you mean?"

"Perfume or powder or something; do you smell it?"

I swallowed and nearly choked on my own pulse. "Yeah. I smell it."

I flung back the extra blanket and threw the lumpy pillow across the room.

Larry swung his legs off the love seat. "What is wrong with you?"

I went to the window and flung the drapes open. The bedroom door was closed, and Jean-Claude was safely inside. Jason was sleeping in there. I stood in the sunlight and let the heat sink into me. I leaned against the warm glass, and only then realized that I was wearing nothing but an over-sized t-shirt and my undies. Oh, well. I stayed in the sunlight for a few minutes, waiting for my pulse to calm down.

"Serephina sent me a dream. The smell is my mother's perfume."

Larry came to stand beside me. He was wearing a pair of gym shorts and a green t-shirt. His curly red hair stuck up in all directions. His blue eyes squinted when he stepped into the light. "I thought only a vampire that had a connection with you, a hold on you, could invade your dreams."

"That's what I thought," I said.

"How could I smell perfume from your dream?"

I shook my head, forehead against the glass. "I don't know."

"Has she marked you?"

"I don't know."

He touched my shoulder, squeezing. "It'll be alright."

I stepped away from him to pace the room. "It won't be alright, Larry. Serephina invaded my dreams. No one but Jean-Claude has ever done that." I stopped, because that wasn't true. Nikolaos had done it. But that was after she'd bitten me. I shook my head. Either way, it was a very bad sign.

"What are you going to do?"

"Kill her."

"Murder her, you mean."

If Larry's earnest eyes hadn't been staring at me, I'd have said, "You bet." But it's hard to contemplate murder with someone staring at you like you've kicked their favorite puppy.

"I'll try to get a warrant," I said.

"If you can't?"

"If it's her or me, Larry, then it's her. Okay?"

Larry looked at me sadly. "What I did last night was murder. I know that, but I didn't go in planning to kill someone."

"You stay in this business long enough and you will."

He shook his head. "I don't believe that."

"Believe what you want, but it's still the truth. These things are too dangerous to play fair."

"If you really believe that, then how can you date Jean-Claude? How can you let him touch you?"

I shook my head. "I never said I was consistent."

"You can't defend yourself, can you?"

"Defend which one? Killing Serephina or dating Jean-Claude?"

"Either, both. Hell, Anita, if you're one of the bad guys you can't be one of the good guys."

I opened my mouth and closed it. What could I say? "I am one of the good guys, Larry. But I'm not going to be a martyr. If that means breaking the law, so be it."

"Are you going to get a warrant?" His face was very neutral as he asked. He looked older suddenly. Even with his orangey curls sticking up, he looked solemn.

I was watching Larry grow older before my eyes. Not in age, but in experience. The expression in his eyes was older than it had been a few months ago. Seen too much, done too much. He was still trying to be Sir Galahad, but Galahad had had God on his side. All Larry had was me. It wasn't enough.

"The only way I could get a death warrant is to lie," I said.

"I know," he said.

I stared at him. "Serephina hasn't broken any laws, yet. I won't lie about that."

He smiled. "Good. When do we meet Dorcas Bouvier?"

"Three."

"Have you figured out what you can sacrifice to raise the zombies Stirling wants done?" he asked.

"Nope."

He stared at me. "What are you going to tell Stirling?"

I shook my head. "I don't know yet. I wish I knew why he's so hot and heavy to kill Bouvier."

"He wants the land," Larry said.

"Stirling and Company have been saying the Bouvier family, not Magnus Bouvier. That means he's not the only one suing them. So killing Magnus won't solve their problems."

"So why do it?" Larry asked.

"Exactly," I said.

Larry nodded. "We need to talk to Magnus again."

"Preferably without Serephina around," I said.

"Amen to that," Larry said.

"I'd love to talk to Magnus, but before we tackle Mr. Bouvier again, I'd like to find some fairie ointment."

"Some what?"

"Didn't you take any classes on fairies?"

"It was an elective," he said.

"Fairie ointment makes you proof against glamor. Just in case whatever else Magnus is hiding is nastier than Serephina."

"Nothing nastier than that," he said.

"True, but just in case, he won't be able to work magic on us. In fact, it's not a bad precaution before we meet Dorrie. She may not be as scary as Magnus, but she shines, and I'd just as soon she didn't shine all over us."

"You think Serephina will find Jeff Quinlan?"

"If anyone can, she can. She seemed pretty confident she could take Xavier, but then Jean-Claude had been pretty confident he could take her last night. He was wrong."

He frowned. "So we're rooting for Serephina?"

It sounded wrong, put that way, but I nodded. "If it's a choice between a vampire that obeys most of the laws, and one that slaughters kids, yeah, we're on her side."

"You were talking about killing her just a little bit ago."

"I can stay out of her way until she saves Jeff, and kills Xavier."

"Why would she kill him?" Larry asked.

"He's killing people in her territory. She can say anything she wants, but that's a direct challenge to her authority. Besides, I don't think Xavier will give up Jeff without a fight."

"What do you think happened to him last night?" Larry asked.

I shook my head. "It doesn't do any good to dwell on it, Larry. We're doing all we can."

"We could tell the FBI about Serephina."

"One thing I've learned is that master vamps don't talk to the cops. Too many years of the cops killing them on sight, or trying to."

"Okay," he said, "but we've still got to come up with something big enough to kill for raising the cemetery tonight," he said.

"I'll think on it."

"You really have no idea what to do?" He sounded surprised.

"Short of a human sacrifice, Larry, I don't think I can raise several three-hundred-year-old corpses. Even I've got my limits."

He grinned. "Nice to hear you admit it."

I had to smile. "It'll be our little secret."

He put his hand out, and I slapped it. He slapped mine back, and I felt better. Larry had a way of making me smile. Friends will do that to you.

32

DORCAS BOUVIER WAS leaning on a car in the parking lot. Her hair gleamed in the sunlight, swirling as she moved, like heavy water. In jeans and a green tank top, she was flawless.

Larry tried not to stare at her, but it was hard work. Larry was wearing a blue t-shirt, jeans, white Nikes, and an oversized checked flannel shirt to hide his shoulder holster.

I was in jeans and a navy blue polo shirt, black Nikes, and an oversized blue dress shirt. I'd had to borrow it from Larry after my black jacket had gotten covered in vampire goop. Had to have something to hide the Browning. Makes people nervous if you go around with a naked gun. Larry and I looked like we'd dressed from the same closet.

Dorrie pushed away from the car. "Shall we go?"

"We'd like to talk to Magnus."

"So you can turn him in to the cops?"

I shook my head. "So we can find out why Stirling is so hot to kill him."

"I don't know where he is," Dorcas said.

Maybe it showed on my face, because she said, "I don't know where he is, but if I did, I wouldn't tell you. Using magic on the police is a death penalty case. I won't turn him in."

"I'm not the police."

She looked at me, eyes narrowing. "Did you come to look at Bloody Bones, or to question me about my brother?"

"How did you know to be waiting here for us?" I asked.

"I knew you'd be on time." Her pupils swirled downward to pinpoints, like the eyes of an excited parrot.

"Let's go," I said.

She led us to the back of the restaurant where it nearly touched the woods. A path began at the edge of the clearing. It was barely wide enough for a man. Even though we walked single file, the branches whipped at my shoulders. The new green leaves rubbed like velvet along my cheek. The path was deep and rutted down to naked tree roots in places, but weeds were beginning to encroach on the path, as if it wasn't used as much as it once had been.

Dorrie moved down the uneven path with an easy, swinging stride. She was obviously familiar with the path, but it was more than that. The tree limbs that caught on my shirt didn't get caught in her hair. The roots that threatened to trip me didn't slow her down.

We'd found ointment at a health food store. So the bushes moving for her and not for us was real, not illusion. Maybe glamor wasn't the only thing to worry about. Which was why the Browning was loaded with nonsilver bullets. I'd had to go out and buy some special for the occasion. Larry was loaded up too, and for the first time I wished he had two guns. I still had the Firestar with silver ammo, but Larry was out of luck if a vamp jumped us. Of course, it was broad daylight. I was more worried about fairies than vamps right this minute. There was salt in our shirt pockets, not a lot, but you didn't need much, just enough to throw on the fey or the thing being magicked. Salt disrupted fey magic. Temporarily.

A breeze came up the path. It grew into a wind in one fitful gust. The air smelled clean and fresh. You hoped the beginning of time smelled like that; like fresh bread, clean laundry, childhood memories of spring. It probably smelled like ozone and swamp water. Reality almost always smells worse than daydream.

Dorrie stopped and turned back to us. "The trees across the path are just illusion. They're not solid."

"What trees?" Larry asked. I cursed silently. It would have been nice to keep the ointment a secret.

Dorrie took two steps back towards us. She stared at my face from inches away, then made a face like she'd seen something unclean. "You're wearing ointment." She made it sound like a very bad thing.

"Magnus did try to bedazzle us twice. Nothing wrong with being cautious," I said.

"Well, our illusions won't matter to you, then." She took off at a faster pace, leaving us to stumble after her.

The path led into a clearing that was nearly a perfect circle. There was a small mound in the center with a white stone Celtic cross in the middle of a mass of vibrant blue flowers. Every inch of ground was covered with bluebells. English bluebells, thick and fleshy, bluer than the sky. The flowers never grew in this country without help. They never grew in Missouri without more water than was practical. But standing in the solid mass of blue surrounded by trees, it seemed worth it.

Dorrie stood frozen nearly knee-deep in the flowers. She was staring open-mouthed, a look of horror on her lovely face.

Magnus Bouvier knelt in the flowers on top of the mound, near the cross. His mouth was bright with fresh blood. Something moved around him, in front of him. Something more felt than seen. If it was illusion, the ointment should have taken care of it. I tried looking at it out of the corner of my eye. Sometimes peripheral vision works better on magic than straight-on sight.

From the corner of my eye I could see the air swimming in something that was almost a shape. It was bigger than a man.

Magnus turned and saw us. He stood up abruptly, and the swimming air blinked out like it had never been. He wiped a sleeve across his mouth.

"Dorrie . . ." His voice was soft and strangled.

Dorrie clawed her way up the hill. She screamed, "Blasphemy!" and smacked him. I could hear the slap all the way across the clearing.

"Ouch," Larry said. "Why is she mad?"

She hit him again, hard enough to sit him down on his butt in the flowers. "How could you? How could you do such a vile thing?"

"What did he do?" Larry asked.

"He's been feeding off Rawhead and Bloody Bones just like his ancestor," I said.

Dorrie turned to me. She looked haggard, horrified, as if she had caught her brother molesting children. "It was forbidden to feed." She turned back to Magnus. "You knew that!"

"I wanted the power, Dorrie. What harm did it do?"

"What harm? What harm?" She grabbed a handful of his long hair and pulled him to his knees. She exposed the bite marks on his neck. "This is why that creature can call you. This is why one of the *Daoine Sidhe,* even a half-breed like you, is called by death." She let go so abruptly he fell forward on his hands and knees.

Dorrie sat down in the flowers and cried.

I waded into the flowers. They parted like water, but they didn't move. They were just never exactly where you were stepping.

"Jesus, are they moving out of the way?" Larry asked.

"Not exactly," Magnus said. He walked down the mound to stand at its base. He was wearing the white tuxedo from last night, or what was left of it. The smear of blood on his shirtsleeve was very bright against the whiteness.

We waded through the flowers that were moving and not moving, to join him in front of the mound.

He'd shoved his hair back behind his ears so his face was visible. And no, his ears weren't pointed. Where do these rumors get started?

He met my eyes without flinching. If he was ashamed of what he'd done, it didn't show. Dorrie was still weeping in the bluebells like her heart would break.

"So now you know," he said.

"You can't bleed a fairie, in the flesh or not in the flesh, without ritual magic. I've read the spell, Magnus. It's a doozy," I said.

He smiled at that, and the smile was still lovely, but the blood at the corner of his mouth ruined the effect. "I had to tie myself to the beastie. I had to give him some of my mortality in order to get his blood."

"The spell isn't meant to help you gather blood," I said. "It's to help the fairies kill each other."

"If it got some of your mortality, did you get some of its immortality?" Larry asked. It was a good question.

"Yes," Magnus said, "but that wasn't why I did it."

"You did it for power, you son of a bitch," Dorrie said. She came down the mound, sliding in the strange flowers. "You just had to do real glamor, real magic. My God, Magnus, you must have been drinking its blood for years, ever since you were a teenager. That's when your powers suddenly got so strong. We all thought it was puberty."

"Afraid not, sister dear."

She spit at him. "Our family was cursed, tied to this land forever in repentance for doing what you have done. Bloody Bones broke free last time someone tried to drink from his veins."

"It's been safely imprisoned for ten years, Dorrie."

"How do you know? How do you know that nebulous thing you called up hasn't been out scaring children?"

"As long as it doesn't hurt any of them, what's the harm?"

"Wait a minute," said Larry. "Why would it scare children?"

"I told you, it's a nursery boggle. It was supposed to eat bad children," I said. I had an idea, an awful idea. I'd seen a vampire use a sword, but was I absolutely sure of what I'd seen? No. "When the thing got out and started slaughtering the Indian tribe, did it use a weapon, or its hands?"

Dorrie looked at me. "I don't know. Does it matter?"

Larry said, "Oh, my God."

"It might matter a great deal," I said.

"You can't mean those killings," Magnus said. "Bloody Bones cannot manifest itself physically. I've seen to that."

"Are you sure, brother dear? Are you absolutely sure?" Dorrie's voice cut and sliced; she wielded scorn like a weapon.

"Yes, I'm sure."

"We'll have to have a witch look at this. I don't know enough about it," I said.

Dorrie nodded. "I understand. The sooner the better."

"Rawhead and Bloody Bones did not do those killings," Magnus said.

"For your sake, Magnus, I hope not," I said.

"What do you mean?"

"Because five people have died. Five people who didn't do a damn thing to deserve it."

"It's imprisoned by a combination of Indian, Christian, and fairie power," he said. "It's not breaking free of that."

I walked around the mound slowly. The fleshy flowers still moved out of the way. I'd tried watching my feet, but it was dizzying, because the flowers moved yet didn't, like trying to watch one of them bloom. You knew it did, but you could never watch the actual event.

I ignored the flowers and concentrated on the mound. I wasn't trying to sense the dead, so daylight was fine. There was magic here, lots of it. I'd never felt fairie magic before. There was something here that had a familiar taste to it, and it wasn't the Christianity. "Some kind of death magic went into this," I said. I walked around the mound until I could see Magnus's face. "A little human sacrifice, perhaps?"

"Not exactly," Magnus said.

"We would never condone human sacrifice," Dorrie said.

Maybe she wouldn't, but I wasn't so sure about Magnus. I didn't say it out loud. Dorrie was upset enough already.

"If it's not sacrifice, then what is it?"

"Three hills are buried with our dead. Each death is like a stake to hold old Bloody Bones down," Magnus said.

"How did you lose track of which hills belonged to you?" I asked.

"It's been over three hundred years," Magnus said. "There were no deeds back then. I wasn't a hundred percent sure the hill was the right hill myself. But when they raked up the dead, I felt it." He huddled in on himself as if the air had suddenly grown colder. "You can't raise the dead from that hillside. If you do it, then Bloody Bones will be loosed. The magic to stop it is complicated. Truthfully, I'm not sure I'm up to it myself. And I don't know any Indian shamans anymore."

"You have made a mockery of everything we stand for," Dorrie said.

"What did Serephina offer you?" I asked.

He looked at me, surprised. "What are you talking about?"

"She offers everyone their heart's desire. What was yours, Magnus?"

"Freedom and power. She said she'd find another guardian for Rawhead and Bloody Bones. She said she'd find a way for me to keep the power I'd borrowed from it without having to tend it."

"And you believed her?"

He shook his head. "I'm the only person in the family who has the power. We are the guardians forever as penance for stealing it, for letting it kill." He collapsed to his knees in the blue, blue flowers, his head bowed, hair spilling forward to hide his face. "I'll never be free."

"You don't deserve to be free," Dorrie said.

"Why did Serephina want you so badly?" I asked.

"She's afraid of death. She says drinking from something as long-lived as I am helps her keep death at bay."

"She's a vampire," Larry protested.

"But not immortal," I said.

Magnus looked up, strange aquamarine eyes glimmering out through his shining hair. Maybe it was the hair, or the eyes, or his being nearly covered in the strange moving, not moving flowers, but he didn't look very human.

"She fears death," he said. "She fears you." His voice was low and echoing.

"She nearly cleaned my clock last night. Why's she afraid of me?"

"You brought death among us last night."

"It can't be the first time," I said.

"She came to me for my long life, my immortal blood. Perhaps she will go to you next. Perhaps instead of running from death, she will embrace it."

The skin on my arms twitched, marching in gooseflesh up to my elbows. "She tell you that last night?"

"There is a power involved, hurting her old enemy Jean-Claude, but in the end, Anita, she wonders if your power would make the difference. If she drank you up, would she be immortal? Would you be able to keep death from her with your necromancy?"

"You could leave town," Larry said. I wasn't sure which of us he was speaking to.

I shook my head. "Master vampires don't give up that easy. I'll tell Stirling that I won't be raising his dead, Magnus. No one else can do it but me, so it won't get done."

"But they won't give back the land," Magnus said in his strange voice. "If they simply blow up the mountain, the result might be the same."

"Is that true, Dorrie?"

She nodded. "It could be."

"What do you want me to do?" I asked.

Magnus crawled through the flowers, peering at me through the shining curtain of his hair. His eyes were swirling bands of green and blue, whirling until I was dizzy. I looked away.

"Raise a handful of the dead. Can you do that?" he asked.

"No sweat," I said. "But will everybody's lawyers agree to that?"

"I'll see that they do," he said.

"Dorrie?" I asked.

She nodded. "I'll see to it."

I stared at Magnus for a moment. "Will Serephina really rescue the boy?"

"Yes," he said.

I stared down at him. "Then I'll see you tonight."

"No, I'll be well and truly drunk again. It's not foolproof, but it helps drown her out."

"Fine; I'll raise you a handful of dead. Keep your land safe."

"You have our gratitude," Magnus said. He looked feral, frightening, beautiful crouched in the flowers. His gratitude might be worth something if Serephina didn't kill him first.

Hell, if she didn't kill me first.

33

I CALLED SPECIAL Agent Bradford late in the day. They hadn't found Xavier. They hadn't found Jeff. They hadn't found any vampires that I needed to kill, and why the hell was I calling him? I was not on this case, remember? I remembered. And yes, the two youngest victims had been sexually assaulted, but not the same day they were killed. I probably should have brought Magnus in, but he was the only one who understood the spells on Bloody Bones. He wouldn't be any good to us locked up. Dorrie knew a local witch she trusted. I'd thought that maybe Bloody Bones was our killer. I'd never seen a vampire hide itself so completely from me as the one that killed Coltrain. I'd added it to my list of suspects, but hadn't told the cops. Now I was glad I hadn't. The sexual assault had Xavier written all over it. Besides, explaining that a nursery boggle from Scotland was committing murders on the ethereal plane sounded far-fetched even to me.

The sky was thick with clouds that glowed like jewels. They shimmered and stretched across the sky like a gigantic gleaming blanket that some great beast had shredded with massive claws. Through the holes in the clouds, the sky peeked through black with a few diamond-chip stars bright enough to compete with the gleaming sky.

I stood on the hilltop staring up at the sky, breathing in the cool spring air. Larry stood beside me, looking up. His eyes reflected the glowing light.

"Get on with it," Stirling said.

I turned and looked at him. Him, Bayard, and Ms. Harrison. Beau had been with them, but I'd made him wait at the bottom of the mountain. I'd even told him if he so much as showed his face up top, I'd put a bullet in it. I wasn't sure Stirling believed me, but Beau had.

"Not an appreciator of nature's beauty, are you, Raymond?"

Even by moonlight I could see his scowl. "I want this over with, Ms. Blake. Now, tonight."

Strangely enough, I agreed with him. It made me nervous. I didn't like Raymond. It made me want to argue with him, regardless of whether I agreed. But I didn't argue. Point for me.

"I'll get it done tonight, Raymond; don't sweat it."

"Please stop calling me by my first name, Ms. Blake." He made the request through clenched teeth, but he had said "please."

"Fine. It'll be done tonight, Mr. Stirling. Okay?"

He nodded. "Thank you; now get on with it."

I opened my mouth to say something smart, but Larry said very softly, "Anita."

He was right, as usual. As much fun as it was to yank Stirling's chain, it was just delaying the inevitable. I was tired of Stirling, of Magnus, and of everything. It was time to do this job and go home. Well, maybe not straight home. I wouldn't leave without Jeff Quinlan, one way or another.

The goat gave a high, questioning bleat. It was staked out in the middle of the boneyard. It was a brown-and-white-spotted goat with those strange yellow eyes they sometimes have. It had floppy white ears and seemed to like having the top of its head scratched. Larry had petted it in the Jeep on the drive over. Always a bad idea. Never get friendly with the sacrifices. Makes it hard to kill them.

I had not petted the goat. I knew better. This was Larry's first goat. He'd learn. Hard or easy, he'd learn. There were two more goats at the bottom of the hill. One of them was even smaller and cuter than this one.

"Shouldn't we have the Bouviers' lawyers present, Mr. Stirling?" Bayard said.

"The Bouviers waived having their attorney present," I said.

"Why would they do that?" Stirling asked.

"They trust me not to lie to them," I said.

Stirling looked at me for a long moment. I couldn't see his eyes clearly, but I could feel the wheels inside his head moving.

"You're going to lie for them, aren't you?" he said. His voice was cold, repressed, too angry for heat.

"I don't lie about the dead, Mr. Stirling. Sometimes about the living, but never about the dead. Besides, Bouvier didn't offer me a bribe. Why should I help him if he doesn't throw money at me?"

Larry didn't call me on that one. He was looking at Stirling, too. Wondering what he'd say, maybe.

"You've made your point, Ms. Blake. Can we get on with it now?" He sounded reasonable, ordinary suddenly. All that anger, all that mistrust, had had to go somewhere. But it wasn't in his voice.

"Fine." I knelt and opened the gym bag at my feet. It held my animating equipment. I had another one that held vampire gear. I used to just transfer whatever I wanted into the bag. I bought a second bag after I showed up once at a zombie raising with the wrong bag. It was also illegal to carry vampire slaying stuff if you didn't have a warrant of execution on you. Brewster's law might change that, but until then . . . I had two bags. The zombie was my normal burgundy one; the vampire bag was white. Even in the dark, it was easy to tell them apart. That was the plan.

Larry's zombie bag was a nearly virulent green with Teenage Mutant Ninja Turtles on it. I was almost afraid to ask what his vampire bag looked like.

"Let me test my understanding here," Larry said. My words fed back to me. He knelt and unzipped his bag.

"Go ahead," I said. I got out my jar of ointment. I knew animators who had special containers for the ointment. Crockery, hand-blown glass, mystical symbols carved into the sides. I used an old Mason jar that had once held Grandma Blake's green beans.

Larry fished out a peanut butter jar with the label still on it. Extra-crunchy. Yum-yum.

"We have to raise a minimum of three zombies, right?"

"Right," I said.

He stared around at the scattered bones. "A mass grave is hard to raise from, right?"

"This isn't a mass grave. It's an old cemetery that was disturbed. That's easier than a mass grave."

"Why?" he asked.

I laid the machete down beside the jar of ointment. "Because each grave had rites performed that would tie the dead individual to the grave, so that if you call it you have a better chance of getting an individual to answer."

"Answer?"

"Rise from the dead."

He nodded. He laid a wicked curved blade on the ground. It looked like a freaking scimitar.

"Where did you get that?"

He dipped his head, and I would have bet he was blushing. Just couldn't see it by moonlight.

"Guy at college."

"Where'd he get it?"

Larry looked at me, surprise plain on his face. "I don't know. Is something wrong with it?"

I shook my head. "Just a little fancy for beheading chickens and slitting a few goats open."

"It felt good in my hand." He shrugged. "Besides, it looks cool." He grinned at me.

I shook my head, but I let it go. Did I really need a machete to behead a few chickens, no, but the occasional cow, yeah.

Why, you may ask, didn't we have a cow tonight? No one

would sell Bayard one. He had the brilliant idea of telling the farmers why he wanted the cow. The God-fearing folk would sell their cows to be eaten, but not for raising zombies. Prejudiced bastards.

"The youngest of the dead here are two hundred years old, right?" Larry asked.

"Right," I said.

"We're going to raise a minimum of three of these corpses in good enough condition for them to answer questions."

"That's the plan," I said.

"Can we do that?"

I smiled at him. "That's the plan."

His eyes widened. "Damn, you don't know if we can do it either, do you?" His voice had dropped to an amazed whisper.

"We raise three zombies a night every night routinely. We're just doing them back to back."

"We don't raise two-hundred-year-old zombies routinely."

"True, but the theory's the same."

"Theory?" He shook his head. "I know we're in trouble when you start talking about theories. Can we do this?"

The honest answer was no, but the thing that dictated more than anything else what you could raise and what you couldn't was confidence. Believing you could do it. So . . . I was tempted to lie. But I didn't. Truth between Larry and me.

"I think we can do it."

"But you don't know for sure," he said.

"No."

"Geez, Anita."

"Don't get rattled on me. We can do this."

"But you aren't sure."

"I'm not sure we'll survive the plane ride home, but I'm still getting on the plane."

"Was that supposed to be comforting?" he asked.

"Yeah."

"It wasn't," he said.

"Sorry, but this is as good as it gets. You want certainty, be an accountant."

"I'm not good at math."

"Me either."

He took a deep breath and let it out slowly. "Alright, boss, how do we combine powers?"

I told him.

"Neat." He didn't look nervous anymore. He looked eager. Larry may have wanted to be a vampire executioner, but he was an animator. It wasn't a career choice, it was a gift, or a curse. No one could teach you to raise the dead unless you had the power in your blood. Genetics is a wonderful thing: brown eyes, curly hair, zombie raising.

"Whose ointment you want to use?" Larry asked.

"Mine." I'd given Larry the recipe for the ointment and told him which ingredients you couldn't mess with, like the graveyard mold, but there was room for experimentation. Every animator had their own special recipe. You never knew what Larry's ointment would smell like. For sharing powers you used the same ointment, so we were using mine.

For all I knew, we didn't have to use the same ointment, but I'd only shared my powers three times. Twice with the man who trained me as an animator. Each time we'd used the same ointment. I had acted as a focus all three times. Which meant I was in charge. Where I liked to be, right?

"Could I act as a focus?" Larry asked. "Not this time, but later?"

"If this comes up again, we'll try it," I said. Truth was, I didn't know if Larry had the power to be a focus. Manny, who taught me, couldn't do it. Very few animators could act as a focus. Those who could were mistrusted by the rest, and most wouldn't play with us. We would literally share our powers. A lot of animators wouldn't be willing to do that. There is a theory that you could permanently steal another's magic. But I don't buy it. Raising the dead isn't like a magic charm that someone can take with them, and leave you without. Animating is built into the cells of our bodies. It's part of us. You can't steal that.

I opened the ointment, and the spring air suddenly smelled like Christmas trees. I used a lot of rosemary.

The ointment was thick and waxy and always felt cool. Flecks of glowing graveyard mold looked like ground-up lightning bugs. I smeared ointment across Larry's forehead, down his cheeks. He untucked his t-shirt and raised it so I could dab it over his heart. Which is harder than it sounds with a shoulder holster on, but we'd both worn a gun apiece. I had left both knives and my backup gun in the Jeep. I touched his skin and could feel his heart pounding under my hand.

I handed Larry the Mason jar. He dipped two fingers into the thick ointment. He traced ointment over my face. His hand was very steady, face blank with concentration. Eyes utterly serious.

I unbuttoned the polo shirt and Larry slipped his fingers inside to touch my heart. His fingers rubbed the chain of my crucifix, spilling it out of my shirt. I slipped it back inside next to my skin. He handed the jar back to me, and I screwed the lid on tight. Wouldn't do to let it dry out.

I'd never heard of anyone doing exactly what we were about to attempt. Not the age part, but the scattered bodies. We only wanted three, but there weren't three intact bodies. Even doing them one at a time, it was chancy. How to raise just so much dead and no more when they were lying jumbled together? I had no names to use. No gravesite to encircle with power. How to do it?

It was a puzzlement.

But for now we just had to close the circle. One problem at a time.

"Make sure both of your hands have ointment on them," I said.

Larry rubbed his hands together like he was putting on lotion. "Aye, aye, boss; what next?"

I drew a deep silver bowl out of my bag. It gleamed in the moonlight like another piece of sky.

Larry's eyes widened.

"It doesn't have to be silver. There are no mystical symbols on it. You could use a Tupperware bowl, but the life of another living creature is going in here. Use something nice to show some respect, but understand that it doesn't have to be silver, or this shape, or anything. It's just a container. Okay?"

Larry nodded. "Why not have the other goats up here on top? It's going to be a trek to get them up here every time."

I shrugged. "First, they'd panic. Second, it seems cruel for them to watch their friends bite the dust, knowing they're next."

"My zoology prof would say you're humanizing them."

"Let him. I know they feel pain, and fear. That's enough."

Larry looked at me for a long moment. "You don't like doing it either."

"No. You want to help hold or feed the carrot?"

"Carrot?"

I dug a carrot, complete with leafy green top, out of the bag.

"Was that what you got in the grocery store while I waited in the car with the goats?"

"Yeah."

I held the carrot up in the air. The goat strained to the end of its picket line, towards the carrot. I let the goat lip the leafy top. It bleated and strained towards me. I let him get a little more leaf. His stubby little tail started wagging. Happy goat.

I handed Larry the silver bowl. "Put it on the ground under the throat. When the blood starts coming, catch as much as you can."

I had the machete behind my back in my right hand, carrot in my left. I felt like a child's dentist. No, nothing behind my back. Pay no attention to that huge needle. Except this needle was permanent.

The goat yanked most of the leaves off the carrot, and I waited while it snaked them up into its mouth. Larry knelt beside it, bowl on the ground. I offered the meat of the carrot to the goat. It got a taste of it, and I drew the carrot out, out, until the goat strained its neck out as far as it could, trying to get more of the hard orange flesh.

I laid the machete against the hairy throat, not cutting,

gentle. The neck vibrated against the blade, straining for the carrot. I drew the blade across the neck.

The machete was sharp, and I had practice. There was no sound, only the shocked, widened eyes, and blood pouring from the neck.

Larry picked up the bowl, holding it under the wound. Blood splashed down his arms onto the blue t-shirt. The goat collapsed to its knees. Blood filled the bowl, dark and glinting, more black than red.

"There's bits of carrot in the blood," Larry said.

"It alright," I said. "Carrot's inert."

The goat's head fell slowly forward until it touched the ground. The bowl sat under its throat, filling with blood. It had been nearly a perfect kill. Goats could be sort of pesky, but sometimes, like tonight, it all worked. Of course, we weren't done.

I laid the bloody knife against my left arm and sliced it open. The pain was sharp and immediate. I held the wound over the bowl, letting the thick drops mingle with the goat's blood.

"Give me your right arm," I said.

Larry didn't argue. He just held out his bare arm. I'd told him what would happen, but it was still a very trusting gesture. His face turned up to me was without any trace of fear. God.

I sliced his arm. He winced but didn't draw back. "Let it drip into the bowl."

He held his arm over the bowl. All the blood was red-black in the moonlight.

The beginnings of power trickled over my skin. My power, Larry's power, the power of a ritual sacrifice. Larry looked up at me with wide eyes.

I knelt beside him and laid the machete across the mouth of the bowl. I held out my left hand to him. He gave me his right. We clasped hands and pressed the wounds in our forearms together, letting the blood mingle. Larry held one side of the blood-filled bowl and I held the other. Blood trickled down our arms to drip off our elbows into the bowl, onto the bloody naked steel.

We stood still clasped together, still holding the bowl. I withdrew my hand from his slowly, then took the bowl from him. He followed my every movement like he always did. He'd be able to close his eyes and mimic me.

I walked to the edge of the circle I had in my mind and plunged my hand into the bowl. The blood was still amazingly warm, almost hot. I grasped the handle of the machete with my bloody hand and began using the blade to sprinkle blood as I walked.

I could feel Larry standing in the center of the circle that I walked like there was a rope stretched between us. As I walked, that rope stretched tighter and tighter like a rubber band being twisted. The power grew with each step, each drop of blood. The earth was hungry for it. I'd never raised the dead on ground that had seen death rituals before. Magnus should have mentioned that. Maybe he hadn't known. Charitable of me.

It didn't matter now. There was magic here for blood and death. Something that was eager for me to close the circle. Eager for me to raise the dead. Hungry.

I stood nearly where I'd begun. I was a sprinkle of blood away from closing the circle. The line of power between Larry and me was so tight it hurt. The potential power was frightening, and exhilarating. We'd awakened something old and long dormant. It made me hesitate. Made me not want to finish the circle. Stubbornness, and fear. I didn't completely understand what I was feeling. It was someone else's magic, someone's spell. We'd triggered it, but I didn't know what it would do. We could raise our dead, but it would be like walking a tightrope between the other spell and . . . something.

I felt old Bloody Bones in its barrow miles away. I felt it watching me, urging me to take that last step. I shook my head as if the fey creature could see me. I just didn't understand the spell well enough to risk it.

"What's wrong?" Larry asked. His voice sounded strangled. We were choking on unused power, and damned if I knew what to do with it.

I caught movement out of the corner of my eye. Ivy stood

at the edge of the mountain. She was wearing hiking boots with thick white socks folded over them, baggy black shorts, and a skin-tight neon pink top, with a checked flannel shirt over it. The chain of her dangling earring gleamed in the moonlight. She'd dressed herself tonight.

All I had to do was drop that last bit of blood, and the circle would close. And I could hold this circle against her, against them all. Nothing would cross it that I didn't want to cross it. Well, within reason. Demons and angels could probably cross it, but vampires couldn't.

I felt a surge of triumph from the thing trapped in its mound. It wanted me to close the circle. I tossed the bowl and machete behind me towards the center of the circle, away from the outer edge so no blood would fall on it. Ivy started towards me in a faster-than-light display, a blur of speed. I went for my gun, felt it slide from the holster, and she smashed into me. The impact knocked the Browning out of my hand. I hit the ground with nothing in my hands but air.

34

IVY REARED BACKWARDS, fangs flashing. Larry screamed, "Anita!" I heard the gun go off, felt the bullet hit her body. It hit her in the shoulder, twisted her body, but she turned back to me with a smile. She dug fingers into my shoulders and rolled us over, putting me on top, with one of her hands leeched to the back of my neck. She squeezed until I gasped.

"I'll snap her spine unless you throw that toy away," she said.

"She'll kill me anyway. Don't do it."

"Anita . . ."

"Now, or I'll kill her while you watch."

"Shoot her!" But there wasn't a clear shot. He'd have to

walk around me and fire point-blank. Ivy could kill me twice over before he got to us.

Ivy forced my neck lower. I braced my right arm on the ground. She'd have to break something to get me down to her. If she broke my neck, it'd be over; a broken arm would just hurt.

I heard something hit the ground, a dull, heavy thump. Larry's gun. Damn.

She pressed harder on the back of my neck. I dug the palm of my hand into the ground hard enough to leave an imprint.

"I can break that arm and bring you to me. Your choice: easy, or hard."

"Hard," I said between gritted teeth.

She grabbed for my arm, and I had an idea. I collapsed forward on top of her. It caught her off guard. I had a handful of seconds to pull the chain around my neck out of my shirt.

Her hand slid through my hair like a lover's, pressing my face against her cheek, not hard, almost gentle. "Three nights from now you'll like me, Anita. You'll worship me."

"I doubt that." The chain slid forward, the crucifix pooled against her throat. There was a blinding flash of white, white light. A rush of heat that singed my hair.

Ivy screamed and clawed at the cross, scrambling from underneath me.

I stayed on all fours with the cross dangling in front of me. The blue-white flames died away because it wasn't touching vampiric flesh anymore, but it glowed like a captive star, and she backed away from it.

I didn't know where my gun was, but the machete gleamed against the dark earth. I wrapped my hand around it and got to my feet. Larry was behind me with his own cross out, held in front of him to the length of its chain. The white light with its core of blue was almost painfully bright.

Ivy screamed, shielding her eyes. All she had to do was walk away. But she was frozen, immobile in the face of the crosses, and two true believers.

"Gun," I said to Larry.

"Can't find it."

Both guns were matte black so they wouldn't reflect light at night and make us a target; now it made them invisible.

We advanced on the vampire. She threw both arms up before her face and screamed, "Nooo!" She'd backed up nearly to the edge of the circle. If she ran, we wouldn't chase her, but she didn't run. Maybe she couldn't.

I shoved the machete up under her ribs. Blood poured down the blade onto my hands. I drove the blade upward into her heart. I gave it that last little wrench to slice it up.

Her arms fell away from her face slowly. Her eyes were wide, surprised. She stared down at the blade in her stomach, as if she didn't understand what it was doing there. The flesh of her neck was black where the cross had burned her.

She fell to her knees and I went with her, keeping my grip on the machete. She didn't die. I hadn't really expected her to. I jerked the blade out of her, doing more damage. She made a low gurgling sound, but stayed on her knees. Her hands touched the blood flowing out of her chest and stomach. She stared at the gleaming darkness as if she'd never seen blood before. The blood flow was already slowing; unless I killed her soon, the wound would close.

I stood over her and brought the machete back in a two-handed grip. I put everything I had into that downswing. The blade bit into her neck, down to the spine, catching on the bone.

Ivy stared up at me with blood streaming down her neck. I swung back for another chop, and she watched me do it, too hurt to run now. I had to struggle to get the blade out of the spine, and still she blinked up at me. If I didn't finish her, she'd heal even this.

I brought the blade down one last time and felt the last edge of bone give. The blade came out the other side, and her head slid off her shoulders in a spray of blood like a black fountain. That black blood poured over the circle and closed it.

Power filled the circle until we were drowning in it. Larry fell to his knees. The light from the crosses faded like dying stars. The vampire was dead, and the crosses couldn't help us now.

"What's happening?"

I could feel the power like water on every side, choking close. I was breathing it in, soaking it up through my skin.

I screamed wordlessly and fell to the ground. I fell through layers of power, and the moment I hit the ground I could feel the power below me, stretching downward, outward.

I was lying on top of bones. They twitched like something moving in its sleep. I crawled to my knees, hands digging into the earth. I touched a long, thin arm bone, and it moved. I scrambled to my feet, slow, too slow through the pressing air, and watched.

Bones slid through the earth like water, coming together. The earth heaved and rocked underfoot like giant moles were crawling.

Larry was on his feet now, too. "What's happening?"

"Something bad," I said.

I'd never seen the dead coalesce. They always came to the surface of the grave all in one piece. I'd never realized it was like putting together a macabre jigsaw puzzle. A skeleton formed at my feet, and flesh began to crawl over it, flow like clay, molding itself back to the bones.

"Anita?"

I turned to Larry. He was pointing at a skeleton at the far edge of the circle. Half the bones were on the outside of the circle. Flesh crawled over this side of the bones and pushed against the blood circle. The earth gave one last heave, and the magic poured out over the ground. I heard it pop inside my head like a release of pressure. The air spread out, not so drowning-thick. It poured over the hillside like invisible flame, and everywhere it touched the dead formed bodies.

"Stop it, Anita. Stop it."

"I can't." The killing magic in the ground had stolen the reins. All I could do was watch and feel the power spreading outward. Enough power to ride forever. Enough power to raise a thousand dead.

I knew when Rawhead and Bloody Bones burst its prison.

I felt the power sag as the thing escaped. Then the power lashed back into this bit of ground and drove us to our knees. The dead struggled from the earth like swimmers dragging themselves to shore. When nearly twenty dead stood waiting with empty eyes, the power flowed outward. I felt it seeking more dead, something else to raise. This I could stop. The fairie was gone, out of the loop; he had what he wanted.

I called the power back. I drew it into me, back through the ground, like pulling a snake by its tail out of a hole. I flung it into the zombies. Flung it into them and said, "Live."

The wrinkled flesh filled out. The dead eyes gleamed. The tattered clothing mended itself. Dirt fell away from a long gingham dress. A woman with midnight hair, dark skin, and Magnus's startled eyes looked at me. They all looked at me. Twenty dead, all over two hundred years old, and they could have passed for human.

"My God," Larry whispered.

Even I was impressed.

"Very impressive, Ms. Blake." Stirling's voice was wrenching, as if he shouldn't have been there. He was a different part of reality from the near-perfect zombies. The fairie was out, but I'd do my job, for what good it would do any of us.

"Which of you is a Bouvier?"

There was a murmur of voices, most of them speaking French. Nearly all of them were Bouviers. The woman introduced herself as Anias Bouvier. She looked very alive.

"Looks like you'll have to move your hotel," I said.

"Oh, I don't think so," Stirling said.

I turned and looked at him.

He had a big shiny silver gun out. A nickel-plated .45. He held it like it was a movie, kind of out in front of him, waist-high. A .45 is a big gun; you don't hit much from a waist shot. Or that's the theory. With it pointed at us, I wasn't eager to try the theory.

Bayard was pointing a .22 automatic vaguely in our direction. It didn't look like he'd held a gun before. Maybe he forgot and left the safety on.

Ms. Harrison had a nickel-plated .38 pointed very steadily at me. She stood with her legs apart, balanced on her ridiculous high heels. She held the gun in a two-handed grip like she knew what she was doing.

I flashed on her face. Her eyes in her thick makeup were a little wide, but she was rock steady. Steadier than Bayard and a better stance than Stirling. I hoped Stirling paid her well.

"What's going on, Stirling?" I asked. My voice was even, but there was an edge of power to it. I was still riding the power, enough power to put the zombies back in the ground. Enough power to do a lot of things.

He smiled visibly in the bright reflected light. "You've released the creature; now we shall kill you."

"Why the hell do you care if Bloody Bones is out?" I saw the guns and still didn't know why.

"It came into my dreams, Ms. Blake. It promised me all the Bouvier land. All of it."

"The fey breaking out won't get you the land," I said.

"It will with Bouvier dead. The deed that got us this hillside will be found to include all the land, once there's no one to fight it."

"Even with Magnus dead, you won't get the land," I said, but my voice didn't sound so sure.

"You mean his sister?" Stirling said. "She'll die just as easily as Magnus."

My stomach was tight. "Her children?"

"Rawhead and Bloody Bones loves children best of all," he said.

"You son of a bitch." It was Larry. He took a step forward, and Ms. Harrison's gun swung to him. I grabbed his arm with my free hand. I still had the machete in my hand. Larry stopped, and the gun stayed on him. I wasn't sure that was an improvement.

Tension sang down Larry's arm. I'd seen him angry, but never like this. The power responded to that anger. The zombies all turned to us in a rustle of cloth. Their glittering eyes, so alive, were waiting for us.

"Move in front of us," I whispered. The zombies began walking towards us. The closest ones moved in front of us immediately. I lost sight of the gun-toting trio. Here was hoping they'd lost sight of us.

"Kill them," Stirling said, loud, almost a yell.

I started to drop to the ground, still holding Larry's arm. He resisted. Gunfire exploded around us and he kissed dirt, flat.

With the side of his face pressed to the ground, he said, "What now?"

Bullets were hitting the zombies. The bodies jerked and twitched. Some of the very alive faces stared down, alarmed as holes appeared in their bodies. But there was no pain. The panic was reflex.

Someone was yelling; it wasn't us. "Stop it, stop it. We can't do this. We can't just kill them."

It was Bayard.

"It is late for an attack of conscience," Ms. Harrison said. It may have been the first time I'd heard her voice. She sounded efficient.

"Lionel, you are either with me, or against me."

"Shit," I muttered. I wormed forward, trying to see what was happening. I pushed aside a billowing skirt just in time to see Stirling shoot Lionel in the stomach. The .45 gave out a booming sound and nearly jerked itself out of Stirling's hand, but he held on. From less than ten inches away, you could shoot nearly anything with a .45.

Bayard collapsed to his knees, looking up at Stirling. He was trying to say something, but no sound came out.

Stirling took the gun from Bayard's hand and put it in his own jacket pocket. He turned his back on Bayard and walked out onto the hard, dry soil.

Ms. Harrison hesitated, but she followed her boss.

Bayard fell onto his side with a dark flood draining out of him. His glasses reflected the moonlight, making him look blind.

Stirling and Ms. Harrison were coming in after us. Stirling pushed among the dead as if they were trees and he was wading through. The dead didn't move for him. They stood there like stubborn, fleshy barriers. I hadn't told them to move, so they wouldn't.

Ms. Harrison had stopped trying to force her way through. Moonlight glinted on her shiny gun as she used a zombie's shoulder to sight on us.

"Kill her," I whispered.

The zombie she was using as a sighting post turned towards her. She made an exasperated sound, and the dead closed on her.

Larry looked at me. "What did you tell them?"

Ms. Harrison was screaming now. High, frightened shrieks. She fired her gun again and again. It clicked empty. Slow, eager hands and mouths latched onto her body.

"Stop them," Larry said. He grabbed my arm. "Stop them."

I could feel the hands tearing bits of flesh from Ms. Harrison. Teeth sank into her shoulder, tore that tender neck, and I knew when blood flowed into that mouth.

Larry was along for the ride. "Oh, God, stop it!" He was on his knees pulling at me, begging.

Stirling hadn't fired a shot. Where was he?

"Stop," I whispered.

The dead froze like automatons, stopped in mid-action. Ms. Harrison slid to the ground in a moaning heap.

Stirling came in from one side, the big gun pointed very steadily at us, out in a two-handed grip like it was supposed to be held. He'd made his way behind us while the zombies worked over Ms. Harrison. He was standing nearly on top of us. It took a lot of nerve to come that close to the zombies.

Larry's fingers dug into my arm. "Don't, Anita; please don't." Even staring down the barrel of a gun, Larry stuck to his morals. Admirable.

"If you say a word, Ms. Blake, I will kill you."

I just stared up at him. I was so close to him I could have reached out and touched his pants leg. The .45 was pointed very solidly at my head. If he pulled the trigger, I was gone.

"Careless of you not to have the zombies attack both of us."

I agreed with him, but all I could do was stare up at him. I still had the machete in one hand. I tried not to tighten my grip on it. Not to draw attention to it.

I must have made some betraying motion because he said, "Take your hand away from the knife, Ms. Blake, slowly."

I didn't do it. I stared up at him and his gun.

"Now, Ms. Blake, or . . ." He thumbed back the hammer on the gun. Not necessary but always dramatic.

I let go of the machete.

"Hand away from it, Ms. Blake."

I moved my hand away. I didn't move away from him and the gun. I wanted to, but I made myself be still. A few inches wouldn't make the gun less deadly, but it might make a big difference if I tried to jump him. Not my first choice, but if we ran out of other options . . . I wouldn't go down without a fight.

"Can you lay these zombies to rest, Mr. Kirkland?"

Larry hesitated. "I don't know."

Good boy. If he'd said no, Stirling might have killed him. If he'd said yes, he'd have killed me.

Larry let go of my arm and moved just a little away from me. Stirling's eyes flicked to him, back to me, but the gun barrel never wavered. Damn.

Larry was on his knees, still moving away from me, forcing Stirling to keep an eye on both of us. The .45 moved an inch from the center of my forehead, towards Larry. I took a breath and held it. Not yet, not yet . . . If I tried something too soon, I'd be dead.

Larry lunged for something on the ground. The .45 swung towards him.

I did two things at once. I slipped my left hand behind Stirling's leg and pulled, and I grabbed his groin with my right and shoved with all I was worth. I was doing the wrong thing to cause a lot of pain, but it tipped him over. He fell flat on his back with the gun swinging back towards me.

I'd hoped he'd drop the gun, or be slower. He didn't, and he wasn't. So I only had a split-second to decide whether to try to pull his privates out of his body, and cause as much pain as possible, or go for the gun. I went for the gun, not trying to grab it, but sweeping my hands into his arms. If I could control his arms, I could control the gun.

The gun went off. I didn't look. No time. Larry was either hit, or he wasn't. If he wasn't, I had to get that gun. Stirling's arms were on the ground, my hands keeping them there, but I had no leverage. He raised his arms off the ground, and I couldn't stop him. I shoved my feet into the ground and forced his arms over his head, but it had become a wrestling match now, and he outweighed me by sixty pounds.

"Drop the gun." Larry's voice behind me. I couldn't look. Couldn't take my attention from the gun. We both ignored him.

"I will shoot you," Larry said.

That got Stirling's attention. His eyes flicked to Larry; for just a moment his body hesitated. I kept my grip on his wrists and shoved myself forward, up his body. I dug my knee into his groin, trying to reach the ground through him. He let out a strangled cry. His hands spasmed.

I moved my hands up and touched the gun. His grip tightened. He wasn't letting go.

I came up beside Stirling's arms and braced his arms against my hip. I pulled the arm against my body, just one quick movement, and snapped his arm at the elbow. The hand went numb, and the gun fell into my hand.

I crawled away from him, the gun in one hand.

Larry was standing over us with a gun pointed at Stirling. Stirling didn't seem to care. He was rocking back and forth over the ground, trying to cradle both injuries at once.

"I had a gun. You could have just moved away from him," Larry said.

I just shook my head. I trusted Larry to shoot Stirling. I just hadn't trusted Stirling not to shoot Larry. "I had my hands on the gun. Seemed a shame to let it go," I said.

Larry pointed the gun at the ground, but kept a nice two-handed grip on it. "It's yours; you want it?"

I shook my head. "Keep it until we get to the car."

I looked up at the zombies. They were watching me with

calm eyes. There was blood on the mouth of the dark-haired woman. It had been her teeth that tore into Ms. Harrison's neck.

Ms. Harrison was lying very still on the ground. Passed out, at the very least.

The power was beginning to unravel at the edges. If I was going to put everybody back in the ground, it had to be now.

"Go back into the ground. Back to your graves. Go back, all of you, go back."

The dead walked upon the earth, moving among one another like children in a game of musical chairs. Then one by one they lay down upon the earth, and it swallowed them like water. The earth moved and buckled in waves, until they were all tucked out of sight.

There were no bones protruding from the earth. The earth was smooth and soft, as if the entire top of the mountain had been dug up and smoothed over.

The power shredded, flowing back into the ground, or wherever the hell it came from. We had to get down to the Jeep and start making phone calls. There was a rampaging fey on the loose. We at least had to get cops out to the Bouviers' place.

Larry knelt beside Ms. Harrison. He touched her neck. "She's alive." His hand came away stained with blood.

I looked at Stirling. He'd stopped rolling around and was just sort of huddled on his side, his arm held at an obscene angle. The look he gave me was part pain and part hate. If he ever got a second chance, I was dead.

"Shoot him if he moves," I said.

Larry got to his feet and pointed the gun dutifully at Stirling.

I went to check on Bayard. He lay on his side, half-crumpled around the wound in his belly. A wide black circle showed where his blood had soaked into the thirsty ground. I knew dead when I saw it, but I knelt on the far side of his body so I could keep an eye on Stirling. It wasn't that I didn't trust Larry. I just didn't trust Stirling.

There was no pulse in his neck. The skin was already cooling in the soft spring air. It hadn't been an instant death.

Lionel Bayard had died while we were fighting. He'd died alone, and he'd known he was dying, and that he'd been betrayed. It was a bad way to die.

I stood up and looked at Stirling. I wanted to kill him for Bayard, for Magnus, for Dorrie Bouvier, for her kids. For being a heartless son of bitch.

He'd witnessed me using zombies as a weapon. Using magic as a killing weapon was punishable by death. Self-defense was not an acceptable plea.

I stared very calmly across at Stirling and the unconscious Ms. Harrison, and realized that I could have crossed that ground and put a bullet in both of them, and slept just fine.

Sweet Jesus.

Larry glanced my way, gun still steady, but he'd taken his eyes off Stirling for a second. Not fatal, tonight, but I'd have to break him of it. "Is Bayard dead?"

"Yeah." I started back towards them, wondering what I was going to do. I didn't think Larry would let me shoot them in cold blood. Part of me was glad. Part of me wasn't.

Wind blew against my face. There was a rustling sound in the wind, like that made by trees or cloth. There were no trees on top of this mountain. I turned with the big .45 in a two-handed grip, and Janos was just there, on the edge of the mountain. Staring at his skeletal face, I think I stopped breathing. He was dressed all in black; even his hands were hidden inside black gloves. For one wild moment he looked like a floating skull. "We have the boy," he said.

35

THE CROSSES WERE still in plain sight. They glowed with a soft white radiance. No burning light, not yet. We weren't in active danger, but the cross grew warm even through my shirt.

Janos put a hand in front of his eyes, the way I would

guard my eyes from the sun in the car. "Please put those away, so we may talk."

He hadn't asked us to take them off. I could live with tucking my cross in my shirt. It could come out again later. I spilled the chain back down my shirt one-handed, keeping the .45 ready. I realized then that I didn't know if the gun had silver ammo. Now was not the time to ask. Stirling would probably lie anyway.

Larry slipped his own cross out of sight. The glowing night was just a little dimmer.

"Alright, now what?" I asked.

Kissa came up behind him, Jeff Quinlan in front of her like a shield. His glasses were gone, and he looked even younger without them. She had his arm behind his back, at an angle that could be painful with just a tug.

He was wearing a cream-colored tuxedo with a cummerbund done two shades darker to match the bow tie. Kissa was in black leather. Jeff stood out against her in wonderful contrast.

I swallowed; my pulse threatened to choke me. What was going on? "You alright, Jeff?"

"I guess so."

Kissa gave a little tug.

He winced. "I'm okay." His voice was a little higher than it should have been, a little scared.

I held out my hand to him. "Come here."

"Not yet," Janos said.

I'd tried. "What do you want?"

"First drop your guns."

"If we don't?" I thought I knew the answer, but I wanted him to say it.

"Kissa will kill the boy, and you will have done all this for nothing."

"Help me," Stirling said. "She's mad. She attacked Ms. Harrison with zombies. When we tried to defend ourselves, she nearly killed us."

That was probably what he'd say in court, too. And a jury would believe him. They'd want to believe him. I would be the big, bad zombie queen, and he would be the innocent victim.

Janos laughed, his paper-thin skin threatening to split, but never quite doing it. "Oh, no, Mr. Stirling, I watched from the darkness. I saw you murder the other man."

Fear flashed across his face. "I don't know what you mean. We hired him in good faith. He turned on us."

"My master opened your mind to Bloody Bones. She freed him to whisper in your dreams about land, money, and power. All that you desire."

"Serephina sent Ivy to kill me, or rather for me to kill her. So she'd be sure to have Bloody Bones free," I said.

"Yes," he said. "Serephina told her she had to rid herself of the disgrace of losing to you."

"By killing me."

"Yes."

"What if she'd succeeded?"

"My master had faith in you, Anita. You are death come among us. A breath of mortality."

"Why'd she want the thing freed?" I seemed to be asking that a lot tonight.

"She wishes to taste immortal blood."

"This is all sort of elaborate for a little extra kick in your food."

He gave another rictus grin. "You are what you eat, Anita. Think upon it."

I did, and my eyes widened. "She thinks by drinking immortal blood, she'll be truly immortal?"

"Very good, Anita."

"It won't work," I said.

"We shall see," he said.

"What do you get out it?" I asked.

He cocked his skeletal head to one side, like a decaying bird. "She is my master, and she shares her bounty."

"You want immortality, too?"

"I want power," he said.

Great. "And it doesn't bother you that the thing will kill children? That it's already killed some?"

"We feed, Bloody Bones feeds, what does it matter?"

"And Bloody Bones is going to just let you feed off it?"

"Serephina has found the spell that Magnus's ancestor used. She controls the fairie."

"How?"

He shook his head and smiled. "No more delays, Anita. Drop the gun, or Kissa will taste him before your eyes."

Kissa ran a hand through Jeff's short hair, a caressing gesture. It pushed his head to one side, baring a long smooth line of neck.

"No!" Jeff tried to pull away, and Kissa yanked on his arm hard enough that he cried out.

"I will break the arm, boy," she growled.

The pain held him immobile, but his eyes were wide and terrified. He looked at me. He wouldn't plead, no begging, but his eyes did it for him.

Kissa's lips pulled back from her teeth in a flashy snarl, fangs visible.

"Don't," I said, and hated it. I tossed the .45 to the ground. Larry threw my gun down. Disarmed twice in one night. It was a record even for me.

36

"NOW WHAT?" I asked.

"Serephina awaits us at the party. She sent suitable clothing for you. You can change in the limousine," Janos said.

"What party?" I asked.

"The one we have come to invite you to. She is delivering Jean-Claude's invitation in person."

That didn't sound good. "I think we'll pass on the party."

"I don't think so," Janos said.

Another vampire stepped out of the trees. It was the brunette that had tormented Jason. She stalked forward in a long black dress that covered her from neck to ankle. She slid her arms around Janos, nuzzling his neck, giving us a glimpse of her pale back. Only a fine webbing of black straps covered her back. The dress moved like it would slide down her body at the least movement, but somehow it stayed in place. Fashion-plate magic. Her dark hair was in a looping braid to one side of her face. She looked good for someone I'd seen ripped to rotting bits of flesh.

I couldn't keep the surprise off my face.

"I thought she was dead," Larry said.

"So did I."

"I would never have risked Pallas if I truly thought your werewolf could kill her," Janos said.

A second figure came out of the dark woods. Long white hair framed a thin, fine-boned face. His eyes glowed blood-red. I'd seen vampires with glowing eyes before, but they always glowed the color of their irises. No one who had ever been human had red irises. He wore a proverbial black tux and tails, complete with a nearly ankle-length cape.

"Xavier," I said softly.

Larry looked at me. "This is the vampire that's been killing everyone?"

I nodded.

"Then what's he doing here?"

"That's how you found Jeff so quickly. You're working with Xavier," I said. "Does Serephina know?"

Janos smiled. "She is master of all, Anita, even him." He said the last like it impressed him.

"You won't get to munch on your fairie for long if the cops trace Xavier to you."

"Xavier was following orders. He was on a recruitment drive." Janos seemed to like saying that last bit like it was an in-joke.

"Why did you want Ellie Quinlan?"

"Xavier likes a bit of young boy now and then. It is his one weakness. He turned the girl's lover, and the boy wanted her with him forever. Tonight she will rise and feed with us."

Not if I could help it. "What do you want, Janos?"

"I was sent to make your life easier," he said.

"Yeah, right."

Pallas uncurled herself from Janos. She glided over to Stirling.

Stirling stared up at her, cradling his broken arm. It had to hurt like hell, but it wasn't pain on his face now, it was fear. He stared up at the vampire; all the arrogance had slipped away. He looked like a kid who'd discovered the thing under the bed was really there.

A third vampire moved out of the trees. It was the blonde half of the pair. She looked fine, like she'd never rotted right before our eyes. I'd never known a vampire that could look so dead, and not be.

"You remember Bettina," he said.

Bettina wore a black dress that left her pale shoulders bare. A throw of black cloth went over one shoulder and down the front of the dress. A gold belt held it in place, cinching her waist tight. Her yellow braid was wound in a crown atop her head.

She walked towards us, and her face was perfect. The dry, rotting skin had been a bad dream, a nightmare. I wish. Fire, Jean-Claude had said, fire was the only surety. I thought he'd meant just Janos.

Janos reached over and grabbed Jeff from Kissa. He gripped the boy's shoulders with both black-gloved hands. His fingers were longer than they should have been, as though they had an extra joint. Against the white of Jeff's jacket, you could tell that the index finger was as long as the middle finger. Another myth that was true, at least for Janos. Those long, strange fingers dug into Jeff just a little.

Jeff's eyes were so wide it looked painful.

"What's going on?" I asked.

Kissa was dressed in the same black vinyl outfit she'd had on in the torture room, though it couldn't be the exact same one, because the first one had Larry's bullet hole in it. She stood beside him, her hands in fists. She stood very still, as only the dead can, but there was a tension to her, a wariness. She wasn't happy. Her dark skin was strangely pale. She hadn't fed yet tonight. I could always tell . . . with most vampires. There are always exceptions.

Xavier moved in a shadow of that impossible blurring

speed past Stirling, to stand beside the still unconscious Ms.
Harrison. Larry shook his head. "Did he just appear there, or
did I see him move?"

"He moved," I said.

I expected Janos to send Kissa out to join the others, but
he didn't. A figure crawled over the lip of the hill, dragging
itself into sight like it hurt to move. Pale hands dug into the
naked dirt, pale arms bare to the spring night. The head
drooped towards the ground, short dark hair hiding the face.
With one upward motion, the face raised into the moonlight.
Thin, bloodless lips drew back from fangs. The face was
ravaged with hunger. I knew the eyes were brown only because I'd seen them staring lifelessly at the ceiling of Ellie
Quinlan's bedroom. There was no pull to her eyes, but down
in the dark depths a flicker of something burned. It wasn't
sanity; hunger, maybe. An animal's emotion, nothing
human. Maybe after they'd let her feed for the first time,
she'd have time for emotions; now everything had narrowed
down to one basic need.

"Is that who I think it is?" Larry asked.

"Yeah," I said.

Jeff tried to run to her. "Ellie!"

Janos jerked him tight against his chest, one arm around
his shoulders like an embrace. Jeff struggled against that
arm, tried to run to his dead sister. I was with Janos on this
one. The newly risen have a tendency to eat first and ask
questions later. The thing that had once been Ellie Quinlan
would have gladly torn out her baby brother's throat. She'd
have bathed in the blood, and minutes, or days, or weeks
later, she would realize what she'd done. She might even regret it.

"Go, Angela; go to Xavier," Janos said.

"A new name won't change who she was," I said.

Janos looked at me. "She is two years dead, and her name
is Angela."

"Her name is Ellie," Jeff said. He'd stopped struggling,
but he looked at his dead sister with fresh horror, as if just
beginning to really see her.

"People will recognize her, Janos."

"We shall be careful, Anita. Our new angel will see no one that we do not wish."

"Well, isn't that cozy?" I said.

"It will be," he said, "once she has drunk her fill."

"I'm impressed that you dragged her this far without feeding her first."

"I did it." Xavier's voice was surprisingly pleasant. It was disturbing hearing that voice coming from that pale, ghostly face.

I looked at him, careful to avoid his gaze. "Impressive," I said.

"Andy brought her over, and I brought Andy over. I am her master."

Since Andy hadn't shown up, I was betting I'd killed him in the woods with Sheriff St. John. Probably not a good time to bring that up. "And who is your master?"

"Serephina, for now," Xavier said.

I glanced at Janos. "You haven't worked out which of you is top dog, have you?" I smiled.

"You waste our time, Anita. Our master awaits you eagerly. Let us finish this. Call our angel."

Xavier held out one pale hand. Ellie made a noise low in her throat, and scrambled on all fours over the raw dirt. The long black dress tangled around her legs. She tore at it impatiently. The cloth ripped like paper in her hands, the skirt shredding around her bare legs. She grabbed Xavier's hand like it was a lifeline. She bent over his wrist, and only his hand in her hair kept her from trying to feed on him.

"There is no sustenance for you from the dead, Angela," Janos said. "Feed on the living."

Pallas and Bettina knelt on either side of Stirling. Xavier fell gracefully beside Ms. Harrison, his black cape spread out around him like a pool of blood. He kept hold of Ellie's hair the whole way down, forcing her snarling face to touch the dirt. Her hands dug at his hands, mewling sounds crawling from her throat. Nothing that was human should have made sounds like that.

"Ms. Blake," Stirling said, "you're the law. You have to protect me."

"I thought you were going to see me in court, Raymond. Something about me attacking you and Ms. Harrison with zombies."

"I didn't mean it." He glanced up at the kneeling vampires, then back to me. "I won't tell. I won't tell anyone. Please."

I just looked at him. "Begging for mercy, Raymond?"

"Yes, yes, I'm begging."

"Like the mercy you showed Bayard?"

"Please."

Bettina caressed Stirling's cheek. He jerked like it had burned. "Please!"

Shit.

"We can't just watch," Larry said.

"You have another suggestion?"

"You never give anyone over to the monsters, not for any reason. It's a rule," he said.

It was my rule. I'd believed in it once, back when I'd been sure who the monsters were.

He was pulling the chain out from inside his shirt.

"Don't do this, Larry. Don't get us killed for Raymond Stirling."

His cross spilled out in the open air. It glowed like Serephina's eyes. He just looked at me.

I sighed, and brought out my own cross. "This is a bad idea."

"I know," he said. "But I can't just watch."

I stared at his earnest face, and knew it was true. He couldn't just watch. I could have. I might not have enjoyed it, but I could have let it happen. More's the pity.

"What are you doing with your little holy objects?" Janos asked.

"Stopping this," I said.

"You want them dead, Anita."

"Not like this," I said.

"Would you have me let you use your gun and waste all this blood?"

He was offering to let me shoot them. I shook my head. "I don't think that's an option anymore."

"It was never an option," Larry said.

I let that go; no need to disillusion him. I walked towards Pallas and Bettina. Larry walked towards Ellie and Xavier, cross held outward to the length of its chain, as if that made it work better. Nothing wrong with a little dramatic gesture, but I'd have to clue him in that it didn't really help. But later.

The cross's glow grew until it was like wearing a 100-watt lightbulb naked around your neck. I saw the world as a black circle outside the glow.

Xavier was on his feet facing Larry, but the others had crawled away from their prey, beaten by the light.

"Thank you, Ms. Blake," Stirling said. "Thank you." He grabbed my leg with his good hand, fawning over me. I fought an urge to shake him off.

"Thank Larry; I'd have let you die."

He didn't seem to hear me. He was nearly crying with relief, slobbering all over my Nikes.

"Back away from them, please." The voice was female and honey-thick.

I blinked over the glow of the cross and saw Kissa holding a gun. A revolver that looked like a Magnum; hard to tell in the glow. Whatever it was, it'd make a big hole.

"Move away from them, now."

"I thought Serephina didn't want me dead."

"Kissa will shoot your young friend."

I stopped in mid-breath and let it out. "If you kill him, I won't cooperate with whatever you have in mind for tonight."

"You misunderstand us, Anita," Janos said. "My master does not require your cooperation. Everything she wants from you can be taken by force."

I stared at him over the shining light. He had Jeff cuddled against him; most heartwarming.

"Take off your crosses and throw them far out into the trees," Janos said. He ran a gloved hand along both sides of Jeff's face, planting a kiss on his cheek.

"Now that we know you would give up your safety for both young men, we have one more hostage than is absolutely necessary." He put his hands on either side of Jeff's neck, just holding, not hurting, not yet.

"Take off your crosses and throw them into the woods. I will not ask a third time."

I stared at him. I didn't want to give up my cross. I glanced at Larry. He was still facing off against Xavier, his cross glowing bravely. Shit.

"Kissa, shoot the man."

"No," I said. I undid the chain. "Don't shoot him."

"Don't do it, Anita," Larry said.

"I can't watch them shoot you, not if I can stop it." I let the chain pool in my hand; the cross shone with a blue-white flame like burning magnesium. It was a bad idea to throw it away. A real bad idea. I tossed it into the woods. The cross glittered like a falling star and died out of sight in the dark.

"Now your cross, Larry," Janos said.

Larry shook his head. "You'll have to shoot me."

"We'll shoot the boy," Janos said. "Or perhaps I'll feed upon him while you watch." He pinned Jeff against himself with one arm, while his other hand dug into the boy's hair, holding him immobile, neck exposed.

Larry looked at me. "What do I do, Anita?"

"You have to decide this one for yourself," I said.

"They'll really kill him, won't they?"

"Yeah, they will."

He cursed under his breath and let the cross fall against his chest. He undid the chain and threw it out into the woods with a lot of force to it, as if he could throw his anger with it.

When the light from his cross died away, we stood there in the darkness. The moonlight that had seemed so bright before was a dim substitute.

My night vision returned in stages. Kissa stepped closer, the gun still pointed at us. The first time I'd seen her, she had exuded sexuality, power; now she was docile, quiet, as though some of her power had been drained away. She looked pale and drawn. She needed to feed.

"Why haven't they let you feed tonight?" I asked.

"Our master is not a hundred percent sure of Kissa's loyalty. It needed testing, didn't it, my dark beauty?"

Kissa didn't answer. She stared at me with large, dark eyes, but the gun never wavered.

"Feed, children, feed."

Pallas and Bettina walked over to Stirling. They stared at me over him. I stared back.

Stirling grabbed my leg. "You can't let them have me. Please, please."

Pallas knelt by him. Bettina walked around to the side I was on. She pulled Stirling's hand off my leg. The vampire's lower back brushed my legs. I took a step back, and Stirling started screaming.

Xavier and Ellie had already started to feed on the blessedly unconscious Ms. Harrison. Larry looked at me, hands out, empty, helpless.

I didn't know what to say.

"Don't touch me, don't touch me!" Stirling batted at Pallas with his good hand, and the vampire caught it easily, held it.

"At least put him under," I said.

Pallas looked up at me. "After he tried to kill you? Why show him mercy?"

"Maybe I don't want to hear him scream."

Pallas smiled. Her eyes flashed dark fire. "For you, Anita, anything."

She grabbed Stirling's chin, forcing him to meet her gaze.

"Ms. Blake, help me. Help . . ." The words died in his mouth.

I watched everything slide out of his eyes, until they were empty and waiting.

"Come to me, Raymond," Pallas said. "Come to me."

Stirling sat up, his one good arm embracing the vampire. He tried to use the broken arm, but it wouldn't bend at the elbow.

Bettina bent the broken arm backward and forward, laughing. Stirling never reacted to the pain. He snuggled against Pallas. The look on his face was one of happiness, joy. Eagerness.

Pallas sank fangs into his neck. Stirling spasmed for a second, then relaxed and began making soft noises in his throat.

Pallas moved Stirling's head to one side, sucking on the wound but leaving enough room on the other side for someone else. Bettina sank fangs into the exposed flesh.

The two vampires fed, heads so close together their hair mingled, gold and black. And Raymond Stirling made happy noises while they killed him.

Larry walked away to the edge of the clearing, hugging his arms tight across his chest.

I stayed where I was. I watched. I had wanted Stirling dead. It would be cowardly to look away. Besides, I should have to watch. I needed to remember who the monsters were. Maybe if I forced myself not to look away, not to blink, I wouldn't forget again.

I stared at Stirling's happy, eager face, until his arm dropped away from Pallas's back, and his eyes closed. He passed out from blood loss and shock, and the vampires hugged him tight, and fed.

His eyes flew open wide, and a gurgling sound crawled out of his throat. Fear screamed out of his eyes. Pallas raised a hand and stroked Stirling's hair, a gesture you'd use on a frightened child. The fear died out of his eyes, and I watched the last light die with it. I watched Raymond Stirling die, and knew I would remember that last look of terror in my dreams for weeks to come.

37

THERE WAS A rush of wind that raised a fine cloud of dirt. Jean-Claude appeared as if conjured from the air itself. I had never been so happy to see him. I didn't run to his arms, but I moved to stand near him. Larry followed me.

Jean-Claude wasn't always the safest refuge, but right now he looked pretty damn good.

He was dressed in one of his white shirts. This one had so much lace on the front it looked fluffy. A short white jacket hit him just at the waist. More lace peeked from the sleeves of the jacket. He wore tight white pants with a black belt. The belt matched his velvet black boots.

"I did not expect you here, Jean-Claude," Janos said. I couldn't tell for sure, but he sounded surprised. Goody.

"Serephina delivered her invitation in person, Janos, but it was not enough."

"You surprise me, Jean-Claude," he said.

"I surprised Serephina, as well." He sounded terribly calm. If he was afraid standing outnumbered on the hilltop, it didn't show. I'd have loved to know how he'd surprised Serephina.

Jason walked up the far side of the hill, from the direction of the Jeep. He wore black leather pants that looked like they'd been poured on him, short black boots, and no shirt. There was what looked like a silver-studded dog collar around his neck, and a black glove on either hand, but other than that he was naked from the waist up. I hoped Jason had chosen his own outfit for tonight.

The right side of his face was bruised from chin to forehead as though something large had hit him.

"I see your pet joined the struggle," Janos said.

"He is mine in every way, Janos. They are all mine."

Just this once I let it go. If my choice was belonging to Jean-Claude or to Serephina, I knew what my vote would be.

Larry moved so close to me that I could have taken his hand. Maybe he didn't like being included in Jean-Claude's menagerie.

"You have lost that air of humbleness that I found so appealing, Jean-Claude. Have you refused Serephina's invitation altogether?"

"I will come to Serephina's party, but on my own with my people around me."

I glanced at him. Was he crazy?

He frowned. "Serephina wanted you at the party in chains."

"We can all live with this choice, Janos."

"Are you saying you would challenge us all here and now?" There was an edge of laughter in his voice.

"I will not die alone, Janos. In the end you may have me, but it will cost you dearly."

"If you will truly come of your own free will, then come," Janos said. "Our master calls; let us answer that call." Janos, Bettina, and Pallas were just suddenly airborne. It wasn't flying, or levitation. I had no word for it. Larry whispered, "Dear God." The first time you see a vampire fly is a red-letter night.

The others scattered into the trees in that blurring motion that made them disappear almost as fast as flying. Ellie Quinlan had vanished with the rest of them. Her brother had been carried away by Janos. Until that moment I hadn't known a vampire could carry more than its own body weight while "flying." Learn something new every night.

We found our guns and walked down the mountainside. Our crosses were well and truly lost. Even Jean-Claude walked, and I knew he had other methods of transportation. Was it considered impolite to fly when others couldn't?

The Jeep was still where I'd parked it. The night was still thick. It was hours until dawn, and I just wanted to go home.

"I took the liberty of choosing clothes for you to wear tonight," Jean-Claude said. "They are in the Jeep."

"I locked the Jeep," I said.

He just smiled at me.

I sighed. "Fine." When I tried the handle it was unlocked. Clothes were folded in the passenger seat. They were black leather. I shook my head. "I don't think so."

"Your clothes, *ma petite,* are on the driver's side. Those are Lawrence's clothes."

Larry peered over my shoulder. "You've got to be kidding."

I walked around the Jeep and found a clean pair of black jeans. The tightest pair I owned. A bloodred tank top that I didn't remember buying. It felt like silk. There was a black duster coat that I had never seen. When I tried it for length it hit me at mid-calf, and billowed capelike when I moved. I liked the coat. The silk blouse I could have done without.

"Not bad," I said.

"Mine is bad," Larry said. "I don't even know how to get into these pants."

"Jason, help him dress." Jason picked up the bundle of leather and carried them to the back of the Jeep. Larry followed him but didn't look happy.

"No boots?" I said.

Jean-Claude smiled. "I didn't think you would give up your jogging shoes."

"Damn straight."

"Change quickly, *ma petite;* we must arrive at Serephina's before she decides to kill the boy just for spite."

"Would Xavier let her kill his new toy?"

"If she is truly his master, he has no choice. Now, dress, *ma petite,* quickly." I walked towards the far side of the Jeep but that brought me within earshot, and nearly eyesight, of Larry. I stopped and sighed. What the hell.

I turned my back on Jean-Claude and slid out of my shoulder holster. "How did you guys get away from Serephina?" I slipped my shirt over my head. I fought the urge to look back. I knew Jean-Claude was watching; why check?

"Jason jumped her at a crucial moment. It was distraction enough for us to flee, but little else. I'm afraid the room is something of a mess."

His voice was so mild I had to see his face. I slid the red tank top on and turned. He was standing closer than I'd thought, nearly within touching distance. He stood there in his white clothes, spotless and perfect.

"Step a few paces back, please. I'd like a little privacy."

He smiled, but he did what I asked. A first.

"Had she underestimated you that badly?" I asked. I changed jeans as quickly as I could. I tried not to think of him watching. It was too embarrassing.

"I was forced to flee, *ma petite.* Janos calls her master,

and he defeated me. I cannot stand against her, not in a fair fight."

I slipped the shoulder holster back on, threading the belt I'd been wearing back through it. The straps chafed a little with no sleeves but it was better than not having it. I got the Firestar from under my seat and tucked the inner pants holster down the front of my jeans. It would show, even with the duster. I finally put it at the small of my back, though it wasn't my first or even second choice of places. I got the silver knives out of the glove compartment and strapped them to my forearms. I also got out a small box. It held two extra crosses. Vampires seemed to always be taking them from me.

Jean-Claude watched it all with interest. His dark eyes followed my hands like he was memorizing the movements.

I put the duster on and walked a few steps to get the feel of everything. I drew both knives just to make sure the coat sleeves weren't too tight. I drew both guns and still didn't like the Firestar. I finally shifted the inner pants holster to one side. It dug into my side hard enough to bruise, but I could draw it in a reasonable time. That was more important than comfort tonight. I slipped an extra clip for both guns in the coat pockets. They were loaded with nonsilver bullets. It made me nervous to only have the silver bullets that were in the guns, but Rawhead and Bloody Bones was going to make his appearance sometime tonight. Magnus might even be there. I wanted ammo for everything I'd meet tonight.

Larry came out from behind the Jeep. I bit my lip to keep from laughing. It wasn't that he looked bad, he just looked so uncomfortable. He seemed to have trouble walking in the black leather pants.

"Just walk naturally," Jason said.

"I can't," Larry said. He had a silk tank top that was the twin of mine except it was blue instead of red. He had short black boots on. The black jacket he'd borrowed from Jason last night completed the outfit.

I looked at the boots.

"Black jogging shoes perhaps, *ma petite,* but white jogging shoes with black leather? I do not think so."

"I feel ridiculous," Larry said. "How can you wear this all the time?"

"I like leather," Jason said.

"We must be off," Jean-Claude said. "Anita, if you would drive?"

"I thought you might want to fly," I said.

"It is important we arrive together," he said.

Larry and I added salt to our pockets. With the extra ammo clips in one pocket and salt in the other, my coat hung a little crooked, but hey, we weren't going to a fashion show. We all slid into the Jeep. There was a lot of protesting from the back seat. "These pants are even more uncomfortable sitting down."

"I will remember your dislike of leather in the future, Lawrence."

"My name is Larry."

I drove the Jeep down the rutted road that led out of the construction site. "Serephina wants to be immortal." I turned onto the main road and headed back towards Branson, though of course we'd be stopping at Serephina's on the way.

Jean-Claude turned in his seat to stare at me. "What are you saying, *ma petite*?"

I told him. I told him about Rawhead and Bloody Bones, and Serephina's plan. "She's mad."

"Not entirely, *ma petite*. It might not give her immortality, but it would give her undreamt-of power. The question remaining is, how did Serephina grow powerful enough to snag Janos before she fed off Magnus and Bloody Bones?"

"What do you mean?"

"Janos was in the old country. He would not have left voluntarily. He followed her. Where did she get the power to subjugate him?"

"Maybe Magnus isn't the first fairie she's fed off," I said.

"Perhaps," he said, "or perhaps she has found other food."

"What other food?"

"That, *ma petite,* is the question that I would very much like answered."

"Thinking of changing diets?" I asked.

"Power is always tempting, *ma petite,* but for tonight I was thinking of more practical matters. If we can discover her source of power, we might be able to undo it."

"How?"

He shook his head. "I do not know, but unless we can find some trick to pull out of our hats tonight, *ma petite,* we are doomed." He sounded remarkably calm about it. I wasn't calm. My pulse was thundering so fast I could feel it in my throat and wrists. Hear it like a rushing in my ears. Doomed: it had a bad ring to it. With Serephina waiting at the other end, it had a very bad ring to it indeed.

38

WE WALKED UP the stone steps to the porch. Moonlight and soft darkness filled the porch. There were no thick, unnatural shadows, no hint of what lay inside. It was just an abandoned house, nothing special. The nervous flutter in my stomach didn't buy it either.

Kissa opened the door. Candlelight spilled behind her from the open door to the far room. No pretense tonight that the empty room was all there was. Sweat beaded on her face, golden drops in the warm light. She was still being punished. I wondered why, but it wasn't my biggest problem.

Kissa led us through that open door without a word. Serephina sat on her throne in the corner of the big room. She was dressed in a white ball gown like Cinderella, her hair piled atop her head. Diamonds like a string of fire glimmered in her hair as she nodded her greeting.

Magnus was curled at her feet in a white tux and tails. Gloves, a white top hat, and a cane were laid next to his knees. His long chestnut hair was the only color in the picture. Every master vamp I'd ever met had been into dramatic presentation. Janos and his two females stood in black behind the throne, like a living curtain of darkness. Ellie lay on her side in the cushions, looking almost alive. Even in her torn and stained black dress she looked content, like a cat that was full of cream. Her eyes sparkled, lips curled with a secret smile. Ellie, alias Angela, was enjoying being undead. So far. Kissa stalked to them, and knelt on the side away from Magnus. Her black leather blended with Janos's cloak. Serephina stroked Kissa's sweating face with a white-gloved hand.

Serephina smiled, and it was lovely until you glimpsed her eyes. They glowed with a pale phosphorescence. You could still get a hint of pupil, but it was sinking fast. Her eyes matched her dress. Now that was color-coordinating.

Jeff and Xavier were missing. I didn't like that. I opened my mouth to ask, and Jean-Claude looked at me. For just this once, the look was enough. He was the master; I was playing servant. Fine, as long as he asked the right questions.

"We have come, Serephina," Jean-Claude said. "Give us the boy, and we will leave you in peace."

She laughed. "But I will not leave you in peace, Jean-Claude." She turned her softly glowing eyes to me. It was like being looked at by twin flashlights, and just as human. "Niña, I am so happy to see you."

I stopped breathing for a second. Niña: it had been my mother's nickname for me. Something flared in her eyes, like a distant glimpse of fire; then the light banked back to a cool wavering light. She wasn't trying to capture me with her eyes. Why? Because she was that sure of me.

My skin suddenly went cold. That was it. I would have said it was arrogance, but I believed it. She offered something better than sex, more fulfilling than power. Home. Lie or not, it was a good offer.

Larry touched my hand. "You're shaking."

I swallowed hard. "Never admit how scared you are out loud, Larry; ruins the effect."

"Sorry."

I stepped away from him; no sense in huddling. I glanced at Jean-Claude, sort of silently asking if I was about to break vampire protocol.

"She has acknowledged you as she would another master. Answer as one." He didn't seem bothered by that; I was.

"What do you want, Serephina?" I asked.

She stood, gliding across the carpeted floor. It looked like whatever was under that full skirt wasn't legs. Feet just didn't move like that. Maybe she was levitating. However she managed it, she kept coming closer. I wanted desperately to back away. I didn't want her close to me.

Larry moved a step behind me. Jason moved a step up to Jean-Claude's other side. I stood my ground. It was the best I could do.

Something flickered in her eyes, like a distant glimpse of movement through a fringe of trees. Eyes didn't do that. I looked away and realized I didn't remember looking at her eyes. So how was I looking away?

I felt her move towards me. Her gloved hand came into view. I jerked back and looked up at the same time. I barely glanced at her face, but it was enough. Her eyes had fire burning down a long dark tunnel, as if the inside of her head fell away into an impossible darkness, and some small creatures had lit a fire against that darkness. I could warm my hands by that flame forever.

I screamed. Screamed and covered my eyes with my hands.

A hand touched my shoulder. I jerked away and screamed again. "*Ma petite,* I am here."

"Then do something," I said.

"I am," he said.

"I will have this one by sunrise." She motioned to me. She took a gliding step towards Jason. She caressed her gloved hand down his bare chest. He stood there and took it. I wouldn't have let her touch me on a dare.

"I will give you to Bettina and Pallas. They will teach you to enjoy rotting flesh."

Jason stared straight ahead, but his eyes widened just a little. Bettina and Pallas had moved from behind the throne to stand a few feet behind Serephina. Dramatic gestures are us.

"Or perhaps I will force you to change into wolf form until it becomes more natural than this human shell." She slid a finger under the collar on his throat. "I will chain you to my wall, and you will be my guard dog."

"Enough of this, Serephina," Jean-Claude said. "The night bleeds away. These petty torments are beneath one of your power."

"I am feeling petty tonight, Jean-Claude, and soon I will have the power to be as petty as I feel." She glanced at Larry. "He will join my flock." She stared up at Jean-Claude. I hadn't realized he was taller. "And you, my lovely catamount, will serve us all for all eternity."

Jean-Claude stared down at her, utterly arrogant. "I am Master of the City now, Serephina. We cannot torture each other. We cannot steal each other's possessions, no matter how attractive they are."

It took me a second to realize the possessions he was referring to were us.

Serephina smiled. "I will have your businesses, your money, your lands, and your people before the night is out. Did the council really think I would be content with the crumbs from your table?"

If she challenged him officially, we were all dead. Jean-Claude couldn't take her, and neither could I. Distraction, we needed a distraction. "You're wearing enough diamonds to buy your own businesses, your own house."

She turned those glowing eyes to me, and I half wished I had kept quiet. "Do you think I live in this house because I cannot afford better?"

"I don't know."

She glided back to her throne and settled onto it, smoothing her skirts. "I do not trust your human laws. I will remain the secret we have always been; let others walk in the spotlight. I will be here when such modern thinkers are no more." She suddenly slashed out with one hand.

Jean-Claude staggered. Blood flew from his face, splattering on his white shirt and jacket in bright crimson flecks. Drops of it clung to my hair and cheek.

She slashed again, and another cut exploded on the other side of his face, splashing Jason with Jean-Claude's blood.

Jean-Claude stayed on his feet. He never cried out. He

didn't touch the wounds. He stood there utterly still; except for the blood there was no movement to him. His eyes were drowning pools of sapphire floating in a mask of blood.

Naked muscle twitched in his cheek. Bone glistened at jaw and cheek. It was a frighteningly deep wound. But I knew he could heal it. Horrible as it looked, it was a scare tactic. I kept telling that to the pounding of my heart. I wanted to go for a gun. To shoot the bitch. But I couldn't shoot them all. I wasn't even sure Janos could be shot.

"I don't have to kill you, Jean-Claude. Hot metal in your wounds, and they'll be permanent. Your beautiful face ravaged for all time. You can still pretend to be Master of the City, but I will rule. You will be my puppet."

"Say the word, Serephina," Jean-Claude said. "Say it and be done with these games." His voice was bland, as normal as it ever was. His voice gave nothing away, not pain, or fear, or terror.

"Challenge: is that the word you want to hear, Jean-Claude?"

"It will do." His power crawled over my skin like cool fire. The power lashed out suddenly; I felt it sweep past me like a giant fist. It slammed into Serephina, scattering the air currents. Kissa caught the edge of it and fell back from the throne, thrown nearly prone among the cushions.

Serephina threw back her head and laughed. The laughter died in mid-motion, gone like it had never been. Her face was a mask with eyes of white fire. Her skin seemed to grow paler, whiter until it was like translucent marble. Veins showed under her skin like lines of blue flame. Her power flowed through the room like rising water, deeper and deeper until when she released it we would all be drowned.

"Where are your ghosts, Serephina?" I asked.

I thought for a second she would ignore me, but that masklike face turned slowly, slowly towards me.

"Where are your ghosts?"

Even though she was looking straight at me, I couldn't tell if she heard. It was like trying to read the face of an animal; no, the face of a statue. There was no one home.

"Can't control Bloody Bones and your ghosts at the same time? Is that it? Did you have to give up one of them?"

Serephina rose to her feet, and I knew she was floating, rising on tiny currents of her own power to hover above the cushions. She floated slowly upward towards the ceiling, and it was impressive. I was babbling, trying to buy time, but time for what? What the hell could we do?

A voice echoed in my head. "Crosses, *ma petite*; do not be bashful on my account." I didn't argue or hesitate.

The cross spilled out of my shirt in a ball of light so bright it was painful. I squinted and looked away, only to find Larry's cross behind me blazing to life.

Jean-Claude cowered beside me, hunched away, arms shielding his face. Serephina shrieked and half-fell to the floor. She could stand before a cross, but she couldn't do tricks in front of one. She landed in a heap of silken skirts. The other vamps shielded their faces, hissing.

Magnus rose from the cushions. He stalked towards us. Jason stepped in front of Jean-Claude, moving to stand in front of me. He glanced at me with amber eyes; his beast stared at me over the glow of the cross, and had no fear. For a heartbeat I was glad I had silver bullets just in case.

Serephina said, "No, Magnus, not you."

Magnus hesitated, staring at Jason. A thin growl crawled out of Jason's throat. "I can take him," Magnus said.

There was a sound from the open door to the basement. Something was coming up the stairs. Something heavy. The stairs creaked in protest. A hand came out of the darkness, large enough to palm my head. The fingernails were long and dirty, almost clawlike. Ragged clothes clung to huge, square shoulders. The thing was at least ten feet tall. It had to bend sideways to come through the door, and when it stood, its head brushed the ceiling, and you couldn't pretend it was human anymore.

Its huge, oversized head had no skin. The flesh was raw and open like a wound. The veins pulsed and throbbed with blood flowing through them, but it didn't bleed. It opened a mouth full of broken yellow teeth and said, "I am here." It was shocking to hear words out of that mouth, that face. Its voice was like the sound at the bottom of a well; deep, and rough, and lost.

The room suddenly seemed small. Rawhead and Bloody Bones could have reached out one long arm and touched me. Not good. Jason had moved back a step to rejoin us. Magnus had moved back to Serephina's side. He was staring at the creature as wide-eyed as the rest of us. Had he never seen it in the flesh before?

"Come to me," Serephina said. She held out her hands to the creature, and it moved towards her, surprisingly graceful. It had a liquidness to its walk that was all wrong. Nothing that big and that ugly should move like quicksilver, but it did. In that movement I saw Magnus and Dorrie. It moved like something beautiful.

Serephina cradled its huge, dirty hand in her white-gloved hands. She pushed back the ragged sleeve, laying the thick, muscled wrist bare.

"Stop her, *ma petite*."

I glanced down at Jean-Claude, who was still cowering before the crosses' fire. "What?"

"If she drinks from it, the crosses may not work against her."

I didn't question him; there was no time. I drew the Browning and felt Larry draw his gun.

Serephina bent over the fairie's wrist, mouth wide, fangs glistening.

I pulled the trigger. The bullet smacked into the side of her head. The force rocked her, and blood dribbled down. She could be shot. Life was good. Janos threw himself in front of her, and it was like trying to hit Superman. I pulled the trigger twice, staring at his dead-eyed face from just over a yard. He smiled at me. Silver bullets just weren't going to do it.

Larry had stepped around Jean-Claude. He was firing at Pallas and Bettina. They kept coming. Kissa stayed on the floor. Ellie seemed frozen in the face of the crosses.

Bloody Bones stood there like it was waiting for orders, or didn't give a damn. It was staring at Magnus like it recognized him. It was not a friendly look.

Serephina's voice came from behind Janos's protective body. "Give me your wrist."

The fairie gave a ragged smile. "Soon I will be free to kill you." It looked at Magnus when it said it.

I didn't really want something the size of a small giant mad at me, but I didn't want Serephina to have its power either. I fired into its raw head, and I might as well have spit at it. The shot did earn me a dirty look. "I have no quarrel with you," the fairie said. "Do not make one."

Staring into its monstrous face, I agreed. But what could I do? "What'll we do?" Larry asked. He'd moved to stand nearly back to back with me. Bettina and Pallas had stopped just out of touching range, held at bay by the crosses, not the guns. Jean-Claude had gone to his knees, face cradled away from the glare of the crosses, but he didn't crawl away. He stayed within the protective touch of that light.

Silver bullets wouldn't hurt the fey, so . . . I hit the button on the Browning and popped the clip out. I fished in my pocket for the extra clip and slid it home. I aimed at the thing's chest, where I hoped the heart was, and pulled.

Bloody Bones bellowed. Blood blossomed on its ragged clothes. I knew when it felt Serephina bite into its flesh. Power whirled through the room, raising every hair on my body. For a heartbeat I couldn't breathe; there was too much magic in the room for something as mundane as breathing.

Serephina rose slowly from behind Janos's dark form. She levitated to the ceiling, bathing in the light of the crosses, smiling. The bullet wound in her head was healed. Her eyes licked white flame around her face, and I knew we were going to die.

Xavier appeared in the door to the basement. He held a sword in his hands, but it was heavier, softer-edged than any blade I'd ever seen. He stared at Serephina and smiled.

"I have fed you," Bloody Bones said. "Free me."

Serephina threw her hands skyward, caressing the ceiling. "No," she breathed, "never. I will drink you dry and bathe in your power."

"You promised," Bloody Bones said.

She stared at him, floating; her eyes of fire were even with his raw face. "I lied," she said.

Xavier cried, "No!" He tried to come closer, but the crosses kept him just out of reach.

I threw a handful of salt on Serephina and Bloody Bones. She laughed at me. "What are you doing, Niña?"

"Never break your word to the fey," I said. "It negates all bargains."

A sword appeared in Bloody Bones' hands, just appeared like the fey had grabbed it out of mid-air. It was the one I'd seen Xavier carrying at the Quinlans' house. How many scimitars as long as my upper body could there be? He stabbed it through Serephina's chest, spitting her in midair like a butterfly. Normal steel shouldn't have touched her, but backed by the fairie's magic, it could. He pinned her to the wall, driving the hilt into her chest. He tore the sword out of her, twisting it, doing as much damage as he could.

She shrieked and slid down, leaving a bloody trail on the naked wall.

Bloody Bones turned back to the rest of us. It touched fingers to its bleeding chest. "I will forgive you this wound, because you freed me. When he is dead, there will be no more wounds." He drove the sword into Magnus. The move was so quick, it looked like stop action. He was as fast as Xavier. Shit.

Magnus fell to his knees, mouth wide with a scream he had no breath to make. Bloody Bones drew the sword upward like he had with Serephina, and it reminded me of the wounds that the boys had had.

If Bloody Bones would help us escape Serephina and company, I had no problem with that, but then what? It drew the sword outward, and Magnus was still alive, staring up at me. He reached out to me, and I could have let him die. Bloody Bones raised the blade back for a final blow.

I pointed the Browning at it. "Don't move. Until you kill him, you're mortal, and bullets can kill you."

The fairie froze, staring at me. "What do you want, mortal?"

"You killed the boys in the woods, didn't you?"

Bloody Bones blinked at me. "They were wicked children."

"If you get out of here, will you kill more wicked children?"

Bloody Bones looked at me, blinked, then said, "It is what I do. What I am."

I fired before I could think. If it moved first, I was dead. The bullet took it between the eyes. It staggered backwards, but didn't go down.

"*Ma petite,* the crosses, or I cannot help you." Jean-Claude's voice was a harsh whisper.

I slipped the cross inside my shirt; a second later Larry followed suit. The room was suddenly darker, colder with just the candlelight. Bloody Bones raced forward, and it was just a blur. I fired into it and didn't know if I hit it or not.

The sword swung out to meet me, and Jean-Claude was suddenly there hanging onto the arm, sending it off balance. Larry moved up beside me, and we both fired into the fey's chest.

It shook Jean-Claude off, sending him skittering into a wall. Larry and I stood our ground, shoulder to shoulder. I saw the sword coming like a blur of silver, and knew I couldn't get out of the way in time.

Xavier was suddenly in front of me, the strange sword blocking Bloody Bones' blade. The steel blade stopped an inch from my face. Xavier's sword was notched where the steel had bit into it. The strange sword shoved upward through Bloody Bones' chest. The fairie bellowed, slicing at Xavier, but he was in too close for the fairie's giant sword.

Bloody Bones collapsed to its knees. Xavier twisted the sword as if hunting for the heart. He jerked the sword out in a wash of gore. The fairie collapsed on its stomach, shrieking. It tried to raise itself. I pressed the barrel of the Browning against its skull and fired as fast as I could. From point-blank range you didn't need to aim. Larry moved up beside me and fired. We emptied the clips into it, and it was still breathing. Xavier drove the sword through its back, pinning it to the floor. Its chest rose and fell, struggling for air.

I switched the Firestar and changed its clip to nonsilver.

Three shots more, and as if a critical mass had been reached, the head exploded in a rush of bone and blood and thicker, wetter things.

Xavier was on its back when it blew. We stood there covered in bloody brains. Xavier drew the sword out of its back. The sword came out notched, dented from contact with bone. We stood there by the dead giant, the two of us isolated in one clear moment of understanding.

"The sword's cold iron, isn't it?" I asked.

"Yes," he said. The pupils of his eyes were scarlet as a cherry, not the blood color of an albino, but truly red. Humans didn't have eyes like that.

"You're fey," I said.

"Don't be silly. The fairie can't become vampires, everyone knows that."

I stared at him, and shook my head. "You tampered with Magnus's spell. You did this to him."

"He did this to himself," Xavier said.

"Did you help Bloody Bones kill the teenagers, the children, or did you just give him the sword?"

"I fed him my victims when I grew tired of them."

I had eight shots left in the Firestar. Maybe he saw the thought move behind my eyes. "Neither lead nor silver bullets will harm me. I am proof against both."

"Where's Jeff Quinlan?"

"He's down in the basement."

"Get him."

"I don't think so." And suddenly there was sound again, movement again, besides us. He'd bespelled me, and bad things had been happening while I'd been caught.

Jason was coughing blood on the carpet. If he'd been human, I'd have said he was dying. Being a lycanthrope, he might live to see morning. One of the vampires had hurt him badly. I didn't know which one.

Jean-Claude was lying under a pile of vampires made up of Ellie, Kissa, Bettina, and Pallas. His voice came out in a thundering yell, echoing through the room. It was impressive, but not enough. "Do not do it, *ma petite.*"

Janos stood near the throne with Larry. They'd tied his

hands behind his back with one of the cords that held the drapes. A piece of cloth was shoved in his mouth. Janos had one pale spider hand around Larry's neck.

Serephina was propped on her throne, black blood pouring out of her. I'd never seen anyone lose so much blood so quickly. Her chest was torn open so wide I had a glimpse of a frantically beating heart.

"What do you want?" I asked.

"No, *ma petite*." Jean-Claude struggled to move and couldn't. "It is a trap."

"Tell me something I don't know."

"She wants you, necromancer," Janos said.

I let that sink in for a minute. "Why?"

"You have stolen her immortal blood from her. You will take its place."

"It wasn't immortal," I said. "We proved that."

"It was powerful, necromancer, as you are powerful. She will drink you up and live."

"What about me?"

"You will live forever, Anita, forever."

I let the "forever" part go; I knew better.

"She will take you and kill him anyway," Jean-Claude said.

He was probably right, but what could I do? "She let the girls go."

"You do not know that, *ma petite*. Have you seen them alive?" He had a point.

"Necromancer." Janos's voice jerked me back to him. Serephina lay propped on the throne beside him. Blood had drenched the white dress, turning it black, plastering it to her thin body.

"Come, necromancer," Janos said. "Come now, or the human suffers."

I started forward and Jean-Claude yelled, "No!"

Janos slashed outward with one pale spider-hand, just above Larry's body. Larry's white shirt sliced open, and blood soaked it. He couldn't scream with the gag, but if Janos hadn't held him, he'd have fallen.

"Drop all your weapons and come to us, necromancer."

"*Ma petite,* do not do this. I beg you."

"I have to do this, Jean-Claude. You know that."

"*She* knows that," he said.

I looked at him, struggling helplessly under three times his body weight in vampires. It should have been ridiculous, but it wasn't.

"She doesn't just want you for herself. She doesn't want me to have you. She will take you to spite me."

"I invited you to come play this time, remember?" I said. "It's my party."

I walked towards Janos. I tried not to look behind him, not to see what else I was moving towards.

"*Ma petite,* don't do this. You are an acknowledged master. She cannot take you by force. You must consent. Refuse."

I just shook my head and kept going.

"Your weapons first, necromancer," Janos said.

I laid both guns on the floor.

Larry was shaking his head furiously. He made little protesting noises. He struggled, falling to his knees. Janos had to release his grip on his neck to keep from strangling him.

"Now your knives," Janos said.

"I don't . . ."

"Do not try to lie to us here and now."

He had a point. I put the knives on the floor.

My heart was hammering so hard I could barely breathe. I stopped just in front of Larry. I stared into Larry's blue eyes. I pulled out the gag, somebody's silk scarf.

"Don't do it. God, Anita, don't do it. Not for me. Please!"

Fresh slashes cut his shirt; more blood flowed. He gasped, but didn't scream.

I looked up at Serephina. "You said this slashing only works with an aura of power."

"He has his own aura," Janos said.

"Let him go. Let them all go, and I'll do it."

"Do not do this for me, *ma petite.*"

"I'm doing it for Larry; doesn't cost any more to throw everybody in."

Janos glanced at Serephina. She was slumped to one side, eyes half-closed. "Come to me, Anita. Let me touch your arm, and they will release them all, my word, one master to another."

"Anita, no!" Larry struggled not to get away but to come after me.

Janos slashed his hand through the air, and the sleeve of Larry's jacket flew with blood. Larry screamed.

"Stop it," I said. "Stop it." I stalked towards him. "Don't touch him again. Don't ever touch him again."

I spit the last words in his face, staring up into his dead eyes and feeling nothing. A hand brushed my arm, and I jerked, gasping. I'd let anger carry me those last few steps. What I was about to do scared me too much to think about it.

Serephina had lost a glove. It was her bare hand that encircled my wrist, not too tight, not painful in the least. I stared at her hand on my arm and couldn't talk past the beating of my own heart.

"Release him," she said.

The minute Janos let him go, Larry tried to come to me. Janos gave him a casual slap that knocked him to the floor and sent him skidding back a couple of yards.

I stayed frozen with her hand on my arm. For one awful moment I thought they'd killed him, but he moaned and tried to get back up.

I glanced past Larry, and met Jean-Claude's eyes. He'd been after me for years; now here I was letting another master vamp sink her fangs into me.

Serephina jerked me to my knees, squeezing the bones of my arm so hard I thought she'd broken it. The pain brought me up to meet her eyes. They were solid perfect brown, so dark they were nearly black. Those eyes smiled at me gently.

I smelled my mother's perfume, her hair spray, her skin. I shook my head. It was a lie. It was all a lie. I couldn't breathe. She knelt over me, and when her face came forward it was my mother's thick, black hair that fell against my cheek.

"No! It's not real."

"It can be as real as you want it to be, Niña." I stared up into those eyes, and I fell down the long black tunnel of her eyes. I fell towards that tiny flame. I reached towards it. It would warm my flesh, comfort my heart. It would be all things, all people, everything to me.

Distant and dreamlike I heard Jean-Claude scream my name, "Anita!" But it was too late. Her fire warmed me, made me feel whole. The pain was such a small price to pay.

The black tunnel collapsed behind me until there was nothing but the darkness and the flicker of Serephina's eyes.

39

I DREAMED. I was very small. Small enough that I fit all in my mother's lap, only my feet stuck off the edge of her knees. When she wrapped her arms around me I was so safe, so sure that nothing could ever hurt me as long as Mommy was here. I laid my head against her chest. I could hear the beat of her heart against my ear. A strong, sure rhythm that pounded louder and louder against my face.

The sound woke me. But I wasn't awake. The darkness was so complete it was like being blind. I lay in my mother's arms in the dark. I'd fallen asleep in bed with her and Dad. Her heart pounded against my ear, and the rhythm was wrong. Mommy had a heart murmur. The beat of her heart was a fraction of a second slow, a hesitation, then two quick thumps to catch up. The heart beating against my skin was as regular as a clock.

I tried to raise up, off her, and bumped my head against something hard and firm. My hands slid over the body that I was pinned to. I touched a satin dress with smooth jewels sewn into it. I lay there in the absolute dark and tried to roll off her. I slid into the crook of her arm. Her naked flesh slid along my bare shoulders, boneless as the dead, but her heart filled the darkness even with me struggling not to touch her.

Our bodies were molded against each other. It was not a coffin built for two. Sweat broke out on my skin in a rush. The dark was suddenly chokingly close, hot. I couldn't breathe. I tried to roll onto my back. Tried to roll off her, and I couldn't. There wasn't room.

Every small struggle made her boneless body move, jiggling the soft, loose flesh. I couldn't smell my mother's perfume anymore. I smelled old blood, and a stale, neck-ruffling smell that I'd smelled before. Vampires.

I screamed and tried to do a push-up to get some distance, and the lid moved. I stayed on my arms, shoving my back into the satin and wood. The lid slammed backwards, and I was suddenly straddling her body, my upper body raised in a half push-up.

Dim light edged the lines in her face. The careful makeup looked wrong, like a badly made-up corpse. I scrambled out of the coffin, nearly falling to the floor.

Serephina's coffin sat on the stage in the Bloody Bones bar and grill. Ellie lay curled at the base of the stage. I stepped around her, half-expecting her to grab at my ankles, but she did not move. Not even to breathe. She was the newly dead, and with the sun up she was truly dead.

Serephina wasn't breathing either, but her heart was pounding, beating, alive. Why? For my comfort? Because of my touch? Hell, I didn't know. If I got out, I'd ask Jean-Claude. If he was alive. If she had kept her word.

Janos lay in the middle of the floor, on his back, hands folded on his chest. Bettina and Pallas were snuggled up against him, one on either side. A coffin lay on the floor. I had no way of knowing what time of day it was. I would have bet that Serephina didn't have to sleep all day. I was getting out of here.

"I told her you wouldn't sleep all day."

The voice jerked me around. Magnus was behind the bar, leaning his elbows on its smooth surface. He was slicing a lime with a very sharp-looking knife. He looked at me with his green-blue eyes. His long auburn hair spilled around his face. He straightened up suddenly, stretching his back. He was wearing one of those frilly shirts that you rent for wearing with a tux. The shirt was pale green and brought out the green in his eyes.

"You scared me," I said.

He leaped over the bar easily, landing on his feet light as a cat. He smiled, and it wasn't a friendly smile. "I didn't think you scared that easy."

I took a step back. "You recovered damn fast."

"I drank immortal blood; it helps." He stared at me with a heat in his eyes that I didn't like at all.

"What's wrong with you, Magnus?"

He swept his long hair to one side. He pulled the collar of his shirt until the first two buttons popped, spinning to the floor. There was a new bite mark on the smooth skin of his neck.

I took another step back towards the door. "So what?" I ran my hand over my neck and found my own bite marks. "So we've got a matching pair. So what?"

"She forbade me to drink. She said you'd sleep all day. That she'd keep you sleeping all day, but I thought she'd underestimated you."

I took another step towards the door.

"Don't, Anita."

"Why not?" But I was afraid I knew the answer.

"Serephina told me to keep you here until she wakes." He looked at me, and it was a sad, woebegone expression. "Just have a seat. I'll fix you something to eat."

"No, thanks."

"Don't run, Anita. Don't make me hurt you."

"Who's in the other coffin?" I asked.

The question seemed to surprise him. He let his hair fall back over his neck. The shirt gaped open over his chest. I didn't remember noticing his chest this much last time, or the way his hair swept over his shoulders. The ointment must have worn off.

"Stop it, Magnus."

"Stop what?"

"Glamor won't work on me."

"Glamor would be a more pleasant alternative," he said.
"Who's in the coffin?"

"Xavier and the boy."

I ran for the door. He was suddenly behind me, impossibly fast, but I'd seen faster. Most of them just happened to be dead. I didn't try to open the door. I turned into his body, and it surprised him. He fell into a shoulder roll almost textbook perfect. I tried to throw him three feet under the floor, everything I had.

He lay stunned for a second. I flung open the door. The spring sunlight poured in and fell on Janos and his women. Janos's face twisted away from the light. I didn't wait to see more. I ran.

Screams followed me out into the sunlight. I heard the door slam behind me, but didn't look back. I hit the gravel parking lot running with everything I had. I heard him pounding up behind me. I wasn't going to outrun him. I waited until the last second, stopped running, and kicked him. He saw it coming and dived under it, taking my other leg out from under me, sending us both to the ground. I threw a handful of gravel at his face, and he hit me in the jaw with his fist. There is a frozen moment after a really good shot to the face. A moment of shock, of paralysis where all you can do is blink. Magnus's face appeared over me. He didn't ask if I was alright; that had been the point. He picked me up and flung me over his shoulders. I got a nice view of the ground about the time I was able to move again.

I walked my hands up his back, trying to get enough leverage to swing a two-handed grip at his shoulders. I let him brace my lower body, but before I could try it, he kicked the door open and tossed me to the floor, none too gently. He leaned against the door and locked it.

"You just had to do it the hard way, didn't you?"

I got to my feet and backed away from him, which took me closer to the vampires. Not an improvement. I backed towards the bar. There had to be a back door. "I don't know any other way, Magnus."

He took a deep breath and pushed away from the door. "It's going to be a long day, then."

I put a hand on the smooth wood of the bar. "Yeah," I said. The half-sliced lime and the knife lay just a few inches away. I stared at Magnus, trying very hard not to look at the knife again. To not draw attention to it. Which isn't nearly as easy as it sounds.

His eyes flicked to the knife. He smiled and shook his head. "Don't do it, Anita."

I put my hands on the bar and pushed myself up on it. I heard him coming, but I didn't look back. Never look back; something is always gaining on you. I grabbed the knife and rolled over the bar at the same time. Magnus's face appeared above the bar too fast. I wasn't ready. All I could do was look up at him with the knife gripped in my hand. If he'd been just a little slower, I'd have stabbed him in the throat, or that had been the plan.

Magnus crouched on the bar, staring down at me. His aquamarine eyes glittered. Lights and colors played in them, reflecting things that were not there. He stayed on the bar above me, swaying slightly on the balls of his feet, one hand on the bar for balance. His hair had fallen forward, trailing thick strands across his face. He was going all feral on me, like he had at the mound. But this time he wasn't trying to be one of the good guys. I expected him to leap down on me, but he didn't. Of course, he wasn't fighting me, he was just trying to keep me from leaving.

I glanced at what was under the bar. Liquor in bottles, clean glasses, a tub of ice, some clean towels, napkins. None of it looked helpful. Shit. I got slowly to my feet, back pressed to the wall, as far from Magnus as I could get. I began to inch my way towards the side of the bar towards the door. Magnus paced me, sidling on the bar, making the awkward movement graceful.

He was faster than me, stronger than me, but I was armed. The knife was good quality, made for slicing food, not people, but a good knife is a good knife. It's versatile. I had to force myself not to squeeze too tight on the handle, to relax. I'd get out of this. I would. My eyes flicked to Serephina's open coffin. I thought I saw her breathe.

Magnus jumped me. His body slammed into mine, and I

drove the knife into his stomach. He grunted, and his weight rode me to the floor. I drove the knife in hilt-deep. His fist closed over my hand, and he rolled off me, taking the knife with him.

I scrambled around the edge of the bar on all fours. Magnus was there, yanking me to my feet by one arm. Blood had soaked the front of his shirt. He raised the bloody knife in front of my face. "That hurt," he said. He laid the edge of the blade against the side of my throat. It felt like my pulse was jumping out to meet the blade. He started backing up, pulling me with him.

"Where are we going?" I asked.

"You'll see," he said. I didn't like that he wouldn't tell me.

His feet bumped against Ellie's body. I could glimpse Serephina's coffin behind him, if I rolled my eyes. Hard to move your head when a knife's at your throat. He pulled on my arm, and I didn't go. I leaned back on my heels, just a little, aware of the knife, but I was more afraid of Serephina than any blade.

"Come on, Anita."

"Not until you tell me what we're doing." I spoke very carefully around the knife.

Ellie lay motionless, boneless, dead at our feet. Magnus's blood dropped onto her empty face. If it had been one of the others, they might have licked the blood off even in their slumber, but Ellie was well and truly dead. She was the newly risen, empty, waiting for her "personality" to rebuild, if it ever did. I'd seen vamps that never recovered. Never became close to the human being they'd once been.

"I'm going to put you in the coffin and lock it until Serephina wakes up."

"No," I said.

Magnus squeezed my arm like his fingers were searching for the bone. If he didn't break it, it would be a hell of a bruise. I didn't cry out, but it was an effort. "I can hurt you, Anita, in all sorts of ways. Just get in."

"Nothing you can do to me scares me as much as getting in that coffin again." I meant it. Which meant unless he was really going to kill me, the knife didn't work anymore. I turned my head into the blade. He was forced to move it away from my skin before I drove it into myself.

I stared at him from about a foot away, and saw something in his eyes that I hadn't seen before. He was afraid.

"Bloody Bones died because he shared your mortality. Were you harder to kill before, Magnus? No immortality to draw from, is that it?"

"You are just too damn smart for your own good," he said softly.

I smiled. "Mortal just like the rest of us; poor baby."

He smiled, a quick baring of teeth. "I can still take more damage than you can dish out."

"If you really believed that, you wouldn't be putting me back in the coffin."

His hand moved in a blur of speed that was almost vampire-quick. He hit my arm, and it took a handful of seconds to realize he'd cut me. Blood welled from the cut and dripped down my arm. He switched his grip from my upper arm to my wrist, faster than I could take advantage of it.

I watched the blood drip down my arm towards my elbow. It wasn't much of a cut, might not even leave a scar; of course, on my left arm, who could tell? "Couldn't you have cut the right arm? I haven't got nearly as many scars on that one."

He made one quick slice downward and opened my right arm from my shoulder damn near to my elbow. "Always happy to oblige a lady."

The slice hurt and was deeper than the first one. Me and my big mouth. Blood ran down my arm in a thin crimson line. Blood on my left arm trembled on my elbow and fell with a soft *plop* onto Ellie's cheek. The blood slid down her skin, into her mouth. A tingle of magic went up my spine. I held my breath. I could feel it. I could feel the body at our feet.

It was broad daylight. I shouldn't have been able to raise even a zombie, let alone a vampire. It was impossible; yet I could feel the body feel the magic. I knew it was mine if I wanted it. I wanted it.

"What's wrong?" Magnus jerked my arm, bringing my eyes back to his face. I'd been staring at the vampire. Hadn't meant to, it was just so damn unexpected.

I could feel the magic just out of reach, almost there. But how to push it over the edge? How? I smiled at Magnus. "You planning to just whittle me down until I get in the coffin?"

"I could."

"The only way I'm going in that coffin is dead, Magnus, and Serephina doesn't want me dead." I stepped into him; he started to move back, but forced himself to stand his ground. Our bodies were nearly pressed against each other. Great. I ran my hand under his shirt, along his bare skin.

Magnus's eyes widened. "What are you up to?"

I smiled, and traced the trail of fresh blood upward to the wound. I trailed the edge of the wound, and he made a small sound like it had hurt. I smoothed my one free hand over his skin, smearing his blood across his flesh like finger paints.

"You saw the murder scene when you touched me and still wanted to have sex with me, remember?"

He took a breath, and it trembled when he let it out between his lips.

I drew my blood-coated hand out from under his shirt. I held it up to him, let him see it. His breath came just a little quicker. I knelt, slowly; he didn't let go, he didn't put down the knife, but he didn't stop me. I smeared the blood on Ellie's mouth. The magic flared, sparked down my skin like cool fire. It crawled up my arm and onto Magnus.

"Shit!" Magnus swung the knife at me.

I blocked his wrist with my arm and came up under him, driving up from my knees. He was balanced across my shoulders, but he still had the knife. I flung him on top of Ellie.

I stood over him, breathing hard. "Ellie, rise."

The vampire's eyes flew open wide. Magnus started to push away from her.

"Grab him," I said.

Ellie wrapped her arms around his waist and held on. He stabbed her with the knife, and she screamed. God help me, she screamed. Zombies didn't scream.

I ran for the door.

Magnus came after me, dragging Ellie behind him. He was moving faster than I'd thought he would, but not fast enough. I flung open the door, and a long bar of sunlight spilled in through the door. I was a step out the door when the screaming started. I glanced back; I couldn't help it. Ellie was on fire. Magnus tried to loosen her arms, screaming. But nothing holds on like the dead.

I ran out into the parking lot.

"Niña, don't go."

The voice stopped me at the edge of the parking lot. I looked back. Magnus had dragged himself out the door and onto the gravel. Ellie was burning white hot. Magnus's shirt and hair were burning.

I screamed, "Go back, you son of a bitch!" But the same voice that kept me pinned to the edge of the parking lot kept him coming out into the light.

The voice came again. "Come back to bed, Anita. You're tired. You must rest."

I was suddenly tired, so tired. I felt every cut, every bruise. She would make it all better. She would touch me with her cool hands and make it all better.

Magnus collapsed in the middle of the driveway, shrieking. The vampire was melting into him, burning him alive. Sweet Jesus.

He reached one hand out to me. He screamed, "Help me!" The vampire was melting into his flesh, eating it away.

I ran. I ran with Serephina's voice whispering in my ear: "Niña, Mother misses you."

40

I FLAGGED A car down on the highway. I was covered in dried blood, cut, scraped, bruised, and still an elderly couple picked me up. Who says there are no more good Samaritans? They wanted to take me to the police, and I let them.

The nice policemen took one look at me and asked if I needed an ambulance. I said no, and could they page Special Agent Bradford, and tell him it was Anita Blake.

They tried to get me to go to the hospital, but there was no time. It was mid-afternoon. We had to move before dark. I asked the police to send a two-man car to make sure that no one moved the coffins. I told them there might be a hurt man in the parking lot and if he was still there to call an ambulance, but under no circumstances go inside the place.

Everybody nodded and agreed with me. Most of the cops in the area had been through Serephina's house last night and today. The cops told me Kirkland had brought the cops back to the vampire's lair after they took me. It took me a second to realize that Kirkland was Larry. Which meant Serephina had kept her word and let them go. The relief at knowing for sure that Larry was alive made me weak-kneed, and I was wobbly enough as it was.

The cops had found over a dozen bodies buried in the basement of Serephina's house. She should have buried them in the woods. For all I knew, she'd raised their ghosts. I didn't know. It didn't matter. All that mattered was that we had a warrant of execution, and the cops were listening to me today.

They sat me in an interrogation room with a cup of black coffee, thick enough to walk on, and a blanket to wrap around me. I was shivering and couldn't seem to stop.

Bradford came in and sat down across from me. He stared at me with eyes that were just a little too wide. "The locals say you found the master vampire's lair."

I laughed, and it came out wrong, almost like a sob. "I wouldn't say I found Serephina's lair. More like I woke up in it." I raised the coffee to my mouth and had to stop in mid-motion. My hands were shaking so badly I was about to slosh coffee onto the table. I took a deep breath, blew it out, and concentrated on taking a drink of coffee. Just concentrated on the simple physical movement. It helped. I got coffee, and calmer at the same time.

"You need to go to the hospital," Bradford said.

"I need Serephina dead."

"We've got warrants for all of them. All the vampires involved. How do you want to do it?"

"Burn them out. Block off everything but the front door. If Magnus is inside, he'll come out."

"Magnus Bouvier?" he asked.

"Yeah." There was something about the way he said it that I didn't like.

"The cops found what's left of him in the parking lot. It looks like something melted the lower half of his body. Would you know anything about that?" He looked at me very steadily when he asked it.

I took another careful sip of coffee, and met his eyes without blinking. What was I supposed to say? "The vampires were controlling him. He was supposed to keep me in the bar until nightfall. Maybe they punished him for failing." What I'd done to Magnus and Ellie was enough to earn me a death sentence. I wasn't admitting that to the Feds.

"The vampires punished him?" He made it a question.

"Yeah."

He looked at me for a long time, then nodded and changed the subject. "Won't the vampires try to make a break when the fire starts?"

"Sunlight or fire," I said. "Just a choice of how well done you want your vampires to be." I finished the last of the coffee in my cup.

"Your protege, Mr. Kirkland, said you were kidnapped from the graveyard. Is that your story, too?"

"It happens to be the truth, Agent Bradford." It was the truth as far as it went. Omission is a wonderful thing.

He smiled and shook his head. "You are hiding more shit from me than you're telling me."

I stared at him until the smile wilted around the edges. "Truth is a mixed blessing, Agent Bradford, don't you think?"

He stared at me for a moment, then nodded. "Maybe, Ms. Blake, maybe."

I called the hotel, and no one answered in Larry's room. I tried my room, and got Larry there. There was a moment of stunned silence when he realized it was me.

"Anita, oh my God, oh my God. Are you alright? Where are you? I'll come get you."

"I'm at the police station in town. I'm alright, sort of. I need you to bring me some clothes to change into. The ones I have on smell like vampire. We're going after Serephina."

Another silence. "When?"

"Now, today."

"I'll be right there."

"Larry?"

"I'll bring the guns and the knives, and an extra cross."

"Thanks."

"I've never been so glad to hear anybody's voice in my entire life," he said.

"Yeah," I said. "Get here soon. Wait, Larry."

"You need something else?" he said.

"Are Jean-Claude and Jason alright?"

"Yeah. Jason's in the hospital, but he'll live. Jean-Claude's in the bedroom asleep. After Serephina bit you, she hit Jean-Claude with some kind of power, energy. I felt it, and it was awesome. She knocked him out and left. The others went with her."

Everyone was alive, or as alive as they had started out. It was more than I'd hoped for. "Great; I'll see you soon." I hung up the phone and had a horrible urge to cry, but I fought it off. I was afraid if I started to cry I wouldn't be able to stop. I couldn't have hysterics just yet.

As agent on site, Bradford was in charge. Special Agent Bradley Bradford, yes Bradley Bradford, seemed to think I knew what I was doing. Nothing like getting almost killed to give you credentials. For once, badge or no badge, nobody was arguing with me. A refreshing change, that.

I did not hug Larry when he brought my clothes; he hugged me. I pushed away sooner than I wanted to, because I wanted to collapse into his arms in tears. To just let a pair of friendly arms hold me while I melted down. Later, later.

A huge bruise had blossomed on the side of his face from

jaw to mid-temple. It looked like he'd been hit by a baseball bat. He was lucky Janos hadn't broken his jaw.

Larry had brought me blue jeans, a red polo shirt, jogging socks, my white Nikes, an extra cross from my suitcase, the silver knives, the Firestar complete with inner pants holster, and the Browning and its shoulder holster. He'd forgotten a bra, but hey, except for that it was perfect.

The wrist sheaths stung going over the cuts, but it felt wonderful to be armed again. I didn't try to hide the guns. The cops knew who I was, and I wasn't fooling any of the bad guys.

Barely two hours after I'd crawled out of Serephina's coffin, we pulled up in front of Bloody Bones. There were ambulances, and more cops than you could shake a stick at. Local cops, state cops, federal cops; it was a smorgasbord of policemen. A fire truck plus fire emergency services completed the official list. Oh, Larry and me.

With Magnus dead, Serephina and company were unguarded. Not helpless. Oh, no. Nothing this side of Hell would have gotten me inside that building voluntarily. But there were alternatives.

The gas truck pulled around to the back and busted out a window. I watched them snake the hose into the window of the back door and turn on the juice.

I stood there in the warm sunlight, a cool breeze playing on my skin, and whispered, "May you rot in Hell."

"Did you say something?" Larry asked.

I shook my head. "Nothing important."

The hose shivered to life, and the sharp, sweet smell of gasoline filled the air.

I felt her wake up. I felt her eyes open wide in the dark. I breathed in the sweet smell of gasoline, felt my hands gripping the coffin edges.

I put my hands over my eyes. "Oh, God."

Larry touched my shoulder. "What is it?"

I kept my hands pressed to my face. "Take the guns, now."

"What . . ."

"Do it!" My hands came down and I looked at him. I looked at his familiar face, and Serephina saw him, too.

She whispered, "Kill him."

I ripped the knives out of the sheaths and let them fall to the ground. I started backing up towards the cops. I needed people with guns around me, right now.

The voice in my head said, "Anita, what are you doing to your mother? You don't want to hurt me. Niña, help Mommy."

"Oh, God." I ran and nearly collided with Bradford.

"Help me, Niña. Help me!"

My hand closed on the Browning. I balled my hands into fists at my side. "Bradford, disarm me now. Please."

He stared at me, but he took the guns from their holsters. "What's wrong, Blake?"

"Cuffs, you got cuffs?"

"Yeah."

I held my hands out to him. "Use them." My voice sounded squeezed, my throat so tight I couldn't breathe.

I smelled Hypnotique perfume, tasted my mother's lipstick on my mouth. The cuffs snapped into place. I jerked away from him, stared at the handcuffs. I opened my mouth to say "Take them off," and closed it.

I could feel my mother's hair tickling my face.

"I smell perfume," Larry said.

I looked at him with wide eyes. I couldn't speak, I couldn't move. I didn't trust myself to do anything at that moment.

"Oh, my God," Larry said. "You're going to feel her burn."

I just looked at him.

"What can I do?"

"Help me." My voice was squeezed down to a whisper.

"What's happening to her?" Bradford asked.

"Serephina's trying to get Anita to help save her."

"The vampire's awake in there?" he asked.

"Yes," I said.

Serephina was out of her coffin. The full skirt of her ball gown brushed the edges of the door that led to the kitchen. She couldn't go closer, because there was a spill of daylight from the window. Gasoline was pouring across the floor towards her.

"Anita, help Mommy."

"It's a lie," I said.

"What's a lie?" Bradford said.

I shook my head.

"Anita, help me, you don't want me to die. You don't want me to die, not when you can save me."

I collapsed to my knees, cuffed hands digging into the gravel of the parking lot. "Stop the gasoline."

Larry knelt beside me. "Why?"

It was a good question. Serephina had a good answer. "Jeff Quinlan is in there. He's inside."

"Shit," Larry said. He looked up at Bradford. "We can't torch the place. There's a kid inside."

"Stop the gas," Bradford said. He walked away from us, towards the truck, motioning them off.

And I felt a surge of triumph from Serephina. It was a lie. Xavier had brought Jeff over last night. There was nothing alive in that building.

I gripped Larry's arm with my cuffed hands. "Larry, it's a lie. She's lying to me. Through me. Get me in the back of a squad car, now, and torch the place."

He stared at me. "But if Jeff . . ."

"Don't argue with me, just do it!" I screamed it, burying my face between my arms, trying to ignore the voice in my head.

I could taste Hypnotique on my tongue. It was too much. Serephina was scared.

Larry called Bradford back, and they half-carried me to a marked car. I started to struggle when they tried to shove me in the back, but I did my best not to fight, and they closed the door. I was in a metal and glass cage. I gripped my fingers through the mesh in front of me, digging it into my skin until it hurt. But even pain didn't help.

The gasoline was everywhere, soaking into everything. Serephina was choking on it. "Niña, don't do this. Don't hurt your Mommy. Don't lose me again."

I started rocking back and forth, hands digging into the

wire. Back and forth, back and forth. It'd be over soon. It'd be over soon.

I felt a gentle touch on my face, a memory so real it made me turn and look for someone. "My death will be as real, Anita."

Somebody lit it. The flames roared to life, and I screamed before they hit her. I slammed my cuffed hands against the glass and screamed, "Nooo!"

Heat washed over her, crumbled the cloth of her dress like a melting flower, and ate her flesh.

I pounded my hands against the glass until I couldn't feel them anymore. I had to help her. I had to go to her. I fell to my back and kicked the window. I kicked it and kicked it, feeling the shock all the way up my back. I screamed and kicked the glass, and it cracked. The glass cracked and fell outward.

She was screaming my name. "Anita! Anita!"

I was halfway out the window before somebody tried to grab me. I let them grab my arm, but pushed my legs free of the window. I had to get to her; nothing else mattered. Nothing.

I fell to the ground with someone holding my arm. I got halfway up and threw them in a shoulder roll onto the ground. I ran for the fire. I could feel the heat now, rippling along my skin. I could feel the heat inside eating us alive.

Someone tackled me, and I beat at them with my hands made into one fist. The hands let go, and I scrambled to my feet. Shouting, and someone else holding me. He lifted me off the ground, arms wrapped around my waist, pinning my arms. I kicked backwards, and hit his knees. The arms loosened, but there were more arms. More hands. Someone lay on top of me. A hand the size of my head pressed the side of my face against the rocks. Hands pinned my hands against the rocks, his full body weight on just my wrists. Someone was sitting on my legs.

"Niña! Niña!"

I screamed with her. I screamed while I choked on the smell of burning hair and Hypnotique bath powder. I saw the needle coming in from the side, and started to cry, "No, no! Mommy! Mommy!"

The needle sank home, and darkness swallowed the world. A darkness that smelled like burning flesh, and tasted like lipstick, and blood.

41

I SPENT A few days in the hospital. Bruises, cuts, some stitches, but mainly the second-degree burns on my back and arms. The burns weren't that bad; there wouldn't be any scarring. The doctors just couldn't figure out how I'd gotten burned. I didn't feel like explaining, mainly because I wasn't sure I could.

Jason had broken ribs, a punctured lung, and other internal damage. He healed perfectly and in record time. There are benefits to being a lycanthrope.

Jean-Claude healed. His face was once again that perfection that had attracted Serephina to him so long ago.

Stirling's company rebought the land from Dorcas Bouvier, and made her wealthy. With Bloody Bones dead, she can leave the land. She's free.

The Quinlans are still suing me. Bert has lawyers that promise to keep us out of court, though I'm not sure how. If I'd walked the house personally, checked every inch of it myself, maybe . . . Hell, even I might not have protected the doggie door. Maybe I do deserve to be sued. I told the Quinlans Ellie was dead. They had to take my word for it; there wasn't anything left of Ellie to prove it. When vampires burn, they burn; no dental records, no nothing. Jeff was well and truly dead, too. Both their children were lost to them. It had to be somebody's fault; why not mine?

I'd raised a vampire like a zombie, which wasn't possible. Necromancers were supposed to be able to control all types of undead. But that was legend, not real. Right?

Serephina is dead, but the nightmares live on. The nightmares are tangled with the real memories of my mother's death. They are a bitch. For the first time in my life, I'm having insomnia.

What to do with the two men in my life? How the hell do I know? In Richard's arms, breathing in the warmth of his body, is the closest I've ever found to my mother's arms. It isn't the same, because I know that though Richard would give his life for me, even that might not be enough. When I was a child, I believed it would be. There is no real safety. Innocence lost can never be regained. But sometimes with Richard I want to believe in it again.

There is nothing comforting about Jean-Claude's arms. He doesn't make me feel safe in the least. He's like some forbidden pleasure that you know eventually you'll regret. I've decided not to wait; I'm regretting it now, but I'm still seeing him.

Somehow Jean-Claude has crossed that line that a handful of other vampires have crossed. I don't think of him as a monster anymore.

God have mercy on my soul.